THE
FOLKUNGS

M. E. JAVITS

BARRINGTON BOOKS

Barrington Books
www.thefolkungs.com

Print ISBN : 978-1-09836-953-8
eBook ISBN: 978-1-09836-914-9

Printed in the United State of America on SFI Certified paper
First Edition

Chapter 1

It was a typical Swedish winterday with pale sunlight reflecting on crisp, white snow--so bitter cold that icicles formed on eyebrows and hair. Young Erik shivered as he trailed behind his two brothers. Not even his well-oiled, lambskin-lined boots could keep the numbness from his toes, nor could his thick woolen hose and high boots protect his legs from the biting wind. He pulled his leather cap lower over his ears and wrapped his fur-lined mantle closer to his body, silently cursing as he pushed on against the wind to catch up to his brothers.

Erik's displeasure was due not just to the biting cold. All three boys were disappointed with their hunting luck that day. Only Erik had felled a hare and it was a skinny one at that. Even this meager achievement had greatly annoyed his elder brother, Birger, who sullenly led the way along the meandering river below Nykoping castle, his eyes searching eagerly among the snow-covered bushes for any sign of wildlife. Their younger brother Valdemar followed close behind him.

The three royal brothers had been hunting for several hours and now longed to be in front of the castle's warming fires but felt that they could not possibly return without a more impressive bounty. Although King Birger was only eleven, Prince Erik nine, and Prince Valdemar eight years of age, they were acutely aware of the importance of living up to their stations. Birger, in particular, resented being unable to outshine a younger brother in any game or sport, but Erik was the tallest, quickest, and strongest of the three.

Each had brought along their hunting dog and the three mastiffs were roaming around the area sniffing in the snow for game. The animals were treasured gifts from their late father; and with the help of their teacher, Father Nils, they had searched the classics for suitable names for their dogs. Young King Birger had named his dog Brutus,

Erik named his Ajax, but Valdemar had insisted on calling his Cupid. Erik and Birger had been merciless in their teasing, while their two sisters had thought the name adorable.

Suddenly Birger's dog, Brutus, flushed a beaver from among tree roots by the riverbank out onto the ice. Brutus dashed after the animal. Birger urgently called him back, knowing the ice was always thin on the fast-flowing river. But it was too late. Brutus had raced out, skidded, and slid into the rushing water. He tried to swim back, but was caught in a swirling pool, unable to clamber onto the slippery surface. Without thinking, Birger ran out to reach his dog. For a few steps the ice held, then broke under his weight. The current quickly dragged him under. Erik acted instinctively. Rushing downstream to an opening in the ice, he lay down belly first and crawled onto the fragile surface. Submerging his arm into the icy water, he grabbed Birger around the neck as the current dragged him by.

"Valdemar!" Erik yelled in desperation. "I cannot hold him alone!"

Valdemar, who had stood nearly paralyzed, broke from his spell and rushed to help. Erik was aware that their combined weight on the ice could send the three of them to their deaths, but as if by divine intervention, or more probably good luck, they were able to haul Birger from the freezing water.

"Brutus..." gasped Birger. "Save Brutus!"

The dog was still caught in the whirlpool, barely managing to keep his head above water. Erik knew the neighboring ice would not hold and looked at the frantic animal in dismay. Then he noticed a branch of a large tree projecting over the water. He threw his wet gloves on the ground, jumped up and caught the limb with his stiff, cold fingers. Hand over hand, he made his way to a spot above the drowning animal and stretched out his leg to where he could feel the dog's muzzle touch his boot.

"Seize!" he commanded the well-trained animal. The dog's jaws clamped shut on his foot with a gnashing sound. In excruciating pain, Erik mustered every ounce of his remaining strength to move back along the limb with the burden of the huge mastiff. He succeeded in dragging the dog onto the ice where Brutus released his bleeding foot on command. As Erik fell to the ground, he felt Brutus' tongue lick his face.

2

Enough of the incident had been seen from the parapets of the royal castle that the wet and freezing boys were soon surrounded by servants and soldiers assisting them into the warmth of the Great Hall.

Dowager Queen Helvig, summoned from her chamber, entered the Hall in a rush of red brocade and ermine. Servants rolled in portable wooden tubs and placed them close to the fire. When she saw her three shivering sons being stripped of their wet clothes, while hot water was being poured into the tubs, she breathed a sigh of relief.

"Thank God you are all safe," she said, crossing herself.

"Brutus chased a beaver onto the ice and fell into the river. I went to save him," Birger stammered between chattering teeth, hoping to elicit praise rather than a reprimand from his mother. Stiffly, he lowered himself into the steaming water.

Queen Helvig knelt beside his tub and stroked his cheek before she turned to Erik who was wrapped in fur skins and grimacing in pain as Father Nils, who had joined the commotion, was swabbing his bleeding foot.

"He will be fine," assured the priest after carefully examining Erik's wounds. "You might want to go to the chapel, your Majesty, and give thanks for the princes' safety. We will do our best to care for them."

The Queen quickly left the Hall. She fervently disliked anything interrupting the normal course of her day.

After their baths the boys were bundled up in dry clothes, given hot broth, and put to bed--Erik and Valdemar in their chamber, and young King Birger in his.

"Everyone thinks Birger was a hero," Valdemar muttered as he snuggled under the covers next to Erik. "Why did you not say something?"

"If Birger wants to look like a hero when he was not, let him. Father Nils must have guessed what happened when he saw the fang marks in my foot."

"I will tell everyone."

"You do not have to," yawned Erik, drowsy from the painkilling potion Father Nils had given him. "The guards probably saw what happened, and when the truth is known, Birger will look quite stupid."

Suddenly a heavy weight pushed against their door. It swung open and Brutus appeared in the doorway. Ajax and Cupid, who were stretched out on the floor, stood and wagged their tails. Ignoring them, Brutus went straight to the bed, licked Erik's face, and lay down by the bedside. The two boys looked at each other and then at the doorway where Birger stood.

"Brutus! Come back!" he commanded. But the beast, which seldom disobeyed his master, remained where he was. Erik could not suppress a smirk.

"How are you going to explain," he asked Birger, who was now pulling at the dog's collar, "that your dog, that you so bravely rescued, came to sleep with me?"

Birger released Brutus' collar and stood looking at the floor. "I am sorry," he finally muttered. Erik looked at him, realizing how awful it must be to be the eldest, and the king, and yet be outdone by a younger brother. He flipped open the fur covers.

"You must be freezing. Come to bed!" Birger's face softened with gratitude as he crawled in and the three dogs settled down on the floor.

The boys were allowed to sleep late the following morning. After morning prayers Father Nils came to their room to look at Erik's foot. When he opened the door, he was almost thrown down by the three mastiffs as they raced past him. Regaining his balance, he entered, approached the bed, and pulled the bed curtains aside. As he lifted the fur covers to examine Erik's foot, the boy winced and awoke.

"Stand up and see if you can walk on it." Erik sleepily stood, leaning on his teacher's arm for support. As he put his full weight on the foot he gasped in pain.

"Sit down and I will change the bandages."

Erik did as he was told and watched his badly swollen foot emerge from the swaddling.

"Good," said Father Nils approvingly, "You will be fine in no time."

Erik doubted the priest's prediction but stood up again to test his bare foot on the cold stone floor. It hurt, but he had to admit that it was not as painful as the earlier step had been. Nevertheless, he decided that Birger, who was still sleeping soundly, did not need to know that, so he let out a loud groan and sat down on the bed with a thud. His theatrics had their desired effect. Both Birger and Valdemar opened their eyes and saw Father Nils bending over Erik's wounded foot.

"It looks terrible!" cried Birger looking at the deep, red puncture wounds in his brother's bruised and swollen foot. Erik only sighed.

"Can he walk?" asked Valdemar as he put his arm around Erik's shoulders.

"He will be fine," Father Nils answered, aware of the boys' deep affection for one another, and of the games they played. "Because this is not a day to stay in bed, we will get him a cane. The Regent arrives today. But first you must see your mother. She has asked for you several times."

Erik had looked forward to this day for weeks. Since his father's death a few months earlier, the only man to whom the boys could turn for guidance had been Father Nils. But Father Nils, for all his learning and other sterling qualities, was not the powerful, worldly man their father had been, nor was he a great warrior like the Regent, the Lord High Constable, Torgils Knutsson. Today Lord Torgils would come to live with them, just as King Magnus had wished, and the boys had high hopes that the new Regent would fill the void created by their father's passing.

"Come!" called Valdemar excitedly, realizing that there would be no lessons that day. He jumped off the bed and reached for his clothes that had been folded neatly on a bench by the wall. Once Father Nils had finished applying clean bandages over a foul smelling herbal concoction, Erik limped over to the bench, groaning loudly. Birger observed his brother guiltily before he crawled out of bed to go to his own chamber.

"I will be right back," he mumbled as he closed the door behind him.

Father Nils bent down by the foot of the bed and opened a large chest. "You are to wear your good tunics today." He lifted out two folded garments and handed them to the boys, rummaging around until he found two gold chain belts with ornamental daggers. "You will wear these, as well."

The boys donned their hose and shirts before they pulled on their finely embroidered, long tunics. They fastened the chains around their waists, and Father Nils helped them adjust the daggers. Valdemar eagerly pulled on his boots, but Erik could not get his boot over the bandages.

"I was afraid of that," said Father Nils while Erik angrily tugged at the soft boot, unwilling to appear at Lord Torgil's homecoming without his knightly finery. "I brought a pair of your father's. They are similar to yours so you can use the left one without anyone being the wiser."

Erik smiled gratefully as he pulled on the larger boot that fit well over the bandages. His face darkened, though, when he saw the cane Father Nils held out to him. With it he would look like a weakling! But he knew that he would be unable to stay on his feet for any length of time without it, so he took it reluctantly. If he had to have a cane, at least it was a finely crafted one.

"Are you ready?" asked Birger as he came back into the room. The young king was wearing a tunic embroidered with gold, a thick stone-encrusted belt, and a thin gold band around his head. Despite his more elaborate outfit, he seemed almost inconsequential beside his taller and striking-looking brothers. But this morning, each of the princes felt well attired for the occasion and did not reflect on their differences.

Father Nils nodded his approval. "Come."

The Queen's chamber was a spacious and well-appointed room. Most of the time it was illuminated by torches held by wall brackets, since its windows were purposely small to prevent the winter cold or, in the event of an armed attack, flaming arrows from entering. The boys had grown up in that chamber, but now they considered themselves far too adult to spend much time there.

In one corner, surrounded by heavy curtains edged with gold braid, stood the queen's bed. There each of the five royal children had been born. Thick fur skins covered the stone floor, while royal banners and tapestries adorned the walls. In the center of the room stood a long table where the queen and her ladies-in-waiting toiled at their daily work. Embroidery frames and spinning wheels stood nearby, and piles of wool mixed with silk skeins in all colors littered the table. Erik remembered staging battles with his toy soldiers beneath that table. He recalled how he had often fallen asleep while listening to a soothing voice singing a ballad or recounting a tale. It was here he had learned about politics and intrigues as the ladies gossiped about current affairs. He wondered why men treated women as if they knew nothing, when in fact they seemed to know everything--and often well before their men.

Now the ladies were busy assisting one another in preparing to receive the new Regent. The two princesses, Ingeborg, ten years of age, and Rikissa, seven years old, sat patiently on a bench having small crowns braided on top of their heads, while the rest of their hair cascaded down their backs as was befitting young ladies. An air of exultation filled the room, and Erik appreciated how beautifully all the ladies were dressed -- in their finest tunics and under-dresses embellished with their most valuable jewelry and fancy headdresses. But then, it was no secret that the Lord High Constable was a widower.

"Ah, there you are!" exclaimed Queen Helvig. "How are you feeling, Erik?" Without waiting for his reply, she continued, "Lord Torgils should be here shortly. I have received a note from him." She turned and lifted her embroidery yarn off a small table looking for the message. "Ah, here it is. He writes that he will bring his younger daughter Kristina to live with him. His older daughter has just married, which leaves little Kristina quite alone. I think she is about nine years old, so she should be a perfect companion to Ingeborg and Rikissa."

Queen Helvig stood back and studied her sons. Erik could see from her expression that she was proud of them. But he knew she would never tell them so.

"Pull a comb through your hair." She took a comb from her table and handed it to Valdemar. "All three of you." The boys did as she asked when a voice called from the corridor, "Riders approaching the castle!"

Kristina Torgilsdotter rode beside her father on the road to Nykoping castle. Her legs were sore from long hours of riding, her face chapped from the harsh winds. Yet she would never complain as her father had no love for weakness. They had been traveling for almost three weeks, and each night was spent in a different house belonging to allies of her father. Each lodging had seemed grander than the last; and in each they had been treated with the utmost respect, given the best beds, and served the finest foods. The lords of those manors had bowed deeply to her father, the newly designated Regent of Sweden, a country whose territorial vastness Kristina was only beginning to comprehend, as it had taken such a long time just to traverse it at its narrowest point. And now they were nearing their destination. She noticed that the squire who preceded them had straightened his back to sit even more proudly in his saddle as he held her father's banner. When she glanced around she saw that the fifty knights and soldiers who followed behind them in their new winter tunics emblazoned with her family's coat of arms had done the same.

When Nykoping castle finally rose from the snowy landscape, Kristina's startled exclamation formed a thick vapor cloud in the chill winter air. She had never seen a royal fortress, and the massive rectangle of high stonewalls surmounted by a host of towers took her breath away. One of the towers was round and much taller than the rest. It seemed to reach almost to the sky like some grim symbol of power.

As they approached the castle, the only access Kristina could discern was by means of a drawbridge over an encircling moat supplied with water from the river flowing along one of its walls. Following her father's stallion, Kristina's mare started across the drawbridge where heavy gates led to a busy entrance court. Kristina could see kennels, stables, servants' quarters, and a forge as they rode among servants going about their business. Lord Torgils' mount scattered a flock of hens as they entered the main courtyard. There, within the quadrangle stood wooden buildings, easier to heat than stone structures through the cold winters, containing kitchens, living quarters, and the Great Hall.

"What do you think?" asked her father with an inquiring glance. "Grand, is it not?"

"What is that tower, father?"

"Soldiers' barracks and prison cells. A dungeon lies deep in its bowels," he answered. "This castle was built as a military stronghold, but gradually has been converted to living quarters for the royal family. I am sure that you will be comfortable here."

Lord Torgils dismounted and then helped Kristina down. Stable boys came running to tend to their horses. Lord Torgils headed for a large wooden building with high narrow colored glass windows and wood-carved double doors. Kristina stared at the carvings depicting huge dragons snaking around the surface of each door. Frightened by the loathsome-looking monsters, she hastened after her father and entered the Great Hall with her small hand securely engulfed in his massive grip.

The chamber was the largest indoor space Kristina had ever entered, save for the cathedral in Skara. Official royal banners hung along the walls over built-in benches, intermingled with large shields, emblazoned with the royal family's coat-of-arms dating back over several generations. Gracefully crafted wall brackets held flaming torches. A huge oblong fire pit, burning immense logs of wood, commanded the center of the Hall, surrounded by long tables that were filled with beautifully attired courtiers. The tables were set with white linen, fine silver and gold chalices, knives and platters--the kind that her own mother had only removed from storage chests for special occasions.

The Great Hall fell silent as Lord Torgils entered. Kristina could see that everyone in the room knew who he was, and the ease with which he nodded his greetings to those nearby showed how familiar and comfortable these strange surroundings were to him. He traversed the Hall in long strides, while she had to run to keep up with him, until they reached the royal dais, which was considerably higher than the other tables in the Hall. It was occupied only by the dowager queen, who sat in one of two high chairs decorated with the royal coat-of-arms, and by young King Birger, who sat in the other. In front of them stood the most beautiful carved silver bowl Kristina had ever seen and she knew that it contained precious salt. The king and the dowager queen looked down on her, while she trembled from nervousness.

The queen was a stern, majestically beautiful woman, dressed in a magnificent green embroidered tunic, partly hidden by a panoply of gold jewelry. She wore a gold band around her headdress paved with precious stones that flashed in the light of the fire and candles. Kristina sank down in a deep curtsy as her father bowed. She looked over to the young king and dipped in a second curtsy. "I wish you welcome," King Birger said importantly.

"Yes, we do wish you welcome, Lord Torgils. And you, little Kristina," echoed the queen, smiling dutifully. "I hope you both will be happy here with us."

Lord Torgils straightened up and replied in a commanding yet gentle voice: "Thank you for allowing me to bring Kristina. She has been lonely at Lena without her mother and sister. And I am told she already does good needlework, so she should be of help to you, gentle Lady."

"I am sure she will, Lord Torgils. Come, sit here beside me so that we may enjoy supper together," she commanded graciously as she pointed to a seat by her side. "And you, Kristina, sit down with my children."

Kristina looked over to a slightly lower table where the royal children sat. The two princesses scrutinized Kristina nodding briefly. They were both pretty, clad in resplendent long silk tunics which made Kristina feel self-conscious about her own attire which was clearly not of the latest court fashion. The two princes were handsome boys. They had proud chiseled faces and thick manes of light hair. While the young king sat in the High chair and wore a crown, his darker looks could in no way match his brothers'. But the princes seemed oblivious to Kristina's shy glances, and only momentarily looked her way with slight bows. Taking her place, she felt awkward. Though she was sitting at the table with the royal children--placed in an honorable position judging from her father's satisfied nod at the queen's suggestion--they paid her no heed but left her sitting in silence while they spoke intimately amongst themselves.

An army of servants offered countless courses of delicacies, none of which Kristina was able to swallow. Nor could she enjoy the sweet voice of the master bard or follow the lyrics of the ballads with so many table rituals to follow. When to eat and when not to, whether to wait for the king to start--or was it the queen? When to drink a toast, and how to wash one's hands in the rose-scented water brought by the Ewerer? She was terrified of doing something wrong and shaming her father. Her first meal in the beautiful Hall was an interminable nightmare, and when her father finally came to take her to their quarters, she could not have been more grateful.

In spite of her extreme fatigue, Kristina did not sleep well. She awoke on her first morning at Nykoping castle with a feeling of despair. She was lying in a small, windowless cubicle adjoining her father's chamber that had been used by the king's page. Other than the narrow cot on which she had tossed and turned all night, it contained no furniture. Had it had a window, that would not have helped much in telling the time, since the Nordic winter nights lasted late into the day. When her father had brought her back after supper he had told her to present herself in the queen's chamber on the morrow before prayers, and she was afraid to over-sleep her first duty.

The cubicle was slightly damp from the cold, and Kristina shivered beneath the fur skin covers. She had almost cried when she saw the cramped and unwelcoming space that was to be hers. Fondly she remembered the cozy, warm hall at Lena where, throughout her childhood, she had slept with her sister in one of the built-in beds along the wall. Kristina could remember awakening at Lena to the familiar sounds of the slaves lighting the fire and setting the table for the morning meal. And there had always been Suma, her wet nurse, who would come and pull the curtains aside with a cheery greeting to help her dress. Here, there was no one to wake her.

Kristina, having eaten nothing the night before, suddenly realized how hungry she was. Her stomach was churning, and she began to rub the sleep from her eyes. She sat up and touched her toes to the cold floor. She shivered and quickly wrapped a fur skin around her naked body while her feet searched for the slippers she had left by the bedside. She found them, slipped them on, and quietly opened the door to her father's chamber. It had been the king's audience chamber but had been refurnished with a large bed to house the Regent in style. The parted bed curtains revealed that her father was already gone. Kristina felt a surge of panic. How was she to find the queen's chamber?

She walked over to the time candle burning by her father's bedside and looked at it closely. She knew how to read the hour by the markings and could tell that she had almost a full hour before morning prayers commenced. She breathed a sigh of relief.

It was warmer in her father's chamber. The heat came from a small fire in a far corner grate, its smoke trailing up along the wall and out through a hole in the ceiling. She stood close to the grate until she felt the heat loosen the stiffness in her limbs. Then she went back to her cubicle to get her clothes. She stood in front of the fire as she slowly pulled on her under-dress and slipped her tunic over it. Taking a comb from its holder on her belt, she sighed. No comb could control her curls however much she tugged and pulled, so she finally let them fall in whatever way they would.

With her preparations finished, she opened the door to the corridor that was dimly lit by wall-mounted torches, spaced so widely apart that frighteningly long shadows danced across the floor. She did not know which way to go, so she listened for sounds to guide her. Hearing noises from a far end of the corridor she quickly ran in that direction, trying to ignore the shadows twirling around her like grey hands tugging at her skirts. At the end of the corridor a staircase led down, and she started to descend the dark stairwell. Halfway down, she realized that she had not taken the staircase leading to the Hall. She was debating whether to go back up to the opposite end of the corridor where the Hall staircase had to be, when she heard voices below the stairs. She decided to follow the sounds. As she reached the bottom of the stairs she found a narrow corridor leading to the huge castle kitchen.

She drew a deep breath of relief. Here, finally, was light and life. She smelled the fresh straw on the floor and the wonderful aroma of bread baking in the ovens. As she stepped through the doorway she marveled at the size of the room where at least forty people scurried around to prepare the first meal of the day. Fires were lit in the large center pit over which a pig was already roasting. A small boy sat near the ashes at the pit's edge, slowly turning the spit. Huge pots and kettles hung from hooks fastened on chains suspended over the fire. The ovens in a far corner sent up clouds of smoke that trailed out through the ceiling holes, blackening the walls on their journey.

In the midst of the frenzied activity stood a fat major domo shouting orders in a loud voice. Boys and girls were hurrying with staples to the different cooks who worked in their assigned areas of the kitchen. The cooks, in turn were calling out orders to their helpers. The kitchen was busy, noisy and warm; Kristina felt her spirits soar and her stomach contract from hunger.

When the major domo noticed Kristina in the doorway, he stopped talking in mid-sentence. He stared at her and slowly everyone in the kitchen turned to see what he was looking at. Kristina felt her mouth go dry as the kitchen became silent but for the hissing sounds of the boiling pots and crackling of the fire.

"Lady Kristina," said the major domo, looking confused over her appearance in his domain. "What do you wish?"

Kristina became speechless since everyone stared at her as if she had broken some rule forbidding her to be in the kitchen. She had always done it at Lena and had always felt welcome.

"Can I be of service?" inquired the major domo. His tone was respectful but unwelcoming.

There was no place where she belonged now. In the Hall, she was too lowly for the royal children to speak to her; and here she was too highborn to fit in. She felt her throat contract and she wanted to cry, but then she reminded herself that she was the daughter of the Regent of Sweden. She straightened her back and spoke in a calm voice.

"I am hungry, and I would like something to eat."

"I am sorry, my lady," said the major domo, "but no one is allowed to eat before morning prayers ... the queen's orders." Kristina thought that the big man looked almost frightened at the mention of the queen. He gestured towards a door at the opposite end of the kitchen. "The ladies are assembling in the queen's chamber now."

Kristina knew that she had no choice but to sit through chapel services before she would get anything to eat, and she began to cross the kitchen with all eyes following her. She looked straight ahead, trying to appear composed, and exited with her head high. Once out in the corridor she took a deep breath and headed for the lights in the Hall. Before she had gotten very far, she heard a voice behind her.

"My lady, please wait." Kristina turned around and saw a girl her own age in a large white apron. "I am the baker's assistant," the girl said as she reached out a warm bun. "This was just baked. But, please, do not tell anyone I gave it to you."

Kristina felt near tears again. This time it was not from loneliness, but from simple gratitude for the first kind gesture anyone had shown her since her arrival.

"What is your name?"

"Ragna. I am the prison warden's daughter, and I am serving my apprenticeship with the baker," she added proudly.

"I will not forget your kindness, Ragna."

"Whatever I can do, just ask me. I am up with the slaves, so you always know where to find me in the morning. But I better get back before anyone misses me." With that, she turned and ran back towards the kitchen.

Kristina ate the bread, relishing every bite before she wiped her mouth and carefully brushed off the front of her tunic before setting off towards the Hall. Just as she entered, the queen came down the stairs, followed by her ladies-in-waiting. Kristina was relieved to see that the ladies were no longer dressed in their finery, but in everyday tunics similar to her own. However, what little self-esteem she felt was quickly crushed.

"There you are," said the queen accusingly. "Tomorrow, I expect you in my chamber promptly, not roaming around the castle."

The queen turned and began to walk across the Hall followed by her ladies who glanced at Kristina with something resembling pity. The two princesses did not even look her way, and she dutifully took a place at the end of the procession as it moved towards the chapel.

The young princes sat waiting impatiently for the morning prayers to end. Father Nils looked sternly at them as they fidgeted in their seats. He purposely slowed his words until the boys caught the hint and settled down. Still, Erik was unable to concentrate on Father Nils' sermon. He and his brothers were to participate in the knight's practice session for the first time that morning, and he could hardly wait. Realizing, however, that there was nothing he could do to speed up the service, he began to look around the chapel. His eyes fell on Kristina

Torgilsdotter who sat with her head bowed. Her face was hidden by a halo of light curls cascading down her shoulders. Erik remembered from the previous night that she was a comely girl with frightened blue eyes. Close beside her sat Lord Torgils who, along with all his other duties, was to supervise Erik and his brothers in martial training.

Lord Torgils looked every inch the powerful man he was reputed to be. He was tall and massive, conveying the impression that the ground moved under his feet when he walked. Though his face was scarred from many battles, he was still a handsome man--not handsome in a charming manner since he rarely smiled or showed emotion--but handsome in an imposing and almost frightening way. His face exuded strength and pride, his eyes were dark and piercing, and the strong line of his jaw was not lost under his short-cut beard.

Eavesdropping on conversations through the years, Erik had learned much about Torgils Knutsson. He knew that Lord Torgils descended from an old noble clan, and that he had made so forceful an entrance into the world that it had caused his mother's death. Torgils had been such a large baby that it had taken two wet nurses to sate his appetite. At the age of eight, despite his size and strength, he was stricken with a paralyzing illness. The attending physician predicted that he would not survive, but in that withering body resided a will of iron. Since he was impatient by nature, long before the physician gave him leave, he crawled out of his bed to learn to walk once again. Torgils not only survived but rigorously exercised every limb of his body until it returned to full strength. When he was finally able to walk and ride, he realized how far his friends had surpassed him at knightly skills, so he practiced incessantly until he was able to vanquish them in every category.

Together with many young knights, Torgils entered the service of Erik's father, King Magnus, and quickly distinguished himself from the rest--not only as an invincible jouster and soldier but as a leader of men. His authoritarian manner went unchallenged, and before long he was put in command of the Swedish army. He made his name as a great warrior during his many tours in Finland where he converted heathens while gaining valuable land for the Swedish crown. The late King Magnus had enjoyed the company of his loyal Marshal who was not only a talented story teller able to drink the strongest of men under the table, but who also exhibited a true talent for politics. A deep friendship had evolved between the two men over the years until Lord Torgils became the only one, beside the late king, privy to all affairs of state. It seemed natural that he was appointed Lord High Constable and later was chosen by the King's Council to serve as Regent until young King Birger came of age.

Erik was pulled out of his reverie the moment the sermon was over, and together with his brothers raced out of the chapel and into the courtyard. He hardly felt the pain of his bandaged foot in his hobbling dash for freedom. However, their haste was wasted. The Lord High Constable did not leave the chapel immediately, but cordially stood waiting for the queen and her ladies to precede him. Expectantly, the boys watched him walk towards them.

"I am pleased that you are so eager, but do not ever let me see you run out of chapel like that again," he chastised them. Birger opened his mouth to remind him who was king but closed it as Lord Torgils signaled for one of his men to bring forward a large chest. As he lifted the lid, the boys saw that it was filled with weapons and armor. "I had the best smith in Stockholm fit these to your size," he explained as he bent down and picked up a breastplate with the royal coat of arms, topped by a golden crown, hammered into it.

"For you, your Majesty," he said to Birger. Then he brought forth two more breastplates, decorated with the royal crest alone--a standing golden lion on a blue field diagonally crossed by three white bars. "And these, my princes, are for you."

Slowly he emptied the chest of its contents--suits of armor, chain mail, swords, shields, clubs, axes and maces--all made to fit the boys. The princes' pleasure knew no bounds over finally receiving their own knightly gear. Previously, they had practiced with wooden swords and lids from huge pots that they had purloined from the kitchens--to the major-domo's perpetual carping. Still they had learned much and were already proficient fencers and riders for their ages.

The boys started to get outfitted with the help of some knights who showed them all the adjustments. Erik omitted the metal boot on his wounded foot so that he could move with greater ease. Once they were attired, and Lord Torgils called for sword practice, the boys were already feeling the weight of their chain mail and armor and the cold that came from wearing metal in the freezing Swedish winter. They walked awkwardly to their places in the line of fully armed knights.

"Commence!" bellowed Lord Torgils, and the men lifted their swords to go through the prescribed exercises. As Erik tried to perform the graceful moves, his shoulders and arms began to ache from the unaccustomed weight of the sword and armor, but at least he became warmer. It was with his last ounce of strength, and terrible pain in his foot, that he finished the final swift strokes with his new weapon.

As the knights turned to face one another for hand to hand combat, Lord Torgils called out: "Your Majesty, Your Highnesses. I think you would gain valuable knowledge from watching some of Sweden's finest knights at practice, so please sit down and observe."

Grateful and sore, the three brothers sank down on a bench by the wall. They looked at each other. Cold sweat was running down their pale faces and they were deadly tired. Erik caught the Lord High Constable looking in their direction with a brief sign of concern before he quickly turned his attention back to his men. As in a fog, the boys watched the knights gracefully attack and defend until Lord Torgils called a halt to the exercise. The knights removed their helmets and went to a table where large pitchers of beer stood waiting to quench their thirst. One of the knights walked over to the boys with a large mug and handed it to Birger.

"You deserve this, all of you," he said with a warm smile. "The first time I wore my armor I could not finish all of the moves."

The boys grinned at one another while they eagerly passed the mug. They had felt so miserable about their pitiful lack of endurance, but now they were receiving praise from Lord Abjorn Sixtensson, the closest advisor and friend of Lord Torgils.

Lord Torgils joined them. "From now on you wear your chain mail--day and night. You must get used to it. On a campaign you would not be able to take it off for weeks. It will feel heavy at first, but soon it will feel like a second skin." He grinned when he added "Which one of you is ready to cross swords with me? I want to see what you have learned today."

The boys stared at him in disbelief. Did he think that they could even lift their arms after doing the full practice? They glanced at one another uneasily. Did the Lord High Constable want to make King Magnus' sons look like weaklings?

"No one, hmm?" said Lord Torgils, feigning disappointment.

"I will," said Erik weakly as he hobbled up from the bench.

"Ah, Erik! But can you fight with your wounded foot?"

Erik did not answer but took up his position with his sword raised as he felt anger energize him. Lord Torgils quickly tapped Erik's sword with his own to show that he was ready. In excruciating pain, Erik took three quick steps forward. His attack totally surprised Lord Torgils who had to step back to keep his balance.

"Well done," he said as he countered, forcing Erik to retreat. Erik could feel the pain in his foot make him lightheaded, but his anger kept him countering. After a few more ripostes, Lord Torgils nailed his sword on Erik's breastplate and Erik stood still in defeat.

"I like that," smiled Lord Torgils. "Despite your exhaustion and injury, you would not let a challenge go unmet." Erik could only breathe in gasps as Lord Torgils turned to rejoin his men. He saw Birger frown in frustration that he had not been the one to take the challenge.

One day, thought Erik grimly as he looked after the Lord High Constable, I will beat you.

After the morning prayers and after breaking fast, the queen, her ladies, the princesses and Kristina adjourned to the queen's chamber.

"Did you sleep well, Kristina?" asked the queen. As was her habit, she did not wait for an answer before she continued. "From now on you will work alongside us, and you will take religious lessons with my children. So, let us start spinning the wool that arrived yesterday," she instructed curtly. "You have to finish your allotment before supper."

The ladies were already at their spinning wheels, while the queen, who detested spinning, sat down before her embroidery frame. Lady Constance motioned for Kristina to sit down by an empty spinning wheel next to the princesses. Kristina stared into the basket on the floor beside her. There was more wool than even a skillful spinner could work in two days. Then, to her relief, she realized that she was sharing the basket with the two princesses. Without acknowledging Kristina, Ingeborg bent down and took a handful of the fluffy wool and started her wheel with a sigh. Kristina took a handful as well. It was fine wool and it spun into a thin and even thread between her fingers. At the touch of the wool, she felt herself relax.

One of the ladies began humming a tune in which everyone joined. The tune was like a magical spell that followed the sound of the spinning wheels, and Kristina felt surprisingly comfortable in her new environment, humming along with the other women. They sat working for a long time without talking, almost hypnotized by the soft, monotonous sounds.

After a while, Kristina cast a glance at the princesses' wheels and saw that not only were they spinning slowly but their threads were uneven. For a moment she felt triumphant, but she quickly realized that she would have to spin even faster if they were to finish before supper.

As the hours wore on, the women began to gossip. Kristina listened with interest as they discussed who was to marry whom, and of what their dowries consisted. Lady Borg Ulfsdotter was to leave the court the following month to marry the powerful, and considerably older, Lord Abjorn Sixtensson. Lady Borg was a member of Kristina's own clan, but Kristina had never met her, as their estates were far apart. The bride-to-be was a rotund and cheerful woman whom Kristina liked on sight; and Kristina was happy that Lord Abjorn was to be her husband. Lord Abjorn was her father's closest friend and had been a frequent visitor to Kristina's home. She had known and loved him for as long as she could remember. Even Kristina, as young as she was, realized that a marriage alliance between two such powerful clans was a fine marriage indeed. She could also sense that Lady Borg would be sorely missed at court when she left to become mistress over Lord Abjorn's domains.

"It will not be long until Ingeborg leaves us, as well," said the queen.

"Not until I am fifteen," protested Princess Ingeborg.

"She is to marry King Erik Menved of Denmark," chimed in Lady Constance while glancing at Kristina, proud to bear such splendid news to someone who might not yet have heard it.

"It is hardly news," said Ingeborg dismissively. "I have been betrothed for so many years already, just like Birger. He is to marry King Erik Menved's sister so the Danish and the Swedish royal families will be doubly tied to one another. This way we will have no more wars," she concluded. The words sounded well-rehearsed to Kristina, but she wondered how the young princess really felt about these arrangements.

"And who will Prince Erik marry?" Lady Borg wondered aloud.

"Nothing has been decided," replied the queen. "But he will be the Duke of Sweden when he comes of age, so he can pick among any of the princesses. It is unfortunate that the Norwegian king and queen do not yet have any children. That would be the ideal match. The whole of Scandinavia would be allied then."

"And Prince Valdemar? And Princess Rikissa? Do they know whom they are to marry, your Majesty?" ventured Kristina bravely.

"Not yet," said the queen. "Rikissa could marry any of the North German princes. But Valdemar is not as fortunate. As he is the third son and will not receive a title nor the lands that go with it, he could probably do no better than to marry some Scandinavian nobleman's daughter. He must find a rich girl who wants a royal connection. And you, Kristina? Has your father found you a husband yet?"

Kristina blushed and shook her head. "Not yet, your Majesty."

"Lord Torgils is rich and powerful. He should have no problem arranging a fine marriage for you."

"Yes, Ma'am." Kristina knew that the queen was right. And yet, she had always hoped to marry for love, as in the ballads.

Lady Borg was the first to finish all the wool in her basket, and when she had, she came over to examine Kristina's handiwork. "You are a fine spinner, Kristina," she said with open admiration.

Kristina blushed at the compliment, mumbled her thanks, and bent over her work with renewed eagerness. But her efforts did not save her and the princesses from having to stay after the other ladies had left for supper. The queen had said nothing as she left, but her parting look was a burning accusation of incompetence. Silently, the three girls spun as fast as they could, and before long they were finished.

Princess Ingeborg looked appraisingly at Kristina. "You certainly did your share," she admitted. "Without you, we would not have gotten any supper." Before Kristina could respond, the princesses left the room.

Later that night, Kristina snuggled under the covers in her frigid cubicle. Her father had been too busy to bid her good night. Again, she felt tears burn her eyes. How she wished that she were back at Lena.

Chapter 2

Some days later, Birger, Erik and Valdemar collapsed at a table by the welcoming fire in the Hall to begin their lessons. Father Nils surveyed their pallid faces and chain mail shirts. His thin, angular face took on a look of disapproval.

"Ever since the Regent arrived you have been falling behind in your studies. How can you concentrate when you are this tired?" he asked, shaking his head. "And why do you come to me dressed in armor? This is a place of learning, not a soldiers' camp."

"Lord Torgils has ordered us to wear the chainmail at all times," ventured Birger. "We are even to sleep in it."

"I do not pretend to understand soldiers' ways, but I do know how difficult it is to learn anything when one is uncomfortable and tired."

"Father Nils," pleaded Erik. "Lord Torgils has given us an order as our teacher, and you, if anyone, will understand that we have to obey his command."

Father Nils looked at Erik who had clearly won the point. "You had better stay awake, or the queen will hear of it," he said tersely. The boys straightened up and did their best to look alert. "Now that you have begun your martial training, do you know why you are doing it?"

"To become the best jousters in Sweden?" suggested Valdemar.

"No," Father Nils fervently objected. "A Christian knight takes up his sword to serve God. He fights to protect his Christian brothers and to help anyone who is weaker and cannot defend himself against injustice. Lord Torgils, like other crusaders before him, fights to make heathens discover the true God, to enable them to enter His kingdom, thereby saving them from eternal damnation. You, King Birger, will fight to keep your people safe from those who attempt to conquer them and starve their families. You, my princes will fight to support your brother in his noble cause. If you become great jousters along the way, that is good sport, but hardly the reason for learning weaponry."

"King Birger, you head a great and proud country," he continued as he unfurled a large map which he fastened to the wall. "You know this map of Scandinavia well by now, but I do not think we have ever looked at it from a military standpoint. The large Scandinavian Peninsula belongs to three countries. Sweden holds the eastern part, Norway the western, while Denmark holds the southern tip as well as land and several islands on the other side of the Ore Strait. Geographically, Norway is the largest country. Norway is not, however, the mightiest of the three. That honor belongs to the smallest of the Scandinavian countries, Denmark, since she has as many inhabitants as Sweden and Norway combined; and her location, as you can see, is the most advantageous. She has territory on both sides of the waterway leading into the Baltic, through which those who wish to trade with the North German principalities, the Hansa cities, the Swedish eastern seaports, Finland and Russia, must sail. She can demand tribute from any one who wants to enter her waters, and her coffers are much richer than Norway's and ours combined. In addition, Denmark has close alliances with the North German principalities and the Hanseatic trading cities, all of which would be landlocked should Denmark decide not to allow their ships to pass."

"Sweden is fortunate to have Lodose as a sea port on its west coast so that we are not totally dependent on passage through Danish waters. Nevertheless, most of our trading ships come from our largest and most important town, and as Stockholm is located on the east coast we frequently need to sail through the Danish straits. With the two approaching royal marriages between Sweden and Denmark, our friendship is sealed. This will be beneficial to both countries. For us, trade becomes easier and less expensive. For Denmark, she gets a reliable ally on her northern border, an ally who in the past has exhibited strong interest in ruling the Danish territory on the southern tip of the Scandinavian peninsula. Sweden might not be as powerful as Denmark; but Sweden could, if so inclined, give Denmark a long and costly war--a war Sweden could win were she to ally herself with Norway--a possibility that these marriages should now eliminate.

"Sweden is, however, presently on good terms with Norway, so today, but for the war in Finland to the east, we live in peace. And that war will end as soon as the heathens there discover the true God. So, you might ask who are our enemies? Who could attack us? Hardly the Finns, since they have neither the martial skills nor the central authority to assemble a large enough army.

"But this peaceful picture can change at any moment, as you well know," continued Father Nils. "The slightest provocation, intentional or otherwise, can set off a war. One consolation is that Sweden is difficult to conquer as she is a large nation and has many fortified castles. Your father, King Magnus, left you a strong and united country, King Birger," Father Nils concluded. "So, while martial training for you lads is not aimed at creating fine jousters, I pray for your sakes that it is all for which you will ever use your skills."

The days had passed one very much like the other, and Kristina had become accustomed to the routine. No one was unkind or disrespectful. Everyone simply kept their distance, as if they did not know how to treat her. She was not a royal family member, but because of her father's position she ranked above the other noble ladies. Her unclear status isolated her, leaving her terribly lonely. Every meal she sat at the far end of the children's table, listening to them talk among themselves. She worked alongside the princesses in the queen's chamber, and she took religious lessons with all the royal children, yet none of them spoke to her, nor did she dare to initiate a conversation herself. She did not think they meant to be unkind. They just did not care if she were there or not. As soon as the lessons were over, the three princes would run off together and the two princesses would whisper together at their spinning wheels.

The only friend she had was the baker's assistant. The morning after Ragna had given her the piece of bread, Kristina had gone down to the kitchen very early to find Ragna alone, lighting the ovens. She had thanked her and given her the finest silk ribbon she owned. The girl had been flabbergasted by the beautiful gift and had almost cried with excitement as she let the soft material glide between her fingers.

"I have never owned anything so lovely," she had whispered over and over.

After that, Ragna had made sure that Kristina had everything she could wish for. She spoke to her friends among the servants and they saw to it that Kristina had new, thick down covers and pillows on her bed, a warm drink beside it at night, and someone to wake her in the morning--all creature comforts for which Kristina would never have dared to ask. From Ragna she also learned about everyone in the castle, and those short moments of gossip before the kitchen filled with people became the best moments of Kristina's day.

At meals, when the household gathered in the Hall, Kristina would sit quietly listening, learning as much as she could about what was occurring in Sweden and abroad. She loved the musicians who played during meals, and was fascinated by the lavish courses of pheasant, wild boar, pig, moose, venison, reindeer, hare, trout, salmon, eel, herring, hake, sole, halibut, goose, capon, pigeon, swan, heron, and any other game that could be hunted in the country. Every day the meals ended with wonderful and rare sweets: almond cream, hot apples and pears in sugar candy, wafers, dates, dried fruits, and an infinite variety of other confections.

The many courses were served from heavy platters and placed in front of each guest on large slices of bread used as eatable plates. These "trenchers" were baked with different spices to color them: saffron for yellow, sandalwood for pink, and parsley for a green shade. Kristina had learned that the uneaten bread slices soaked with juices from the different courses would later be consumed by the servants. Since most of the food was eaten with the fingers, bowls with rose-scented water were offered intermittently for the guests to wash their hands. Kristina did not remember the name of the nobleman who served as the Ewerer--the one who carried the washing bowl and towels to the king and the royal family--but she assumed he must be from a high-ranking clan to hold such an honorable position. She saw that Lord Abjorn attended as the Cupbearer serving the wine; and another powerful lord acted as the Panter, cutting and serving the king's bread; and still another nobleman served as the Carver of the meat and fowl for the dais tables.

On Kristina's birthday, her father was away and no one else knew the significance of the day for her. As she sat by the supper table, her silver goblet filled with fine wine and a freshly roasted quail on her trencher, she felt an uncontrollable urge to cry. Unnoticed, she stood up and left the Great Hall. She ran up the stairs and sat down on the cold floor of the upstairs corridor to allow her tears to flow freely.

She did not know how long she had been sitting there, crying unabashedly, when she heard a low growl by her shoulder. She lifted her head and saw the gleaming teeth of a huge dog only an inch from her face. She froze, and instantly stopped crying. Another large mastiff, growling even more ferociously, came to join the first. She had no idea how to placate them.

"Ajax! Cupid! Here!" a boy's voice commanded. The dogs moved away. Slowly, she looked up to see Prince Erik standing in front of her with the dogs by his side. "I am sorry if they scared you. They were just protecting their territory. You are sitting outside my door," he added in explanation. Kristina remained paralyzed and unable to speak. "They really meant you no harm, I promise," he said.

Kristina met the steady blue gaze of her savior. Erik stood tall beside the dogs, his silver blond hair reaching to his shoulders, dressed in a rich, blue tunic with a silver dagger in his belt. His smile was comforting, and Kristina thought that she had never seen a more handsome boy. Though he was only slightly older than she, he seemed so very grown-up.

"Come," he said as he reached out his hand and pulled her to her feet. "The dogs do not know you very well. Ajax! Cupid! Come here and meet Lady Kristina!" he commanded. The dogs obediently moved closer. They started wagging their tails when Kristina reached out to pet them, and she felt her fear melt away. "Why were you crying?" Erik asked bluntly.

"I was feeling lonely," she confessed aloud to her total surprise.

Erik looked at her and smiled. "This is the first time I have heard your voice. We thought you could not speak since you never said a word to us."

"You did not say very much yourself," Kristina shot back.

"And you have a temper, too," laughed Erik. Kristina looked down at the floor, feeling embarrassed. "But you are right. We probably have not made you feel very welcome. We are so used to just being amongst ourselves. We have never been with other children."

She had been correct in thinking that they did not mean to hurt her feelings, and she was grateful to hear Erik say so.

"Are you going to stop crying now?" he asked. "If you want, you can come and watch us practice at arms on the morrow," he offered as he walked down the corridor.

Kristina felt as if her body was blushing all the way from her head to her toes. Finally, one of the royal children had spoken to her. That was the best birthday present she could have wished for.

Erik noticed Kristina the moment she sat down on a bench by the wall from which she could observe the knights in training. She was impossible to miss, with her bright red, fur-lined cape tightly wrapped around her, and her blond curls sticking out from under the hood. At first, Lord Torgils looked surprised by her presence, but then he seemed pleased at her interest.

"You must put more aggression into your moves," he called to his men. "Think about someone you loathe, or someone who has sworn to kill you. Anything that makes you move with something resembling vigor."

The knights redoubled their attacks, which brought a satisfied grunt from the Lord High Constable as a reward for their efforts. When he finally called off the exercises, the knights rushed to the refreshment table.

"Hello Kristina," Erik called as he walked past her towards the Hall for the lessons with Father Nils. She smiled shyly. His brothers looked at him in surprise before they mumbled their own greetings and disappeared into the warmth of the castle.

The following morning when Kristina took up her customary last-place position in the procession to the chapel, Princess Ingeborg turned toward her and beckoned, "Walk with us, Kristina." The princesses said nothing further, but Kristina assumed that they must have noticed their brothers' greetings and did not want to behave differently. Kristina felt as if she had broken through some invisible wall.

Later in the morning, as the ladies returned to the queen's chamber after breaking fast, Kristina noticed that Ingeborg looked unusually pale. She was slower than ever at her handiwork and she kept closing her eyes and pressing her fingers hard against her temples. Naturally, the queen noticed and came over to look at Ingeborg's embroidery frame.

"You have hardly done any work during the past hour, and what you have done is not fit for an altar cloth in our chapel," she scolded. "What is wrong with you?"

"My head aches terribly," said Ingeborg in a frail voice.

"We will ask the herb woman to give you something that you can finish in time for the Archbishop's visit."

Rikissa volunteered to visit the herb woman. She returned with a mug full of steaming liquid that she gave to Ingeborg who swallowed the foul-smelling brew while wrinkling her nose.

As the hours went by Kristina could see that Ingeborg was feeling no better. On the contrary, she looked quite ill. When the ladies were ready to go down for supper, the queen again scrutinized Ingeborg's work. "No improvement, I see," she chided. "You better stay here and keep on working. I will have some food brought to you."

Kristina was sent back up with a tray of food, and as she entered she found Ingeborg vomiting by the window.

"Let me get the surgeon." Kristina exclaimed, "You need something much stronger than what the herb woman gave you." she turned to run out, but Ingeborg stopped her.

"No, please. Mother will be furious with me. She thinks that I pretend to be sick to avoid my work. And look at what I have done. I tried to be sick out the window, but I did not make it in time."

"Do not worry," said Kristina softly. "I will clean it up. Just lie down and rest."

Ingeborg sat down on the queen's bed, her face ashen. Slowly, she closed her eyes and lowered herself against the many pillows. Kristina fetched water and napkins from the queen's commode and cleaned up Ingeborg's mishap. After she had run down to the kitchen to secure Ragna's help in having the napkins cleaned, she went to the Hall where everyone was seated and would be enjoying supper for hours to come. Discreetly, she approached Brother Gregory to request his help.

"Why all this secrecy?" he asked kindly once he had joined the girls in the queen's chamber.

"Mother will think that I am exaggerating," Ingeborg whimpered as she tried to sit up.

"I do not think you are exaggerating," said Brother Gregory after examining her. "I can see that you have a fearsome headache, but I have a remedy. I will be back shortly," he said as he stroked Ingeborg's cheek.

Kristina, who had stood back from the bed, was studying Ingeborg's embroidery frame. The queen had been right. The work was pitiful. Kristina sat down and started to pull at the threads to correct the mistakes.

"Kristina, are you still here?" asked Ingeborg in her pained voice.

"Yes, I am here," answered Kristina and walked over to the bed.

"Please, do not leave me," pleaded Ingeborg.

"I will not leave you," said Kristina as she sat down next to her.

Brother Gregory returned with a cup of liquid that he helped Ingeborg to swallow. She had difficulty not vomiting again, but she drank it slowly to the last drop. "Now you go to sleep, little one," he said soothingly. "You will feel better when you awake." Brother Gregory smiled at Kristina. "I will inform the queen that I gave Princess Ingeborg an ergot brew and that she needs to rest. You should eat the food on the tray and stay with her."

He left the chamber on silent feet and Kristina ate hastily from the tray before she returned to Ingeborg's embroidery frame. Later, when she heard footsteps in the corridor, she quickly put aside Ingeborg's frame and turned to her own. As the queen came bursting through the door Kristina looked up innocently.

"It was good of you to stay with Ingeborg," said the queen nodding her approval. "Brother Gregory told me that she suffers from the Devil's Curse. My poor mother used to get those headaches too. And Ingeborg can make up for her lost work tomorrow."

Ingeborg was eventually carried to her room where she slept through the afternoon and night. Kristina, on the other hand, spent much of the night at Ingeborg's embroidery frame, which she brought to her father's chamber, her needle tracing the intricate pattern until she had done more work than Ingeborg could have done in an entire day.

The following morning she heard Ingeborg take a deep breath as she sat down by her frame. "Did you do this for me?" she asked in an astonished whisper.

"I did not want your mother to remain cross with you," said Kristina dismissively.

"How can I ever thank you?" whispered Ingeborg. "No one has ever been so kind to me."

Saturday was Kristina's favorite day, a preference the princesses shared. The morning was taken up bathing and caring for one's clothes. Once supper was over they would have to work for only two hours before their religious lessons.

The three girls sat in front of the fire in the princesses' chamber, combing their wet hair before the warming flames. Ever since Ingeborg's illness, Kristina had been welcomed in their circle. After Ingeborg's hair was partly dried she twisted it around rolls of linen cloth to make it wave the way she liked. Rikissa was the first to finish since her long straight hair only required the minimum amount of brushing to fall soft and shiny down her back. Kristina tugged at her myriad curls that defied her efforts, until Rikissa took over and formed them into long spiraling ringlets.

Later Kristina mended their dresses where needed, Rikissa brushed and sponged out spots on their tunics, while Ingeborg polished their everyday silver jewelry.

"Kristina," said Ingeborg suddenly turning serious. "I asked one of the servants where you slept, and she told me you are staying in that miserable little cubicle next to the audience chamber. Rikissa and I would love for you to share our room, if you would like to."

"I would like nothing better," exclaimed Kristina with a gasp of pleasure.

"There is plenty of room in our bed," Ingeborg added pointing at their large bed in the corner of the room.

"Let us go and pick up your things," offered Rikissa.

"But what will the Queen say?" asked Kristina, looking worried.

"She will have no objection," said Ingeborg. "She thinks that you have been a good influence on us. Even I sew better now after you spent time to teach me."

"Then let us get my things," called Kristina as she rushed out with them following her down the corridor to her cubicle. Together they collected Kristina's few worldly goods and hurried back.

"You can put your chest next to ours," instructed Ingeborg. "And you can put your shoes over there. And your jewelry box can go here," she continued as she went around arranging Kristina's belongings about the room.

Later that night, lying in the large, comfortable bed with Ingeborg and Rikissa sleeping next to her, Kristina put her hands together and thanked God for answering her prayers. She had a new home, surrounded by new friends. She was living like a real princess. What possible ill could befall her in such a safe and beautiful place?

Birger absentmindedly scratched himself under the chain mail that touched his neck.

"You are still not used to your chain-mail?" asked Lord Torgils.

"I do not think one ever gets used to it," answered Birger as he studied the chessboard between them. "But at least you are not forcing us to wear it all the time, as you did at first."

"Check mate," said the Lord High Constable as he moved his last bishop.

"Oh, no!" protested Birger. "How could I have missed that?"

"You relaxed after you took my queen and my other bishop. That was a great mistake."

The princes were sitting by the fire in the Hall after supper. Between them and Lord Torgils stood a magnificent chess board that the Lord High Constable used as a teaching tool, as much for logic as for chess. Again and again, he drilled them in the fundamental principles of the game: Make a plan, be willing to sacrifice, and never, ever be taken by surprise. Easy rules, but terribly hard to follow, thought Erik, who so far had lost every game he had played against Lord Torgils. Still he loved these times together with his brothers and the Lord High Constable.

Lord Torgils had spent as much time with them as he could manage, and Erik sensed that he was proud of their progress in the knightly skills, though he was short on praise. He took great pains in explaining everything about which they asked. They all admired him greatly, and unhesitatingly followed whatever he bade them to do. The only one who had any reservations was Birger. As he was fully aware of his own youth and inexperience, he resented Lord Torgils' fluent command of every decision as well as his occasional failure to ask Birger's royal permission to act, even though Birger knew that for the Regent, obtaining consent was only a matter of etiquette. He confessed these feelings to Erik and Valdemar one night.

"Think about how lucky you are to have someone like him to learn from," countered Valdemar. "Father trusted Lord Torgils completely and there is no competition between the two of you. You are the king and he is an experienced statesman who is temporarily in charge. Learn, until you surpass him one day."

Erik had been impressed by Valdemar's sensible advice, and he saw that Birger was, too.

"You put it very clearly. It is just that because I am king I feel I must show that I can lead . . . that I already know the answers. I have no idea if I will ever be as good as our father or Lord Torgils."

"Not everyone thinks Lord Torgils makes all the right decisions," said Erik as he supportively put his arm around Birger. "The Church thinks he does everything wrong. During Father's reign the Church paid no taxes, and they had other privileges, which Torgils has now revoked. The nobility, on the other hand, thinks he is an excellent ruler because he has given them greater privileges than before. It all depends on where you stand. But I think that Lord Torgils is a clever ruler because he has succeeded in keeping a balance between the factions. You will eventually learn to do the same."

After that rare conversation in which he had openly confessed his insecurities, Birger never brought up the subject again. Together with his brothers, he hung on every word Lord Torgils uttered and tried to absorb as much as he could.

"Now one last game. It is your turn, Erik, is it not?" Lord Torgils asked.

This time Erik planned to use the move he had seen Father Nils open with a day earlier in the game he had won against Lord Abjorn, a skillful opponent. Erik quickly played his knight forward and Lord Torgil's looked puzzled as he sat back to ponder the move. It did not take long for Erik to cry out "Oh, damnation," as Lord Torgils again checkmated him.

"It was an interesting opening, though," said Lord Torgils as he stood up and stretched his long legs.

The Hall was busy as usual at this time of night. Father Nils was deeply engrossed in a conversation with a visiting bishop at one of the tables while six knights were throwing dice. The queen, a few of her ladies, and the three girls were listening to a visiting bard singing a new ballad about a young knight saving his lady from some dreadful fate only to learn that he was not high-born enough for her. The girls looked deeply disappointed.

"He should be able to marry her after all he endured for her sake," lamented Ingeborg.

"There are rules, my dear," insisted the queen. "But let us hear a song which ends happily, otherwise the girls will not sleep."

Kristina and Ingeborg looked at one another. Did the queen know how late they whispered in bed at night? Or how they would sit by the window on moonlit nights and dream? She would surely be furious if she knew, and would berate them for wasting so much time fantasizing about what love would be like. Even Rikissa grew testy when she could not sleep because of their giggles and whispers. But as the queen said nothing more, the girls guessed their secret was safe and smiled at Rikissa in gratitude. From Rikissa's expression, they knew that she expected something very special in return for her silence and loss of sleep.

The bard began to sing of the Blue Knight and the Lady of the Glen, the most romantic of ballads, and Ingeborg let her embroidery fall into her lap. The queen cleared her throat and shot a glance at her eldest daughter who quickly bent over her work while Kristina and Rikissa started to sew even faster.

"Sing some new ballad," said Lord Torgils, turning to the bard who had finished his last tale, leaving the women teary-eyed. "You have been all the way down in Italy, I hear."

"Still, some of the best ballads are from the North," smiled the bard. He struck a chord on his lute and started singing the ballad of The Evil Prince. Lord Torgils grimaced as if to stop him, and the queen almost spoke, but both remained silent as he strummed his instrument and his clear voice intoned the sad tale. It told of a prince who killed his older brother, the king, and then took over the rule of the kingdom. Not only did he murder his brother, but he also refused to honor the dowry payments of the dead king's daughters.

"I think it is bedtime for you girls!" said the queen once the bard had finished.

The children started to protest but knew the look on their mother's face well enough not to argue. Reluctantly they left the Hall while the queen drilled her eyes into the bard.

"You surely know that my daughter is to marry King Erik Menved of Denmark. How could you sing about the Danish royal family's misdeeds? She will be frightened to death."

"I am sorry if I erred," said the bard. "But it is an old ballad, and it never mentions Denmark. I am surprised if she has not heard it before. Also, it is about the present kings' granduncles. It has little bearing on life at the Danish court today."

"Let us not forget that the present king's father was murdered as well!" snapped the queen. "We have forbidden the ballad at our court so as not to frighten Ingeborg before she is old enough to understand why things happened as they did."

"Ingeborg is a levelheaded girl," interjected Lord Torgils. "I am sure she will understand that incidents long past will not necessarily be repeated."

"Why were we so suddenly sent to bed?" asked Rikissa as the girls entered their room.

"Perhaps it was the ballad," ventured Kristina. "Both the queen and my father did not seem to like it."

"I know why they asked us to leave," said Ingeborg as she closed the door behind them. "The incident in the ballad took place in Denmark. I heard them speak of it as we left."

"In Denmark?" asked Rikissa looking concerned. "Will you live among people like that?"

"It seems so," said Ingeborg as she sat down on the bed.

"I am sure it will never happen again," said Kristina supportively.

"I would loathe to live in a family where they think so little of women that they stain their honor for lack of a dowry," said Rikissa. "Why would the new king be so vengeful when he had gained the kingdom and its riches? Maybe an evil streak runs in the family?"

"Rikissa!" exclaimed Kristina with unusual sharpness. "Please, do not talk like that when you can see how frightened Ingeborg is."

"If you marry King Erik Menved it is the will of God," said Rikissa firmly. "If that is what He demands of you, you must obey."

"I know my duty," said Ingeborg. "It is just that I am afraid of going to Denmark alone, without anyone I know."

"I will come with you," Kristina offered.

"I doubt Mother would allow that. You are the best spinner and the quickest one with the needle, she will never let you leave."

"It is for my father to decide," suggested Kristina hopefully.

"He will do what mother wants," said Rikissa bluntly.

"Rikissa is probably right," said Ingeborg. "Only when it comes to your marriage will your father decide."

The girls went to bed. Rikissa, as usual, put her crucifix beside her on the night table.

"Dear God," she whispered touching it. "Please let Ingeborg be happy in Denmark and find true friends there who will love her as much as Kristina and I do. Amen."

"Thank you," said Ingeborg. "I pray He hears you."

Kristina could not concentrate on Father Nils' words when she saw the blue skies and the sun shining outside the windows of the Great Hall. She could feel that almost irrational yearning Northerners experience when the days get ever longer and warmer in the spring. She had already seen delicate flowers poking up their colorful heads wherever the sun had melted the snow. The earth on the open fields smelled fertile and rich, and the pine scent from fir trees floated into the courtyard. Though the sun was shining brightly, it was still cold, and the air held a deliciously fresh chill, just perfect for running and frolicking in the forest, Kristina thought longingly. She and the other children could not wait to get outside the castle in which they had been virtually imprisoned during the long and dark winter months. Of course, they had played outdoors making snow castles and giant snow knights to which they had added Lord Torgil's spare armor to frighten any unwelcome visitor. But the days had been short with only a few hours of light, so just as they began to enjoy their games it was time to go inside, as bears and wolves roamed closer to human dwellings under the cover of darkness.

Even darker had been the mood of the people within the castle, testy from the lack of daylight, fresh air, fresh meat and vegetables, and the over-abundance of salted food. The air in the castle was stifling, heavy of human smells and smoke. How Kristina longed to escape it all! She looked around and noted that she was not the only one who found it difficult to concentrate on Father Nils' lesson on this glorious day.

"I will only ask one more time," said Father Nils, raising his voice in an attempt to command their attention. "Which one of Jesus' followers betrayed him before the rooster had crowed three times?"

"It was Peter," Rikissa answered quickly.

"Thank you, little one," said Father Nils. "It seems that only you have read your text for today. You may be excused while I continue my lesson with these other five." The children's faces took on such gloom that he laughed out loud. "All right. Go, all of you. It is a lovely day, and I cannot blame you for not paying attention. But do read your text for tomorrow!"

"Thank you, Father Nils," they sang in chorus as they ran to don their mantles and draw on thick boots. Laughing, they ran out into the courtyard.

"Let us go and pick flowers," suggested Ingeborg. "The sunny field behind the castle should be filled with them by now."

"You do that," encouraged Birger. "We will go hunting."

The girls were about to leave when they heard their mother's and Lord Torgils' voices behind them. "Why are you not with Father Nils?" Queen Helvig demanded.

"He let us go early since it is such a lovely day," Rikissa answered with a sweet smile. "I suppose it was a reward for our diligent studies."

"We will pick some flowers for you" volunteered Ingeborg.

"Do not venture beyond the large meadow, though," Lord Torgils warned. "The wolves are still roaming abroad."

"We promise," called the girls as they ran towards the drawbridge.

"The same applies to you, lads," called Lord Torgils. "Stay out of the forest!" The boys looked at one another. Where else but in the forest could they hunt? Sometimes older people showed so little sense.

The three girls raced down the castle hill and along the muddy road. They climbed over a stone fence leading to the sunny meadow where they had always found snowdrops in the spring. This year was no different, and they happily gathered the fragile flowers into bouquets. Ingeborg called out from the far side of the meadow with excitement in her voice: "Look, there are wood anemones here. So early."

Rikissa and Kristina eagerly joined her in picking the pretty white flowers. Before they realized it they found themselves on the forest path, which was lined with the delicate flowers.

"We are forbidden to go into the forest," said Rikissa as she stood up to look around. "I think we better go back to the meadow."

"Let us pick just a few more," Ingeborg pleaded as she bent down to add to her bouquet.

Kristina did not see the harm in gathering just a few more, and eagerly followed Ingeborg, as did Rikissa, finding more and bigger flowers. The next time they looked up, however, they were deep in the forest.

"We are almost by the pond," said Ingeborg. "We might as well see if any of the hepatica are blooming on the other side."

"We have gone far enough as it is," said Rikissa.

"Rikissa is right," said Kristina. "If we go back now nobody will find out that we disobeyed." As she spoke she caught a movement out of her left eye, but when she turned her head she saw nothing, only the wind rustled the fragile branches of the bushes. Kristina felt a shiver down her back. "Let us go now," she said aloud.

"What was that?" asked Rikissa at almost the same moment. "I saw something move over there."

"So did I," confessed Kristina with heightened anxiety, as the movement had come from behind them, blocking their escape back to the meadow. Just then Kristina caught a movement again, only this time when she looked it did not go away. There, not twenty yards behind them stood an enormous wolf. "Behind us!" she whispered frantically.

The three girls stood still, frozen next to one another. They knew that wolves rarely traveled alone, so if one was near, others were not far away.

"Can we go back?" asked Rikissa in a whisper.

"No," whispered Ingeborg as the wolf moved behind a stone farther down the path.

Kristina knew that the animal must be at least as cautious as they were, but the difference between them was that he looked hungry and would soon overcome his restraint.

"We must do something quickly," she whispered, not knowing what it could be.

"Rikissa, can you remember where the cave is that the boys showed us last year?"

"It is right about there," pointed Rikissa. Kristina saw nothing but moss and boulders on the high sloping rock wall. She felt her heart sink.

"You are right," nodded Ingeborg. "Let us walk there slowly."

Kristina forced herself not to run as fast as she could, because if they ran the wolf would follow his instinct and pursue them, and she had no doubt which would be the swiftest. Slowly and close together, they moved toward the rock wall, all the while gripping their bouquets and looking towards the spot where they had last seen the wolf. Once they reached the rocky wall they started to climb up the boulders. Several times they saw the dark shadow of the wolf cautiously glide ever closer between trees and bushes.

They continued to climb, and Rikissa who was in the lead sighed in relief: "It is here, just as I remembered." Kristina saw her disappear behind a huge stone, closely followed by Ingeborg. It was dark behind the boulder and Kristina could not see much when she entered the cave through its low opening. As her eyes became accustomed to the darkness she saw that it was a small cave and that snares and traps were piled up against the back wall.

"My brothers use this for storing hunting gear. Let us hope they left something with which we can defend ourselves," Ingeborg said hopefully.

Kristina momentarily peered from the safety of the cave and saw the wolf standing down by the foot of the rock wall, staring up at her with hungry eyes. Kristina quickly drew her head in, her heart beating faster. When her eyes readjusted to the darkness of the cave, she could see that Ingeborg and Rikissa were holding long staves that were used for setting up snares. "This is all we have to fight him. If we poke him in the nose he will stay at a distance," said Ingeborg trying to sound valiant.

Kristina knew that the princesses were as frightened as she was, and she wanted to make them all feel better. "He is still at the foot of the rockpile."

"Just wait until it gets dark," mumbled Ingeborg.

"We must call for help," said Rikissa. "Some hunter might be nearby."

Desperately they called for help, and when Kristina next looked down she saw the large wolf gracefully jump up on the boulders and slowly move up towards them, his eyes now gleaming fearlessly.

Armed with bows, arrows, and hunting knives, the three princes had set out for the forest. It was still light, so they had no fear of any wild creatures. They had succeeded in killing four rabbits as well as a white weasel, which Erik had nailed with a swift knife-throw as it raced in front of them, nearly invisible against the snow. As they were leisurely returning towards the castle they heard a faint cry. They listened carefully and heard it again.

"It sounds like Rikissa," said Valdemar, concerned.

They found a path and ran along it. Before long they reached the pond. There the cries were clearly audible, but still there was no sign of their sisters or Kristina.

"Where are you?" shouted Erik.

"Here, in the cave," the brothers recognized Ingeborg's voice, trembling with fear, ". . . there's a wolf outside . . ."

The boys looked up towards the sound of the voice, which came from the cave where they kept their traps, and they saw the large beast pacing outside it.

"We are lucky that the wolf is alone and not in a pack," said Erik softly. "But still, a rogue male used to hunting alone is the most ferocious."

"He is big," said Valdemar

"My God," Birger whispered. "What are we going to do?"

"I have an idea," mumbled Erik. Loudly he called to the girls. "Do not worry, we will get that old devil." Then he proceeded to give his brothers instructions.

Birger turned to run deeper into the forest to shinny up a tree and climb out on a limb overhanging the path. Valdemar moved cautiously to a position near the foot of the rock wall to wait for Erik's signal. Erik, in turn, slit the bellies of two of the rabbits and dragged them along the path towards Birger's tree, leaving a trail of blood and guts behind him. When he was just beneath the spot where Birger lay in wait, he left the rabbits on the ground. Then he quickly returned to the pond and saw the huge beast pacing back and forth by the cave at a more agitated speed. Erik raised his arm and Valdemar quickly cut up his rabbits and tossed a few pieces up to the wolf. After a moment of initial surprise, the large beast sniffed them and unhesitatingly devoured them. Valdemar tossed more pieces at different points leading towards the path where Erik had started to drag his rabbits. The smell of blood caught the full attention of the wolf. It quickly descended the rock wall, eating his way down to the path where he picked up the scent and followed it eagerly.

"Hurry!" Valdemar called to the girls. "Get out of the forest." The girls came out pale and shaken and started down to where Valdemar waited for them. "Run back over the field and down to the road. We will catch up with you there," Valdemar called as he ran after the wolf.

The wolf was moving swiftly now, and Valdemar had to put all his strength into the pursuit. Once the wolf came upon the two rabbits in the middle of the path, he stopped and began to tear into the carcasses. Valdemar could see Birger in the tree readying his bow to shoot, when an arrow came flying from the side of the path, striking the large wolf in his ribcage. The beast howled in pain and was immediately struck with an arrow from above that pierced its back. Valdemar's arrow hit its target as well. With a yell of exhilaration, Erik jumped from his hiding place and ran towards the wounded animal that in his pain and rage never saw him. Erik's knife speedily cut its throat, leaving the beast twitching on the ground.

The boys roared in triumph, and Birger jumped to the ground. "What a kill!" he screamed pounding Erik on his back.

"Everyone will be mighty impressed," said Valdemar as he bent down beside the kill.

"We cannot tell anyone," Erik said softly.

"What do you mean?" asked Birger incredulously. "We cannot tell anyone that we killed the largest wolf ever seen in this forest?"

"Precisely," said Erik.

"We were not supposed to be here, remember," said Valdemar. "If Lord Torgils finds out that we disobeyed his orders we will be in serious trouble."

"But we saved the girls," objected Birger.

"We will get them into trouble, as well, if we tell the truth," said Erik.

The three boys stood looking down at the greatest hunting trophy of their lives, heartbroken.

The girls had been too shaken to do anything other than what Valdemar had ordered. They had run through the forest and over the meadow as fast as their legs could bear them until they stood by the roadside, out of breath. Kristina looked down at the bouquet of flowers she was still clutching in her hand. She started to laugh. She had not let go of them through the entire ordeal. Ingeborg and Rikissa looked at her.

"The flowers," laughed Kristina hysterically. "I still have all of my flowers."

The princesses noticed that they, too, were still gripping their bouquets tightly even though they had picked up the long sticks to fight the wolf.

"We are holding ours as well!" exclaimed Rikissa before all three girls began to cry from relief, their arms around each other. Soon, though, they composed themselves, knowing they had to calm down before they got back to the castle lest they be found out. Before long, they saw the boys walking towards them across the meadow.

"You saved our lives," said Ingeborg when her brothers reached them. Her eyes shone with admiration. The boys looked proudly at one another, and then Birger told the girls how they had killed the beast.

"You are so brave!" exclaimed Kristina breathlessly. "And you cut his throat," she said to Erik with a look of adulation.

"We cannot tell anyone what happened today," Erik said sternly.

"You saved our lives and nobody will know?" Rikissa asked in wonderment. She turned to Ingeborg and Kristina. "I would be willing to take whatever punishment Mother can think of, but everyone must know how brave you were."

"The punishment would not be worth the glory," said Erik knowing that Lord Torgils would be unmerciful if he found out they had defied his orders. "This has to remain our secret. But to remind us of what happened today, I took something from the wolf." Erik opened his palm to reveal six enormous and bloody wolf teeth. He ceremoniously handed one to each of them. Then he said: "Repeat after me: I swear always to defend my sisters and my brothers--and that includes you, Kristina--against anyone who threatens them in any way."

The children repeated the oath before Rikissa cried out:

"Look, it is getting dark. We must get back."

They managed to slip unseen into their chambers where the boys washed the blood off their hands and clothes, and just to be safe, changed for supper. The girls arranged the flowers and placed them around the castle.

After the evening meal Kristina noticed that the boys had cleaned their wolf teeth, bored through them, and hung them on their neck chains. "That looks wonderful," she said admiringly.

"We girls cannot wear them like that or Father Nils will accuse us of being pagans," sighed Rikissa. "I guess we will have to hide them in our jewelry boxes."

"Maybe not," said Kristina with a mysterious look.

A few weeks later she presented Ingeborg and Rikissa with her solution. She had asked the blacksmith, a skilled artisan, to carve each tooth into the shape of a fish, the symbol of Saint Peter, so it could be worn on the same chain as their cross.

"You are very clever," Erik whispered to Kristina when the girls proudly showed their new amulets to the boys. Her heart pounded with pleasure and pride.

Chapter 3

Nykoping, Sweden 1293

The royal family returned to Nykoping after passing the summer at Visingso castle, following a year and a half spent in Stockholm, the seat of government.

Erik was happy to be back at his old hunting grounds and looked with pride at the large rabbit he had killed earlier that day and was now skinning. He glanced up at Nykoping castle's guest quarters where he thought he could see a figure standing at a small barred window, looking out at the courtyard.

"That must be Uncle Valdemar," he said aloud.

The boys had heard many stories of how their father had usurped the crown from his older brother, King Valdemar, who was still imprisoned right here in the castle. The boys never grew tired of listening to the tales about their father's coup, even though they knew they had never been told the full story.

"Tell us about Uncle Valdemar," Birger at one time had begged Father Nils.

"That story is not for me to tell you," Father Nils had answered evasively. "Suffice it to say that your father had right on his side when he removed his brother from the throne. Your uncle committed an act so heinous that I find it disturbing even to think of it!"

"If you will not tell us, we will ask him ourselves!" Birger had retorted, intrigued by Father Nils' air of mystery.

"Unless your mother orders it, I doubt you will be allowed to visit him," Father Nils had added.

"I am the king, so if I want to see my uncle I should be able to."

"When you are older you may indeed do as you wish. But for now, you must follow the advice of your mother and Lord Torgils," Father Nils stated before he turned away.

Valdemar followed Erik's gaze up to old King Valdemar's prison window. "I want to hear the full story. Why not make a wager of it? The first one who gets to see him wins," he whispered.

Birger and Erik nodded enthusiastically.

Erik crouched behind a large pillar on the second floor of the guest quarters. He had tried for six days to learn the guard's schedule, but it was not until Kristina introduced him to Ragna whose father was one of the prison guards that he had learned the different shifts. It had been easy to get to the upper floor, but now it seemed their schedule was off as he had been waiting for far longer than anticipated. Just when Erik thought his legs would give out, the guard down the corridor rose from his seat, stretched and yawned before descending the stairs. Erik dashed to the door at which the guard had been posted, took the key from the hook, unlocked the door, and hung the key back before he quietly entered the chamber.

It was a large room, richly decorated in hues of deep blue. Tapestries adorned the walls and fur skins covered the floor. On a table by the open window stood a vase of fresh flowers and a platter of red apples. The room resembled a nobleman's chamber more than a prison cell.

Across the room, King Valdemar rested on a wide bed. As Erik approached, he opened his eyes. "Who are you?" he asked, focusing upon Erik. "I am glad for the company, whoever you are."

Erik smiled uneasily at the sight of the former king, so grateful to chat with any stranger. Erik had only seen his uncle once before, five years earlier, when he arrived to Nykoping castle in chains. Erik could clearly remember his father's face, hard and withdrawn, as he stood in the Hall overlooking the courtyard while his brother was led to captivity.

"Why did you keep up the fight?" his father had mumbled. "Why were you not satisfied with your riches and your freedom in Norway?" Erik thought he had seen the glimmer of a tear in the corner of his eye, but he must have been mistaken because King Magnus had turned away, saying "May that traitor rot in his cell!"

Erik walked over to his uncle. "I am Erik Magnusson, your nephew."

"Ah, you are indeed a Folkung," nodded old King Valdemar, referring to their clan name, as he scrutinized the eleven-year old boy standing tall before him. This youth had the air of a boy who knew he was special, a secure, uncompromising bearing. "You look like a young lion," he continued. "Like my father, Birger Jarl, when he was young. The same look of a true ruler. I pray you will be a good king."

"You are mistaken, uncle," Erik said. "It is my older brother, Birger, who is the king."

"Indeed," smiled the old man. "But then, things can change," he seemed to disappear into his own world before he asked, "Why have you come?"

"My brothers and I want to know why my father dethroned you."

"Your elders did me a kindness not to tell you," chuckled his uncle. "You see, I did something quite shameful. Something which I regret every waking moment of my life . . ." He drifted away again. Erik thought he appeared quite ill. His skin was grey and his face sunken. The deep red of his worn tunic made him look paler still. Regaining his awareness, he continued, "I have never lacked for anything here. Though I do miss my son and my daughter. But you have come to hear my story. So sit, Erik."

Old King Valdemar pointed to a pair of chairs by the window and slowly got up from his bed. He sat down in one of them and gestured toward a carafe of wine on a small table. "Let us have a cup together," he suggested, and Erik went over and poured two silver chalices to the brim. "I often sit here and watch you practice at arms," said Valdemar as he took his cup and lifted it to his nephew. "I always assumed you were the king since you were the tallest of the boys." He chuckled again and drained his cup. "I was indeed king once, but I did not have the strength of my father, and when the power was placed in my hands, I lost it to my younger brother. He was more like the old man. And now I see you have that same look in your eyes."

"I do not understand," Erik blurted out. "The crown was yours. How can you ever forgive my father?"

"When you have lived over sixty years, as I have, you see things differently. I have had much time to reflect. It is not that I forgive him,

I simply understand why he did what he did. He had a passion for power. I had a different passion . . .Growing up as the chosen king, I was used to having things decided for me, including whom I was to marry. As Regent of Sweden my father, Birger Jarl, believed that our country would benefit from an alliance with our neighbor, Denmark. Well, of course, you know that your grandfather never was King of Sweden, even though he was married to the old king's sister. Still, he managed to have me elected king and he was the interim ruler until I came of age.

"The Danish King, Erik Plogpenning, who had been murdered by his brother, Abel--sometimes called the Evil Prince--had left four daughters. Another uncle of the girls, Kristoffer, who became king after Abel died, was anxious to marry the girls off, but was equally intent on keeping most of their dowries. The oldest princess, Ingeborg, had been promised to Magnus of Norway, and my father picked Princess Sofia for me as she was rumored to be the most beautiful. I married her when I was twenty-one years old, and truly Sofia was beautiful. But she demanded endless praise and attention, and after a few years I tired of her vanity, and turned my attention to other women.

"Despite the fact that I had long come of age, my father continued to rule Sweden as if I did not exist, and by the time he died, the Council was accustomed to ignoring me. My brother Magnus – your father - warned me, but I paid him no heed. I was the king. I had a competent Council to run the affairs of state, and a never-ending choice of women. My life seemed perfect. I saw no need for change. Then Jutta arrived at the Swedish court . . ." old King Valdemar's voice trailed off as he leaned back in his chair and closed his eyes, reliving the moment as if it had been yesterday, rather than so many years ago.

"She was Sofia's younger sister, and from the very first time I saw her I was helplessly drawn to her. She and another of her sisters had become nuns. Their calling was hardly a matter of choice, but rather the result of their insultingly paltry dowries. Jutta had been living at Saint Agnes convent in Denmark. Knowing how unhappy Sofia had been with my father's second wife ruling the household until her death--not to mention the ridicule to which I had exposed her as a result of my philandering--I could hardly object when Sofia implored me to let Jutta stay with us.

And she was an unusual woman. In the convent she studied the classics and kept up with the happenings of the outside world. She was an intelligent and skilled defender of her views and became a favorite of the court not used to a woman with skills usually thought of as a exclusivity within a man's domain. She was not as beautiful as Sophia; but with her knowledge, wit and charm she was nothing but beguiling. She introduced me to my library and all its treasures, which had held little interest to me before.

I fell deeply in love with her, a nun. I made every effort not to let Jutta know how I felt about her, and for some time I was content just to be near her. Everything seemed quite blissful until I realized that she, in turn, loved me. That changed what was placid emotion to turbulent yearning, yet we both knew that we could not consummate our love until she had been released from her vows to the Church.

"I had been chosen King of Sweden--the title was not heredi-tary--so the people, through the Council, could unseat me, were they dissatisfied. Were anyone to discover that I had made love to a nun I would certainly lose my crown. I had nightmares as I thought of the ancient sacrificial rite of killing the king when the country suffered some disaster.

"I wrote a dispatch to the Pope. The reason I gave for my sister-in-law's desire to leave her Order was simple: She wanted to continue serving God, but no longer as a nun. And to prove her sincerity, she wanted to bestow upon the Church a generous gift.

"But in those days no one could be trusted at the court. Your father was searching for something that would enable him to seize the crown, as he thought me poorly equipped for my role as Sweden's ruler. His spies were everywhere, and one of them was the messenger taking my dispatch to Rome. After reading it, Magnus must have suspected the real reason behind my Papal request. He instructed the messenger to proceed at a snail's pace, hoping that I would create a scandal if given enough time. And he was right. We succumbed to our passions. For a time we cunningly outwitted all eyes and ears. But one night one of Magnus' spies caught us making love in the library.

"The gossip spread like wildfire through the court and through-out the country. Already having strong support among the nobles, your father got the churchmen on his side. The kingdom on which

I had spent so little effort and attention was rapidly slipping away from me. I called together the few men I trusted, and their advice was clear: Jutta had to return to her convent and repent for her sins, and I must go on pilgrimage to Rome to seek absolution and prevent my excommunication.

"There are no words to describe the pain I felt when Jutta left our court. I could not envision my life without her, so I wasted no time departing for Rome. The Pope expressed his willingness to consider retribution for my soul if I allowed Holy Mother Church her 'rightful position' in Sweden, a position of formidable power, even over certain decisions of the crown. I saw no alternative. Were I excommunicated, Magnus would have had every justification for dethroning me. Most importantly, the Pope promised that when enough time had passed for the scandal to die down, he would release Jutta from her vows."

"The news of my pact with the Pope reached Sweden before I did, and that was all my brother needed. The nobles did not cherish sharing power with the Church and stood solidly behind him; and the Danes, who were outraged at my heretical actions, joined the Swedish forces. When again I set foot on Swedish soil, I found myself confronted by a formidable army. I fled to Norway from where I tried to regain my crown with the help of some Danes and Norwegians to whom I promised liberal rewards. Together we conquered part of Sweden, but could not hold it for long.

"The Pope did not honor his promise to release Jutta from her vows; and when I found out that she had died, nine years later, I was inconsolable, and my only remaining interest was to regain my crown. I renewed my attacks on Sweden with little success. When Magnus' armies finally captured and imprisoned me, it may seem strange, but I was grateful. Very little outside my prison walls meant anything to me. My wife had died a few years earlier, a deeply embittered woman; and I must have been an embarrassment to both my son who also lived in Norway, and my daughter who was living in Holstein with her husband Count Gerhard. Both had been close to their mother, and neither expressed any desire to see me. But, at least, in my prison, your father, and later Lord Torgils, always treated me well."

With that the old king ended his tale and Erik could see that his eyes were clouded with tears. He sat silent for a long time before he smiled softly. "So, now do you see why I do not really care about losing the crown, when I lost something so much more precious?"

Erik was fascinated by his uncle's tale; but to allow a crown to slip from one's head for a woman, was not only inconceivable to him, but ridiculous. He studied the old man sitting in his chair, calmly sipping his wine, lost in his memories. In the dim afternoon light, it could just as well have been Erik's father sitting there, so strong was the resemblance. But, as Erik well knew, King Magnus had been a man of action, strength, and resolve. King Valdemar was still a dreamer. Erik had always felt that of his brothers, he was the one best suited to rule Sweden. But Birger, being the oldest, was the king and had been chosen when he was only four years old; and Erik had never contemplated any alternative. But now, his uncle's story stirred emotions deep within him. He quietly rose to go to the window, hoping not to disturb the old man who seemed to have fallen asleep. Slowly his uncle opened his eyes.

"It was good of you to visit, my boy," he said nodding. "Please, come back again."

"I managed to sneak past the guards today, but I doubt I will be so lucky again," said Erik as he looked for Ragna who periodically came out into the yard. "I must leave here unseen, or Mother will have me flogged."

"Queen Helvig is as formidable as ever, I see." Valdemar laughed. "She used to have the bravest of knights shaking in their boots."

"She has not changed," said Erik as he spotted Ragna emerging from the kitchen. She looked up and he waved at her. She nodded, and slowly walked over to the guard by the foot of the tower. He could not hear her from the window, but he knew she was luring him and his colleague guarding the door away with the promise of hot tea and fresh bread in the kitchen so that Erik could make his escape. "I must leave," said Erik.

"It is said that every man is the creator of his own destiny," said old King Valdemar with a shrug. "So, you should not feel sorry for me. I live with my memories and they are beautiful."

Erik saw the two guards walking across the yard towards the kitchen. He knew that he had to be quick if he was to leave undetected. He bent down beside his uncle's chair and covered the old man's hand with his own. "I wish you well," he murmured, not knowing what else to say to his kinsman who was imprisoned right under his own roof.

"Go with God," said the old king. "And good luck," he added with a glint in his eye.

"Your Majesty," said Lord Torgils as he seated himself next to the queen in the Hall. He looked over to where the children were huddling, their heads together and talking excitedly. "I am sorry to tell you that one of the princes defied your order not to visit the former king. One of them, I do not know which one, visited him today."

"He will regret that!" she said, readying herself to take the guilty party to task.

"Your Majesty," countered the Regent softly. "Maybe we should not make an issue out of it. The children have no friends besides each other, and naturally they are looking for novel experiences. In many ways they are not like children, but rather like adults in children's bodies. The princesses seem to have benefited from Kristina's arrival. Maybe the princes also need a friend their own age. With your permission I will look for someone suitable."

"Please do," replied the queen with a sigh as she bent over her embroidery.

"You prevailed again," proclaimed Lord Torgils as Erik collapsed on a bench after a grueling hand-to-hand combat. "You have bested both your brothers and every one of your contemporaries, even some of my knights. However, I have another opponent for you."

Erik looked at Lord Torgils with anticipation. This was the moment he would finally beat his mentor, something he had promised himself a long time ago.

"No, it is not me," laughed Lord Torgils as if he had read Erik's thoughts. "You're not ready for that. No, it is someone else."

Lord Torgils' gaze turned to an unfamiliar figure walking toward them across the courtyard. He was at least a head taller than Erik, and his body appeared muscular and lean under his chain mail. The coat of arms on his tunic indicated that he was Lord Kettilmund's son, Mats. He was about the same age as King Birger, and already spoken of with great respect. He bowed deeply to Birger and Valdemar who were resting on a bench nearby.

"I am happy to meet you," Erik said as he reached out his hand.

"And I you, my prince," said Mats as he took Erik's hand in a firm grip. "You have a reputation as a good jouster, and I consider it a privilege to test my sword against yours."

"You flatter me," said Erik modestly, yet pleased with the compliment. "From what I have heard, my humble talents are nothing compared to yours. Now I presume I will discover that to be true. Hand-to hand with swords?"

"My pleasure," smiled Mats as he unsheathed his massive weapon.

Valdemar lifted Erik's sword off the bench and handed it to his brother. The two combatants stood before one another, saluted and faced off. Slowly they circled, gripping their swords with both hands, studying one another, until Erik made a quick attack from which Mats retreated unscathed before he countered and his sword bit into Erik's chain mail with a clang. As Mats' sword was lowered momentarily Erik moved in and ripped into Mats' tunic.

"This is good sport," grinned Mats as he launched another attack causing Erik to retreat. Then Erik quickly stepped to the side and hit Mats hard on the arm with the flat of his blade. Mats' brow furrowed from the sudden pain. He turned and pursued Erik mercilessly with attack after attack. Barely able to defend himself, Erik countered fiercely and forced Mats to step back.

The courtyard was silent; the only sounds to be heard were those of heavy breathing and metal striking metal. Servants and stable boys who had left their chores stood mesmerized behind the knights. Finally, the combatants slowed their furious pace. Their strikes became heavier and more deliberate. Sweat poured down their faces and their breathing turned into grunts. Then suddenly, Mats picked up the pace and managed to strike the sword from Erik's hands with a mighty blow. They both stared as Erik's weapon flew to the ground, halfway across the courtyard. Erik opened his arms in a gesture of defeat, then bowed to Mats.

"You are indeed as great as they say," he admitted. "I have never fought so hard in my life."

"Nor have I, my prince," said Mats with a broad smile as he wiped his forehead. "Any time you want revenge, I will be ready."

Erik, breathing heavily, gestured for Mats to follow him to the refreshment table where he unceremoniously lifted a full pitcher and drank so greedily that the beer poured down his tunic. Mats followed his lead and they finished at the same time. Laughing, they put the pitchers down and wiped their chins.

"My pupil has met his match," Lord Torgils said as he joined them, holding a more moderate mug of beer. "Since Mats has promised a rematch I think we better keep him here with us. What do you think, your Majesty, will he make a worthy addition to our circle of knights?"

"Absolutely!" agreed Birger. "Erik has become unbearably cocky, and we need someone to keep him humble."

"It would be my honor. My king, my princes," Mats said with a deep bow.

Life at Nykoping castle changed from the moment Mats arrived. Birger, Erik, and Valdemar immediately took a liking to the self-effacing and skillful fighter, and the four of them spent most of their waking hours together.

As the men were practicing at arms one morning a rider galloped into the courtyard. Mats lowered his weapon when he saw his family's coat of arms on the rider's tunic. He left his exercise opponent and ran towards the steaming horse. He knew instinctively that his father was dying. "Is he still alive?" he asked of the rider, who nodded.

"But he is badly off," the messenger said, trying to catch his breath.

"Then there is not a moment to waste. Let the princes know where I have gone," Mats called as he ran for the stables.

As he rode on the narrow paths his mind flashed back to life with his father.

The powerful and eccentric nobleman, Lord Kettilmund had taken a careful look at his newborn son and from that moment had centered his whole existence around Mats. His good wife had been surprised by his fatherly devotion since he had shown little interest in his beautiful daughters. But she presumed that fathers and sons formed special bonds. What she did not know was that Lord Kettilmund had seen a special mark on his son, the sign his family had been expecting for generations. When she had suggested that the boy be baptized, her husband had offered some lame excuse to delay it, and when she again reminded him that ill could befall the child were he not under God's protection, he had roared at her to let him handle the boy's welfare. Some time later, when he had returned from a trip to Upsala with young Mats, he mentioned having had the boy baptized at the cathedral. Somehow, she had doubted him, but she did not dare to question his word.

Mats grew to be a handsome and strapping youth. He had a quick mind and an even temper, and was loved by all. His sisters and mother doted on him, while Lord Kettilmund spent every free moment teaching him the martial arts. He also filled Mats with ancient tales about the powerful, magical, yet mortal Viking Gods, and Mats was fascinated. To die with a sword in his hand, to go to Valhalla where he could do battle by day, be healed from deadly wounds by night, and enjoy fabulous feasts with the Valkyries and the greatest warriors the world had ever known, was more exciting than anything he could imagine. His young mind absorbed the tales of pagan heroism and adventure - - all the while hiding his fascination from the priests who were his teachers and who railed against the heathen gods. Sharing that secret world created an unbreakable bond between father and son.

Lord Kettilmund lavished gifts upon his cherished son: swords, knives, spears and lances made by the finest craftsmen in the world. He would bring them back from his travels, which were frequent. Whenever a beleaguered relative needed help against an enemy, they would send for Lord Kettilmund who took it as his calling to defeat any man who wronged one of his clan. He would don his legendary silver armor, polished to perfection, and ride at the head of his knights to wherever he was needed. Mats begged to accompany him as his martial skills evolved, but Lord Kettilmund shook his head and smiled softly. "Not yet, my son, not yet."

Mats was disappointed. Yet he never protested, so he stayed home, counting the days until his father would return. His mother thought it a pity that Mats had no friends his own age and arranged some introductions, but Mats was not interested. When Lord Kettilmund returned from one of his forays, his wife complained about their son's solitary existence. Again, he insisted that he knew what was best for Mats. But he must have reflected upon it, because after he went to join the Lord High Constable and his army in Finland he brought back the finest gift for which a boy of thirteen could ever wish--a beautiful Finnish girl.

Mats' mother was incensed and berated her husband at the top of her lungs. This was certainly not what she meant when she suggested that Mats needed friends his age, but she grew quiet when Lord Kettilmund threatened to bring a handsome Finnish savage to each of their daughters on his next foray. She knew that he would do so just to spite her, and she did not like the gleam in their daughters' eyes when the idea was mentioned.

The Finnish girl was stunning, with long golden hair cascading down her back. She looked just like Mats had envisioned Thor's wife, Sif, the goddess of the fields, with her hair of pure gold. "Welcome, Sif," Mats said when they met for the first time.

She did not answer him, not because she could not understand his language, but because she could not speak at all. She just gazed at the handsome youth before her, understanding that he was her master, and she smiled such a sweet smile that Mats forgot everything but her. He reached out, took her hand, and led her out of the hall, away from his hysterical mother and chuckling father.

Joyfully she followed her young knight towards the forest, never questioning where they were going. They stopped beside a small, deep lake where they sat on a rock overlooking the dark, tranquil water. Mats shyly glanced at her. She was dressed in a long, soft leather dress with a thick rope around her small waist that held a hunting knife, and with soft, low leather boots on her feet. She wore no ornaments of any kind, but Mats thought her the most magnificent creature he had ever seen. Once in a while she would look at him and smile, but then her concentrated gaze would go back to the lake and the near shore. Suddenly she leapt up and quick and quiet as a cat, moved towards the water's edge where she disappeared into a stand of bushes. Soon its branches began to shake, and when she came out she held a dead rabbit in one hand and a bloody knife in the other. She walked back to Mats and laid her kill at his feet before she dropped to her knees.

"No!" protested Mats. "Never kneel to me."

As he spoke she looked at him with a bewildered look, and her expression showed concern that she had offended him. He reached out and patted the rabbit while smiling and nodding. Sif immediately relaxed, and her smile again became radiant.

"I have never had a close friend except for my father," Mats told her, despite the fact that he knew she did not understand, so strong was his desire to speak his thoughts and feelings. Sif listened attentively as he spoke of his life. He did not know if it was to please him; only that it was wonderful to have her sit there before him so he could gaze at her face. Suddenly she shivered, and he realized that it was time to return so she could sit by the warm fire.

Everyone in the hall stared at them when they walked in. Mats glared at anyone daring to look unkindly at her until they averted their eyes. He turned to the major domo. "The lady killed a rabbit for supper. Prepare it well."

The major domo looked at Mats' mother for permission, but Lord Kettilmund said curtly, "It is about time the women here do something other than just twiddle their yarn. Prepare your fine stew with the animal." The major domo quickly left for the kitchen with the rabbit in hand, and Mats sat down on the edge of the fire pit. "You should see her hunt, father. She is swift as the wind."

"Wait until you see her use her sling," said Lord Kettilmund. "I just gave her the knife."

The lady of the house got up and left the hall. Mats could almost guess her thoughts: Imagine admiring such savage, unwomanly behavior. But Mats' sisters did not leave. They were curious to know more about her, as was he. "Where is she from, father?" he asked.

"She is from a small village we passed on our way back. I bought her from her father for two of my best hunting knives. It was a fair price since she was the most beautiful girl in the village. The fact that she does not speak, I hardly consider a shortcoming in a female."

"She should dress more like a woman," said one of Mats' sisters. "With some decent clothes she would look quite acceptable."

"I like her just the way she is," Mats objected with unusual sharpness making his sister keep any other thoughts to herself.

"Where is she going to sleep?" asked another sister. "Not in my bed!"

"Do not fret," said Lord Kettilmund. "She will sleep with her master."

While the girls had a basic understanding of men and their need for lowborn women; to have such a permanent arrangement with their father's consent, in a good Christian home, was more than any decent woman could accept. They began to voice their objections.

"Stop your sniveling!" snapped Lord Kettilmund. "Your mother begged me to arrange for Mats to have a friend. And I have done so. Not only is she pretty to look at, she is the best hunting companion a man could wish for. Treat her decently, all of you!"

The girls lowered their gaze, and Mats could feel how they despised the intruder who received praise from their father as well as the undivided attention of their brother. Rather than expose Sif to more icy glares from his sisters, Mats decided to withdraw. After bowing to his father and his sisters, he led Sif to his chamber. He lit a candle as he entered and looked at his room with new eyes. It was littered with weapons and armor and was in no way inviting to a woman. He started to clear off the tables and stools, but Sif touched his arm and shook her head. Then she looked around and nodded her approval as she touched each of his fine knives and swords. Mats could not believe his fortune--a woman who liked a man's world. And best of all, a woman who was not a Christian, and to whom he would not have to feign Christian beliefs. He smiled gratefully at her.

Sif smiled back. She came over and put her arms around his neck and brought her lips close to his. Mats had never kissed a woman like this before, but when her lips parted under his, he instinctively knew what to do, and he pulled her closer. He had never experienced such an exhilarating feeling as her strong, slender body pressed against his, and he kissed her again and again. Slowly she pulled away from him and started to untie the rope around her waist. He stared at her, almost afraid to breathe, lest she vanish as quickly as she had appeared. Slowly she pulled her leather dress over her head and stood naked before him. He took a deep breath and felt how dry his mouth was. She was perfect. Not that he had seen many naked women before, but he had sometimes succeeded to peek when the women had taken their summer baths in the lake, and he knew what he liked. Without taking his eyes off her, he hurriedly pulled off his tunic, his boots, his hose and shirt. She looked appraisingly at his well-trained physique and he could sense that she approved of what she saw. He walked over to the bed and reached out for her. She joined him among the many pillows and they sank down together, kissing each other with animal-like fury. If she guided him or if he found his own way, he would never know, but the feeling of moist friction made him almost go mad. He moved wildly until he heard himself roar when he could no longer endure the pleasure. And for the first time he heard Sif make a sound, a deep purring sound, the most beautiful sound he had ever heard.

The following morning Mats went to the knights' quarters and asked if there were any Finns among them. One of the knights told him that there was a Finnish squire, named Toivo.

"I want you to teach me Finnish," said Mats.

"I would be glad to, but I have other chores to do," answered the squire, hoping that if he had to teach, it would be in the hall, with the best food and little heavy work. Lord Kettilmund did, of course, allow Toivo to teach his son how to communicate with Sif.

As time went by, the household grew accustomed to the lovely savage who followed Mats like a shadow. If he were practicing at arms, she would sit curled up watching him with the intentness of an owl. If he went hunting, she would be a few steps ahead, scouting for animal tracks which she had an uncanny skill of discovering. Never did the two of them return home empty handed. Even Mats' mother grew used to Sif, not that she approved of her being there, but the quiet girl who was always smiling at her son obviously made him happy. Most satisfied was Lord Kettilmund who had dreaded that his son would become closely involved with devoutly Christian companions, and through them would become a believer. As it was, Mats knew all the Christian scriptures and rituals, which he followed as a matter of course, but his soul had not been won by the Church. Sif's presence had, if anything, strengthened his beliefs in the ancient ways.

Mats loved the way Sif dressed, and he had more leather dresses made for her, as well as a belt of silver encrusted with large amber stones. He gave her a long string of matching amber beads that she happily wound around her neck. He loved her natural manner and total honesty of feeling. She was easy to make happy, quick to anger and tears or to forget a wrong, and unabashed in her lovemaking. She was utterly different from his mother and his sisters who he had always found difficult to understand since they showed their feelings in masked and covert ways. Were they angry, they would berate someone else for something unrelated to their discontent. Were they happy, they would keep it to themselves and just smile mysteriously. Mats knew that he did not even remotely comprehend women, except, of course, his Sif.

One day, the son from the neighboring estate came with his parents to pay a visit for a possible marriage alliance with Mats' younger sister, Ragnhild. Mats' mother outdid herself in preparing for the visit, since their neighbors were everything she wanted for her daughter--rich and devoutly Christian. The hall had been cleaned until every piece of wood was shining, and the best silver wares were set out on the tables.

The visit began well enough. The neighbors' son seemed to like Ragnhild, and she looked delighted with the possibility of marrying him. As the lavish meal progressed, the lord of the adjoining estate kept gazing at Sif with curiosity. As the hours went by, he drank more of Lord Kettilmund's wine and became visibly more fascinated with Sif's wild beauty. Finally, the two lords departed the hall for a private conversation. Those left behind looked pleased since it seemed only to be the size of the dowry that had to be settled. Mats alone felt a twinge of foreboding. He signaled to Sif to stay, while he left the hall to eavesdrop on the meeting.

"I cannot promise you the Finnish girl since she is not mine to promise. She belongs to my son," he heard his father protest firmly as he neared his chamber.

"If I cannot have her, there will be no marriage," slurred their neighbor angrily.

"I have given you a generous dowry proposal," replied Lord Kettilmund soothingly, "I think you should be glad to accept it. Both our families will benefit from this alliance, and our children seem well suited to one another."

"Without the slave girl there will be no marriage," insisted the neighbor.

"I can ask my son, but I think I know his answer already. He will say no."

"Why should you have to ask him? I thought you were the master of your house."

Mats knew that the man could just as well have slapped his father's face as utter those words. He stepped through the doorway and strode into his father's room. Lord Kettilmund appeared glad to see him even though he must have guessed that he had been eavesdropping.

"Lord Hjalmar wants to have Sif as part of the dowry agreement," said Lord Kettilmund softly, but Mats could hear the anger in his voice. "Of course, he does not want his family to know. That would not suit his image as a righteous Christian. I assume he will keep Sif in one of his hunting lodges and visit her there when the mood strikes him. This might not be the future you had envisioned for Sif, but if you refuse it, your sister will not marry, and that would be sad because I can see that Ragnhild and Lord Hjalmar's son like one another."

Lord Kettilmund became silent and Mats could see the lecherous leer on Lord Hjalmar's face. Mats looked at his father quizzically, trying to guess what he wanted him to do, but Lord Kettilmund's face was impassive and Mats knew he was alone with his decision.

"Father, if you want me to give up Sif you have only to say so. I have never treasured anything more than her, save our friendship, yours and mine. That goes beyond anything else."

Lord Kettilmund looked lovingly at his son and turned towards Lord Hjalmar. "You may return home then, neighbor. You cannot have the girl. But should you reconsider, my offer still stands, and we will forget this whole incident."

"I told you what I wanted; and if I cannot have it, you, my lord, be damned forever!" Lord Hjalmar's vehemence seemed to startle him out of his drunken stupor, and he became furious at the realization that he had allowed his lust for this heathen beauty to deprive his son of a wife with such a generous dowry. However, his pride did not allow him to change his mind.

"Then," repeated Lord Kettilmund coldly. "You may leave my house."

As they returned to the hall everyone looked expectantly at them, but Lord Hjalmar gestured for his family to leave with him as he departed the hall without so much as a goodbye. His wife and son reluctantly followed him, looking at their hosts with concern while calling hurried words of farewell. Mats' sister rose in alarm. "Why are they leaving like that?"

Lord Kettilmund went over to his daughter. "You should be glad not to marry into such a family," he said trying to comfort her. "You would never have been happy in their house."

"But I want to marry him," she cried out.

Her mother put her arms around her and looked at Lord Kettilmund. "What did happen?" she demanded.

"I do not think you want to know," he said softly. "Let it suffice to say that we will never have anything to do with them in the future. Is that understood?"

"Is it something I did?" asked Ragnhild despairingly.

"No, my dear," said Lord Kettilmund with unusual tenderness. "It had nothing to do with you, or with their son. His father just made demands that I could not meet."

"You are a rich man," protested Mats' mother. "You could pay him whatever he asked."

"You do not understand," shouted Lord Kettilmund, letting his anger strike his wife. "That lecherous hypocrite wanted Sif without his family knowing about it." The hall was silent as everyone looked at Lord Kettilmund and then at Sif. She, in turn looked at Mats who said something in Finnish as he put his hand softly on her shoulder.

"You are right. I do not understand," said the lady of the house angrily. "Why would such a fine man as Lord Hjalmar, who is highly thought of by the bishops, want Sif? Did she tempt him in some way?"

"Sif has done nothing. I doubt if she even looked at the stupid brute. And just because a rich man gives of his plenty to the Church, that does not make him virtuous."

"Then, why did you not give Sif to him if that would have sealed the marriage agreement? I suppose it was Mats who did not value his sister's happiness - only his own."

"You know your son very little, if you think that," Lord Kettilmund replied. "The truth is that Lord Hjalmar insulted me in my own house, and no man of honor can accept that!"

None of the women said anything. A man's honor could never be questioned. Ragnhild broke into tears and rushed from the hall, followed by her sisters.

"You have to do something!" Mats' mother warned her husband with a chilling glare before she sailed out of the hall to console her daughter.

The spring passed slowly, without the mood in the house becoming any less somber. Ragnhild cried as if her life were over, fearing that no one would ever want her if gossip spread that the young man had found her wanting. When she learned that her younger sister was to be married early that summer, she was beyond consolation and spent most of her time sitting sullenly in the hall, spinning her yarn.

Mats and Sif escaped from the house as often as they could to avoid the accusing looks the women shot at Sif who was clearly considered the cause of all the sadness. Once they were away from the house, Sif and Mats were happy, hunting and making love in the great forest surrounding the estate.

Finally, the day of the wedding feast arrived. Mats' sisters decided that Sif could not attend such a formal gathering in her habitual leather garb but had to be dressed like a lady--especially since most of the wedding guests had heard about her and were curious to see her. The sisters, except for Ragnhild, dragged Sif into their mother's chamber, stripped her of clothes and amber, and pulled a dress and a lavishly embroidered tunic over her. Sif stood mute, looking at them with trepidation in her eyes.

"This will not hurt you, silly girl," snapped one of the sisters. "We are just doing you a favor by not having people think you are a barbarian."

They forced her to sit down and succumb to their nimble fingers braiding her hair. They wove strings of fine silk ribbons in her blond tresses, placed an embroidered belt around her waist, and hung a large crucifix around her neck before they stood back to look at her. "She actually looks beautiful," said the youngest of the girls.

"Yes, she looks quite passable," agreed the older.

When they finally entered the hall, most of the wedding guests had assembled. Mats stood among them looking for Sif. When he saw her, his mouth fell open. His beautiful, natural Sif looked just like any of the silly, pious women whom he could not tolerate. Then he noticed that she was wearing a cross around her neck. Sudden anger welled up in him against his sisters for transforming the woman he loved into something she was not. At that moment, Sif caught his eye. She smiled shyly, seeking his approval. But all she saw in his eyes was anger--an emotion so shockingly strong--that she felt her heart cringe. She had never seen him express such feelings before, whatever she had done. She felt trapped in her unaccustomed finery, trapped by the curious looks directed at her, and most of all, trapped by Mats' sudden revulsion. She turned, pushed her way through the guests, and fled from the stifling hall.

Mats realized how she must have interpreted his look, and he wanted to race after her to explain that he was simply angry with his sisters. He could not rush through the crowd for fear of appearing rude to the guests, and when he finally reached the doors she was gone. He raced along the path they normally took into the forest hoping to overtake her, but she was not by the lake when he got there. He called her name, and in his now passable Finnish, shouted that he was not angry with her. He followed another of the paths they usually chose, calling her name as he ran. After an hour of searching he returned to the lake and collapsed on the rock on which they had sat on the first day of her arrival. She had to come back here at some point, he thought. He sat and waited for a long time before he suddenly remembered that his sister was being married! His family would never forgive him. He stared into the darkening forest and called Sif's name again and again before he reluctantly ran back to the house.

As he stepped into the hall, the wedding feast was in full progress. He caught his father's eye across the hall, and Lord Kettilmund gestured for him to wait in his chamber. Mats went there, filled with worry for Sif's safety. "Did you find her?" Lord Kettilmund asked as soon as he entered. As usual, he had not missed anything happening.

"She ran away when she saw how distasteful I thought she looked in ladies' clothing," said Mats. "I have looked everywhere, but she is nowhere to be found."

"At least you need not worry about her. If anyone can take care of herself, it is Sif."

"Normally I would agree," said Mats sadly, "But this time she is dressed in awkward skirts, and she has no weapons."

"You realize that there is little we can do now. I cannot even send out a few knights, or your mother would notice. I promised her that nothing would interrupt this wedding, and I must keep my word. She was looking for you in the chapel, but I told her you were helping to carry your sick uncle to his seat, and that you probably stayed with him in the back. She thought that was kind of you," chuckled Lord Kettilmund.

"What should I do?" asked Mats in despair.

"Join the festivities and pretend that you are having a pleasant time. Tell your mother what a fine wedding it is and compliment your sister on how well she looks as a bride. Be attentive to everyone so that they notice your presence. When everyone is too drunk to notice, I'll go with you. But until then, my son, you must pretend to enjoy yourself."

Mats knew the wisdom of his father's advice and did his best to follow it although he could feel that Sif needed him. Mustering all his self-control he continued to talk to the guests. He could see that his mother was pleased with him, and equally pleased by Sif's absence.

The passage of time was painfully slow. When Lord Kettilmund finally left his guests, Mats gratefully slipped out of the hall to join him. They donned their chain mail, strapped on their swords, and slipped extra knives in their bootstraps.

"I have an awful feeling that Sif has lost her way and is now on Lord Hjalmar's lands," said Mats in anguish.

"You might well be right," said Lord Kettilmund pensively, trusting his son's intuition. "She probably would have crossed at the river bend to enter his property. That is quite a way off, so let us ride there. Odin seems to be helping us - it is a moonlit night."

Very quietly, they led their horses out of the stable and into the forest. There they mounted and rode along the path at high speed. Once they reached the river and found the crossing, they let their horses wade to the other side. Slowly, since they were unfamiliar with the terrain, they followed a narrow path. They had not been riding long before they saw a flicker of light between some trees. They dismounted, tied their horses, and quietly approached the light. There, in an opening, lit by a campfire, they saw Sif tied, spread-eagle, to a big tree. In front of her stood Lord Hjalmar with his sword in hand. Behind him were three other knights.

"She is a witch," cried Lord Hjalmar angrily. "She made me ruin my son's life. He has hardly spoken a word, mourning the loss of the girl he wanted to marry. I cannot think of a way cruel enough for her to die. This is God's will. He sent her to me, to receive her punishment by my hand." As Lord Hjalmar lunged forward and thrust his sword into Sif's heart, Mats roared at the top of his lungs as if the sword had pierced his own heart. He dashed from among the trees with drawn sword, a terrifying sight in all his fury. Mats and his father slew two of the knights before they had their swords out of their scabbards.

"You have insulted my family for the last time!" Lord Kettilmund cried as he turned to the surprised Lord Hjalmar.

"He is mine," hissed Mats.

"No, my son," said his father with deadly calm. "You should not soil your hands with this lowly boor. This is between him and me."

The last knight attacked Mats, confident against one so young, but in his fury Mats countered and drove the knight back towards the forest where he desperately fought to regain control. But he was no match for the unknown strength Mats found in his grief. His' sword kept attacking the retreating knight until it found a spot between the man's chain mail and helmet that brought him heavily to the ground and to his death.

"You are an unchristian pagan to house a savage witch!" roared Lord Hjalmar angrily as he moved towards Lord Kettilmund who stood waiting for his onslaught.

Mats had only seen his father fight at practice, and he watched in awe his father's display of combat skills. From Lord Hjalmar's first attack, Lord Kettilmund merely toyed with him, savagely cutting him wherever the chain mail left him vulnerable. Lord Kettilmund's speed, strength and aim left Lord Hjalmar, who was considered a fine swordsman, looking like a clumsy oaf. Soon Mats could see fear in Lord Hjalmar's eyes when it became evident that Lord Kettilmund had tired of the unchallenging game. He stepped forward to slash open his opponent's throat. He took a step back as the body fell forward, blood spurting from severed arteries.

Lord Kettilmund looked at the fallen corpse. "What I would give for us to have arrived just moments earlier," he said sadly. Mats went up to Sif and gently untied her from the tree. He held her body close and placed her reverently on the ground. Even in death she was beautiful. He slowly removed the cross from around her neck and loosened her hair.

"Lord Kettilmund watched his son. "Mats, I must ask you a favor. You know now how it feels to lose someone you love, so I ask you to help Ragnhild marry the man she wants. If we tell no one what really happened here but say that all of us fought together to free Sif from a band of outlaws, your sister will be able to marry Lord Hjalmar's son, and we will secure a friendly neighbor. Can you accept the world thinking well of this villain?"

Mats sat silently rocking Sif in his arms. "Nothing will bring her back," he said with a sadness that tore at Lord Kettilmund. "I have felt pity for my sister, and if what you suggest will make her happy, I certainly do not object."

Together they laid Sif on Mats' horse and Lord Hjalmar on his father's. As they led their mounts slowly through the trees, Lord Kettilmund could hear the stifled sobs from his son as he vented his grief in the dark, primeval forest.

No one at the wedding had missed them. So, it was with shock and concern that the guests gathered on their arrival. Lord Kettilmund told them about the outlaws' attack, then sent one of his squires to Lord Hjalmar's house to bring his family the sad news.

Ragnhild came up to Mats. "Did father and Lord Hjalmar make up before he died?"

"Yes," said Mats trying to smile. "Now you can get married."

"Oh!" she exclaimed excitedly before her face took on a sad expression. "But you have lost Sif. I am so sorry."

Since no one else seemed to take note of his grief, Mats slipped out of the house to sit by the lake until the first rays of the morning sun broke through the clouds. There he shed his last tears in memory of the most wonderful year of his life. He awoke from his thoughts as his father touched his shoulder. "It is time to come home, Mats. Your sisters have laid out Sif's body, and you and I will bury her in the forest she loved so well."

Mats rose and numbly followed his father home. The wedding party had gathered in the hall where Sif's body was laid out on a pallet. She was dressed in her leather dress with her amber necklace around her neck. Her hair was loose and brushed to a shine. In her hands was placed a bouquet of wild flowers. Mats was touched by his sisters' efforts.

Lord Kettilmund picked up one end of the pallet and Mats the other to carry Sif to her forest. Lord Kettilmund led the way to the lake where he stopped at a rock formation on which they set the pallet down. He rolled away one of the large stones that hid the entrance to a small cave. By the cave wall, they dug a deep grave into which they lowered the pallet. Together, and in silence, they filled it with dirt.

"Do you regret that we lied about Lord Hjalmar?" asked Lord Kettilmund. "Looking at the pain on your face, maybe the truth would have made you feel better."

"No, father," whispered Mats. "It was the will of the gods. It was her time. But I must leave this place. It has become unbearable. Please, father, arrange somewhere for me to go."

Mats finally reached his ancestral home two days after leaving Nykoping and having changed horses when he passed estates belonging to his clan. He breathed a sigh of relief when he saw no funeral banners by the doors. He left his horse in the yard and raced into the hall. His mother stood to greet him as he came in.

"Thank God you are here in time!" she exclaimed as she threw herself into his arms. "Your father refused to take his last rites before you came, and we were so worried that he could not hold out and would be damned in hell forever."

Mats smiled to himself. His father would grasp any excuse to avoid the priests. Mats gently pushed his mother aside and walked to his father's chamber. Lord Kettilmund was lying in his bed with his eyes closed. He had bandages around his head and left shoulder, and his face was ashen grey. He had miraculously survived the long journey home from Germany where he had fought alongside some beleaguered kinsmen. Mats walked up and touched his hand gently. Lord Kettilmund opened his eyes slowly and smiled when he saw his son.

"I have been waiting for you, my son," he said with considerable effort. "Close the door. I want to talk to you alone." Mats did as he was bid, and then sat down by his father's bedside.

"After I am buried, I want you to secretly dig me up from my Christian grave, take me to the lakeshore where you will burn my body on a pyre and throw my ashes to the winds--just as they did for the Viking chieftains. Promise me that," he said weakly. "But right now, please go to the cave by the lake. You will see a pile of rocks that you must move, and then dig down about three feet where you will find a long box. Bring it here to me."

Lord Kettilmund closed his eyes, drained by the effort of speaking. Mats caressed his hand and left the chamber. He went to find a shovel, and then ran into the forest. When he came to the cave he rolled away the entrance stones, entered, and walked over to the pile of large rocks, which he laboriously removed, one by one. He dug ferociously, fearing that his father might die at any moment. When his shovel finally struck a wooden object, he continued to dig more carefully so as not to damage it. He extracted the oblong box and ran back home.

His father appeared asleep when Mats, still out of breath, quietly closed the door behind him. Lord Kettilmund opened his eyes and whispered for Mats to open the box and bring its contents to him. Mats did as his father instructed and found a sword in an old leather scabbard that had begun to disintegrate from age. He could see the beautifully worked haft protruding at one end. The haft of the double-edged sword was forged in the shape of a dragon; its mouth ferociously gaping at the top, its coiled body comprising the handle, while the tail faded into the thick blade of the weapon.

"This sword was used by our forefathers for centuries," Lord Kettilmund explained, "but for the past two hundred years--since the damned priests took over--it has lain buried. Now you will head the family and the sword will be your responsibility." Lord Kettilmund took a labored breath and continued. "Our clan served the old gods, and this sword forged by the dwarf smiths was their gift. It rarely needs sharpening and never has to be polished! It has a balance like no other weapon. No mortal can use it before the true gods return, except for those destined to become rulers. A clear sign is written on those men, a star-shaped patch of silvery white hair by the left temple."

Mats unconsciously touched his left temple where a patch of white grew in his dark-blond hair. He felt a shiver down his spine.

"But I am not of royal blood, father," he protested. "How could I ever become a ruler?"

"Do not question the gods, my son. I do not doubt for a moment that you will become a ruler. That is why I felt that you needed the proper surroundings and training, and why I agreed with the Lord High Constable that you should be a companion to the princes. Use this sword wisely, or it will become a curse rather than a blessing. It is called Gram after the one with which Sigurd slew the dragon." The dying man tried to pull himself up against the pillows before he whispered anxiously. "Let me hold it one last time."

Mats carefully drew the blade from its crumbling scabbard. It was shining as if it had just been polished, and it possessed an incredibly sharp edge. Mats had never seen metal glisten like that before, and he carefully placed the sword on his father's bedcovers. Lord Kettilmund touched the cold surface and a smile spread over his face. "I will meet you in Valhalla," he whispered. Within the hour he was dead.

Chapter 4

Nykoping, Sweden 1296

Three years had passed since Mats had returned to the court, during which time he and the princes had become inseparable, accomplished in weaponry, fluent in latin, and skilled in politics. Their development had actually been furthered due to Lord Torgils' frequent absences in Finland that gained ever more land for Sweden. Not only had they learned to rely on themselves and each other, but also how to handle themselves as true courtiers.

Kristina and the princesses had each evolved into young ladies abiding naturally by the most stringent etiquette rules. However, when alone together they acted like all girls of their age, and were fiercely loyal to one another. Not even the queen could find any fault in their behavior.

This evening, Princess Ingeborg, celebrating what was to be her last evening in her childhood home, had no appetite. With the queen relentlessly directing the hectic preparations for their imminent departure for Ingeborg's wedding in Denmark, everyone at Nykoping castle had been left exhausted. While the members of the royal party chatted through the meal about the upcoming voyage, the bride-to-be sat quietly pushing her food about the plate.

"Are you not hungry?" asked Kristina who was sitting beside her.

"I cannot remember what my betrothed looks like," said Ingeborg morosely.

"You met him only twice when you were just a little girl. How can you expect to remember? And if you did it would be of a young boy and not the man he is now. He is seven years older than you - an accomplished warrior and a ruling king in the prime of his life. Had you seen him even four years ago you would find him changed today."

"Ingeborg," called the queen who had noticed her daughter's ashen pallor. "If you would like to withdraw, you may leave the table."

Ingeborg gratefully arose from her seat. Kristina and Rikissa began to rise, but Ingeborg motioned for them to stay. They joined her as soon as they had swallowed the last of the delicious dessert of poached apples in almond cream. Kristina brought Ingeborg's portion to her, as it was Ingeborg's favorite sweet, and had probably been prepared with that in mind.

"I do not want to leave," Ingeborg lamented. "I am frightened." She did not even touch the dessert they set before her.

"You will be the queen," said Rikissa as she sat down on the bed beside her sister. "Everyone must do as you bid."

Just then the queen entered to check the girls' traveling attire and their travel chests that were piled high to the ceiling. Satisfied, she turned to the girls. "Ingeborg, I have decided that Kristina can remain with you in Roskilde."

"Oh, Mother," cried Ingeborg gratefully as she threw herself in her mother's arms. "Thank you."

The queen blithely removed her daughter's arms from around her neck. "I know from my own experience how difficult it can be to live in a strange household, and I think Kristina will be of help to you." Turning to Kristina who was flushed with excitement, the Queen continued, "In two years, you will accompany Princess Marta back here for her wedding with Birger, and then you will remain here, Kristina, to be of support to Sweden's new queen."

"I am so grateful, Mother," Ingeborg exclaimed with tears in her eyes.

"What about me?" asked Rikissa. "I will be here all by myself!"

"I know," said the queen in an unusually gentle voice. "But in two years you will get a new sister in Marta, and Kristina will be back. Time will pass quickly. But for now, go to sleep, as we are sailing early on the morrow."

The following morning the girls awoke early, dressed, and went down to the Hall. Servants were carrying chests out to wagons to be taken to the docks, and the courtyard was filled with noise and excitement as the girls walked to the chapel where the entire household gathered for morning prayers.

Father Nils smiled at Ingeborg. "Today, Lord, we offer a special prayer for our beloved Princess Ingeborg who is to leave us to assume the position of Queen of Denmark. We pray that You will protect her and make her strong so that she can support her husband, and that You will bless her with many and healthy children. Dear Lord, we will miss her, and we pray that You will let her feel our abiding love through Your protection. Amen."

Kristina saw tears run down Ingeborg's cheeks, and both she and Rikissa reached out to take her hands. Kristina wondered how it would feel to leave one's family and one's country forever. She remembered how badly she had felt when she had to leave Lena.

Ingeborg cried through all the embraces and farewells from those in the castle, servants and nobles alike. "I will come back for Birger's wedding," she sniffled as she climbed into her litter and waved at her childhood friends. She was grateful for its window curtains so she could cry in peace, even though she had thought it unfair that Kristina and Rikissa were allowed to ride on horseback to the harbor instead of being carried, as she was, like an old woman.

"You are to act like a queen, my dear," her mother had said with finality when she had protested.

When the royal party reached the dock area where the ships were just finishing loading their cargo, a brisk wind promised to hasten their voyage. Kristina and Ingeborg overheard one captain say to Lord Torgils that if their luck held, they would sail past Kalmar in less than two days.

Once aboard, the royal family settled in for the journey. Their vessel resembled a large trading ship. It was deep and wide in the beam with lofty aft and forward decks. Below, where cargo normally would be stowed, were the quarters for the royal passengers. The ladies were housed in the stern and the men in the bow. In the ladies' cabin, which was the largest and most comfortable, fur skins had been spread on the floorboards and a table with benches had been bolted down in the middle. On one side of the cabin were wide bunks, and on the other hung hammocks for those who preferred that mode of sleeping. At the rear of the cabin were stacked the few travelling chests they would need during the voyage, the rest were aboard one of the cargo ships.

Erik and his brothers were thrilled about the impending journey. They had sailed innumerable times from Nykoping to Stockholm and Kalmar, even as far as Lodose on the west coast, but they had never been to Roskilde in Denmark. They promptly investigated every corner of the spanking new ship, built especially to transport the future Queen of Denmark to her new homeland. When the ship finally hauled anchor and unfurled its sails, the youngsters stood on the high aft deck as the small armada got under way for Denmark. Twelve flag-decorated and newly overhauled ships escorted them on their journey. The companion ships were carrying nobles who had been invited to attend the wedding, as well as soldiers and cargo.

Everyone remained on deck to view the small islands they passed. Large seagulls screamed their good-byes from the cliffs, and multi-hued wildflowers waved theirs from the crevices in the rocks. The blue water played around the prow of the ship, and the sound of the sea lulled the passengers into a state of peaceful expectation. Many hours later when it was time for supper, the crew slackened the sails to slow the vessel so the meal could be enjoyed in comfort. The royal family, Lords Torgils and Abjorn, Lady Constance and Fathers Nils and Gregory assembled in the aft cabin, said their prayers, and ate with healthy appetite. Even Ingeborg, who was now fully enjoying the adventure, emptied her dish of the very last morsel.

The sun did not set until after ten o'clock that night. When it passed below the horizon it was with an explosion of breathtaking colors.

"I have never seen anything so beautiful," sighed Ingeborg as she and Kristina stood beside Erik on the aft deck.

"A good omen," suggested Erik.

"I hope so," Ingeborg answered, turning serious.

"Are you frightened, then?"

"Would you not be? After hearing all those stories . . ."

"And that is what they are, sister; stories of what happened a long time ago."

"Erik Menved would not be king today if his own father had not been murdered."

"At least it was not brother killing brother. King Erik Klipping was murdered by his political enemies."

"Does that make it any better?"

"Well, at least you do not have to look on Kristoffer, your future brother-in-law, with the thought that all royal brothers kill one another in Denmark."

By the time they had rounded the Scandinavian Peninsula and entered the quieter waters of the Ore Straight, the excitement of the voyage had worn off, and everyone was longing for solid ground beneath their feet. This feeling was amplified as they sailed once more in open waters around the northern tip of Sjaelland when huge dark clouds massed on the horizon. In just a few hours the sea began to boil with high waves. Rain and roaring wind mercilessly drove all the passengers inside the ladies' cabin where they were tossed against the table and benches if they tried to move about. Only the hammocks were safe to rest in, as they swayed with the violent heaving of the ship.

The queen and Rikissa became ill the moment they entered the cabin. Kristina and Lady Constance did what they could to make them comfortable, attending them with bowls in which to vomit and wiping their foreheads with cool, fresh water. Even Valdemar and Birger who rested in hammocks got a greenish tint to their skin. Lord Torgils, unable to stay confined, left the cabin. The two priests sat mumbling over their prayer books, while Erik and Mats peeked out the portholes to monitor the progress of the ferocious storm. They caught an occasional glimpse of a companion ship being tossed about by the towering waves.

Suddenly they heard the fearful sound of wood shifting and the groaning, high-pitched sound of planks fighting the irrepressible sea.

Erik and Mats looked at each other. "That does not sound good, does it?" asked Erik.

"I am not a seaman," answered Mats. "But even I can see that this is a bad storm."

"Let us join Lord Torgils on deck," suggested Erik. "I cannot stay cooped up here. I am beginning to feel nauseous." The youngsters edged toward the cabin door, holding on to the walls to keep their balance. As they opened the door the wind blew in with such ferocity that most of the candles in the cabin were extinguished. As the boys struggled to close the door behind them they heard the queen wailing her objections over the roar of the sea. As they emerged on deck, Erik felt a huge wave collapse over him, almost sweeping him off his feet. Had it not been for the railing-rope he grasped with one hand, he would have been pulled over the side, and he coughed from the water he had unintentionally swallowed.

"Let us get back in," screamed Mats behind him.

"No. I want to see what is going on," insisted Erik as he pulled himself toward the ladder leading up to the aft deck where the captain was stationed.

Every step was a struggle as the ship heaved violently, but they finally made it to the top deck. Again, they pulled themselves along the railing rope until they reached the captain, Abjorn, and Torgils, all of whom had lashed themselves to cleats in the deck floor.

"What in the name of damnation are you doing here?" roared Lord Torgils over the wind.

"We were getting sick in the cabin, and we wanted to know how serious the storm is," Erik screamed back.

"It is deadly serious!" Lord Torgils yelled. "Get back and . . ." He was interrupted by an ominous creaking sound. The captain, who had been struggling with the tiller, fell to the deck as the tiller snapped. Seconds later, a massive wind gust snapped the main mast with a thunderous crack, toppling it, and spilling its furled, wet sails onto the main deck.

"Go back and take charge of the women," called Torgils over the wind. "Erik, you help Princess Ingeborg. Tell your brothers and Mats to assist Princess Rikissa, Kristina and Lady Constance. Lord Abjorn and I will get the queen, the gold, and the royal seals to safety. Go!" he shouted, as he looked anxiously towards the rocky coast that was rapidly approaching. They made their way down the ladder and across the deck. Their journey was slow and perilous, but finally they tore open the cabin door and pulled it closed behind them. They were soaking wet.

"I do not want to alarm you, but we are drifting towards the coast," said Lord Torgils, attempting to sound calm. "Should we not make it to the protected waters of Roskilde fjord, and should our ship crash against the rocks, do not take anything with you, just get to the shore."

The queen's pale face was marked with fear as she attempted to bring herself to a sitting position despite the violent heaving of the ship. "Do not forget the jewelry," she called.

"We will take care of that, your Majesty," said Torgils who was already opening one of the chests and removing small boxes which he gave to Erik, Lord Abjorn and Mats to secure to their bodies under their tunics.

The two priests were frantically praying for salvation when they suddenly heard an explosion and saw the cabin wall break away to reveal the ferocious sea.

"I wonder how they weathered the storm," King Erik Menved of Denmark asked without expecting an answer. The reports had said only that there was a sudden squall, and that the Swedish ships were caught by surprise. But he could not just sit by and wait for news. He had to find out what happened and so he had boarded one of his swift longboats to investigate. He pulled his mantle tighter against the strong headwind.

"Let us hope they did well, or you will have a seasick bride on your hands, which would not make your wedding night merry," commented his younger brother who was sitting beside him in the stern of a sleek oar-driven vessel.

"It is hardly time for your tasteless jokes, Kristoffer," retorted Erik Menved curtly.

"Ah, the lovelorn . . . " snickered Kristoffer as he took a swallow from his flask of wine.

"This has nothing to do with love, as you damn well know. Only with the future of Denmark. I pray nothing has happened to them, and so should you."

Their search vessel had been under way for hours, and it was with visible relief that the king sighted a group of Swedish ships anchored by the mouth of Roskilde fjord. The rain had long since stopped, and the wind was finally dying down. "Ahoy!" called the Danish helmsman as they approached one of the ships. "The King is nearing. Which is the royal ship?"

"It is lost," called back a voice. "We have several ships out looking for it."

Erik Menved's boat pulled up alongside the vessel and the king called out anxiously, "Was the ship lost or wrecked? Do you know?"

The captain of the Swedish ship leaned over the railing and saluted the man who, he realized from his regal attire, must be the Danish king. "I do not know, Your Majesty. Our ships got separated during the storm, and we are still missing three of them. So far we have sighted no wreckage, so we are hoping that they are still afloat."

"Continue to search for the royal ship!" ordered the king as he sat back down and his vessel quickly moved out along the coastline of Sjaelland.

The sun broke through the grey clouds that had obscured it and once again the coast basked in the warm rays. It was difficult to imagine that a violent storm had ravaged it only hours before. Prince Kristoffer sat humming a drinking song, contentedly sipping from his flask, while the king was impatiently tapping his fingers on his knee. As their vessel passed swiftly along the shore, they could see Swedish ships sailing ahead of them scanning the beaches. The king kept an eye on their mastheads to see if any flags went up to signal the sighting of wreckage. His vigilance was rewarded when one of the ships hoisted a red and white flag. Erik Menved shouted to his oarsmen to pick up speed, and they caught up with the ship that had raised the signal flag.

"What do you see?" called the helmsman as they drew alongside the Swedish vessel.

"There is wreckage in there," pointed a sailor from aloft. The Danish helmsman ordered his men to race towards the beach. As the boat touched the rocky coast, Erik Menved was the first to leap ashore, followed by his brother who seemed to enjoy the adventure immensely. Erik Menved dropped his mantle on the rocks and ran anxiously along the water's edge. Prince Kristoffer sat down on a boulder and took another draught from his flask. The rowers took up their weapons and half of them followed the king, while the other half went searching in the opposite direction.

"I have found it! Here!" the king called as he rounded a bend on the rocky shore where half a ship was lying intact on the boulders. All around it lay the splintered timbers of what must have been the rest of the ill-fated vessel. Its size indicated that it could indeed be the remains of the royal ship, and Erik Menved vaulted over several large rocks to reach the wreckage. As he came around to peer inside the hulk, he found it deserted. Wedged between some debris he noticed a prayer book which he lifted carefully so as not to tear its soggy pages. He opened it to the frontispiece where he discovered the Holstein coat of arms. He closed it and turned to the men who had joined him.

"This is the royal ship. I just found Queen Helvig's prayer book. Let us split up into search parties. Go along the shore, and if you find nothing, continue searching inland. The royal family might have sought shelter away from the sea." If they are still alive, he wanted to add, but kept the words to himself.

"Wuh," slurred Kristoffer as he caught up with his brother. "They did not have much of a chance, did they now? We will have a fine funeral instead of a wedding."

"Cease your drivel" blasted Erik Menved. "Get back to the boat and stay there. You are good for nothing in your present condition."

"As Your Majesty orders," Kristoffer bowed mockingly. "I have another flask in the boat. This one is almost empty."

Erik Menved sighed. The three princes and Lord Torgils had, in all likelihood, been on the same ship; and if they had drowned, so had the entire leadership of Sweden. Erik Menved could just imagine Sweden's nobles feuding for power and the turmoil that would ensue in all three Scandinavian countries, pitting one clan against another, according to age-old enmities and alliances. He shuddered. Dear God, let at least one prince survive.

Ingeborg slowly returned to her senses. When her eyes opened she found herself resting in an unfamiliar forest glen, and once she sat up and looked around she found that she was alone. Her body was aching, and she noticed black and blue marks on her hands and arms. She tried to remember where she was and how she had arrived here. Foggy pictures of towering waves and sounds of wood crashing against craggy rocks flickered through her mind as she began to panic, thinking of her family. While she was trying to put her thoughts together, she heard soft footsteps behind her in the moss. She turned her head to see a man standing close by her.

"Do not worry," he said gently with a Danish accent. "I will not hurt you."

She looked up at him. His clothes were those of a nobleman. His face was kind, and his eyes mirrored his concern. He bent down close to her. "Are you hurt?" he asked gently.

"I am fine, " she answered numbly, transfixed by his vibrant green eyes. Still she felt her throat constrict and tears burn her eyes.

"Are you alone?" asked the man kindly.

"I . . . we were in a storm," she began haltingly as her memory slowly returned. "Our ship broke up . . . I was thrown onto the shore . . . but where are the others?" She looked around anxiously. She struggled to get to her feet. The man gently helped her gain her balance until she stood unsteadily in front of him. She looked down to see her dress and tunic torn. She touched the ripped fabric absentmindedly, and then looked again at the stranger.

"Where am I . . . and where are the others?"

"I do not know where the rest of your party is, but you are in a forest on the north coast of Sjaelland."

"They must all have drowned," she cried in panic, clutching at her tunic. She could no longer contain her tears and the stranger took her gently into his arms where he let her cry, comforted with his arms around her until her confusion settled.

"I never should have come. I should have known something terrible would happen. There is a curse on them, and those who get near them. . ."

Suddenly voices from among the trees could be heard in the distance.

"Kristina," she called. "Are you there?"

Ingeborg began to run on wobbly legs toward the voices, leaving the stranger standing where he had found her. As she ran she heard Kristina's voice.

"I am here. I am here," she cried out in relief as she crossed the glen.

Through the trees appeared Rikissa, her mother and Kristina.

"Thank God you are safe," called the queen as she enveloped Ingeborg in her arms. "Do not cry, dear child. Our family is safe, as are Lords Torgils and Abjorn and the Fathers. Poor Lady Constance was lost, though, God rest her soul."

Ingeborg turned to look back at the glen, but the stranger had vanished. She felt strangely disappointed.

Once the royal family gathered aboard one of the escort ships, the fleet again set sail for Roskilde. A large Danish ship had come alongside and refilled their freshwater supply to permit those aboard to wash away the sea salt that covered their bodies.

The queen attempted to sound brave as she scrutinized her family. "Apart from some cuts and bruises, no one would know how close we came to almost perishing in that storm. Or becoming lost," she said as she looked at Ingeborg. "Whatever happened to you?"

"I have no idea, Mother," said Ingeborg shaking her head. "All I know is that I heard that terrible crashing sound before I fell onto the rocks. I think I just walked away. I do not remember."

"Well, do not walk off like that in the future," muttered the queen irritably.

"I was not alone," Ingeborg whispered to Rikissa and Kristina who were seated beside her.

"You keep saying that," Kristina whispered in return. "But who was with you?"

"I am not sure. Maybe he was a nobleman out hunting."

"It is time to get dressed, girls," the queen ordered. "Perhaps not in the dresses I had planned, as they are at the bottom of the sea, but I had your other clothes chests brought here so you can choose something else. You may change later," said the queen as she dismissed her sons and the rest of the men from the cabin with an imperious wave of her hand. Kristina marveled at how well the queen had taken their near encounter with death--but then she probably viewed the storm as just another inconvenience to be promptly dismissed.

Ingeborg scrubbed herself down and washed her hair in the cold, fresh water. After she was dry she was helped into a silk underdress and a new tunic made of thick blue brocade. She chose to wear the most magnificent of her jewelry hung from a thick neck chain--the heavy cross that had been worn by her ancestor, Erik the Holy. When the queen fastened an elaborate gold belt around her daughter's waist as a finishing touch, Ingeborg exclaimed, "But this is yours, Mother. It was given to you by your father!"

"That is why I am giving it to you now. He gave it to me when I left Holstein to become Queen of Sweden. I have always felt that it protected me."

"Thank you so much," Ingeborg exclaimed happily as her mother stood back to examine her. The queen was clearly pleased. Ingeborg was a striking young woman, flaunting the same proud profile as her brothers. Tall and naturally erect, she was reminiscent of the fabled Valkyries. Her thick, strawberry blond hair cascaded over her shoulders and down her back in soft, damp waves. She looked very much like a queen, and would look even more so once she covered her hair with a regal headdress.

"Now the rest of you get ready," ordered the queen as Rikissa and Kristina brought in more buckets of fresh water. Everyone in the party had finished their preparations in good time before their ship reached Roskilde. The sun was shining brightly as they sailed leisurely down the waterway framed by green shores. The royal family stood grouped on the deck as they caught their first glimpse of Roskilde castle. It was larger than any of the royal castles in Sweden, and Ingeborg felt a wave of excitement sweep over her.

"It is very impressive," Kristina commented, remembering how she herself had felt when she saw Nykoping castle for the first time.

As they drew near the dock and could see the many members of the Danish court waiting to greet them, the full meaning of Ingeborg's new role struck them.

"We will surely treat you with respect from now on, sister," Erik quipped.

"At long last," Ingeborg bantered back as she tried to pick out Erik Menved in the crowd.

"Which one is he?" asked Kristina trying to guess from the clothing who could be the king. But it was impossible to tell since everyone was beautifully attired.

"I told you I do not remember what he looks like," insisted Ingeborg as she kept searching for her future husband.

The passengers were momentarily jarred as the ship touched up against the dock and the air filled with calls from the seamen to those ashore as they threw the lines to secure the ship. Before long a gangplank was laid permitting the Danish Chancellor to climb aboard.

He stepped in front of Ingeborg who was standing slightly ahead of her family.

"I have the honor of welcoming you in His Majesty's name since he has not yet returned from the search to see if you were safe after the storm. He will, of course, see you this evening at the welcome celebrations."

Ingeborg at first felt humiliated that her future husband was not meeting her in person, as it would be an unforgivable slight to her and her family, but the Chancellor's explanation satisfied her. She smiled politely as they greeted the Danish king's two sisters and an endless line of nobles, before they were finally escorted to the castle and shown to their quarters.

"Now that we are on firm ground after two weeks on the ship, it feels as if this floor is moving under my feet," Kristina observed as she looked longingly at the wide bed in Ingeborg's chamber.

Kristina had never seen a more beautiful private abode. It had uncommonly large windows that allowed the sun to shine directly into the room. Beyond the windows stretched the glittering waters they had just navigated. The windowpanes were of differently tinted glass positioned in lovely patterns. Under the windows ran built-in benches covered with plush cushions. Rikissa sat down among the pillows and pulled her legs up, looking over the green lawn sloping down towards the water. "I, too, feel sick," she admitted.

"That happens sometimes when one gets off a ship after a long journey," said the queen as she inspected every corner of her daughter's new chamber. The floors were covered with fine woven carpets, and the walls were hung with tapestries depicting female figures in garden settings.

"It is indeed a lovely room, Ingeborg. You will be comfortable here. Now you should all rest before the welcome feast commences. I heard that the Hall will be filled to capacity."

Once Queen Helvig left the room the three girls began to undress. When they had carefully draped their tunics over a bench they heard a soft knock on the door.

"Come in," called Ingeborg and the door opened to reveal Princess Marta of Denmark.

"Am I disturbing you?" she asked when she saw them in their under-dresses.

"Not at all," said Ingeborg warmly. "Do come in."

Marta, two years Ingeborg's senior, slipped into the room, peering out in the corridor before she closed the door as if she did not want anyone to see where she was going. She turned around to face the new arrivals. " I have looked forward to your coming," she said as she took Ingeborg's hands in hers.

She was far shorter than Ingeborg, petite and almost fragile in appearance. Her face was thin, and her hands were long and narrow. Her pale reddish hair hung to below her waist, making her look as though she was wrapped in a protective blanket. The reddish hue made her flawless skin appear even paler than it was; but her eyes that were huge for her small features, reflected the energy of a physically larger person. She imparted a sense of strength and frailty at the same time.

"I have so longed for someone my own age since my sister, Rigitze, married. Her words came rapidly, a little nervously. "I heard there was a storm. Was it terrible?" she asked without a pause. Ingeborg twice opened her mouth to answer, just to close it again. "But now you are here, safe and sound, and that is what matters." She stood back and looked at Ingeborg with approval. "You look just like I have always dreamt of looking. So tall and imposing, just as a queen should be." She bent forward and gave Ingeborg an impulsive kiss on the cheek. Then her eyes wandered towards Rikissa, and she let go of Ingeborg's hands. "I am so happy to meet you, too; and I do look forward to being with you in Sweden." She beamed as she looked toward Kristina. "And you, Kristina Torgilsdotter, I welcome you as a sister too."

The three Swedish girls were transfixed by Marta's energy that seemed to fill the room. But as she sat down on the window bench it seemed as if the light suddenly left her eyes. They were still large and compelling, but her exuberance had vanished. She looked distant.

Ingeborg was the first to respond. "I am delighted to have both you and Kristina near me. It will make me feel so at home."

As suddenly as Marta had withdrawn, just as suddenly she came back with a big, warm smile. "Now, do tell me about your journey. Was it terrifying?"

Later that evening Ingeborg stood before a large mirror in her new chamber, turning from side to side and scrutinizing herself. She was ready to meet the Danish court.

"I am proud of you," said her mother, making the rare compliment sound like a demand to become even better.

"Thank you, Mother," Ingeborg said resignedly.

A soft knock was heard before the door opened to reveal the Father Confessor at the Danish court. "His Majesty has asked me to spend a few moments alone with Princess Ingeborg before she joins the festivities," he explained.

"We have our own Father Confessor," objected the queen.

"Naturally, Your Majesty," said the priest with a kindly smile, which was hard to accomplish since he had a warrior's harsh face. "But His Majesty especially asked me to see the princess alone," he persisted in such a soft, yet commanding tone of voice that the queen could no longer object.

"Let us proceed to the Hall," she said to the others with ill-concealed annoyance. She marched out of the room trailed by Rikissa, Kristina and two ladies-in-waiting.

"I apologize if I displeased your mother, or you," said the priest, "but King Erik Menved wanted to see you alone before the festivities."

Ingeborg nodded and looked towards the door. The man who walked in moved with purpose. He was dressed in the finest tunic

Ingeborg had ever seen. It was elegantly cut and thickly embroidered in gold. Over it he wore an elaborate thick chain of office draped upon his shoulders. His belt and sword scabbard were made of pure gold, and even the tops of his soft boots were decorated in gold. His straight-cut red hair reached to his shoulders and was encircled with a thick band of gold. Finally, her eyes were drawn to his face, and she gasped in recognition as she saw his clear green eyes.

"May I introduce His Majesty, King Erik Menved of Denmark," said the priest as he quietly withdrew from the chamber. Ingeborg stared at her future husband, unable to speak.

"It was you, my Lady?" asked Erik Menved, equally surprised.

"It was you . . ." was all she could say.

"Are you glad?" he asked.

"Oh, yes . . ." she confessed, blushing at her own forthrightness.

"I am glad, too," he said as he pulled her towards the window bench and gestured for her to sit down. "How could I be this fortunate?" he asked shaking his head.

"I never even pondered that it could be you."

"Nor did I think it was you, but rather some beautiful lady in your entourage whom I would have to admire from a distance."

They sat silently looking at one another. "What did you mean when you said that they were cursed, and that everyone who got near them became cursed. Who are 'they'?" he asked.

"Did I say that? I remember so little. But if I said it I meant your family."

"You must explain, my Lady."

"All through my childhood I heard stories whispered about your family. How brother murdered brother."

"Well, it is true, so I do not blame you for being concerned. My grandfather was killed by his brother; and while my father was murdered, it was not by a brother, even though there were several relatives involved. I have blood on my crown, Ingeborg, but I have lived with that fact all my life, so to me it seems absurdly normal." He reached over and took her hands in his. "I promise you that I will do everything I can to protect you from any harm. I can do no more than that. Should you, however, desire to break our betrothal, I will relieve you from your promise because I already care enough for you to wish you no unhappiness."

"I could not do that. This is an important alliance for both our countries."

"I admire your sense of loyalty, but I am repeating my offer."

"My Lord, would you prefer that we broke the betrothal?"

Erik Menved smiled. "No, my Lady, I most certainly do not."

"Then, in memory of our meeting in the glen, I will trust you and stay by your side whatever may happen."

"I am indeed a lucky man to be promised such a brave wife," he said as he pulled her up from the bench. "Let us swear, here and now, to be loyal to each other, to trust and share. It will be just the two of us against the power-hungry throng out there," he gestured towards the Hall.

"I swear," whispered Ingeborg, again feeling all her fear melt away under his open gaze. She felt so utterly protected by him, and over-joyed that he saw her as a partner.

"Let us join the others," Erik Menved said. "They have been patiently awaiting their new queen. I know they will be very pleased."

Ingeborg adored the puzzled look on her mother's face when she entered the Great Hall with her hand comfortably in Erik Menved's. She felt so relaxed and so at ease that she hardly recognized herself. She seemed to be saying just the right things to everybody without trying. She was feeling so lighthearted and exuberant that she never even noticed the expression on her future brother-in-law's face.

Kristina stood on the dock below Roskilde castle with Ingeborg, Rikissa, and Queen Helvig, observing sprays of flowers gliding slowly away on the water. Kristina tossed her roses after the others and watched them follow along with the current. After Father Nils concluded the final prayer for Lady Constance and the sailors who were lost in the storm, the small group genuflected. The girls and the priest then started to go back toward the castle while the queen remained motionless at the end of the dock.

"We should stay with Mother," whispered Ingeborg. The three girls returned quietly to the queen who stood with her head bowed, not seeming to notice their approach. Without warning, she threw her head back and let out a cry of anguish. Tears flowed down her cheeks. Ingeborg, stunned by her outburst, anxiously touched her mother's hand. The queen turned and wrapped her arms around her daughter, clinging to her and crying from the depth of her soul. Kristina had never seen her display such emotion.

"I did not know that you cared so much for Lady Constance." was all Ingeborg could say.

"How could anyone know," uttered the queen as she tried to collect herself. "A queen must never display her feelings, never show her vulnerability. Not even to those close to her." She withdrew a handkerchief from her sleeve and dabbed at her eyes. "Constance was with me when I arrived in Sweden. She was by my side during the twelve years of agony when the Pope withheld his blessing on my marriage to your father because of our close family relationship. I could have been cast aside; and you, my children, would all have been bastards, but she stood by me. She was with me when there was an uprising against your father and I had to flee to a convent. She was always there, caring for me, protecting me. Now she is gone."

The queen straightened her back and composed herself. She wiped away the last of her tears and looked at her daughters. "If you girls remember nothing that I have taught you, remember this: find someone, just one person, you can confide in so that you are not alone. Constance meant so much to me. May her soul rest in peace." The queen crossed herself, put her arms around her daughters, and walked with her head high toward the castle.

The girls had collected in Ingeborg's chamber, preparing themselves for supper.

"Are you still feeling nervous, Ingeborg?" Rikissa asked.

"Not as much as before."

"I would not be nervous if I were about to marry someone as attentive as Erik Menved," said Kristina.

"He has been kind," Ingeborg admitted with a smile.

Their conversation was interrupted by a knock on the door and Marta entered peering carefully in both directions of the corridor before she closed the door, carrying a small chest before her.

"My brother sent me," she began. "He did not want you to be surprised by the weight of the official crown, so he thought you might want to get used to it gradually by wearing it for a time each day." She placed the chest on the table and opened it.

The girls jumped off the bed and looked inside. Cushioned on a soft pillow, lay a massive crown, encrusted with precious stones. Marta lifted it out carefully and approached Ingeborg to place it on her head. After she adjusted it Ingeborg went over to the mirror to view herself. Not only the flattering reflection but the weight of it reminded her that in just a few days she would become the Queen of Denmark. As she smiled at her image she remembered her mother's words. She would not only be the most powerful and most envied woman in Denmark, she would also be the loneliest. She turned and looked at the beaming faces admiring her.

"Will I always be able to trust you?" she asked. The happy faces looked puzzled. "Will you always be my friends?"

"Of course, we will," Kristina assured her, looking confused.

"You can certainly trust me," said Marta. I need a friend just as much as you do. One cannot trust anyone at court. I should know."

"Is that why you always look behind you like a scared rabbit?" blurted Rikissa.

Marta hesitated a moment before she spoke again. "I was only seven years old when my father, King Erik Klipping, was assassinated. He had gone off on a hunting trip, and when the weather turned bad he and his chamberlain took cover from the rain in a barn in Finderup. During the night, while they were sleeping, some men—close friends of my father--crept into the barn and stabbed him to death. They brought his body home in the early morning hours. The pealing of bells awakened me, and I immediately sensed that something terrible had happened. I wrapped myself in a blanket and raced downstairs on bare feet. I saw my mother as she stood in the middle of the Hall with her ladies-in-waiting huddled around her. She was staring at the door through which they bore my father's body on a rickety, wooden pallet. Everything was so quiet; no one moved or said a word while the pallet was placed on a long table. I started to scream and ran to throw myself on my father's mutilated body. The Lord High Constable tried to pry me off, but I clung to my father's bloodied clothes. My mother tried to reason with me, but I could not bear to let go of him. As long as I held on to him I did not have to look at him and know that he would never again smile at me.

"Finally, my brother, Erik Menved came in, and everyone bowed deeply to him. At the age of twelve, and without any warning, he was King of Denmark. His first act as a monarch was to loosen my arms from my father's corpse and hold me close while he murmured calming words in my ear.

"It took days for me to truly comprehended what had happened. It was not because I did not understand. It was because I did not want to understand that a mighty king could be killed by his most trusted friends.

"No one has actually stood trial for the murder, although seven men were declared guilty in absentia for committing the crime. They fled to Norway once the court, under the jurisdiction of our Lord High Constable, found them guilty and sentenced them to death. Quite a few of the nobility felt they were innocent, including some devoted allies of my father. They felt it was a maneuver by the Lord High Constable to get rid of some potential troublemakers and consolidate power for the young king. Whatever the case may have been, my brother does not have to contend with these men who were once ruling large areas of Denmark."

"My mother became a changed person from that moment on. She thought that everyone was plotting to kill her and her children. She only trusted those servants who had been with her for most of her life, so we rarely saw anyone who was not stooped over with age. She kept all her valuables packed in case she had to leave in haste. I can remember one cold and rainy night when she hid us beneath some fir trees amidst her boxes to wait for imaginary assassins to assault the castle. For years, we were virtual prisoners locked in for weeks during the short summer months when the sun glowed so magically in the meadows. She prevented us from playing with other children who she suspected were relatives of would-be assassins. My brothers soon rebelled, but Rigitze and I were required to remain indoors unless we were under the protection of armed guards. After a while, Rigitze and I begged to be sent to a convent, since that seemed wonderfully permissive in comparison to life with Mother. We were sent away, and those years were actually happy ones for both of us, but as you noticed the fear I learned from her has never entirely left me." Marta looked forlorn as she finished her story.

"I have not seen Queen Agnes since our arrival," said Rikissa.

"Mother does not live at court anymore," Marta replied. "Once my brother became de facto king, she left Roskilde. I think she imagines that she is distracting our "enemies" by living elsewhere. I know that she is happier away. So much so that she has not been back for years. We have stopped inviting her since she always declines."

Ingeborg had hoped that hearing the whole story from Marta would somehow reassure her. Instead she felt a shiver run down her spine.

"I have taken the liberty of selecting a lady-in-waiting for you, Ingeborg," Marta said, changing the subject. "Lady Brigitte served my mother before she left, and she has been with Rigitze and me since we were born. I have chosen her because she has such a pleasant way about her, and she has very sound judgment. Lady Brigitte will start attending you on the morrow, and she will stay on if you approve."

"How very kind of you," Ingeborg replied gratefully. "I was worried about how to choose my first lady-in-waiting without insulting anyone, and now you have solved that for me."

Erik lifted a blue and white silk veil from the table in his and Valdemar's chamber. "And to whom does this belong?"

"Kristoffer told me that those were the colors of the sister of the marshal," answered Valdemar as he joined Erik by the table. "And that one belongs to none other than the bishop's sister."

Erik chuckled. "You seem to have made an impression, brother." He quickly counted almost a dozen delicate silk squares.

"You have not done badly yourself," Valdemar said as he pointed to a sizeable pile on a bench nearby with no trace of envy in his voice.

He had been surprised to find any silks at all in his own tunic pockets on different occasions when they arrived back in their chamber. How the women managed to slip them there was a mystery to him. Not once had he caught anyone doing it--to him or to Erik. "So, whom will you pick?" he asked.

"No one. You know as well as I do that they want marriage."

"I am sure several of them would settle for a secret tryst with the greatest of pleasure."

"The problem is to figure out who those would be. It is easier to dally with one of the lesser ladies, especially a married one who would be thrilled by attention from a royal."

They left their chamber to mingle in the Great Hall and to partake in the daily supper. Erik once again surveyed the huge room. It irked him to compare the majesty of Roskilde castle to the castles in Sweden. He swore to himself that on becoming master of Nykoping castle in a few years, he would refurbish it. He disliked the idea of living like a poor relation to Erik Menved whom he had come to hold in high esteem.

And how could he not admire his future brother-in-law? Erik Menved exuded an aura of strength and power. Erik sensed the keen intelligence beneath his composure. He was surprisingly attentive to detail, and nothing seemed to escape him. He would even chastise a poorly attired servant or have wine cups changed for his guests if the wrong ones had been placed on the tables. These were not normal concerns for a king, but they had an impact on his court. No one spoke carelessly in his presence, and all deferred to him as if he could read their minds and might punish them if their thoughts displeased him. He commanded great respect, if not always affection, and his courtiers gossiped about him only with the greatest caution.

Kristina was listening to the guests chatting around her. It seemed, strangely enough, that the busy meals in the Great Hall were the only moments she could relax and not have to smile and talk to everyone who wanted to endear themselves to her as one of the persons close to their future queen. She knew how important her role as Ingeborg's shield would be for the next two years, and she took her position most seriously. She had to discern which of the courtiers were insincere, as they were all displaying utmost kindness. The smirk on someone's face when they turned their back on Ingeborg could signal of whom to be wary.

The banquet was winding down in the Great Hall, and the noble ladies had long withdrawn. "This party is getting dull," slurred Kristoffer as he reached over to nudge Erik sitting beside him at the end of the dais table. "Let us seek some real entertainment."

"I am having a good time where I am," answered Erik, amazed that Kristoffer could still sit up, let alone speak in coherent sentences after all the wine he had imbibed. As Erik studied Kristoffer, he was again struck by the physical similarity between the two Danish brothers who were so different in character. Kristoffer, like his brother, had red hair and green eyes, but both his hair and eyes were paler than his brother's, as if touched by a shade of grey. While Erik Menved's face was open and resolute, Kristoffer's was guarded and secretive. He exuded negativism, and often sounded sarcastic, even angry. But Kristoffer was also a man of action, which Erik thoroughly enjoyed. They had been hunting and riding together during every free moment since their arrival.

Kristoffer drew himself up on unsteady legs and motioned for his friend, Anders Hojby, to join him. "Come along!" he coaxed as he left the dais table.

Erik and Valdemar stood up and were joined by Mats who had been sitting next to Lord Anders at a lower table. "Where are we going?" he inquired.

"I have no idea," Erik answered, "but let us see what Kristoffer has in mind." Erik glanced over to the center of the dais where Birger was deep in conversation with Erik Menved. " Birger will not be joining us," he concluded as he followed Kristoffer out of the Hall.

The five men exited the castle and walked over to the large, round prison tower where Kristoffer banged loudly on the door. They heard the turning of keys in several locks before the warden held the door ajar and smiled in recognition.

"Back with us again, eh," he chuckled as he motioned for the group to enter.

They came into a large area, occupying the entire diameter of the tower, where one circular stone staircase followed the curve of the wall upwards and another wound downward. Even though it was a warm summernight, the walls were gleaming with moisture and the straw on the floor was damp under their feet. Eight guards, sitting by a table at the far end, rose to their feet as the princes entered and smiled in anticipation. They quickly lit more candles to light up the dark space, while four of them descended the spiral staircase. The remaining guards moved forward the benches they had occupied to permit the princes and their friends to sit down. Kristoffer, who had brought a flask of wine, took a slug before he passed it around.

"Now, you are going to see the sport of our forefathers," he chuckled. "You shall watch real berserk fighting." Erik had heard stories of Viking warriors who went wild after drinking a special brew, and who fought with superhuman strength until they were either victorious or dead. He had also heard about their form of hand-to-hand combat, but he had never witnessed it, and he felt a chill of excitement.

"My brother does not countenance this and would be angered to learn we are here," continued Kristoffer. "But we have an understanding here," he said as he winked at the warden.

Erik could hear the rattling of chains, and soon two prisoners were brought up the stairs. The warden went over and unlocked their fetters. The men blinked their eyes to get accustomed to the light and began massaging their wrists and ankles. Despite their imprisonment, they were muscular and appeared in good physical condition.

"You know the arrangement," said the warden. "You fight each other, and the winner is set free. And as a special privilege you get to have a drink with Prince Kristoffer himself."

One of the guards returned with a keg of beer from which he filled two large tankards. Out of the prisoners' sight the warden added a few drops to each tankard from a small vial he had taken from his pocket. "Drink to your savior," he nodded toward Kristoffer.

The two prisoners grasped the tankards, bowed to their prince who lifted his flask in response, and emptied their contents to the last drop.

"I would not mind another," burped the one who had finished first.

"You can have as much as you want," mused Kristoffer as the guard poured the tankards full again.

After downing yet another refill the two men declared themselves ready to fight.

"It is betting time, my friends," Kristoffer said to the guards. If you win I will pay double your wager. You, too," he said, turning to his Swedish guests.

Valdemar nudged Erik. "Let us leave. Erik Menved would not be pleased to find us here, and I do not relish slaughter like this."

"We are guests here," Erik whispered, despite his feeling that the whole experience would be a tawdry one. "Stay, brother, we cannot insult Kristoffer."

Valdemar reluctantly settled back, while Erik pulled out some silver coins that he dropped on the floor between his feet. "Let my bet be for the three of us," he said quickly as he realized how much he had dropped in the straw. He looked at his brother and Mats. "You pick the winner."

The guards had just placed a red belt around the taller of the two combatants and a blue one around the waist of the stockier one.

"Well," said Mats pensively. "I think we should wager on the one wearing the red belt."

"He looks fine," agreed Erik.

After ascertaining who was right-handed and who was left-handed, the guards took a thick leather thong, carefully measured its length, cut it to the right size, and tied one end to the left wrist of the red fighter and the other end to the right wrist of the blue fighter. The two prisoners stood in the center of the arena, dressed only in torn pants and bound to one another by the short restricting tether. The guards held up two hunting knives with long sharpened blades. "Whenever you say, your Highness," said the warden to Kristoffer.

"You say when," offered Kristoffer graciously to Erik, who silently nodded to the warden.

The combatants were handed their knives and the guards stood back. The two started to circle, studying each other intently. The eerie silence and the fighters' huge shadows dancing on the walls mesmerized the viewers. The blue fighter took two quick steps forward, slashing his opponent on the chest. Erik realized that every assault would result in cuts since the opponent could not escape his attacker's reach. The red fighter became infuriated by the pain and assaulted his adversary with cut after cut on his arms and chest. The blue fighter roared in fury and renewed his attacks with equally bloody results.

The fighters' eyes were burning with hate, and Erik had never seen such raw fury as that which emanated from these men. After only a few minutes both fighters were dripping with gore and screaming at the top of their lungs. They seemed impervious to the pain they were suffering and totally focused on how to inflict the most horrendous damage on the other. They reminded Erik of hunting dogs fighting over a scrap of meat when they were at the point of starvation, madly attacking with total disregard of their own safety.

The sweet smell of blood mingling with that of sour sweat was overpowering, and Erik felt his stomach start to heave and the hair on his neck stand up. He sat on the edge of the bench, spellbound by every knife thrust. The crazed combatants kept moving, circling and attacking, cutting each other ever more viciously. They no longer looked human. Every part of them was oozing blood. Before long, entrails were spilling from a deep cut in the blue fighter's stomach. Bones were laid bare where blades sliced more than once, and their roars were deafening as they kept up their insane assault. The straw beneath their feet became red from dripping blood. They slid around in the mess as they wildly stabbed at one another. The red fighter suddenly managed to pull the blue one off his feet into the slimy straw. He jumped on him and quickly slit his throat. The blue fighter's body shook spasmodically, his knife hand stabbing in the air as if he did not comprehend that he was no longer alive. As the red fighter roared triumphantly and turned to Kristoffer to lift his arm in victory, his eyes glazed over and he fell unconscious across the body of his vanquished foe.

"They will both die," reflected Valdemar aloud.

"That is the idea," grinned Kristoffer grimly. "If they do not bleed to death, they die from the potion they drank. Keeps our prison nice and empty. " He leaned down to pick up the bets from those that had lost and tossed the proper amounts beside the winning bets. Erik collected his generous pile of coins and gave half to Mats and half to Valdemar before he quickly left the tower and its powerful stench of death.

After the wedding festivities that had lasted three long days, the Swedish entourage stood on the dock bidding their farewells. Ingeborg, Marta and Kristina had their arms entwined around Rikissa who was crying helplessly. "I cannot imagine what my life back in Sweden will be like without you," Rikissa whispered, which brought Ingeborg to tears as well.

"I will see you soon," responded Ingeborg as her mother gently led Rikissa away towards the gangplank.

Kristina then turned to her father who pulled her into a powerful hug. "I am so proud of you, and I know that you will be of immense help to Queen Ingeborg," he said, "But damn my soul, I will miss you fiercely." Kristina looked up at him. The pain of knowing that he would not be close by tore at her, and she buried her face in his huge, safe chest. "Two years will pass quickly," he added consolingly.

She nodded and took a step back. "Of course, father" she answered bravely as he turned to board the ship.

Kristina remained on the dock watching Birger bid farewell to Marta. He kissed her hands gently before he scaled the gangplank. Kristina wished that Erik had bid goodbye to her in the same way; but he had not even said farewell, and now she did not see him anywhere. Suddenly she heard his voice behind her.

"I saved you for last," he added as he swung her around and transfixed her with his intense blue eyes. Just then the sailors were about to raise the gangplank and cast off from shore.

"Take good care of Ingeborg," he said as he leaned down to give her a hasty kiss on the cheek before rushing away to board the ship.

Chapter 5

Kristina soon discovered that she enjoyed living in the ladies' quarters at Roskilde castle. Not that the spacious dormitory was as comfortable as the royal chambers she had shared in Sweden, but it was the place where every secret in the castle became known. The atmosphere was always intriguing as new visitors came and went.

The sleeping areas consisted of wooden platforms running along the walls where each of the ladies had a thick straw mattress with fine linen sheets and soft pillows, and beneath which each lady kept her clothes chest. In the center of the lengthy room stood a long table where the ladies would read and embroider by the light of a multitude of candles. The south wall had several small windows through which traces of daylight filtered into the dark room. As the first ladies to the queen, Kristina and Lady Brigitte enjoyed honored places in a quiet corner of the room. The other ladies treated Kristina and Lady Brigitte with great respect and made every effort to ingratiate themselves in the hope of being privy to news from the royal chambers. None were successful, however, as Kristina and Lady Brigitte never allowed personal news of their mistress to be pried from them.

Kristina had never imagined that so many intrigues could be devised in a single day as were hatched at the Danish court. Most often they were petty and involved only the vanity or ambition of the courtiers, but sometimes they were dangerous and could sully or ruin an innocent. Kristina remembered how one of the ladies-in-waiting had spread lies about a rival who had captured the attention of the man she loved. Through skillful manipulation the lies became "truth" and the other woman was banished from court. Though the heartbroken man had to renounce his affection for the exiled woman to save his own good name, the lady-in-waiting never regained his love.

It had not taken Queen Ingeborg long to sense webs being spun around her and to decide not to become ensnared in any of the seemingly innocent games played to break the boredom of the long and dark winters. The courtiers, who instinctively sensed her resolve, soon ceased to involve her or Kristina in their frivolous pursuits. Erik Menved praised Ingeborg for her determination to stay aloof, even if it meant distancing herself from potential friends and valuable information. Lady Brigitte, who had spent most of her adult life at court, understood just what her new mistress wished; and her protective and capable handling of Ingeborg's everyday life was a blessing for the new queen. But while Lady Brigitte served as a shield, she could not protect her mistress from other members of the royal family.

Four months after the wedding it became evident to Ingeborg that Prince Kristoffer was far from pleased about the joyful news that she was with child. While everyone doted on her and the king beamed with predictable pride, Kristoffer skulked around the periphery. Whenever he inquired about Ingeborg's condition he looked disappointed to learn that she was in excellent health.

"He loathes me," lamented Ingeborg one night after she had withdrawn to her chamber.

"No, he does not," objected Kristina who was alone with Ingeborg. "He wants to rule some day, and he could become king if your husband perished in one of his many wars. But if you have one, or several sons, his chances of reaching the throne are slim."

"I do not like the way he looks at me with his malevolent eyes," said Ingeborg.

"You are especially sensitive now, Ingeborg. Do not worry so. Just ignore him."

Kristina wondered if her reassurances did not ring hollow as she, too, was troubled by Kristoffer's obvious lust for the crown. She hoped that Ingeborg was unaware of her and Lady Brigitte's special vigilance over her food. They supervised its preparation and served it themselves. Not that this was unusual, but was normally done as a matter of custom, not out of real concern. But Lady Brigitte had immediately insisted when the court physician announced the happy tidings.

"I have known Kristoffer from infancy, and from the moment he could understand anything, he wanted to be king," Lady Brigitte had whispered to Kristina. "His brother is aware of his ambition but seems to regard it as the normal and innocent dream of any king's younger brother. Kristoffer has always done whatever he pleased. He killed a little kitten just for fun that Princess Marta had when they were children, and he has beaten servants who displeased him within an inch of their lives."

At first Kristina had been shocked, but she realized that Ingeborg' first lady-in-waiting had come to love her new queen and would do anything to protect her. Still, Kristina had never noticed anyone trying to interfere with Ingeborg's food or drink, and as the months went by she began to feel that Lady Brigitte had exaggerated the need for precautions.

But then, one day when Kristina was in the bustling kitchens to heat some tea for Ingeborg, she saw Kristoffer pass the door and look in the direction of the herbal woman's corner, but once he noticed Kristina he turned quickly and left. He could have needed a remedy for any small illness of his own she thought, but then why had he left so suddenly upon seeing her? Although Kristina despised the suspicions that were overtaking her, she reminded herself that she had to do whatever was required to protect Ingeborg and the baby. She carried the tea up to the queen's chamber to find Ingeborg lying on her bed, her face an ashen gray.

"We have called for the physician," explained Marta anxiously as she stroked Ingeborg's forehead. "At first we thought she had one of her headaches, but this seems different."

Father John came though the door and immediately went to the bedside. He leaned over to examine Ingeborg. "The queen needs rest. I will give her something to sleep," he said as he left to find the herbalist monk.

Kristina, Marta, and two ladies-in-waiting helped Ingeborg remove her tunic before pulling a down-filled coverlet over her. As Kristina plumped up the pillows a small amulet fell by her feet. She picked it up and saw it was a tiny metal Thor's hammer--the kind worn by pagan Vikings--which must have been hidden among the bed-curtain folds. She felt intuitively that it had been placed there with evil intent, as Thor was the god of thunder and lightning. She quickly put it in her tunic pocket.

Father John returned and helped Ingeborg swallow the potion the herbalist had prepared. "Now you rest," he ordered calmly, but Kristina could see that he was concerned.

As soon as Kristina was able to gesture discreetly to Lady Brigitte, the two women quietly left the room. Not for a moment had it occurred to her to share her discovery with Princess Marta, although Marta was equally devoted to Ingeborg. But Kristina knew that Marta would only become frightened which would help no one.

"This fell from among the bed curtains," Kristina confided.

Lady Brigitte looked at the tiny charm with alarm. "Let us talk to Father John. He might have some remedy if it was meant to cause harm," she suggested as they hurried along the corridor and down the stairs towards the chapel. They reached the chapel where Father John was sitting alone, reading.

"Is the queen getting worse?" he asked when he saw their concerned expressions.

"We found this in the queen's bed," said Kristina holding out the small amulet.

"Thor's Hammer," Father John mumbled as he took it from her hand. "It was often used for protection in battle, but also to wreak destruction on an enemy. We should not underestimate the power of dark Viking magic. How long has this been in the queen's bed?"

"I do not know," said Lady Brigitte searching her memory. "It has been a fortnight since we changed the bedding, so it could have been there for some time"

"That is troubling," said Father John, looking grave. "Evil penetrates deeper with the passing of time. You must change the bedding right away and inspect it every day. I will sprinkle it with holy water, which should take care of any immediate threat. That is, if any harm was intended in the first place. I have to confess that I suspect it was, because I could find nothing wrong with the queen and yet she is sick."

Father John's instructions were followed faithfully, but during the night Ingeborg lost her child, leaving the new bedding soaked with blood and tears. The king looked pitifully sad when he was called to his wife's side. "I am so sorry," Ingeborg whispered.

"It was the will of God. He will grant us a son in time, have no fear," he said softly. He stayed by her bedside until she drifted off to sleep.

Kristina would never forget the sadness in Ingeborg's eyes as the weeks and months passed. The cloud only lifted half a year later when Father John pronounced that she was again with child. The entire court, which had keenly felt the queen's distress, came to life; while the cheerful smile Kristoffer had sported for so many months vanished.

Although Kristina had no proof that the amulet had been placed to harm Ingeborg or that Kristoffer had anything to do with her miscarriage, she turned Ingeborg's bedding inside out every morning and night. Ingeborg noticed her taking those precautions, but she remained silent. Having become disciplined in her role as queen, Ingeborg observed whatever custom and duty prescribed, regardless of her preference or feelings.

Then, just as suddenly, Ingeborg fell ill again. She was put to bed and to sleep with the help of the herbalist monk's concoctions. But nothing could save the baby, which was stillborn two days later. The king sat by his wife's bed, night after night, holding her hand while she cried herself to sleep.

Father John suggested that the queen's chamber should be locked every time the ladies left it for meals or entertainment, and he would sprinkle the room with holy water every morning and night. That was, of course, if the queen ever got with child again. To facilitate that likelihood, Father John suggested that they hold morning prayers in the queen's own chamber instead of in the chapel in order to make her room as inviting for God's generous deeds as possible.

Quite close to Kristina in the ladies' quarters, slept a pretty young girl by the name of Lady Irmgaard, the daughter of a powerful North German count who was an ally of King Erik Menved. Rumors quickly circulated that her dowry was wanting due to her father's costly wars. It was understood that her family had sent her to Roskilde hoping that she would beguile some wealthy Dane with her grace and beauty, if not her dowry.

Lady Irmgaard was thirteen years old and truly lovely to behold. Fine-boned, willowy, yet shy as a result of having been reared in a rural setting where few travelers journeyed, she had no idea how comely she was with her big eyes and sultry mouth. Ingeborg, Marta, and Kristina had not failed to note the interest aroused amongst the male courtiers the first time Lady Irmgaard entered the Great Hall.

It was soon apparent to all what a fine girl Irmgaard was--hard-working, self-effacing, and always eager to please. Unbidden, Irmgaard had taken it upon herself to wait on Kristina and Lady Brigitte. Kristina had grown exceedingly fond of her and hoped that her prospects for a felicitous alliance would be realized.

Kristina had watched Kristoffer ogle Irmgaard at moments when he thought he was not being observed. The lecherous glint in his eyes was unmistakable as he touched himself under his tunic. Kristina's dismay came from the realization that the lovely maiden was not high-born enough to marry into the royal family, so if Kristoffer seduced her it would never be in a marriage bed, and the sweet girl's prospects for a respectable marriage would be ruined. She promised herself to keep a watchful eye on Irmgaard.

In the days that followed, Kristina was grateful not to be the target herself of Kristoffer's attention as she watched him in the Great Hall continuing to ogle Irmgaard, his eyes hazy with desire. If Irmgaard was aware of his feelings, she gave no indication of it.

As was the custom before the Easter celebrations, the ladies went into the garden with their spades to dig up spring bulbs so that they could be potted and enjoyed indoors. Kristina and Irmgaard partic-ipated by preparing a large silver trough for the chapel. They added dirt and lovingly arranged the tender white and purple buds in an intricate pattern. Once Ingeborg gave her approval, they lifted the heavy trough between them to carry it toward the castle. They had to stop several times to rest before they entered the courtyard where they sat down on a bench, out of breath and laughing at themselves.

"Let me help you, ladies," said Kristoffer who suddenly appeared in the courtyard.

Before Kristina could protest he had lifted the large container and started towards the chapel, apparently remembering where he had seen it every Easter through his childhood.

"Your Highness, please do not concern yourself," pleaded Irmgaard as she raced after him across the yard. "Lady Kristina and I were managing quite well, even if we were a little slow."

"Just show me where you want it," said Kristoffer, ignoring her protests as he moved on with long, rapid strides.

Kristina hurried after them, but by the time she reached the chapel, Kristoffer had kicked the heavy door shut behind them.

He could not possibly have anything evil in mind, thought Kristina as she touched the door latch. Not in a House of God.

As she pushed against the door and at the same time tried to lift the latch, she was unable to open it. When she nervously pushed harder against the door, relieving the pressure on the latch, she finally managed to open it. She saw Kristoffer holding Irmgaard close to him.

"Thank you very much, Your Highness," Kristina called as she walked quickly towards them. "We will arrange the altar ourselves."

Kristoffer turned to her as he slowly released Irmgaard. He looked amused and his mouth was curved in a sarcastic smile.

"How officious we are, Lady Kristina. One would almost think that you suspected me of impure thoughts here in this holy chapel." He laughed as he walked out.

Irmgaard looked ashen and Kristina reached out to touch her arm. "Are you all right?" she asked.

"He frightens me," was all Irmgaard could whisper.

"Has he tried to be alone with you like this before?" asked Kristina.

"Yes, he creeps up behind me when I least expect it, and I do not like the way he touches me. He always smells foul from wine and horse spill. Oh, Lady Kristina, I am afraid of him, but I cannot push him away as he is the king's brother."

Irmgaard's eyes filled with tears and her words came hesitantly. "Lord Kjell has shown an interest in me and we have spent time together talking in the Hall, and I could not be happier if he wanted to marry me. But now that Prince Kristoffer has indicated his interest, not one of the men will speak to me. And I am not a fool, nor is anyone else, to think that it is marriage he wants from me. I feel so unclean, and yet I have done nothing wrong."

She broke into tears as Kristina protectively put her arms about her. "Do not cry, my dear. I will watch out for you."

After that incident Kristina kept Irmgaard near her. In the Great Hall Kristina made certain that Lord Kjell, a young and strapping knight, was asked to sit nearby, invitations he gratefully accepted since he dared not approach Irmgaard on his own. Kristoffer kept shooting hungry looks in Irmgaard's direction, and Kristina knew that he was simply waiting for the right moment to be alone with her. Many a night Kristina prayed that the king or the queen would discover what was brewing and tell Kristoffer to direct his attention elsewhere, but he was careful in their presence and they did not seem to notice his interest. Ingeborg and Marta might have wondered why Irmgaard was never out of Kristina's sight, but they did not seek an explanation nor would Kristina volunteer one. As close as the women were, Kristoffer was part of their family and it would not do to gossip about him.

With the fickle spring weather came the usual seasonal ailments. Coughs and sniffles were heard from every corner of the castle. Living in close proximity, no one escaped this disabling spring rite. Both the king and queen were stricken along with the ladies, knights, soldiers and servants. Everyone who could still stand erect, or who had recovered, was dispensing warm broth, honey-laced drinks, and cooling water to friends and superiors. The Father herbalist worked ceaselessly to ease fevers and pain, to calm coughs, and to induce healing sleep.

Irmgaard, who was strong and young, was one of the first to recover in the women's quarters. She began to work as soon as she could to attend the queen, Marta, Kristina, and Lady Brigitte, all of whom suffered from high fevers. Kristina had given strict orders to the kitchen staff, to the surgeon, and to the herbalist monks that they were not to send Irmgaard to Prince Kristoffer who specifically had asked that she serve him.

Late one night, Irmgaard happened to be alone in the kitchen, preparing some herbal tea to sooth Kristina's nagging cough. She was tipping the hot water kettle that hung from a chain above a mound of glowing coals, using an iron poker to pour boiling water into a beaker. She became aware of the fact that she was not alone by instinct rather than from any sound. As she slowly turned she saw Prince Kristoffer leaning against the doorway dressed only in a long, rumpled shirt and carrying a wine carafe in his hand.

"What luck," he grinned as he sauntered toward her. "All I wanted was some wine to soothe my fever but look what I found instead. An even better remedy."

Irmgaard carefully pushed back the chain holding the kettle over the coals and faced him with the poker in her hand.

"Do not look so frightened, my dear. Fear attracts predators."

She could see that he was already drunk. She tried to figure out how to escape since he was blocking her way to the Great Hall.

As he came closer she could smell the sour wine on his fevered breath. The stench made her weak with nausea. She backed away as he reached out and snatched the poker from her hand. Quickly she ran around the large fire pit to try to reach the door, but she underestimated his agility. His hand grasped her wrist just as she tried to flee the kitchen.

"Not so fast, my little one. Now, when we are finally alone I want to get to know you. Really well."

Brutally he pulled her around, causing her to drop the pitcher on the floor with a crash.

"Do not make so much noise. We do not want to wake up all those poor sick people when they need their rest so badly," he wheezed as he pulled her close to kiss her.

She fought desperately to escape his strong arms, his foul mouth and probing tongue; but he held her firmly in place. Suddenly he picked her up and walked over to the long kitchen table where he lifted her and sat her on the edge. She was struggling as he pushed her down on her back and pulled her legs towards him, one on each side of his body. He pinned her arms and held both with one of his hands while he pulled up her skirts with the other. He eagerly fumbled under his shirt for his member that was thick with excitement. Forcefully, he thrust himself into her while covering her mouth with his to muffle her screams. Beyond himself with desire over her tightness and the warm blood his thrusts brought forth, he moved wildly back and forth with moans of pleasure. He did not see the tears streaking her face or hear her muffled screams of pain as he mercilessly rode her. His pleasure was intense, but he did not end his assault until much later when he pushed her hard against the table, holding her legs and roaring with relief.

As he slowly pulled away from her she lay still on the table with her eyes closed, hardly breathing.

"You bitch," he mumbled under his breath. "You should not have tempted me the way you did."

He stumbled toward the pantry, grabbed the wine carafe that he had left by the firepit, and filled it from a large cask. He gulped the wine until it ran down his chin and onto his shirt where it mingled with her blood. He glared with contempt as she lay motionless on the table before he left the kitchens with a loud burp.

Irmgaard, in shock, fought against regaining consciousness. She did not want to awaken as she had done intermittently to find her body being brutally violated. But this time she was surrounded by stillness. Although her body was wracked with pain, at the same time it felt numb. She was unable to suppress her nausea and she vomited on the table. She felt strangely separated from her body as she pitied the girl laying there in puddles of blood, semen and vomit. Suddenly she slid off the table, and to her surprise when her feet touched the floor she could stand by leaning up against it. She was alive. Yet she wished she were dead.

She stood there for a long time, not remembering why she was there or what she should do next. Her first rational thought went to Kristina. She had to talk to someone. Her legs were weak and shaking and her whole body was trembling, but she managed to reach the firepit where she sank down to rest. She did not know how she would reach the women's quarters. But she had to get there.

By leaning against the walls for support, she staggered into the Great Hall and labored up the stairs. Quietly, she reached Kristina's bed and touched her.

"Please, come with me," she whispered pleadingly.

Kristina awoke from her fevered sleep, saw Irmgaard's disheveled state, and instantly sensed the urgency. She threw off her covers, wrapped a shawl around her shoulders, and pursued the girl who was already stumbling down the dark stairs towards the kitchens. When they entered the oven area lit by the glowing coals and a night candle, Irmgaard collapsed on the side of the firepit. Kristina's eyes flew over the room, and upon seeing the mess on the table she knew that Kristoffer had had his way with her. She drew a deep breath to fortify herself before she leaned down close to Irmgaard.

"Do not worry, my sweet. We will get through this together. Just do as I say."

Moving quickly, Kristina filled a basin with hot water and removed Irmgaard's only garment, her underdress. Gently she sponged off the young girl's shivering body, cleaned her vaginal area, wrapped her in her own shawl, and sat her down with a cup of steaming herbal tea while she cleaned up the table. Her anger made her utterly efficient and clearheaded.

"Irmgaard, listen to me. No one need know about this. That beast is not going to ruin your life. You will marry, have children, and live a wonderful life."

"How can I?" Irmgaard asked in a broken voice. "I have to be a virgin to marry a man of standing."

"Neither one of us know much about this, but being at court has taught me many things, and I have heard there are herbs that make you swell up inside to make a man think that he is bedding a virgin."

But Irmgaard was now crying with abandon and shaking her head. Kristina sat down beside her and enfolded her in her arms for a long time before she finally calmed down.

"Remember what I said," Kristina persisted. "That beast is not going to spoil your future. I know that you have had a horrifying experience, but we must keep this to ourselves and pretend that you had a sudden relapse of ailing so you can stay in bed and get some rest. Let me see what the herb woman has on her shelves."

Kristina found some herbs that she had seen Queen Helvig use when she could not sleep. She brewed them into a strong concoction that she gave Irmgaard to drink. Together, they walked up the stairs with Kristina supporting the still shaky Irmgaard whom she caringly put to bed. As Kristina crawled into her own bunk, she reached out to Irmgaard who eagerly held her hand before she fell into a deep and healing sleep.

Irmgaard remained in bed for the next several days. Kristina, who still had a fever, recuperated beside her and tried to make her talk about what had happened, hoping it would help clear her mind of the horrid memories before they festered there to torment her permanently. Quietly, so that no one could hear, Irmgaard allowed herself to relive those awful moments, damning the man who had shattered her peace of mind. Then came the healing tears, hours and hours of them. When Irmgaard finally left the confinement of the women's quarters, no one knew the true reason for her being so pale and her eyes so swollen. They just assumed that her 'relapse' had been severe.

When Irmgaard entered the Great Hall for the first time after the assault, knowing she would have to face Kristoffer again, Kristina could see that she was frightened. But just as Kristina had predicted, Kristoffer paid her no heed. Once the chase was over he had lost all interest. For that Irmgaard was grateful, but the hatred she felt when she saw him shocked her. Still, she knew she had to hide her feelings and go on with her devastated life.

Her anguish and despair intensified when she and Kristina realized how long it had been since her last monthly flow. A few months after that horrible episode left no doubt in either of their minds that Irmgaard was pregnant. They sat together on a stone bench in the garden one early summer eve, Irmgaard in tears and Kristina trying to console her.

"Now it does not matter if I keep up appearances, because my body will soon betray me," Irmgaard sobbed in desolation.

"There are remedies for that, as well. I will talk to the herbal woman."

"What happened to me was God's will. If He wills me to have a child, I will have a child."

"God does not wish an innocent to suffer, of that I am sure."

"I wish I could just go to sleep one night--never to awaken," cried Irmgaard.

It took Kristina a long time to calm Irmgaard enough to get her to bed; and finally, with the help of a strong potion, to sleep. No longer could Kristina contain her fury at what had befallen the young girl. Resolutely, she strode down the corridor to the queen's chamber.

Ingeborg noticed Kristina's expression the moment she entered, and immediately dismissed the ladies-in-waiting who were assisting her to undress. "Princess Marta and Lady Kristina will help me."

"What is it?" she asked with concern once the three of them were alone. "You look pale and upset. Come, Kristina, tell me what is bothering you."

Ingeborg took Kristina's hands and sat her down on a bench, all the while watching her. Marta sat down opposite them.

Kristina remained silent for a moment to consider the wisdom of telling not only Ingeborg, but also Marta, what had transpired. But the memory of Irmgaard's battered body made her break her silence and she told them the sad tale. "I could not tell you before, but now I have to. The poor girl is considering ending her life. We cannot allow that to happen."

Kristina could see the shock on Marta's face. "Kristoffer has always done whatever he pleased. He is ruthless and selfish. But to do this to sweet Irmgaard. . ." Marta had tears in her eyes as she shook her head in disbelief.

"I do wish that you had come to me earlier, even though I understand why you did not. Let me see what I can do to help," Ingeborg offered resolutely.

Later that night Ingeborg asked her husband, "If anyone would harm Lady Irmgaard while she is here under your protection, what would happen to that person?"

"Who would dare to harm a royal ward?" asked Erik Menved in turn.

"A member of the royal family perhaps," Ingeborg responded softly.

Erik Menved looked searchingly at his wife. "What are you trying to tell me?"

"Kristoffer raped her and she is pregnant," blurted Ingeborg tearfully. "That poor, innocent creature."

Erik Menved looked sternly at her. "This is a very serious accusation with dire consequences. Are you absolutely sure?"

Between sobs, Ingeborg related what had transpired and his face hardened as she spoke. "I will handle this," he vowed grimly, his jaw jutting out as he clenched his teeth.

"Why do you wish to see me at this ungodly hour, brother?" asked Kristoffer yawning widely as he entered the audience chamber.

"What happened between you and Irmgaard?" demanded Erik Menved who was standing with his back to his brother as he looked at the dawn's first light through the open window.

"What do you mean?" asked Kristoffer, his voice taking on a guarded tenor.

"Answer my question."

"Nothing, really . . ."

"What happened?" pressed Erik Menved in a commanding tone.

"Well," laughed Kristoffer. "We had a moment together, you know."

"In which she was a willing participant?"

"Of course," replied Kristoffer.

" She in no way objected to your advances?"

"Well, you know how young girls are. They lead you on and then they become concerned at the last moment."

"You should know, should you not?" asked Erik Menved coldly. "You seem to find only very young girls attractive."

"We all have our preferences," answered Kristoffer.

"Since young girls are usually quite romantic I assume that they would only part with their virginity in a well chosen, private and romantic place, would they not?"

"Most of them, yes," answered Kristoffer lamely.

"Is a kitchen table a private and romantic place?" roared Erik Menved as he turned around, his eyes glaring with anger. "Or is it just a convenient place for a beast like you to rape an innocent girl?"

Kristoffer did not reply but looked decidedly uncomfortable.

"Because you are my brother, you get away with many unchivralous acts, but to rape a ward of the crown is something that cannot be overlooked. What do you have to say?"

"It is all quite exaggerated. . . "

"How exactly? She asked you to make love to her?"

"Not in so many words," said Kristoffer, wondering how his brother had found out.

"Not even in a single word, brother. You raped someone under my personal protection."

"Maybe I was a little insistent, but it was all in the heat of the moment."

"I know many of the despicable things you have done over the years. Rumors reach me like they reach everyone else at court. I have ignored them because I have not always been a model of virtue myself, but this time you have gone too far. Do you know the punishment for your transgression?"

"No."

"In the past I, like our father, have stripped men of their titles and properties for lesser infractions against a royal ward."

Kristoffer looked at his brother in disbelief. "You would take away my privileges because of what a silly girl tells you?"

"Lady Irmgaard has told me nothing. But maybe I should confer with her before I pass judgment."

"Someone is lying to you," said Kristoffer emboldened by the fact that Irmgaard was not the informer.

"This someone is far more believable than you are, brother," cautioned Erik Menved. "Do not lie to me on top of what you have already done."

Kristoffer was fuming over having been found out, but he tried to look contrite as his brother studied him in cold fury.

"Irmgaard's father is our good friend and ally, and there is little I could do to make up for what has happened which would satisfy him. Except one thing," Erik Menved concluded with sudden sweetness.

"And what is that?" asked Kristoffer eager to put the incident behind him.

"Marry her!"

"I cannot marry her," cried Kristoffer. "She comes from a much lesser clan!

"You are right when you say that her good and honest family does not deserve to have a prince like you in their midst, but that is nevertheless the punishment you will accept since the girl is with child."

Kristoffer bridled at his misfortune in getting her pregnant and at having to marry beneath his station without enough of a dowry to make up for it. "How do you know that the child is mine? You cannot do this to me," he cried in despair.

"I can do this and a lot more if you continue to argue with me," Erik Menved said sternly. "If I had dealt with you earlier this might never have happened. So, because I am partly to blame, I will let you keep your privileges. But you will have to learn to take responsibility for your actions. That is all." He turned away dismissively when he saw Kristoffer begin to open his mouth to protest further.

Kristoffer glared at Erik Menved's back, but he knew that he was lucky to have gotten off so lightly. He had been stupid to lust after that girl and to force himself upon her since there were hundreds of others willing to provide whatever a prince would wish. He cursed himself when he realized that he would have to live with the consequences of his actions for the rest of his life--or the rest of hers . . . He straightened up before he bowed deeply toward Erik Menved.

"I do apologize for having placed you in this position, my brother. I did not think beyond the moment, and I will, of course, obey your directives."

Erik Menved's face softened as he turned around and walked up to Kristoffer to put his hand on his shoulder.

"You are a member of the Danish royal family, and it is time that you start to behave in a manner suited to your position. Next time I will not be so lenient. I will announce the betrothal when her father next visits us."

It was a warm and lovely day, and apple trees in full bloom encircled a long table that the servants had carried out for the ladies. The gentle breeze carried the delicate white flower petals to the ground, creating a snowy carpet over the soft grass.

"Kristina, I have the most wonderful news," whispered Ingeborg as the women sat down to do their daily chores in the garden rather than inside the castle. "The king has commanded Kristoffer to marry Irmgaard to set the situation right. It will be announced when her father arrives in a few weeks."

Kristina stared at her.

"Why do you look so displeased," asked Ingeborg. "It is a finer marriage than her family could ever have hoped for."

"But Irmgaard loathes and fears him."

Ingeborg replied slowly and deliberately "Then it will be your task to make her deal with her feelings. I think my husband showed a commendable sense of justice with his decision."

"Oh, I am impressed by the king's gracious justice, Ingeborg. I was just commenting on how Irmgaard feels about Kristoffer."

Later that afternoon, Kristina took Irmgaard for a walk down to the dock to feed the swans.

"You were sent here for one reason only, Irmgaard, and that was to find a good marriage despite your small dowry," said Kristina. Irmgaard nodded. "Well, you have found an alliance that should please your family beyond their wildest imagination."

"I will never be married. No one will want me now."

"The father of your child is going to marry you."

"Kristoffer?" asked Irmgaard perplexed. "Why should he want to marry me?"

"The king has learned what happened, and he has commanded Kristoffer to marry you."

"If what you are saying is true, it will be the unhappiest union ever. He will hate me for having to marry below his station, and I will hate him for the brute he is." She broke into tears.

"Try not to allow your feelings to enter into this, Irmgaard. You will do more for your clan by this marriage than your valiant father could do in three lifetimes."

Irmgaard just shook her head. "I would rather kill myself than share my life with that monster."

"I know how you feel now, but time will place everything into perspective. Please, do not show your displeasure since it was the queen herself who intervened on your behalf. You have a few weeks to grow used to the idea."

Kristina left Irmgaard to collect herself, but as she walked back across the lawn to rejoin the ladies she thought how cruel the twists and turns of Fate could be.

Irmgaard did her utmost to look happy whenever she was in the presence of the royal family. As no one else knew of her impending wedding, she did not have to pretend at other times. Kristina could hear Irmgaard crying every night, but there was little she could say or do to make her less miserable.

Kristina was amazed to find Kristoffer speaking kindly to Irmgaard whenever their paths crossed. But what could he do, she asked herself, other than make everyone believe that the beautiful young girl had utterly beguiled him, or they would soon figure out that the king had forced him into the alliance--and why. His insincerity made good sense.

As days passed, Kristina could not rid herself of the feeling that Irmgaard might do something foolish rather than go through with the marriage. She watched her carefully, but when Irmgaard did nothing suspicious she began to relax and hope that everything might end well.

One night, as Kristina prepared to go to bed, she realized that Irmgaard was not in the women's quarters. She became concerned as it was quite late, and she had not seen Irmgaard since supper.

"Please step outside with me," she whispered to Lady Brigitte who followed her obediently. "Have you seen Irmgaard?" she asked as they emerged into the quiet corridor.

"Last time I saw her she was leaving the Hall with Prince Kristoffer."

"Oh, no!" cried Kristina as she rushed along the corridor and down the stairs to the deserted Hall where only a few servants were still cleaning up.

"When did she leave?" Kristina asked Lady Brigitte who ran behind her.

"Hours ago. Why do you ask?"

"I am worried about her," said Kristina as she suddenly slowed down and faced Lady Brigitte. "I have to tell you, something which you must swear never to repeat to a living soul."

Lady Brigitte shook her head with sadness when Kristina had finished. "Poor little Irmgaard. We have to find her."

They went to the kitchens and asked some servants, but no one had seen Irmgaard. They searched every corner of the castle where they could expect to find her, but to no avail. They were becoming truly alarmed. They decided to look in the gardens.

It was still light despite the late hour when they searched through the garden, the apple orchard, and then ran down to the dock, but they could not find Irmgaard anywhere. Aimlessly they walked along the water's edge.

Suddenly Kristina cried out. "No, dear God, let it not be Irmgaard!"

Lady Brigitte followed Kristina's gaze and saw a dark shape floating in the water quite near the shore. Quickly they ran closer, and to their horror they saw a lifeless body, clothed in Irmgaard's familiar dress, floating face down in the water.

Lady Brigitte ran back to the castle for help while Kristina knelt and reached out to try to pull Irmgaard in. But she could not get near her, and since the water was deep she could not wade out to her.

Within moments, soldiers came running with torches. Two young men jumped into the water and brought Irmgaard onto shore. When they laid her down on the grass, Kristina noticed a deep wound on the side of her head.

"She must have slipped on the dock, fallen into the water, drowned, and floated down here," said the captain of the guard as he carefully inspected the wound.

No, thought Kristina sadly, she did not want to live anymore. She must have jumped and hit her head against something. Kristina took a deep breath of relief. At least, if that had caused her to lose consciousness, her death must have been quick.

Kristina knelt beside Irmgaard, arranged her dress and tunic sedately over her body and legs, and folded her arms across her chest. Soldiers then placed her body on a pallet where Kristina whispered to her while she stroked her long hair. Had it not been for the severe head wound she would have appeared to be asleep.

More footsteps and calls were heard behind Kristina as the tragic news spread around the castle, arousing everyone from their beds. When, finally the king and queen joined the large group on the lawn, Father John had already finished kneeling at Irmgaard's side to recite his prayers.

Ingeborg and Marta went over to Kristina and gently led her away from the pallet. As Kristina took a last look at her young friend, her eyes shifted for a moment to Kristoffer who was standing behind the dead girl. She caught his fleeting victorious smile as the pallet was carried away.

Chapter 6

Stockholm, Sweden 1297

Rikissa had been working for hours at her spinning wheel in the queen's chamber in Stockholm castle. The ladies-in-waiting had ceased gossiping for the moment allowing Rikissa to perform her monotonous task in silence.

All at once and without warning the "feeling" invaded her. She could "feel" her sister, Ingeborg, in agonizing pain. Rikissa doubled over and almost cried out from the cramps she felt in her stomach when, as suddenly as they had gripped her, they let go. She took a deep breath in relief as she felt cold sweat break out on her forehead. Looking around, she saw that her episode had gone unnoticed, so she walked out onto the parapet where she could be alone in case the pain returned.

She had been haunted by the "feeling" ever since her early childhood. She remembered clearly when she had felt it for the first time. She had been six years old, sitting on the floor of her mother's chamber playing with some discarded yarn, when she had been struck by the horrifying knowledge that one of her brothers was in mortal danger. "Birger!" she had screamed at the top of her lungs. "Birger!"

"What is it, child?" Lady Borg had asked gently. But before anyone could find out why she was screaming, the door had burst open and a guard shouted, "The king has fallen into the icy river!"

Rikissa would never forget the look on her mother's face as she hurried from the chamber to learn the fate of her eldest son. A moment later Rikissa's panic had loosened, and her feeling of being asphyxiated had disappeared. But a lingering trace of anxiety had been revived when her mother later took her aside and asked, "Why did you scream yesterday?" Rikissa could not find an answer. "Did you know that Birger was in trouble?" she pressed. "Could you feel it?" To which Rikissa could only nod.

Queen Helvig had sighed, "So I have passed the "feeling" on to you." Her mother had looked so sad at that moment that for years Rikissa had dared not broach the matter with her. As it happened rarely, she took great care not to show when the "feeling" came over her, yet she always sensed when anyone close to her was in trouble. On another occasion while half-asleep, she had been overcome with the irrefutable knowledge that her favorite old nurse was dying. She had sat up in bed, her heart cringing in pain. She must have called out, since both Ingeborg and Kristina had awakened and asked what was wrong. Rikissa had blamed her outcry on a nightmare, and she had not lied; the "feeling" was indeed like a horrible dream. Later, when she found out that the old nurse had indeed passed away during the night, she finally became frightened enough to ask her mother what she had meant by passing on the "feeling".

"You are not the first to have this ability," the queen had answered dolefully. "Several women in my family have known intuitively when anyone close to them was in danger or dying. Not only did they know when misfortune was befalling those to whom they were close, but they experienced the same pain. These were sad women, Rikissa. I prayed that none of my children would inherit this ability."

"But I am not sad, Mother," Rikissa had objected. "If it is God's will for me to have this "feeling", I will simply learn to live with it."

"I hope you can," the queen had said in a hollow voice.

When Rikissa confided in Ingeborg and Kristina, they both looked at her askance. While she realized that they could not possibly understand what she experienced, and although they tried to empathize with her, she had felt hurt nonetheless. It was with renewed resolve that she decided never to reveal when the "feeling" overcame her. She had indeed grown accustomed to living with her strange ability and its different levels and facets. More convinced than ever that hers was a God-given gift she had become a deeply religious child.

While her family might not have understood the phenomenon, they began to heed her warnings and ask what she foresaw. By now they had all grown accustomed to the fact that she had abilities for which, were the Church to learn of them, most women not of royal birth could be put to death. As a protection, but also because it was true, she had impressed on Father Nils and other churchmen that she was sincerely devout.

Now as she stood against the parapet wall she could again sense the "feeling" bringing her back to Ingeborg. She did not know what was befalling her sister; but she guessed it had something to do with childbearing.

"What are you doing out here?" Mats asked from behind her.

"I was thinking of Ingeborg and Kristina, and how much I miss them."

"You are not the only one. We all miss them," he offered kindly as he approached and noticed tears in her eyes. "Do not cry, Rikissa, they will be back soon enough."

He reached out to enfold her in his arms. She sank into his broad embrace, feeling safe and protected. So overpowering and peaceful was his presence that she stopped crying and buried her face in his tunic, despite the hard chain mail beneath it.

"Rikissa!" Valdemar's voice boomed from somewhere down the corridor. "Where are you?"

"Here," answered Rikissa as she ran towards the sound of his voice.

Stockholm castle was in many ways similar to Nykoping except that is was constructed on a larger scale. The Great Hall was at least double the size of Nykoping's; there were many more and larger chambers, and the corridors were longer and darker. She ran down the staircase to the Great Hall. "We are going hunting," said Valdemar who was waiting for her by the foot of the stairs. "It is a sunny day and you need to get out."

Rikissa knew her brothers missed Ingeborg and Kristina. When they sat down for their lessons in the Great Hall they would at times look expectantly towards the staircase as if the two girls were simply late in arriving. The boys had begun to include Rikissa in many of their pursuits as if she, too, might disappear if they did not keep an eye on her.

"I do not know what Mother will say about my going hunting," Rikissa objected meekly.

"Birger has talked to her already. Come now, they are waiting for us."

They ran into the courtyard where Birger, Erik and Mats were already mounted, with their hunting birds on their gloves. She jumped up on her horse and they set off for the forest, riding through Stockholm at breakneck speed and hollering their approach, as people and animals scattered before them. They spent a happy time together, and at the end of the day they sat down by a small forest lake, watching their horses drink.

Mats looked excited and bursting with pride as he seated himself beside her while her brothers plucked and cleaned the birds their hawks had killed. She looked up at him, and asked why he was so happy, quite unprepared for what he was going to tell her.

"Lord Torgils has asked me to accompany him to Finland as his aide! Can you imagine what an honor that is?" His face crinkled with a broad smile, while Rikissa could feel her heart shrink. Countless knights had perished in the Finnish wars, yet here he was, happier than she had ever seen him, eager to join in the bloody endeavor. But he was right. It was a great honor to go with the Lord High Constable, and who else would the Regent choose but the devoted, and talented Mats Kettilmundsson? And it was part of Mats' appeal that he seemed to have no concept of his own formidable skills. She made an effort to smile encouragingly.

"It is indeed an honor."

Mats absentmindedly was breaking some twigs unable to contain his excitement. "My father told me so much about Finland. Now I will see the places he visited." He stopped himself and looked at her. "I want to fight in your honor, Rikissa. That is why I wanted to talk to you . . . to ask for your colors." He looked at her with tenderness.

She was the total opposite of Sif. She was not interested in hunting and killing. But she was kindness and goodness personified, and he had come to care for her deeply. It was surprising to him that he had not been revolted by her deeply held religious belief, but that must have been because she actually lived by its commands and did not break them when it suited her. He reasoned that he must have become more accepting of the new God once his father had passed.

"I will be proud for you to wear them," Rikissa replied.

"Thank you," he said softly.

She tried to allay her concern for his safety with the knowledge that he was a superb swordsman. He had a better chance than most to return alive. "When are you leaving?" she asked, trying to sound as happy as he was.

"In just a few days."

"Then you have much to attend to," she said briskly. "Let me help you. Mother says that I am a good organizer."

"You are good at everything," he said admiringly as they stood to join her brothers who were ready to leave. Rikissa looked at the trees' vivid fall colors. How beautiful nature is before dying, she thought before shaking herself out of her morbid thoughts.

The days that followed were busy, as everyone in the castle prepared for the upcoming departure of the Regent and his army. Birger, Erik, and Valdemar envied Mats for going off to his first war while they had to wait, as Lord Torgils explained, until they were older.

"I am sixteen," Birger had protested. "My father had already fought a war at my age."

"But he was not King of Sweden then, his brother was," counseled Lord Torgils. "We must protect our king, and it is far more important for you to study and learn how to be an effective ruler than to risk being killed or maimed. When you actually rule Sweden, you can do as you wish. However, for now you have to follow my directive."

On the day of departure, Mats and Rikissa withdrew to the privacy of the parapet.

"I will pray for your safety."

"Your beautiful banner will protect me. " He could not possibly have guessed the amount of time and effort it had taken her, with her limited skills, to finish it. But she felt that her time had been wisely spent. He would be well protected by his coat of arms, fluttering above his head and made by her own hands, since it carried with it every prayer she knew.

"And thank you for this," he said as he tied her silk around his arm. "I will be fighting for the loveliest lady in the realm."

They stood close to one another until he leaned forward and kissed her gently on the lips.

"God speed," she whispered, her throat constricting.

It took many months for Rikissa to adjust to living not only without Ingeborg and Kristina, but also without Mats. Every morning she would wake to let the "feeling" travel to him and then to Ingeborg. While she could sense that much was happening to Mats, she felt no immediate threat to him. Around Ingeborg she could sense only darkness, and she wondered what it might signify; but since she felt no urgency she reasoned that all must be well. Even so, she rose early each day to go to the chapel before morning mass to offer private prayers for those she loved.

However, as time passed, other disquieting sensations began to reach her. Something was evidently afoot in the King's Council since Queen Helvig had been invited to attend its last two meetings. Rikissa sensed that these somehow concerned her, and she was proved right when her mother sat down with her by the small fire in her chamber.

"It is time for you to get married, my dear," Queen Helvig said kindly as she pulled a parchment from under her tunic. "Lord Torgils and the members of the Council have made a list of the prospects, and I wanted to see if you have any special preference. You did meet some of these men at the Danish court, and others you have met here."

Rikissa stared at the list, unable to focus on the names. She knew that there was only one man she wanted to marry. She prayed that his name would be on the list but feared it would not. "Would you really take my preference into consideration?" she asked.

"Well, we must choose carefully for the sake of Sweden. But if we have two equally qualified candidates, we will naturally pick the one you prefer," her mother said benevolently.

Rikissa looked down the twelve names. There were several princes and dukes, a count, two barons, and the rest came from rich and powerful clans. Rikissa recognized some of the names and recalled with horror the face of one of the princes that had looked so cruel. The count had been fat and slovenly. Slowly her eyes went down the column before she handed the list back to her mother.

"Birger makes the final decision?" she asked.

"Naturally. But he will, of course, be guided by Lord Torgils and myself."

"May I think about it, Mother?"

Queen Helvig nodded. "Of course. After all, we are considering your future life companion." Rikissa thought that her mother sounded as if they were selecting a new stallion to lead the tournament parade.

Later that evening Rikissa cornered Birger in the Great Hall and pulled him aside. "I must talk to you about the list of my suitors."

"There are some fine names on it, and you deserve the very best," he smiled.

"The man I want to marry is not on it!"

"If he is not, then he is not worthy of marrying you."

"He certainly is," insisted Rikissa. "You, yourself, have said that Mats can be matched by no other, either as a knight or as a man, and you cannot have failed to notice that we care about each other."

"While Mats is one of the finest men I know, his position is certainly not as prestigious as those listed, all of whom have expressed an interest in an alliance with our family," Birger replied. Rikissa looked him in the eyes, all the while pointedly fingering the small carved fish hanging on her neck chain. Her gesture was not lost on Birger.

"I will give it some thought," he said as he left her to join his brothers.

"What is bothering you?" Erik asked as he arranged the pieces on the chess table.

"It is the list of Rikissa's suitors," Birger replied as he sat down on the other side of the table. "According to Rikissa, the right candidate is not on it."

"You mean Mats," said Erik looking up from the chessboard.

Birger nodded. "While he is our best friend, he hardly ranks as highly as the others."

"The fact that he is our closest friend places him above all others," said Erik simply.

"Our personal preferences should not govern the decision," insisted Birger.

"With our Danish marriage alliances, Sweden sits in a very secure position. Had there been a Norwegian prince available, I would agree with you, but rumor has it that Prince Hakon of Norway is to be married to a Scottish princess, so as it stands, none of the candidates is of critical importance to Sweden," Erik countered.

"Mother and Lord Torgils . . ." Birger began. Erik looked sharply at him.

"You are the king."

Birger looked miserable.

Rikissa bolted upright in bed with sweat streaming down her face. Mats is in mortal peril! She clasped her hands and bowed her head. "Dear God, do not let anything happen to him," she pleaded. She sat in agony for hours, wringing her hands and praying loudly. "Please protect him, Father, and I will serve you for the rest of my days." Her whole body was aching, but she could feel Mats' life force weakening as she fervently continued her prayers. "Dear Lord, if you save his life I will serve you full heartedly as one of your brides."

As suddenly as it had caught hold of her, the "feeling" left and she sank back against the pillows in pure exhaustion.

Shaking, she lay awake for the rest of the night, again and again sending the "feeling" to visit him, but she could sense nothing. She kept praying for his life.

In the morning she went to see Birger in his chamber. "When is the army expected back?" she asked simply.

"We received a message some days ago that Lord Torgils plans to return for reinforcements shortly."

She took a deep breath of relief. If Lord Torgils was coming home, so was Mats.

Rikissa had to wait another month before three Swedish warships sailed into the harbor. As the news of their arrival spread through the castle, she slipped out of the queen's chamber and rushed down the corridor to her room. There she pulled on a new tunic and hurriedly braided ribbons into her hair. Pleased with the results and trying to appear calm, she walked down the stairs to join her brothers in the courtyard where they waited for the soldiers to come riding over the bridge.

She saw him right away. Mats was riding just behind Lord Torgils, looking fit and tanned but slumping in his saddle. She caught his eyes and saw a smile break over his face. Forgetful of everything she rushed forward, whereupon Mats leaned down to scoop her up on his horse. Surrounded by his strong arms she felt calm at last. "Welcome home," she whispered happily.

"That was an unseemly display of affection, Rikissa," admonished the queen as the ladies joined the men in the Great Hall for the welcome celebration.

"Mother, he almost died in one of the battles, and I was simply overjoyed to see him alive."

"You felt it?" asked the queen.

"Yes, and it was agony."

"I see," said the queen in a softer tone of voice. She turned to the major domo as they took their places at the dais table. "Prepare a seat for Lord Mats next to Princess Rikissa," she ordered.

Mats sat down next to Rikissa. He was already well fortified from homecoming toasts. "You must forgive me..." he started, embarrassed by his overindulgence.

"It is a time for celebration," she said sweetly to put him at ease.

Mats was now eighteen years old, but appeared younger with his unruly dark blond hair, sparkling eyes, and warm smile. Sometimes he reminded her of a cuddly puppy, but she knew that was not the case on the battlefield where, armed with his fear-inspiring Gram, he was known as an awesome fighter. When everyone had withdrawn from the Great Hall, Rikissa seated herself with her brothers and Mats by the fire pit.

"Tell me about your battles," coaxed Birger.

Mats told them of their raids against the Finns and of the vast lands the Swedish army had captured. The campaign had been successful from the outset, and the Swedes had suffered very few losses. Rikissa could envision everything he described as they sat by the crackling fire. She could not remember a single moment in her life when she had felt more at peace.

"But there was one battle I will never forget," Mats related eagerly as Erik refilled his wine goblet. "One night our camp was overrun by the enemy, and we fought them for hours. It was the largest force we had encountered, and we were taken by surprise. At times, I stood alone against four or five opponents and it was a wonder that I survived." He was lost in the stirring memory. "You should have seen me, Rikissa," he said shyly but proudly. "It was as if I had been given the strength of seven men, as if Odin himself, was fighting by my side. And in the midst of that battle, when I had been dealt a blow that shattered my helmet, I even thought that I saw you, Rikissa."

All at once she remembered: her promise to God. She had forgotten it. Being with Mats again had made her think of nothing but him. Her body turned heavy with the knowledge of what she had to do. Numbly, she stood up and tried to smile at her brothers and Mats.

"You must forgive me," she began. "I am terribly tired. The excitement of the day..." She stopped, unable to finish the sentence.

"It is me tiring you . . . talking on and on," said Mats apologetically, starting to get up.

"I love to hear your stories. It is just that I am exhausted," she said as she walked towards the stairs, followed by Mats. Her brothers politely turned their backs.

"This has been the best day of my life," said Mats. "Coming home to you . . ."

"And it has been the best day of mine," she said, knowing it to be true.

"Good sleep," he said as he took her hands in his and looked into her eyes.

She saw his love and she felt her own. "Thank God for your safe return," she said before she quickly turned to run up the stairs, her eyes filling with tears.

Mats returned to the fading fire where Valdemar handed him his refilled goblet to drink yet another toast to his bravery. Mats sat down on a fur-covered bench and took a large swallow.

"You deserve an immense reward for your accomplishments, no doubt," said Birger.

"At least half the kingdom," laughed Mats in jest.

"You know what this is?" asked Birger, waving a parchment in front of Mats.

Mats took the parchment from Birger and studied it. "It is a list of some powerful men," he said looking at Birger, and when he did not respond, at Erik and Valdemar.

"It is a list of prospective husbands for Rikissa," answered Erik.

Mats stared numbly at the document.

"You love her?" asked Birger.

"With all my heart," was Mats' immediate answer.

"That was all I wanted to know," nodded Birger. "As a reward for all your brave deeds, you will marry her."

"But these are men of great power. How could my suit be of any interest at all?" Mats' face became anguished. Reality had not touched him until now as he had been so filled with happiness by seeing Rikissa again and his success fighting for his Fatherland.

"It would serve Sweden well if you married Rikissa," replied Birger resolutely.

Mats was quiet for a moment. "You mean that?"

"Yes, I do."

Mats stood up, his goblet clattering to the floor. "Well, in that case . . . I have to tell her . . . I mean, I have to ask her . . ."

The brothers laughed as Mats started towards the stairs. "Let that wait for the morrow. You are not going to barge into her chamber, are you? And you could use a good night's sleep."

"How can I sleep? I am much too happy to sleep."

Birger settled back in his chair. "Then tell us another story," he suggested as Valdemar put new logs on the fire.

"Have you seen Rikissa?" the queen asked her ladies when her daughter had not shown up for morning prayers. No one had, and one of the ladies-in-waiting was sent to the princess' chamber only to find it empty. After several hours of not being able to concentrate on her embroidery, the queen ordered a search of the castle. Even the princes, who were practicing at arms, stopped to join in the search.

By the time the evening meal was served Rikissa still had not been found. No one in the royal family had much appetite and Mats did not touch his food. After the meal everyone lingered quietly without the will to go to their chambers. Lord Torgils had ordered his knights to search the city, and every hour one of his men came in to report. Each time they shook their heads; Princess Rikissa was nowhere to be found. Father Nils had long since withdrawn to the chapel to pray for her safety, and the queen was pacing nervously in front of the fire.

Then a thin, dark shape became visible in the doorway to the Great Hall. As the person moved into the light everyone assembled could see that it was the Mother Superior from Santa Klara convent. She approached the queen and offered her greetings.

"I come with a message from Princess Rikissa," she said calmly. "Would you like to receive it in private?"

Lord Torgils gestured for everyone except the royal family to leave but did not object when Mats stayed behind.

"Please tell me where she is," pleaded the queen. "Is she well?"

"Yes, your Majesty. She is safe in God's house."

"Thank the Lord," said the queen crossing herself. "We have been besides ourselves with worry. But why did you not bring her here with you?"

The nun accepted the stool that Erik pulled up. She reached out and took Queen Helvig's hands in hers. "Princess Rikissa is not coming back, your Majesty. She wants to stay with us."

Father Nils crossed himself, while the queen stared in disbelief.

"It cannot be true! She might as well be dead," cried Mats in utter despair.

"She is far from dead, my son," said the nun looking sharply at Mats. "I think she will be very content living with us and serving our Lord."

The Hall fell silent while Rikissa's family tried to comprehend the step she had taken. Mats, who could not bear the oppressive atmosphere, left the Hall with long strides.

"I want to talk to her," cried the queen.

"I am sorry, your Majesty, but the princess is in seclusion of her own wish. When she is ready to see anyone, I will send a message."

Queen Helvig shook her head. "I cannot believe it. Why would she leave without telling us of her decision?"

"Maybe she was afraid that you would talk her out of it," ventured Erik. "I, for one, would have done my damnedest to stop her."

"But why?" asked the queen again.

"She chose to marry Christ instead of a man of the world," said the Mother Superior tenderly. Then she unobtrusively removed a small roll of parchment from under her long tunic and handed it to Erik who stood next to her. "Please give this to Lord Mats," she whispered.

Erik quietly left the Great Hall. He climbed the stairs to the place where he knew he would find Mats. His friend was standing by the parapet, his head lowered. He looked up when he heard Erik approach. Without a word, Erik gave him the parchment and turned to leave.

"Do not go," pleaded Mats. He unrolled the parchment and read it slowly before he handed it back to Erik who read his sister's short message.

> My dearest,
> You mean more to me than anything on this earth. The fact that you are safe and alive is my reason, as well as my reward, for doing what I am now doing. I cannot explain more than that for now. I will always be praying for you with eternal love.
> Rikissa

"I still do not understand how she could choose to become a nun when I know that she loves me," said Mats in a broken voice.

Erik placed a strong hand on his friend's shoulder. "Maybe it is for the best," he said gently. "She has a calling to God, and you have a calling to War."

Chapter 7

Kristina stood before a mirror in the dimly lit cabin of the ship carrying her back to Sweden. Breathless with expectation, the two years of homesickness, the miscarriages of Ingeborg, and her loathing of Kristoffer were momentarily forgotten. The only things on her mind were seeing her father, her friends, and most of all, Erik.

As she studied the reflection of her face, all she had experienced in Denmark was etched there. The effect, she realized, was not disagreeable. She looked mature, grown up. She had made her newly washed hair fall in orderly curls, just as Rikissa had taught her. Her soft rose tunic embroidered in the latest fashion pleased her. She turned towards the cabin door with a satisfied smile. She was only moments away from home.

She went out on deck to join Ingeborg and Marta who stood side by side, Ingeborg pointing out the sights. They watched the verdant islands floating by until finally the fortified island capital came into view. The Stockholm harbor looked welcoming as a section of the protective screens of sharpened poles surrounding it had been opened to allow them safe entry.

"Oh, what a beautiful town!" called Marta excitedly.

Ingeborg and Kristina smiled proudly. Stockholm was basking in the midday sun with its proudly presiding castle flying Danish flags from all its towers. Marta clapped her hands with pleasure while Kristina could vaguely discern the royal family standing on the end of the dock--Queen Helvig, Birger, and Valdemar . . . but not Erik. Rikissa also appeared to be absent. Then she spotted her father among the throng and she waved to him.

It seemed forever before the ship docked, but finally the royal family came on board. Ingeborg threw herself into her mother's arms, scarcely able to hold back her tears, while Birger walked up to Marta to gently kiss her cheek. Laughter and greetings were exchanged as the kings and princes embraced each other. All the while, Kristina stood in the background looking for Erik. Why had he not come to greet them? Had something happened to him? Then she saw her father walking toward her with his long heavy stride to enfold her in his giant embrace.

"Welcome home, my sweet Kristina," he said, holding her at arms length to study her. "I have missed you more than I can say." She looked into his eyes and was overwhelmed tenderness.

"I have missed you, too," she whispered as she happily hugged him.

"We will talk later, my little one," he said as he then turned to greet the rest of the party. Once again, she stood alone anxiously looking for Erik. Then, finally, she saw him making his way through the throngs on the dock. Kristina stood staring at him while he greeted the travelers. She tried to think of something clever to say when would reach her. He had grown into the most handsome man she had ever seen. He was taller than when they had parted, and his face was thinner and manlier. His eyes shone with the same intense blue and that humorous sparkle she had always loved. His body was lean and well trained, and when he moved to greet Ingeborg his stride was as graceful as ever. Then he caught her eye, and a soft smile slowly illuminated his face.

"Kristina?" he said as he walked slowly towards her, his eyes filled with pleasure. "Is this really you?"

When he reached her, he swept her off her feet, hugging her and whirling her around in his strong arms, making her dizzy. He smelled of fir trees and grass, and she closed her eyes to savor the feeling of his arms around her and hers around him. She took a deep breath. She was home.

Gently he put her down with a broad smile that softened again as he stared at her. "You look beautiful," he said, sounding a little overcome. He seemed to want to say something more, but he just kept looking at her.

"Welcome home, Kristina," she heard Valdemar say before he closed his arms around her. "You have been sorely missed." he smiled warmly as he let her go, but Kristina could say nothing in response, as her whole being was concentrated on Erik.

"You look so grown up, Kristina," said Birger who had joined them. "I hardly recognized you."

"What does that imply?" she heard her own voice say as she hugged him. "Do I look that old?" She heard them laugh as they turned to greet more Danish guests. Erik was the last to turn away, and she felt lightheaded from the intensity of his gaze.

The rest of the day was a blur of activity. The castle was filled with noise and commotion, with servants carrying chests, unpacking them, and trying to organize the many guests who attempted to settle in and ready themselves for supper.

Kristina looked over to where Ingeborg sat on the deep window-sill of the chamber they had occupied as children, admiring the sunset reflecting in the water that surrounded the castle on two sides. The window was open wide, allowing the summer breeze to carry the sounds from the busy docks into the room. Ingeborg's strawberry blond hair hung casually plaited in a thick waist-long braid, free from the confinement of her headdress which she had carelessly dropped with her tunic and crown on a bench near the window. Marta stood in the center of the chamber amidst a disarray of traveling chests, trying to organize her clothing. The women were silent allowing each other the privacy of their own thoughts, but their minds were all on Rikissa.

She had not been at the dock to greet them but had merely sent a message that she would be in seclusion for another year and so would not attend the wedding. Ingeborg and Kristina felt deeply wounded that Rikissa had not shared with them her decision to enter Santa Klara convent. Her absence was painful and made Stockholm castle seem different.

But then Ingeborg and Kristina were different, as well. Kristina knew that the two years in Roskilde had changed them both. The innocent openness of their eyes had been replaced by a guarded look. The transformation had not been lost on Queen Helvig.

"You look like me now," she had said with a sad smile when she greeted them. "But you both look beautiful." She did not flatter them idly. The riding and swimming during the previous balmy months had made their bodies slim and firm; and their fair skin, which had turned golden, emphasized their blond hair that had become paler from the sun. Ingeborg was looking more queen-like than ever with her back erect and her head held high. Kristina's sweet face framed by cascading curls still resembled that of an angel, but a more worldly one.

"Come over here Marta," coaxed Ingeborg still curled up on the windowsill. "There is nothing like a sunset over the Malar waters." Marta walked over to the window. The waters were sparkling as if painted with pink gold. Lush green islands contrasted with the deep blue sky, and the harbor was filled with fishing boats returning with the day's catch. Marta rested her hand on Ingeborg's shoulder and absorbed the view that would be a daily part of her new life.

"It is beautiful," Marta agreed, "I understand why you miss this place. I am sure I will learn to love it just as much."

Ingeborg stepped away from the window and slowly closed it. "We must get ready now." She laughed as she tried to walk across the room. "That is, if we can make it down the staircase on our sea legs." Kristina could feel her own legs disobey her and her head swim with fatigue from the journey, yet nothing would stop her from seeing Erik and her father again.

All three women dressed themselves with rapt concentration. Ingeborg, because she wanted to look her best as the Swedish-born Queen of Denmark; Marta, to show the Swedes what a stately queen they were getting; and Kristina, to convince Erik that she was indeed as special as he had made her feel when he welcomed her home. As they descended the stairs, the Hall fell silent as those assembled turned to look. The cheering began spontaneously as the three comely ladies descended. Even Queen Helvig smiled with pride as they proceeded to the high table.

Fate, or protocol, had been kind to Kristina. She found herself seated between Erik and Valdemar from whom she received the undivided attention of both during the meal. She could not remember feeling more exuberant. She drank deeply from her wine chalice while laughing at the stories of what had transpired in her absence. As soon as the meal was over, they asked her to accompany them to visit their new hunting birds.

"You always had a deft hand with them," Erik recalled as they slipped out of the Hall. Kristina blushed in spite of herself.

She had enjoyed the falcon and the hawks from the time she was a little girl. When she was six years old she had slipped into her father's aviary alone for the first time. She had taken an instant liking to a brown hawk that had sat very still, staring at her. She had pulled up a stool, crawled onto it and loosened the leather thongs that bound the bird to its perch. It had instantly soared up towards the lofty ceiling in search of escape. Her father had arrived just in time to see the hawk fluttering among the rafters.

"Did you let him loose?" his voice boomed. Kristina could only nod as her father whistled for the bird to settle on his glove. But the bird refused to come down. "He is supposed to hunt with us tomorrow, and he will be exhausted from flying around to find a way out," grumbled Lord Torgils between whistles. "He will be useless by the time he returns to his perch."

Kristina looked down, cowed by her father's displeasure. "I am sorry," she stammered.

"You should be!" her father said angrily as he threw his glove on a shelf. "I will go and get Hans, maybe he will have better luck getting the damned bird down."

He left with furious strides, slamming the thick wooden door behind him, leaving Kristina sobbing. Slowly she went over and picked up her father's huge glove and put it on. It reached almost to her shoulder and her hand fit into two of the leather fingers. She wiped her eyes and tried to imitate her father's whistle. The third time it sounded quite similar; and to her surprise, and fear, the bird slowly spiraled down to settle heavily on her gloved arm. She could feel his sharp claws through the leather gripping around her thin forearm. Instinctively, she took hold of the leather straps around his legs and cooed calmingly as she supported her arm against her body to hold his weight. Just then her father returned with the falconer, and both stopped short by the door.

"Now how did you do that?" Her father sounded amused as he came over to take the heavy bird from her arm. "Do we have a bird elf among us?" He did not sound a bit angry as he placed the hawk back on its perch. "You will always be welcome in the aviary with that talent, Kristina. They have not had a gifted one here for a long time."

From that day on, she spent much time in the aviary, but she declined to deal with the torturous training there. She had been horrified as she listened to proud birds screech from pain and frustration during the first days and nights of training, and she was grateful the initial process was not of longer duration. She had seen what transpired after their capture to quench their strong wills and resistance to confinement. In order to break a bird's spirit, a thread was pulled through its eyelids to close the lids tightly, rendering it totally dependent on the falconer. Around the bird's feet were wound leather thongs, and these jesses were used to secure the bird to its perch or to the hunter's gloved hand. Those were loosened only when the bird was thrown into flight. Small bells were often attached to the feet to alert the falconer when the bird became unruly during training. The first day and night of training the falcon was starved while continuously staying on the trainer's gloved hand. To calm the bird, it was often necessary to bind its two feet together. Every time it tried to bite, it would be given a stone to quickly break it of that habit. As man and bird became used to one another, the thread through the eyelids would be loosened to allow the bird partial vision as the training proceeded, until it was removed altogether. Once the birds were fully trained, each to respond to its special call, the birds would only be brought outdoors wearing a hood that would be removed once they were sent into flight.

The royal brothers were in constant competition as to who owned the best hunters. Each took great pride in training their own birds. When Kristina, Erik, and Valdemar entered the royal aviary, the falconers had just finished feeding their charges, and the birds were contentedly ripping at the raw meat. The falcons and hawks were of varying sizes and many colors: black, reddish, white; one even had hyacinth-colored feet.

Kristina spotted the new birds and asked excitedly as she pointed, "That wonderful gold-colored falco sacer, to whom does he belong?" Erik did not look entirely pleased as he answered. "It was a wedding gift to Birger from the British king. As you know, it is a rarity for us to have one here, and he is truly a fine hunter. But that grey and white one is Valdemar's new peregrine, captured far up north. He promises to be a powerful high flyer. And this," he said as he proudly pointed to a large bird digesting its meal on a high perch, "is my new falco montanarius. He can out-fly any I have ever owned, and he cost me a king's ransom. I had to trade six white falcons for him. You will see tomorrow, Kristina. He is the best bird here."

"Exaggerating, as always," chided Valdemar amicably as they stood watching the birds.

"My small black falcon is very nervous of late," continued Erik, turning to Kristina. "Maybe you could handle him tomorrow." He smiled when he saw her pleasure at his suggestion. "He might be unhappy because he has missed you," he added, and then quickly looked away.

They left the aviary and crossed the courtyard to rejoin the festivities in the Great Hall. It was still light, and the sky was an almost iridescent blue. "It looks like fine hunting weather," Valdemar predicted before he stepped aside to let Kristina precede him into the Hall.

"Ah, there you are my dear," Lord Torgils called out as he spotted his daughter. "Come and sit by me and tell me all about your stay in Denmark."

For once Kristina was sorry that her father asked for one of their rare and cherished talks. She saw Erik look briefly disappointed before he chivalrously escorted her to her father's side.

Kristina tried not to think about Erik as she told her father about Roskilde castle and the many people living and visiting there. She omitted most about Ingeborg's miscarriages and the fear she had of Kristoffer. She wondered why she held these things back since she had always told her father everything. She assumed it had to do with growing up.

Before she got a chance to talk further with Erik, Ingeborg and Marta rose to withdraw, blaming their early departure on the long sea voyage. Kristina kissed her father goodnight and joined the ladies leaving the Hall. They all began talking the moment the door to Ingeborg's chamber closed behind them; Marta about Birger, and Kristina and Ingeborg about how happy they were to be back in Sweden. When Queen Helvig unexpectedly entered the room, they fell silent.

"I think you better go to sleep and save your gossip for tomorrow," she said in her usual commanding tone.

Kristina saw a look of concern float over Marta's face before she went over to kiss the queen on the cheek. "You are right, of course. We are all very tired."

Marta dragged Kristina with her to the adjoining chamber they were sharing, closing the door behind them. "Does she treat everyone like that?" she asked, looking troubled. "I thought I was to be in charge, but with Queen Helvig around that does not appear likely."

Kristina did not envy Marta's position, as she knew how Marta abhorred confrontations. "Let us not think about that now but instead concentrate on your wedding. We only have a few days left, and so much to do."

"And a lovely hunt on the morrow for which we must be rested," yawned Marta, and Kristina could hardly disagree.

As the hunt master's first call echoed in the corridors, Kristina was already up, dressed, and tugging at her boots. Marta was still lingering in bed, but Kristina did not want to wait so she quietly left their room to run downstairs.

Birger, Erik, and Valdemar were already there, eager to get under way. Erik had his new falcon balanced on his glove.

"You go ahead," said Birger benevolently. "I will stay with our guests for morning prayers. We will join you later."

A falconer brought forward the restless black falcon and Kristina took its jesses and held the bird down on her glove while she stroked his back and cooed softly. After a while the bird settled down. "See how he responds to you already," said Erik. "I knew that you would put him right again."

The three mounted their horses and set out for the northern gate of the sleeping city. As they rode through the narrow lanes they encountered not a living soul, and they had to wake the guard to open the city gate before they rode over the bridge to the mainland. Once on the other side they took off at full speed toward the forest that was basking in the pale morning sun.

Kristina relished the speed of her mount and the tight grip of the bird clutching her wrist. It was just like when they were children together. Erik and Valdemar slowed their horses as they passed the hill behind which the foreign wedding guests were camping, so as not to disturb them. But their caution was needless since the guests in the camp had risen well before those billeted in the castle. Smoke could be seen billowing from the cooking fires, and the clanking of armor mixed with the baying of hunting dogs. Erik picked up speed again and they followed him towards their favorite glen.

Kristina watched in awe the flights of Erik and Valdemar's hunting birds as they spiraled to the skies. Once they were out of sight she concentrated on her black falcon. Knowing that he was trained as a low flyer she gently let him off and called him back for a treat once he had circled the area. She kept sending him off and calling him back to reward him until he picked up speed and flew low and fast over their heads searching for small animals. Within the hour he behaved as he always had, and he appeared so content to perch on Kristina's glove that she did not even have to hold the jesses. In the meantime, Valdemar's bird had alerted him to some prey in the forest, and he left Erik and Kristina watching Erik's falcon attack a small dove at lightning speed. The falcon dropped the dove with a victorious screech not far from Erik's feet, and Erik rushed forward to kill it.

"He seems worth everything you spent on him," Kristina said as she stroked the black bird on her wrist.

Erik called back his hunter and rewarded it with a bread ball as it touched down on his glove. He pulled the jesses tight while the bird struggled to get free again. Satisfied that the bird was ready for another flight, Erik threw it in the air where it quickly gained altitude. "We will not see him for a while," Erik said. "Let us sit in the shade while we wait."

Kristina pulled the hood over the black falcon's head and it rested on her glove as they slowly walked over to the edge of the forest and seated themselves on a large stone. Kristina felt happier than she had in years. Just sitting beside Erik and sharing this moment as he watched the small spot in the sky was all she had ever wished for.

He turned his gaze on her. "I did not know how much I had missed you until now," he said softly. She held her breath. Was this real, or was she still asleep in the ladies' quarters in Roskilde castle, dreaming as she had for the past two years? But she knew it was real when he moved closer. She looked into his eyes to see them filled with caring and need. He touched her face tenderly, following the curves of her features as if to become accustomed to her new face. He leaned forward when, suddenly, they heard a low whistle from among the trees. The whistle was repeated more urgently, and Erik stood up.

"Could that be Valdemar in trouble?" he asked as he pulled Kristina to her feet. "We better go and see," he said as he headed into the forest with long strides.

Kristina followed him, still in a daze, along a small footpath while he called Valdemar's name. They heard no answer, but the whistling continued and Erik hurried deeper in among the trees. Without warning he stopped so abruptly that Kristina almost walked into him. In front of them, on a log, sat a tall man, dressed in fine hunting clothes. He was immobile, looking down at his left arm that rested beside him. Across his hand lay a snake coiled in attack position. The zigzag band on its back signaled that it was poisonous, and the man had no choice but to remain motionless if he wanted to avoid a lethal bite. Kristina could see beads of perspiration on his forehead, and she wondered how long he had been sitting there without moving.

Without even thinking, she pulled off the falcon's hood and threw the bird in the direction of the man. The falcon's sharp eyes quickly spotted the adder and silently dove at its prey. The bird's sharp claws grabbed the head of the reptile, which had slowly turned at the sound of fluttering wings, and pulled it up in the air, only to release the heavy burden a few yards away. Both the man and Erik rushed forward to kill the snake. The man reached the reptile first and quickly severed its head with his hunting knife. He collapsed to the ground beside the writhing headless coils.

"You came just in time," he said as he struggled to his feet. "I could feel my body start to twitch. I must have sat there for an eternity." Kristina heard his Norwegian accent as he continued: "Such an idiotic thing for me to do; to sit down and lose myself in reverie without paying attention to my surroundings. But thank you. And special thanks to your splendid bird." He bent his neck back and forth and stretched his arms above his head to relieve the tension. "Please forgive my manners. To whom do I owe my life?"

"The lady is Kristina Torgilsdotter," said Erik gesturing towards Kristina who was stroking the bird that had landed on her glove. "And I am Erik Magnusson."

The tall man burst out laughing. "Imagine, to have come upon you this way, cousin. I am Hakon Magnusson of Norway, here for your brother's wedding."

Erik looked at the Norwegian prince. "I did not recognize you, but then I have not seen you for many years. What a welcome you had to our forests."

"The incident was entirely of my own making. Thank you, kind lady," Hakon said as he walked forward, taking Kristina's free hand to gently kiss it while looking deeply into her eyes. "I am forever in your debt."

Kristina studied him with curiosity. Duke Hakon was tall and imposing, with unusually dark hair and complexion for a Norseman. The strong character of his face was enhanced by his sharply observant, light grey eyes. He had an almost solemn look that gave the impression of preoccupation with serious thoughts, but when he smiled his face became radiantly warm and open. Erik had once mentioned how he had admired Hakon's astute grasp of Scandinavian politics. Kristina knew that Duke Hakon was twenty-eight years old and still not married, though it was rumored he was betrothed to a Scottish princess. As Hakon kissed her hand, his eyes shone of admiration.

"You must be a great source of pride to your father," he said gently.

Erik moved quickly between them with his hand outstretched. "Again, Hakon, welcome to Stockholm. I am very happy that you arrived so early. This way, we have two days of hunting before the wedding."

Kristina enjoyed the attention they paid her, and especially the way Erik had so demonstratively taken hold of her elbow as he greeted Hakon.

She could not help wondering how Hakon could have been caught unawares by a snake, since she had heard much about his skill and zest in hunting. It was rumored that he would leave the royal castle in Norway at a moment's notice, accompanied by only a few of his most trusted friends. He would return days later, always with a surfeit of game. It was said that he had single-handedly killed four wolves when he became separated from his friends while hunting moose. Just looking at him, one sensed his confidence. As she turned, she could see Erik admiring Hakon's exquisite boots, and she assumed that Hakon had adroitly hunted down the animals that had given their lives to keep his feet warm.

"I better get back to the glen to see how my bird is doing," said Erik as Hakon went over to recover the decapitated snake. "Come with us and meet Valdemar."

Hakon put the body of the snake on the log where he had been sitting and with one swift motion opened its belly. He scraped out the innards and held up the long skin. "A fine memento, is it not?" he laughed before he became serious. "Could I count on your discretion not to tell of this incident? It would destroy my reputation."

"We promise," Erik and Kristina said with conspiratorial smiles as they made their way back to the glen.

There they met the hunting party that arrived with Birger and Erik Menved in the lead. Kristina noticed the cold formality exhibited between the Danish king and the Norwegian duke which reminded her of what she had heard at the Danish court about the animosity generated between the two countries after Norway sheltered those Danes accused of murdering King Erik Menved's father.

"You were solely responsible for saving his life, you know," whispered Erik who had come to stand beside her. "That bird has refused to follow directions for weeks, but today he did just what you wanted him to do."

Kristina felt herself blush from pleasure. "You were the one to trust me with your bird," she modestly replied.

"Because no one will ever know about you saving Hakon's life. The least I can do is to gift him to you."

She turned to him in surprise. "Truly? He is mine? Oh, thank you. I know of no woman at the Swedish court who has a bird of her own."

"It is a small gift indeed," said Erik as he smiled into her eyes. "And he needs to be flown often . . . every time I go hunting might you accompany me?" Kristina stood still, as if she would wake from a lovely dream if she moved or uttered a word.

140

"Kristina!" Queen Helvig called out sharply from behind as Kristina was about to descend the stairs to the Great Hall. "You will not have time to go hunting today. We are preparing for a wedding, and everyone is needed to assist with the work."

Kristina froze on the spot, not turning immediately to face the queen as she had habitually done all her life. For the first time she felt a burning resistance to complying with the queen's demand. She could only hear Erik's loving voice asking her to join the morning's hunt. Why should she still have to obey the dowager queen when a new queen was about to replace her? She felt the full force of rebelliousness as she turned to face Queen Helvig. As she looked into the queen's eyes she saw them momentarily narrow in surprise.

"I should think you would take your duties more seriously at a time like this. We saw little of you yesterday, and you were tardy in leaving the Hall last night, lost in conversation with Duke Hakon and Prince Erik, and utterly oblivious to your responsibilities to your queen-to-be."

"Your Majesty," Kristina stammered, again feeling like a disobedient child. "Princess Marta is partaking in the hunt, and she asked me to do the same. As for leaving the Hall late, I am sorry, I did not notice when the ladies left."

"Very unseemly behavior for the Lord High Constable's daughter. But since you are up so early, there is a rip to be mended in the altar cloth to be used for the wedding ceremony. By the time everyone else has risen, you should be finished with it. If you hurry," snapped the queen as she turned with a haughty swish of silk to walk back to her chamber.

Kristina had little choice but to obey, her heart heavy with disappointment. She knew that Erik would be waiting for her, and she had hardly slept during the night in anticipation. Now she was unable to let him know why she would not join him. She looked around the queen's chamber as she entered to see if any servant was there to carry a message to him. But no one was in sight, and she had to seat herself by the table under the icy stare of the queen. Kristina sighed when she saw the long tear in the altar cloth. It would take the better part of the day to mend it properly.

If it had been the queen's intention to wake her from her dream world filled with Erik, her new falcon, and a budding friendship with Duke Hakon, she had been quite successful. And maybe Queen Helvig was right; her behavior was unworthy of a lady in her position. Besides, there would be many days of hunting and many nights in the Great Hall to be enjoyed once the wedding was over. She resolutely threaded her needle and began work with utmost care; the cloth had to be perfect for Marta's wedding. She became absorbed in her work, and when she finally looked up she caught a sad, faraway look on the queen's face as she sat immobile over her embroidery frame. Kristina felt guilty, as if she had caused the queen some unintended pain. She took a measured breath before she continued her task.

On the eve of the royal wedding, the lavish supper lasted over six hours. Because the ladies took their meal separately on this occasion, the assemblage in the Great Hall consisted only of boisterous and carousing men. Many were too drunk to hold their wine, and urgently rushed to the privies hidden by hanging curtains. Erik pushed away from the table for a visit, as he was about to burst from too much drink. He claimed his royal privilege and pushed some equally needy court-iers out of his way to enter one of the "private rooms" protruding from the castle walls like a small enclosed balcony. There he relieved himself through a hole in the floor directly into the water below. With a satisfied grunt he returned to the festivities.

Some of the guests had fallen asleep at their seats, blissfully unaware of the clamor around them. The king's hunting dogs roamed under the tables searching for discarded bones. When no one prevented it, the hounds snatched food off the platters, noisily pulling down tableware in the process.

Erik had been on edge the whole day, wondering why Kristina had not joined the hunt without a word of explanation. He was afraid that she had not joined it because she did not feel about him as he had begun to feel about her. Might she have found someone in Denmark, or did she prefer the attention of Duke Hakon? Or had he simply mistaken childhood adoration for more than that?

142

He had had no idea how he would react to seeing her again. Naturally he had looked forward to her return, as had all the members of his family, but he had not been prepared for his reaction. The moment he had seen her all else had disappeared. She was beautiful. She had grown at least a head taller, and her body looked temptingly perfect under her pale rose garments. Her angelic face had become sensual, and her eyes drew him to her with a forceful magnetism. He had felt both surprise and boundless joy as he spontaneously ran to lift her up and whirl her around. The caring and closeness he had always felt for her had morphed into passion in a matter of moments. But all this emotion on his part did not mean that his feelings were reciprocated.

He told himself not to read anything into her absence as Kristina had probably not joined the hunt because she had to assist with the wedding preparations. He resolved to put the quandary out of his mind and concentrate on the present. He downed yet another cup of wine as he went over to where Birger and Erik Menved were sitting at the head of the dais table watching a group of young women who had begun dancing between the long tables to the accompaniment of musicians.

"It is your last night of unwedded bliss, dear Birger," smiled Erik Menved. "Tomorrow you will have a wife by your side." He lifted his cup for a toast, his eyes beaming at Birger.

"Marta is even more beautiful than I remembered," said Birger, looking a little embarrassed while returning the warm gaze over the rim of his cup. "And according to Ingeborg and Kristina she has a lovely, quiet way about her. I am very lucky."

Erik knew how important Erik Menved's friendship was to Birger, and how Birger's admiration for the Danish king had grown during the past years as he closely followed developments in Denmark under Erik Menved's successful rule. Both men had assumed the role of king as children; but unlike Birger, Erik Menved was now a powerful ruler. Erik understood Birger's longing for equal dominance, and how daunted he felt by the legendary strength of his father and grandfather, not to mention Torgil's overpowering presence. Erik sincerely hoped that the double wedding bonds between Sweden and Denmark would strengthen Birger's position once he became de facto ruler.

"What are you two talking about?" asked Erik, as he sat down beside them. "Are you giving my brother last minute advice?" He winked at Erik Menved. "I am sure Birger can handle it. He certainly has broken enough hearts in his days."

"Second only to you, dear brother," added Birger as he gestured for the dancers to draw nearer. The group was comprised of seven girls in long flowing dresses. They wore colored ribbons in their blond hair, except for one who had auburn hair surrounding her serene face.

"Now that one I fancy!" mumbled Birger. "She is a beauty, is she not?"

"I had an eye on her myself," said Erik, "but this being the night before your wedding, I will let you have her," he said in jest.

Birger's face suddenly froze. "What do you mean "let" me have her?" He glared at his younger brother.

Erik looked back at Birger, his eyes turning cautious. Then he quickly smiled: "Well, she certainly is beautiful enough to fight over, even with a king. But on the eve of your wedding I do not want you to spend your strength by having to defeat me."

Birger looked steadily at Erik and realizing that he was being cajoled back to good humor, he relented. "Let us have more wine! And go on dancing. Especially you!" he said pointing to the dark-haired girl who giggled as she joined her friends in a dance celebrating the summer harvest.

Erik rose and walked over to Valdemar who was sitting at the end of the dais. "One is obviously not to forget who is king!" he muttered under his breath.

"You have both been drinking, and you know how touchy he is," replied Valdemar who had overheard the exchange. "It is his obsession to beat you just once. At anything. Actually, you should let him do it."

"Why should I? Let everyone see who is stronger."

"Everyone already knows," Valdemar observed quietly, pouring some wine for his brother who was still seething. "Why let such minor matters upset you? Soon, as Duke of Sweden, you will have your own domain to rule, and that means power, wealth and independence. The only one who will end up with nothing is me -- the lowly third son. In my blissfully drunken state, I should be wishing an early end to you both so I could inherit the whole kingdom."

"I always thought your position unfair," reflected Erik more calmly, "and I would like to see it changed."

"How could I possibly be granted a dukedom? Every parcel of crown property means income to Birger. To his Council members, crown land means possible rewards for loyal service, and they would laugh themselves silly if I dared ask for even the smallest, swampiest part of Sweden."

"You might well be right," Erik agreed. "However, we must find some way to rectify your situation." He looked at Valdemar's resigned expression, knowing that a positive solution was quite unlikely.

Duke Hakon ambled toward them. "Why such glum faces?" he asked.

"Sit down with us," the princes offered warmly as they had come to like their Norwegian kin during the past days of hunting and feasting.

"We were just discussing the plight of younger brothers," said Erik, realizing that Hakon, too, was in a similar position. He was present at the wedding to represent his ailing older brother, King Eirik of Norway. "How is your brother faring?" asked Erik.

"Not well," answered Hakon morosely. "We fear the worst."

"I am very sad to hear that," said Erik. Since King Eirik had no male heir and Hakon would succeed him, Erik in all honesty did not know whether to condole or congratulate him. Instead, he asked "Will you drink a toast with us?"

Hakon lifted his cup and grinned, "To a wonderful wedding, but most importantly, to a lasting friendship. Especially between us younger brothers."

Chapter 8

Marta awoke in the early morning hours of her wedding day to find the summer sun already high in the sky, as was the custom in this land of the midnight sun. The birds were chirping loudly, as if to remind the world how foolish it was to waste such magic hours in sleep. She stretched, savoring the beautiful morning which she took as a sign that God approved of her impending marriage. Marta saw that Kristina was still asleep. Careful not to wake her, she swung her legs over the edge of the bed, wrapped herself in a long, padded gown, and tiptoed to the window. The stone floor and the thick stonewalls retained the night chill, so that when she opened the window the rush of outside air was warmer than that in the bedchamber.

Everyone here had treated her with such kindness and respect that despite her nature all her fears had vanished, and she was filled with eager expectations. She knelt in front of the large golden crucifix she had brought from Denmark and prayed for God to grant her the happiest day of her life. Then she went over to an archway leading to a tiny cubicle where her first lady-in-waiting slept.

"Wake up, Lady Astrid. The sun has been up for hours. Fetch us some food. Immediately!"

The lady-in-waiting, jolted upright by the unusually authoritative voice of her mistress, hurried to dress, while Marta walked into the adjoining chamber and parted the heavy curtains surrounding the bed where Ingeborg was sleeping. "It is a beautiful morning. Wake up!"

Ingeborg's eyelids twitched, but she did not open her eyes. "Go back to bed. It is the middle of the night," she mumbled. " She tried to pull the covers over her head, but finally Marta's infectious joy made her relinquish her warm bed to be dragged into Marta's room. There they woke Kristina who likewise objected, but quickly succumbed to Marta's irresistible happiness.

Torgils Knutsson, the Lord High Constable, stood outside his tent overlooking the sleeping town of Stockholm. His pavilion was pitched beside those of other wedding guests on the hillsides north of the town. Today, three large groups dominated the placement of the tents--the Swedes, the Danes, and the Norwegians. The distances between them indicated their delineation, but their proximity also showed this to be a friendly occasion. Other clusters of pavilions and marquees belonged to visiting princes and nobles from Holstein, Mecklenberg, Rugen and other principalities. Brightly-hued banners gently billowing in the wind among the many striped and colored tents, made a festive sight.

But the picturesque scene did not interest the Lord High Constable. He was studying the island town of Stockholm spread out below, pondering how difficult it would be for a potential enemy to conquer it surrounded by the Malar waters and approachable from land by two bridges only--one from the south and one from the north. Both were guarded, and at night the huge gates in the wall that encircled the city were closed. The castle itself was well protected; its north and east walls rising directly from the water, while its west and south walls facing the town were separated by a deep moat accessible only by a drawbridge. The island itself was cordoned off by a stockade of sharpened poles making it impossible for ships to approach the harbor unless special gates were opened to allow their entrance. Fortunately, Stockholm constituted a secure place from which to run a government. Unfortunately, that government was no longer to be run by him.

As he frowned over the inevitable, he heard someone approaching from behind. He quickly swung around to find Abjorn Sixtensson walking towards him. He relaxed.

"You startled me. I thought I was the only one up at this hour." Torgils looked at his friend with affection. Abjorn was younger by several years, but he had been Torgils' most trusted advisor for as long as Torgils had been Lord High Constable. Abjorn was head of the powerful Tofta clan and enjoyed the rare distinction of being a man without enemies. His and Torgil's alliance had been permanently sealed when they became kinsmen through Abjorn's marriage to Lady Borg.

"Today is an important day for Sweden," said Abjorn while he studied Torgils. "Important, but not a happy one for you. As King Birger is of age, and will have a queen by his side, the Coronation Day must be set. It cannot be postponed any longer. It is a damn pity. You have been a skillful ruler; you have enlarged our domains in Finland, and you have enjoyed amiable relations with our neighbors. Sweden has prospered under your watch, and now you have to step aside for a young, and to my mind, weak king. I imagine you must feel resentful."

"To say the least," admitted Torgils, amazed at how Abjorn always seemed to know what was on his mind. "There are a few more things I would have liked to accomplish before I stand aside . . . as well as a few items I would like to acquire!" he added wryly. He hated to admit that he had found no way to prolong his tenure, but he vowed to himself that if there were a way to do it, any way at all, he would find it.

Abjorn put his arm around Torgils' shoulders and shook him warmly. "My servants have prepared some food. Come, let us break fast, and enjoy the peace and quiet. In an hour or so, all will be madness."

Birger sat facing Father Nils in his tent. He, like his brothers and Lord Torgils, had moved out of the castle to allow the female guests more comfortable accommodations. It was dark in the tent even though the entrance flaps had been opened wide to the sun outside. Birger was in the process of dressing and fidgeted on the edge of his chair.

He observed his teacher--tall, thin, always calm and dignified --seated opposite him in his gray robe. Though he had been the royal family's confessor long before Birger was born, he still looked amazingly youthful. Not only was he devout, but also so well versed in the intricacies of worldly affairs that his knowledge had earned him the honest admiration of Birger and his brothers. Now Father Nils' grey eyes were resting on his eldest pupil.

"Your Majesty seems a little tense, but one does not marry every day," he said kindly.

"I do not want to make any mistakes during the lengthy rituals," sighed Birger.

"I will be there to guide you every step of the way," assured Father Nils. " It is only the anticipation that is unsettling. Everything will go well, I assure you."

Birger noticed that Father Nils was treating him in a different manner now, and he assumed that it had to do with the fact that he would be the actual ruler of Sweden when his coronation took place later in the year. He could already feel other friendships, like that with the priest, had changed to more formal ones. He suddenly felt lonely.

"If Your Majesty please, may I speak freely?" Father Nils asked after a long silence during which he was studying the young king before him.

"You have never been anything but forthright, Father."

"As you well know, the Church is eager for you to become the de facto ruler. Your father was the Church's benefactor; he exempted us from taxes and granted us many other privileges, but when he died Lord Torgils allied himself with the nobles by reconfirming their privileges, not ours. Now we are taxed, and Church property has even been reclaimed and given to nobles loyal to Lord Torgils. We pray that you will follow in your father's footsteps and restore the Church to her rightful position. We feel that you can rule the nobility as did your father, with firmness."

"Dear Father Nils, you know that I have promised the archbishop to restore the Church's privileges. What is it you really want to say?" Birger looked searchingly at his tutor.

"It would be unwise to have Torgils Knutsson remain your Lord High Constable after your coronation," replied Father Nils gravely. "He will not easily relinquish his position, especially when he has such a solid following among the nobles--and their armies."

"My father trusted Lord Torgils," answered Birger curtly, "and he has ruled Sweden quite capably." It struck him with sudden force how little he knew about leading a large kingdom despite all his eavesdropping and Lord Torgils' formal instructions; and he wondered why he had not insisted on learning more. He now realized that Lord Torgils never had shared the day-to-day decisions and responsibilities with him.

"The man your father knew and trusted worked for him--he was not the ruler of Sweden then. Now he is. My suggestion is for you to neutralize his power before it weakens yours."

"I will consider what you have said," Birger responded in a dismissive tone, reflecting on how everyone around him was maneuvering for power. His father had been able to keep a balance while supporting the Church, and so had Torgils while favoring the nobles. Now he had to decide how to maintain the balance; and he realized, to his dismay, that he had no idea how he would. To his relief, a guard announcing the arrival of Erik Menved interrupted them. They rose to greet the Danish king.

"Good morning," Erik Menved said as he approached his brother-in-law to embrace him. Birger knew that Erik Menved enjoyed their alliance as kinsmen and neighboring kings. He especially seemed to relish Birger's current weaker position that would hopefully make Birger follow his lead in regard to political matters.

"And a good morning to you," Birger replied warmly, returning the embrace.

"If your Majesties permit, I will take my leave and meet you at the cathedral later," said Father Nils as he withdrew.

"More last-minute instructions, I assume," observed Erik Menved looking after the departing priest. "Father Nils appears to care deeply about you, which is natural since he has known you from childhood . . . and his own fortune has not exactly suffered from the connection. I hear he is being considered for appointment as Bishop."

"He has certainly earned the promotion," said Birger before changing the subject. "You have no idea how grateful I am to have you here, my friend, and I will feel even better when Erik and Valdemar join us. As brothers we have been together for every important event in our lives; and today is yet another one for us to share."

Lady Astrid smiled with pride as she stepped back to admire her ward. Having been with Princess Marta since birth she knew all the royal family members intimately, so she regretted that Queen Agnes would not see how radiant her daughter looked on her wedding day;

but the fear-ridden dowager queen would not leave her country estate even to attend her daughter's nuptials.

"We are ready now," called Marta who was accompanied by Ingeborg, Kristina and their retinue as they descended to the Great Hall. When they entered the court yard a groom led forth a large white gelding adorned with flowers and draped with dark blue velvet edged in gold. Carefully the captain helped Marta mount and adjust the reins before her ladies-in-waiting impatiently brushed him aside to assist with her skirts and to arrange the saddle blanket. Ingeborg deftly mounted a dappled mare, while Queen Helvig had already been helped into a flower-bedecked wagon where she was seated on a specially built throne surrounded by her ladies-in-waiting. Other wagons adorned with birch leaves were already filled by noble ladies and their retinues. Kristina quickly took her place in the leading carriage.

"You will be riding alone," Ingeborg called softly to Marta. "But I am right behind you. God speed!"

Marta straightened her slender back "Ready!" she announced. The captain gave the order to march, and the long, perfectly paired column of soldiers rode out before her into the heart of Stockholm.

The houses along the narrow streets were decorated with garlands of flowers draped around their windows and strung across the streets from one rooftop to another. The royal banners of Sweden and Denmark were billowing everywhere in the warm summer breeze. All shops were closed, and the streets overflowed with people dressed in their finest. Waving arms and enthusiastic cheers greeted Marta, and she could scarcely conceal her own excitement as she waved back, doing her utmost to appear regal. All too soon they reached the open area in front of the cathedral where they dismounted.

Marta was ceremoniously ushered into a side vestry to prepare her entrance into the main cathedral. A long formal mantle was hung around her shoulders, and her simple gold crown was replaced by the official one. She closed her eyes and felt her knees buckle under her. Where was the courage that she had felt earlier? The Danish archbishop observed the petrified look in the eyes of the young woman and he reached out, took her hands, and pressed them warmly. He saw her lips quiver and felt her small hands shake as she took her first steps towards the main aisle. The choir burst into song as the archbishop guided her towards the altar where the bridegroom waited.

When Birger and Marta's eyes met, she felt strengthened by his warm smile. Then she was irresistibly drawn into another world as the ceremony proceeded. Slowly, she returned to reality as she listened to the familiar chants and prayers. After the vows, when she finally rose from her kneeling position and stood next to Birger, she found that she had unconsciously reached out to grasp his hand. Walking down the aisle, she felt a warm rush as his hand squeezed hers.

"My queen," he whispered, and her eyes filled with tears. With her hand in his, they walked out of the dark cathedral into the bright sunshine. The bells were tolling, and people cheered and waved. Marta silently prayed that by becoming Birger's wife and Sweden's queen, she would magically shed the last of her childhood nightmares.

Kristina went to the vestry while the cathedral was still slowly emptying of wedding guests who were returning to the castle to enjoy a lavish banquet and tournament to follow. She closed the door behind her and went over to where Marta had left her own crown in exchange for the official one. Kristina opened the leather box that had housed the official crown and placed Marta's in it before she closed the box to bring it back to the castle. As she turned to leave, the door opened, and Erik entered.

"Was it not a lovely wedding?" Kristina exclaimed.

"It certainly was," he said as he closed the door behind him. He looked searchingly at her. "What happened yesterday? Why did you not join the hunt as you promised?"

"Your mother caught me on my way down and insisted that I help with the preparations. I could not get a message to you."

"Is that all?"

"Of course. Why do you ask?"

Erik looked flustered. "I thought that I might have assumed too much."

Kristina smiled at the thought of the many hours she had spent longing to be near him during these last years. If only he knew how she had suffered under Queen Helvig's burning gaze while stitching as quickly as she could in the hope of finishing her work before the hunt was over. "I wanted to come, but the altar cloth needed repairing."

"Thank the Lord," he blurted. He walked over and pulled her close. She lifted her head and looked into his eyes. Slowly their lips met.

After the lavish wedding supper, Birger stood up to announce the departure for the games that were to take place between the champion knights on the tournament field north of Stockholm. By the time Birger and Marta took their seats in the royal pavilion, all of Stockholm had gathered at the tournament field. Though comfortable canvas-covered structures shielded spectators from rain or sun, many onlookers dared to perch on perilous tree limbs for the best view. Outside the spectators' circle, young girls were busy dispensing free beer from huge barrels and the mood was festive and expectant.

Birger declared the competitions open, and knights from several countries competed in archery, lance throwing, and weapons handling on horseback. The Swedes graciously accepted their defeat when the Danes prevailed in the overall competition. Was not their new queen from Denmark? Was it not fitting that her knights should win? The crowd cheered and drank more free beer. While awaiting the main event of the day--the jousting between champion knights--the arena filled with acrobats, jugglers, and musicians.

Erik and Valdemar were sitting on the corner of the royal dais, idly watching the entertainment.

"Do you boys think we will win the joust?" Torgils asked from his seat behind them.

"Of course," Erik replied with conviction as he pulled his chair around to face the Lord High Constable.

"They claim the Danish champion is invincible," Torgils shouted over the music.

"They better be wrong," huffed Valdemar as he turned his chair to be included in the circle. "I have placed a huge bet on Birger's champion."

Erik leaned towards Torgils. "I would like to discuss something with you . . . and this is as good a place as any. No one can hear what we say."

"I am listening," said Torgils, intrigued.

Erik looked on the man before him with the greatest respect. Not only was he the actual ruler of Sweden and Kristina's father, but he was also a formidable master strategist who had taught him and his brothers everything they knew about statesmanship and warfare. Still, Erik felt that the moment had come to test himself. Though he had not consulted Birger on the matter he wanted to broach, he felt sure that Birger would agree with what he was about to attempt.

"The time has come for Birger to take charge of his kingdom," he began cautiously, "and he wants me to take over my dukedom as well--even though I am not yet of age." Then, more boldly, he added, "I have heard that you are not in favor of my ruling my dukedom until I am eighteen."

"To be precise," answered Torgils, "I have expressed objections to a divided kingdom in general. Your dukedom will be a separate domain, and a divided country is not a strong country."

Erik studied Torgils with his steel blue eyes. Despite his nervousness, a slightly arrogant smile played on his lips. "I have also heard that you are not particularly eager for Birger to take over the rule of Sweden." Torgils made a gesture in protest, but Erik pressed on. "Why would any man in his right mind want to yield his position as Regent? Especially to an inexperienced young king? Birger and I have still more to learn before we take over our new responsibilities" Erik smiled broadly at Torgils, who for once looked puzzled. Erik, who had never seen Torgils look anything but confident, felt a surge of encouragement as he continued. "Maybe a division of Sweden at a later date would indeed be better . . . and do you not agree that since it inevitably will be divided, it would not matter whether it was split into two . . . or three parts? I know that the third son's customary lot is to receive nothing, but both Birger and I find it unfair to Valdemar. However, if again I have heard the rumors correctly, the Council feels that this royal cub's share is already too large."

"How can that be denied?" countered the Lord High Constable calmly. "Had it not already been declared before your father's death that you be given the dukedom in the east, I doubt you would ever get to rule it." Torgils' eyebrows arched questioningly. "Are you now proposing that Sweden be divided even further? That would never pass the Council, even if the king insisted!"

"Well," began Erik slowly, relishing the moment and looking straight at his mentor. "The members of the Council might accede if the idea were presented to them in a very convincing way. Let us assume that the king was the one to suggest it, and that the second dukedom he suggested was Finland. It lies across the waters, is difficult to govern in absentia, et cetera. And let us further assume that you wholeheartedly supported the idea, Lord Torgils."

"Me? They would never believe that!" countered the Lord High Constable, frowning, and wondering why this boy could think he would support something that went totally against his frequently expressed principles? The idea was preposterous.

Erik continued softly, "But then Sweden would remain undivided and under your rule until we all come of age. You would have three more years to rule--until Valdemar becomes eighteen!"

Torgils looked at Erik in astonishment. How had he missed this talent for intrigue? Not that he had underestimated Erik's intelligence, far from it, but for this young whelp to find the bargaining point so precisely was undeniably impressive. Torgils felt the frustrating confusion of a proud teacher and a vanquished opponent. His head swam at the thought of keeping his position for another three years. He took a large gulp from his wine goblet and stared at three jugglers tossing flaming torches through the air.

Erik broke the silence. "Perhaps you would like to consider your answer?" he asked gently, savoring the exquisite feeling of impending victory.

Aware that he had betrayed his acceptance of the bribe, Torgils knew he would lose all dignity if he did not answer directly. "You have a good point, my prince," he said smoothly, "The country will be divided in any event, and it would be helpful to have someone with the status of a Swedish prince govern Finland directly. And of course, it would benefit Sweden to have three well-trained rulers taking over the reigns simultaneously. As for my remaining as Regent, I would, as always, do my best to serve Sweden."

Torgils' prayers had been answered. He had gained exactly what he wanted, but at what price? He had abandoned his well-known stand against a divided kingdom for a bribe from a boy. No one would ever know the humiliation he felt at that moment.

Without further comment Erik pulled his chair back to its original position. Valdemar followed suit, a stunned look on his face. "Some more wine . . . Duke Valdemar?" whispered Erik as his stupefied brother numbly held out his cup.

Erik had bested the master! The victory was intoxicating, especially since he had been uncertain of the outcome, but he had correctly measured Torgil's thirst for power. All at once he regretted the years lost before he would take over his own dukedom. But as chess had taught him, sacrifices are necessary, and for Valdemar he was willing to sacrifice that lost time . . . and, not to forget, Valdemar would be forever beholden to him. Erik glanced over at his brother who still looked stunned but who turned towards him sprouting a happy smile. "Thank you," he mouthed as he lifted his cup to his brother. Well, ruminated Erik as he drank deeply, one could always learn more while waiting.

A hush fell over the crowd as the two champion knights rode towards the dais. One was the Danish king's champion, and one was Birger's new champion knight, Johan Brunkow. Johan's father, who had emigrated to Sweden from Brandenburg, had risen to become an advisor to the late King Magnus despite the fact that he was foreign-born.

The Swedish and Danish queens favored their knights with their colors and personally tied the delicate silks around their champions' arms. The competition was something that would long be remembered, and by the time the Danish champion yielded to Johan Brunkow there was no limit to the joy amongst the spectators, especially those who had won their wagers.

Johan Brunkow received the victor's sword from Queen Marta as he knelt before her.

"I was honored to have you wear my colors," she said formally as she looked upon the ruggedly handsome face below her.

"To fight in your honor made my victory possible. May you grant me the privilege again," said the young champion as he gazed up at his queen.

Erik could guess what he was thinking. To serve her and to shield her from harm would be his life's goal. Tonight as the victor, Brunkow would be seated beside Marta at supper. He hardly seemed to notice the beautifully crafted sword she placed in his hands, or the cheers of the crowd, so dazzled was he by her soft smile.

Birger had just finished washing off the road dust after riding back to the castle. As he adjusted the seal of office upon his shoulders, Erik entered the chamber.

"Congratulations on your champion's victory. Valdemar made a fortune betting on him. It has been a spectacular day." Erik went over to his brother. "Are you going to announce the date of your coronation at supper?"

Birger looked uncomfortable at the very mention of impending responsibilities. "I wonder if I will ever feel ready, but as you say, it is time to take over."

Erik was well aware of his brother's insecurity and that Birger would welcome any honorable excuse to delay his accession to the throne. "Birger, I have been thinking about what you and I so often have discussed: Valdemar's unfair situation. Would you consider making him Duke of Finland? It would be good for Sweden to have a member of the family overlooking our interests over there."

"It is a good idea, and I would gladly do it if it had the slightest chance of being supported by the Council."

"If Torgils supported it the Council members--most of whom are his allies--would go along with him," said Erik as he paced the floor. "You could offer him a deal. Since he is not eager to relinquish his position, you could let him keep it for a while."

"You know that I cannot do that! I am of age now, and I would look ridiculous if I allowed him to continue to rule."

"There were discussions," interjected Erik, "about me taking over my dukedom now at the time of your coronation, but most members of the Council opposed it until I become of age. If they would grant

Valdemar a dukedom now, you could offer Torgils continued rule until we are all of age, giving them a few more years to build their fortunes undisturbed by us. Even if they grow stronger during the interim, they would never sanction a coup by Torgils who is not of royal blood, so there is little to fear from the delay. Naturally, the Church will not be pleased, but with continued assurances of future tax abatement you can manage them. Especially if you explain that Valdemar's role is to spread the Christian faith among the heathens in Finland!"

Birger glared at his younger brother. Birger's efforts to find an excuse to delay his coronation had been embarrassingly unimaginative, and Erik correctly guessed that Birger would not reject a solution just because it was not his own.

"I assume Lord Torgils is equally enthusiastic about the idea?" Birger said finally. "You have spoken to him, have you not?"

"Well, I did try it out on him," admitted Erik uneasily, knowing that he had overstepped his bounds. He should have consulted Birger first. He was the king. Then he felt angry. Damn it! Because of his intervention, both his brothers would get exactly what they wished for, while he would be delayed for several years from ruling his dukedom.

Birger, realizing that Erik had nothing to gain from the deal, conceded. "It is an excellent idea. And, in the meantime, you will both join me in the Council. We can still wield some influence while we wait."

Erik, deeply relieved, went over to hug his brother. "This also means we will live together for a few more years."

"That is the best part," said Birger, returning Erik's hug with a wry smile. "I will tell Valdemar about MY decision to make him Duke of Finland!"

Marta was amazed that she was not tired. It was already early in the morning and she was still seated at the long dais table flanked by the royal families. At her left Birger presided, and on her right sat her triumphant champion. Giddy from all the attention, she wished the festivities would never end. Just then, Birger rested his hand on her arm.

"It is time to withdraw," he whispered quietly. She hesitated, but then quickly stood with her husband waiving to the cheering guests. Young girls tossed flower petals over them as they left the Great Hall.

In the quiet corridor, Marta's ladies-in-waiting stood outside the Queen's chamber. Birger bowed. "I will see you shortly, " he mumbled as he continued on to his own quarters.

Marta stepped into her new chamber. She was amazed to see the transformation it had undergone during the day. Queen Helvig's possessions had been removed and hers had been put in their place. She smiled with pleasure when she saw her own things looking as if they belonged there. The walls were hung with her tapestries, the floor was covered with woven Danish rugs, and in front of the fire were thrown soft fur skins. The bed was now encircled by her own gold-trimmed, luxurious curtains. A multitude of exquisite pillows, embroidered by Marta and her ladies over the years, made the hard benches and stools appear welcoming. On the wall opposite the bed hung a new banner bearing the Swedish and Danish coats of arms. Marta drank it all in. This was her new world, and it was lovely. Her ladies-in-waiting would be there to work, read, sing, and to play with any future children. This room would be her true home.

Except for Lady Astrid who stayed behind to brush her long hair, the other ladies-in-waiting withdrew. Dressed only in her simple robe she felt suddenly insignificant, as if her stature had diminished with the shedding of her regal attire.

Some time after Ingeborg had arrived in Denmark to become its queen, Marta had summoned the courage to ask her what the nuptial bed had to offer. Ingeborg replied that it was not bad--after all it was a wife's duty to please her husband, since that was how children were created. Marta had not questioned Ingeborg's point of view since she adored her, but she preferred the breathlessly whispered versions among the servant girls. In any case, she was not frightened since God commanded women to perform wifely duties, but she was not sure whether she would please her husband.

"Enough brushing, Lady Astrid," Marta said. "Leave me now." She hoped she sounded confident and did not betray her nervousness. Lady Astrid curtsied and left the room. Marta noticed that her hands were shaking. She looked over to where several pitchers of wine stood on a table. She quickly went over to fill a cup. Rarely, if ever, did she drink more than a few sips, since she was afraid to say or do anything silly. Once, when she was younger, she had drunk too much and had made a fool of herself according to her sister who, thank heavens, was the only one who had seen her. But she did remember how light-hearted and carefree she had felt before a terrible headache left her immobile the next morning. She picked up the cup and slowly drained it. It burnt going down, and she gasped as she sank down on a bench in front of the fire. Once she caught her breath a lovely warmth spread through her body. She began to relax.

She did not know how long she had been sitting in front of the fire watching the glowing embers changing shape and form, when she heard a knock on the door and Birger entered, wearing a soft linen tunic over his hose and soft leather shoes on his feet. Gone were his crown, sword, and neck chain. Still, he appeared very manly in his simple attire.

Birger looked at her seated on a narrow bench with her slender hands clasped in her lap. Her long, reddish hair reflected the glow of the fire and made her resemble an iridescent forest siren. She seemed at peace with herself, and her smile was warm. He went over to the table where the wine pitchers were standing.

"Would you like some?" he asked, turning to see her nodding with that smile. As he poured, he realized that for the first time in his life he felt insecure, even foolish in front of a woman. He had never before considered whether he would be a pleasing lover, but only what the lady of the moment could offer him. Were he too drunk, were he spent too quickly, it had never mattered. He was the king, and a woman was there to please him and to be gone the next morning. But this woman would remain by his side, and she would know whether he was a real man or not--and treat him accordingly. As he picked up their goblets, he tried to push the disquieting thought from his mind.

"Let us drink to a long and happy life together."

She took her cup and touched it to his before they both drank. He settled down on a large pillow beside her bench. He did not know what to say, so he remained silent. Damn it, why was he not like Erik--self-assured and in command of every situation?

"This is the first time we have had a chance to talk together since you arrived," he said.

"Yes, it is," she answered, and again they fell silent.

"I do not know what to say to you," he blurted. "I want to say all the right things, but nothing seems to come to mind."

"I feel the same way," she confided, and they both started to laugh.

He studied her small and lovely face and realized that he was happy just to be with her, feeling released by his confession.

"Tell me all about yourself. I know so little about you except what Ingeborg has told me. Which was all wonderful," he added quickly when he saw her concern. "She loves you very much."

"And I her," said Marta warmly. "My life has not been very interesting," she began talking hesitantly about her childhood. After a while the words came more easily, and the two of them laughed at her anecdotes. She also shared the sad story of her father's assassination, and the feelings of loneliness and fear she had experienced after the incident.

Birger stood up to pour more wine for them, then put the pitcher down on the floor beside him. He told Marta of his own childhood, about his closeness to his brothers, and how happy he was that they were going to stay at court for a few more years. He was amazed at the ease with which he talked to her. He had never spoken openly to any woman--not even to his sisters--only to his brothers, Father Nils and to Lord Torgils. But this was different. He felt intoxicated by her attention and quiet praise. Sitting here with her in front of the small fire seemed the most perfect thing in the world.

As they talked, he put his hand on hers, which she did not withdraw, but opened for him to hold. After a while she sat down on the floor beside him, and he moved closer to put his arm around her shoulders. Together they leaned back against the large fur-covered pillows on the skins spread out on the floor. She peacefully leaned her head on his shoulder to look at the flickering fire while listening to his voice. As she turned to say something, he turned his head at the very same moment. Their faces almost touched, and they both caught their breath. Then their lips slowly met. Birger was amazed at how intensely he felt the warmth of her body and smelled the subtle rosewater scent on her skin. He marveled at her every detail. Slowly and lovingly, he guided his virgin bride to more and more daring kisses and caresses. Soon they both rested naked on the furs, and not for one moment did she hesitate, but rather urged him on. He felt an excitement he had never experienced before. Still, he felt no sense of urgency. So naturally did they come together that he was utterly surprised when she cried out in pain. He froze as he saw her tears, and he gently kissed her eyes. After what seemed like an eternity she moved against him carefully, searchingly, and signaled him to resume their lovemaking with a passion that almost shocked him. For a while they played the exquisite game until he finally gave in to the inevitable. His body and his mind exploded with uncontrollable joy. As he gently moved away to look at her, she was crying. When he looked worried, she shook her head--these were tears of happiness: she knew she had handled becoming a wife even better than becoming a queen. He lifted her in his arms and brought her to the bed where he gently wrapped her in the down-filled cover and curled his body next to hers.

"You are a miracle," he mumbled into her hair. "A pure miracle."

He pulled her closer and held her as if never to let her go. This woman was his to love and by whom to be loved. She had no allegiance or duty to anyone but him. For her he was the center, and Erik, Valdemar, Torgils and all the rest were just part of the scenery. What a wonderful thought. He was not a bit tired, even though the morning sun painted long golden streaks on the floor. He wanted simply to lie there, holding her and knowing a whole life awaited them. For the first time he was reminded of words of the poets. He was tempted to quote a love ballad he had found perfectly silly just a few days earlier. Feeling her warm body next to his, he felt his excitement grow; and gently their lovemaking resumed anew.

Chapter 9

Kristina was amazed at how silent Stockholm castle was when she awoke the morning after the wedding. The sun was already shining brightly; but she realized that the guests who had gone to bed only a few hours earlier, were still fast asleep. Reluctant to leave the warmth of the covers, she finally got up to put on her hunting garb. This day she would not miss flying her falcon, even if Erik slept all morning. She quickly dressed, went out into the corridor, and headed for the stairs. As she passed one of the guest chambers, Queen Helvig appeared in the doorway.

"Good Morning, Your Majesty," Kristina said, wondering why the queen was in that room, until she reminded herself that Marta was now occupying the queen's chamber.

"Come in for a moment," the dowager queen requested.

Kristina went in and closed the door. She noticed that the chamber was filled with chests and trunks. "Can I help you unpack, your Majesty?" she asked immediately.

"No, my dear," said the dowager queen quietly. "I am not unpacking, I am leaving."

"Leaving, your Majesty? I have heard nothing about that."

"I have always known that two women cannot rule under the same roof, but until the other day I had blissfully ignored the fact that it applied to me as well. You, my little Kristina, were the one who reminded me. When I saw how reluctant you were to follow my directions, I knew my time had come."

"My poor behavior is no measure of your authority here," protested Kristina.

"It is, Kristina," interrupted Queen Helvig. "You, if anyone, have always obeyed my wishes. But let us not talk about that now. I am leaving, although I have told no one else."

"Surely you are not taking your leave without saying goodbye to your children!" Kristina blurted out in disbelief.

"It was painful to bid farewell to Ingeborg last time, and now Rikissa . . ." The queen fell silent. She looked at Kristina and drew a deep breath. "I am going to my estate at Dovo, and my children can visit me there whenever they like." Again, Kristina tried to protest.

"Everything I have done in my life has been out of duty. Would I ever have left Holstein to come to this cold, barbaric North to marry a man I had never seen had it not been out of duty? Would I have suffered miscarriages and labored to bear five children, had it not been my duty? And now, when Birger has a wife, is it not my duty to allow her to rule over the royal household?"

Kristina could not object to the logic of her words, but she still pleaded "Please bid farewell to your children, your Majesty. Rikissa's abrupt departure still hurts them."

"My boys are grown men now. Besides, it will be many hours before they arise. I cannot wait. I have to start my journey now if I am to reach my destination before nightfall."

"You could leave on the morrow," pleaded Kristina.

"I have written a letter to Ingeborg," said the dowager queen as she handed Kristina a sealed parchment. "And do not forget that you, too, have duties to fulfill--whatever pain that may cause you." Kristina swallowed. Did the Queen Helvig know of her feelings for Erik, warning her not to hope for marriage? But the queen just said, "Fetch some servants to take my cases to the docks. Everything else is already at the harbor. I have had a ship waiting to cast off since early morning."

After Kristina had done as she was told, she walked to the chapel where the dowager queen had gone to pray. As she silently approached, she saw Queen Helvig on her knees in front of the small altar, her body heaving with sobs. Kristina discreetly left as silently as she had entered. When the queen finally emerged, she looked as composed as ever.

Kristina insisted on accompanying the dowager queen and her three ladies-in-waiting to their ship. As they stood on the dock, Queen Helvig turned to Kristina and said with unusual softness. "You have always been a blessing to my children, Kristina. Help them when you can." She embraced Kristina, then turning her face away, boarded the ship. Once the wind filled out the sails, the ship quickly pulled away. Kristina could not see the dowager queen's face, but she felt her unspoken sadness.

On her return Kristina entered the aviary, went over to her black falcon and gave him a lard-dipped piece of bread. He eagerly climbed onto her glove.

"My dear Soot," she whispered as she spoke his name aloud for the first time. Though it was considered bad luck to name a hunting bird, she was convinced that custom did not apply to birds owned by women. "Everything is changing around here. I never thought that I would miss Queen Helvig, but now . . . It is as if everything has lost its balance."

She continued talking to the bird quietly while she slipped on its hood and waited for the stable boys to bring her horse. Once she had mounted, she rode through the town's narrow lanes, eager to reach the silence of the forest.

Imparting the news of Queen Helvig's departure had to wait until after the hunt when all were assembled in the Great Hall for the final supper before the wedding guests would depart for their respective abodes. "Your mother will not be with us tonight," was all Kristina could say when Birger asked where the queen was.

"Is she ill?" asked Ingeborg as she stood with her brothers by the high table.

"Queen Helvig has left for Dovo . . . to live there," Kristina said as she handed Ingeborg the dowager queen's message.

"Without saying good-bye?" Valdemar asked in disbelief.

"She said that she could not do it in person . . ."

"That does not sound like Mother," objected Erik.

"But I think it is true," said Ingeborg as she handed Birger the message she had just read.

In silence, he read and then passed the parchment amongst them. "Still," said Birger looking terribly hurt, "she should have said her farewell in person."

"That is the very least she could have done," Ingeborg agreed. "We are not children anymore, and she owes us the respect accorded adults. All my life I have felt as if I could do nothing to please her, but I now know that I am a capable woman in my own right. And still, she makes me feel like a miserable child, as if I do not even merit a proper farewell. Damnation on her!"

"Ingeborg!" protested Birger.

"No, I agree with Ingeborg," said Valdemar. "A word of caring and encouragement would have strengthened us on so many occasions in the past. But as she never said them, we had to rely on each other and on ourselves; however maybe that was what she wanted for us."

"Whatever she intended," said Ingeborg in a broken voice, "I cannot forgive her for leaving like this!"

They stood silently together as Marta entered the Hall, oblivious to their mood. She rushed toward Birger who enfolded her in his arms. Then gently he held her at arm's length.

"My mother has just left court to live at her estate at Dovo."

Marta looked confused. "I am sorry that I did not get to say good-bye to her." She pondered the news for a moment before she smiled gaily. "It is most kind of her to allow me to preside singly over the household from the very first. You have a wise mother," she said as she again moved into Birger's arms.

One by one Erik, Valdemar, and Ingeborg turned away, the hurt etched on their faces.

"Marta has questioned me about the significance of the wolves' teeth we wear around our necks," Birger said to Erik and Valdemar as they waited for the rest of the hunting party to join them in the glen a few days later.

"And what did you tell her?" asked Erik.

"That we wear them as a secret token of loyalty. She said that she had been curious about them ever since she saw them on Ingeborg and Kristina, but that she had never wanted to ask. She thought it was a lovely idea and said that she would like to have one as well."

"It was only a childish gesture," said Erik evasively.

Birger stiffened. "You mean that she should not have one?"

"No, I am not saying that at all," hastened Erik. "I simply mean that it was a gesture made at a specific moment when we were children. Its significance comes from what we experienced then. We made each other feel close and strong in our otherwise regimented lives."

"Well, whatever the case, Marta wants one, and we should all go hunting together to get it, just like last time," beamed Birger.

"We will get her one," promised Valdemar.

As Birger, Marta, Erik, Valdemar, and Kristina rode out early the next morning they were laughing and singing when they dismounted their horses to walk the final distance on foot. The princes carried snares and nets; and Marta and Kristina followed with an array of knives and bows. They quieted down to pass silently through the cool forest, enjoying the sun that drifted through the crowns of the trees to slowly dry the dew on the forest floor. The silence was filled with the hum of insects and the crackling sounds of twigs breaking under their feet. They saw a startled pheasant, roused from its perch on a low tree branch, flutter away with heavy wing strokes. The forest smelled of pine and moss; and they all became lost in its beauty.

As they finally neared the slope by the lake where the wolves' presence had been reported, they took a circuitous route to prevent the wind from carrying their scent to the wolf den. They found a vantage point downwind on higher ground from which they could look down on the opening of the den that had been inhabited intermittently over the years. Erik whispered that they were lucky that the wolves were still there at this time of the year since their young must already be a month old. The pack would soon move out through the forest to range over a wider territory where it would be much harder to track them.

"It is so quiet," whispered Marta once they had settled down and deposited their weapons beside them in an orderly fashion.

"The pack is out hunting now," Erik explained. "Only the mother and the pups are here, and they are probably sleeping. That is exactly the way we want it, since they would have discovered us immediately if we had arrived when they were up and about. But from now on we have to be quiet and move as little as possible since the wolves have very sensitive hearing and smell."

They settled down to wait, deciding to take turns to see what was transpiring at the den.

Marta rested against Birger who had his back against a wooden log. Valdemar lay on his back studying the clouds racing across the skies, while Erik and Kristina took the watch. They were lying on their stomachs, looking expectantly towards the den. Erik gradually moved closer until his arm was touching hers. She could feel his warmth through the leather sleeve of his hunting garb, and she was filled with peace and excitement at the same time.

They had waited for more than an hour, when suddenly Erik nudged her. A small furry cub emerged from the opening. Kristina drew her breath. "I have never seen a wolf so small," she whispered excitedly. "It is adorable!"

She motioned to the others who quietly moved into position on their stomachs to observe five more cubs emerge from the den. The young animals, dazed by the bright daylight moved clumsily about, pushing and biting each other playfully in the process. The mother wolf emerged and led them down to the water where they all drank their fill. She nudged them back to the mouth of the den where she lay down, surrounded and overrun by the yelping and cavorting pups.

The blissful domestic scene was interrupted as a huge grey wolf emerged from the woods. He stood motionless for a moment, perhaps sensing something unfamiliar. But after a while he approached the den, followed by five adult wolves in single file. As he stood tall and proud in front of the den, the other wolves surrounded him with their bellies low to the ground, pushing their heads towards him, nuzzling his muzzle while whimpering and wagging their tails. After this demonstration of subordination, the small pups rushed up to the adults and pulled on their muzzles. Kristina saw the big wolves regurgitate some half-chewed meat that the pups attacked with squeals of pleasure.

"It has been a successful hunt," whispered Erik. "That means they will loll about for the rest of the afternoon."

They all studied the wolves with fascination. It was not hard to discern which was the dominant couple. The mother was obviously the mate of the lead wolf, the largest one that had arrived first. Then there was another adult couple helping with the pups, all of which seemed to belong to one litter. The other two wolves were adolescent males, strong but clearly subjugated, as Kristina saw them roll on their backs exposing their bellies in front of the alpha wolf.

Despite all the frightening stories Kristina had heard about them, the wolves seemed unusually kind towards one another. Once the lead wolf had lain down, he tolerated the pups playing all over him, pulling at his ears without any sign of irritation.

"So, what do we do now?" asked Birger. "Should we trap one in a net?"

Marta, who was thoroughly absorbed by the peaceful scene, objected. "But you cannot kill any of them, they look so happy together."

"We came here to get you a tooth," said Erik.

"But you cannot kill them!"

Erik's faint smile did not escape Kristina. "So how will we get you a tooth?" he asked.

"I do not need one," Marta replied resolutely. "When you got yours, it was from a wolf who was threatening you, and you deserved your memento. But these . . ." she said with a soft smile. "These are just a happy family."

"You mean that we came all this way for nothing?" asked Birger.

"Oh, but this is wonderful," exclaimed Marta. "I could stay here all day just to watch."

After a while Birger suggested that they start their long trek back. Birger and Valdemar quietly gathered their weapons, while Erik indicated that he and Kristina wanted to watch some more before following them.

"You knew all along that Marta would not insist on killing one of the wolves to get a tooth of her own once she saw them as a family," Kristina said knowingly. "You never wanted her to have one to start with."

"That is not quite true," Erik said. "I just did not think it made sense that she should wear something that meant absolutely nothing to her, while for the rest of us it represented a lifelong pledge. She behaves like a child."

"Erik, that is not fair," Kristina protested. "She has had a difficult life at the Danish court. She behaves like a little girl so that no one will consider her an adversary."

Erik's face softened. "You see the good in everyone, Kristina. That is one of the reasons I love you so very much."

So naturally did his words come that they did not immediately catch her full attention. But as they made their impact she looked at him incredulously.

"This is the first time I am saying it aloud, Kristina. But you must know what I feel."

"I . . ." she began, but he interrupted her by leaning forward, his lips slowly touching hers. When her mouth opened under his he gently turned her on her back. Slowly, then more passionately, they kissed until his hands moved down her shoulders and closed around her back. Their bodies moved together while their embrace became fierce.

Suddenly, without warning he pulled back and shook his head. "As much as I want you, it will not happen unless we are married."

"As I cannot offer an alliance of importance to Sweden, a marriage will never occur," she protested. "Why can we not be happy now until we both have to marry someone else?"

"Because, my love, you must be unsullied. Your marriage will be an important . . ."

"I know how a woman can feign virginity on her wedding night," she interrupted. When she saw his raised eyebrows she quickly added. "I heard about it at the Danish court where the women were not reluctant to impart their secrets."

He laughed. "Maybe you could fool someone who knows little of women, but I do not think your likely future husband will be that innocent. I do not think you heard me when I said that I love you. That means that I want the best for you in every way."

"So, what are we going to do?" she asked, bewildered. "Just go on, stealing glances, touching when nobody watches, hoping for a moment alone together?"

"That is what we will have to do until we marry," he answered with a warm smile. "You see I intend to do everything in my power to make you my wife."

Kristina felt her heart pound so hard that all she could hear was blood rushing through her head. "That will not happen," she said, while an irresistible force of hope pervaded her being.

"Yes, it can, if we have a little luck on our side. Nevertheless, you have to remain untouched in the event that we are unlucky. However, I can still kiss you," he grinned as his lips again touched hers.

As they reluctantly left their outpost and walked slowly into the forest, Erik kept looking carefully at the ground. He searched for a long time before he suddenly dropped his weapons to kneel at the base of a large fir tree. He parted the dense lower branches, enabling Kristina to see the totally decomposed carcass of a large wolf.

"I knew that we would find some bones around the area since the wolves have kept returning here for such a long time. Now Marta can have her tooth," he said exultantly as he pried one of the large teeth from its jawbone.

Kristina smiled. "You are not as cynical as you sometimes appear. Maybe that is one of the reasons I love you so much."

Erik kicked a large log to reposition it so that it would ignite from the glowing coals beneath. They had just finished supper and were settling in around the hearth in the Great Hall. Several weeks had passed since that magic day in the forest.

Marta and Birger were sitting and whispering together, while Valdemar and Kristina were setting up a checkerboard. Milling about were the same courtiers, telling the same stories, and singing the same ballads. But to Erik everything had changed. While his mother's and sisters' departures had left a deep void in his life, his love for Kristina had filled that empty space, and more. He longed to be with her every moment of the day, and he was envious of Birger's open happiness with Marta while he and Kristina had to hide their feelings.

Finding a wife for Erik was a much-discussed topic at court. Many of the nobles vainly hoped he might choose a member from their clan even though they knew that the bride of a prince had to bring to their union a powerful alliance for the country as a whole. Members of the Council had made recommendations of suitable foreign princesses, but Erik found that they were either too young or too drab for him to even feign interest. As he looked at Marta and Birger laughing softly together, he shuddered at the thought of long winters in Nykoping castle together with an ugly, chatting wife--however rich and power-ful. No, he wanted to sit by the fire and look over at the beautiful and vivacious Kristina, just as he was looking at her now, caught in concen-tration at the checkerboard.

As usual, Valdemar had sensed early on what Erik was feeling, and had suggested that they thoroughly investigate who would make a suitable wife for Erik before he made any stupid mistakes which would ruin Kristina's future.

"If you find the right woman you will stop thinking about her," Valdemar had insisted. Erik chose not to contradict him, as he needed his support.

They had sat down together with the names of all the eligible ladies. They found that there were at least a dozen names and method-ically collected information on each of the twelve leading candidates.

"The daughter of King Eirik of Norway is the strongest candidate, even though her father is mortally ill, and the line will most likely pass to her uncle, Duke Hakon, in the near future," concluded Valdemar after studying the list. "But she is far too young to marry now, so she could not help you out of your present predicament. The same holds true for little princess Sofia of Werle, the niece of Erik Menved, and we already have strong ties with Denmark."

Slowly they went down the list, and after rejecting most only two candidates remained, both from powerful German houses.

"They would definitely not help you forget Kristina," concluded Valdemar.

Erik had to agree with him since he had met the young ladies at Ingeborg's wedding in Roskilde and found them both dull and unat-tractive. "Why not show Birger and the Council that we have found no candidate of true importance for Sweden except King Eirik of Norway's daughter? We could argue that she is far too young at the present and that we should wait," Erik suggested, hopeful that the search for a wife would be abandoned for, at least, some time to come.

Erik was sure Lord Torgils would be more than pleased with, and thoroughly supportive of, his desire to marry Kristina, as would Birger and Marta. If he held out for a while, other eager suitors might wed the two German candidates, offering the possibility that he could have Kristina for a wife in view of the Norwegian princess' tender age.

He smiled to himself as he remembered how he and Hakon had been sitting by the fire for many hours of drinking together with their friends the night before Hakon was to return to Norway. In the wee hours of the morning he had asked Hakon how, as a Norwegian duke, he had been able for so long to avoid marrying.

"Not easily," had been Hakon's answer. "I was nearly married off to an English princess, but after struggling for years with my brother and our nobles to avoid a loveless marriage, I prevailed. But my dear sister-in-law, Queen Margaret, who was very fond of her niece in Scotland, pressed her niece's suit and managed to get my brother on her side with enthusiastic descriptions of the sweet little girl. Moreover, the young lady had a huge dowry, so I was finally forced to visit her, or Margaret would have lost face in front of her relatives," recollected Hakon.

"The Scots are a wild people. They even impressed me, a descendant of Vikings, with their warlike demeanor and fierce pride. But that did not discourage me as much from marrying such wealth as did the girl herself. She seemed twice my size. And I am not a small man. Her welcoming grip could have snapped a stout limb, and her voice could have awakened the dead. Her manners were those of a son her father never had, and while he beamed with pride over her martial skills, he did not have to bed such a woman. I did not know how to act, so I tried just to keep my good manners. I went through the first meal without being able to swallow my food while watching her devour a shank of venison with the grace of a starving farmhand and pour down more wine than the best of my drinking companions. There was nothing feminine or even remotely attractive about her, except if one were seeking a comrade in arms."

Erik had laughed at Hakon's description, but Hakon looked deadly serious. "I dreaded insulting those fierce Scots, and I was far from sure that I could continue to hide my true feelings. So, I feigned fatigue from my journey and withdrew with my entourage. I ordered my men to be ready once the castle was sleeping for a quiet and hurried escape from that frightening woman and her clansmen. It was with the greatest sigh of relief that I hauled anchor and sailed back to Norway."

"Of course, I had insulted Margaret's clansmen beyond redemption, and they threatened to exact revenge, until my brother interceded and wrote to explain how I had taken sick and was ashamed to expose my frailty to them, such perfect and powerful specimens, and so had simply left in shame. This they seemed to accept, and peace was restored between our clans. I did, however, get to speak my peace; and I refused ever again to meet with any young lady he, or Margaret, suggested. I am sure that I missed some fine opportunities, but my adamant refusal proved a blessing in disguise since recently I met Euphemia of Rugen, and we are to be married soon. It is a provident alliance for Norway, and she is truly lovely."

Erik, who had been greatly amused by the story, had tried to hide his smirk when he realized how embarrassed Hakon was over his cowardly behavior.

"I do not want to rush into anything myself," Erik had countered quickly. "There are some suitable alliances available to me, and while the ladies certainly are not as valkyriean as the one you encountered, they hold little interest for me. If I hold off, they will be spoken for; and then I, too, will be able to wait for the right woman."

Erik was grateful that Birger had not insisted that he make his choice immediately. Although he felt more and more hopeful that one day he would marry Kristina, he said nothing to anyone but Valdemar. Erik was determined to bide his time while he silently admired that comely profile across the flames of the fire pit.

Chapter 10

Stockholm, Sweden 1299

It was silent in the queen's chamber as Kristina let the wool glide steadily through her fingers. She had been back in Sweden for a year now and she was happier than ever before. Her secret love for Erik--and their stolen moments together--made every day precious. Even the long, dreaded winter months had flown by this year. She had actually enjoyed being cloistered in the castle while snowstorms raged without and the inevitable influenza raged within, almost as much as she had relished riding out to hunt with the courtiers and Erik on clear and sunny days.

She was relieved to have left behind Roskilde's countless intrigues. Naturally, intrigues existed in Stockholm as well, but life was much less complicated at the smaller Swedish court. Marta was distrustful of the new people around her, so she often left important decisions to Kristina or Lady Astrid. No one seemed to dwell on the lax exercise of her acknowledged authority. Instead, everyone was delighted by the deepening love between her and Birger that had already resulted in Marta becoming heavy with child.

Everything would have been quite idyllic had it not been for the fact that Rikissa no longer lived at court. Simply by looking at Mats, whose face was etched with loss, Kristina was constantly reminded of her. And she worried about Ingeborg. To console herself, she had taken to writing a diary, installments of which she sent to Ingeborg whenever couriers traveled between the courts. Ingeborg began to do the same, and Kristina read aloud most of Ingeborg's writings in Marta's chamber to the ladies' great delight, omitting only those things meant for her alone. To her great sadness Ingeborg had suffered yet another miscarriage, but she had written little of the circumstances.

As Kristina looked up from her spinning, she noticed that Marta, whose baby was due any day, appeared clearly uncomfortable, shifting her position every few moments. The only thing that dampened Marta's excitement about giving birth to her first child was that Birger had to leave for Norway to attend the wedding of King Hakon to Euphemia of Rugen. Hakon had become King of Norway earlier that year following the death of his brother. Birger had postponed his departure until the very last moment, but finally he had to take his leave. The birth of a child would have been a poor excuse for a king not to attend an event as important as a royal wedding. After all, birthing was women's business.

Suddenly Marta took a deep breath and doubled over in pain. "The baby!" she cried.

Lady Astrid calmly went over and together with Kristina, helped Marta to her bed.

"You all know what to do," Lady Astrid said softly to the women who quickly cleared the table of their handiwork. Two of them ran to the kitchens for hot water and swaddling. Another went to find the surgeon monk. "You do not have to rush," continued Lady Astrid with the self-assurance of a commander in battle. "This will take time."

It had indeed taken time--hours and hours, but finally Marta was stretched out in her bed, a picture of blissful contentment for delivering a healthy and beautiful son. Her ladies-in-waiting had aired out her stuffy chamber, changed her linens, sponged her body with flower-scented water, and brushed her hair. Brother Gregory, the surgeon-herbalist, persisted in fussing over her, the sleeves of his grey tunic fluttering about her like protective wings. He had her drink a mild solution of nightshade to help her rest. Satisfied that his patient was beginning to feel the calming effect of the drug, he left the chamber.

According to Lady Astrid who was experienced in assisting at birthings, the delivery--with the help of Brother Gregory's ergot concoction--had been easy considering it was a first child. Marta had vehemently disagreed; from her point of view it had been incredibly lengthy and painful. She had felt utterly embarrassed, being encroached upon by so many people crowded into her stifling chamber, but custom prescribed that representatives of the King's Council and the Church witness a royal birth.

Her body was covered in sheets under which the midwife assisted the birth. In the middle of her worst pains, she had to suffer the presence of the bishops and selected nobles staring uneasily into space. Kristina was convinced that Marta had screamed with abandon only to make them feel even more uncomfortable. They had eagerly fled the chamber once the prince was born and declared healthy. And as promised, only moments after the baby's birth, the swiftest rider had been dispatched to Norway with the news of a crown prince.

Kristina could see a change in Marta from when she had first arrived. Then, she had appeared petrified by the commanding presence of the Lord High Constable, and she had expressed fear that he would never willingly yield his power. Kristina had spent long hours trying to convince Marta that Lord Torgils had no choice but to cede the reigning power to Birger.

Marta had also expressed a fear of Erik and Valdemar. She had confessed to Kristina that however much she loved Birger, she could clearly see that his two younger brothers were stronger physically, intellectually, and by force of personality. She felt that the brothers could easily outmaneuver her husband if that was their aim. But what had finally comforted her was that they showed no wish to do so. The three brothers spent much time together, and in many ways acted as one. And the day Erik had given Marta the wolf's tooth carved into the shape of a fish, Kristina felt that Marta had finally come to believe that the Swedish court was a safe home. And however close Birger was to his brothers, Marta had confided that he had become closer still to her, and that he had even started depending on her advice in minor matters.

Kristina was touched by the trust and caring Marta showed her. Although they had very different personalities--Marta, insecure and overly frightened, Kristina the opposite--they had become close, sharing every event of their lives. The one thing Kristina kept to herself was how deeply she and Erik cared for one another, although she was sure Marta sensed that something had developed between them.

Kristina came smiling to Marta's bedside with the newborn babe in her arms. "He is beautiful! The loveliest baby I have ever seen."

"You must be exaggerating," said Marta as she took the swaddled infant from Kristina's arms. She looked down on the little face resting on the soft linen wrapping and took a deep breath. "You are right. He is adorable, and he looks like his father and a little like my brother. Like two kings. That is a good omen, is it not?"

"Then he will have a king's name. Which one? Erik, Magnus, Valdemar . . .?"

"He will be called Magnus, after his paternal grandfather." Marta yawned, feeling the effect of the sleeping potion. "I think I can rest, now that I have held him." She looked down at the baby in her arms. "I will see you soon, Prince Magnus." She kissed the infant gently before returning him to Kristina.

Kristina went over to the royal crib and gently put down the little prince. She lovingly wrapped a soft blanket around him and again checked that a knife, wrapped in a linen cloth, had been placed beneath the bedding. No evil trolls are going to exchange you for one of their own, she thought as she left the chamber knowing that the trolls could not tolerate the presence of the blade's metal, and therefore would be unable to make a changeling of the heir to the Swedish throne.

Erik and Valdemar had arrived in Norway a few days ahead of King Hakon's and Euphemia of Rugen's wedding, in order to join Hakon and his friends at the hunt before the festivities.

A roaring fire blazed in the center pit of the log cabin where the hunting party was warming their frozen limbs near the flames. Wet boots, clothing, bloodied spears and knives were strewn about the floor. Servants were passing around mugs of hot, spiced wine that were quickly emptied.

Their hunt had been for bear that, for some reason, had come out of hibernation early and wreaked havoc and destruction upon the farmers. After two uneventful days, they had startling success by killing four of the enormous rogue beasts. King Hakon, who had been in the lead, killed the first bear single-handedly before the others felled the remaining three. The hunting party had every reason to feel exuberant about their trophies.

"Would you go and skin our bounty?" Hakon asked when his guests had finally warmed themselves. "We will gamble later to determine who gets the pelts since there are not enough for all of us. I have some matters to discuss with my cousins." The men rose politely and left.

"I am so pleased we have become good friends," Hakon began warmly, "So I want to share some concerns with you." Erik and Valdemar beamed proudly at being considered intimates of the intelligent and fearless king. They had envied Birger's friendship with Erik Menved, a relationship from which they felt excluded, and this new friendship with Hakon redressed the imbalance.

From where Erik was standing by the fire his attention was drawn to a map of Scandinavia painted on a huge moose hide, hanging on the wall behind Hakon. Erik looked intently at the map. In the southwestern corner of the Scandinavian Peninsula--the only point where the borders of Norway, Sweden, and Denmark met--each country had built a sentinel fortress. Marked on the map was the Norwegian fortress, Kungahalla; next to it Lodose, which guarded Sweden's only western port; and south of these, the Danish fortress, Hunehals.

"Sweden has very close ties with Denmark," Hakon continued, bringing Erik out of his reverie, "but Norway does not enjoy a similar friendship--we seem to be on the brink of war with the Danes--and if it comes to pass, I pray it remains a matter strictly between Norway and Denmark, without Sweden becoming involved."

Erik was familiar with the long-standing feud between the Norwegians and the Danes that had been triggered many years earlier when the Danish king, Erik Plogpenning, was murdered by the "Evil Prince, Abel". Hakon's mother had been one of Erik Plogpenning's daughters, as had been Sofia, the wife of old King Valdemar of Sweden, and his beloved mistress, Jutta. All of them had been denied their proper inheritance.

"Before my mother died," Hakon continued solemnly, "she made me swear to reclaim her rights. I have to honor that oath, whatever the cost or consequences."

But there was much more to it, as Erik well knew. The Danish Count Jacob of Northern Halland, who had royal blood running in his veins although he had been born "on the wrong side of the blanket," had been a close friend of Hakon's Danish-born mother. Count Jacob, in turn, had been denied his inheritance because of his close ties to the Norwegian royal family. However, after careful deliberation, the Danish crown allowed him to repossess his lands in the hope of wooing him away from his Norwegian allies. That gesture had been to no avail and the count remained devoted to Hakon. This was a great disappointment to the Danes since Northern Halland was an extremely strategic piece of property located in the very area where the three Scandinavian countries met.

Further complications had arisen many years later when some dissident Danish noblemen assassinated Erik Menved's and Marta's father, King Erik Klipping. The ruling group in Denmark had summarily condemned some nobles for the crime, among them Count Jakob, without a trial. However, before the executions could take place, those accused had managed to flee to Norway where they were given sanctuary. Despite the Danish accusations, Count Jakob continued to rule Northern Halland and Fort Hunehals; and the Danish "rebels"--as they were referred to in Denmark—were given the use of the Norwegian fort, Kungahalla. The Danes clearly felt threatened with those "rebels" on their border.

"Erik," Hakon continued, instinctively turning to the older of the two brothers, "you understand that this is a war Norway has no chance of winning if Sweden were to support Denmark. I ask you to help me by persuading Birger not to actively assist Erik Menved. And if you are successful in doing so, you and Valdemar will always have a special friend in Norway--no matter against what or whom."

"You know that the Danes are furious about Norway harboring Erik Klipping's murderers," said Erik, trying to conceal how much Hakon's promise of friendship appealed to him. "They claim that Norway wants to conquer Denmark and is enlisting anyone who can help her."

"That is ridiculous!" exclaimed Hakon. "We would not stand a chance against their armies. I am glad that the rebels' sanctuary here galls them, since I had hoped to use that as a way of getting justice done in regard to my mother's inheritance, but not as an act of war. Still, if the Danes do not come to terms with us, we will have to stand up to them--against all odds."

"Should they ask for help from Sweden, I will try to convince Birger that they are perfectly able to handle it themselves," said Erik as he walked around the fire. He knew Birger would be delighted to stay out of the conflict in any case. "I do not know if he will listen," Erik continued loudly, "but I will do whatever I can."

"That is all I want," Hakon smiled. Then he stretched his long legs. "I am going to wash up before we eat. I will see you back here in a little while," he concluded as he left for the washhouse.

"Not much chance that Birger, or should I say Lord Torgils, would join another war just now, is there?" asked Valdemar, already knowing the answer.

"Not much. Our dear Lord High Constable and his friends are busy filling their coffers in Finland while they can. They are not eager to squander money on a neighbor's squabble." Erik fell silent again while he studied the wall map, his gaze resting on that point of the Scandinavian Peninsula where the three countries met. "You know, Valdemar," he mused. "Northern Halland is a very interesting piece of property."

On the third day after the magnificent Norwegian wedding, the three brothers sat together in the large chamber that had been assigned to the Swedish king during his stay in Norway. Since the arrival of the messenger announcing the birth of his son, Birger had been beside himself with excitement and impatient to return home. He had roused his brothers at an ungodly hour to break fast before his departure. Erik and Valdemar judged it a timely moment to share Hakon's concerns about an impending war with Denmark.

"I have no choice but to support Erik Menved," Birger declared resolutely. "I do not want to ruin our friendship with Norway, but if asked, I have to take sides."

"Of course, you have to support your ally. I am not questioning that for a moment. I just thought we might be able to stay out of this squabble and maintain our alliances with both countries. And with our armies over in Finland, I doubt Erik Menved would expect you to move them from there to support him," said Erik.

"He would never ask unless it were a dire emergency," agreed Birger.

"Lord Torgils had planned on sending home some troops now that heavy fighting has ended and we have the territory we set out to conquer," noted Valdemar, following Erik's train of thought. "Still, it might be wise to keep those troops in Finland until this neighborly dispute is resolved. What Erik Menved does not demand you do not have to volunteer, and we can remain on good terms with everyone."

"We could use some more territory in Finland," Birger mused as he jumped up. "But now I have to leave to see my son."

Erik and Valdemar accompanied him out to the courtyard where his entourage was waiting. Valdemar gave him a hand up in mounting his horse. "Give Marta our love and tell her we are looking forward to seeing her and little Magnus," Valdemar slapped Birger's boot affectionately. "Have a safe trip."

Birger signaled his guards to move out and waved as he rode away.

"It feels strange that he has to go off somewhere without us," said Valdemar to Erik. "But then our lives are changing."

Erik hoped that change would include his marriage to Kristina, but so far only one of his two marriage prospects had become betrothed. If he were lucky, the second one, who was already fifteen, would not remain unpledged much longer.

"Erik, I do not know what to do," Kristina confided one night several months later as they were sitting by the fire in the bustling Great Hall of Stockholm castle. "I have received a note from Rikissa. She is no longer in seclusion, and she has asked me to come and see her, alone. I feel strange about her request. I am not a blood relative. She should have asked for one of you."

"I am not surprised that she wants to talk to you. You were like sisters," answered Erik. "Rikissa probably does not know that Mother has left court, and she might want to see you before dealing with her. I will take you to her right now. Nobody needs to know and feel left out."

Without waiting for her reply, he stood up, took her hand and started to walk towards the courtyard where he asked her to remain by the door while he got his horse saddled. Once mounted, he lifted her up in front of him, wrapping her in his mantle.

"Hide your face against my chest. The guards will think that I am out for some amusement. They will not guess that it is you."

He was right. The guards only gave him winks and smiles as they rode across the bridge. Erik avoided the commercial streets where people were milling about despite the late hour, and he took the longer route to Santa Klara convent by way of deserted lanes. Kristina did not mind the lengthy trip as she rested comfortably against his chest. When they reached the convent, Erik freed her from his mantle and lowered her to the ground. He led his horse to the gate where he pulled a chain that sounded a bell. After a while, a nun came to the gate to inquire about their business. Once Erik explained, the nun unlocked the gate to admit them.

They entered a large courtyard where Erik tethered his horse. Then they followed the nun to the visitor's area where she asked them to wait. They seated themselves on a cold stone bench and marveled at the stillness. Kristina realized that she had never actually heard silence until that moment, and she did not dare to break it, so she sat immobile, looking at the columned corridor stretching out before them. After a while they could hear singing and a bell began to toll.

When Rikissa finally appeared, she wore the gray habit of a novice; and while her face was still Rikissa's it had changed. Last time, Kristina had seen a girl. Now she was looking at a woman.

"Thank you for coming. I am glad you are here too, Erik," Rikissa said as she kissed him on the cheek and embraced Kristina with her usual warmth.

Both Kristina and Erik felt confused by the familiarity and at the same time, the strangeness of this new Rikissa. They moved like puppets as she took their arms to lead them out into the convent garden.

"I am not happy about the way I left you without a word of explanation, but I could do it no other way. You would have tried to stop me. I love you all so much, but it was here where I belonged. Please, forgive me if I hurt you with my long silence, but it was necessary."

"Was it because of Mats?" asked Erik, unable to restrain himself.

A shadow seemed to pass over Rikissa's face before she responded. "Whatever the reason, I should not have left without telling you of my decision. For that I am sorry. And yes, it was because of Mats." She told them how she had to keep her promise to God if Mats' life was saved. Her love for Mats made it impossible for her to break that promise.

"If you are happy here, Rikissa, then we are happy for you," said Kristina while Erik nodded his agreement. "Still, we cannot help but miss you."

Kristina saw tears begin to well up in Rikissa's eyes as she said, "I could not face Mother. I cannot even imagine her visiting me here in the stillness. One day I will have to talk to her, but not now." Rikissa took a deep breath. "I asked you to come here for a reason. You know how I can feel things as they happen, or sense warnings about the future. This "feeling" has become even stronger here; and I must warn you, Erik. Our family is in danger. I do not know exactly how or why, but I can sense that it is very much up to you to save it. I have debated if I should tell you, and that is why I asked Kristina to come here to find out what she thought. But since you are here, I can tell you directly. It is an awesome burden to place on someone's shoulders, but I must, if I am to live in peace."

Erik looked troubled since he had never known her premonitions to be wrong. "I am glad you are telling me so that I can be vigilant," he mumbled.

"Also, please tell Birger that I would be grateful if he gave my dowry to the convent so that I may be consecrated as soon as possible."

Erik nodded as they strolled around the peaceful garden. No one spoke; and as they again came to the portal through which they had entered, Rikissa took their hands and smiled at them.

"In you two, I feel love, and that makes me happy." She reached up to kiss Erik and she held Kristina close for a long time. "My thoughts and my love will always be with you."

Soundlessly, she disappeared down the corridor leaving Kristina and Erik in the doorway. They walked slowly, burdened in thought, towards the courtyard gate where Erik untied his horse. Its hooves clopped loudly against the stones as he led the animal from the convent. Erik mounted first before he gently pulled Kristina up in front of him. He turned his stallion around and allowed it to walk slowly along a narrow lane.

"I wonder what is to happen to my family, and what I can do to prevent it," he sighed.

"She would not have warned you if she did not think you could prevent it, whatever it is," Kristina opined trustingly.

"And which of us will it befall?" continued Erik. "We are spread out all over Scandinavia now. Mother is at Dovo, Ingeborg is in Denmark, soon Valdemar will be living in Finland I will be moving to Nykoping, leaving Birger here in Stockholm. How will I know what is happening everywhere?"

"I would think it has to do with you, Birger, and Valdemar," said Kristina with conviction. "The three of you are like one."

They rode on in silence until they reached the drawbridge of the castle.

"In a little more than a year we will all live apart. I feel lonely at the very thought of it . . ."

Chapter 11

Stockholm, Sweden 1300

Erik had to restrain himself from taking the castle stairs two at a time, keeping a dignified pace towards the women's quarters where the spring cleaning was in its final stage. He spotted Kristina across the large chamber, her hair in disarray, dust clinging to her clothes, and a cheerful smile that lit up her face when she saw him. When he signaled to her urgently her curiosity propelled her to follow him, attempting to arrange her curls and to pat the dust off her tunic. She felt a bit guilty about abandoning the others who were changing the straw in the mattresses and the down in the pillows and covers.

Without explanation, Erik dragged her up onto the parapets where the chilly spring air whipped through her thin work clothing. He put his arms around her to shield her from the cold and looked into her inquisitive face.

"I have the best news ever," he said excitedly as he guided her out of the wind behind a tower wall. "One of the Danish bishops who arrived this morning brought us news from the Danish court. He mentioned in passing that Euphemia of Pomerania is getting married to Kristoffer of Denmark. Euphemia was the last candidate who I would have had to accept if Birger insisted. And the Norwegian princess is of less interest now that her father has passed away and the power has moved to her uncle."

"You really think that we could marry?" asked Kristina, her eyes wide with excitement.

"Wait, I am not finished! Your father approached me although he has been back for only for a few days. He said that he could hardly miss your radiant glow, or the way I looked at you, and that nothing would make him happier than to see us as man and wife. He whispered a shockingly large dowry figure in my ear."

"Thank God that we have my father on our side," said Kristina radiantly. "There might be a chance for us after all."

"I told you! Now, all we have to do is to convince Birger and the Council; and then, finally, I can get my hands on you," Erik grinned. She rested her head against his shoulder. He could not remember experiencing a more blissful moment. Slowly he lifted her face to his and kissed her with more passion than he had ever dared to allow himself.

Kristina was humming to herself as she threaded her needle. The queen's chamber was no longer a place of toil and discipline but a joyous workplace where little Prince Magnus crawled on the floor and got into all sorts of mischief. At the moment, however, he was sleeping blissfully on a fur skin close to the fire, which afforded the women a moment of peace.

"Ladies, it is time for our supper," Marta announced. The women rose to leave. "Stay," she motioned to Kristina who was preparing to join the others, "I want to talk to you."

Kristina sat down. "What is it, Kristina?" asked Marta when they were alone. "You have been wearing a mysterious expression all day."

"At last I can tell you," whispered Kristina, her eyes shining with joy. "The last lady ahead of me on Erik's marriage list is now betrothed, and my father will propose marriage between Erik and me!"

Marta impulsively reached for Kristina's hand. "I could hardly have missed that you were in love with Erik, but since I feared that there was little chance for marriage I never mentioned anything. No one can be happier for you than am I."

"I am not of royal blood," Kristina said, voicing her main concern. Although the royals had always treated her as one of them, the servants and the courtiers had, in many subtle ways, never let her forget she was not a member of the family.

"Still, your father is Regent of Sweden," protested Marta. "And as such he is the undisputed leader of the nobility."

"Dare I hope the king and the Council will agree?" Kristina asked.

"How large is your dowry?" countered Marta pragmatically. She nodded in appreciation at Kristina's answer. "Very few candidates could match that. And let us not forget," she added quickly, "how much Erik cares for you. I am not blind, you know. Why would not the proposal be accepted?"

Kristina's eyes filled with tears as she pressed Marta's hand in hers. "If I marry him," she whispered, "I will be the happiest woman in the world."

"Together with me," smiled Marta. "I think I am with child again!"

The two friends sat silently together, embroideries abandoned in their frames. No words were needed. Each was immersed in the other's happiness.

"Good news, I hope," said Abjorn Sixtensson, as he entered the Lord High Constable's field tent in Finland to find Torgils reading a message that had just been delivered.

"Indeed!" exclaimed Torgils as he walked over to his portable desk that was littered with architectural drawings. As he ceremoniously filled two cups with beer he mentally regretted having run out of wine several months earlier.

"Let us drink to Prince Magnus of Sweden--the healthy baby boy birthed by the Queen some weeks ago."

Torgils handed a cup to Abjorn that he drained in their toast to the prince.

"That is splendid news," exclaimed Abjorn. "That, with your latest victories here in Finland, is doubly so. And the completion of Landskrona fortress will crown your achievements."

"Capturing additional territory was an unexpected bonus, especially since I came to Finland this time to give King Birger a chance to rule Sweden without me and, hopefully, to gain some experience."

"But," observed Abjorn, "you are Regent for still another year."

"Indeed," agreed Torgils studying his longtime friend. "But the way I managed to keep my position made it clear that I am not in control. I had always assumed the three brothers would act as one, and that I would only have to deal with the king, but now I must also contend with two clever dukes who have a strong influence over the king."

"The dukes thought it a splendid idea that I capture more territory for Sweden, and thereby for Valdemar who soon will rule these lands. That is why I allowed Valdemar to come along on this trip though I have ordered him to stay back in battle as he is still young with little combat experience.

"It was actually Erik who suggested this particular piece of land. He had no problem in convincing me of its strategic value, or profitability since the Hansa merchant ships have to sail by this point of the Neva river to reach the Russian trading cities. They will have to pay us tolls to pass the range of our catapults once the fortress is completed."

Torgils stood and paced restlessly in the tent. "But I was hoping for something more than glory and gold if this mission succeeded. I have not dared to mention it to anyone, but if Erik marries Kristina I would be safely ensconced in both camps in the event of a schism. I venture the king might agree to their marriage because the queen would be delighted to have Kristina in the family. And whatever makes the queen happy makes the king happy. And Kristina, of course, would like nothing better."

Abjorn followed Torgils' train of thought. If Kristina were to marry Erik and if Erik rebelled against Birger, she could well become Queen of Sweden one day. Abjorn looked at Torgils whose face wore a slightly wicked smile.

The two men were interrupted by a commotion outside the tent. They hurried outside to see what was happening. A group of young warriors were staggering up from the shore, laden with heavy chests and evidently fortified by large quantities of beer. One of them stopped abruptly in his tracks when he saw the formidable Lord High Constable emerge from his tent.

"We did well, my Lord," slurred Mats Kettilmundsson with an impishly satisfied grin. He had been given the honor, together with Valdemar, of "exploring" the area surrounding the newly established Swedish stronghold being constructed.

Lord Torgils walked closer to peer into the chests that the young men had thrown open. He whistled softly when he saw the rich spoils of gold and silver coins, jewelry and tableware.

"Not bad," he nodded approvingly. "Come and tell us about your incursion," he said as he gestured for Mats and Valdemar follow him into the tent.

Mats, aware of his need to sober up, hesitated but entered. Torgils refilled his own and Abjorn's cups, and poured two for Mats and Valdemar who protested weakly as they prepared to relate their adventure.

Mats had volunteered for every scouting mission the Swedes had undertaken. He abhorred being idle as his thoughts would invariably wander to Rikissa and the futility of loving her. Anything that could keep his mind off those thoughts was welcome. He was happy to have Valdemar with him, eager to participate in their first armed foray.

Mats began to relate what had transpired during the preceding two weeks. They had left Landskrona in one of their swiftest ships with forty men. Since they had perfect winds, he had decided to sail to Novgorod on the far shore of Lake Ladoga. If the favorable wind held, he planned to descend on the town and loot the harbor warehouses before the Russians could organize an effective resistance. The soldiers had been doing little else but working on the fortress and were aching for action, but just as their ship neared the town and they could hear the sentinels calling out warnings to the inhabitants, the skies turned dark and the wind shifted. Within minutes the waves grew high and a thick mist rolled over the lake.

Suddenly they found themselves in the midst of a ferocious storm. Desperately they tried to turn around to avoid crashing on the now invisible shore, but their ship was out of control even though the helmsman tied the rudder to secure their course. The sea and the winds tossed their vessel around like a nutshell. The waves rushed over the decks and the men were knocked off their feet, grasping for anything to avoid being swept overboard. Mats could hear the soldiers praying for salvation while the storm continued unmercifully. He looked over to the helmsman who shook his head, crossed himself and began praying to Njord, the Viking god of the Sea. Then, as suddenly as it had begun, the storm subsided, the mist lifted, and the huge lake was ablaze with sunshine. It took a while before they could get their bearings, and when they did, they realized that they had been blown almost clear across the lake. Everyone on board was glad to sight land since many had been severely battered by the violent heaving of the ship. Luckily no one had been lost overboard, but Mats decided that they should land for a rest.

By the following day most of the men had recovered, so Mats gave the order to haul sails. For a couple of days they ravaged villages along the coast without much reward, but then they spotted a large Russian merchant ship. They pretended to pass peacefully alongside before they unexpectedly attacked. The element of surprise paid off.

"Congratulations," said Lord Torgils after Mats had finished his account and downed another mug of beer. "Your and Valdemar's share of the spoils, as well as your men's, will be quite handsome." Silently, Lord Torgils congratulated himself, as well.

During the ensuing monotonous months, the construction of Landskrona fortress continued. Mats and Valdemar worked tirelessly along with everyone else. Even though the Swedes had emptied the nearby villages of able men under threat of death, every Swedish soldier and knight had to put in long days of bone-tiring work. Tall trees had to be felled in the deep forest, shaped into poles, and hauled to the shore site. There they were raised and fitted together to form the protective walls or to build dwellings within. The impressive wooden structure was erected on a narrow peninsula cut off by a deep trench filled with water from the Neva. Only a drawbridge linked Landskrona to the mainland. When Lord Torgils and his men finally folded their tents and took possession of their new stronghold, they were well satisfied with their efforts.

But soon thereafter, from a passing merchant ship, the Swedes learned that Mats' attempt to attack Novgorod had so infuriated the Russians that they were rumored to be gathering their forces for revenge. Lord Torgils gave orders to double the guard and that proved to be a wise precaution because early one morning out of the fog the Russians emerged and approached Landskrona with an impressive fleet, towing dozens of large wooden structures behind their ships.

"I have never seen such structures before. They are not high enough to be scaling towers, nor wide enough to work as moat bridges," Lord Torgils mused quizzically as he stood on the parapet overlooking the approaching fleet.

As the Russians maneuvered their ships into a line away from the fortress, the Swedes were still trying to figure out the use of the towers. The answer became frighteningly clear when the Russians set them afire and cut them adrift. The winds blew the burning structures toward the peninsula and the newly built fortress.

Lord Torgils quickly ordered his men to form a human chain to pass water up to the parapets to be ready to quench the approaching fires. Some of the men were ordered to leave the sanctuary of the fort to fend off the floating pyres with long poles before its timber walls could ignite. The water did little to affect the tongues of fire that were flickering dangerously from the tar soaked floating structures. The poles were not long enough to save the men from having their eyelashes singed, their hands scorched, and their faces blackened from the flame and smoke.

All this activity did not allow the Swedes much time to use their own catapults against the attackers. It was backbreaking work--pouring heavy buckets of water on the voracious flames while arrows and stones showered them from the enemy ships. But just when it looked quite hopeless--the weather changed. The winds turned and blew the floating pyres away from the peninsula, forcing the Russians to break off the attack in order to maneuver their ships out of harm's way.

The same quirk of nature that had saved Novgorod now saved Landskrona. The Swedes cheered at their luck, but quickly sobered down when they counted their casualties. Many soldiers had died from smoke inhalation and burns, while arrows that had found their way between chain mail and armor had taken the lives of others. The dead were collected, and a mass grave dug outside the fortress while sentries kept a wary eye on the Russian fleet that had sailed out of catapult range--awaiting the burnout of the smoldering towers barring their way.

Still numb from the surprise attack, the Swedes held a brief service for their dead and closed the grave. Inside the fortress, the surgeons and herbalist monks busied themselves with the wounded. The surgeons carefully removed arrows and set broken bones, while the herbalists applied soothing and healing ointments. They ran among the moaning men with pots filled with salve of arnika, lotion of snake-weed, poultices of comfrey, sweet coltfoot and bloodwort, which they gently applied to burns and cuts. Kindly but firmly, they forced down foul tasting draughts of nightshade and allheal to relieve pain and induce sleep.

Against the orders of Torgils and Mats to stay back and not partic-ipate in the defense Valdemar had crawled up towards the parapets to view the ensuing battle. Nobody had noticed him keeping low behind the protecting wall or when he suddenly stood up to get a better view, or when Valdemar took an arrow in his neck that dropped him close to the parapet.

Valdemar was discovered quite some time later in a dark puddle of blood. He was carried down to Lord Torgils who was barking orders to soldiers fighting the fires.

"I told him to stay safe," grunted the commander as he saw the unconscious figure covered with blood. He noted Mats some distance away and ordered the soldier who was cradling Valdemar in his arms to carry him over to Mats.

Mats blanched when he saw his friend slowly bleeding to death. He, in turn, carried him over to the monks who tried every remedy at their disposal, but it soon became clear that only a miracle could save Valdemar, so the monks quickly turned their attention to others who might better use their services. Mats knew the monks had done what they could but was frustrated by their lack of success. Then he remem-bered the stories his father had told him about the magical medicine men in Finland, so he impulsively left the fort and set off in search of a village with a medicine man.

He walked for a long time as fog overtook the forest, painting everything a lifeless gray. It began to get dark and he started to despair. Then, suddenly he saw a light flicker behind some trees, and he soon entered a tiny village. Crooked huts leaned against one another, and in the village center a large fire burned to dispel the dense fog. Mats loomed like a giant over the seated villagers sharing their evening meal by the fire. They instinctively huddled closer together, staring in fear at the metal-clad warrior. Mat's eyes rolled over the scrawny peasants until he spotted the shaman.

He was an old man dressed in leather hides layered down to his feet with a strange cap pulled down over his forehead and ears. His face was surprisingly free of wrinkles, and his dark skin stretched tightly over his bony face. He gazed steadily at Mats with his deep-seated, slanted eyes, betraying no surprise or fear over the intruder in his small and remote village.

"One of my friends will die if you do not help him," Mats pleaded in Finnish.

"Then tell your monks to heal him," scoffed the shaman.

"They have tried, but there is nothing they can do."

"What makes you think I can help you?" asked the shaman, his eyes narrowing.

"You can go to Manala," whispered Mats.

The shaman, somewhat taken aback, betrayed his interest by asking, "What makes you think that I would go there for help? You Swedes have conquered my people and used them like slaves. Why should I help?"

"Because you are a healer. You have the magic gift that you cannot deny," said Mats knowing it would be difficult for the shaman to refuse the request of a man who respected his power.

The shaman sat silently as his people watched him in awe for speaking so boldly to an armed enemy.

"I will come with you," said the shaman finally as he rose to follow Mats.

It was dark when Mats returned to Landskrona with his strange companion. The shaman followed him into the fort. Most of the soldiers were asleep, and only the crackle of campfires and the moaning of wounded men could be heard in the stillness. Mats gestured for the shaman to follow him towards a corner of the yard where Valdemar lay.

"Who is that?" asked one of the wounded knights nearby as Mats led the shaman to Valdemar.

"He is a sorcerer, a healer," answered Mats. "He can go to Manala--the land beneath the earth--to find a cure for one who is dying."

"The monks will never allow him to help," whispered the knight anxiously. "You should not have brought him."

"You want Prince Valdemar to die?" hissed Mats. "The shaman is our last chance. Let us see what he can do."

Mats watched the shaman bend over the stricken and unconscious Valdemar. The shaman's dark eyes scrutinized his patient before he sat down beside him with folded legs and pulled a drum from under his leather wraps. The skin of the drum was decorated with cabalistic signs, and he reverently placed it between his knees. He took what looked like toadstools from under his clothes and put them in his mouth. He produced a beater, shaped like a spoon, and slowly and rhythmically began beating the drum while chewing the toadstools.

Mats looked nervously around the yard, praying that the monks would be too exhausted from their day's work to wake up from the drumbeats. No one seemed disturbed by the soft rhythmic sound, so after a moment's hesitation Mats settled down next to Valdemar.

The shaman closed his eyes and experienced the spicy earth taste of the mushrooms that filled his mouth. His heartbeat changed to the rhythm of the drum, and he and the sound became one. As the mushrooms took effect, the beat left his body and became a guiding light before him. The sound and the light slowly began pulling his spiritual essence forward on his journey to Manala.

He had been there many times before, and he unhesitatingly followed the pulsing light. It and he flowed rather than walked along a riverbank until he reached a whirlpool where the river disappeared into an icy cave. This was the entrance to the underworld. He remained still for a moment, preparing for the descent into Manala. Slowly he went across the water and down along an underground path. The throbbing light leading his way was the only source of illumination in the pitchblack cave. He knew he had to move quickly, lest he attract the attention of the giants guarding the underworld spirits whose sole existence was to cause suffering to mortals. Still, the spirits would never refuse to answer the shaman's questions. Why, he did not know. Perhaps an answer was simply the reward for traveling into the bowels of the earth and risking everything to seek their knowledge.

Suddenly he heard thunderous noises that told him a giant was on his way. Without reflecting, he changed himself into a long black snake, gliding quickly along the steep path. But the giant who saw the light preceding the shaman's snake form was not fooled by the disguise. The shaman avoided looking at the horrible giant who was trying to mesmerize him with glowing eyes; then darting to the right and left to avoid the giant's huge feet, but finally became pinned between a foot and a boulder. The giant roared with pleasure as he tore off one of his own arms to hold the bloody limb in front of the snake. The shaman could feel his snake form longing for the meat, yet he knew that swallowing even one drop of the giant's blood would kill him. Struggling against his reptilian desire for the raw flesh, he willed himself to change into a bird. He felt his wings flap against the cave stones as he desperately sought to get lift under them. As he managed to fly towards the cave ceiling, avoiding the giant's healthy, thrashing arm - he heard the giant scream a warning to the other sentinels. When the shaman looked down he saw the giant push his dismembered arm back into his shoulder socket where it miraculously rejoined itself.

Swiftly the shaman flew down the passageway, avoiding the giants as they spotted his guiding light and tried to capture him with their long arms or with nets they threw at him. But he had flown this course before, and he successfully averted every trap they set for him. By now the caves resounded with the hideous howling of infuriated ogres.

Suddenly the cave ceiling abruptly lowered, and it was no longer practical to fly, so the shaman changed himself into a large rat and scurried down the slippery path. Soon he heard flowing water, and he knew he did not have far to go. Then, without warning another figure loomed up in the darkness. As fast as he could, he darted between the giant's feet, but became trapped between them. The giant reached down to scoop up the pinned rodent that wriggled away only to be blocked by the cave wall. The shaman morphed into his own shape for a confrontation. As he regained his human form, the giant was momentarily thrown off guard. The shaman raced past him, but not quickly enough--the giant caught his left arm and held him firm. The shaman closed his eyes and let the giant pull off his arm at the elbow. It hurt no more than a bee sting, and as he fled down the path away from the flabbergasted giant--who thought he was the only one who could do such tricks--the shaman started to grow a new arm. By the time he reached the safety of the island of the underworld, fingers were sprouting on his new hand.

The underworld island sat in the middle of a turbulent river lit only by an opal moon high in the cave sky. The forbidding island looked empty, but the shaman could feel the energy of beings in the darkness. As he slowly flowed across the river, still preceded by his pulsating light, shadows began to emerge, pale shapes of human forms floating above the ground. He could feel them passing him in cold bursts of air. He moved towards the center of a huge space where a towering stone formation rose. On its highest crag was seated the ruling spirit of Manala.

"You are back," said the shadow ruler in a voice sounding like wind howling through a narrow space.

"How do I cure the young Prince?" asked the shaman directly, knowing the spirits had knowledge of everything occurring in the world of man.

"Seek the foul-smelling plant with the small yellow, purple veined flowers in the new god's garden," rustled the spirit. "Put seven leaves in a measure of water and boil. Add a pinch of the white powder we gave you many moons ago. Finally dilute it by three measures of water and let the man drink it. Apply it to his wounds, as well."

"May I depart in peace?" asked the shaman as always, never sure what the answer would be. A murmur, as if a storm were rising, filled the space as the spirits gave their consent. Without another word, the shaman left the underworld by changing himself into a black raven flying up to the icy entrance of the cave without interference from the giants. Exhausted, he started his journey back to Landskrona along the riverbank, guided by the pulsating light that was growing ever fainter.

Mats, who had been dozing, bolted upright--awakened by the drumbeats changing and becoming sporadic. Finally, they stopped. He walked over to the shaman who was rocking back and forth, mumbling words Mats struggled to comprehend. At last he understood what the shaman was saying. Mats woke two knights who had not been wounded in the battle and asked them to accompany him on an excursion.

"We will be damned in hell if the priests find out," predicted one of them after Mats explained what they had to do.

"Do we have a choice?" asked Mats in frustration. The knights reluctantly shook their heads and ordered two trusted friends to guard the shaman who was already asleep beside his unconscious patient. No one was to go near them.

"We will be back soon," was the only explanation Mats gave as they ran over the briefly lowered drawbridge and into the dark forest, guided by torches. Mats knew only vaguely where he was heading, but he followed the shaman's directions. It took them many hours in the darkness to locate the burned-out monastery the shaman had described. In its overgrown garden Mats found the needed plants.

"How do you know which plant to pick?" one of the knights asked.

"My grandmother often took me to the garden in the monastery near our home. She was as knowledgeable in the use of plants as the herbalist brothers themselves. They used to have long conversations, none of which I understood," smiled Mats, "I was just a small boy then, but there is no way I can forget the smell of henbane."

"That is poisonous," said the other knight. "It will kill Prince Valdemar."

"Do not worry, the shaman has been told exactly how much to use," said Mats resolutely.

Mats carefully picked enough of the herb to fill a small sack, and they started on their way back. It was growing light by then, so they extinguished their torches. As they neared the edge of the forest bordering Landskrona, they saw to their horror that the Russians had landed and were making camp facing the fortress moat.

"Now, what in damnation are we to do?" one of the knights wondered aloud.

Crouching down behind some low bushes, they looked over the area in front of Landskrona that had been painstakingly cleared of trees to give those in the fortress a clear view of anyone approaching. There was no way anyone could cross the open space without being detected by the Russians. And if they waited for darkness as a cover, their own men might shoot at them thinking they were enemies.

"The three of us are no match for all of them," said the other knight grimly. "We simply cannot get back."

"We have to," insisted Mats. "We will wait until it gets darker and hope that we do not become victims of the sure aim of our own men."

When darkness was soon to fall, Mats whispered that the moment had come. Receiving consenting nods from his companions, he resolutely gave the signal for a dash to the fortress. They sprang out of hiding, but halfway across the open space, one of the Russians spotted them and called out.

Mats and his knights were only twenty yards from the moat when ten Russians cut them off. Mats unsheathed Gram, which flashed in the setting sun like a beam of lightning as the Russians furiously assaulted the young Swedes.

The three Swedes were fighting for their lives. All were fine swordsmen, so they were able to hold the attackers at bay as they inched towards the drawbridge. More Russians joined their brethren in the fierce assault but were unable to put any of the Swedes out of action. Russians were falling left and right as Gram's shining blade cut a lethal swath through a wall of bodies.

"What is going on?" asked the Lord High Constable as he arrived on the parapet to survey the fighting. In a flash he analyzed the situation and turned to the commander. "Why are you not lowering the drawbridge?"

"We cannot lower the bridge now! We might as well surrender the fort to the Russians!"

Torgils knew the commander was right, but as he watched Mats and his knights valiantly resist the onslaught he realized that it was only a matter of time before they fell. Torgils knew then that he could not countenance losing young Mats. If he had had a son of his own, he would have wanted him to be like Mats.

"Lower the bridge!" he roared above the din of clashing metal.

Mats and his companions were nearly exhausted as they stood, back to back, fending off Russians attacking from all sides. After what seemed like an eternity, a group of Swedish knights leapt from the still-descending bridge to help Mats and his friends beat back the Russians who were now storming toward the only entrance to the fortress. With the help of the others, the three men reached the safety of the wooden bridge just as a large crew in the fortress began to winch it up. The Russians who tried to jump on were shoved into the water, along with two Swedish knights who met their deaths while valiantly fighting off the Russian horde.

Once the bridge was raised, Lords Torgils and Abjorn rushed forward to assess the damages. Apart from some deep cuts and ugly bruises the young men were fine, as were most of the knights who had supported their rescue.

"Where have you been?" boomed Lord Torgils like an angry father relieved to see his children safely home. "I did not give you permission to leave the fort." Torgils glared furiously at the young men who kept their eyes sheepishly fixed on the ground. "Your stupidity cost us two men! I will deal with you later!" he vowed as he turned and walked away.

Mats felt relieved to have gotten off so lightly for the moment. He quickly ran over to where Valdemar lay, his body contorted in pain, with the shaman still sitting motionless beside him. Mats placed the bag of herbs in the shaman's hands, causing him to wake. The shaman requested a small fire to be kindled in front of him as well as a clean cooking pot and water. Once the pot was boiling on the fire, the shaman dropped the leaves into the bubbling liquid. From the folds of his sleeves he pulled out a small container of white powder, carefully adding some to his concoction.

While the shaman was absorbed in his work, the monks who had been wondering about the presence of the strange little figure officiously drew near.

"A heathen medicine man," whispered one of the surgeons. "Who let him in?"

"I have no idea," answered the herbalist, "But his presence is an affront to God."

Indignantly the monks came closer, and one of them asked loudly, "Who has invited this shaman to touch our Christian patient?"

"I have," said Mats belligerently as he stood up, towering over them. "You gave up on Prince Valdemar. You said you could do nothing for him."

"If God's servants cannot cure him, then it is God's will that he join Him in Heaven," retorted the herbalist. "It is blasphemy to think that a heathen can defy God's will."

"But if the shaman saves the prince's life, then that must be God's will," argued Mats. "What can we lose by letting him try?"

The monks were momentarily speechless before one of them stepped forward to point an accusing finger at Mats, "You will be excommunicated for your lack of faith!"

"I have faith," Mats bellowed, "I believe Prince Valdemar can be saved. Now leave us alone," he commanded, putting a menacing hand on Gram. The monks took a step back, but then angrily stood their ground, all the while looking at the shaman stirring his brew.

"What herb is it?" whispered one of the surgeon monks.

"Henbane," answered the herbalist in a low voice, recognizing the aroma rising from the pot.

"That is hardly a new remedy."

"Of course not, but he is brewing an unusually strong concoction, and he added a strange white powder."

"Good, that will kill the patient," snarled the surgeon between his teeth.

Mats stood guard as the hunched-over figure prepared the herbs. The shaman requested a cup and poured some of the hot liquid into it, then added cool water to dilute it. He gently approached the semiconscious Valdemar, lifted his head, and helped him to down two cupfuls. The shaman then took some of the remaining solution and applied it to Valdemar's wound. Within minutes he stopped gritting his teeth, and after awhile seemed to drift into deep sleep. Once he was resting comfortably, everyone who had gathered around drifted away. The monks, too, walked away, anger etched on their faces.

Finally, the shaman sat down for his meal. As payment for his services, the small man ate everything in sight and drank copious amounts of ale.

Despite his initial anger, Lord Torgils never punished Mats and his friends. Perhaps out of respect for their effort to save the prince for whom Mats had sworn to take responsibility. But he could not fathom why the large Russian army decided not to seize the moment to attack. He reasoned that the enemy may have realized how little food the Swedes had stored, and so preferred to wait them out until the fortress had to surrender.

The waiting continued, while Valdemar's health miraculously improved—much to the monks' dismay. After many long days had passed, the shaman approached Mats with a request to leave the fort.

Mats tried to explain that the Russians would probably kill him if he left. The shaman sadly shook his head. He had to return to his people. Mats told him he could not leave. They were all prisoners.

With the passing days, the soldiers, and especially Mats, became increasingly edgy and restless. In his idleness, Mats' thoughts unfailingly returned to Rikissa, reopening the emotional wound he had tried to heal through incessant activity. He hoped that she had found the peace that eluded him.

Finally, in an act of desperation he approached Lord Torgils hoping to atone for his disobedience. With the Lord High Constable's blessing he donned his meticulously polished armor, and wearing a sign of truce on his sleeve, rode alone over the drawbridge to speak to the Novgorodians.

Their chieftan came forward followed by a guard of powerful warriors. The chieftan was not a young man, but he was tall and muscular enough to dwarf his soldiers. His gray hair was tied tightly behind his head and hung down his back. He wore his heavy chain mail uncovered by a tunic on his tanned skin. His hose was made of leather and his legs were encircled by metal plates that rattled as he walked. He stopped in front of Mats and stared at him with fierce eyes.

"I am Mats Kettilmundsson," Mats called out in Finnish, hoping one of the Russians would understand. "I challenge your best warrior to one-on-one combat. If your champion wins, we will surrender our fortress and leave. But if I prevail, you will withdraw peacefully."

The chieftan looked questioningly at his men and one hurried forward to translate what Mats had said. The tall leader stood looking at Mats with his arms folded over his chest. Finally, he spoke in a deep voice and his words were repeated by the translator.

"Our great leader asks you to unsheathe your sword."

Mats wondered why but obliged by lifting his sword in one sweeping motion high over his head. Gram caught the rays of the sun and flashed a million dazzling reflections over the enemy. The chieftan looked intently at the lone Swedish knight on his mount and again spoke to the translator who quickly relayed the message.

"Our great leader will confer with his men and let you know on the morrow."

"I will return then," said Mats as he replaced Gram in its scabbard, wheeled his horse and galloped back over the drawbridge.

Mats related the conversation to Lord Torgils who had overheard, but not understood, the exchange.

"Why did he ask you to unsheathe your sword?" asked Torgils.

"I do not know," answered Mats, equally confounded.

Mats felt no anxiety over the impending combat. As he rose early the next morning to participate in a special mass for his victory, a sentry came running across the yard, his face aglow.

"They have left!" he screamed at the top of his lungs. "The Russians are gone!"

The rudely awakened soldiers raced to the parapets as fast as their sleep-stiffened legs could carry them. The sentry was right. The Russians had left, ships and all. Their camp was deserted.

While Mats stood bewildered, the soldiers began to whisper, "Lord Mats scared them away. They dared not fight him and his magical sword!"

As Mats looked over the empty camp, he heard the drawbridge being lowered. The frail, huddled shaman quickly ran across the bridge towards the forest. As if he sensed someone was watching, he stopped and turned to look back towards the parapet where Mats stood. The shaman's piercing eyes beamed across the still space and his lips moved without any sound. But Mats heard the words in his head, "Farewell, Leader of Men" before the small figure disappeared into the dark forest.

His last conversation with his father reentered Mats' mind. Gram could only be wielded by one destined to rule, one who wore the special mark of the old gods. Mats wondered, not for the first time, if there was any truth to the legend.

Chapter 12

Stockholm 1301

Erik had been deeply distraught after reading Mats' dispatch reporting on Valdemar's near death experience. When he finally learned of his brother's miraculous recovery he was utterly relieved, and when the Lord High Constable's ship returned from Finland he was the first on the dock in Stockholm harbor to greet his brother, to hug him and make sure that he was, indeed, whole again.

Erik was saddened to learn that the Russians had renewed their attacks on Landskrona. For almost a year, the tolls--which represented a considerable asset to the Swedish Treasury--had caused some merchant ships to turn back rather than to trade in Novgorod. Naturally the Russians were desperate to eliminate this mercantile impediment. Thus far, the Swedes had withstood the furious attacks of the Novgorodians, but their renewed assault on the fort had made Lord Torgils urgently request reinforcements. The situation had become grave enough for the Lord High Constable to decide that he himself had to return to Finland even though he had just arrived in Stockholm.

Erik was practicing some chess moves in his chamber when he heard a knock, and a messenger entered carrying a leather pouch.

"Why did you not give it to the captain of the guard?" asked Erik, irritated that his train of thought had been interrupted.

"King Hakon charged me to deliver it to you personally," the messenger explained.

"In that case, thank you. Go to the kitchens and have something to eat. I shall call for you if I need to reply." The messenger bowed and left the room. During the previous two years the Norwegian king and the Swedish princes had frequently and openly exchanged correspondence. Their friendship had deepened when Hakon's attack on

Denmark brought no response from Sweden, a fact Hakon attributed to Erik. The Danes had been unprepared at the sudden onslaught and were consequently forced to return to the negotiating table, which was where Hakon wanted them in order to discuss his maternal inheritance. Erik, intrigued by the unusual secrecy of this delivery, quickly unfolded the message.

> *Dear Erik,*
>
> *It is with great happiness I write you about the birth of my first-born, our daughter Ingeborg. The child is beautiful and healthy, though unfortunately Euphemia has been quite ill. Our physician is positive she will recover fully, but he does not hold any hope she will ever have another child. This is tragic, as you can imagine. Since Ingeborg will, in all likelihood, be my only legitimate child, I plan to make her pretender to the throne. The man she marries could therefore become ruler of Norway, so I have to make my selection carefully. Still, it is an easy choice for me. I would like you to marry my daughter. Your position in Sweden would be of immense benefit to Norway, and I am sure the Norwegian crown would be welcome on your head. As you see, my dear friend, it pays to wait for the right opportunity. Please send me your immediate answer. If it is in the affirmative, which I hope it will be, let us keep it to ourselves for a time until I have made the right political and diplomatic gestures.*
>
> *Yours,*
> *Hakon R.*

Erik stood motionless. The Norwegian crown. He was stunned. Deep within, he had always felt that he was meant to rule, and now, if he accepted Hakon's offer, chances were, he would.

He took a deep breath. While he had not yet replied affirmatively to Torgils' offer, he had planned on doing so the moment he received the blessing from Birger and the Council. But now...? Now he was offered the possibility of becoming King of Norway, which placed everything in a different light. Whatever he felt for Kristina could play no part in whether or not to accept a proposition so beneficial to Sweden.

Yet the lure and promise of the Norwegian crown was replaced by the image of Kristina's face in his mind's eye. Had the decision been his to make, he would have felt no hesitation. He wanted Kristina with his whole being, and no crown or glory could tempt him away from her. But the decision was not up to him, and he knew what the outcome would be once the proposal was presented to the Council. He felt sick from disappointment. He desperately tried to look at the bright side of his future as King of Norway--a prospect which would have excited him immensely just a few years ago--but nothing could ease the pain he felt, knowing that he would not spend the rest of his life with Kristina.

Barely able to breathe, he started pacing the floor to collect his thoughts. After a while he became calm enough to sit down at his desk. This proposal was one he had to answer immediately since he knew that Birger would enthusiastically welcome so powerful an alliance. He carefully removed a sheet of parchment from a leather folder. He sat with his quill poised for a long time before starting to write. His hand trembled and the ink dripped, smudging the parchment. He threw it away, took out a new sheet, and within the hour he had finished his letter of acceptance and pressed his seal on the parchment. As he was about to place it in the leather pouch he felt a small parcel that had escaped his attention earlier when he had removed Hakon's letter. He unwrapped its cloth cover and found an exquisite ladies' belt pouch made of snakeskin with silver clasps. The message attached bore Kristina's name, but he did not hesitate before reading it:

> *My Dear Lady Kristina,*
> *This small gift is long overdue, so please accept my humble apologies for the delay. It is fashioned out of the skin of the snake from which you and your bird saved me, and I am sending it with gratitude. You impressed me as a woman of singular courage. Hakon R.*

Erik wondered if Hakon knew of his and Kristina's feelings for one another, and if this gift was Hakon's way of showing Kristina respect while he simultaneously destroyed their chance to marry. Or was it simply intended as a grateful acknowledgement of her swift reaction two years ago, the timing only a painful coincidence? Erik looked at the exquisite little pouch. It would tear him apart to see her wear it, as it had accompanied the one offer he could not decline, one that would end their hopes for a life together. But wear it she would, as she would consider it an honored gift.

Finally, he sent for the messenger. "This letter should be given to no one but King Hakon himself. I wish you a safe trip," he said as the man bowed and withdrew. Erik went to the window overlooking the courtyard where he saw the messenger mount a fresh horse and ride away.

Unseen by Erik who had turned away to fill a chalice with comforting wine, a knight rushed into the courtyard and gave agitated orders to the grooms. A few moments later a strong stallion was led forward, on which the stable boys were still fastening the saddle. The knight, impatient for them to finish, hastily mounted and rode off at full gallop.

Lord Abjorn was dirty, tired, and out of breath. He stood in the Lord High Constable's chamber in Stockholm castle drinking water from a cup Torgils had twice refilled.

"Relax and take your time. I can wait," said Torgils in a voice betraying his impatience. Abjorn sat down and drew a deep breath.

"I followed the messenger as you ordered. He was riding at full speed for several hours before he stopped at an inn. He was exhausted and barely awake in the common room, waiting for a bed to be prepared. I sat down and struck up a casual conversation, offering him a mug of beer. We drank by the fire, chatting idly. After a while he began to nod off, and I offered to help him to bed. He was asleep before his head hit the pillow, and while I pretended to make him comfortable, I slipped the leather pouch from under his jacket and returned to the deserted common room. I succeeded in loosening the wax of the seal with the help of a candle, and after reading the message I carefully resealed it. I went back to the sleeping messenger and started to pull off his boots. He woke up briefly, unaware of the passage of time and thanked me for making him comfortable. He was fast asleep when I replaced the letter under his jacket. I returned here immediately."

"So, what did the message say?" pressed Torgils.

"Prince Erik's letter was the acceptance of a marriage proposal King Hakon had made on behalf of his newborn daughter. From the tone of it, I assume that the princess is to be heir to the throne, and that Erik could one day become ruler of Norway."

"That is news, indeed," mumbled Torgils. "It must have been determined that the queen will have no more children. Why else would King Hakon make his daughter successor?" The Lord High Constable pondered the news before he concluded, "Erik is the obvious choice for a husband. With such a connection, Norway no longer stands alone against the Danish-Swedish alliance. Once Erik takes over his dukedom he will be powerful in his own right—and someone King Birger will continue to listen to. Erik is indeed a wise choice." Then he added with a frown. "I have just lost a prospective son-in-law."

Abjorn finished another cup of water before he ruminated, "But there is another prince . . ."

The following day when Lord Torgils left Stockholm castle to embark for Landskrona fortress in Finland, Erik and Valdemar accompanied him to the harbor where troops were busy boarding the ships.

"Please, Lord Torgils, allow me to sail with you again," pleaded Valdemar.

"I have already told you: not this time. I would have thought the last visit had been enough for you. And this war is my responsibility," said Torgils resolutely. "Once the fort is yours, you can fight for it." When they reached the harbor, there was still time before the fleet hauled anchor, so Torgils suggested they share a cup in his cabin.

"I am concerned about what is awaiting us," he said as he poured wine for them. "The reports indicate that the Russians have assembled a very large armada." He took a deep breath. "If anything were to happen to me, I would like to know that Kristina's future is secure." He saw Erik stiffen. "I do not mean to press the issue," he continued smoothly. "But since you have not indicated any interest in my proposal of marriage to Kristina, Prince Erik, I presume you are considering some offer more beneficial to our country. Please, I am not offended in any way," he added quickly as Erik was about to speak. "I do understand the obligation of royal duties and if that is the case--and as I am about to sail into battle--I will repeat the same offer to you, Prince Valdemar."

Erik felt as if he had been kicked in the stomach. He was grateful when, following a knock, the captain entered. "We are ready for the final inspection, Lord Torgils."

"Would you excuse me," said Torgils as he left with the captain.

The two brothers looked at each other. Erik felt the full, devastating impact of losing Kristina. The wine he had swilled during the past two days had numbed both his reason and pain, and had pushed the inevitable from his mind. Now it returned full force. The woman he loved was to marry his brother.

"A perfect solution, Erik. You do not even have to insult Torgils by turning down his proposal," said Valdemar with irony in his voice. He had been sworn to silence the night before as Erik had drunkenly confided his new betrothal. "You will wear the crown of Norway, and Torgils is giving me the generous dowry instead. I truly care about Kristina and I would gladly marry her, . . . except it is you she loves."

Erik could hear his own hollow answer. "She knows what is expected in a royal family. She will do what is best."

Valdemar walked over to Erik and placed his hands on his shoulders. His face bore a pained expression. "Do not think me callous if I say that I always felt it made little difference who one marries, as long as one's true love is nearby, to be cherished and revered from a distance."

"Chivalrous love," scoffed Erik in pain and anger.

"The highest kind of love," objected Valdemar. "But if this marriage will cause you pain I will, of course, not contemplate it."

"She could not marry a better man than you," said Erik with conviction. If Kristina had to marry someone, a thought he had firmly pushed from his mind before, Valdemar was the best choice from every point of view. "If you want to say yes, do so. Birger will be delighted," he managed to say while feeling his chest constrict.

Valdemar looked at Erik. "You mean that?"

"Yes, yes, I do!" cried Erik.

Torgils returned just then, looking questioningly at the two brothers.

"It will be an honor to marry Lady Kristina," Valdemar said with a formal bow. "You can go into battle knowing she will be well cared for. All you have to worry about is winning this war for all of us."

"I shall do my utmost," promised Torgils, delighted with the outcome he had never doubted. "To yours and Kristina's future," he added, raising his cup.

"To the success of your mission," chorused Valdemar and Erik before putting down their empty cups and heading for the cabin door.

"God speed," called Valdemar as they descended the gangplank. "I have you to thank for so much, Erik", he continued as they turned to mount their horses. "You alone made it possible for me to become a duke rather than living off your and Birger's graciousness. You gave me pride and independence. I will be grateful to you for the rest of my life. And now I am to marry Kristina with her vast dowry. It is hard for me to accept my good fortune, because I know how you feel about her." Valdemar glanced at Erik who looked sadder than he had ever seen him.

"You are right, of course, I love her. And I know that she loves me in return."

"Talk to her, Erik, before I do."

"I will," promised Erik, not having any idea how he would tell his beloved that he had single-handedly shattered their dream of a future together.

For several days he avoided his responsibility, making the excuse to Kristina that he was busy in the Council discussing the situation in Finland. More than once he caught Valdemar's disapproving glances. Finally, he decided to join the ladies and some courtiers for a boat trip and a picnic supper on a nearby island.

It was a large and joyous group that embarked the long skiffs at the king's dock. The day was sunny, and spirits were high. As soon as the oarsmen dipped their blades into the water the passengers joined in their singing to help them keep pace. Erik looked over to where Kristina sat next to Marta. Her golden locks were blowing in the wind and she sang merrily along with the others. She looked beautiful in her simple linen tunic, with only a few ribbons to keep her hair under control. How he loved her way of moving, so confident yet so gentle. He knew her better than he knew his own sisters, and there were few things they could not easily talk about. Except that with which he had to confront her today. His heart ached as he had felt her excitement when he announced that he would join the excursion.

After landing on the island and being helped ashore by the oarsmen, the company settled down for their meal. Large cloths were spread over the green grass; each was covered with masses of platters containing one delicacy after another. Large casks of wine and cider were placed under a shady tree, and the ensuing hours floated pleasantly away under the cloudless blue skies. Once the meal was finished, Erik motioned for Kristina to accompany him for a walk. Her face was expectant when she joined him among the wildflowers, but he remained silent as they walked across the small island.

Suddenly Erik turned to her and blurted out, "I know no other way to say this, Kristina. I have to marry King Hakon's newborn daughter, Ingeborg of Norway." He looked at her face, which betrayed total disbelief. "How I wish it could be otherwise." Haltingly, he related to her what had transpired. "You will get the best husband in the world, Kristina, and Valdemar is happy about the alliance."

Kristina had not spoken. She looked straight at him appearing not to comprehend what he was saying. Erik repeated himself, but with no reaction from her.

"Kristina, speak to me," he pleaded finally.

"What can I say?" she asked in a whisper. "I love you and I am to marry Valdemar."

Erik was taken aback by her bluntness. How simple it sounded and how incredibly it hurt. He leaned forward and touched her face. His fingers followed its curves and she closed her eyes. He ached to take her in his arms and when he saw the tears well out from under her thick eyelashes he pulled her to him, holding her close. After a long while she pulled away. "Perhaps I should join Rikissa."

"Not you!" cried Erik in frustration. "You would never be happy in a convent. You are life itself. You should never be closed in, nor live without children of your own. Do not ever say that again!"

"But it would not be fair to Valdemar."

"He will be marrying someone he adores. What more could he, or you for that matter, expect if we consider our positions. Valdemar is the son of a king, and you are the daughter of a Regent. We must each do our duty, however difficult it may be."

Kristina heard Queen Helvig's parting words ring in her ears.

"We can never again be alone together," Erik said gently as he lifted up her face. "You will be the wife of my brother, and as I love you, I will honor you above all women."

But as they looked into each other's eyes the longing and the love that had grown since childhood welled forth, while their lips met in a kiss so heartbreaking that it mingled with their tears. Erik abruptly broke away and ran back over the fields towards the rowboats where he ordered one of the rowing masters to take him back to the castle. Kristina collapsed in the grass, pulled herself into a fetal position as if it would soothe her pain to press her knees hard into her chest, and there she lay until Lady Astrid found her hours later when it was time to leave the island.

From that day on, the quiet chapel became a place of refuge for Kristina as it was the only place in the castle where people were not always coming and going. Marta had tried, unsuccessfully, to cheer her. Father Nils, now Bishop Nils, had come all the way from Vasteras, and spent much time with her, with similar results. He was clearly saddened for her, and at the same time expressed his admiration as she attempted to do her duty and bear her pain with dignity.

Many young noblemen had been noticeably disappointed over the rumors of her betrothal to Valdemar. A marriage to Lady Kristina would have meant a fortune, and even more important, it would have meant power. Though she could not marry Erik, she knew that she should be grateful not to be exploited by some ambitious young suitor attempting to marry the Lord High Constable's daughter. Not that her life with Valdemar would be free of intrigue, but at least she would operate from a most privileged position.

She had already decided that upon her father's return from the wars in Finland she would make it easy for him by keeping her composure. Especially since her father had shown his caring by requesting that her wedding to Valdemar take place before the coronation of Birger and Marta to enable Kristina to attend as duchess at that solemn occasion. While she appreciated the gesture, it was of little importance to her. All joy had vanished, even though her father had left behind part of her dowry--chests of jewelry and bolts of embroidered dress fabrics, luxurious items of such beauty that the women who saw them paled with envy. Kristina gave Marta the choicest fabrics, as these fabulous gifts meant little to her now.

She also had learned from Marta that Valdemar would not be living in his Finnish dukedom, but with Erik at Nykoping castle. Apparently, that had been decided quite some time back, but she had been deeply shocked when Marta told her. At first, she was at a loss to understand why Erik would want to encounter her on a daily basis until she realized just how seriously Erik must have taken Rikissa's warning. He would not allow his younger brother to disappear from view. But would the three of them be able to lead their lives together?

She forced herself to think about her good fortune in marrying a prince, but it was difficult when she knew how close she would be to the man she loved. She could picture him sitting in front of the fire, playing chess with his brothers and concentrating intently on the next move. Or she could see that infectious smile spread across his face when the bard sang a droll ballad; and she could clearly remember the concern in his eyes when recently she had fallen from her horse. But the image of his face would not wane; it remained etched in her mind--especially the way he had looked at her on the island. His eyes had shown his love more clearly than any words could express.

Today, she would see Valdemar for the first time since learning of their betrothal, as he had been visiting his mother at Dovo. Though Kristina had known Valdemar all her life, she felt nervous about being alone with him. She had to be in control to show everybody, especially herself, that she was worthy of becoming a duchess.

Suddenly the heavy chapel door creaked open, causing her to jump in surprise. It was Valdemar. Already! She had spent endless hours rehearsing for this moment. She had planned to meet him in the privacy of the queen's chamber, in her most imposing gown, with her hair in gold combs and King Hakon's pouch on her belt. Instead, she was wearing her everyday dress, and she felt at a loss without her few prized possessions.

"You are here early," she heard herself say in a voice that did not waver. She realized that he had come to see her directly, since he was still short of breath from his ride and his clothes and hair were covered with dust.

"I hope you will forgive my unkempt state; but we must talk," he began hesitantly. "I have thought about this moment . . . I know you are disappointed, and I understand your feelings . . ."

He was unable to continue, but Kristina looked at him with gratitude. Maybe he did understand. He must have known how she felt all these years, so she did not have to pretend. Her relief came in an uncontrollable gush of tears. She threw herself into his arms, oblivious of the dust clinging to him. She had cried on his shoulder many times when she was little, and his arms felt comforting around her now.

"I will do my best to be a good husband to you," he whispered. "I will never be Erik, but I will do my best."

"When I thought I was going to marry Erik," confessed Kristina between sobs, "my most secret wish was about to come true. That is why the disappointment is so devastating. I am telling you this, so we can live a life of honesty together. But believe me when I promise to be a good wife to you."

"I know you will," said Valdemar, softly stroking her hair. "And I am glad you have told me what is in your heart. I am not surprised you love Erik; there is no one I admire more."

"You are making this easier for me," said Kristina as she pulled away to dry her tears. "I am glad you are my friend."

"I will always be that." He suddenly was reminded of his disheveled appearance. "I must wash and change," he said as he searched for something he had placed under his cape. He brought forward a small leather case that he placed in her hands. "This is from my mother. " He bent forward, kissed her gently on the temple, and was gone as quickly as he had appeared.

Numbly she opened the case, revealing the gold time glass she remembered vividly from the large table in Queen Helvig's chamber. It had stood there day after day, year after year, counting the dutiful hours of its owner. Now it would count hers.

As Torgils regained consciousness, the first sensation he experienced was an excruciating pain in his right leg. He also felt nauseous from the heaving of his ship, and his head was exploding. He carefully touched his forehead, only to feel it bandaged. Another battle scar for his collection. Yet worse than the physical pain was his mental anguish. Landskrona fortress was lost.

"Drink this," Abjorn's voice demanded as Torgils felt a cup with hot broth being pressed to his lips. He was surprised he could swallow even a mouthful, but the strong brew tasted remarkably good. "Thank God you can take some nourishment. You have been unconscious for days now. The physician has been worried because you lost so much blood. Mats and I have taken turns looking after you, but we have been unable to give you anything other than a little water and pain-killing draughts. How do you feel?" asked Abjorn while he carefully removed the cup from Torgils' lips.

"Everything hurts, especially my leg" whispered Torgils, too weak to speak in a normal tone of voice. "How did it end? I know we lost, but how bad was it?"

"Are you strong enough to hear the truth?" asked Abjorn. Torgils nodded. "It was a disaster. We were badly outnumbered and most of our men who were able to escape and get back to the ships are gravely wounded. I am afraid the dream of Landskrona fortress as the perpetual purse has ended. We should be satisfied with what else we have in Finland and leave the Russians in peace."

"That is not good news to carry home," Torgils moaned.

"You should be grateful that you are going home at all--with your head bashed in and your leg almost severed. But stop thinking about this for now," said Abjorn as he pulled the blankets higher over Torgils chest. "Try to sleep."

It was not until several hours later that the heaving of the ship subsided. When Torgils stirred, Abjorn, who was sitting by the desk, poured some herbal tea, which he brought over to the bunk.

"I cannot take my mind off our defeat, I keep dreaming about it," sighed Torgils between sips of the warm liquid. "This was to be my greatest victory before I stepped down as Regent. I needed that to impress the king with the wisdom of keeping me on as his principal advisor. But I failed miserably."

"The king will surely keep you as his Lord High Constable. You have too much support among the nobles for him to do otherwise," said Abjorn. "And this is not the time to fret over such matters."

"I have to find some way to retain my position," groaned Torgils. Then his pale face lit up. "No one is aware that I know of Erik's marriage plans; so this still-secret future alliance between Sweden and Norway offers me the perfect moment to proclaim myself willing to serve as the peacemaker between Denmark and Norway, which will make me a hero in all three countries. Then my position would be more secure." Torgils gestured for another cup of tea, which Abjorn brought. "You know, I suddenly feel better," he mumbled before lapsing back into semiconsciousness.

"It is a boy," the midwife cried triumphantly as she pulled the infant from Marta's loins and handed it to Father Gregory who deftly severed the umbilical cord.

Marta's scream of relief that the ordeal was finally over sounded almost like one of pleasure. Through her teeth, so that only Kristina could hear her, she whispered, "Never, but never again will I have another child! I cannot endure the pain."

Kristina heard the felicitations from those crowded in the stifling chamber as Birger hurriedly ushered them out to allow Marta some privacy.

"You are magnificent, my love," he said as he returned to her bedside. He bent over to kiss her drenched forehead. "Another son. Thank you."

"Please go and celebrate, your Majesty," ordered Lady Astrid with the authority of one never contradicted in matters of birthing. "We must tend the queen in peace and quiet!"

Birger tenderly kissed Marta's hand before he reluctantly left the chamber.

While the room was being aired the medicinal monk finished administering his herbalist concoctions, and Marta was finally able to rest against freshly changed linens while awaiting the arrival of her second born. Without a word Kristina placed the baby in her arms and stood back.

Marta looked down on her swaddled child. "He is smaller than Magnus was, but his features are perfectly formed. How is it possible that two infants can be so different? Magnus was full of energy, while this baby emanates an awesome calm." As she studied the infant, he opened his eyes and looked straight at her with shocking clarity. Marta looked up, bewildered.

"Yes, he is remarkable," Kristina agreed. "He appears to understand everything already."

Kristina turned as Bishop Nils quietly entered the chamber. "May God bless you and your son," he said making the sign of the cross over Marta.

"Have you seen him?" asked Marta, still bewildered.

"Yes, I have. He is a most unusual child . . ."

"He is not a changeling? He is normal, is he not?" she interrupted anxiously.

"Most certainly, your Majesty," said Bishop Nils. "He is a special child of God. I could feel it the moment I blessed him. You are most fortunate."

"Rest now," Kristina urged in her caring voice as she left Marta's bedside.

It was the morning of the third day after the birth of the new prince that the three royal brothers remained at the dais table long after all the guests had retired. They had drunk countless toasts to little Prince Erik Birgersson and had loudly lamented the loss of Landskrona fortress.

"Next year will be good!" slurred Birger happily. "I will be coronated . . . you will become dukes . . . and we finally get to rule Sweden!" Then he looked downcast. "But that is also the sad part; dividing the kingdom will separate us. We have always lived together, and now you both will move to Nykoping." He fell quiet. "We must all start planning for the future," he added as he poured them more wine.

"Most important for our future is for the Scandinavian countries to live together in peace," Erik responded somberly. He had been spending most of his waking hours attempting to concentrate on affairs of state and planning for his new role as Duke of Sweden. It was the only way he knew of not thinking about Kristina. "Sweden and Denmark already have a secure peace through family connections, and the same opportunity is now presented with Norway. As we are on good terms with both parties, why do we not act as mediators between Hakon and Erik Menved to see how we can resolve their grievances?"

"Torgils has proposed the very same idea," Birger said eagerly.

"That is curious," remarked Erik, "as we are the only ones who know about my future connection with Norway," noted Erik.

"Torgils merely said that as he would no longer be Regent, with more time at his disposal, it would be a worthy undertaking to be a peacemaker," related Birger. "That is, if and when he recuperates from his injuries."

"He is stronger than the devil. He will be fine," Valdemar interjected. "And now that Kristina has gone home with him to tend his injuries he will heal in no time, you will see. And when he learns that Erik is pledged to marry Ingeborg of Norway, he will be surprised how timely his suggestion was."

Birger looked pleased, but Erik turned pensive and suggested an end to the festivities. They stood up, and with arms around each other for support, stumbled down the corridor. After depositing Birger by his door, Erik and Valdemar continued on to their chamber.

"Twice Torgils has surprised us with cooperation," muttered Erik. "I think he already knew about my impending betrothal to Ingeborg when he offered you Kristina's hand in marriage. It seems we have a spy in our midst." Erik was in no way insulted by the fact that the Lord High Constable had him under observation. On the contrary, he was pleased that he had finally reached a position worthy of the attention. He smiled. "I wonder what Torgils is up to."

"He is simply trying to stay in good grace with us all," yawned Valdemar as he staggered over to the bed and fell headlong onto it.

"That is my side," protested Erik; but when he saw that Valdemar was already fast asleep, he covered him, disrobed himself, and climbed into the other side.

Chapter 13

Solberga, Sweden 1302

September arrived dressed in breathtaking colors, while the warmth of the summer still lingered. The morning sun broke through the clouds just as Lord Torgils emerged from his tent overlooking the encampment at Solberga. The tents of the Swedes were arrayed on one side, the Norwegians' on the other. Between them stood a huge tented pavilion that would serve as their meeting place and banquet hall. The peace talks that Torgils had initiated were to be held during the coming two days with a tournament to follow. He gazed enviously down at the fit young soldiers plunging into the Gota River that flowed nearby. He yearned to join them, but his leg still gave him pain. He shifted his weight with a sigh.

Torgils thought back to the many months he had been bedridden at Lena, his estate, while he slowly and painfully regained his strength under Kristina's loving care. Once he was able to move about his hall with the help of two canes he had suggested she return to resume her duties at court. While she had been with him he had not felt the boredom and restlessness which now filled his every waking hour. As long as he had been serving as Regent, messengers had been coming and going wherever he had been. That was no longer the case. Weeks could go by without any visits, and when a message arrived it was not to seek his decision on some intricate political matter, but merely a note from the king to inform him that everything was going well in the Council. His initial annoyance at not being needed had turned to smoldering resentment. After all, he had left King Birger with a strong and rich country. He could not stomach the young king's smugness over his unremarkable accomplishments, since he was merely coasting on Torgils' hard work.

Upon his return to Stockholm from Finland the king had visited him at his sickbed before his departure to convalesce at Lena.

"My brothers and I have discussed my coronation," the king explained, "and we agreed that it should take place in Soderkoping, in the beginning of December."

"Most suitable, your Majesty," Torgils had agreed. "Your parents' coronation took place there, and the date gives us ample time to pursue the peace talks."

"Splendid," Birger had said before continuing. "While I finally feel prepared to take over the reign, I will still need your support. I want you to remain my Lord High Constable."

Torgils had drawn a deep breath of relief. "Thank you, your Majesty," he said, honestly moved. "I shall continue to do everything in my power to justify your trust."

Despite his intention to restrain himself in the future, he could not resist offering a suggestion. "It has occurred to me that Duke Erik has no chancellor to assist him when he takes over his dukedom. My closest advisor, Abjorn Sixtensson, is knowledgeable and trustworthy; and while I would miss his sound counsel immensely, he could be of great help to the duke."

"What a generous gesture," Birger exclaimed. "Lord Abjorn is indeed a good man. I will speak with Erik."

Torgils had smiled. Would he be so lucky as to place his loyal friend at Erik's shoulder, thus to always know what was happening at Erik's court? Torgils knew that he was fortunate, but as the nights had passed he realized that he would find it difficult not to be in command. It was not that he disliked the king or his brothers, but governing was a game he had played and mastered for too long. He doubted he could change now.

A young boy wearing the colors of Northern Halland jarred Torgils out of his reverie as he approached, bowing deeply. "Count Jakob wonders if you would care to break fast with him."

"It would be my pleasure," replied Torgils. "Lead the way, young man."

Torgils' limped across the campground with the aid of his cane, delighted to see his newfound friend again.

He had met Count Jacob for the first time in Norway some months earlier when Torgils went there to initiate the peace effort. Since Jakob ruled the Danish Northern Halland, his position at the Norwegian court was unique. Torgils and Jakob, both realizing the precariousness of their positions, sensed that a link would be propitious for them both. Consequently, they had spent much time together, and on the eve of Torgils' departure they had sealed their friendship as blood brothers. Torgils, in the age-old ceremony, had drawn his dagger across his wrist with measured pressure, causing the blood to flow without severing the vein. Jakob repeated the procedure, then flattened his arm on the table while Torgils placed his wrist on top, allowing their blood to mingle while, with their other hands, they raised their cups and vowed an oath loyalty.

Now, as Torgils approached Jakob's tent, he found a sumptuous table inside already set.

"What a pleasure to see you again," Jakob said as he reached out with both arms to embrace Torgils before gesturing toward the table.

A servant brought forward a stool on which Torgils seated himself with a groan, extending his leg before him. Jakob lifted his tankard to propose a toast to their friendship. Torgils was aware that they were a study in contrasting types. While he himself was large and powerfully built, looking every bit a knight, Jakob was slender and elegant; at least a head shorter, with finely chiseled features, looking as if he had never wielded a heavy weapon. His skin was fair, bordering on pale, but his grey eyes revealed strength that his frail physique seemed to deny. His clothes had a continental flair, and he was considered by his admirers to be the best-dressed man at the Norwegian court. Others thought him a bit of a dandy, but Torgils had immediately appreciated the cunning mind of the count, dandy or not. Jakob, too, had not been misled by the Lord High Constable's warrior-like appearance, but respected the logical intellect beneath the powerful demeanor. The two men beamed at each other.

"We do not have much time before the meeting starts," Jakob began. "And I would like to understand some of the details of the peace plan." He passed a platter of herring to Torgils who helped himself to a generous portion. "All we know at the Norwegian court is that the Swedes are offering to serve as peacemakers between

Denmark and Norway. That is most commendable; but as we also know how closely allied the Kings of Sweden and Denmark are, the Norwegians naturally are suspicious of how impartially the Swedes can mediate the upcoming talks."

"Then you do not know about King Hakon's marriage plans for his daughter?"

"No. Has anything been decided?"

"King Hakon will announce the betrothal of his daughter to Erik of Sweden today."

"That is news, indeed. King Hakon certainly knows how to keep a secret. Our nobles were opposed to this meeting as they felt it would be an exercise in futility, but Hakon convinced them to attend. I think they came just to participate in a good joust." Jakob laughed, and then his face took on a pensive look. "Now where does that leave our plans, my friend?"

"We will have to wait," sighed Torgils, wiping his mouth with the back of his hand.

Jakob lowered his voice and leaned closer. "I had hoped that we could act sooner rather than later . . ." He stopped speaking as a servant brought another plate that Jakob pushed toward Torgils with a polite burp. "I cannot eat another mouthful, but I am sure you can manage some of this beautiful venison."

"With no trouble at all," smiled Torgils as he filled his platter.

Birger, Erik, Valdemar, and their entourage approached the wide striped pavilion in the middle of the field, both ends of which were open to form a long tunnel. An honor guard of knights lined their way as they neared the east end, at the same time as the Norwegian king and his followers reached the west entrance. Judging the pace well, the two kings entered at the same time. The two groups then solemnly filed into their places opposite each other at the long table before the tent flaps were dropped.

The Norwegian king sat on a large, wood-carved chair. He cut an imposing figure in a red tunic emblazoned with his coat of arms--a single golden lion clutching a battleaxe. Around his neck hung his thick chain of office, and on his dark hair sat a heavy crown.

As usual, he exuded composure and his smile was warm. He was the first to speak. "I am delighted to be here today at the invitation of our Swedish neighbors. This meeting could well be the first step toward peace and unity in Scandinavia." Hakon looked at Birger over the wide table. "To prove the seriousness of Norway's intention to strengthen its ties with Sweden, I have offered my daughter, Ingeborg, in marriage to Prince Erik of Sweden."

A murmur of surprise was heard from all except the members of the royal families. Torgils and Jakob feigned surprise as they eagerly nodded their congratulations to Erik.

"Prince Erik has gracefully accepted my offer," continued Hakon, "So I feel we can begin our talks knowing that our two countries are united in spirit."

The discussions lasted for several hours with no insurmountable issues being raised. A document reflecting the points agreed upon was needed for the kings' signatures; so Torgils, representing Sweden, and Jakob, representing Norway, volunteered to compose it.

While the royal party was enjoying a splendid supper, the two men settled down in Torgil's tent, assisted by two scribes. Torgils, though fluent in Latin, preferred to dictate in Norse, which the monks resented as they had to do double duty by transcribing his words into Latin; but they had no alternative since most formal agreements were written in that international language, simplifying communication among the literati of Europe. Jakob, who possessed a special talent for putting thoughts into words, dictated the third and final draft. He did it speedily and in perfect Latin, to the great relief of the scribes who, nonetheless, had difficulty keeping up with him. By the time they were finished, Torgils' leg had stiffened so Jakob offered to join him on a walk.

"I have thought about our plans," Jakob began as they slowly strolled toward the riverbank, "And I realize that the one great obstacle is money. While we are by no means poor, we are not rich enough to support our undertaking without additional funds. You have been a widower for many years. Maybe you should remarry." Jakob was amused by the bewildered look which came over Torgils' face. "A relative of mine, Count Otto of Ravensberg in Northern Germany, has a beautiful daughter, and she will receive a huge dowry once he is satisfied with the groom's prospects. Should I approach him? It would be a fine match," Jakob beamed.

"I never contemplated remarriage," said Torgils. " I have been consumed with finding a good marriage for my daughter, but I had not thought about one for myself."

"You certainly achieved an excellent match for her," said Jakob. "I, on the other hand have thought about possible candidates for you, but I have come up with no one who could rival Hedvig of Ravensberg. However, I do understand your reluctance. I married once and did my duty. Now, as a widower, I am grateful not to have my days disturbed by a woman's chatter and demands."

"I am not hesitating because the thought of a wife is unpleasant; rather to the contrary, when I think about it," said Torgils pensively. "Granted that I shall have more time now, and, of course, I am not getting younger. While I could pick and choose women in my youth, I am afraid I have come to the age, and condition," he smiled as he tapped his leg with the cane, "when I have to ask nicely, and reward the kind lady with expensive gifts. In fact, marriage might be good for this old man."

Jakob laughed. "I will write to Count Otto then. It would be a pleasure to have you as a relative."

Birger was reading at his traveling desk as Erik and Valdemar entered. He looked up, smiled broadly, and gestured for them to be seated.

"Please look over the final document summarizing our morning meeting so we can give our opinions on the morrow."

Erik and Valdemar read the document carefully. When they finished, Erik looked at Birger. "Since I am to marry the heiress to the Norwegian throne, no one could be more interested than me in a close relationship between Sweden and Norway, but even I find this wording too strong. Here, for example: The monarch of Sweden will join with the Norwegian monarch, and vice versa, against enemies threatening either country. That is almost a declaration of war against the Danes who the Norwegians feel threaten their country. And here further down it says that you will impartially, and to the best of your ability, represent the claims of the Norwegian royal family to their rightful inheritance from their Danish ancestors. First it must be proved that the claims are indeed rightful. And there is no mention of the demands the Danes have expressed."

"The language does seem partial," Birger agreed as he picked up the document.

"The Lord High Constable is not accustomed to you scrutinizing his papers. He was expecting you just to sign," said Erik.

"I think you are being unfair," objected Birger as he reread the document. "Maybe Torgils is too eager to assure Hakon of our impartiality, but I do not see any intentional wrongdoing. Oh, by the way," continued Birger with a broad smile. "I have given some thought to whom you might consider as chancellor when you take charge of your dukedom, Erik--or I should say; both of you, since you have decided to rule your dukedoms jointly. I have an excellent candidate in mind: Abjorn Sixtensson."

Erik did not respond immediately, and whatever emotions he felt, he willed his face to betray none of them. "I am grateful for your interest," he finally said with a smile. "I would be delighted to consider Lord Abjorn- if Torgils can spare him." Erik went around the narrow table, placing his hand on Birger's shoulder. "Thank you for your concern."

Birger was clearly proud to find Erik pleased with his suggestion.

"Are you out of your mind?" hissed Valdemar when they left Birger's tent. "We both have serious doubts about Torgils' loyalty to anyone but himself, and Abjorn owes everything to Torgils--his position, his wealth, everything!"

"Right now, yes," said Erik quietly. "But things change. Everyone respects Abjorn, and he has experience. He is an excellent choice for the position, and if he becomes dependent on me, on us, his loyalties will change. And when they do; we will have a spy in Torgils' court, and not the other way around. I only have to figure out Abjorn's price. But if, for some reason I cannot turn him, he will not stay. Are you willing to try?"

"You might be right," Valdemar relented.

The members of the conference assembled for the meeting early the following morning. After agreeing to correct the points and wording that Birger requested, the meeting concluded. Everyone seemed pleased except Lord Torgils and Count Jakob, who Erik noticed exchanged quick glances as if to express their surprise over Birger's careful reading of their paper. But they forced themselves to smile, and together with the other members left for the tournament field. Hakon gestured for Erik to follow him. As they walked through the camp, Hakon turned to his future son-in-law.

"Your brother is more astute than I thought. He did a careful analysis of the document." Erik did not reply. Hakon, who took his silence for consent, switched the subject. "I want to tell you something that I would like you to keep between the two of us for the time being. Should you then deem it necessary to tell Erik Menved, you have my permission--but only to him." Erik nodded before Hakon continued.

"If Count Jakob was one of King Erik Klipping's killers I do not know, but as I told you before, I have allowed those accused of that murder to stay at our court because they were sentenced without due process. If Erik Menved consents to a proper trial, I would consider extraditing them if that were the only way to buy peace between our countries." They reached the edge of the tournament field. "I would be saddened to send Jakob back for trial," Hakon continued. "There is no one I trust more in my Council. He is extremely intuitive. And he is my friend."

Everyone had taken their places at the tournament field, and it was a noisy and expectant crowd that surrounded the dais where Erik took his seat. As the initial heat was about to begin, two entrants, one from each nation, anxiously awaited the starting signal. At the blare of the trumpets, the knights spurred their horses to full gallop, lowered their lances, and charged with a thundering noise. Crashing sounds reverberated as lances made contact with opponents' shields. Cheers went up from the spectators as one of the knights was toppled from his steed. The victor proudly returned to his side of the field, to be congratulated by his comrades, while squires quickly removed the fallen warrior from the arena. The many remaining heats produced two Swedish finalists--Johan Brunkow, Marta's champion, and Mats Kettilmundsson.

Erik was elated that Mats had acquitted himself so proudly. Erik had been tempted to enter the competition, but he knew it was far wiser to select a champion to represent himself and Valdemar, rather than to risk a personal loss to the Norwegians.

But Mats had paid a price for his success. He was bleeding from wounds he had not felt in the heat of battle, and when he rode to his side of the field he slumped over his horse. He was helped off his mount and relieved of his heavy armor to rest and be attended by a physician.

Meanwhile the field was prepared for the archery competition. Big bales of hay were dragged in and painted wooden targets were rested against them. Ten targets were lined up about fifty feet away from the spectators. The competition was open to anyone, which offered a rare opportunity for a commoner to win fame and a purse of gold.

Erik gestured for Valdemar to follow him. They walked across the field to the tent where Brother Gregory was ministering to Mats who was lying on a cot, stripped to the waist. His broad and powerful body was gleaming with sweat, his face cringing in pain. The physician looked up from his work. "Your champion came through well enough," he said with a smirk, having little admiration for men risking life and limb in peacetime for the ephemeral prize of glory. "He has an impressive assortment of bruises, but nothing is broken."

Erik bent over Mats. "You were magnificent! How do you feel?" he asked, casting an annoyed glance at the physician.

"Now that it is over, I feel as if I spent the day in a torture chamber. But I will be fine."

"This is as good a moment as any to ask you if you would like to be Valdemar's and my Marshal. With you in command of our armies, we shall be invincible."

Mats tried to sit up, but Erik gently pushed him down. "I will do everything I can to meet your expectations," whispered Mats. "And to show my gratitude, I will win this tournament!"

"You do not have to win to convince me that we made the right choice. I know we have. And now you should rest." Erik stepped back, and Valdemar walked over to add his own congratulations. Then they left with a final nod to Brother Gregory.

When they returned to the dais, the final archery heat was under way with only two contestants remaining. One of the finalists was a knight, and the other a commoner. Erik's eyes were drawn to the wiry figure dressed in hunter's garb. The man had a sharp, weather-beaten face with alert blue eyes. He moved with catlike speed and grace and handled his bow with the ultimate confidence of a master marksman. "Who is the man in hunter's green?" Erik asked the Norwegian in charge of the archery competition.

"His name is Alf Arvid of Smaland. They call him Alf, your Highness," the knight replied after checking his score sheet. "According to many in this region he is a sensational shot; but he will never beat Lord Tomas from Norway."

"Then you would not mind taking my bet against Lord Tomas? I have a feeling this Alf of Smaland will be the winner."

"I shall be happy to, but remember I warned you," said the Norwegian with a wide grin.

"One hundred marks?" asked Erik.

"With pleasure. I will be able to buy a new tournament horse."

"Do not be too sure," said Erik as he studied the green-clad man preparing for the next round, sensing his quiet air of calm. Alf evinced no trace of nervousness, whereas Tomas was pacing back and forth while waiting for the starting signal. Erik could sense the knight's concern about living up to his reputation.

The targets had now been moved to seventy-five feet from where the archers stood. Each finalist shot five arrows. Erik noticed how rhythmically Alf strung his bow, and that he was considerably faster than the knight. The scores were tallied anew, and both men scored perfectly. "The hunter is worth a bet," said Erik to his brothers. "He is the best I have seen."

"It would be a sporting bet to make," said Birger who turned toward Hakon. "What would you say about a bet against Lord Tomas?"

"I would be a poor friend if I took it. Tomas has not lost for as long as I can remember."

"Then you would not mind my placing a thousand marks on the hunter?" asked Birger.

"It is your money! Of course, I will take it," grinned Hakon.

A leaf-covered screen was carried out on the field, and a strange looking contraption was placed behind it. The device was a small catapult, normally used in battle to hurl flaming, oil-drenched balls over fortress walls. Now the catapult would launch wooden target disks. It had been adjusted to throw neither too high nor too rapidly. Should the bowmen need further challenge; the angle, height and speed would be adjusted. Since the catapult was positioned behind the screen, the exact moment of release was obscured.

The spectators settled down for the final test. Tomas was first to shoot. The target flew in a wide arc through the air and Tomas' arrow pierced it with a splintering sound. Alf readied himself, and his arrow found its target with equal accuracy. The crowd went wild, cheering and stamping their feet, delighted to see a common hunter pressing a knight. The two kings conferred and decided that the disks should be thrown at higher speeds. Adjustments were made in the catapult's mechanism, and the archers readied themselves for a second round. Both were successful. The speed was adjusted for the third time using smaller disks. The archers shot again. Neither missed. After asking the monarchs' consent, Count Jakob rose to pull off the thick gold chain he was wearing around his neck. On the chain hung a large round pendant with a hole in the middle about an inch in diameter. "As a final test," he called out. "We shall hang this pendant on a wooden plank one hundred feet away. The one who places an arrow in the hole with the fewest shots, will be the champion."

With the crowds' noisy approval, the target was stationed farther down the field. Tomas was the first to try. Suspense filled the quiet afternoon air. The first arrow missed. Erik, who sat quite close to the disappointed knight, could see the perspiration break out on his forehead. Tomas was shaken. He took his time preparing for the second shot, and as the arrow sped towards the target he closed his eyes not to see it miss again. His eyes flew open when he heard the crowd roar. He had done it! The only way he could lose was if Alf succeeded on his first attempt. Tomas turned around and waved to the spectators as Alf calmly took an arrow from his quiver, notched it and rested it on his left forefinger. He slowly pulled the string, sighting as he tensed his bow, and let his arrow fly. The point of the feathered shaft found the tiny hole of the pendent with a thunk that could be heard across the silent field.

The crowd came to their feet, and soldiers had to protect the victor from being crushed by the onslaught of the delirious throng. They were finally pushed back, leaving Alf standing in front of Birger to receive the reward. Birger raised his hand for silence, but it took a long time before the cheers died down. He lifted a golden arrow from a pillow and stood before the hunter.

"Alf Arvid of Smaland, it is with great admiration for your skill that I present this golden arrow as a token of your accomplishment. As a prize, I hand you these five pieces of gold and request your presence at my table tonight. I also commission you to teach my sons the art of bowmanship."

The crowd was impressed. Five pieces of gold was an enormous purse, and the honor of instructing the princes was rarely bestowed on a common man. King Birger invited Alf to sit on the platform for the grand finale of the tournament. A soldier returned Jakob's neck chain, and the count scrutinized it carefully before he exclaimed: "There is not a scratch on it! You two fellows certainly know how to hit a target, though you could hardly see it for the distance."

Erik offered Alf the seat beside him. "You won me a lot of money. Thank you."

"My pleasure, your Highness. My own rewards were generous," said Alf of Smaland. "Especially defeating a knight."

Erik looked at him with curiosity. "You do not seem overly fond of knights."

"If your Highness will forgive me, not particularly."

"Explain!"

Alf took a deep breath before starting his tale. "I was just married and had a tiny farm in a Smaland village consisting of only eight homesteads. We were pitifully poor, and our land could barely carry us through the winters, even if we put bark meal in our flour. Still, my wife and I were happy, and my wife's younger sister, Anna, came to live with us since my wife was pregnant and we needed someone to help on the farm. The harvest did not come out well that year, and as the first snow fell, we could only pray that we would survive the bitter months to come. A rich farmer began courting Anna, and we all rejoiced since he brought gifts whenever he came to visit: a smoked ham, a string of sausages, a leg of venison. We felt as if we were rich ourselves, and I was grateful that my pregnant wife was getting good nourishment.

"Then one day a group of knights and their men-at-arms came to our village. They needed provisions and feed for their horses. The knights settled down in the largest farmhouse and ordered their men to go to every farm and take the best food they could find. The village elder begged them not to empty the larders because the village was on the brink of starvation, but the knight in charge laughed and sent his men out to search each house.

"No one in the village dared stop them. As the villagers stood shivering in the snow, they saw their scanty provisions brought to the knights. After the soldiers had eaten everything worth eating and drunk several kegs of beer, they were too tired to ride on, and decided to stay in the village for the night. My wife and I made a place for ourselves to sleep on the floor by the hearth so the two knights who were billeted at our house could take our bed. I had asked Anna to stay in the attic and not to show herself, but as the drunken knights came reeling into the house, pushing furniture over and screaming with laughter, she looked down to see if we were harmed. One of the knights caught a glimpse of her and alerted his friend. They both grinned, and one of them staggered up the ladder to the attic. She tried to escape her pursuer, but we could hear his heavy reeling footsteps as he followed, and her petrified whimper as he caught her. From the sounds we knew she was trying to fight herself free, and from her screams we knew she did not succeed. I started to move toward the ladder without thinking but took a savage blow to my head as the other knight struck me with his heavy gauntlet. He ordered me to stay, and not to interfere. It seemed like an eternity before the rapist began his wobbly descent. Gloating, he told his friend that she was a beauty, and the second knight eagerly climbed to the attic. Not a sound was heard from the girl, only the rhythmic movement of the heavy body on top of hers. We waited in agony until the second knight came down. Satisfied with the evening's exercise, he threw himself down beside his friend and slept like an innocent child. My wife quietly climbed up the ladder to minister to her sister.

"I found myself sitting frozen by the hearth, staring at the sleeping knights. These men would have fought to kill if another man had as much as touched one of their women or merely insulted them. I just had to sit there, powerless against their brutality. After a while my wife came down, and my heart cringed with pain when she whispered that her sister had been badly battered. My wife went up to her again, to sleep beside her, to keep her warm, and to try to make her feel secure. I sat down by the hearth and felt tears stream down my face.

"I did not sleep at all that night. Finally, a knock was heard on our door, and a soldier announced it was time to move out. The two knights awoke, ill tempered and hung over. They collected their weapons and left without a word. The villagers collected and told of their experiences during the night. Several of the women had been raped, and the larders had suffered badly, so that everyone would have to be on harsh rationing. But, as the village elder said, our hamlet had not been burned, and for that we should be grateful.

Reality moved in fast enough. We were hungry every day, never eating enough at any meal. My wife feared that her sister was pregnant, and she was right. And soon the whole village knew it, as well. The eager suitor stopped visiting and started courting another girl.

"My wife had lost weight and was in poor health. When her time was due, there was nothing to be done to save her or our child. They both died. My wife's death devastated my sister-in-law, and two days later she threw herself off the high cliff by the lake. We found her body washed up on the shore.

"A year later, our village had a visit from another large group of men-at-arms. I will not bore you with the details, but this time a few of the villagers tried to stop a knight from raping a young girl. They succeeded, but in his anger the knight burned down the nearest farm. The rest of the drunken visitors followed his example and set fire to the entire village before they rode away in the night. As hard as we tried, we could not save three of the children and two elderly people, along with many of our animals. When the dawn approached we were looking at what was left of our village: ashes and charred beams. That was the moment I decided that I could no longer live like a helpless animal.

"It was then a few young men and I took to the woods. We struck up with a band of highwaymen who were eager to teach us the art of ambush. I became a good archer and a respected member of the band. When the leader was killed, they selected me to be their new chief. While I enjoyed attacking a solitary knight or squire and taking their money, I did not like to confront defenseless people. As one with the power to deprive others of what they had worked for, I was not proud of my actions, so I left the outlaws. Still, I had learned about forest survival, so I went to the nearest town to become a hunter in the service of a nobleman. At the nobleman's court there were several knights who often practiced at arms on the field below the castle. Every time I saw them I felt angry, but more often than before, the anger would give way to sadness over the loss of my loved ones. Slowly, I began to think more clearly. I asked to shoot with them and I beat them all. It was an exhilarating moment, and I knew that I could no longer hate all knights. Since that day, I have made a good living from my bow. Still, I enjoy humiliating one who thinks his lofty status entitles him to vanquish a lowly hunter. "

Alf looked at Erik, again aware of the world around them. Erik gazed back, but he was still in Alf's world. "The knights who ravaged your village still do not know, or even care about the results of their actions," said Erik. Then he added, "But I am a knight. Why are you confiding in me?"

"I noticed you appraising me earlier as worthy of consideration solely because of my ability. You judged me as a man. And there are good knights and bad knights, and, to me, you turned out to be . . . a man." Alf laughed, embarrassed.

"I confess that I often act without thought of others. I am afraid that is the curse of privilege. But as you might know, my father instituted a law that travelers must recompense common people for food and shelter."

"Such a law will never work. To whom should we complain? Who will stand up for us?"

It was late in the day when the preparations were finished for the grand finale of the tournament and the two knights stood mounted in the middle of the field. Erik was relieved to see that Mats looked fit and showing no trace of pain.

Johan Brunkow, as usual, was wearing the colors of Queen Marta as he had done ever since he won his first tournament in her honor. Birger was fond of their champion, especially since he had won many bets on Johan's tournament skills over the years. But today his young knight looked edgy. This would be the first time Johan was to meet Mats on the field, and Erik knew that he had great respect, bordering on envy, for his opponent. Mats was the quintessential knight: he possessed superb ability with weapons; and coming from an old line of Viking chieftains, without a drop of foreign blood, he had the background Johan had yearned for all his life. Mats was respected by every noble family, while Johan had always been treated as a German upstart. If Johan could vanquish Mats today, people would have to treat him with more respect. This was the most important joust of his life.

The two knights spurred their horses out on the field. Facing off for battle, both had chosen the mace as their first weapon of attack. After bowing to one another, they closed on horseback and the battle began. Their blows were vicious and effective. Suddenly, after a long round of relentless fighting, Johan struck a perfect blow against Mats' shoulder that sent him reeling to the ground. Mats still had his mace clutched in his hand, while Johan lost his in striking his opponent. Before Johan could turn his horse and attack the fallen man, Mats managed to get to his feet and unsheathe his sword. With a mace in one hand, the eerily shining Gram in the other, and his shield slung over his shoulder, he waited for Johan's attack. Johan quickly drew his horse to a stop. With his opponent standing firmly on the ground armed with two weapons, while he himself had only his sword, he knew that his horse would have to take the blows. A good battle horse was worth a fortune, and rather than having the animal's legs crushed by his opponent's weapons, Johan dismounted. The crowd went wild. They loved watching a fallen knight regain the upper hand. As Johan dismounted and drew his sword, Mats threw away his mace, and the spectators again roared their approval. This was chivalry at its best.

Both knights appeared to be of equal strength, and as their hand-to-hand combat continued, the spectators became less certain of who would emerge victorious. The ferocious pair kept the crowd breathless. The only sounds to be heard were the clashing of sword against shield and armor, and the heavy breathing of the combatants. Finally, Mats moved against his opponent with unexpected speed, and as Johan retreated before the onslaught, Mats struck a savage blow to his right shoulder that split the armor and penetrated the chain mail. Johan, stunned by pain, fell on his back. Mats quickly put Gram under Johan's neck mail, lifted it, and exposed his throat to the sword tip.

"Do you surrender?" he asked as he looked down on his prostrate opponent.

"Not unless my queen and king wish me to," grunted Johan between heavy breaths.

Mats looked towards King Birger and gestured with his head towards the fallen knight. The king made the sign of surrender. Mats withdrew his sword and the crowd roared. A group of Mats friends rushed forward, lifted him onto their shoulders, and carried him jubilantly in circles while Johan, now unconscious, was carried towards the physicians' tents.

Erik could see that Mats was straining to climb a platform to get onto his horse again, and he had difficulty sitting upright in the saddle when he rode toward the royal platform. As Sweden had won, King Hakon made the presentation, consisting of a gold chain with a pendant bearing the Swedish and Norwegian coats of arms. Mats, because he was almost doubled over, did not have to bow to receive the victor's chain that Hakon hung around his neck. Hakon handed him the prize--a beautifully crafted silver box containing a generous purse of gold.

Mats struggled to sit erect to savor the proud moment. After allowing the crowd to laud him with their seemingly endless cheers, he rode back toward his side of the field. Luckily his horse knew where it was going, since Mats lost consciousness and was found by his squire at the physician's tent, slumped over his mount. Hastily the squire and two soldiers got Mats down and into the tent.

Erik was enthusiastically lauded for his champion's victory, and he collected his bets with unconcealed pleasure. As the royal brothers walked towards the tents, Valdemar turned to Erik and whispered, "Did you see the look on Birger's face when Mats had Johan on the ground? He had all he could do to give the sign of surrender."

"It is the same old story," sighed Erik. "Mats is my champion, so Birger lost to me again."

Chapter 14

It was late November, and a heavy snowfall blanketed the sleeping city of Stockholm. Duchess Kristina had lost all track of time as she sat in her chamber, warming herself before a small fire in a portable grate and listening for steps in the corridor outside. She was waiting for Valdemar, but not hearing his characteristic walk, she wrapped the fur skins tighter around her and settled back in the chair.

Four nights earlier on her wedding night she had sat just like this, waiting for her husband to arrive. She had undressed and prepared herself, not with the nervousness or anticipation of a young bride, but rather with the calm resolve of a soldier going into battle for king and country. She had waited for Valdemar while going over in her mind every detail of the lavish wedding Marta had arranged. She had resisted Marta's insistance on making a big wedding for her because Birger and Marta's coronation was to take place so soon thereafter, but Marta had dismissed her protests.

She knew that she had been a beautiful bride. Her wedding dress, sewn from one of her new silks, drew gasps of admiration. Valdemar had given her a crown wrought of gold and encrusted with pearls, and she had been touched by the generous gift, resolving again to be the perfect wife. Her father had added an intricately carved gold belt, and the king and queen had given her three long strands of rare and precious pearls that were fastened at the shoulders with ornate gold clasps. The jewelry had set off her fair complexion, and her eyes had taken on the soft luster of the pearls.

She was surprised at how much she had enjoyed being the focus of attention. Valdemar had beamed at her proudly, while she had avoided looking at Erik's stony countenance. But then her day of glory had ended. When the long-awaited bridegroom finally had arrived in their quarters, he was drunk and supported on the arms of two friends. Giggling foolishly, they deposited his body on the bed and scrambled for the door, slamming it shut behind them. Not even its loud bang registered with Valdemar, who was flat on his back with his boots on the silk coverlet. Kristina was not naive enough to think that a man so drunk would soon regain consciousness; but it was her wedding night, and she felt obliged to wait.

In truth, she was relieved that Valdemar was in no condition to consummate their marriage. She knew it was her wifely duty to conceive children, but she was grateful that her initiation was not to occur that night.

Still, she waited most of the night in case he did awake. But knowing that Valdemar would be called to the morning hunt, she realized she had to do something. It would be embarrassing if a servant were to enter and find him fully dressed. She could not allow him to suffer that humiliation.

She rose from her place by the hearth and went to the bedside where he was sleeping. She began to pull off his boots. It was no easy task, and she almost fell backwards when the first boot came off. After more tugging and great exertion, she succeeded in getting the second one off. The belt and dagger were easy, and she felt encouraged as she attacked his tunic that had been her wedding gift to him. She had fashioned it of thick gold brocade, appliqued with his coat of arms. The shield was of dark blue velvet, its cross bars of white silk, and the standing lion had taken her months to embroider with fine gold thread.

Valdemar had been pleased with her gift and insisted on wearing it for the wedding. Now it was rumpled and stained with wine. She had to struggle to get it up to his shoulders. As she lifted his arms to pull it over his head, she prayed she would not strangle him. She exhaled with relief as she finally held it in her hands. Valdemar continued sleeping with a blissful smile on his face. Next came his shirt. She removed it with ease, having practiced with the tunic. She folded the clothes over a bench before attacking the final garment--his long hose. That was difficult because of his bodyweight. By lifting his hips, she got the hose over his buttocks, but something else in the front seemed to be preventing it from coming down. The duke, in his drunken stupor, boasted a proud erection. Had she been a woman of experience, she would have been gratified that he was so generously endowed; but instead she simply stared with a child's curiosity. She tried to make sense of all the gossip she had heard, and she was still transfixed as the cold night air shrunk the object of her attention. Finally, she pulled the blanket from under his body to cover him.

She went back to the fire, added some wood, and sat down to think about what to do next. If the seduction scene were to be convincing, she needed some blood. She had witnessed the morning ritual that inevitably followed a wedding in a royal household: the women of the castle would discreetly inspect the bed sheets, and everyone would soon know if the bride had been a virgin. Kristina was certainly a virgin, but she had to prove the opposite. She had to cut herself somewhere not easily detected by her ladies-in-waiting. Her solution was a nosebleed. She scratched her nose and went over to the empty side of the bed to lift the covers. She allowed the blood to stain her fingers, and then smeared it on the sheets halfway down the bed. Satisfied with the results, she went over to the basin to wash her hands. Now they could inspect as much as they pleased.

Once the nosebleed had stopped, she pulled off her robe, and crept under the covers. She glanced at Valdemar who had his face turned towards her. He looked like a peaceful child. She smiled to herself. She had done her initial wifely duties rather well, even if they were not those she had anticipated.

She was awakened from a fitful sleep by the master huntsman loudly announcing in the corridor that the royal hunt was soon to commence. Valdemar sat up, grabbed his head with a groan, saw that he was naked, and looked over at Kristina. His expression was one of total disorientation. He opened his mouth, but then closed it again, trying to remember what had occurred the night before. She was not about to help him.

"Good morning," he began hesitantly. "I seem to have lost my memory. I know I was drunk, and I apologize if I behaved badly. What happened?" he pleaded helplessly.

"We got married," she said innocently. "Do you not remember?"

"Of course, I do. You looked beautiful," he said with a soft smile, making her feel guilty for being so uncooperative.

"Are you referring to what happened after the banquet?" she relented.

"Exactly! Here we are undressed, and .. I think there's something I should remember, but I do not!"

She decided to help him out of his predicament. It was, after all, she who had been relieved over the fact that they had not made love.

"There is nothing to remember, Valdemar. You were carried here by two friends who dropped you on the bed where you promptly fell asleep."

"You mean . . . I did not . . . we did not. I should never have drunk so much . . ." he groaned. "How did I get out of my clothes?"

"I assumed that you did not want the world to know that you spent your entire wedding night asleep, so I removed them."

As if to illustrate her point, a knock was heard; and without awaiting permission, one of her new ladies-in-waiting entered followed by servants carrying trays of refreshment. One started the fire while the others busied themselves setting the table. The lady-in-waiting's eyes darted around the room to see what gossip she could bring to the kitchens.

"I think she was satisfied," smirked Valdemar after she and the servants had left. "Thank you for protecting my reputation."

"Your reputation is now my reputation," Kristina said seriously. "I bloodied the bedsheets, as well." Feeling suddenly embarrassed by her nudity, she reached for her robe before she stood up. She felt better being covered. She could see that Valdemar was hesitating, so she discreetly turned her back, allowing him to get out of bed to put on his robe.

"You have thought of everything," he said gratefully as he came up behind her to put his hands on her shoulders. "Thank you."

Feeling awkward, he let go of her and served himself a mug of beer. Then he devoured some eggs, venison and bread. The servants had placed his hunting gear on a bench, which he donned hastily. The silence was oppressive. Kristina kept her back to him, pretending to eat. She was not hungry and longed to be alone. He came over to kiss her cheek. As he left the room, she fought the urge to cry.

On their second night together, Valdemar was sober and in a good mood. As they lay in bed and he put his arms around her, she felt an involuntary shiver down her spine. She could not go through with it. She could not make love to him. She turned to face him to tell him so when she saw his profile in the dim light of the solitary candle by the bedside. She was stunned. In the soft light he looked like Erik. She closed her eyes to dispel the vision, but when she opened them again, the image was still there, and she marveled once again at how similar the brothers were. She was going to spend the night with Erik after all. As Valdemar kissed her, she acted as if in a trance. He was tender and gentle, and his kisses and caresses began to excite her. She responded to his every move, seeing Erik through her half-closed eyes. But as Valdemar was about to make love to her, he was not able.

He appeared surprised and he was clearly embarrassed. "I do not know what is wrong with me. This has never happened before." He took a deep breath while searching for an explanation. "Maybe I had too much to drink last night . . . maybe I need a good night's sleep."

She nodded and curled under the covers. She cursed herself for being so ignorant in these matters, not knowing what to do. She lay awake for a long time, feeling a tingling sensation in her body and debating her dishonesty in pretending it was Erik who had touched her. But she had to bear children, and she might as well conceive them with pleasure.

The next evening her radiance prompted some to hint to Valdemar that he had turned his bride into a ravishing beauty. She observed their surprise when he abruptly cut them off. That night he again was late in coming to their chamber, and when he walked through the door she could see that he was in a dark mood.

"Let us go to sleep. I am no good to you anyway," he said angrily as he tore off his tunic.

"Do not say that, Valdemar," she pleaded, not knowing what more to say. She sat quietly in the bed with her eyes locked on the covers until he climbed in next to her. She tried to caress him, but he turned his back to her. She spoke caringly and encouragingly, and after a while he relented. They began to kiss, and before long she could feel his strength against her body. She knew he wanted her, but again it was not to be.

He slammed his fists against the pillows. Tears of frustration filled his eyes. He left the bed and poured a cup of wine that he drained in one long gulp. She pleaded with him not to be so angry with himself. There must be some simple explanation. But he did not hear her as he downed one cup after another. When he returned to bed he promptly passed out. She saw a tear still wet on his cheek and wiped it softly with her finger. What could she do?

The same question was on her mind when she woke up the next morning to find that he had already slipped out of their chamber. She felt so helpless that she was ready to cry. Then the door opened, and to her astonishment in walked Ragna with two servants to light the fire and set the table for the morning meal.

"Good Morning, Lady Kristina," Ragna said with a small wink of caution. "I am to be one of your ladies." Speechless, Kristina looked on as the servants went about their chores.

"Stay, please," Kristina said to Ragna, as the servants were about to leave.

When the two women were alone, Kristina looked in disbelief at her old friend from Nykoping castle. "What are you doing here?"

"Duke Valdemar sent for me since he felt that you would need someone you could trust, now that you are a duchess. I arrived from Nykoping yesterday. Duke Valdemar did not think it wise for anyone here to know how well we knew each other because then I might not be trusted by the servants, and I would be unable to bring you the gossip you should know."

"Ragna, you have no idea how grateful I am to have you here," said Kristina as she hugged her. "Your arrival is so timely. If you only knew."

"I have been taught how to act and serve by Lady Borg herself. She said she was very pleased with me," beamed Ragna.

"I know I will be too, Ragna. I am so very happy to have you with me. Both Ingeborg and Rikissa are gone," Kristina lamented with tears in her eyes, "and there are certain things that I cannot talk to Queen Marta about, or I will betray my husband." Kristina stopped when she saw the bewildered look on Ragna's face. Then she sat down and told Ragna the story of her short marriage.

"I always knew that you loved Duke Erik," said Ragna. "Still, you are Lord Torgils' daughter so you must do what is expected, and that is to bear children for Duke Valdemar. I think I might have a solution. There is someone who could help you, but she lives in town, and we cannot leave the castle unescorted. Maybe before you married a prince, but now we cannot."

"I will go anywhere to find a solution," insisted Kristina. "We will dress like merchants' wives, so we can move about the town freely, without appearing of too high status to do our own shopping. Can you arrange that?"

"Of course," smiled Ragna, eagerly.

"Let us leave after the morning meal," Kristina said as she sat down at the table. Ragna hurriedly left the chamber. Kristina hardly noticed how her food tasted. She was upset, confused and expectant, all at the same time. After what seemed like an eternity, Ragna, who had already changed her costume, arrived laden with clothes. Kristina looked at her and laughed.

"You look extremely respectable. Let me see what you have."

Ragna had selected warm garments as it was a cold day, and she helped Kristina pull on a full-length, green wool dress, and over it a dark blue wool tunic. Around Kristina's waist she hung a leather belt with a bunch of keys, put on a blue and green headdress, tying it under Kristina's chin, and then helped her on with a pair of thick boots. To complete the outfit she threw a long, fur-lined, green wool cape over Kristina's shoulders, fastening it with a silver clasp. Kristina looked at herself in a mirror. "The very image of a cloth merchant's wife," she smiled. "You have done well."

"We should hurry now while the servants are having their morning meal in the kitchens. I told everyone that you looked tired this morning and did not wish to be disturbed. No one will miss us for hours."

Kristina opened the door and peered down the corridor. Seeing no one, they ran quickly towards the Great Hall, but before entering, they descended a small staircase toward a narrow corridor below. Following it, they arrived at a thick wooden door that Ragna unlocked and then re-locked behind them. They reached the outer courtyard, passed through the main gate and over the drawbridge without attracting much attention other than the routine stare of the guards.

All at once they found themselves in a different world of sounds and smells. The snow crunched under their feet in the cold, and Kristina experienced an exhilarating feeling of freedom as they turned onto the main street leading to the Big Square. Kristina had been there many times before, but she never ceased to be fascinated by the commerce.

The low buildings housed shops of every kind. The two women slowed their pace to survey the offerings. One storekeeper displayed fragrances from all over the world, although most women could not afford the expensive, exotic oils for their baths. Still, the place was busily selling rose water and crushed lavender, which was a favorite among the merchant class. The shop next door contained leather goods; and Kristina, who loved the smell of the fresh hides, inhaled deeply. Its counter was crammed with satchels, boots, saddlebags, belts, tunics and slippers of all kinds and shapes. The shop beyond offered cloths and fabrics, some as thin as spiders' webs and some embroidered with gold. Slowly they progressed towards the Big Square. While the street selling finer goods had been relatively quiet, the sound level that met them at the food stalls was deafening. Every merchant was hawking his wares in a voice louder than his competitor's, and bargaining was done at the same noise level.

Amidst the stalls burned fires where the merchants and their customers warmed themselves while exchanging gossip. Kristina smiled when she heard comments about the royal wedding and how beautiful the bride had been. But mostly the merchants were complaining about the difficulty of having goods delivered when the seas were frozen, and as always, the women complained about the high prices. Kristina passed a spice stand where the smells of cardamom, cloves, thyme, marjoram, saffron and sandalwood hung heavy in the air. Not even the sight of two thieves manacled in the stocks and being spat upon by passers-by at the far end of the square--one with his ear cut off and the other branded on the forehead for their offenses--could dampen Kristina's excitement.

They passed stands offering ornamental wares--wreaths made of pinecones, garlands braided in straw, and wooden depictions of the holy family. One stand had candles in every different size and scent, and Kristina insisted on buying some for her room. She put them in a basket that Ragna carried over her arm and paid the merchant after bargaining only briefly. The merchant shrugged his shoulders as they left, surprised that a woman in her position had not bargained harder. But who was he to complain over small favors?

They turned down the street toward the harbor. Here they found the stores of the copper smith, the weapon smith, and the jeweler. They were fascinated by the selection of beautiful, everyday items displayed in the jeweler's store. Kristina could not resist buying a silver belt for herself, and she bought Ragna a silver cape clasp. They walked giggling down the narrow street and turned to the right by the harbor. Here, they were met by new smells--fish, oil, and tar. Some shops were still offering fresh fish; but the selection at this time of year was limited and expensive, and most of the customers were buying from large casks of salted herring. Though it was early in the day, some men were already drunk, loitering around the doorways of the taverns. The boats and ships were creaking at their moorings as if anxious for the ice to melt and let them sail away again.

"Where are we going?" Kristina asked anxiously as they left the market area and Ragna walked confidently along the harbor.

"You will see," was the answer.

They struggled along the wharf against a cold wind and had to step aside as two ragged beggars sitting by a small fire outside the communal bathhouse reached out to them. They passed stores selling rope and sails before they came to a small, low stone building where Ragna stopped and knocked on the door. After a while they heard slow, shuffling steps.

"Who seeks me on this cold day?" whined a querulous voice.

"We are here to ask your advice," answered Ragna, shivering in the cold wind.

"Then you are welcome," came the reply, and a bent old woman opened the door.

They had to lower their heads as they entered the dimly lit room. The old woman lived in a clean and comfortable house. A fire was flickering on the hearth, and iron pots filled with sweet smelling herb concoctions bubbled over the flames. An owl sat on a shelf blinking its eyes, scrutinizing the new arrivals. A black crow screeched and flapped its wings as they approached its perch that protruded from the wall. Two black cats were stretched out on the floor, peacefully sleeping the day away. The old woman gestured toward a bench on one side of a long table as she seated herself on the other side. As her face came into the light, Kristina jumped.

"The witch," she whispered almost inaudibly, pressing close to Ragna who did not seem afraid. Kristina, like everyone else in Stockholm, had heard stories of the old crone and her powers. Kristina felt frightened, but her trust in Ragna calmed her somewhat, and gradually the kind eyes of the old woman made her feel at ease in the warm, cozy room. The walls were hung with tapestries from floor to ceiling, woven so skillfully by the old woman that they had become legendary throughout the town. They depicted forest settings with trolls, elves, gnomes, and every animal imaginable. The scenes, despite a few evil-looking giants and dwarfs, were filled with peace and harmony. The colors were chosen with great skill; and after one studied the tapestries for a while, they seemed to come alive. Many would-be purchasers had offered the old woman handsome sums, but she refused to sell any of them.

Kristina reluctantly turned away from the haunting tapestries exclaiming "They are exquisite!"

"I am glad you like them," said the old woman kindly. "But that is not why you came."

Kristina hesitated, bit her lower lip, and remained silent.

"I will leave you two alone," Ragna said quickly.

"Go into my weaving room," replied the old woman pointing to a door in the far shadows of the room. Ragna took a candle and closed the door behind her.

"I do not know where to start," said Kristina close to tears.

"Now, now, my girl," said the old woman soothingly. "Nothing can be that bad. Let's see if I can help you."

"I am just married, and my husband cannot make love to me," whispered Kristina. "I think he wants to, but he is not able to. I do not know why, and I do not know if it is my fault, or what I can do about it."

Little by little, the old woman coaxed the details out of the blushing bride, and then sat silent for a moment. "You are a lovely young woman and of a high-born family. That I can plainly see. Any man would take a fancy to you, and your husband has, if I understand correctly. But something is preventing him from fulfilling his desires. That barrier is within him, my dear. I have an herb all the way from Constantinople, which has been used for as long as anyone can remember. It allows a man to enjoy what is before him, and to forget all else for that moment. If your husband is successful once, that should break the spell. I will prepare some, and we shall see what happens," the old woman finished with a kindly smile on her wrinkled face.

She shuffled over to an open cupboard, which held hundreds of jars and bottles, and searched until she found what she was looking for. She brought a jar to the table and opened it. It contained small brown lumps. She poured some on the table, selected one and returned the rest to the bottle. She put the lump in a small iron pot and heated it over the fire, watching the contents slowly soften. She carefully added some liquid and stirred, removing the pot from the fire before it began to boil. She took an empty vial from her large collection, poured the liquid into it, corked it, and gave it to Kristina.

"At night, when you are alone, add a few drops to his wine. He will not taste it."

Kristina, who had been totally absorbed in the preparation of the love potion, took the precious little vial and put it in her tunic pocket. "Thank you. I am so grateful," she said before hesitantly continuing. "Would you tell me about my future? I do not mean to impose . . ."

"With pleasure, my dear," said the old woman as she stood up to fetch a deep silver dish that she placed on the table. She poured some hot water in the dish and once more went over to her cupboard. She returned with two jars, and from one she poured out a white powder that sizzled as it mixed with the water. From the other jar, she sprinkled thick black powder that swirled around the dish. When the sizzling stopped, the black powder sank, depositing itself over strange figures carved into the bottom of the silver dish.

"The configuration of the black substance over the magic symbols will tell me about your life that has been, and your life that will be," whispered the old woman. One of the black cats soundlessly jumped up on the table and sat down, folding his tail around his front paws and looked intently into the dish as if he were following every detail of the ritual.

"You have lived in a large household surrounded by many people," said the old woman in a monotonous voice, almost as if she was chanting. "You have lost people important to you, and you will lose more. I see betrayal and death among those close to you. But when life seems at its darkest, you will find happiness." Her voice faded as she sat looking in the plate. "Remember: when all seems dark, happiness will enter your life, and you will be at peace. I can tell you no more than that," the old woman concluded, as she looked up with tenderness and pity in her eyes.

Kristina wondered what more the wise old woman had seen in the water, but she knew it would not help to ask, so she shakily called for Ragna who emerged, shivering, from the unheated room. Kristina put a small gold coin on the table and stood up.

"You have been extremely generous, my lady," said the wise old woman. "But even before you showed your gratitude, I had planned to give you a small gift." She shuffled across the room and disappeared into the weaving chamber. When she returned, she held a small tapestry in her hand. It was no larger than a foot square, but it depicted in great detail a woodsman holding a wounded doe in his arms. Kristina drew a deep breath in admiration.

"It is lovely. I have heard that you refuse to part with your tapestries at any price."

"That is so," smiled the old woman. "But I sometimes give them as gifts. If you ever feel sad, just look at it, and it might ease your pain."

"Thank you . . . for everything," said Kristina as she prepared to leave with Ragna.

Kristina held the tapestry tightly under her mantle and imagined that it warmed her in the driving wind as they hurried along the wharf and turned up the street leading towards the square. They returned to the castle undetected. After changing her clothes and asking Ragna to bring her something to eat, Kristina busied herself with exchanging the candles in the room for those she had bought. When she had eaten and was alone, she took out the small vial. She smiled as she put it back. Everything was going to be fine. She actually felt happy as she dozed off in front of the fire with the lovely little tapestry spread out on her lap.

From the moment he had awoken after his wedding night Valdemar had felt the full impact of his humiliating failure. He had stood in the corridor outside their chamber for a long time, trying to compose himself. When he had finally descended to the Great Hall, he spotted Erik, and for the first time in his life he was not happy to see his brother. He slowed his pace to allow Erik to reach the courtyard first where the hunting party was gathering. Once Valdemar was mounted, his horse quickly took the lead at the head of the group of eager young men determined to reach the edge of the forest before the rest.

However fast he rode in the cold winter morning through the soft snow, he could not escape his feelings of remorse. Kristina's resolute little face when she had told him of the measures she had taken to hide his inability to consummate their marriage burned in his memory. What a lucky man he was to have found such a wife, and what a cad he was to have taken her from the one she loved and who loved her in return. He had caught a glimpse of Erik's face during the wedding ceremony and had actually felt his pain. These were the two people he cared for above all others, and he had brought them nothing but unhappiness. Dear God in Heaven, he prayed silently, let everything be as it was between us, let us remain friends. But even as he prayed he knew that everything had changed. He felt isolated, distanced from his brothers, apart from Kristina, and indescribably lonely.

He had not wanted to admit it but now, after three unsuccessful nights, it seemed painfully clear that he was useless in the marital bed. If Kristina had not been attractive he could have understood it; but she had been both alluring and loving. He had always enjoyed women, and they seemed to enjoy him. Even dead drunk he had performed adequately in the past. While he seemingly took part in today's activities with enthusiasm, his tormented mind was hunting elsewhere, asking questions that found no answers.

Later that afternoon, when the hunting party returned, he did not go to their chamber, but went instead to Erik's. Having avoided Erik for the past three days, he now felt a desperate need to recapture their closeness.

He found Erik sitting in front of a small fire, stripped of his sweat-soaked hunting gear and wrapped in a thick robe, warming his feet.

"What a nice surprise," Erik exclaimed warmly, though in a guarded tone. He gestured to a small table. "Have some hot wine. It was just brought in. And while you are at it, kindly refill my cup."

249

Valdemar complied, and told the servant who was removing Erik's soiled attire to have a change of his own clothing brought there. Erik gave Valdemar a curious look. "Is anything wrong?"

"You might say that," answered Valdemar as he pulled off his wet boots. "But I would rather not talk about it. Later, maybe, but not now." He sat down next to Erik. Then suddenly he put his face in his hands.

Erik looked at his brother who had not moved and put his arm around his shoulders. "Would you like to get away from here? Away from all these people we have been cooped up with for the past days. Would that make you feel better? How about the two of us spending a night carousing like we used to?"

Valdemar nodded his head without moving his hands. He was shamefully close to crying, and he did not want Erik to see him this way. Erik must have sensed Valdemar's despair, so he stood up to stoke the already briskly burning fire.

"We have not been to the Black Cat in ages. What do you say we go?"

"Fine," answered Valdemar without enthusiasm.

Valdemar composed himself and took a long drink of wine while Erik studied him with concern. Valdemar guessed that Erik was not eager to pry into the reasons for his unhappiness, since Erik himself had looked miserable since the wedding. As they always had in the past, they would try to cheer each other up without too many questions.

By the time they had changed their clothes, they were already a little drunk. Erik left word that they would not attend the evening meal, and they walked through quiet castle corridors since most of the guests were resting and the servants were in the kitchens and the Great Hall preparing for the evening's festivities. When they reached the guard's quarters they requested an escort to accompany them to the Black Cat tavern. The captain had no difficulty finding ten volunteers for the excursion. After leaving the castle grounds, they entered the quiet street that earlier had been filled with bustling commerce. The counters had been pulled up over the shop openings and light spilled through the cracks as the merchants and their families, who lived within, enjoyed their supper. They emerged at the Big Square that was never quiet. On one side was a tavern that commonly closed by early morning, and across from it was an inn where people came and went at all hours. Its patrons' horses were stabled on a side street into which the princes and their escorts turned.

Some twenty yards from the stable hung a wrought iron sign depicting a hissing black cat. Two of their escort went into the tavern and returned, gesturing for Erik and Valdemar to enter. This was one of the best taverns in the kingdom; and Anskar, its owner, had become wealthy from the constant flow of customers. Anskar, named by his devout mother for the monk who brought Christianity to Sweden, made his living selling sin rather than salvation. While for most the tavern was a place for good food and drink, for men of wealth it was also a brothel.

The princes were respectfully greeted by two giant doormen whose task was to eject unwanted or unruly customers. The captain of the guard and his men stamped the snow off their boots and settled down by one of the fires. Part of their job was to have a good time and behave as would any customer. Unfortunately, they would only be served one beer an hour so as to remain alert if any kind of trouble developed. Still, this was coveted duty since the Black Cat was a place the soldiers could rarely afford at their own expense, and where danger was quite unlikely to ensue. Yet no man was without enemies, and one never knew what could happen on the way home.

Anskar came running as fast as his corpulent physique permitted to greet his esteemed guests. "What a pleasure, what a pleasure to have you here again. Please follow me." He led them, beaming, in a half trot across the tavern which, as usual, was filled to capacity.

Anskar opened a small green door in the far wall and gestured for the princes to enter. They had to lower their heads as they went through into a high-ceilinged room with a huge fire roaring on the hearth. Comfortable chairs draped with fur skins were placed around the fire, and tables of varying sizes were scattered about the room. A few customers were already enjoying the famous foods and wines of the house. "Would you like some supper, your Highnesses, or some company perhaps?" Anskar smiled as he wrung his fat hands.

"We will start with supper," replied Erik after a consenting nod from Valdemar.

"Would you like it in here, or would you prefer a private room?" inquired the eager host, as he gestured towards some drawn curtains that concealed private dining areas along the far wall.

"I would like to sit right here," said Valdemar with a look at Erik who concurred. It would give them a clear view of the balcony that ran over the private dining rooms and along both sidewalls. It was connected to the large room by an open staircase. Small rooms were hidden in the shadows of the balcony where the ladies of the house entertained their guests. When they were free, they would often walk from one room to another, giving the customers a chance to look them over while dining.

"I hope you will have an enjoyable evening, your Highnesses," said Anskar. "What can I bring you to eat? The full menu or the small supper?" Knowing that the small supper contained six different dishes, Erik and Valdemar decided it would suffice. They ordered some of Anskar's fragrant Spanish wine that was a rarity anywhere but at the Black Cat.

As usual the tasty fare was a pleasure, and Valdemar gradually felt better. Before long the two brothers were laughing at memories of former escapades. All the time they kept their eyes on the balcony, and after a while Erik asked. "Are you interested in visiting upstairs? If you are, we should tell Anskar before the other guests make their choices."

"The dark-haired one in red looks just like what I could use tonight," answered Valdemar.

"I think that tall, blonde girl in green looks very much to my liking." Erik told a servant to get Anskar. When the proprietor arrived, the princes expressed their preferences.

"Ah, the lovely senorita for you," mused Anskar to Valdemar. "You have excellent taste. And for you," Anskar was beaming as he turned to Erik, "The snow maiden from Iceland. Nothing but the best." His face took on a serious expression. "Your excellent taste, however, will cost you . . . but . . ." he added rapidly as Erik's steel blue eyes bore into him, "being old customers of the house I will charge you nothing extra for these exquisite ladies."

"I would think so," mumbled Erik, as he gave Anskar the sum in advance. Anskar happily trotted off to inform the ladies of their good fortunes. Erik and Valdemar settled down to enjoy the rest of their meal.

Since the time Birger had started to build a separate life for himself, Erik and Valdemar had grown even closer, and it was only the events of the past months, and especially the last few days, which had kept them apart from one another. Neither of them had liked it, and without voicing their innermost feelings, they both knew that their fraternal bond was stronger even than the strained situation in which they presently found themselves. So, despite their inner turmoil, they enjoyed their dinner together.

After they finished eating, they went upstairs for the pleasures of the balcony. Valdemar found the small room belonging to the sultry senorita, bid Erik good night, and closed the door behind him. The girl was sitting on the only piece of furniture in the room, a wide bed. She had a fringed black shawl wrapped around her that she coyly let drop from one shoulder, exposing one huge white breast. She smiled at the handsome man standing in front of her.

The girl was more voluptuous than any woman Valdemar had ever seen. His immediate response made his hose tighten around his groin. Slowly she let the shawl drop all the way down to her waist and Valdemar stared at both large breasts and provocative nipples that tightened from exposure to the cold air. He walked over to her and sat down. She took his hand and brought it to her breast. The softness under his palm brought forward all the desire he had not been able to release over the past nights.

He savored her warm skin before he slowly stood up and pulled off his clothes. She was eyeing him with appreciation as she allowed her shawl to slip open to reveal that she was totally naked underneath. Valdemar did not dare to wait another minute, fearing he might falter again, so he lowered himself over her as she slid down to accommodate him. As he dove into her wet, soft body he felt himself harder than ever. And he lasted so long that the girl went against her professional principles and climaxed with him.

"Ah, Dios mio!" she exclaimed as Valdemar rolled down beside her.

Valdemar relished her tone, even if he did not understand the words. He was relieved beyond belief. There was nothing wrong with him, thank the Lord. He asked the girl, who understood Norse quite well, to bring them some of Anskar's Spanish wine. Happy at the prospect of drinking her costly native brew, she wrapped herself in her shawl and left the room.

Not only had he succeeded in making love to the girl, he had done a marathon job of it. He shut his eyes in gratitude. But then the gnawing question returned. Why had he not been able to make love to Kristina?

The girl returned with a large carafe of wine. She poured a cup for him and filled one for herself. In her halting Norse, she told him about her warm and sunny homeland. He felt at ease as he listened to her tales, and they became quite drunk as they continued filling and emptying their cups. She invited him to more lovemaking, and he eagerly accepted--to reassure himself that he had fully recovered from his temporary lapses. He celebrated his second success with more wine. The girl stumbled into her shawl once more to refill the pitcher.

He continued to ponder why he could not make love to his bride when he was so successful with this girl, but still he could find no answer. The girl returned with the wine, and they embarked on more drinking and lovemaking. Finally, she fell asleep, leaving Valdemar with his carafe and his questions. Why, with a woman sated by his side, should he be anguished by thoughts of another with whom he had failed?

He knew the answer. It had slowly come to his conscious mind. He had begun to care about Kristina in a new and different way. He stood up from the bed, spilling wine on the floor. He lurched over to where his clothes had been thrown, put them on with considerable effort, and then he opened the door to the balcony. Only a few guests were still in the dining room below, but he could hear moans and laughter coming from the small rooms off the landing. He knew that he was very drunk when he tripped upon the stairs and the remaining guests politely pretended not to notice. He opened the low door into the tavern and headed for the exit. The captain of the guard hurried over to ask him if they should wait for Erik, but Valdemar angrily brushed him aside and stumbled out into the street. The captain quickly ordered five of his men to escort Valdemar home.

Kristina awakened from her fitful sleep in the chair as the door opened.

"Erik?" she asked in her half sleep.

Valdemar flung the door closed behind his back and stood staring at her. Then he staggered closer, pointing a wagging finger.

"No, this is your husband, my lady. I am sorry to disturb your precious dreams," he said infuriated by her one word. "I am here to inform you that there is nothing wrong with me. I have just bedded three times, so there is nothing, whatsoever, the matter with me!" He stopped in front of her, breathing heavily. "It is your fault. The whole thing is your fault. You love Erik and not me!"

She stared at him. "I told you how I felt, Valdemar. You said you understood."

Valdemar rocked back and forth, trying to control his frustration. "I will not bother you henceforth, my lady," he slurred. "You will be safe from me here in your bedroom with your precious dreams!" He turned and stumbled out of the chamber, slamming the door behind him.

She was shaken, unable to understand what had triggered this outburst. It was common practice, she knew, for even happily married men to pay for women of lower station. Out of respect to one's wife, however, these things were never to be mentioned. Obviously, her husband did not even care enough about her to observe common courtesies. She surrendered to the welling tears. She felt ashamed and alone. She had already lost the man she loved, and now she was losing her husband.

She looked at the untouched chalice of wine that held a few drops from the Wise woman's vial. She cried for hours and did not get to sleep until shortly before Ragna came to awaken her. She told Ragna not to disturb her for the rest of the day, and upon seeing her mistress' swollen face, Ragna promptly withdrew, taking the wine cup with her to be cleaned.

The young manservant who found the wine-filled cup in the kitchen looked to see if anyone was watching. No one saw him drain it dry. After a while he got an irresistible urge to take one of the scullery maids to the haylofts. As she had work to do, she followed him only after considerable protest, but she did not regret her decision as the amorous fellow displayed endless inventiveness to his love-making. The young man wondered fleetingly what had possessed him; but he was too sated by the wine laced with hashish to give it a second thought.

Stockholm castle was shrouded in darkness when Valdemar awoke the following morning. Pain from heavy drinking pounded his head and tore at his stomach, but the ache he felt in his heart was far worse. He tried to review what had taken place the night before at the Black Cat and thereafter with Kristina. He groaned in anguish. When he sat up, he realized that he was in the chamber he and Erik used to share. He looked over toward his brother's side of the bed, but Erik had not returned. Valdemar stood up and went over to the bucket in the corner to splash some water on his face and to drink deeply from the cup attached by a long cord. The cool wetness made him feel a bit better, and he walked over to a large mirror only to see his tired, unhappy face staring back at him. He took off the shirt in which he had fallen asleep and pulled on one of Erik's which he found neatly folded in his brother's locker. As he silently walked down the corridor to his and Kristina's chamber he tucked the shirt into his hose and pulled his fingers through his hair. This was one conversation that could not wait.

He quietly opened the door to their chamber and walked in. The candle by the bedside was burning and Kristina was asleep. As he walked closer he could see that she had been crying, for her face was still swollen. He was filled with remorse as he looked at her. But before he could speak or move closer she awoke and sat up with her hair falling over her face and flowing down her shoulders. As she pulled the cover close around her and tried to adjust her eyes to the light, she seemed so small and vulnerable. He must have hurt her incredibly, and he felt like a knave as he sat down at her bedside.

"Please forgive me, Kristina," he pleaded as he took her hand in his. "I have treated you shamefully. I assure you that I will never act that way again."

"How am I to behave?" she asked directly.

"We have always been friends, let it stay that way," he said softly. "We should live together as friends . . . not as man and wife."

"You mean that we will never have children?" she asked, incredulously.

He had avoided thinking about the need to produce an heir. "Well . . . not now anyway," he mumbled, skirting the subject.

"I always wanted to have children," she whispered as her eyes blurred.

He reached out and took her other hand. "I do not understand what is happening to me, Kristina, but I know I cannot be a real husband to you now. Maybe with time . . ."

"Meanwhile we should continue to live together as we always have. Is that what you want?" she asked. He nodded. She let out a sudden sigh of relief. "I did not know what you expected of me, I was so confused. I felt that you hated me last night."

"Kristina, we are in a situation much more complex than we first thought. Had I known how difficult this would be maybe I would not have accepted your father's offer. But it seemed so natural that we would always be together. You have been like a sister to me. Now . . . I am confused. But I certainly do not hate you. If I hate anyone it is myself.

She put her hand on the small fish hanging around her neck and reached out to touch the wolf fang hanging around his. "We made a promise once; to be friends, always," she said and leaned over to kiss him on the cheek.

He still could not find words, but he looked at her with deep gratitude. She patted his side of the bed. "You need some sleep. You look terrible, as I expect I do."

Valdemar stood up and took off Erik's shirt before he sat down to pull off his boots and hose to crawl under the covers. Kristina turned towards him. She smiled sadly, but with tenderness, as he murmured "Good sleep, my sweet wife."

Erik sat back in his chair with his feet up on the edge of the fire pit in the Great Hall. He was not feeling his best even though he had slept most of the day, recovering from the final night of Birger and Marta's coronation festivities. Most of the guests from far and wide had departed, but still the Great Hall was crowded and busy around him. Music could be heard amidst laughter and shouts from the game tables. He looked over to where Birger and Marta sat in their chairs-- the same chairs in which his father and mother had been sitting when he was the age of little Magnus who was now playing by his parents' feet. Both Birger and Marta were laughing at their son's antics, and the domestic scene looked utterly blissful. Valdemar and Kristina sat close by, and Erik felt a pang of jealousy when he saw how relaxed and at ease they looked together.

The urge to escape the tranquil scene was almost irresistible; to be with his comrades drinking and gambling, without a serious thought. He knew that manner of relief was only temporary, yet he had accepted Hakon's invitation to get away and visit the Norwegian court, hopefully to gain perspective on his present situation.

His suggestion that Valdemar should come to live with him at Nykoping had been a wise one after all. He craved that closeness. Even though he hurt at the very thought of seeing Kristina every day, knowing that she shared his brother's bed at night; that thought was less threatening than living alone, without a single family member. And, in truth, he wanted Kristina close as well. He had arranged for carpenters, masons, and painters to refurbish Nykoping castle as he wanted Kristina to be happy in her role as its mistress. Still, he was not ready to confront that situation just yet. He had to concentrate on the future he himself had chosen. The future of ruling a kingdom that any sane man would choose.

Chapter 15

Norway

Erik was suitably impressed when he beheld Akershus, the newly built Norwegian royal castle standing proudly on a peninsula surrounded by water on three sides. King Hakon intended the huge fort, parts of which were still under construction, to one day be the mightiest fortress in all Scandinavia.

The boat trip to Norway had passed uneventfully. The weather had been mild, so the ship easily found passage through waterways not yet frozen. Abjorn and Mats had done what they could during the voyage to cheer Erik's mood, and by the time their ship reached Oslo, he was in lighter spirits and looking forward to spending time with his prospective in-laws.

Once their ship had docked, the travelers approached the castle through its only entrance in the Maiden's tower, then continued up through a steep covered walkway appropriately named the Dark Passage. They emerged through the Birdsong Gate turret into the spacious North courtyard that was dominated by the huge Daredevil tower, still under construction but destined to reach an incredible height of sixty feet.

The Great Hall in which King Hakon received them was no less impressive. Its cathedral-like ceiling and its fire hearths were enormous. Intricate and vividly colored woodcarvings spread like wings from the ceiling rafters and walls. The painted patterns that were reminiscent of Viking runes gave the huge chamber an imposing, almost eerie feeling of being both a church and a pagan place of worship.

On a large, finely carved chair sat King Hakon with the beautiful Queen Euphemia beside him. The courtiers crowding the Hall bowed deeply as Erik and his men passed the many long tables lining the walls to approach the monarch. Erik became acutely aware that the obeisances were not those normally accorded a high-ranking visitor, but more like obeisance made to a king. Or, thought Erik with pleasure, a future king.

Seeing so many Norwegian courtiers gathered together strengthened his impression that they more closely resembled their Viking forebears than either the Danes and the Swedes who had adopted a more continental style. The Norwegians all favored silver jewelry covered with rune inscriptions and their clothes were closely fashioned after the traditional Viking garb, making them appear fiercer than their Scandinavian neighbors. Inspired by the respect in these men's eyes, Erik in turn bowed deeply to their king. That evoked a murmur of approval, and as he straightened up he saw Hakon come forward to embrace him warmly. The shouts of hail that rang through the cavernous Hall told him that he was, indeed, the accepted heir to the Norwegian throne.

Once the courtiers drew away to allow their king and his guests some privacy, Erik greeted the men Hakon had chosen to attend him during his stay. The first to come forward was Count Jakob of Northern Halland. King Hakon's gesture of allowing his most trusted advisor and friend to be Erik's guide while in Norway was, in itself, a great compliment. A Norwegian of Erik's own age, Bjarne Lodinsson, who was to serve as his chamber man and squire was introduced next, and Erik immediately took a liking to the tall and open-faced knight.

The third man to come forward piqued Erik's curiosity as he waited for an introduction. This man was older, in his thirties, thin, tall and somber looking. He reminded Erik of someone, though he could not think of who it could be. The man's eyes were guarded when he looked at Erik, betraying a strange mixture of curiosity and disdain.

"This is your and my cousin, Erik Valdemarson," smiled Hakon looking kindly at the man. "It is high time the two of you got to know one another since I value both your friendships."

This must be old King Valdemar's only son, Erik thought, realizing why the face looked familiar. Erik could well understand the look of dislike as the man greeted him with a bow as slight as possible without insulting both Erik and King Hakon. Had his father not fallen in love with a nun he would now be the King of Sweden instead of having to grow up in a foreign court, the object of his cousin's generosity without riches or power.

"I welcome you, my kin," Erik Valdemarson offered with a perfect Norwegian accent. "I trust you had a pleasant journey."

"Thank you, cousin, we did." Erik answered in the customary exchange of politesse while wondering why Hakon had brought them together without even a hint or warning. During King Hakon's wedding, Erik Valdemarsson had not been present--for whatever reason--but now he was thrust upon Erik in a manner uncomfortable for them both. He found it impossible to express his sympathies for old King Valdemar's passing earlier in the year in this akward situation.

"Tomorrow we will go hunting, just a small group of us," Hakon quickly announced as if reading Erik's mind. A few men, banding together against nature, could more easily forge friendly bonds. "Now, you must be fatigued after your long journey. Bjarne will show you to your chamber."

The following morning when the hunting party set out it had started to snow gently. The day was cold and crisp, and steam from the breath of men and horses floated about their faces. All the men were dressed for the weather in fur-lined clothes, hats and boots, and prepared to stay outdoors as long as necessary. They rode in file on a small path at a good pace, and after they had ridden for an hour to reach the depth of the forest, the snow suddenly became heavier and the wind strengthened.

"This does not look good," King Hakon said as he studied the dark sky "I think we might be in for a bad storm."

"Then I suggest we seek shelter in my hunting lodge while we can still find our way," called Erik Valdemarsson over the increasingly strong wind. "We are only a short distance from there," he added before King Hakon nodded his assent.

The short distance turned out to be another hour of slow riding though blinding, gusting snow. The storm clouds blocked most light, and they rode in virtual darkness while snow drifts piled up on the path making it harder and harder to navigate among the trees. The icy snow blew in under their hoods and up their sleeves, and they were all grateful when they finally could see lights flickering in the distance. They came upon a scattering of small huts that Erik Valdemarsson, riding at the head of the line, passed before he called a halt at a large house situated in their midst.

The men dismounted, and four young stable boys took their horses. After stamping the snow off their feet, and brushing it off their clothes, the men entered the cold, dark house. Erik Valdemarsson shouted for his servants in an impatient voice, and they came running from the huts to build fires and light candles.

Once the fire in the center pit was burning brightly, Erik looked around. The house consisted of one large hall with built-in beds lining the walls. Two long tables were standing close to the fire, flanked by long fur-covered benches. The walls featured elaborate carvings painted in brightly colored traditional Viking patterns, and they were further decorated with fine weapons. The tables were being set with finely wrought silver plates and cups. It clearly was the house of a wealthy man. Erik wondered if old King Valdemar had been able to smuggle such riches out of Sweden for his son.

As if he was reading Erik's thoughts, Erik Valdemarsson explained "This estate was my wife's dowry--she is dead now--and I only come here with hunting parties, as it is quite out of the way. But the farm does give me a good living."

"It is a fine place," Erik said quickly to conceal his uncharitable thoughts. He accepted a cup of hot, spiced wine offered by an old woman servant. "To your good health, my lords, and a special 'thank you' to our host for this most welcome shelter," he added as he savored the warmth of the drink.

The men toasted their host before they settled down in front of the fire. As the old servant woman went around refilling their cups, Erik heard Erik Valdemarsson speak to her in a hushed but angry tone.

"Why are you not living in the main house, as usual? It felt utterly inhospitable to enter this cold and empty place."

"It is the vetters," she hissed before she scurried away to replenish her pitcher.

Before Erik could ask his host what the old woman had meant, Erik Valdemarsson became engrossed in a conversation with Jakob and Abjorn. Erik forgot the incident as the evening wore on during which they enjoyed a fabulous feast of fine and varied roast game, and the best beer Erik had ever consumed.

"This mead tastes as if Odin himself had brewed it," Mats said enthusiastically, alluding to the most powerful of the Viking gods. The others readily agreed.

"Where did you get it?" King Hakon asked as he motioned for one of the servants to refill his mug.

"We brew it here," Erik Valdemarsson replied.

"Then what is your secret?" continued the king. "I thought I had the best brew master in the land. Clearly I was wrong."

"Believe it or not, that woman has done it for as long as I can remember," said Erik Valdemarsson with a nod towards the old woman who had just entered carrying a small cask on her hunched shoulder.

"You must give me your recipe," said Hakon kindly as the woman put the cask on the table and removed the plug from the bunghole.

"That, I cannot do," she snapped, and then she quickly left the house.

"She did not know who was asking her," said Erik Valdemarsson embarrassed. "Once she realizes that it was her king's request, she will be delighted to give the recipe to Your Majesty."

"I would hope so," said Hakon, not knowing whether he should be annoyed or amused as he leaned back in the chair of honor. "But meanwhile, let us enjoy her brew."

The servants brought in cask after cask in a seemingly endless parade. The brew intoxicated the men in the most delightful manner, and they thoroughly enjoyed the evening, completely forgetting their disappointment over the cancelled hunt.

After a while, Erik stood up to relieve himself. As he opened the door he saw that the snow had piled high outside and that the servants had had to dig a walkway to their huts.

"I need to, as well," slurred Bjarne Lodinsson who passed Erik and positioned himself in front of a snow bank at the side of the house.

"Look out, vetters," he called as he relieved himself with a big sigh.

Erik, desiring some fresh air, walked farther away from the house into the icy night. Just as he finished his task and was about to escape the cold whirling snow, the old woman came along the path.

"They will appreciate your consideration," she said as she passed him, carrying yet another small cask of beer into the house.

"She must be insane," Erik muttered to himself before returning to the warmth of the large room where he was quickly drawn into the animated conversations of his friends.

It was late when the men finally went to sleep in the beds along the walls while the servants slept on the floor. As Erik reposed on the soft, fresh straw mattress and pulled the down covers around him, he felt happy for the first time in a long time. Despite all the beer he had consumed, he did not feel drunk. He felt only a glorious haze of bliss, and it was with Kristina's face smiling lovingly before him that he drifted off while the wind and snow whirled around the house.

Interspersed in his dreams of victorious battles against great warriors were dreams of little people looking down on him with curious eyes. When he awoke he felt refreshed and rested, without the slightest trace of discomfort from the copious quantity of beer he had consumed the night before.

"I cannot believe how well I feel," said King Hakon who was already sitting by the brisk fire the servants had prepared. " I am glad you are up, Erik, so that you can help me open the door. I am ready to burst."

Erik realized that no one had yet been outside where the snow had piled high against the walls and door. Erik had to climb out through a small window to shovel the snow away from the portal so he could force it slightly ajar.

"That is all I need," said Hakon as he relieved himself in the snow.

"Not there!" protested the little old woman sternly.

"Do you know to whom you are speaking?" Erik asked her as he stood brushing snow off his clothes.

"They do not care who you are," she persisted. "King or beggar, it is all the same to them."

"I think you had better explain to me who "they" are," said Erik as he, too, prepared to do his business.

"She is talking about the vetters," said Hakon. "They live a reclusive life on our farms, just like your tomtes, helping us with chores in exchange for a place to live. But instead of living in our barns they live underneath our houses. When you heed the call of nature, or pour out dirty water next to your house, it leaks right down to their dwellings which they do not appreciate."

"I see," said Erik, as he remembered the many stories he had heard since childhood about the small tomtes who lived on an amicable basis with humans by sharing their daily chores. The only form of retaliation he had heard tomtes take against humans for mistreatment was to leave the farm where they lived, thereby forcing the farmer to do all the chores himself.

"Their retribution can be fearsome," said the old woman with passion.

"Let them be angry," concluded Erik Valdemarsson who had just arisen. "My guests should not have to be inconvenienced during their short visit here."

The old woman shook her head as she went about her business, and the men sat down to break fast and drink more of the fabulous beer. However, as snow was still falling and the wind was still howling, the group realized that they would not be able to go out hunting. Rather than being disappointed, they settled in for a lazy day of story-telling and gluttony. Erik saw, to his pleasure, that there were several casks of beer piled up at the end of the room.

The day passed most pleasantly as more beer was consumed, and many visits were made to the door step. It was late in the afternoon when a deeply apologetic and disappointed Erik Valdemarsson announced that the last cask was empty.

"We need some more beer, old mother," he said to the woman.

"We do not have any more," she said glumly.

"Surely, we do," insisted Erik Valdemarsson irritably. "There are always casks in the larder."

"How will I get there and bring any back through all this snow?" she asked.

"I will help you," volunteered Bjarne.

"We will all help you," suggested the king. "This heavenly brew is too good to be missed."

The men took any item they could find which could be used for digging, pulled on their gloves, mantles and boots, and ventured outside. With much laughter and joshing, thigh-high in snow, they finally dug their way to the storage hut. Tired and out of breath, they scraped away the icy snow to free the door which they eagerly pulled open. They did not want to believe what their eyes beheld. In a frozen mass of brown ice lay the wooden splinters of twenty smashed casks.

"Hell, and damnation!" cried Erik Valdemarsson.

"I told you," said the old woman behind them. "They do not like to be mistreated. That is why we moved out of the house, so as not to disturb them further after the last time the master came home with his friends."

"How dare you talk to me like this?" roared Erik Valdemarsson.

"Both of you, calm down," ordered King Hakon. "Could there not be another explanation?"

"The casks were untouched last night," the old woman said with a frown.

The men stood glumly surveying the disaster before Hakon sighed, "What else can we do but return to the house and wait out the storm?"

Sullenly, the men walked back through the wind and snow and silently disrobed. Erik realized that they might be there for days, and he could well imagine how ill tempered everyone would become without anything decent to drink.

"We will have some wine then," suggested Erik Valdemarsson trying to lift the pall.

"It all disappeared during the night," said the old woman. "Look, all the shelves are empty," she said as she pointed to the far wall where her master had kept his precious hoard.

"And all of this because we obeyed the call of nature outside my own house, on my own land," cried Erik Valdemarsson angrily.

The warm and comfortable atmosphere had suddenly evaporated around the seven men. Now the house seemed like a prison as they sat quietly around the fire. Erik could see that Erik Valdermarsson's anger had turned to despair over displeasing his king who sat staring into the flames with a sullen look.

"What can we do to make peace with your vetters?" Erik asked his host. When he got no answer, Erik looked demandingly at the old woman. "Your king is here. Would not the vetters want to honor him, however inconsiderate we have been?"

"They liked you," she finally said to Erik. "You showed them respect and consideration. Maybe they will listen to you."

"What should I do?" Erik asked. "Promise that no more noxious liquids will seep into their dwelling?"

"You have to decide for yourself how to appeal to them," said the old woman.

"How can I reach them?" he asked, in spite of himself. If these vetters existed at all, what would he say to the elusive creatures? The situation was utterly ridiculous.

"They will come to you," said the old woman as she went outside to fill her pitcher with snow to melt for the men to drink with their meal.

The supper did not turn out as merry as the one the night before. The king was annoyed that they could neither go hunting nor enjoy the visit, and the rest of the guests were subdued and uncomfortable. They all retired to their beds at an early hour.

Again, Erik had vivid dreams, and once more he saw one of the little people standing upon his bed and looking down on him.

"Come with me," said the creature jumping to the floor and motioning for Erik to follow him. Erik felt himself leave his comfortable bed and descend a staircase, which he had not noticed before that led under the house. Once he reached the bottom of the stairs he came into a large earth chamber filled with little people. As large as the room was, Erik still had to bend over to prevent his head from touching the ceiling, and he gratefully accepted a place on the floor next to a long low table.

The small man, less than four feet tall and with a long gray beard, stood before Erik with his hands on his hips.

"So, you are to be our new king?" he asked with solemn curiosity.

"Maybe, one day," said Erik.

"Then let us see how you will dispense justice," said the man who was obviously the spokesperson for the group that had drawn near and was eyeing the stranger in their midst.

"The only reason we are talking with you and not just burning the house down is that we have been happy here, and we do not want to move anywhere else. We have lived here ever since this house was built, many generations ago. But since our last mistress died and Erik Valdemarsson took over nothing has been the same. He shows us no respect even though we, together with the old woman, brew him the best beer in the land. Whenever he comes here with his rowdy friends, they make our life unbearable," he said as he motioned towards a part of the earth chamber where Erik could see the walls were damp, and from whence came a penetrating stench.

"I will talk to him," said Erik. "I am sure he is not aware of how disruptive his behavior is to you."

"Oh, he knows," said the small man, angrily. "He is just an arrogant, uncaring man."

"As I see it, you are not asking much in return for your magic brew, and I am sure the message you sent him in the storage house and on his empty shelves has been received. If that was not enough, then the king's displeasure with him certainly was."

The little people laughed with glee.

"The beer was ours to make, and ours to destroy, and we did not steal the wine," objected the little man. "We just hid it."

"Well," said Erik. "I am sure neither Erik Valdemarsson, nor his friends, will ever insult you again."

"If that is truly the case, we shall continue to do our chores in exchange for the right to occupy and enjoy our home, but we will never again brew our beer for him."

"Your brew will be greatly missed. Is there anything I can do to change your mind?"

"No, my prince, nothing. But the day you become King of Norway we shall brew it again."

"That is a great honor. I hope I will be worthy of your generosity."

"We hope so, too," said the little man, and the people around him sounded their agreement.

When Erik woke up the following morning he remained in his bed reflecting on his dream. It had seemed amazingly real, but he doubted that it could be anything but a figment of his imagination.

When he sat up in his bed he saw Erik Valdemarsson scrutinizing his wine shelves

"Look, the wine is back," he said when he noticed Erik was awake. "I assume I have you to thank for that."

Erik was dumbfounded when he saw the shelves lined with bottles and containers.

"I am very grateful to you," said Erik Valdemarsson with genuine warmth. "And never again will I antagonize the vetters."

Erik did not know what to say, but the old woman smiled kindly as she passed him. "The storm has subsided," she said. "You can go hunting today."

When they arrived back at Akershus, laden with white hare, ermin and snow fox, the rumors of Erik's intercession with the elusive and vindictive vetters spread around the castle.

"Tell me," begged Queen Euphemia who was seated next to him at the dais table that night. "Did you really threaten them with extinction if they did not do twice their normal chores?"

Erik could only laugh because his dream had been so vivid that he almost believed that he had met the vetters. But now he strongly suspected that the old woman had hidden and later replaced the wine, and that the whole episode was nothing more than a hoax.

"I did no such thing," he objected.

But Erik Valdemarsson who had overheard their conversation assured the queen that only Erik's intervention had saved his homestead from even harsher retribution.

On a cold and sunny Swedish winterday some weeks later, Erik rode over the drawbridge of Nykoping castle. At last, he was its master. Accompanying him were Lords Abjorn and Mats and a retinue of fifty knights and soldiers. Valdemar who had taken up residence there in his absence, greeted them as they rode into the courtyard.

"How wonderful to see you again!" Erik exclaimed as he embraced his brother, all the while looking over Valdemar's shoulder to see if Kristina would come outside, but she was not to be seen.

"I have missed you, and I am glad that you are finally here." Valdemar replied as he returned Erik's hug with great warmth. "Kristina will join us as soon as she has finished the preparations for your homecoming."

The two brothers headed for Erik's chamber to settle down where they constantly interrupted each other with stories of what had transpired since they last met. "How is our brother?" Erik finally asked.

"Birger is very happy with Marta and his sons. You know how well he did presiding in his first Council meeting when you were present; and the next meeting--while you were in Norway--went equally well." Valdemar weighed his words as he continued, "But I know Birger, and I have listened to Torgils enough to know whose words Birger spoke then. It follows that the Church has not regained its tax-free status, and the bishops are disappointed. It is also common knowledge that petitioners must approach Torgils with their requests before Birger reads them. This way Torgils can encourage petitions suited to his interests while discouraging those he opposes. Still, he is careful. He does not push his views on Birger but lets him deal with most issues as he wishes; and because Torgils rarely gives unsolicited advice, Birger listens to him when he does and repeats his words almost verbatim. Torgils is still in total control."

"I thought that he would be," said Erik. "But Torgils was a good ruler; and while he enriched himself, he did not deplete the treasury. If he does not interfere with our dukedoms, as far as I am concerned he can run Birger's life any way he pleases."

"I agree," nodded Valdemar before switching the subject. "How was your trip?"

"It was interesting . . . and listen to this. I learned that Torgils is getting married."

"What?" blurted Valdemar in surprise. "To whom?"

"The lady in question, Hedvig of Ravensberg, is a relative of Count Jakob's. She is not only beautiful, but she comes with an enormous dowry. What surprises me is that her father would countenance Torgils for a son-in-law as he always wanted a crown for his daughter. But maybe Count Otto of Ravensberg had to find her a husband before she gets too old."

"It is a fine match for Torgils, whatever the reasons," mused Valdemar. "By creating close ties with Counts Jakob and Otto, both allies of King Hakon, Torgils will be held in high regard in Norway."

"I hope you remember that we are expected to go to a meeting on Bull's Island to ratify the concord of the last peace meeting with the Norwegians in order to meet next with the Danes."

Their discussion was interrupted by the announcement of the arrival of Valdemar's Finnish chancellor. Valdemar stood up. "There is always something going wrong over there. If it is not the Finns resisting taxes, then it is a poor harvest or some other problem. And I never seem to have enough money to solve them all."

"That sounds rather familiar," chuckled Erik as Valdemar withdrew.

A few moments later he heard a knock and the servant announced Kristina in a ceremonious voice. Erik stood up and felt his heart race as she entered the room. She looked as lovely as ever and he ached to hold her close, but instead he just stood looking at her.

"You look beautiful," he whispered. "Just as I pictured you would when I came home." He could hear his own voice sound strained. "But I should not forget that you are not my wife." He immediately loathed himself for saying those words as he saw her lips quiver. "I am sorry, Kristina. I was simply overwhelmed by seeing you again. Forgive me."

"It has not been easy to work in your home, Erik. To constantly hope that everything I do here should meet with your approval."

"You do not need my approval for anything. You are the lady of this house."

"Thank you," she whispered, while looking down at the floor.

"I want you to be happy here."

"I suppose I am trying to say the same thing," she replied softly as tears welled in her eyes.

He walked over to her and kissed her chastely on the cheek. "You have my undying love, my sweet sister-in-law."

Kristina looked up at him and he saw her sadness mirroring his own, so deep that it cut him to the core. "And you have mine, dear brother-in-law," were the only words she said before she quickly left the room.

One by one, Erik was introduced to the men who were to handle his affairs as he sat by the fire in the Great Hall. For hours, he enjoyed the parade of bailiffs, soldiers, stewards, treasurers, overseers, game wardens and village elders who each bowed deeply before him to explain their duties and reported on the current state of affairs.

"This is a far richer dukedom than I thought," Erik exclaimed exuberantly when the last visitor left. "Next year, let us not raise taxes. I wish to be known as a benevolent ruler."

As they sat down for the elaborate welcoming dinner Kristina had arranged, Erik nodded to one of the older servants. "I am pleased to see so many familiar faces here. How long have I known you, Harald?"

"Ever since you were a boy, your Highness, I served your father and grandfather."

"Then you should be my chamber man, because I enjoy having old friends around."

During the meal, Harald took the position of sentinel behind Erik as his new position prescribed. No servant was to approach the dais table without his permission, and he meticulously supervised those who served his master.

Later that night, after the homecoming celebrations were over, Erik remained in the Hall with only Abjorn and Mats. Kristina and Valdemar had already bid them good night, and Erik tried not to think about their being alone together.

"I am finally home," he said while surveying the Great Hall with unconcealed pleasure. The walls had been washed in white to give the large room a lighter look during the dark winter days. New wall sconces and banners adorned the freshly painted surfaces, and the tables had been polished to reflect the candles placed upon them.

"I will drink to that," said Mats as he lifted his cup. "To your future here, Duke Erik."

"And to yours, my friends," replied Erik, before he continued pensively. "I know, Mats, that I can call you 'friend'. But how about you, Lord Abjorn?"

"Your Highness? Have I given you cause to believe otherwise?"

"Not yet . . ." said Erik, as he put his elbows on the table while scrutinizing his new chancellor. "But is it not safe to assume that you will inform your old friend and benefactor, Lord Torgils, of whatever goes on here?" Abjorn offered no reply but looked steadily at Erik. "You are not contradicting me," noted Erik as he sat back in his chair.

"Still I am deeply honored that you have come to work with us. You are knowledgeable and skillful, and I will value you as my advisor . . . and friend. To express how strongly I feel in that regard, I am giving you the estate of Knivsta." Erik pulled a scroll from under his tunic and unrolled the deed on the table.

"Your Highness!" exclaimed Abjorn, stunned by the unexpected and exceedingly generous gift that was at least double the size of his present domain. "I am honored." His face was momentarily torn by conflict. "I had hoped to be able to serve two men, both of whom I greatly respect, if that were possible. However, being close to you these last months, I know that dual loyalty cannot exist without complications, so I had already made my choice. While I want to remain Lord Torgils' friend, I am in your employ now, and I will serve you without reservation. I hope to earn the privilege of also being your friend."

"I think you already have," smiled Erik as he rolled up the document and handed it to Abjorn. "I am going to bed now to enjoy my first night as lord of this castle. Good sleep."

As he walked up the stairs to his chamber, Abjorn turned to Mats. "I think we have tied our lives to the right man."

"I know I have," Mats agreed.

Chapter 16

Kristina and her ladies had set up their spinning wheels and embroidery frames in the queen's old chamber in Nykoping castle in which Kristina was now ensconced. She prayed she would make it a cheerier place than the one she remembered from her childhood, but she realized that in order to get her household into perfect condition she was driving her ladies just as hard as had Queen Helvig.

"Am I demanding too much?" she asked anxiously. "I hope you understand that we must get everything ready, since we will have many visitors during the warm months."

Ragna smiled and replied; "We all take great pride in making the castle come to life again."

"So we suffer," Lady Borg bantered with a wink. She had volunteered to help Kristina, while her husband, Lord Abjorn, was assisting the dukes with the business of governing. "As long as you work harder than anyone else, my lady, you will shame the rest of us into doing what is expected."

"I am so grateful to have you here despite the needs of your many children," replied Kristina affectionately.

"I can use the rest," said Lady Borg before she went over to supervise two young girls who had begun to labor over a large wall banner. Once all the women had settled down to their daily work, Lady Borg turned again to Kristina. "Tell us about Hedvig of Ravensberg," she said.

"I know nothing of the lady," replied Kristina, thinking back on her conversation with her father. He had seemed uncharacteristically uncomfortable when he had broken the news to her of his impending marriage, and then had added almost as an excuse,

"I feel a little lonely now that you are moving away, Kristina, especially as I am no longer working day and night as Regent. I need some company." Somehow, she had had the feeling that he was not telling her everything.

"Lady Hedvig is supposed to be very beautiful," she said finally. "I have never seen her, but Ingeborg extolled her looks in her last letter, and was very complimentary about Count Otto having chosen my father for his son-in-law. But Ingeborg said nothing more."

"It will be good for your father to have someone to take care of him," opined Lady Borg.

"Of course. Still, I cannot imagine when we will find time to make new dresses for father's wedding this fall," Kristina sighed.

She glanced at the unused time glass that she had relegated to a side table. Under Queen Helvig's sharp gaze it had measured seemingly endless hours of work, but in those days it had also shown Kristina how much time remained before she would see Erik again. When the last grain of sand had trickled down on the fourth turn of the timeglass she had been free to leave the queen's chamber. It was then that she would rush down to see if Erik had returned from the day's hunt, to find him reading by the fire, or playing games with Valdemar and their friends. Whenever she had entered the Great Hall, Erik's eyes had lit up before he re-busied himself with the task at hand so as not to betray his feelings. She used to seat herself by the fire until eventually he came and sat down close to her. Then the hard work and problems of the day would be forgotten. His closeness was all she had ever craved.

All those years she had spent wishing they could have a life together had been realized, but not the way she had hoped. Though both Erik and Valdemar made every effort to make her life pleasant, and always treated her with respect and kindness, their living arrangement was not an easy one. The brothers never seemed to stay at home for more than a few days before they left for Council meetings, peace meetings, or hunts. Perhaps they absented themselves because they, too, could feel the tension. So she had reconciled herself to being alone or amongst her ladies, since that, after all, was a woman's lot.

Nevertheless she could not help daydreaming about Erik. She never envied women who entered the Hall after she had withdrawn, or the women Erik met at other estates with his drinking friends, but she did feel pangs of jealousy on occasion, such as the time when he had retrieved a fallen glove for a comely visiting princess. His smile, as he handed over the glove, had made Kristina's heart constrict. But the most painful moments were when their eyes met as they laughed together at something amusing. Their laughter would die and they would quickly look away in sadness.

Still, against all reason, she had accepted her lot. Valdemar was the kindest husband a woman could wish for, and she would rather live in the same house as Erik than not see him at all.

Abjorn threw on his mantle before he left his tent. It was a cold, clear evening in March and the sky glittered with stars. He had just arrived on Bull's Island in the Gota River and was heading for Torgils' quarters. He was eager to share a private supper with his old friend since they had only seen each other briefly in recent months, and then always in the company of others at Council meetings or banquets. As he reached the Lord High Constable's tent he heard a ferocious growl in the dark, but Abjorn smiled.

"It is me, Odin," he called.

Torgils' dog immediately ceased growling and started wagging his tail. Odin was a huge mastiff whose size inspired awesome respect. He had been trained by Torgils from puppyhood, and had maimed more than one man who threatened his master. Occasionally, when Torgils wanted to be sure that his conversations were not overheard, he would station the sentries off at a distance and have Odin guard his tent. If anyone came within earshot, Odin would have him by the throat. The fearsome animal would not permit even the sentries to approach, and only the captain of the guard could come and go as he pleased. But Abjorn was one of those to whom Odin allowed access, and now he put his paws on Abjorn's shoulders, towering over him while licking his face with a huge, wet tongue.

"Enough Odin!" cried Abjorn, as he fended off the beast and staggered backwards into the tent, leaving the dog outside, happily wagging his tail.

"I see you have been properly greeted!" laughed Torgils as Abjorn made a hurried entrance wiping his face. "Odin always liked you."

"I am flattered," grimaced Abjorn as he rubbed his face a final time before saying warmly to his friend, "How good to see you again."

"It is mutual," beamed Torgils, as he walked over to fill two cups with wine. He had begun to walk without a cane, but his limp was still severe. "Are you happy working with Duke Erik?" he asked.

"Very much. I am grateful that you suggested me."

"Are you working on any special tasks?" Torgils asked innocently.

"Nothing of special interest," answered Abjorn, grateful that he could tell the truth.

The Lord High Constable smiled. "Let us have something to eat," he suggested, as he walked over to a table where food was already laid out.

After finishing their repast, they were comfortably relaxing, when one of the sentries called out the approach of Count Jakob of Northern Halland. Torgils stood up, went over to the tent opening, and ordered Odin to sit. Odin obeyed, allowing Jakob to hurry by.

"Quite a guard you have there," Jakob observed with a shudder.

Jakob gratefully raised the cup of wine Torgils offered in welcoming him. "Your good health, my lords!"

"I have a few things to attend to before I retire, so I shall bid you good night," said Abjorn once he emptied his cup. "I enjoyed spending time with you, Torgils, and I am glad we met again, Count Jakob."

Odin, who had settled down outside, lifted his head as Abjorn left the tent. "You just stay where you are, old boy," said Abjorn as he bent down to rub the dog on the neck. Odin rolled over to let Abjorn scratch his belly.

"A good man, Lord Abjorn," he heard the count say from within the tent.

"That he is. And very useful at Duke Erik's court. I trust him implicitly."

Abjorn felt a twinge of conscience, and he was about to stand up when the conversation continued. "Let us drink to our new kingdom!" he heard the count say. New kingdom? In spite of himself, Abjorn sank back on his heels and continued to scratch the still supine and very contented canine.

"Have you spoken to King Birger about the possibility of consolidating your properties?" asked Jakob.

"Yes, I have explained that I would prefer to visit just one area to oversee my domains, rather than wasting time traveling from one part of the country to another. Since my family estate is in the west, I suggested it would be the best place for consolidation. The king seemed very receptive. I have carefully studied the crown land maps, and some properties are ideally situated for our purposes. And considering the interests of the crown, my present properties are well located, so the king certainly will not suffer in the exchange. Everything looks good, Jakob, once we combine our properties we shall have a kingdom of our own."

A kingdom of their own! Abjorn abruptly stopped scratching the dog. With a grunt and a nudge of his muzzle, Odin encouraged him to resume the treatment, which he quickly did to prevent the animal from making any noise.

"We have never discussed who would be king," continued Torgils.

"Do not worry," laughed Jakob, "Though I come from royal lineage, you will be king. It was on that basis that I negotiated the dowry with Count Otto. All I want is to keep the tax revenues from Northern Halland, and not have to share them with the Danish crown."

Abjorn was so stunned that he felt almost paralyzed, but he realized that he had to leave before he aroused suspicion. He stood up and left the dog lying with its paws in the air. As he passed a young guard, Abjorn heard him mumble, "I would rather die than pet that monster!"

Abjorn lay awake the whole night, torn between duty to Duke Erik and his long and deep friendship with Torgils. But however he tried to rationalize it, secession was an act of treason, and as the morning dawned he knew that duty had to prevail. As he approached Erik's tent, his heart was heavy. It would not matter if Torgils never learned that he had been the informer. He himself knew, and never again would he be able to look his friend in the eye. He lifted the flap of Erik's tent.

"I am afraid I have bad news," he said to Erik and Valdemar who were seated together for their morning meal.

"Dear Abjorn, first of all, get comfortable. You look like you are dying on your feet." Erik gestured for Abjorn to be seated. In a low voice Abjorn related the incident of the preceding night. When he finished, the dukes stared at each other in amazement.

"I will be damned!" exclaimed Erik.

"You have to give him credit, though. It is a clever plan," mused Valdemar. "You always said that that area where the three countries meet would be the strategic strongpoint if one planned to control Scandinavia."

"Yes, Torgils is clever," Erik opined glumly. He turned to look at Abjorn, who was staring at the ground. "I can imagine how you feel. To expose a friend is distasteful, no matter how egregious his actions. But you understand that I must tell Birger . . . without mentioning your name, of course." He looked at his chancellor's ashen face. "You should go and rest before the conference. I will call you when we are ready to begin." Abjorn nodded and left, moving like a sleepwalker. "Well, at least I am convinced of his loyalty, and that is something positive from this rotten mess."

"I do not doubt what he told us is true, but I cannot believe their plan could succeed," said Valdemar, shaking his head.

"Why not? If Torgils can exchange his farflung holdings for land in just one area, and combine that with neighboring Northern Halland, he will have a domain larger than many of the German princes. He could entice his new neighbors to join with promises of high offices and low taxes. Most likely he would then try to conquer Lodose. Control of that harbor town alone would yield an enviable income."

"But if Sweden were about to lose its only western port, would Birger not fight to get it back?" queried Valdemar.

"Of course! But do not forget that some of the strongest fortresses in Scandinavia would lie within Torgil's new domain: Jakob has Hunnehals and Varberg in Northern Halland, and his friends, the Danish refugees, hold the Norwegian Kungahalla, not far from there. In order to dismantle the new kingdom, the Swedish army would have to wage full scale war."

"But would not the Danes and the Norwegians get equally upset about a new kingdom, and support Birger?" asked Valdemar.

"The Danes would obviously want Northern Halland back, but since Erik Menved is preoccupied with his wars against the Hanseatic cities, he might not be able to divert armies to the north at the same time. As far as the Norwegians are concerned, they have nothing to lose if Torgils carves a kingdom out of an area he owns in Sweden plus Jakob's domain in Denmark. The new country would serve as a buffer zone. Hakon will certainly want to continue his alliance with his old friend Jakob, which would pit the Norwegians against the Danes and the Swedes, should they attempt to retake their lands. To answer your question; under the right circumstances, Torgil's and Jakob's plan could well succeed," Erik finished with a sigh.

"I cannot believe what I hear!" objected Birger. He sat down heavily on a bench in his tent as he stared at his brothers. "Who told you such lies?" he demanded.

"I cannot tell you. If Torgils finds out who he is, he will be killed. And what makes you so sure these allegations are lies?" protested Erik.

"If these accusations are true, they would cost Torgils his life, and I do not believe he would take such a risk."

Valdemar intervened. "Birger, I, too, believe they are true."

Birger took a deep breath, trying to control his emotions. "Still, you bring me no proof. How can I believe this tale without any solid evidence?"

"I repeat that the informer risked his life when he told us," Erik retorted.

"All right," said Birger as he raised a hand. "Let us discuss this calmly. I have no reason to think that you are lying, Erik, so I accept that you believe Torgils and Jakob are planning to create a separate kingdom. But you must prove it!"

"The sad truth is that you would not have any proof even if you spoke to the man who overheard the conversation. It would be his word against theirs. He could not provide the evidence you feel you need to act against your Lord High Constable. Still, I had to tell you."

Birger shook his head. "I cannot believe that Torgils would act against Sweden . . . and me. He is the only man I have ever fully trusted, apart from the two of you, and I need his expertise to rule Sweden."

"There is circumstantial evidence pointing to their plan, Birger. Why, for example, do you think Otto of Ravensberg consented to a marriage between his daughter and Torgils, when it is common knowledge that he has been seeking a crown for her? Obviously, because Jakob told him Torgils would soon wear one."

"That is not enough," said Birger after a long silence. "Until I have solid evidence, I cannot let anything ruin my relationship with Torgils."

"If you can work with him after what we have just told you, you are much stronger than I could ever be. So, only the future will establish whether we were right or wrong. Unless . . ." said Erik as his face brightened.

"Unless . . . what?" demanded Birger.

"Unless Torgils does not get an exchange to the land in the west. Then his plans will fail."

"If, indeed, he has such plans. And suppose he does not, I will unjustly have denied a fair request from a man to whom I owe so much.

"I do not envy your position, Brother," Erik said.

Despite the fact that Birger was deadly tired after the long sea voyage to Stockholm, he remained next to the small fire in Marta's chamber, gazing lovingly at his wife. He pulled his padded gown around him against the chill of the night.

"What are you thinking about?" asked Marta as she fastened her needle to her embroidery and leaned back in her chair.

Birger smiled. She always seemed to sense his moods. He wanted to talk about Torgil's and Jakob's alleged plan to create a new kingdom, but he was afraid that she would worry if he confided in her. Instead he smiled and spoke in a casual tone of voice.

"Our negotiations went well. I succeeded in making Hakon agree to present his list of demands essential to a lasting peace, together with what he knew the Danes would demand in return. To convince him,

I offered to personally ensure that the Danish refugees, if extradited, would be under my protection and would receive fair treatment from an impartial court," said Birger proudly.

"That is commendable. But I can sense that you have something else on your mind."

Birger could no longer resist the need to unburden himself, so he told her what his brothers had confided to him. "I have been thinking carefully about what to do," Birger said in conclusion. "Probably the best way to solve the situation would be to exchange Torgils' land-holdings in an area other than in the west."

To his great relief Marta did not seem alarmed. "That is such a clever idea, Birger," she said admiringly, which made Birger feel like a brilliant statesman. "You always have the right solutions," she added with an encouraging smile. "But if I may suggest something, maybe you should give Lord Torgils a little more than what he asked for in the exchange, just in case he never had treasonous intentions."

"And you, my sweet one, are the cleverest of all," said Birger as he went over to kiss her cheek.

Torgils had been working with King Birger at his desk for hours. Piles of documents littered its surface, which the king now insisted on reading before signing.

"Sit down," said Birger suddenly as he gestured to a bench on the other side of the massive table. "I want to discuss your request to consolidate your landholdings."

Torgils felt a shiver of excitement go through his body. The moment had finally come.

"I should have dealt with this earlier, but we have had so much work lately," Birger continued as he studied Torgils' face.

"It is kind of you to find the time to bother with such a trifling matter, your Majesty," answered Torgils, feeling almost faint with expectation.

"This is the time to show my gratitude for all you have done for Sweden . . . and for me," said Birger as he spread a map between them. Torgils, whose breathing had virtually stopped, stood up to view the map. "I estimate that I am giving you a lot more land than what you offer in exchange," said Birger as he looked at the map.

"Your Majesty . . ." whispered Torgils in anticipation.

"You shall receive one third of the crown's land in Vaxjo and Lindkoping counties, and I will allow you to repossess the land in those two counties which the crown previously gave to the Church."

Torgils felt his knees go weak. The area offered was located in the center of Sweden, far from Jakob's domain! He wanted to explode in protest, but he sat down as if overwhelmed by his good fortune. And he was overwhelmed. By disappointment. When they had discussed the exchange before, the king had as much as promised to give him land in the west. Why had he changed his mind? Did he know about their plans? But if he did, he would hardly have been so generous. But if, somehow, he even suspected the scheme, he would be watching closely for his trusted advisor's reaction. Torgils knew that he had to be extremely careful. His dream of a crown was crushed. Now, he had to survive.

Torgils stammered, "I am overcome, your Majesty! Please forgive me for not being able to express my gratitude properly."

"At first I wanted to exchange land adjacent to your family estate, but then I realized that I could be more generous elsewhere," replied Birger with a smile.

"Your Majesty . . ." Torgils began, but was unable to continue, which Birger seemed to take for profound gratitude. Torgils was mortified to feel tears of disappointment burn his eyes, and it was not until Birger came around the table to embrace him, that Torgils realized he had delivered the performance of his life.

"I am so happy you understand what I am trying to express with my gift," said Birger, sounding pleased with himself.

"Thank you, your Majesty. Thank you . . ." Torgils mumbled as they broke from the embrace. "I shall return as soon as I have composed myself. Forgive me!"

He hurriedly left the audience chamber and did not stop until he was well out of earshot. Then he kicked the stonewall in an uncontrollable fit of anger. And while he realized that he must be the most fortunate man in the realm that day, he continued down the corridor with long, furious strides, cursing under his breath.

"I want you to think carefully. Did anyone come near my tent that night on Bull's Island?"

"No one can come close without Odin alerting us. The only ones were your guests, Count Jakob and Lord Abjorn," answered the captain of the guard.

"Are you absolutely sure?" asked Torgils who had concluded that this was the only occasion when any of his conversations with Jakob could have been overheard.

"I am, your Lordship."

"Send in the sentry who was posted by my tent that night!" A young soldier soon entered with a timid look on his face.

"Do not be frightened," said Torgils reassuringly. "I am merely trying to establish if anyone was lurking about my tent the night you were on duty on Bull's Island."

"Nobody was near your tent except Count Jakob and Lord Abjorn, your Lordship," affirmed the young soldier nervously. So, Torgils concluded, the king could not know. Perhaps he should have pressed him for a smaller domain near his family estate.

"Odin frightens everyone, your Lordship," the young sentry rambled on nervously. "Nobody dares to come near him. I can not understand how Lord Abjorn can be so friendly with him!"

"Well, they have known each other for many years." Torgils made a dismissive gesture and the soldier gratefully made for the door when suddenly Torgils stopped him. "Wait! What do you mean by 'so friendly'?"

"After he left your tent he was rubbing Odin's stomach as if he were a house cat. I would not dare do that in a million years!"

"No, I would not recommend it," said Torgils pensively. "How long would you say Lord Abjorn played this dangerous game?"

"For quite a while," answered the young soldier.

"Do not mention a word about this," ordered Torgils sternly. "I do not want anyone to know of Odin's soft spots. Do you understand?"

"Yes, your Lordship!" stammered the soldier as he backed out of the chamber.

Abjorn! Torgils felt a stab in his chest as he realized his best friend had betrayed him. While playing with Odin, Abjorn could not have helped overhearing their conversation, even if he had never planned to eavesdrop. Abjorn must have found his new loyalty stronger than their old friendship and carried the tale to his master; and Erik, in turn, to the king. And what Erik knew, Valdemar knew. That made three people who were privy to his plans, but could prove nothing; and one who merely harbored suspicion--the king. Torgils poured himself a large cup of wine and emptied it in one motion. What now? If he was lucky, the king was no longer suspicious, but the dukes would be following his every move. Well, he would even the score with Abjorn, but all in good time. And he would watch the dukes closely from now on.

But for the moment, the most pressing problem was his upcoming marriage--by which his bride expected to become a queen. He had to get word to Count Otto to release her from the betrothal. He composed a letter to Jakob, glowingly reciting how his beloved sovereign had rewarded him with choice properties in the center of Sweden. He regretted only that the two of them would not be able to see one another as often as he had hoped, had his lands been consolidated in the west. Torgils closed the letter with profound assurances of continued friendship and assigned a messenger to carry it to the count. Jakob would surely understand the underlying message.

Birger read and carefully resealed Torgils' letter to Count Jakob. Here was further proof that he had never conspired to commit treason against Denmark and Sweden. The letter was simply a message from one friend to another.

Birger felt a deep sense of relief. Not one word of query or complaint had come from Torgils' lips when he received his new lands. A man who had just had his dreams crushed would have made some objection, however small, but Torgils had displayed nothing but profound gratitude, and Birger was convinced that he was innocent of any treasonous design.

He ordered the Captain of the Guard to send on the letter, and not to intercept Lord Torgils' future correspondence. He felt at peace for the first time in weeks, and energetically attacked a new pile of documents.

Chapter 17

Nykoping

Half a year had passed since Valdemar and Kristina's wedding. After months of seeming withdrawn, Kristina had become more like her old self and her laughter came easily once again. Erik was proud to have her as mistress of his house. She was beloved by the servants, was kind though strict, addressed each one by name, and never neglected to praise a job well done. He could, in all honesty, not envision anyone running Nykoping more capably.

But his thoughts were not always those of appreciation. Especially at night the demons of jealousy tore at his mind and heart. Had Valdemar claimed not only her body but also her love? It was a struggle not to let such thoughts preoccupy him. Consequently, he forced himself to concentrate on preparing for his future role as King of Norway. Every waking hour was filled with attending to his dukedom and learning all he could about governing. If he were to become a king, he wanted to be a great one. And, apart from memories of times past with Kristina, the memory of the Norwegian nobles bowing deeply to him in Oslo was the only cherished one.

The sun had just dipped below the horizon in a burst of red and gold. Erik lingered by the window of his chamber, enjoying the soft approach of night while listening to Valdemar and Kristina's animated conversation over a game of chess by the fire. Erik had discovered that Kristina had a talent for the game he loved, so the long winter evenings had become more enjoyable with both Valdemar and Kristina as opponents. For months the three of them had played running games, and to his and Valdemar's dismay, Kristina began to emerge the winner. Erik turned from the window in time to see Kristina's jubilant expression as she made the inevitable move against Valdemar's queen. She had planned her game well. There was no way he could save the piece, and he took it off the board with a groan.

"She got you again?" Erik chided as he walked over to the table.

"Not yet," grumbled Valdemar as he captured Kristina's last knight with a vengeance.

"I was hoping you would do that," Kristina exclaimed triumphantly as she moved her tower along the side of the board. "Checkmate!"

"Oh no!" groaned Valdemar. "I was so eager to take your knight that I did not think."

"You always lectured me on the need for sacrifices," Kristina reminded him with a merciless grin as she took the tally sheet and meticulously added her latest score.

A knock was heard, and Harald entered with a bow. "Bishop Nils has just arrived, your Highnesses. Should I bring some food for his Excellency?"

"Please do," Kristina replied. "And some of Duke Valdemar's Spanish wine."

"Yes, my lady," said Harald as he withdrew.

"What a welcome intrusion," Valdemar exclaimed. "I was about to demand a return match, and the blessed bishop saved me."

"It must be the will of God," retorted Kristina smugly.

They all fell respectfully silent as the bishop entered Erik's chamber. "This reminds me of the old days," said Bishop Nils, greeting his former pupils with affection. "I always interrupted some form of recreation when I arrived with my volumes of Latin. But now I could use some recreation myself. That is one of the reasons I came to see you, my children."

Kristina cleared away the chessboard and served the men some wine. While Bishop Nils enjoyed the food that Harald brought, he shared news from Vasteras where he was currently living. When he had finished his repast, Kristina bid the men good night and left.

The bishop sat back. "Dear boys. What I really came to see you about is your brother, or more precisely, your brother's government."

"You mean Torgils?" Erik inquired.

"Lord Torgils is central to my concerns," confessed the bishop. "He and the nobles have ruled this country to the detriment of the

Church. And while your brother promised to rectify the inequity once he became de facto ruler, he has still not done so. Six months after his coronation, Lord Torgils is still in control."

"What specifically has convinced you of that?" asked Erik.

"The king has promised Lord Torgils a vast expanse of land in central Sweden . . .." The two brothers exchanged glances as the bishop continued. "The Lord High Constable wanted to consolidate his properties, and the king gave him a generous exchange. So generous, in fact, that Lord Torgils will be allowed to repossess all Church property within his new boundaries previously gifted by the crown. The anointed King of Sweden, who rules by the grace of God, cannot wreak such wrong against the Church!"

Upon seeing the bishop's angry grimace, Valdemar quickly poured him some more wine. "When did the land exchange take place?" he asked.

"I do not know if it has been signed yet," said the bishop evasively.

"Then you should talk to Birger . . ."

"I am not supposed to know anything about the exchange, so I can hardly object before it becomes official," said the bishop as he lapsed into a brooding silence before defiantly adding, "The Church has only one way to deal with the situation. Excommunication!"

"Are you serious?" demanded Valdemar. "Excommunicate Birger for retaking land which once belonged to the crown?"

"Actually, I had Lord Torgils in mind, since he will be the one to carry out the transfer. And this is not the first time he is doing it. Did you know that Lena, which he calls his "family estate", was actually left to the Church by your uncle, Bishop Bengt?"

"You smite with a mighty hand," said Erik. "Can you legally accomplish his excommunication?"

"In 1296 Bonifacius VIII issued a Clericis Laicos to prevent this kind of behavior on the part of the English and French crowns, and it suits our purpose perfectly."

Erik and Valdemar felt no mercy for Torgils after what they had learned from Abjorn, but neither did they wish him eternal damnation.

"We have been waiting to have our rights restored for thirteen years. Now we will act!"

"It seems the whole situation could be avoided if Birger revised his pledge," Erik noted, imagining Kristina's anguish if her father were excommunicated.

"Naturally," agreed the bishop wryly.

Erik leaned forward. "You actually do not want us to intervene! On the contrary, you want to excommunicate Torgils and thereby force Birger to dismiss him from his post. Am I right?"

"In a crude manner of speaking, yes," confessed Bishop Nils. "There is but one thing which saddens me, and that is how this will impact our dear Kristina." He was silent before he continued with real passion. "But I represent Holy Mother Church. I do not act from worldly lust for power, and I will do everything I can to save the Church from humiliation."

After a long silence Erik asked, "Are there other reasons you are telling us this?"

"Yes," answered the bishop, calm again after his outburst. "I want you to urge the king to keep his promises to the Church once Lord Torgils is removed from office--and I want you to support and guide the king . . ."

"Stop, please!" interrupted Erik. "By asking me, us, to do that, you are making us our brother's keeper . . ."

"Consider carefully, Erik. If your brother allows repossession of Church property and refuses to grant us what he promised, then the Church might be forced to support a change of ruler!" He fixed Erik with his intense gaze. "But the first step, whatever the future holds, is to eliminate Torgils Knutsson."

Erik and Valdemar stared at the distinguished, gray-haired bishop, sitting at the table, resembling a peaceful country priest delivering a message of God's love rather than advocating treason. "I am feeling weary from my journey. I will retire now with the last of my fine wine," Bishop Nils concluded as he took his cup and nodded to the brothers who jumped to their feet. "You need not show me the way. I am staying in my old room. Good night, boys," he said kindly as he left the chamber.

Erik and Valdemar sat down numbly. "What are we going to do? Stand by and let events take their course, or tell Birger?" Valdemar finally asked.

"I do not know," said Erik, preoccupied with the possibility of becoming not only King of Norway, but of Sweden as well.

"I still do not understand why he told us. He does not want us to interfere, but he is giving us the chance to do just that," said Valdemar looking puzzled.

"He is counting on human greed. He is hoping that I will not intervene to save Torgil's soul if there is the remotest chance that I could become king in Birger's place, being the next in line. But most importantly he is testing my devotion to the Church. Still, for Kristina's sake we must give Birger a hint--a tiny hint. If he does not take it, then at least we have done our part," Erik concluded.

The following morning after presiding over mass, Bishop Nils bade his farewells to Erik and Valdemar as if the conversation of the night before had never taken place, but the bishop then brought them back to reality.

"In a few weeks we are opening the casket containing the relics of Erik the Holy at the cathedral in Upsala. We had not planned to invite any of the royal family, but after our talk it might be a good idea if you came to the ceremonies, Erik."

"I would be honored to be present at such a solemn occasion," Erik replied.

"And what have you decided to do in regard to our little discussion?" asked Bishop Nils.

"After Upsala, I will join Birger in Stockholm, and I am sure we shall have many things to discuss other than the land exchange--of which I know nothing anyway," Erik said evasively as the bishop mounted his horse.

"Then I will see you in Upsala," called the bishop as he rode away with his armed escort.

Torgils had just finished reading a dispatch from Count Jakob of Northern Halland brought to him by a trusted friend. Jakob reported that he had been in contact with Otto of Ravensberg who had expressed full understanding for the vagaries of fate and fortune, and consequently considered Torgils' newly enlarged domain quite suitable for his daughter. However, he felt obliged to adjust the dowry by cutting it in half! Torgils would have strangled Otto had he been there yet he had to accept the new terms! If he refused, the count might reveal his failed scheme. Although Torgils had not been anxious to remarry, the need for revenue for a new kingdom had encouraged the prospect. Outraged, he burned Jakob's letter, and in an effort to calm himself, he turned to concentrate anew on the maps he had been studying before the message arrived.

Torgils' initial hurt over Abjorn's betrayal had turned to consuming hatred. Nothing seemed wicked enough for his revenge. He enjoyed dreaming of alternate ways to torture his erstwhile friend before killing him, but he realized that such fantasies could not be acted out without his reasons for seeking such retribution coming to light. He therefore resolved to find some way for Abjorn to lose his wealth or be discredited. He carefully scrutinized the maps to see if there was any flaw in Erik's conveyance to Abjorn of the Knivsta estate, but he could find nothing wrong in the deed. He sat back in his chair with a grunt. Then, all of a sudden he bolted upright, leaned again over the map, and looked more closely at the outlines of Erik's dukedom as it had been drawn up for Erik's father when he became king. What he saw made his heart pound with excitement. This might not harm Abjorn directly, but it would strike someone very close to him. Torgils had all he could do not to run straight to the king.

The right moment arrived a couple of days later when the king was meeting with his treasurer to discuss tax issues. Very discreetly, Torgils picked out the correct map, and innocently asked the treasurer "How much tax do we receive from this town?"

"Please hand me that map and I shall be glad to tell you," replied the treasurer. "You must be mistaken, my lord. This town belongs to Duke Erik. Maybe you meant the one further north?"

"No,'" said Torgils as he pointed to the map. "This one. It is located on crown land. You are mistaken."

The treasurer studied the map carefully and began to pale. Birger, who had been watching the exchange, grew impatient. "What are you talking about?"

"Your Majesty," stammered the treasurer. "I . . . I just assumed . . ."

"Torgils, can you explain what he is mumbling about," demanded Birger irritably.

"Duke Erik seems to think this town is situated on his lands, while most of it is not. It started as a small village within the dukedom, but it grew onto crown property," explained Torgils as he showed Birger the location on the map. "Your brother is presently collecting taxes which should go to you."

"Does he know about this?" asked Birger.

"I do not know, your Majesty," answered Torgils, wishing he could have replied affirmatively. "But it would be strange if he had not noticed. After all, he has only a few tax maps to keep track of. Not like us," said Torgils pointing to the pile of maps on the table.

"Well, that is a surprise," said Birger. "I always assumed the town was his, but obviously it is not. I shall talk to him when I see him. What is next on our agenda?" he asked the shaken treasurer who was still profusely apologizing for his oversight.

Torgils gloated. The king would surely want to claim taxes that were rightfully his, and when he did, it would diminish Erik's revenues. This, in turn, would create a source of irritation between the brothers, and the one to whom Abjorn had pledged himself could lose influence at court. A small but not a bad turn of events.

"I heard you went to Upsala for the opening of Erik the Holy's relics," Birger began with a trace of envy in his voice.

Erik was visiting him in Stockholm on his way back to Nykoping.

"It was a beautiful occasion," Erik replied lightly.

"I see," said Birger tartly. He reluctantly changed the subject when Erik did not elaborate further. "By the way, Erik," he continued, "when we last went though our taxation maps we found that one of your towns has overgrown its boundaries, and that the major part of it is now on crown land." Birger went over and spread a map on his desk.

Erik studied the map and exclaimed in surprise. "I had no idea. The town has belonged to the dukedom as long as I can remember."

Birger was unable to detect the slightest trace of tension or guilt in Erik's voice or manner. "Has your treasurer not looked at the map then?" Birger asked.

"My treasurer is an old man who has been in charge of the dukedom's finances under Lord Torgils' as well as during our father's reign. I suppose he is so used to thinking about the town as part of the dukedom, that he never looked at it closely."

Birger could feel that Erik was telling the truth, and so was unsure of what to do. "Most of the town, and all of its commercial area, is located on my lands; so I should be the one who receives the taxes," he said finally.

"Legally it seems that way," Erik countered. "But those who live there have a longstanding allegiance to the dukedom and feel they belong there."

"That is nonsense," retorted Birger. "The people do not care to whom they pay taxes."

"Still your treasurer is a lot sharper than mine to have picked this up," Erik interjected.

"My treasurer is just as dull. It was Torgils' sharp eye that discovered it."

Erik clenched his fists behind his back. Torgils again! "Just let me know what you decide to do," Erik said in a monotone to mask his ire. "Whatever you want is fine with me. Speaking of Torgils, have you decided how to handle the exchange?"

"Yes, I have. I am fully convinced that he never had any designs against Sweden, and that he never planned anything with Count Jakob except a marriage alliance. I just signed a deed for a generous land exchange in central Sweden and he was overwhelmed. Not once did he protest or ask why I had changed the location, which I venture he would have, were I about to ruin some precious scheme of his."

"So, you think it was all misinformation?" asked Erik.

"Yes, thank God," said Birger with relief. "It would be awful not to trust him."

"Did you include all of the crown's land in the area you offered?" Valdemar asked.

"Much of it, and I also granted Torgils the right to repossess Church property."

"Was that wise?"

"The Church is so rich, Erik, they will not miss those few tracts. Our father was overly generous with them."

Well, thought Erik, if Birger does not care to reconsider, there is nothing more I can do.

The archbishop had not said a word for some time. Bishop Nils did not prod him, but silently waited for his reply. They were sitting in the abbott's cell in the same monastery in Upsala where Bishop Nils had trained for the priesthood. He remembered how fine he had thought this small chamber then--it had a large bed and rugs on the stone floor--however old and worn. But now, after a life in the royal castles and as master of Vasteras cathedral, the cell seemed disappointingly humble. Still, this was the setting he had deliberately chosen, since he wanted to talk to the archbishop alone and away from his habitually opulent surroundings. Bishop Nils had broached excommunicating Lord Torgils several times before with the archbishop, but always it had evoked an evasive answer. He could well understand the archbishop's reluctance to banish the Lord High Constable from the Church since Torgils had a solid following among the nobles--the very same nobles who contributed the wherewithal for building cathedrals for Holy Mother Church. But the archbishop did not seem to grasp that if the crown ceased taxing the Church, she could afford to build her own cathedrals without being beholden to anyone.

After hours of trying to convince him of the obvious, Bishop Nils realized he had gotten no further than to make the archbishop uncomfortable in the small, drafty chamber. However, this time Bishop Nils was not going to take no for an answer. As usual, after vespers the monastery was silent; and he could hear no sound but the labored breathing of the elderly archbishop.

"Excommunication is the ultimate punishment. Do you honestly feel," asked the archbishop finally, "the Lord High Constable deserves it without any warning?"

"He has been cautioned in the past. We must act now, since it is clear that we will never regain our rights as long as he controls the king," Bishop Nils asserted vehemently.

"I am painfully aware of our situation and I, like you, have looked forward to a stronger position for the Church . . ."

"This is the right moment, and the bishops agree with this course of action," argued Bishop Nils impatiently while keeping his withering stare fixed on the old man before him.

His look was not lost on the archbishop, who, more than anything, feared insurrection among his bishops. "I think I heard the dinner gong," the archbishop suggested, stalling.

"I did not hear anything," said Bishop Nils curtly, although he, too, had heard the sound. Whether or not it was the dinner gong, he was not about to let the archbishop leave the chamber.

"We should warn him once more," the archbishop persisted.

"That will not have the desired effect. He must be served with a ban."

"We could, of course, not follow through if he voluntarily withdraws his claim to Church property," speculated the archbishop, looking a little brighter.

"Of course," said Bishop Nils, realizing that he was winning the battle.

The archbishop looked at the parchment on the desk before him. "All the bishops agree, you said?" Bishop Nils nodded. With an air of resignation, the archbishop melted the wax over the flame of the table candle, dripped it onto the parchment, and pressed his seal into it. "Make sure that the situation is handled with the utmost care," he admonished before he stood up and headed for the door.

"I most certainly will," replied Bishop Nils, starting to relax. "Thank you, Lord," he whispered under his breath as he reverently lifted the parchment from the table, and carefully rolled and tied it. "Thy will be done."

Torgils had just returned to Stockholm after visiting his newly acquired properties for the first time. He had been impressed by the rich farmlands of Linkoping and fascinated by the mystery and beauty of the forests around Vaxjo. He had asserted his right of repossession to only a few Church properties so as not to tempt the wrath of the bishops.

He had hardly washed off the road dust when the arrival of a priest from Upsala was announced. "His Excellency, the archbishop has personally requested me to hand you this communication in the presence of at least two persons," he said, his voice quavering.

Torgils glared at the young priest but sent for two scribes who were working in the library. As soon as they arrived he said sternly, "Give me the document and wait outside for my answer."

"It does not require an answer," said the priest as he handed it to the Lord High Constable. Then he backed towards the door and left, followed by the scribes.

Torgils broke the seal and rolled open the document. As he read it his complexion took on a bright crimson hue. He stormed out into the corridor and headed for the king's chamber. He knocked and stepped in without waiting for a reply.

"Torgils, how nice to see you. Did you have a good trip?" Birger asked. When he noticed Torgils' contorted face, he quickly rose from his desk to meet him. "What happened, my friend? Were you not happy with the properties?"

"Oh no, your Majesty. The properties were more than I ever hoped for," said Torgils realizing that he was acting irrationally. "Please read this, and you will understand my rudeness in bursting in on you."

The king took the document and returned to his desk. He read its contents while Torgils sat down heavily on the other side of the table. "They cannot be serious!" Birger exclaimed.

"They are deadly serious, your Majesty," said Torgils, now calm enough to speak normally. "Since your father's death, the bishops have been out for my blood. If they claim they have done nothing but wait for you to restore them to their former glory--do not believe them! They did everything they could think of to induce me to restore their power, and when that failed, they sought to discredit my government. Yet however they tried, they never succeeded. They have threatened, but never before have they served me with formal notice of excommunication. This time they are counting on you to denounce me when

I am excommunicated, or to yield to their demands to save my soul. But you can do neither if you want to control Sweden. Fight fire with fire, your Majesty. Jail the damnable bishops!"

"Torgils, that is unthinkable!" exclaimed Birger. "I agree that excommunication is too severe, and I will not countenance it; but neither will I jail the bishops. The people would rise against me."

"Not if you jail them secretly. You would be surprised how slowly rumors spread if you take precautions. After a Church Council meeting you could seize all the bishops at the same time so they would be unable to come to each other's aid. Then you could announce that they are guests of the crown for the guidance of the king's soul. After just a few days in our dungeons they would withdraw their edict and be grateful they were alive," said Torgils with a chilly smile.

"I will not consider such an idea. But when I signed the land exchange agreement with you, I not only gave you the land; I gave you my solemn oath that you would remain Lord High Constable. For that reason alone, I will make the Church withdraw her ban."

"I am grateful," said Torgils. "And, naturally, I will not press for repossession of any Church property but, please, do not give them anything else."

"Torgils, this might be the time for activating part of my promise to them . . . if they withdraw the ban."

"They will take that as weakness, and they will push to get more," said Torgils throwing his hands in the air. "You are starting to feed a beast that will never be sated."

"That likewise describes the nobility who support us now," said Birger.

"The nobles are only human, your Majesty. The Church rules as God's representative on earth. Her power is of another dimension. If you have a grudge against a nobleman it can be settled between your champions or your armies, and that is the end of it. If you have a grudge against the Church, you might defeat her armies; but she will damn your soul forever or turn your own people against you by branding you an enemy of God. No, your Majesty. I know the strength of the Church, and I will not be caught in her web."

"Do you not believe in God?"

"Of course, I do. But I do not believe that God desires to rule our little kingdom. I very distinctly remember having learned that 'His kingdom is not of this earth.' Obviously, some of the bishops hold a different opinion."

"I, too, am astonished at the ruthlessness and greed of certain bishops who seem ill-equipped to pass on Christ's message of love and salvation. But there are many good men in the Church, and one of them is our friend. I shall send a message to Bishop Nils and ask him to come and see us. I am sure we will be able to solve this problem."

Torgils looked skeptical, but he did not object.

"It has all been arranged, Torgils," said the king happily some weeks later, as he came into the audience chamber where the Lord High Constable was working.

"I just heard from Bishop Nils that the archbishop will lift your ban!" The king exuded satisfaction. "I thought I did rather well in my meeting with Bishop Nils. I told him in no uncertain terms that I intended to keep you as my Lord High Constable whatever happened, and that I would contemplate my promises to the Church for eternity if they insisted on banning you," smiled the king smugly.

"So, what was their final price?" Torgils inquired glumly.

"They requested that you not repossess any Church property."

"That is too generous, your Majesty. They are up to something," said Torgils.

"I think they simply want me to grant them what I promised," concluded Birger. "Be happy, Torgils. You are saved from eternal damnation!" the king said brightly as he left the audience chamber.

Still, Torgils remained in his chair, brooding. He had grave doubts that the king would be able to maintain a balance between the nobility and the Church. He would have to side with one or the other, and regrettably, Torgils guessed, the Church would surely prevail.

Chapter 18

Northern Halland

Torgils had been waiting for several hours in the harbor below Count Jakob's castle in Northern Halland for the ship bearing his bride, and he was growing impatient. He finally decided to seek shelter from the harsh wind in a dilapidated tavern where he quickly developed heartburn from the tainted beer he was served. When, at last, the lookout reported that the ship had been sighted, Torgils was in the foulest of moods. As the boat was about to dock, he strode out onto the pier and was the first to board once the gangplank was laid down. Count Jakob who was accompanying the bride stepped forward to greet him with a friendly hug, before introducing Count Otto of Ravensberg who limply shook Torgils' hand. Count Otto's bony face and thin-lipped mouth wore a smile as weak as his handshake. The count seemed to Torgils just as tight of countenance as he had proved to be of purse. Count Otto turned to bring forward his daughter.

Hedvig was a ravishing beauty. She looked older than Jakob had represented, but she was tall and carried her head proudly. She had black hair, piercing dark eyes, and as Torgils learned when he bowed to kiss her hand, velvety skin.

"It was a horrible journey," was her only comment in greeting her prospective husband.

"Hedvig is prone to get a trifle ill at sea," her father explained solicitously.

"That is regrettable," said Torgils, somewhat taken aback by her caustic manner. "Still, I welcome you to Scandinavia, and hope that you will find it a happy place to live."

"They say it is even colder here than in Ravensberg," the countess lamented as she wrapped her cloak tighter against the wind.

"Please, let us not stand here and get chilled," said Torgils, relieved to have something polite to say. "Horses and sedan carriers are waiting on the dock."

Torgils personally undertook to get his prospective bride settled in a carrier and her lady-in-waiting in another. The soldiers shouldered the sedan chairs and began the ascent to Count Jakob's castle, followed by the mounted escort.

Kristina, who was acting as unofficial hostess for Count Jakob, soon discovered that her prospective stepmother was most difficult to please. Hedvig complained about the size of her room, the firmness of her bed, the temperature of her bath, as well as the facilities for her clothes. Finally, some of the wedding guests had to vacate the chamber adjoining hers so that she would have ample space for the forty-two trunks she had brought with her.

When Kristina had a free moment, she hastened to Marta to report on the bride-to-be. "What is she like?" asked Marta.

"I have known her for only a few hours, but I can safely say she is used to getting her way!" sighed Kristina as she collapsed into a chair in Marta and Birger's chamber, exhausted from trying to please Hedvig. "She is beautiful and exotic-looking, but her face is hard. Even when she smiles, she looks unkind. Her every sentence is a command or a complaint. Maybe she just had a miserable trip, but if this is her true nature I pity my father!"

"They say she brought more than forty trunks of clothes with her," reported Marta.

"You should see them," said Kristina with a laugh. "They are all numbered. And her lady-in-waiting has a long list showing the contents of each. We needed two soldiers to arrange them so that they could all be accessible, as the countess keeps changing her mind about what to wear."

That night at the welcoming dinner Hedvig kept everyone entertained with anecdotes about her trip. She was undeniably witty, but most of her jokes were at someone else's expense. No one seemed safe from her sharp tongue, including her father and Count Jakob.

Kristina noticed that her father was unusually quiet. He was studying his future bride, and Kristina wondered what he was thinking. When the ladies withdrew early that evening, Lord Torgils left as well. He went to his chamber and there, in solitude, got blissfully drunk.

The wedding took place the following day. The afternoon sun was shining from a clear blue sky, the festivities were beautifully arranged, and the guests were truly enjoying themselves. The only ones who seemed to be having a miserable time were the bride and the groom. Torgils could feel the punishment of the previous night's drinking that he was attempting to remedy by consuming more wine, and Hedvig was upset that her new husband did not pay her the attention to which she felt entitled.

When the newlyweds withdrew to the bridal chamber, Torgils sat down on a bench with a heavy sigh. Hedvig crossed the room with a sensuous walk to the bedside where she started to take off her jewelry. She slowly removed each piece with tantalizingly seductive movements, sliding the bracelets from her arms and unwrapping the necklaces from her white throat and ample bosom. Torgils sat mesmerized in spite of himself and followed her every move. As she unbuckled her gold belt and suggestively pulled her tunic over her head he was as aroused as he had ever been. He drank in the gorgeous creature before him, standing in her clingy, silk under-dress, humming and moving her hips to the tune. Before he was aware of what he was doing, he pulled her to him, threw her to the bed and made passionate love to her.

After he was spent, and still groaning from pleasure, he suddenly sat up in the bed and stared at her, smoldering. "You are no virgin! And you are even older than I thought!"

"You, too, are older than I was led to believe, dear husband. And it did not seem to matter that I am older, did it? You could not wait to take me," she gloated.

"You heard what I said," he repeated. "You are not a virgin! That is grounds for annulling this marriage."

"It is hard to remain a virgin after you have been ravished by your own husband," said Hedvig with an angelic smile. "Should we call the physician and have him examine me? A clever man would have been more careful if he wanted to make sure his bride was untouched. But being the lustful brute you are, you just took what you wanted and discovered too late that your wife already knew about love."

Torgils swallowed. She was right, and he felt like an idiot to have been tempted into such mindless lovemaking. "Still, I am owed an explanation," he said brusquely, staring at the half-naked woman resting comfortably against the wall behind the bed.

"Well, Papa has always given me whatever I wanted, and he promised I would marry a king. When he found out that you were not going to wear a crown, he should have broken the contract. But it seems my father felt that I had reached an age when I had to get married, and that you were the best available prospect. I took his word that no better match could be arranged. When I later found out that he had gotten away with paying only half my dowry, I was livid since it was clear that he only had his own best interests at heart. Therefore I decided to look after mine. I had been attracted to a young nobleman for a while so when I learned that I was not going to become a queen I simply succumbed to that delectable swain," she concluded with a nostalgic look on her face.

Torgils stared at her. "You should not talk so brazenly. You should behave like a lady."

"I have been forthright all my life. Why should I change now?" she demanded. "What upsets you is the fact that you are not the very first man in my life. But I fear you will just have to live with it."

Torgils could not believe what he was hearing. No woman of his class had ever spoken to him like this. He desperately wanted to get away from her, but he realized that he could not leave the bridal chamber on their wedding night with his honor intact. He was choking with fury as he stared at her reposing in the wide bed. Then he remembered that she had taken over the adjoining chamber for her trunks. He grabbed a lighted candle.

"Where are you going?" she asked with alarm. "You cannot leave our bed tonight!"

"Do not worry. No one will know," he said as he opened the door to the next room and closed it behind him. Her trunks were piled high, even on the bed. He had to put the candle down so that he could move the heavy chests to the floor. The room was chilly, so he quickly crept into the bed and pulled the covers up around his ears. What a bitch he had married!

Soon the door opened and Hedvig peeked in. "It is freezing in here. I think you should come back. I actually enjoyed you making love to me. You were not bad, you know."

Torgils did not answer at first, but then he realized the absurdity of the situation; trying to sleep in a room full of trunks, while his tantalizing wife was urging him to join her. Grudgingly, he returned to the bridal chamber. Hedvig, who was now totally naked, sat on the bed studying him. "I did not feel like sleeping alone."

Torgils was not sorry to have relented.

Torgils returned to Stockholm some weeks after having installed his bride at his new estate outside Linkoping. While he had thoroughly enjoyed the nights with her, he had been worn down by her daily demands. She wanted his new stallion for her own, she wanted her rooms refurbished, she wanted servants dismissed and new ones hired, and she insisted on running his estate without ever having to seek his approval. Her list was endless, and he found that he gave in to almost everything just to have some peace. He was relieved when he departed since hard work would seem like a vacation from her constant harangue. God forbid he would ever have to deny her anything!

On his first day back in Stockholm, Torgils immersed himself with the king in the audience chamber. "Has your Majesty made any decision in regard to the revenues of the border town we discussed this summer?" Lord Torgils asked casually.

"Not yet. I am considering deeding it to my brother since the town, by tradition, is part of the dukedom."

"It involves a substantial sum of money every year," commented Torgils.

"I have not made a final decision," said Birger, dismissively.

In the silence that followed, a muffled noise came from behind the door that led to the king's private chamber. Birger looked inquisitively at Torgils who started to talk about some invented problem, while with a gesture he encouraged the king to respond and to continue talking. As the king went on speaking, Torgils pulled a dagger from his belt and stole across the room toward the king's chamber. He stood for a moment with his back pressed against the wall, and then he quickly kicked open the door that was slightly ajar. In the small passageway, where the king and his brothers themselves had eavesdropped as boys, there stood a young servant. The Lord High Constable grabbed him by the arm and pulled him into the audience chamber.

"What are you doing here?" he demanded as he shook the man. The eavesdropper did not reply. There was not much he could say in his defense since he was not one of those select servants who attended the king. He had no reason to be where he had been discovered.

"Who sent you to spy on the King of Sweden?" demanded Lord Torgils incensed. The young man remained silent. "You know the punishment for spying on the king? It is death! Still, if you tell us who sent you, the king might find it in his heart to let you live." Torgils again shook the man who silently eyed his captor. "Guards!" shouted Torgils.

As the guards rushed into the room, Torgils pushed the servant towards them. "Put him in a cell. I shall deal with him later," he ordered as the guards dragged the man from the room. The king remained immobile and silent. "Who could have sent him?" Torgils wondered aloud as he resheathed the dagger and angrily paced the floor. "I cannot for the life of me think who would place a spy on you at this time, your Majesty. I really cannot."

"Nor can I, Torgils," said the king. "But you will find out, of that I am confident."

Although he felt deeply violated and threatened, Birger left the audience chamber trying to appear unmoved by the incident, as he could not reveal his insecurity to Torgils.

When Lord Torgils interrogated the castle staff he learned that the eavesdropper who had been employed for less than a year, he had been a good worker, had never given cause for complaint, and had kept to himself. No one was certain where he had worked previously.

When Torgils questioned the prisoner, the young man politely looked him in the eyes without responding. Torgils was tempted to have him tortured right away, but he decided to wait. He hoped the man would realize how unwise it was to remain silent while listening to the bloodcurdling screams of other prisoners under torture. When he still refused to talk, Torgils ordered the Master of the Chamber to personally deal with the matter. The Master was known for his skill in keeping his victims alive for long periods while inflicting horrendous pain.

Torgils was eager to discover the identity of the spy's master, since he suspected the spy was not placed solely on the king, but on himself as well. He could think of only two sources: the dukes or the Church. The Church had good reasons for placing a spy at court. The bishops would always be interested in knowing what Torgils was up to, as well as if and when the king would fulfill his pledge. On the other hand, the dukes would want to know how the king planned to deal with the border town tax matter. If they found out that he had decided to take over the town, they could foment dissent among the townspeople by spreading rumors that the king would charge higher taxes. It would not matter if the king denied the rumors. It would be too late; the townsfolk would not believe him. Taking over a town against the will of its inhabitants would engender acrimony, which might cause the king to deed the town to his brother. Furthermore, since the dukes knew of his own treasonous intentions, they would certainly want to keep abreast of his plans.

Three days after the prisoner was placed in the hands of the Master of the Chamber a guard summoned Torgils to the dungeons. He had to go to the deepest point of the castle to reach the torture chamber. The stonewalls were dripping with moisture, and the stench that enveloped him as he descended the stairs was nauseating. He tried to breathe through his mouth, but it did not help. The Master of the Chamber met him by the massive iron door leading to the torture chamber. Torgils entered and saw the spy stretched out on the rack.

"He said nothing, your Lordship, until just now when he started mumbling. I thought I better send for you." The Master was a gruesome looking man. He was well over six feet in height. His torso was immense, his arms and legs were disproportionately short, but thick as tree trunks. He seemed to have no neck. His bald head appeared to rest directly on his broad shoulders, and his nose had been squashed flat against his face during childhood. His skin was dark and oily, and he was perspiring profusely from his arduous labor. He was dressed in a sleeveless leather tunic smeared with dried blood.

Torgils walked slowly towards the rack that was located at the far end of the chamber. The air in the room was stifling from the fires used to boil oil and to heat pokers and tongs. The chamber had a smell unlike anything Torgils had ever experienced. The very essence of human ugliness had spilled on its floor and walls for decades: urine, feces, blood and guts.

Torgils felt the nausea return as he drew near the rack. What was left of the body covered with blood and gore was almost unrecognizable. The face without eyes showed two black bloodied sockets. The swollen mouth was mumbling so quietly that Torgils had to lean over to try to hear what the poor wretch was saying.

He was praying. He did not react when Torgils questioned him. He did not show the incredible pain he was enduring. In a faint whisper he prayed feverishly. All of a sudden Torgils heard the name Erik mentioned and he leaned even closer to the dying man. As he listened, he heard the man praying to Erik the Holy as well as to God, and by his manner of praying Torgils realized he was a priest. The spy's master was Holy Mother Church. How could he otherwise have endured such agony for three days without yielding up some secret, real or fabricated? Torgils straightened up and summoned the Master and his assistant who had respectfully remained by the door.

"Finish him. I have what I need to know," said Torgils who turned away as the assistant pulled a knife from his belt and deftly cut the man's throat.

The Lord High Constable headed for the door to escape from that abominable place, with the Master following him like an eager shopkeeper making sure his customer was satisfied. Torgils pulled a large coin from his tunic and offered it to the Master who grabbed it, bowing again and again.

Torgils hastened back to his own quarters in strides as lengthy as his dignity would permit. Once inside his chamber, he ordered a servant to draw him a bath. Then he tore off his clothes, which were permeated with that putrid, indescribable smell of the torture chamber. He scrubbed himself until his skin was pink. But even after he had dressed in fresh clothes, the smell of pain and suffering seemed to linger faintly around him.

As he sat down by his desk, one of his squires knocked on the door and entered. "This was left by a man who said that you would want to have it immediately," he said, handing Lord Torgils a small leather pouch before leaving.

Torgils opened it and found a small coin inside. He whistled slowly before he went over to pick up his sword, fastened it around his waist, and threw a hooded mantle over his shoulders. He walked quickly along the corridor, down the back stairs, and exited through the side door. He pulled the hood low over his face as he walked by the guards, quickly crossed the drawbridge and continued towards the cathedral.

Once inside he paused and fell down on his knee to genuflect. The stillness was overpowering. He loved this cathedral with its large wood-carved statues of the saints and prophets. During long sermons he had always enjoyed studying the many windows set with colored glass patterns depicting scenes from the life of Christ. Though he had been there countless times, the place never failed to inspire reverence.

He looked over to the last pew where a man knelt in prayer at its far end. He went over and knelt beside him. "Greetings," Torgils whispered. "I received your message."

"I am sorry I have not been able to reach you before today, my Lord, . . . though I have tried twice . . . I do hope my news does not reach you too late," he rambled on nervously. "But I can only come to Stockholm when I am sent on an errand . . . otherwise it would appear suspicious."

"I understand," said Torgils soothingly. "Just tell me your news."

"I overheard Bishop Nils talking to the dukes . . . just before midsummer when he visited Nykoping castle . . . I could not hear everything which was said . . . now and then I had to leave my post to make sure that no one saw me listening . . . "

"I understand," repeated Torgils growing impatient. "What did they talk about?"

"The bishop said he was going to ban you from the Church!"

"I know all about it," Torgils mumbled under his breath. "What else?"

"The bishop said that the Church might want a new king for Sweden."

Torgils stiffened. "Did he say why?"

"I did not hear . . . I am sorry."

"You have done well," said Torgils as he let some silver coins drop in the informer's palm. Then he stood up to leave. "Thank you, Harald."

It was almost dark, but Torgils had not yet lit any candles as he sat deep in thought at his desk. The situation had changed drastically. He knew now that the Church had gone so far as to contemplate a new ruler. The new king would logically be Erik. Since Erik and Valdemar knew about his plotting with Count Jakob, no doubt, they also knew that it was he who had made the king aware that Erik's village had grown onto crown land. Surely, they would seek to dislodge him from his position. He would have to fight back.

The solution came easily to him. If the king granted the Church her "rights" there would be no need for the bishops to seek a new ruler, and if the brothers could be split apart, Erik and Valdemar would be isolated from the circle of power. This, in turn, would weaken Abjorn's position. There was a way to widen the emerging rift between the royal brothers, and he would not even have to lie--well, not exactly. He was looking forward to his talk with King Birger as he headed for the audience chamber.

Birger sat before the fire, numb from shock over what Torgils had just told him. The Lord High Constable had sworn on his life that the spy had spoken the name Erik during his final moments.

"And," Torgils said, "there is only one Erik I can think of who would have something to gain by spying on you."

Birger had not wanted to believe what he was hearing. Time after time he made Torgils swear on all that is holy that he himself had heard the spy say "Erik" when asked to identify his master. Finally, the look of immovable conviction in Torgil's eyes had convinced him.

Birger felt as if he, himself, was undergoing torture; his breathing became painfully constricted and his heart ached. Why would his brother place a spy on him now? There was no reason for it. Absolutely none. He went to the door; but before he opened it, he stopped himself. While he had consulted with Marta about certain problems, they had never been as grave as this one. Marta would undoubtedly become terrified. He walked back to his chair and sat down heavily. "Why?" was the question that kept entering his mind. He had no answer other than that Erik and Valdemar wanted to know what went on at court in general, and that the spy was not really sent there to keep an eye on him, but on everyone. Or, perhaps, to keep a close watch on the Lord High Constable whom his brothers had come to distrust as of late. That must be it. He felt better at the thought, but then his spirit faded anew. It was his court, and consequently, any spy placed there would be watching him.

But why? Was it to learn in advance about his border town decision as Torgils intimated? Still that did not justify his brothers spying on him. They were his closest, most trusted friends. He felt horribly violated, and again he rose to go to Marta. This time he walked into her room where she was sitting with their youngest son on her knee, singing softly while the child played with her necklaces.

"What is wrong, my dear?" she asked when she noticed his distraught expression.

He could see fear creep into her eyes, and he knew that he could not involve her in his anguish. "Merely affairs of state," he said, trying to sound unconcerned as he sat down beside her and extended a finger that his little son grasped with surprising strength. "Just some problems I have to solve."

"You will do it well, of that I am confident," she smiled encouragingly as Birger took the babe from her knee to hug him close. Why could not life be like this always? Safe and unthreatening. Slowly the atmosphere of the peaceful room engulfed him, but still he could not force the thought of his brothers' betrayal from his mind.

"Erik."

He stopped when he heard Kristina's soft voice behind him. It had that special tone it used to have during that magic year when they had discovered their love for each other. He had not heard her say his name this way since the day he had told her of his forthcoming marriage. He turned around expectantly. Kristina stood in the dim corridor with her arms laden with flowers.

"I must talk to you," she pleaded. "I can feel something is wrong. Neither you nor Valdemar ever mention my father, and when I ask you why, you both evade my questions."

He took a deep breath feeling sadness replace his brief excitement. "Your father and we do not always see eye to eye. Just now, we are not on the best of terms. But these things change, as you know."

He hated himself for avoiding a direct answer. But how could he tell her that her father was a traitor and could lose his life if the king learned the truth?

"I want to believe you," she said as her eyes blurred with tears. "But I can feel something sinister is happening."

He pulled her to him, almost crushing the flowers between them and kissed her on the forehead. Fighting his urge to pull her even closer he reluctantly let her go. He could see that she would not have fought him had he held her in his arms, and again he felt that familiar pain. He wanted to tell her how much he loved her and that he never wanted to hurt her. He opened his mouth, but she turned away and walked down the corridor, her head cast down.

Erik and Valdemar left for Stockholm a week later to participate in a Council meeting. As they dismounted in the courtyard of Stockholm castle, a servant requested their immediate presence in the audience chamber. Erik noticed that Birger was about to burst with emotion, so he kept his greetings brief in anticipation of what Birger had to say. The king sat down in a chair by the short end of the center table where he remained motionless, his lips pressed together as if he were suppressing a scream.

"What is wrong, Birger?" asked Erik finally.

"How dare you ask me what is wrong?" exploded Birger between clenched teeth, his hands grasping at the armrests so hard that his knuckles turned white. "You, of all people, ask me what is wrong?"

"Yes, I do. Would you please tell me?" demanded Erik while he turned to Valdemar with a puzzled look.

"How could you send a spy to my court? To your own brother!" hissed Birger, almost propelling himself out of his chair as he increased the pressure on the arm rests.

"What spy?" Erik retorted, incredulous.

"There is no use denying it, so stop acting innocent. You have used that skill all your life, but it will not work this time," said Birger getting more upset by the moment.

"Birger, I do not know what you are talking about!"

"Stop denying it, and tell me why you did it," insisted Birger, furiously beating his fist on the armrest.

"I did not place a spy on you."

"Neither did I," interjected Valdemar. "Why would we do that?"

"We caught him red-handed, and he specifically mentioned Erik's name before he died," said Birger, unable to control his rage. "You must know he is dead since you have not heard from him lately."

"With the assistance of the Master of the Chamber anyone will confess to anything," said Erik sarcastically. "If the man really was a spy, he was not sent by me."

"Then why would he name you?" insisted Birger.

"I cannot answer that. But have you considered the fact that there are quite a few men, other than me, who bear the name Erik? Did you hear him confess yourself? Or are you relying on what you were told?"

Birger was silent for a moment before he answered, "I did not hear the confession myself, but whom could he have meant but you? No other Erik would have such a burning interest in what transpires at our court. Furthermore, there is no reason to believe anyone would lie about something as serious as a final confession."

"There is every reason to believe someone would lie if it would serve them to do so. May I venture to guess that it was your precious Lord High Constable who overheard the confession?" Erik countered, unable to contain his own rising anger.

"It does not matter who did," answered Birger defensively, verifying that it was, indeed, Torgils. "If there had been nothing to independently substantiate it, I would be skeptical of a tortured man's last words. But there are other coincidences . . ." he ended weakly.

"Listen to me!" said Erik as he slowly walked towards his brother. "Let this idiocy stop right here and now! The spy was not sent by me. If Lord Torgils said he was, he is lying! And he has every reason to split us apart, so he can continue to exert control over you."

"You suspect Lord Torgils of everything," interrupted Birger, getting his second wind. "You accused him of conspiring against Sweden, which I know to be untrue; and now you are accusing him of lying about the spy."

"You take Torgils' word over mine?"

"Precisely so, brother!" retorted Birger fiercely.

Time seemed suspended as the three brothers stared at one another. Nothing but the crackling flames on the hearth could be heard in the eerie silence. Erik was seething, but he drew a deep breath to gain control of himself before he began to speak.

"For the last time, I am telling you that neither Valdemar nor I have spied on you."

"I do not believe you."

"Then tell me what my reasons would be for spying on you."

Birger sat silent before he hesitantly said, "I know why, and I do not want to discuss it anymore."

"I am afraid you have to discuss it," insisted Erik. "Someone has falsely accused me, and we have to find out why." Birger looked as if he wanted to believe Erik, but at the same time was too convinced of his guilt to yield. "You do not even want to listen to your own brother? Are you so completely under Torgils' heel?"

"You do not think I can handle Torgils? You think he is controlling me? Well, he is not. I am the king, and I make all the final decisions!"

"Only an idiot would think that! You are nothing but his puppet!" said Erik in a voice as cold as ice.

Birger rose from his chair grasping his chest as if he was having heart failure. "How dare you talk to me like that!" he screamed.

"Because I speak the truth, and you do not have the decency to listen to me, who have not wronged you," said Erik with furious calm. "I have always thought you weak and easy to maneuver. You possess none of the qualities of an effective ruler. The one and only reason you are king is that you were first born!" By now Erik's fury knew no bounds, and his long-suppressed thoughts poured forth. "This kingdom is functioning only because we have not had a major crisis since you took over, and because you have Lord Torgils by your side to keep you from making the most rudimentary mistakes. And the saddest part of it is that you yourself know how weak you are. Why, otherwise, would you have delayed your coronation for three years? Was it so Valdemar could become Duke of Finland? No, it was simply because you lacked the strength to take command!" Erik felt Valdemar's restraining hand on his arm, but he shook it off. "You again confirm what a pathetic king you are when you refuse to even question this accusation. Instead, you blindly follow what your advisor wants you to think. As my King and Ruler, you have lost my respect." Erik took a deep breath and turned his back on Birger.

"We should talk about this calmly," pleaded Valdemar. "You have been misled, Birger, and we should find out why."

Birger, who heard Erik's tirade with shocked disbelief, rose from his chair. "More than ever—now, when I have heard from your own lips what you really think of me--do I believe what I was told. Henceforth we shall meet in the Council, but that is all that we shall see of one another."

Erik slowly turned to face Birger, his eyes filled with disdain. "You are a patheticly small man, Brother. But let right be right. In regard to the border town, of course you should claim its taxes. It is on your land." Erik bowed derisively to his brother who stood with both fists clenched before he strode from the chamber with Valdemar close behind.

Birger fell into his chair breathing heavily as his eyes filled with tears. The pain in his chest increased at the thought of never again spending close and carefree times with his brothers. He felt alone as never before, but how could he forgive such a despicable act? Erik had been vehement in his denial, and Birger had briefly believed him. But he could not allow himself to be taken in. Erik had always envied his crown.

Chapter 19

Nykoping

The wind was howling against the thick stonewalls of Nykoping castle, and cold seeped like frozen fingers through every crack and crevice. Erik and Valdemar sat drinking in the Hall with Mats and Abjorn, close to the roaring fire. The weather had prevented them from hunting for days, and none of them were in high spirits. Kristina sensed that their somber mood was not just from being confined in the castle. Erik and Valdemar had been downcast all winter. She had asked again and again what was bothering them, but each time they had given cheerful assurances that everything was proceeding just splendidly. She did not believe them. Especially when they had not gone to Stockholm for the customary Christmas celebrations. So, when she bid the four men good night and started up to her chamber, she secreted herself in the shadows of the stairwell.

"Something has to change," she heard Erik say. "Things cannot remain as they are."

"But what can we do? Birger listens to no one but Torgils," sighed Valdemar.

"All of us here are convinced that the spy was sent by the Church. After all, Bishop Nils told you about the land exchange before anyone else knew, and the only way he could have received that information would be from a spy. Why not tell that to the king?" asked Abjorn.

"I just told you. Birger is convinced that we spied on him and is oblivious to any other possibility," Erik concluded bitterly

"Why not ask Bishop Nils to tell King Birger the truth, if indeed, it was their spy?" asked Mats.

"He would never admit to it," ventured Valdemar. "The Church is about to regain her privileges. The bishops cannot risk the king's ire now. And we cannot prove it was the Church's spy, just as we could not prove that Lords Torgils and Jakob conspired."

Kristina's heart began to pound. Spies. Conspiracy. Her father and Count Jakob. What were they talking about?

At that moment she heard a muffled sound behind her. It would not do for any of the servants to find her eavesdropping on her husband and brother-in-law, so she continued quickly up the stairs. As she neared the top, she stood face to face with Harald. She got the feeling that they both were pretending to look unconcerned about having encountered each other in the stairwell.

"Where are you going, Kristina?" asked Valdemar as he entered the courtyard and noticed his wife attired in warm traveling clothes. She and Ragna were arranging her trunks on the cart where his and Erik's chests were already loaded.

"I am sailing to Stockholm with you."

She saw his face register concern. "But . . . it is an uncomfortable journey, my dear. The sea ice has not melted fully, and the voyage might be rough."

"I do not care," she replied, rebelliously. "I have not seen Marta and the boys for months."

Erik entered the courtyard and the brothers exchanged quick glances before Erik said, "We shall be in Stockholm only a short while, Kristina. Would you not be more comfortable here?"

"Why can I not come?" she asked, studying them.

"Who said that you could not come?" asked Valdemar. "I simply think this is the worst time of the year to travel."

"I agree with you. But I have been closed in here longer than you have, and am looking forward to any change, good or bad."

Erik flashed an ingratiating smile while making one last effort. "The captain said that we might encounter a gale strength storm . . ." But he was speaking to her back as she mounted her horse.

"I am ready," was all she said as she turned to look down at him.

Kristina sank gratefully into the warm tub. Erik and Valdemar had been right when they had warned her of an uncomfortable journey. The sea voyage had been windy and blistering cold. Luckily, it was bathing day in Stockholm castle, affording her a steaming bath the moment they arrived. She wondered how long she would need to linger in the tub to feel like a human being again.

"I am so happy you came," exclaimed Marta who had finished her bath and was already combing her long, wet hair by the fire. They were alone in the bathhouse, as the lesser ladies would follow later. " Did you see how the boys have grown?" she asked proudly. Marta seemed childishly happy to have Kristina back again, and Kristina could not sense the slightest tension in her voice. But then, maybe Birger kept problems to himself, just as his brothers did. It was clear that she would learn nothing from Marta.

When Ragna arrived with more hot water Kristina welcomed her with a contented sigh. She closed her eyes and curled deeper into the warmth. Marta slipped on her padded robe, wrapped a towel around her head, and pulled on her slippers. "Enjoy your bath," she said as she prepared to leave. "Come and see me when you have finished."

Kristina nodded and relaxed. She was blissfully dozing when she heard the door open and saw her stepmother enter. "Lady Hedvig," she exclaimed in surprise on seeing her father's wife. "I did not expect to see you here."

"Greetings, Kristina," cooed Hedvig as she threw off her robe and stepped into another tub which two ladies-in-waiting were filling with steaming water. "I got bored at home, so I came to court for a little amusement. Ah, this is lovely," she said as she sank down in her tub.

"How are you finding the Swedish court?" Kristina asked, eager to continue the conversation and guessing Hedvig was the one person who would speak freely if she knew anything of the problems troubling Erik and Valdemar. "Some interesting things are going on," noted Kristina searchingly.

"So, you have already noticed."

"Yes, but I still do not know who sent the spy they all seem so upset about," Kristina ventured audaciously.

"I am sure you do not want to believe that brothers spy on brothers, but it is not uncommon. I imagine that the dukes did not relish being found out and will continue to deny the spy was theirs." Hedvig fell silent as Ragna and the ladies-in-waiting returned with more hot water. "Do not fret, Kristina. Your husband might have lost some influence, but your father is in a stronger position than ever," continued Hedvig after the ladies had left. "Your father's present position almost makes up for what I was originally promised. Of course, nothing makes up for a crown, but your father is almost wearing one, the way the king follows his advice."

Her father almost a king? Kristina was at a loss until she remembered what Valdemar had referred to as a conspiracy between Count Jakob and her father.

"You seem to be taking it well, but how about Count Jakob?" Kristina asked innocently, hoping her question was vague enough not to disclose her ignorance.

"What could he do? Once your father received consolidated landholdings in central Sweden, rather than in the west, their plan fell apart."

Kristina's mind was racing. Had they planned to annex their lands and together create a kingdom? But that would have been treason against the crowns of Denmark and Sweden.

"I assume King Birger never found out about it?" she asked searchingly.

"Evidently not. How otherwise would your father be in such a powerful position?"

"You are not talking to anyone about this, are you?" Kristina asked anxiously.

"Of course not, Kristina. How stupid do you think I am? I am not about to spoil our situation. But you and me, we are family. Come scrub my back," Hedvig demanded as Kristina stepped out of her tub.

After accommodating Hedvig, Kristina excused herself and ran to her and Valdemar's chamber, overtaken by dread. Whatever was to happen, it would hurt someone she loved. She could hear the wise old woman predicting her future: "I see betrayal and death among those close to you."

The Great Hall was hot, smoke-filled, and noisy. A lavish supper was about to be served to the visiting Council members and other guests, and Kristina knew that the festivities would last until late into the night.

When everyone had seated themselves at the dais table, Kristina became acutely aware that she had lost her seat of honor beside the king that was customarily hers on the first night of a visit. In her place sat Lady Hedvig who had also taken note of the subtle rebuke, but who exhibited no reaction to the change that favored her. Marta looked briefly at Kristina with a surprised expression but was quickly engaged in conversation by the archbishop who was seated beside her. As the evening progressed, Kristina could not help but notice that the royal brothers never once exchanged a word or even a glance. While her father had greeted her warmly on their arrival, he had bowed wordlessly to Erik and Valdemar. The situation was unbearably tense. She had to do something.

What that would be she could not fathom as she sat in her bed, aimlessly staring at the walls with her prayer book unread in her lap. Finally, Valdemar arrived.

"What is going on?" she blurted out as he closed the door behind him.

"You should not get involved," was all he would say as he began to undress.

"I thank you for your consideration . . . but I cannot go on like this, seeing you and Erik so unhappy."

"There seems to be nothing we can do to change it right now."

"Please, tell me everything," she pleaded.

"All right," he relented. "It is not fair to keep the truth from you any longer."

Kristina sat silent for a long time after he had finished. "I simply cannot believe that my father would lie like that. He must have misunderstood what the dying man said."

"This is exactly why we did not want to tell you about it," said Valdemar. "You would face a difficult choice as to where your loyalty lies."

"Because I am in the middle, maybe I could help to clear up any misunderstandings," she said hopefully. Valdemar only shook his head. "It is my choice to try," she insisted.

Kristina did not sleep that night. She rose at dawn, and after praying in the chapel with little concentration she settled down by the newly lit fire in the Great Hall to wait. As she had hoped, her father was the first to descend the stairs. He looked surprised when he saw her.

"It is early, my sweet," he said as he came over to kiss her forehead.

"Father, we must talk," she began urgently. Torgils expression turned somber as he sat down opposite her. "I know everything which has transpired during the past year. Everything. About your plans with Count Jakob and your claim that the spy you caught was working for Erik."

Torgils sat studying his daughter before he leaned over to take her hand. "My dear Kristina, you should not concern yourself with these matters. It will only confuse you."

"Please, do not speak to me like a child."

"I understand that you are grown now. But it is unwise to press issues over which you have no control because they will only hurt you."

"But you are my father, and you are causing harm to my husband and my household. How can I just stand by?"

"That is a woman's role, Kristina," Torgils said with finality.

"But why did you tell King Birger that Erik sent the spy? I am sure that he did not."

Torgils stood up. "The spy clearly said Erik's name. I would not lie about that. Put all this out of your mind." He leaned forward and quickly stroked her cheek before he left the Hall.

"My father swears that your name was given, Erik. I can feel that he is telling the truth. Just as I feel that you are truthful when you say that you did not plant the spy," Kristina said, close to tears. "I should not have tried to intercede, I accomplished nothing. I am so sorry."

Erik took her gently in his arms. "You tried, and we are grateful," he said softly as he rocked her in his strong embrace.

She could no longer control her emotions. If she cried because of the enmity between her family members, or because she had longed for Erik to hold her like this for so long, she did not know, but her tears were unstoppable. Erik held her close as they stood in the cold wind on the parapet where they had spent so many hopeful moments.

"When are we going home?" she asked as he reluctantly released her when a guard neared them.

"As soon as we can. And do not cry, Kristina, this will solve itself. But right now, I have to go to a Council meeting," he said as he abruptly let go of her and ran down the stairs.

She again wondered who was telling the truth. Her father, or the man she loved? No answer presented itself, and she realized that she was far too upset to go to Marta's chamber and gossip with the ladies. Instead she went to her own chamber, put on warm clothes and boots, and asked for a horse to be saddled before she went into the aviary.

High on a perch sat her beloved Soot. She had not taken him with her to Nykoping since she had had no time for hunting during the past year. She whistled for him, and he impatiently pulled at his jesses which held him to his perch. She stepped over and untied him. She let him settle on her glove before she took a piece of meat from a jar to feed him. He looked in fine condition, and she carefully pulled a hood over his head before she mounted her mare.

No one paid attention as she rode over the drawbridge with the hood of her cloak drawn over her face. She knew that it was unwise to ride to the forest alone, but she was far too upset to dwell on what was appropriate or safe. Once she had reached the glen, she dismounted, unhooded Soot and threw him into the air. She could almost feel what he experienced in spreading his wings and taking to the skies, untethered and free. She wished she could join him, rather than staying earthbound and filled with fear of what lay ahead.

She stood watching him circle the area until he disappeared over the treetops. She paced back and forth on the frozen ground to keep warm while trying to spot her falcon. She felt the tears running down her face again, but she was unable to stop them. She prayed that the four men who had taken such opposite stands would be able to resolve their differences before something dreadful happened.

Suddenly she saw Soot coming towards her, flying low, and being chased by three hawks. When she whistled for her bird to return to her, she was ignored as her falcon tried to elude his pursuers. But as they were three, at least one of them was constantly hacking at his tail. Soot must have sensed the futility of escaping the hawks in the open air, so he flew in among the trees. Kristina rushed after him, along the beaten path. She heard frantic screeches and she ran even faster. Then she saw the hawks soar up in flight and quickly disappear, but she saw no trace of her falcon. She whistled for him as she ran towards the area from where she had seen the hawks lift off, but she could not find Soot. She ran in and out among the bushes before she again heard a screech from further up the path. Her heart stopped in horror as she saw a large lynx paw at Soot who was flopping on the ground in an effort to escape. The lynx made ready to pounce for the kill when out of nowhere an arrow whizzed through the air to pierce its neck. The lynx fell heavily to the ground and Kristina rushed forward to see how badly her bird was hurt.

"Do not get near the cat until we are certain it is dead!" ordered a hunter dressed in green dashing forward to deftly cut the animal's throat.

"He will make a handsome rug," he said as he released his grip on the lynx and then bent down beside the falcon still thrashing on the ground. Gently he lifted the bird, placed it on its back, and stroked its belly to calm it down before he examined it. "A broken wing, my lady. Let me take him to your falconer so he can tend to him," the man suggested.

"I am here alone . . . " stammered Kristina. The stranger looked quizzically at her, then turned his head and whistled. Kristina heard hoof beats, and soon she saw a horse come down the path.

"Let us see what we can do for him, then," said the man as he looked into a saddlebag when the horse stopped beside him. "Maybe you can hold your bird while I get what we need."

Kristina obediently took the docile bird, while the man pulled out a piece of cloth that he ripped into thin strips. Then he looked around on the ground until he found two twigs that passed his scrutiny. Gently he braced the bird's wing, and carefully wound the strips to hold the twigs in place.

"It is unusual for a falcon to perch so low that a lynx can get to him," commented the man.

"He was being chased by hawks and was flying low to elude them."

"Well, we shall never know what happened, but he will serve you soon again," he said as he bowed to Kristina who was still concentrating on the bird in his hands.

"How do I get him home?" she asked helplessly, realizing that she could not ride and hold the wounded bird at the same time.

"I will be glad to help you home safely. You need not cry, my lady."

Suddenly aware that her tears were still streaming, she looked up at the man's face. The hunter had the kindest and most caring eyes she had ever seen. Had it not been for his garb she would have taken him for a priest, or even a saint.

"You are sad for something other than your bird, then," he said matter-of-factly as he took the falcon from her and whistled for his horse to follow as they made their way back to the glen. Walking alongside him, she straightened her back and felt her courage return. What an amazing effect this man had on her, as if no problem in the world was unsolvable.

"Where may I escort you, my lady?" he asked.

"To the castle."

"That is where I am going," he said with a bow. "My name is Alf of Smaland."

Kristina's face lit up. "I am so pleased to meet you. Prince Magnus has spoken of nothing else but you. He admires you tremendously. And I am Kristina Torgilsdotter."

"Prince Magnus has often and lovingly spoken of his Aunt Ninnie. I am pleased to meet you, my lady."

Kristina untied and mounted her horse, briefly holding the bird while Alf mounted his. Then he took back the bird and cradled it in the crook of his arm as they rode slowly towards Stockholm. Kristina knew that he must be wondering what she was doing alone in the forest flying a hunting bird, but he asked no questions. She felt comfortable riding beside him. In the same gentle manner with which he cradled her bird, he seemed to envelop her with his quiet serenity. In silence, they entered the city and rode through the narrow lanes.

"You must find me very silly to cry the way I did," she finally said.

"Not at all. There are, unfortunately, many painful things in this world, and I think it was wise of you to release your sadness so that it will not fester."

"But crying did not solve my problem. It is still there, making me feel as badly as ever."

"Give time a chance. It has a tendency of solving everything. I know," he said as they rode up over the drawbridge. The guards saluted as Kristina quickly dismounted and reached up for the falcon that the man placed in her hands.

"How can I ever thank you?" she asked, not wanting to leave his calming presence.

"You already have," smiled Alf as he dismounted. "And please do not worry, my lady, your tears will remain my secret," he confided as though he had read her thoughts.

She blushed. "I will take my bird to the falconer," she said as she turned towards the aviary.

Birger was impressed, even astonished, with the results of Alf of Smaland's tutelage of the castle guards and little Prince Magnus. After only a few months of training, the bowmanship of the guardsmen had markedly improved, and little Magnus had learned far more than was to be expected from a four-year-old. Moreover, everyone in the royal household had grown fond of Alf for his quiet, considerate ways. He had a powerful, and at the same time, unassuming manner of command. His almost uncanny way of dealing with people seemed to be based on his instinctively knowing what they were really like. And because he seemed to understand their innermost feelings, people automatically trusted him and listened when he spoke. Even the royal chaplain praised Alf's ethical views on life.

One night, when they were alone, Marta pleaded with Birger to let Alf stay on as Magnus' permanent companion.

"My love, I am fully aware that this is a role normally undertaken by a fully trained knight," she said. "But a prince's training should be more than just weapon skills, and I know Alf would be the perfect companion."

The following day Birger summoned Alf to the audience chamber where the hunter arrived with little Prince Magnus in tow.

"Father, Alf brought me a baby fox. His family was killed, and he would have died if he had been left alone. Alf says that he must return to the forest when he gets older, but I want to keep him, Father, may I?" Magnus asked excitedly.

"I think Alf is right, Magnus," Birger replied.

"You called for me, your Majesty?" Alf asked as he bowed to the king.

"As you know, it is time we select the companion for Prince Magnus. The queen and I have come to a decision. It is to be you, Alf."

"But your Majesty, the companion to a crown prince should be a nobleman with the proper education. I am just a man of the woods."

"I know very well what is customary, Alf, but we feel that you have qualities found in few men. You have the humanity we all admire; and you are wise, though you have no formal education. We have therefore decided that you will receive your education along with the prince. Whatever he learns, you will learn. When you finish, you shall be as educated as any nobleman."

"I am most honored, if serving in that way would gratify your Majesty," said Alf with a low bow.

"Magnus," said the king to his son. "From now on you address Alf as "Master Alf". You obey him as you would me. Master Alf will be with you all the time from now on."

"I like that," beamed the youngster, affectionately tugging on Alf's sleeve. As the hunter and the small boy left the chamber, Birger felt pleased with his decision. Alf had the strength of character any father would want his son to acquire.

But the feeling of pleasure vanished as thoughts of his brothers returned to haunt him. He missed them, and yet he despised them; and he knew that he had to do something to rid himself of the pain of pretending that they did not exist.

Chapter 20

Nykoping, Sweden 1304

The messenger galloped past them down the road splattering mud in all directions. Kristina, Ragna, and the other ladies stepped quickly off the path to avoid being soiled. They all had their arms filled with huge bouquets of wood anemones they intended to place about the castle to announce the long-awaited arrival of spring.

"He was wearing the royal colors!!" Ragna exclaimed excitedly as she stepped back on the road. Kristina's face brightened with anticipation, and she hastened her steps toward Nykoping castle. When she and her ladies entered the courtyard, she handed her flowers to Ragna and raced into the Hall where Erik and Valdemar had been laboring over their accounts. Erik was eagerly unrolling a scroll of parchment. Without looking up he gestured for those in the Hall to leave him and Valdemar alone with Kristina.

"Birger is asking us to come to see him at Aranas. If I remember correctly that is one of your father's estates, Kristina, in order as he puts it 'to clarify our respective positions'".

"He might finally listen to the truth," Valdemar added hopefully.

"Who knows what he has in mind. But we are inconsequential without Birger's support, so I think we should go."

"I agree. Kristina, would you like to accompany us?" Valdemar asked.

"I would have insisted, had you not asked me."

A week later, with an escort of sixty men led by Lords Mats and Abjorn, they set off on their trip to the western part of Sweden where

Aranas was situated. It was a long journey by ship and on horseback, but Kristina would not have minded a trip of any length if it promised to resolve the differences that divided those she loved. She was eager to revisit one of her childhood homes, from where she had dim but sweet memories of her mother.

Upon disembarking their ships in Lodose the travelers delighted in the greening of the countryside. The trees were bursting with swollen buds, and birds were busy building their nests. The earth smelled rich and fertile as they crossed spacious fields, and stately pine trees enveloped them in their fragrant scent as they rode through the forests.

They arrived at Aranas on the last day of April. The estate looked exactly as Kristina remembered it, only smaller. The central building with its single large hall appeared to have shrunk slightly, as did the many buildings clustered around it.

The hall where her family and their servants had spent the cold months of those years was a dark place, with only a few small windows so as not to lose precious heat. In the center of the room was the large fire pit where an endless variety of delicious foods had been prepared. She recognized the long tables, and even found her childishly carved initials on the side of one tabletop. The two large chairs that her parents had used still stood by the fire pit. She spotted her bed; one of the many built in along the walls, and she noticed that the painted cupboard beneath it still bore her name. She recalled how the family would have the hall to themselves during the summer when the servants repaired to the attics of the outbuildings for greater privacy.

Her father welcomed them cordially, and after washing off the road dust, Erik and Valdemar sat down at one end of the hall with Birger and their host. The other inhabitants and guests went about their business with the acquired discretion of people accustomed to living in close proximity. Kristina knew that she would be unable to overhear the conversation at the other end of the hall, so she resigned herself to reminiscing with the servants.

"I have called this meeting to formalize our future behavior towards one another," Birger began. "Please be so good as to read this document and seal it." He hardly glanced at his brothers as he spoke, and Erik noticed he appeared unusually pale. He and Valdemar bent over the document that Birger pushed towards them. They read it with growing astonishment.

Erik was the first to speak. "In your invitation, you said that this meeting was--and I quote you--'to clarify our respective positions'. Now you are presenting us with a formal document which states that we cannot leave the country without your permission; that we cannot see you unless you send for us--and then, only with a limited number of men-at-arms. Now this is ridiculous, Birger!" protested Erik as he threw the document on the table. "This meeting should give us a chance to find out how your misconception arose, Birger," Valdemar added. "Instead you have concluded that we not only spied on you but are now conspiring against you. What has happened to you, brother?"

"Place your seals on the document," repeated Birger.

Erik looked at the Lord High Constable who had not entered the conversation. "Lord Torgils, you were the one who heard the confession of the spy," said Erik. "Could you not have misunderstood?"

Torgils, unsure whether the king had told his brothers that it was he who had overheard the spy's confession, did not answer immediately. Erik might be guessing, but he could not take that chance. "The spy gave your name," he said looking straight at Erik.

"Maybe his real master instructed him to say so, or have you not thought of that?" Erik asked sharply.

"I have thought of that," Birger answered in Torgil's stead. "Seal the document."

"You do not want to hear the truth, Birger, but again I swear that I did not send the spy. I can also swear that I have no intention of conspiring against you. But for your peace of mind, I shall affix my seal to this document as an act of good faith," Erik said as he pulled his heavy ducal chain and signet over his head. Valdemar waited for his brother to drip hot wax on the document and press his seal into it before he repeated the procedure. Erik broke the oppressive silence.

"Birger, I would lie if I said that you have not hurt me deeply with your baseless accusations. We shall be leaving now. No, do not bother being polite," said Erik as Lord Torgils made a gesture of protest. "I do not wish to spend another moment under your roof, Lord High Constable. We shall stay at Sinsta for three days in case you wish to speak to us further. Good-bye."

Erik and Valdemar motioned for their men to follow them out of the hall. Kristina came rushing out after them. "What happened? Where are you going?" she inquired anxiously.

"Birger did not care to listen to us," Valdemar replied, since Erik had turned away, too angry to speak. "We shall go to Sinsta, as planned. Perhaps Birger will come to his senses in a few days. You may do as you wish."

"I will remain here to see if I can make Father and the king understand that you are innocent of spying."

"That is kind of you," said Valdemar. "But I do not think it will do any good."

She watched them mount their steeds and ride off, fearing they were correct in their pessimism.

Birger sat with his head down, listening for the sound of horses, hoping his brothers would return to miraculously set everything right. His hands clasped the golden wine chalice Torgils had handed him and he took one large swig and then another. But as time passed his anger returned. "Why do they keep denying what a witness has already verified?"

"They hope that you will believe them rather than me," answered Torgils softly. "Still, why would I lie to you? I have absolutely nothing to gain and everything to lose by doing so."

"Erik claims that you want to split us apart so you can exercise total control over my decisions."

"That would make sense if I did not already have your trust. And even now you ask my advice only when you want it. I pray you do not feel that I impose my will on you."

"Of course not, Torgils." Birger took another swallow from his goblet before he continued: "Still, Erik pointed out that he is not the only Erik . . ." his voice drifted off.

"Naturally Erik Menved has informants at our court, though you are close allies," Torgils countered quickly. "That is to be expected. But Sweden and Denmark are presently on excellent terms, so he would only risk placing a spy to eavesdrop on you personally if you and he had some unresolved matters. I think we can safely rule him out." Birger nodded slowly. "Then there is Erik Valdemarson in Norway who probably feels that he should be King of Sweden had his father not been usurped, but he has no power or money to go against you. I can see no way to ignore the fact that that leaves only one Erik-- your brother."

"Every court wants to know what is happening at another, and we all have allies who report back to us. Erik has loyal friends in Stockholm and we have our friends in Nykoping, but with the bond we always had between us brothers, it is unforgivable to have someone crawling around listening at my keyhole." Birger stood up. "I am going to bed," he announced abruptly, and as he turned to leave he did not see the victorious smile slowly spread over his Lord High Constable's face.

Once Birger got comfortably settled down, he listened to the voices that filtered through the heavy curtains shielding his bed. Through a slight parting in their drapery he could see the fire flicker on the hearth. He was infused with a feeling of normalcy that reminded him of his childhood. Then he had shared a bed like this one with his brothers, times where they had shared every secret through the hours of the night. They had never sought other friendships as their closeness was all they needed. He had never questioned their loyalty until now. Night after night he had turned in his bed trying to find an answer which would prove that his brothers were still his trusted friends, but he was always left with the memory of Erik's tirade when confronted with the spy's allegations. Birger now knew clearly that Erik thought him pathetically weak as a king, a figure of ridicule even. What audacity for Erik to think himself better suited to rule Sweden.

Erik and Valdemar spent three days drinking and hunting at Sinsta, an estate that belonged to a relative of Lord Mats, but they could not forget their predicament for even one moment. On the morning of the third day a message arrived from Birger. Erik was handed the message in bed. He dismissed the young girl at his side, pulled on his hose and shirt, and threw the curtains aside.

"Birger is requesting a meeting at Visingso castle. We are not to bring more than twenty men-at-arms. What do you think he has in mind this time?" Erik asked, walking over to Valdemar and Mats who were breaking fast at one of the tables.

"Stay away from Visingso, my lord. To be told to bring such a small escort reeks of treachery," Mats said firmly.

"Do you think he is going to harm us?" wondered Erik. "No, he has some perverse desire to humiliate us. After all, he is convinced we spied on him, and the only pleasure he can derive now is to see us crawl before him."

"You have done nothing to merit such treatment," Mats insisted angrily.

"He does not know that, Mats," said Erik. "We must try one more time."

Ten days later Birger received his brothers in the library at Visingso castle together with Kristina. Erik and Valdemar had not seen Lord Torgils anywhere about, which encouraged them slightly. After greetings had been exchanged, Kristina, visibly worried, absented herself at a gesture from Valdemar. If they were going to be further humiliated they wanted to receive Birger's abuse in private. He seemed as cold and distant as he had during their previous encounter, and again he had a document on the table before him.

"You have acted against me on several occasions during the last months," he recited without emotion. "Number one: you have exported grain abroad without my permission. Number two: you have been seen in the company of my enemies. Number three: one of your knights has badly abused one of my servants. Number four: your tournament champions have bested mine too often!"

Erik and Valdemar stared at him, their mouths agape. "Have you lost your mind?" Erik responded, incredulously. "Is this how you spend your time? Have you forgotten that you are a king, and have far more important matters to deal with?"

"Birger, I have never heard such stupid nonsense," Valdemar blurted out. "The grain came from Erik's lands, and was sent to Norway because they had a bad harvest last year."

"Erik's dukedom is in Sweden, and he must first get my permission," countered Birger.

"If Erik and I have been seen with your enemies, we do not know who they are, and therefore we were not with them to upset you," continued Valdemar. "If any of our knights have mistreated any of your servants we are also unaware of it. And, finally, we can hardly be sad that our champions won over yours in fair competition, can we?"

Erik put his hand on Valdemar's arm. "Do not dignify such idiocy with an explanation." He turned to Birger with disdain. "Again, we have come before you to try to solve the riddle of who sent the spy, knowing full well that you would treat us without dignity or kindness. Still, we came. But it is clear that you are blind to the truth!"

Erik gestured to Valdemar to exit the library. Walking down the corridor, they could hear Birger screaming after them, "How dare you leave! I have not finished with you!"

Queen Ingeborg looked up in surprise as her husband flung open the door to her chamber in Roskilde castle where she was at work with her ladies-in-waiting.

"I have a wonderful surprise for you!" he announced as he motioned for her to follow him with a wide grin.

She stood up, causing skeins of yarn to drop from her lap. "What is it?" she asked as she hastened down the corridor behind him.

"Something that will make you very happy," he promised as he took her hand.

Ingeborg descended the stairs to the Great Hall filled with anticipation. She gasped when she saw Erik, Valdemar, and Kristina standing by the foot of the staircase. She let go of her husband's hand as she ran to throw herself into Erik's arms. She hugged Valdemar and Kristina fiercely.

"Why did you not tell us you were coming?" she asked as she embraced Kristina once more. "It has been so long since I saw you, and you should have given me the pleasure of expecting you." She failed to notice the solemn looks on their faces as she hugged them again and again. "Come with me, Kristina, to bathe and rest." Ingeborg swept Kristina along with her as she motioned for servants to help with their travelling chests. "I have dreamt about this day ever since we last saw each other at Birger's wedding," Ingeborg continued without a pause while she dragged Kristina up the stairs.

Erik Menved smiled. "You have made your sister very happy," he said to his brothers-in-law before he ordered his servants to ready their chambers. "Please, come to see me before supper."

Erik and Valdemar washed and refreshed themselves before going to the king's private chamber. Erik Menved, unlike his wife, quickly sensed something was amiss.

"What is the problem?" he asked with evident concern, after exchanging polite formalities.

As concisely as he could, Erik related the latest incidents. Erik Menved listened intently, asking only the occasional question. "We do not know what to do. Birger is acting like a lunatic, and we have come to ask for your advice and possible intervention. You are the only person, apart from Torgils Knutsson, Birger would listen to," said Erik, finishing his tale.

"I will be glad to talk to Birger and tell him what you had no chance to impart. I shall also listen to his side of the story. I do not think he is out of his mind. He is deeply hurt, and he is doing all he can to make you suffer. Childish maybe, but not insane."

"You may be right," conceded Erik. "But it is ridiculous that we have become estranged as the result of a lie or misconception."

"But now you are our guests, and we want you to have a pleasant stay. Try to put this from your minds, and I shall send a message to Birger right away."

"Thank you," Erik responded appreciatively. "I know that you have more pressing concerns, so we are grateful for the time you are giving to our problem."

"We are kin, and that comes before all else," said the king with a warm smile.

After Kristina had finished bathing, Ingeborg sat brushing her hair in front of a small fire just as they had done countless times in their childhood. Kristina wore a pained expression as she confided in detail all she knew of what had transpired between the Swedish royal brothers and her father. "I know that Erik and Valdemar never sent a spy. I can feel that they are truthful. And I am equally convinced that the king believes they did based on what my father told him. What I do not know is if my father could have misunderstood the confession or . . ."

"I can understand that you do not want to believe that your father could be deliberately lying. But politics are politics, and men do things they feel are perfectly justified to achieve their goals, whatever we women may think about it."

"He told me as much," sighed Kristina. "Neither he nor the king paid me the slightest heed when I pleaded with them at Aranas. My father became angry, and the king just stared into space. I felt like a fool."

"Let us see if my husband can help," said Ingeborg encouragingly.

Kristina studied Ingeborg with concern. "I have not once asked how you are faring. I am unforgivably thoughtless."

Ingeborg bit her lip, and Kristina could see tears begin to well in her eyes. "I have yet to carry a babe into this world. I have lost six already, and I am petrified that I will not be able to give my husband an heir."

"Does it happen the same way every time? Or at the same stage of your carrying?"

"No, it happens at different times, but it is always sudden. And as vigilant as Lady Brigitte has been, and as much as I hoped my miscarriages were not caused by any one person, I know that someone must be behind them. If he, or she, has used poison or black magic, I do not know, but I cannot bear for it to happen again. I feel utterly defenseless, Kristina. But without solid proof, I dare not talk to my husband of my suspicions," she said sadly.

"Did Lady Brigitte show you the Thor's Hammers we found during your first two miscarriages?"

"Yes, she did, but they have vanished. And even if I had them, what proof is that of who placed them?" Ingeborg shook her head.

"I wish I could be of help," Kristina said.

"Maybe you can," whispered Ingeborg. "I think I am expecting again, but I have told no one, not even my husband. Together, with Lady Brigitte and your dear little Ragna, we might be able to outwit the culprit this time. We can say that you are expecting, Kristina, so that no one becomes suspicious when the ladies keep extra vigilance over the food we eat. But maybe you really are with child. Do we need to lie?"

"We cannot use that pretext without Valdemar knowing it is untrue."

"Come now. Men never know about these things in the beginning."

Kristina looked at Ingeborg with deep sadness. "You have confided in me, so I will tell you my own secret. I have never lain with a man, not even my own husband."

Ingeborg looked incredulous until Kristina imparted her desolate tale.

"Oh, Kristina," exclaimed Ingeborg pulling Kristina close to her. "We are both to be pitied. But one day we shall become mothers, just as nature intended, despite how bleak it may look now. If I did not believe that, I would go mad."

"Won'erful to have you back in Denmark again," slurred Kristoffer as he lifted his chalice to toast Erik and Valdemar for the sixth time. He was already drunk although the welcome feast had just begun. Erik and Valdemar had kept up with his toasts, but they were too morose to lose their sobriety.

"Things have changed since we last met," mused Kristoffer. "We have received our titles, and we rule our lands. My dukedom in Southern Halland is a rich one, though it took my brother long enough to give it to me," he sneered.

Erik could discern the change in Kristoffer. He had always exuded arrogance, but his visage now betrayed his unmistakably cruel side. He had deep lines etched in his face, far too deep for his age, as if his anger had seeped to the surface. Erik pitied the thin-nosed, flat-chested, and richly dowered Euphemia of Pomerania who had become Kristoffer's wife. Still, he was glad that it was Kristoffer, not himself, who had married her. Kristoffer was abusive towards the servants and had no kind words for anyone. But Erik, like the Danish courtiers, had to smile to his face, as he had become too powerful to ignore. Being Kristoffer's enemy could be lethal--that was made plain by the way the men around him cowered.

"I deserved an even larger dukedom, as I and my armies have supported my brother against his unruly neighbors for years. I almost lost a leg in one of the battles at Rostock. But as a younger brother, one has to be grateful for what one gets. Right?" He grinned at Erik and Valdemar, who only nodded in return. The one-way conversation continued throughout the meal, and by the time the ladies rose to leave, Kristoffer was almost incoherent. "Look there. That is the one person who can make it impossible for me to become king."

Erik looked over to where Kristoffer fixed his hateful stare. "My sister?" Erik asked.

He saw Kristoffer stiffen before he feigned an innocent smile--an effort that was utterly unsuccessful. "I think I have had too much to drink. Let us take a walk and get some fresh air." Erik and Valdemar politely excused themselves, explaining they were tired from their journey.

The first few weeks at the Danish court passed pleasantly enough. The hunting parties for wild boar were exciting, and the feasts were elaborate. But as much as Erik and Valdemar tried, they could not forget their troubles back home, and as the days passed they became less and less interested in leisurely pursuits.

Erik Menved found little time for entertaining visitors as he was constantly closeted with his council, planning new offensives against his contentious neighbors. Because Abjorn and Mats had remained in Sweden to tend to his and Valdemar's affairs, Erik had no one to turn to but Kristoffer. Naturally, Valdemar spent much time with them, but at night it was Kristoffer who remained by the fire. At first, Erik had found his depraved relative difficult to endure. But as the weeks passed Kristoffer held his drinking to more reasonable levels and Erik realized that the cruel exterior hid a surprisingly erudite man; and since Kristoffer spent a minimum of time with his wife, a man who was as lonely as himself.

It took a long time for Erik to trust Kristoffer enough to tell him about his shattered relationship with Birger. Kristoffer listened without comment. When Erik finished he found surprising empathy in Kristoffer's eyes.

"So, we thought that we would finally be our own masters in our dukedoms," Kristoffer ventured. "But our lives will always depend on our brothers' good will."

"I know that now," sighed Erik. "I was both stupid and arrogant to believe that I would always have some influence over Birger."

"Let us hope my brother will be able to clear up the misconception Birger labors under."

"I do not think Birger will be open-minded enough to listen to him. It has been many weeks since Erik Menved sent his message."

"Tomorrow," yawned Kristoffer. "Maybe tomorrow we shall get a reply."

Kristoffer's prediction appeared to be borne out when a messenger arrived the following day with the Swedish coat of arms showing through the dust on his tunic. But then Erik saw that it was his own crest the rider wore, as it did not carry the royal crown above. He felt a stab of disappointment but hoped it would be good news from Mats and Abjorn. He took the pouch from the messenger and walked down to the dock to be alone. He was oblivious to the beauty of the blooming fruit trees and to their sweet smell as he hurried through the orchard. He sat down on a bench running along the side of the dock. He eagerly broke the seal and began to unroll the scroll. What he read made his heart race and his mouth go dry.

After staring numbly out over the water he reread the message, praying that he had misunderstood its content. But as he read it a second time, he felt his entire being burn with fury over what had taken place in his absence. He started toward the castle, but before he entered, he turned to walk back through the orchard to calm himself. He moved quickly through the stand of white and pink flowering trees. He finally stopped and took a deep breath. It was then that he noticed a pair of woman's silk slippers half hidden by a familiar pale green tunic behind a tree trunk. Warily, he approached and discovered

Kristina sitting with her back against an apple tree, a small book resting in her lap, her eyes closed in sleep.

As suddenly as anger had seized him, it now evaporated as he stood gazing at her. She embodied such tranquility reposing there that he felt his entire body relax. She was so beautiful, her face like a child's, utterly at peace. Her long dark eyelashes cast shadows on her cheeks, and her mouth held the faintest smile of contentment. She had placed her headdress beside her on the ground, and her hair cascaded freely down her shoulders, the sun making it appear like spun gold. He felt his suppressed love surge forth. Carefully, so as not to wake her, he walked closer and bent down beside her. Unable to stop himself, he leaned forward and gently kissed her temple. He saw a smile light up her face, and without opening her eyes she reached out to him and he took her in his arms. Forgotten were his promises of never expressing his feelings for her as his lips found hers, and he kissed her with all the love and yearning he had so long resisted. He became so lost in their kiss that she startled him as she pulled back. "I thought I was dreaming," she whispered.

"I am sorry," . . .he said when he saw her eyes widen in confusion. "No, damn it, I am not. I am only sorry I cannot kiss you like that every day."

"But . . ."

"I know. I know," he sighed. "You are the wife of my brother."

Silently they sat looking at one another. He lifted her hand and held it to his lips. "Nothing has changed, Kristina, I love you with all my heart."

"And I, you," she whispered as she moved his hand to her cheek and closed her eyes. He was amazed at her effect on him. Only moments before he had been running like a wounded animal; and now, as he looked at her, he felt only her presence. She smiled sadly as she very reluctantly released his hand. "What is that?" she asked as she saw the scroll on the ground where Erik had dropped it.

"A message from Mats. Birger has seized Nykoping castle!"

"What? He took it by force?"

"With very little resistance. Your father's army arrived unexpectedly. This is an act of war, and for the life of me, I cannot understand how it could have gone this far." Erik felt his anger and frustration return as he contemplated his brother's attack on his home. "Birger has lost all reason. Even if I had placed a spy on him, this action makes no sense."

"He is so hurt, Erik, I could see it in his eyes. As much as he always envied you, he also admired and loved you; and the thought of you spying on him was more than he could endure."

"But how could your father seize our home? How could he do this to his own daughter?" Erik stared at Kristina who was looking dejectedly at the ground. He immediately regretted his words. His heart went out to her and his voice softened. "He was not acting against you, Kristina. You and Valdemar have a home in Finland. It is me he is attacking. Me alone."

They sat in silence as Erik contemplated his situation. He could not allow Birger to take his dukedom without a fight, even though his own army could easily be overpowered by Birger's.

"Does this mean war?" Kristina finally asked.

"How can it mean anything else?" Erik answered bitterly.

"You know that you cannot win against his army. Come with us to Finland."

He saw the pleading in her eyes, but at the moment his anger predominated. "I must fight for my dukedom. I have no choice."

"Before you make up your mind, wait until Erik Menved has spoken to Birger."

"Birger has not even responded to Erik Menved's proposal for a meeting. By seizing Nykoping, he has made clear that his mind is made up."

"I do not want anything to happen to you," Kristina whispered.

Erik realized he was upsetting her, so he turned to other topics. "Ingeborg, how is she? I have not had the opportunity to speak to her in privacy."

"She is heartbroken, not to have given Denmark an heir."

"Is that her fault, or is someone meddling?"

Kristina looked at him in surprise. "What makes you ask that?"

"Let me only say that I have a reason. Please, answer me honestly."

"We suspect that someone has placed a curse on her."

"Do you know who that could be?"

"Ingeborg does not, but I have my suspicions."

"As do I. It is Kristoffer," Erik said.

Kristina nodded. "That is whom I have suspected ever since she had her first miscarriage. Not that I have any proof, but I feel it in my guts."

"He let something slip once when he was drunk . . . it made me wonder . . ."

"If we both feel that way, we should do something."

"There is nothing we can do, except keep an eye on him."

"If you could get him away from court for half a year, we would find out if it is him."

"Should we not wait until Ingeborg is with child again?" Erik asked. Kristina looked uncomfortable and did not reply. "So, she is with child!"

"I did not tell you."

"No, you did not. Well, I will not betray her, and I will do my utmost to get Kristoffer away from here."

"You have at least another month or two before Ingeborg's condition becomes apparent."

"Let me try, then. And Kristina, if it is him, I shall kill him with my own hands."

"I feel better not being the only one who suspects Kristoffer. Not even Erik Menved knows that she is with child," Kristina confessed.

"Then it is our secret. No one will learn it from me."

In the distance they could hear supper being sounded on the large metal triangle hanging outside the kitchen. Reluctantly, Kristina reached for her headdress, gathered her hair on top of her head, and carefully put it on. She fastened the toque under her chin.

Erik helped her to her feet. They stood close together for a moment, smiling at each other with sadness before they slowly walked towards the castle.

A few days later, the long-awaited reply from Birger finally arrived.

"Birger and I are to meet in Fair Valley, on the Swedish-Danish border, in a few weeks," reported Erik Menved. "Birger makes no mention of you as a topic for discussion, only that the meeting is the official election of Prince Magnus as the future King of Sweden."

"Evidently Birger is not inclined to discuss our situation," said Erik.

"He is obviously not willing to let you think so," agreed Erik Menved. "But I am sure the topic will be broached between the two of us. I will bring Ingeborg along so she can keep Marta company, leaving Birger and me to spend time alone."

"Thank you," said Erik. "We shall accompany you to the border and make camp there. If Kristoffer joins you, he can let us know the outcome of your discussion," Erik suggested. Then he turned to Valdemar. "I think Kristina should also go to Fair Valley. She has little to do with our feud, and she would enjoy seeing her father and Marta again."

As Valdemar and Erik Menved nodded their agreement, Erik breathed a sigh of relief. If Ingeborg traveled, Kristoffer would be less likely to suspect her delicate condition, and Kristina would be there to care for her. If only he felt as good about the upcoming talks.

The dukes made their camp by a small forest lake about a mile from Fair Valley. There they eagerly awaited the news that would accompany Kristoffer's arrival, but after two days there was still no sign of him. Every hour seemed eternal, and both Erik and Valdemar became short tempered.

Their mood spread to their men-at-arms. While the tarn was lovely, it was remote, and the men had nothing to do. They became edgy and bored, and their normal bantering and joshing turned to bitter quarreling. When Valdemar's captain assaulted one who had mistakenly taken his cup of beer, Erik and Valdemar had to physically step in to separate them. However, by that time other knights had joined in the fray and were furiously pummeling one another.

Finally, Erik put two fingers between his lips to let out a piercing whistle. The men froze in surprise, while Erik bellowed, "Cease fighting, immediately! Anyone who cannot control himself will have to answer to me and my brother!" Sheepishly, the men separated and returned to their campfires.

Erik and Valdemar returned to their tent where Valdemar found a wad of cloth to stem the nosebleed caused by his captain's reckless flailing. "I cannot blame them," muttered Erik. "Even we are acting as if doomsday were on the morrow. Let us, at least, appear cheerful."

Late the following afternoon, the sentry announced the approach of a knight and six soldiers. When Kristoffer dismounted, Erik and Valdemar almost forgot to greet him in their eagerness to find out what had transpired. Kristoffer held them at bay until he had emptied several goblets of wine and all three were seated on a large stone formation that jutted out into the lake where they could easily spot anyone who came within earshot.

"I am afraid that I bring bad news," Kristoffer reported finally. "Our brothers spent much time together, and according to my brother, their final judgment was that you two are the villains in this affair."

"I cannot believe it!" Valdemar erupted angrily. "How could Torgils and Birger persuade a man as astute as your brother?"

"Lord Torgils never met with them in private. Birger, himself, convinced my brother."

"I told you that he is insane," said Erik, more in resignation than in anger. He looked out over the dark lake, silent and unmoving before him. "Did you find out what Birger plans? Will he take our dukedoms away from us?"

"I have no idea what he plans to do. My brother said nothing about that."

Erik and Valdemar sat brooding. Finally, Erik spoke. "Valdemar, I will fight for my inheritance. You do not have to. You should go to Finland and live in peace."

"We have always acted in concert," said Valdemar. "There is no reason to change now."

Erik smiled gratefully at him. "Then we must begin preparing. If we are to have any chance of success we must surprise them."

"Do you have enough men?" Kristoffer queried.

"I plan to turn to my prospective father-in-law for help," answered Erik.

"Will King Hakon support you?" asked Kristoffer. "If he joins you, he might have to fight Birger's allies as well, which include Denmark."

"Whatever he says about family, Erik Menved has his hands full with the Germans who are Denmark's primary concern," Erik replied, unable to keep the bitterness from his voice. "Aiding Birger will come second to the revenues he would lose if the North German states withdraw from their alliance."

Erik studied Kristoffer. "Will you help us? I will show you my gratitude. You might end up with a larger dukedom than you already have."

"I cannot help you," objected Kristoffer. "If I do, I would be in exactly the same situation as you are in now, and my brother's armies would swallow mine in a matter of hours."

"Let us hope King Hakon has a more cooperative attitude," said Erik with a slight smirk.

"You must understand my position," pleaded Kristoffer. "I cannot join you openly, but I will certainly keep you informed of what is transpiring at my brother's court. That could be of vital importance to you."

"That is true," agreed Erik. Then he remembered his promise to Kristina to keep Kristoffer away from the Danish court until Ingeborg gave birth. His voice softened. "I do understand your position, Kristoffer. But why not come with us to Oslo as moral support?"

Kristoffer lifted his shoulders in a gesture of futility. "I cannot. My brother has spies everywhere, and he would surely find out. Given his feelings about King Hakon harboring the Danish rebels, he would interpret my going there as treason."

"I have always felt that Birger was weak, and overly dependent on others," Valdemar said. "But now I realize that he is completely inept. He is risking a civil war in Sweden that he could easily avoid if he searched for the truth. And even if he wins this war, it will be costly and weaken our country."

The three men sat in silence watching a hawk dive for its prey on the far shore of the lake. As they heard the screams of the animal, Erik concluded grimly, "We will fight for what is ours."

Chapter 21

"**M**y lady!" Kristina could feel the hair stand up on her arms. She collected herself and straightened her back before she turned around to face Kristoffer.

"Yes, my Lord," she said, trying not to show her discomfort at being alone with him. It was late in the evening and she was the last of the ladies to retire to her tent in Fair Valley.

"I have just met with your husband and your brother-in-law at their camp. Your husband asked me to give you this." He handed her a scroll bearing Valdemar's seal.

"Thank you, Duke Kristoffer," she said as she took it from him and prepared to turn away.

"You need not be so formal with me, Kristina," Kristoffer smirked. "We are kin, and we shall be seeing more of each other as you will be quite alone here," he added with a smug grin. She bid him a coldly formal good night before hurrying to the safety of her tent where Ragna was waiting.

Ragna peered out through the tent flap. She saw Kristoffer's broad back disappear from view. "He is gone," she declared. Turning around, she saw Kristina go closer to the lighted candle on the small table between their traveling cots where she carefully scrutinized the scroll.

"I wonder if Duke Kristoffer opened this," Kristina said as she pinched the sides of the scroll to see if the signet wax had been loosened. Satisfied that it had not been tampered with, she broke the seal and unrolled it. While she was reading it, Ragna tried to hide her curiosity by busying herself with her mistress' bed pillows.

"They are going to war," Kristina announced with a sigh of resignation. "Erik and Valdemar are on their way to Norway to seek King Hakon's help," she added while she held the message over the candle. As the flame consumed the parchment, she dropped it on the ground where it shriveled into flaky ashes. "You and I are to remain with Ingeborg at Roskilde until this is over."

"If you are serious about retaking Nykoping and precluding any further erosion of your holdings," Hakon began calmly after he had heard Erik's tale of woe, "You should immediately abandon the idea of outright war. Your armies combined with mine could never over-power Birger's."

The brothers sat facing the Norwegian king who was pacing back and forth in his private chamber at Akershus, shaking his head. "You could, however, place yourself in a negotiating position to regain your property. If I supported your army with a division of my knights, the combined force could easily take Lodose. Since the Gota river passes there, you could conquer the surrounding area all the way to Lake Vanern. That should not take much time or a large force, and it will seriously hurt Birger's position because you would control Sweden's only western port. When he tries to regain Lodose, it will not be all that easy once you are entrenched there, so he will eventually sue for peace and you will have Nykoping back."

"That is a brilliant strategy!" Erik replied, as he and Valdemar looked admiringly at Hakon.

"And to make your task easier, I will let you use Kungahalla fortress as a base of operations," offered Hakon.

"That is most generous," Erik responded gratefully.

"I allowed the Danish rebels to use it when they first arriveed, and it was a fine buffer between Denmark and us," mused Hakon. "Now it is ideal for your purposes since it is so close to Lodose."

"Thank you," Erik reiterated, not knowing what else to say, and realizing that he, like the rebels before him, had no other place to go.

At that moment, the door to the king's chamber opened and a golden-haired little girl peeked shyly into the room. "Ingeborg, my sweet one!" exclaimed Hakon upon seeing his daughter. "Come in and say hello."

The little girl, about three years old, walked hesitantly into the room, all the while studying the two strangers. Then she walked straight up to Erik and appraised him with her big blue eyes. "Are you a saint?" she asked. "You look like one in my picture book."

The men broke into smiles as her words melted the tension over the forthcoming war. "No, Ingeborg, I am not a saint. On the contrary," said Erik, looking at the little girl who would one day become his wife. "But you must be a princess because you are so pretty."

"Yes, I am a princess. And you better do as I say!" she said importantly.

"I shall always obey you," Erik promised solemnly, trying to suppress his smile.

"Then come play with me," ordered the little girl.

"Maybe later, dear," said the king as he gently ushered her out of his chamber. "We have important things to talk about now."

"Good bye," called the girl as her father closed the door behind her.

"That was love at first sight," laughed Valdemar. "A saint! What will I hear next?"

"She seems like a sensible and perceptive girl," bantered Erik, unable to control his laughter.

When Erik and Valdemar entered Kungahalla fortress they felt surprisingly at home. It was purely a military stronghold with none of the comforts of a royal castle. The entire first floor constituted a spacious, crude hall with many narrow wall slits that made it drafty but allowed archers to launch arrows in case of an attack. The hall was crowded with rickety benches and long, well-worn pine tables littered with candles. Huge black cauldrons hung over the large fire-pit and the aroma of long-cooking stews permeated the air. The stone floor was strewn with soiled hay and refuse. The knights were all housed together on the upper floor of the tower. Erik and Valdemar had been assigned the luxury of a large corner space with more than a hundred knights crowded around them. The common soldiers were billeted in long wooden structures lining the interior stonewalls of the stronghold, which Erik knew would be hot in the summer and freezing in the winter.

As time went by, Erik became accustomed to the loud voices, crude curses, and the smell of unwashed bodies, along with the constant clanging of weapons. During the long evenings when the knights would gather around the fire in the hall, he took to listening to the older veterans recounting tales of their valiant battles.

Erik was jubilant when Mats and Abjorn finally arrived from the east coast, riding over Kungahalla's drawbridge with a large following of knights and soldiers. All those in whom he had placed his trust had chosen to join him and Valdemar, instead of their brother who was, after all, their king. Behind the incoming column, pairs of horses pulled heavy wagons bearing large chests. Erik looked at him quizzically. Mats grinned. "Abjorn had a feeling something was afoot, so he had your treasury packed up and buried at his estate before the king's armies took Nykoping."

"Blessings upon you," exclaimed Erik, stunned by his luck. Without monies, maintaining an armed confrontation, however limited, would be difficult.

"Yours are here, too," added Mats as he turned to Valdemar who crossed himself and wordlessly patted Mats on the shoulder. Life was not as dark as it had seemed just a few weeks earlier.

As Mats and Abjorn joined Erik and Valdemar for an evening ride along the water outside Kungahalla, Erik called them to a halt. "Since we are fortunate to have our treasuries with us I want to use our resources wisely. Abjorn, take some trusted knights and your strongest soldiers and ride to where the Gota river flows into Lake Vanern. Look for the best spot of crown land you can find there and construct a stronghold as fast as is humanly possible. Use labor from the surrounding villages to work day and night. The fact that we have the audacity to build on crown land will infuriate Birger, who will lose time and troops in an attempt to destroy it while we entrench ourselves in Lodose and here at Kungahalla. Mats, you continue training our soldiers, while Valdemar and I will stock Kungahalla in case of a siege."

Both Mats and Abjorn voiced their approval of the scheme as they all dismounted and slowly led their horses along the water's edge discussing the details of the forthcoming confrontation. The following morning Abjorn departed with his men and one of Erik's chests, while Mats roused the soldiers early to begin their rigorous daily practice at arms.

One early autumn morning long columns of fully armored knights rode out of the gates of Kungahalla, followed by several hundred foot soldiers, their course set for Lodose. As they neared the town but still under cover of the forest, Lord Mats called the column to a halt.

"You all know what you have to do," he called as the soldiers threw mantles over their armor and tied rags around their legs to conceal their chain mail before they pulled hoods over their helmets and wrapped their weapons close to their bodies. Quietly they left at intervals in groups of threes and fours.

Small groups of men riding towards Lodose gave no cause for alarm to its citizens since it was market day and the harbor town had many visitors. When Erik and Valdemar finally rode through the large town gates, they saw their men loitering along the harbor quays and around the taverns and stalls in the main square. Since it was late in the day, the merchants were in the process of packing up their carts and bundles for the long walk home after a busy day of commerce. Soon it was only Erik, Valdemar, and their knights and soldiers who were about, as the townspeople had withdrawn to their homes for evening supper.

Erik let out a sudden, shrill whistle that was the signal for his knights to assemble. They came walking beside their horses from the side lanes where they had waited so as not to congregate in the square and risk frightening the inhabitants. As they mounted and filled the square in long lines, Mats arrived, leading the foot soldiers who took up their posts around the square. Once Erik was satisfied with their placement, he walked over to the door of the largest house on the square and knocked loudly. After some time, a small man opened the door and peered out.

"Tell your master that Erik of Sweden wishes to speak to him," Erik demanded in a loud voice. The little man was obviously impressed. He quickly stood aside to let Erik and Valdemar into the main room of the house.

"Duke Erik of Sweden," he intoned officiously.

The mayor looked up from his supper and paled. It was apparent that he found two strangers, in full armor and so tall that they had to bend down to get through the door, both surprising and frightening.

While their royal coats of arms seemed to calm him somewhat, his mouth stayed agape.

"We are here to take over the rule of Lodose," Erik said matter-of-factly. "You may continue to serve in your post if you swear allegiance to us, or to leave in peace if you choose not to. I would appreciate it if you would call together the people of the town and tell them that we shall not harm anyone as long as they offer no resistance. It would not profit them to do so anyway, as you shall see," said Erik who motioned for the mayor to follow him.

When the mayor came out through the front door and beheld the sea of soldiers and knights, he looked as if he were about to faint.

"Give the order to congregate at the church," he announced in a shaky voice. The town's bell soon began to toll as his call was repeated by the townspeople who ran along the lanes to alert their neighbors. It did not take long for everyone to assemble. They filled the pews and stood in the aisles of the church, looking nervously around. As Erik strode through the crowded church he could hear anxious questions being whispered between neighbors, and small children crying who had been pulled abruptly from sleep or play to accompany their parents. Erik stood at the altar with Valdemar at his side. He struck an imposing figure in his polished armor as he held his flag-festooned helmet under one arm and rested his other hand on the haft of his sword. He motioned for silence.

"I am Erik of Sweden, and this is my brother, Valdemar of Finland," he demanded in a strong voice. He heard the people start to whisper anew. "I am the new ruler of Lodose, and you will swear me fealty. I do not wish to cause anyone harm, and if you do not want to be under my protection you have until dawn to leave. After that my soldiers will deal with whomever opposes my rule." The silence was absolute, and Erik looked over to where a few men were huddled together, whispering. "Do you have any questions?" he boomed.

"My lord," said one of the men as he hesitantly stood up. "I mean no disrespect, but we have just paid our taxes to the king. Must we now pay you, as well?"

"Not until next year." The man looked relieved, and a murmur was heard from the crowd.

"I leave you to make your decisions," Erik concluded. Then he and Valdemar walked out of the church, followed by the mayor who seemed anxious to talk to them.

"I . . . I would like to stay on as mayor if . . . if that is agreeable to you," he stammered with an ingratiating smile. "And naturally you should stay at my house while you are here," he added.

Which you hope will not be for very long, thought Erik. Aloud he said, "Tomorrow you can show us the town and your accounts. Right now, we would like food and rest."

Erik and Valdemar went to the square where Mats was still standing with his men. "All is going according to plan. Find the men some food and places to sleep, and then join us at the mayor's house," Erik directed.

It was late at night when Erik and Valdemar were joined by Mats. They ate with hearty appetite and quickly finished a large cask of wine.

"Congratulations," said Mats as he lifted his chalice. "You are now the masters of Lodose without the loss of a single soldier."

"Has anyone left town?" asked Valdemar.

"Only a few knights who were in the king's service. The rest do not seem to care who rules as long as they do not have to pay more taxes," said Mats.

"Those knights will spread the news," added Erik with a smile, taking a deep draught from his cup.

It was late in the evening when a lone figure moved furtively along the dim and deserted lanes of Lodose. He circumvented the street leading to the main tavern that was filled with knights, and from what he had been told, Dukes Erik and Valdemar, as well. This meant that the big house on the square would be empty. As the mayor stood in the shadows, he felt his heart constrict with anticipation. The dukes could return at any moment, but then he reminded himself for the hundredth time, he had no choice.

As the square appeared deserted, he walked quickly up to his door and inserted his key. The large lock opened with a heavy clunk, but no one stirred around the square. He withdrew the key, closed the door silently behind him, and tiptoed into the hall. As quietly as he could he walked along the row of beds to see if anyone had stayed behind, but all the beds were empty. Relieved, he lit a candle from the embers in the fire-pit and walked over to the far wall where he knelt down on the floor. With his dagger he pried open a wide floor plank, and then reached in for a wooden chest which he removed with considerable difficulty. He replaced the floorboard and dragged the chest over near the fire-pit. With trembling hands he unlocked the chest. He sighed in relief upon finding its contents untouched.

He put some dry wood on the glowing embers and stoked the red coals until the fire caught on. He took out three large ledgers from which he began to rip pages that he threw on the fire. Once they were burning briskly he added the leather covers. What would the dukes have done to him if they had discovered the real accounts of the city, along with his small hoard of treasure? He shivered, even though pearls of sweat were running down his forehead.

He knew that he could not carry out the chest without appearing suspicious, so he looked around for some alternative mode of transportation. His eyes searched the room anxiously until they came to rest on a large banner hanging on the wall. He walked over and ripped it down. Dust and dirt fell with it, causing him to sneeze as he began tearing it in half. He fashioned one part into a sling and hung it around his neck. Quickly, he began to fill it with the gold coins he had squirreled away over the years. Soon it was filled to capacity and hung painfully heavy over his shoulders. He was not sure the cloth would hold the weight of his treasure, or even if he would be able to carry it. He kicked the empty chest under the table and looked around for a cloak to drape over himself that would hide his loot. He noticed a blue mantle hanging by one of the beds and he pulled it over his shoulders. He giggled nervously with the realization that he must look monstrously fat, when suddenly he heard sounds in the square outside the house. Frightened, he looked around for a place to hide, and as he did, he noticed the last remnant of the banner on the table. Hurriedly, he threw it into the fire and raced towards the kitchen. As he closed the door behind him, he heard steps nearing the kitchen, so he quietly opened the door to the larder and stepped inside.

Hidden in the dark, he did not know if it was the sound of his heart or the sound of a man's footsteps he was hearing, but he realized when he heard swearing that someone had entered the kitchen and had set down something quite heavy. Several other men came in with equally heavy burdens. After they had delivered their cargo, they left the house. He could hear them talking as their footsteps and the sound of a wagon receded across the square. After some time passed he decided it would be safe to leave his hiding place, so he pushed the door to get out. It did not open. He realized that several huge casks of wine that he had ordered had evidently been delivered and placed up against the larder door. He began to push with all his strength. Rivulets of sweat poured down his face, but the door would not budge.

Despondent, he took the sling that was hurting his shoulders from around his neck and set it on the floor. He knew all was lost if any of the knights grew hungry during the night, and he fervently prayed that it would be one of his faithful servants who would let him out in the morning. He would certainly show his gratitude. He was beginning to feel better about spending the night in the larder when he caught the faint smell of smoke. He was puzzled by it and thought it strange since there was no fire in the ovens or the kitchen pit.

But the smell became stronger. Suddenly, in his mind's eye he pictured the last shred of the banner he had thrown toward the fire-pit on his way to the kitchen. Had part of the banner ended up outside the pit? He could picture the tablecloth on the table next to the fire-pit, and the many cushions on the bench adjoining it. If they caught fire, it would be just a matter of minutes before fire raged throughout the hall. He felt his stomach churn and again he threw his weight heavily against the door, but still to no avail.

He continued to frantically push on the door as smoke began to seep in under it. He was gripped by panic and started coughing as he pounded on the door and called for help. What could Duke Erik do to him that was worse than this? His final thought as the smoke overcame him was that he should have married his childhood sweetheart with the plump cheeks and settled on her father's farm.

King Birger's face was ashen. "Are you sure?" he asked his Lord High Constable who nodded. "So now they control our one and only western port? Damn them! How could they do this to me?"

Torgils studied Birger with a stony gaze. What did he think his brothers would do when he seized Nykoping? Stay at the Danish court and lick their wounds? Despite their former intimacy, how little he seemed to know his brothers.

"How strong is their army?"

"From the latest reports, it seems quite large, so I assume they are receiving support from King Hakon. But they can never take Sweden."

"I know that," said Birger irritably. "But they have created problems for us. Why did you not think of that before we took Nykoping?"

"If you remember, Your Majesty, you ordered me to do so."

"You are the one with military experience, you should have known what could happen," Birger whined.

I did, I do, and I hope it continues to happen, thought Torgils. If Birger, Erik and Valdemar did not survive the forthcoming battles, he would again be in control of Sweden, as he would surely be appointed Regent for young Prince Magnus. "They might rattle their weapons," he countered assertively. "But we shall take care of that once we have massed sufficient forces to attack Kungahalla, which is where I hear they have gone now."

"Still it is almost winter and laying siege to a fortress as strong as Kungahalla in cold weather is not an idea I relish. But I am pleased that I spent all that money to build Gullbergshed fortress. Had I not done that, they might have taken over the whole region by the Gota river."

"You showed excellent foresight, Your Majesty. Still it might be wise to ask Erik Menved for support. That would enable us to attack immediately since we would not have to ready the entire force ourselves," said Torgils.

"We shall show them who is the King, once and for all!"

There was no mistaking the preparations underway at Roskilde castle. Kristina observed messengers and soldiers arriving and leaving at all hours, armor being polished, and the forge blazing day and night. The ladies seemed quieter. Some looked downhearted as they sat embroidering new banners for loved ones. Kristina did not know where the Danish army was going until the day when she saw her father's coat of arms on one of the messengers. Then she realized that Erik Menved had decided not only to judge Erik and Valdemar the villains in the brotherly dispute but to actively intervene against them.

After a sleepless night thinking of what might happen to the men she had loved and cared for all her life, she sat listlessly by her spinning wheel, unable to concentrate on her work. She noticed Ingeborg looking her way several times. Finally, Ingeborg dismissed the other ladies and turned to her.

"What is troubling you?" she asked with concern.

Kristina was unsure of how to approach the subject since it would inevitably put the two of them on opposite sides. Yet if there was the remotest chance she could help Erik and Valdemar she had to try. "I realize that your husband is sending an army to support Birger's forces against Erik and Valdemar."

"I am afraid so," confessed Ingeborg.

Kristina had heard persistent rumors that Erik and Valdemar had seized Lodose, and that they were building a fortress on crown land by Lake Vanern--rumors she secretly had relished.

"Why cannot Birger just talk to his brothers," she blurted out. "They would never have taken Lodose if he had sat down with them instead of treating them like traitors."

"Kristina, I am just as sad as you are that my brothers are feuding, but there is nothing whatever you or I can do. They have to resolve their own problems."

"But now your husband is taking sides," complained Kristina.

"He is honor-bound to support his ally, the King of Sweden, who happens to be Birger. You know that. Let us hope that his involvement quells this conflict quickly."

"I pray you are right, Ingeborg."

The news that Erik Menved was readying his troops to assist Birger was not welcome to Erik and Valdemar who had left Lodose in the hands of Mats while they went to Kungahalla to await the impending confrontations. Erik stood by a small window, looking out over the lonely road leading to the stronghold. His eyes followed a rider who was nearing the fortress at full gallop. He tried to identify him but saw no coat of arms on his tunic.

"I pray someone is bringing us good news," he said as Valdemar followed him outside.

The brothers received the messenger in the courtyard where Erik was handed a leather pouch. "Greetings from my master, Duke Kristoffer of Southern Halland."

"Take some refreshment," Erik told the rider as he and Valdemar went back inside the hall. Erik tore the seal from the parchment and unrolled it. Slowly he read the contents to himself while Valdemar waited impatiently. "Erik Menved is soon leaving Roskilde for Sweden with a large army," said Erik with a broad smile.

"I know but what is so good about that?" asked Valdemar incredulously. "His forces will be here before December!"

"Wait, wait, I have not read you the whole message," interrupted Erik. "Kristoffer writes: 'While my brother is offering to come to King Birger's aid, he will most likely not arrive in time because his real aim is to take Northern Halland from Count Jakob whom he sees as a traitor to Denmark. When, and if, his armies reach Sweden, your confrontation will most likely be over.' You understand, Valdemar? We do not have to worry about a Danish army!"

Kristina awoke in the silence. All she could hear was the soft breathing of the women sleeping around her. The hammers at the forge had stilled, and the comings and goings of horses and men had ceased. The troops had left the previous day, and this had been the first night everyone could sleep in peace.

Another reason she had slept soundly was that Kristoffer had left Roskilde with his brother. Though Kristina was sure that Kristoffer knew about Ingeborg's condition now that she was well into her sixth month, the vigilance they had kept had given him scant opportunity to do her harm, if indeed he had intended it. It had pleased Kristina to see Ingeborg finally relaxing during the farewell feast. The fact that Kristoffer was leaving seemed to make Ingeborg glow. She had laughed and joked during the supper like her old self, and she had even drunk a toast with her dreaded brother-in-law.

Kristina's restless nights would certainly resume once the battles were joined, but for now she intended to savour the tranquility. Contentedly, she pulled the down cover around her and closed her eyes. Just as she was falling back to sleep, she felt a tugging at her bedcovers. One of the servants, the girl who lit the queen's fire in the early morning, was urgently gesturing for Kristina to follow her. Kristina got up, stepped into her slippers and wrapped herself in a padded gown to follow the girl quietly out of the chamber.

"Hurry! Please, hurry! The queen has taken ill, and she is asking for you," the girl whispered as she ran ahead of Kristina along the corridor.

As Kristina burst into the queen's chamber she heard moans from the bed. She rushed forward to pull the curtains aside. Ingeborg was ashen, with beads of cold sweat running down her forehead. She stretched out her hands towards Kristina, unable to speak from pain.

"Get Ragna and Lady Brigitte immediately," Kristina ordered the girl who stood shivering in the doorway. Kristina pulled down the covers and saw that Ingeborg was lying in a pool of blood. Quickly she rushed to the door and called the girl back. "Bring the herbalist and the surgeon monks as well," she called frantically.

Kristina returned to the bedside where Ingeborg was looking pleadingly at her while her body shook in pain. "Ingeborg, help will be here soon," Kristina said before she went over to the washbasin, wet a towel with cool water, and gently washed Ingeborg's face. She held Ingeborg's hand firmly, while Ingeborg whimpered through waves of pain. Kristina knew that the child was coming, and the only thing she could pray for was that it would somehow survive.

She heard running in the corridor and Lady Brigitte and Ragna came through the door. Kristina motioned to the bloodied bed linens and Ragna turned to get hot water from the kitchen. Lady Brigitte came closer and touched Ingeborg's stomach while she smiled encouragingly at her mistress. "The baby is coming early," she said in a steady voice, trying not to show the alarm she felt at the sight of the bloodied sheets.

As the medical monks came rushing down the corridor, Lady Brigitte went to meet them to inform them of the situation. The herbal monk ran back to his laboratory for the necessary herbs, while the surgeon put down his implements before he neared the queen. After having examined her he nodded to Kristina to assist him with his instruments by the fire.

"I fear the child is already dead," he said softly. "But if we work fast and are very fortunate we might be able to save the queen. She has lost a dangerous amount of blood already. Keep up a cheerful attitude, Lady Kristina, whatever you do," he admonished her.

With the help of the surgeon's tongs they pulled out a stillborn boy an hour later. Herbal concoctions had stemmed the blood flow, but the queen was unconscious and deathly pale as they wrapped the tiny body in swaddling and Lady Brigitte took it to the chapel to pray for its soul. Since Ingeborg was no longer aware of the people in her chamber, Kristina could not hold back her tears. The herbalist monk took her aside.

"Have courage, Lady Kristina, God will help His deserving children, and the queen is a good woman. You have to give her all your support if there is to be any hope of recovery. She must want to live again."

"Will she ever bear another child?"

"If the queen survives, I believe that she can have a child. This premature birth was not caused by any shortcomings within her body. The child died from poison. I could see it on his nails."

"Are you saying that both the queen and the child were poisoned? How did she survive?"

"The child was weaker and died. The queen might die, as well, if my herbs do not work. But I feel certain that whoever did this did not want her to die, but rather gave her a measured dose just strong enough to cause a miscarriage. I have given her something that will purge her of the poison without causing her to bleed again. But she will require a long convalescence, both physical and mental."

Kristina felt her heart pound as she remembered how Ingeborg and Kristoffer had linked arms and drunk each other good wishes during the farewell feast. Kristina knew that it was not a toast Ingeborg cared to make, but Kristoffer had stood up and showered her with praise, so she could scarcely have rejected his toast. The chalices had looked similar, if not identical. It would have taken little effort to switch them.

Erik wrapped his mantle tightly around himself. Outside the winter winds howled around Kungahalla's thick stonewalls, and the candles on the table flickered in the icy draft of the hall. The fire on the hearth had almost died, though none of the men leaning over the map table seemed to notice, so deep were they in concentration.

"It appears we are being approached from two directions," Valdemar explained, pointing to the map. "King Birger has moved a large army from the northeast against our new Dalaborg fortress at Lake Vanern. King Erik Menved, on the other hand, has marched from the south, and his army has Count Jakob's Varberg and Hunehals fortresses under siege. However, if it is true that the Danish king is not planning to attack us until he has finished his business in Northern Halland, we need only be concerned with King Birger for the moment."

"It does seem that he decided not to attack us here but go to Dalaborg. Though it is not a very large fort, it is strong and well-provisioned so our men should be able to endure a lengthy siege in relative comfort, while Birger's armies will not fare as well in the open winter fields," mused Abjorn.

"If we can wait him out there, he will likely request negotiations."

"Is this a good time for us to attack Gullbergshed fortress?" Valdemar asked tentatively. "Since most of Birger's armies are at Dalaborg, we should have a fair chance to take it from him."

"I would not suggest it," counseled Abjorn. "Storming a fortress of that strength is too costly an undertaking. We only want to force the king to the bargaining table. We are not trying to conquer Sweden."

"Alas, you are right," conceded Valdemar. "But I hate to just sit and wait."

"That, my lord, is also part of warfare," smiled Abjorn.

"Already we are having problems supplying our men with adequate rations. How long must we stay here and stare at these fortress walls?" King Birger asked while he continued pacing his tent and slapping his frozen hands against his thighs. "We must do something!"

"I agree, your Majesty. But we should not attack until the Danish reinforcements arrive," said Lord Torgils.

"Once the Danes get here, what are our chances to take Dalaborg?"

"Excellent."

"I wish Erik Menved would hurry," Birger sighed gloomily.

"As do I, your Majesty," the Lord High Constable replied soothingly.

Their conversation was interrupted by Knut Jonsson, one of Birger's most trusted knights, who entered and bowed deeply before he blurted, "The men are restless, your Majesty."

Torgils cut him off. "That is to be expected," he snapped. "We have been here for more than a month."

"It is not only the inactivity, the bitter cold and lack of food ... but stories about the Huldra have begun to circulate."

"A Huldra? Here?" asked Birger, as a shiver ran down his spine.

"Nonsense!" objected Torgils. "The men will spread any rumor to try to end this freezing siege. They only have to forage a little further afield to find food and firewood."

"That is just it, Lord Torgils, the men refuse to go into the forests."

"That is ridiculous," snapped King Birger. "They will do as they are told."

"I am not so sure," mumbled Knut.

"Men fear the inexplicable, your Majesty," said Torgils finally. "I think we better talk to those who claim to have seen the Huldra."

"Very well," conceded Birger. "Bring them here, Lord Knut."

Lord Knut returned with just a single soldier. The young man looked nervous but showed no fear of standing face to face with his king and the mighty Lord High Constable.

"Was it you who started all this rubbish about a Huldra?" asked Lord Torgils.

"It is no rubbish, my lord. I saw her clear as day."

Birger looked into the open face of the young man who seemed to have no doubts about his experience. "Tell us about it," Birger ordered.

"We were out looking for farms where we could get some food. We had gone quite a distance without finding anything but firewood, and our leader told us to go off in pairs to scout out farms and then meet back to report what we had found.

"I went with my good friend, Per, who works on the farm next to my father's in Smaland. He was the handsomest man for miles around, tall, strong and always wearing a winsome smile. There is not one girl in our parish of marriageable age who would not thank the Lord for a husband like him."

"Keep to the story," snapped Torgils.

"This is part of the story," said the lad unfazed. "In any case, we had walked for a long time and were getting deeper and deeper into the forest. None of us were particularly frightened, as there had been no reports of wolf or bear. As we walked along, we suddenly saw a shadow moving among the trees. All of a sudden, Per, who was walking ahead of me stopped and stared into the bushes. When I came up behind him I saw that he was face to face with the most beautiful girl I had ever seen. What was strange was that she was totally naked in the biting cold, shielded only by her long, thick hair that fell all the way down to her knees.

"We both stood there, like fools, staring at this creature 'til she winked at Per and beckoned him to follow her. As if he had lost all will, he slowly walked towards her. At that very same moment I came out of the spell. I called for him to stay, but he paid me no heed. The girl ran playfully into the forest and Per chased after her. I ran after him, shouting for him to stop. But he was laughing and running after her as she darted among the trees. It was then I noticed that she never once turned her back on us, and I felt the blood freeze in my veins.

"It is the Huldra," I called again and again, but Per did not heed me, and her pace grew swifter. I knew then that she would make it impossible for me to catch up with them as she enticed him to run faster and faster toward her underground lair deep beneath the mountain. I knew she intended to enslave him for the rest of his life. I could just imagine what would happen. She would seduce him into one glorious night of lovemaking when she would break his will forever. Then she would mercilessly whip him to make him work, day and night, in her underground mines until he fell dead.

"Even though I ran as fast as I could they soon vanished, and I never saw Per again. I looked around until dark when I hurried back to the others who were waiting impatiently for me. I told them what I had seen, and that is the God's own truth."

"It might well have been a beautiful woodcutter's daughter who is now enjoying Per's amorous attentions," Torgils said with a laugh.

"No woman would go about naked in this cold," insisted the soldier.

"You have a point there, except if she were mad," pondered Torgils. "In any case, your friend will be severely punished when he returns. For now, however, I want you to tell the other soldiers that you had a fever, or found something strong to drink, and that it was all in your mind."

"How can I lie and expose my comrades to capture, as well? It would not be fair," objected the soldier, stoically.

"You heard what I said," said Torgils. "Either that, or you will become a head shorter!"

The soldier remained silent, staring sullenly at the ground.

"You do as Lord Torgils bids you," said Birger softly. "We can have no rebellion among our men."

"Yes, your Majesty," the lad answered obediently.

After he had left there was a very long silence.

"I suppose," Birger concluded finally, "we best avoid that part of the forest."

"We will not," objected Torgils. "And we will lead the men on the food forages ourselves. They have to see that we have no fear of the Huldra, since they know that she has no preference for knights or paupers as long as they are strong enough to do her bidding."

"Then you lead the men," said Birger to Torgils and Knut.

"I am afraid you have to come as well, your Majesty," Torgils replied. "If you show no fear, the men will quickly forget the story, especially if that young man claims he stretched the truth to help his runaway friend."

Birger paled at the suggestion. He felt faint at the very thought of mounting his horse to lead his men into the forests against a creature he had no hope of conquering unless he saw the empty hollow in her back--a hollow no one had ever seen, though he, like everyone else, had heard about the thousands of men who had been mountain bound by the irresistible Huldra. He shuddered at the very thought, but he knew he had to go.

What a ridiculous war this had turned out to be. He should have tried to reconcile with his brothers and he should never have seized Nykoping castle. Now Lodose was occupied, and he was literally a prisoner before these fortress walls, while Erik and Valdemar sat comfortably in Kungahalla. He had not seen Marta and the children for ages, and to top it all off, he, the King of Sweden, would have to endure freezing forays to the depths of the forests.

He saw Lord Torgils look at him expecting his answer.

"When do we go?" he asked with a sigh.

The following week Birger suffered from a disabling cold with a high fever. He felt more miserable than he could remember and continued to blame his brothers for everything. After a few days he summoned Torgils, who arrived inquiring about his condition. "I shall live," said Birger sniffling. "But we cannot let this siege continue. Tomorrow, we shall attack."

"We should wait for Erik Menved."

"Our scouts have made it clear that he is delayed with his own concerns in Northern Halland. We cannot just sit here and burn up the woods around us and pillage every farm within reach. If we want our men to fight at all, we have to do it now."

Torgils shook his head. "If this is what you order me to do; we shall attack on the morrow."

"Good," said Birger, satisfied that Torgils would follow his orders without further dissent.

Despite its premature timing, Torgils felt confident that an assault could wreak heavy damage on the hastily erected fortress.

Torgils went to inspect his machines of war. The three largest machines stood over thirty feet tall. Their basic configuration was that of a tower on huge wheels, with steps running up the back. At the top of the steps, resting on the tower was a cantilevered extension that projected out about fifteen feet. If one of these towers were pushed towards the fortress its bridge-like extension would reach over to the parapet and the soldiers could race up the steps, over the bridge and onto the parapet.

Other soldiers would pull up long ladders to reach the parapets. The latter approach was more dangerous since those in the fortress would not stand idly by and allow access, but would pour scalding oil on their attackers, shoot at them with deadly arrows, push their ladders away from the walls, and if some finally succeeded in scaling the parapet, overwhelm them before they got their bearings. The attackers were at a clear disadvantage.

To counteract this inequality, Torgils had large catapults that hurled not only stones but fireballs as well. The stones would force the defenders to duck below the parapets and allow those who tried to scale the walls some reprieve. Fireballs had the same effect, but with the added possibility of setting the interior of the fortress on fire. The more soldiers engaged in fighting fires, the fewer to defend the parapets!

The fortress was equipped with catapults as well. But catapults placed behind the high walls were difficult to aim and often missed their targets. A lucky shot from the attackers, on the other hand, could ignite and destroy the granary within the fortress walls.

The battering ram, which Lord Torgils inspected next, consisted of a powerful structure on wheels from which a huge tree trunk was suspended horizontally on thick chains. At one end was a massive metal hood, and the whole trunk could be swung back and forth like a pendulum to crash against the gate.

In response the defenders would again pour hot oil and throw heavy stones on the attackers. Torgils did not think he would have to use that approach since he hoped some of his men would be able to get inside to open the gates.

Torgils checked on the giant wooden shields constructed for his archers. Normally these heavily planked barriers stood upright on the ground at some distance from the walls, shielding the archers who shot upwards towards the parapets through small openings. Their shooting angle diminished the impact of their arrows, so Alf of Smaland had devised upright barriers composed of upright metal-covered planks behind which ran long shelf-like ledges high above the ground, from which the archers could gain an angle of advantage for their arrows.

Movable shelters with walls and roofs, mounted on a multitude of wheels, stood at each side of the planked barriers. Their purpose was to protect men and horses from arrows, fireballs and stones as they dragged the war machines up to the fortress.

Before the sun had risen Birger, clad in full armor, gave the order to attack. Moments later, fireballs streaked from catapults towards the fortress and they could hear frantic calls to arms inside Dalaborg. The next moments would be the most advantageous for the attackers since the defenders had been taken by surprise. All the king's soldiers were busy loading and hurling tarred fireballs with ever more precision into the fort.

By the time the first assault waves of Birger's men hit the walls, the defenders had taken their posts and were catapulting heavy stones down on the attackers. Birger, who had never been involved in an actual assault, stood fascinated, watching the scene before him. It was as if the soldiers were simply actors performing roles of being burned, pierced by arrows, and thrown to the ground. The horrifying screams had no relation to real dismembered living beings but were only part of a play. Birger felt his blood pumping through his veins. He could taste it in his mouth, smell it in his nostrils, and see it like a red haze before his eyes. As in a dream, he moved among the soldiers at the catapults shouting encouragement. Never had he felt so thrilled as at this very moment.

His enthusiasm faded after a few hours when he saw the piles of fallen bodies mounting. Even the vigorously burning fires and the piercing screams of the wounded within the fort gave him no pleasure. The enemy's resistance was fierce, and his troops had been unable to gain entry or to force the gates. Only after heavy losses had they discovered that the fort had double gates and that they could not use the heavy ramrod against the inner gate without being bombarded by burning oil and heavy rocks poured directly from above. Finally, Torgils, who had been in the thick of it, returned to Birger's side. He looked exhausted, his face blackened with soot and his hands charred from oil. "We must call off our men, your Majesty. They were far better prepared than we had expected."

Birger reluctantly nodded his permission and heard horns blown for retreat. Again, he was shocked to see how many of his soldiers remained on the ground in front of the fortress. Were they all dead? Numbly, he stood and watched his men retreat as the reality of the attack hit him. He felt angry that he had never gotten to participate, for he was to have been among the first to enter the stronghold to inspire his men for the final slaughter if they continued to meet with resistance.

Once his soldiers had rested, and while the wounded were being tended, the war machines were pulled back out of range. Soldiers and surgeon monks tied white sashes around their arms and returned to the fortress walls to retrieve the dead and wounded. It was a tedious and painful procedure, but Birger remained frozen in place, watching the heart-wrenching moments as soldiers and knights discovered their dead comrades. A large pit was being dug under an oak tree for a mass burial while a scribe noted the names of the fallen.

Torgils had come quietly to Birger's side. "A battle is something different in reality, is it not?" he asked. Birger only nodded. He was unable to speak.

As Erik awoke and heard the loud snoring of the men around him in Kungahalla he wondered how he could have slept at all. Yet it was not those familiar noises that had disturbed his sleep. It was the hoof beats of a rider approaching the fortress. He threw off his fur blanket and stood up. Quietly he pulled on his boots and stepped over sleeping knights to reach the stairwell. He went down in time to hear the drawbridge being lowered and by the time he arrived in the courtyard the rider came thundering over the bridge. He could see Birger's coat of arms emblazoned on the man's tunic and he was momentarily confused until he realized that it was one of his own men who he had placed with Birger.

"Duke Erik!" the rider saluted as he slid off his horse.

"Come within and catch your breath," suggested Erik knowing that the man must have been on the road for hours in the icy darkness.

"Thank the Lord that it was a moonlit night," huffed the man as he followed Erik into the hall where the fires had been lit and the servants were going about their morning chores. An old servant unceremoniously plunked two mugs of hot herbal tea down on the table where the two men seated themselves.

"King Birger attacked Dalaborg," the messenger reported between sips of tea. When he saw Erik knit his eyebrows with concern he shook his head. "They should have waited for Erik Menved to arrive for they failed miserably in their assault."

"That is indeed welcome news," exclaimed Erik. "I thank you for bringing it so swiftly. Still, I need one more favor of you."

"You only have to name it."

"King Hakon is sending forces to support Duke Valdemar and myself. Please see that King Birger learns of this."

Chapter 22

Kungahalla, Norway 1305

"Did you get everything you wanted?" King Hakon inquired when Erik and Valdemar entered the hall at Kungahalla.

Erik sat down next to Hakon and began pulling off his boots. Then with a contented grunt he put his feet up on the edge of the fire-pit, relishing the warmth of the brightly burning fire. Valdemar took a seat beside him.

"It was a bitter cold journey not even the snow queen would have enjoyed," Erik began in describing the trip from Kolsater where they had met with Birger. "My brother insisted that we surrender Lodose, withdraw our armies, refrain from further hostilities, swear loyalty to his family, and promise not to seek revenge on the Lord High Constable," Erik recited.

"That seems reasonable," Hakon said. "What did he offer you in return?"

"He is returning Nykoping to me, and he will let us retain our dukedoms on condition that they no longer be hereditary but revert to the crown upon our deaths."

"That can change as time goes by. What else?"

"Birger's final requirement was that Abjorn Sixtensson, my trusted chancellor, be banished from Sweden, and that all his properties be forfeited to the crown."

"One could hardly miss the vindictive curl at the corners of the Lord High Constable's mouth when that last demand was mentioned," interjected Valdemar.

"Birger gave you as much as you could possibly expect. Why do you not look happier?"

"Because we will miss Abjorn's capable hand, and we had hoped to re-establish our relationship with Birger. Without it, we remain on the outside even though we sit in the Council," said Erik.

"You cannot expect everything at once," Hakon admonished them. "Birger believes you spied on him, and it will take time for him to forgive you. Have patience. Lord Abjorn is welcome to stay with me in Norway. I can use a man of his talents."

They were interrupted as a servant announced the arrival of Count Jakob of Northern Halland. When the count came into the hall, his clothes were covered with snow. He removed his elegant fur-lined mantle and, after exchanging greetings, seated himself in front of the fire.

"Has Erik Menved given up on conquering Northern Halland?" King Hakon asked.

"Yes, finally!" Jakob replied as he rubbed his hands together near the warming flames. "When he heard about the negotiations between King Birger and the dukes, he just left. If he had maintained his siege for just a while longer, we would have had to capitulate as we were running short on food. But Erik Menved could no longer supply his army because he had already depleted the countryside."

"Northern Halland is in poor condition then?" Erik ventured.

"Disastrous!" sighed the count. "My treasury is empty. The peasants will be starving; I do not have even the means to help them until spring. The Danish troops devoured everything they could lay their hands on, even the planting grain the farmers had squirreled away. So, Your Majesty, I appeal to you. I shall deed you my lands if you promise to help my people survive and provide seed for the spring planting."

"That is not possible. Erik Menved would never allow you to deed your lands to Norway. They are Danish territory," replied Hakon resolutely. "Despite how much I want your properties, I could not accept them, or I would have a war on my hands."

"I will never give them to Erik Menved after what he has done to me!" insisted Jakob. "You are my people's only hope. If I keep Northern Halland, I would be ruling a land with no one to tend it."

"I have a solution which might satisfy everyone," said Hakon slowly.

"What is that?" asked the count.

"You deed your properties to someone else. Someone who is very close to me, and to whom Erik Menved would not object as a neighbor."

"Who is that?"

"Duke Erik . . . with the able help of Duke Valdemar, of course!" said the Norwegian king, flashing a smile.

"Us?" asked Erik, surprised.

"Yes, you! Erik Menved would not resent your ruling Northern Halland if you pledge him your allegiance. You have no quarrel with him, he stayed out of your conflict with Birger, and he knows it will be costly to repair the damage his troops have inflicted. He would welcome someone else footing that bill as long as the land remains allied with Denmark. In all likelihood, Erik Menved would appreciate your replacing the rebellious count," concluded Hakon with a wink towards Jakob.

"Perhaps," said Count Jakob. "But Duke Erik is betrothed to your daughter, and he might be too closely allied to Norway for Erik Menved's comfort."

"You, yourself said you would never cede Northern Halland to Erik Menved," said King Hakon. "If you really mean that, you only have one option left: you could give it to the King of Sweden, who is a close ally of the Danish king. But that would not please me, so I think I have given you the best possible solution."

"Can you afford to restore Northern Halland to a healthy state?" Jakob asked Erik with a tone of resignation in his voice.

"With my help, he will be able to do what must be done," King Hakon quickly volunteered.

"If Northern Halland becomes as prosperous as it was in the past, I would hope that I, or my heirs, would receive some compensation in the future," suggested the count softly.

"That would be fair," King Hakon agreed. "Then, in principle, we are agreed on how the transfer of Northern Halland is to take place," said King Hakon. "I will pay you a handsome sum for Varberg fortress, and I shall give you the amount as soon as you do me one small favor, Jakob," he added.

"But before we talk further, if you will excuse me, I shall change out of these wet clothes to join you for the evening meal." The count stood up and bowed as he left the hall.

"Of course, the dear count is right to question my suggestion" said Hakon as he looked at Erik. "If you get Northern Halland, it will be part of your dukedom; and when you marry my daughter, Northern Halland will automatically become Norwegian. But if the Danish king does not like these possibilities, he can attack the restocked Hunehals and Varberg fortresses again. A rather discouraging prospect for him, I would think, seeing how he failed this time. He will surely accept you as the new ruler, Erik."

Erik, who had been silent, spoke slowly. "I do not know what to say."

"Try a simple 'thank you'," suggested Valdemar with a laugh.

"That is hardly enough," said Erik. "I am overwhelmed."

"Enough," chortled Hakon. "You know very well that I could not take the land myself." Hakon lifted his chalice to the brothers and drank a toast before he continued. "But now we have work to do. Grain, salted fish, and livestock must be sent immediately. That humane gesture will serve you well, Duke Erik. The people will love their new master."

King Hakon was grateful that the Swedish royal brothers had made a truce as he approached the Swedish fortress Gullbergshed, with his army. This stronghold had been the target of his planned intervention on the part of the dukes. The fortress was strong and forbidding, and he had little doubt he would have been forced to withdraw after an extended siege for lack of provisions.

Birger welcomed Hakon in the hall, and as soon as formalities were exchanged, Birger asked those present to leave.

"I am glad for the opportunity to meet with you alone," said Hakon as the two men settled down. "Especially under peaceful circumstances."

"As am I," said Birger. "I respect your decision to aid your future son-in-law, but I am glad we never met on the battlefield. In any event; our countries have no quarrel."

"For which I am grateful," replied Hakon somberly. "Because I have something to discuss with you. It has to do with the suspicions your brothers had about Lord Torgils and Count Jakob. I have brought Count Jakob with me so that you can ask him yourself. May I send for him?"

Birger appeared surprised as Hakon spoke but nodded his assent. As Count Jakob entered, Birger felt his stomach constrict in anticipation. The Danish nobleman stood mute before the kings awaiting questioning.

Finally, Birger asked "Is it true that you and Lord Torgils planned to annex land from Sweden and Denmark to create a kingdom of your own?"

"Yes, your Majesty," said Jakob quietly fingering his rings.

Birger sat back in his chair and took a deep breath. Erik and Valdemar had spoken the truth! "It is difficult to believe Lord Torgils would contemplate such treachery against Sweden," Birger said aloud.

"Nevertheless, he did," affirmed Count Jakob with a shrug. "Why else do you think he married Hedvig of Ravensburg? Her father was willing to pay a huge dowry for a crown for his daughter, and Lord Torgils needed the money to finance the new kingdom. It was you, your Majesty, who unwittingly put an end to our dream."

"Oh, I suspected it, but I did not want to believe it! I switched the land exchange just to make sure the plan, if there was one, would go nowhere," groaned Birger.

"I am sorry, your Majesty," mumbled the count. Hakon silently nodded his dismissal, and the kings were alone once again.

"So, what will you do?" asked Hakon.

"I am not going to do anything," snapped Birger. "I was foolish to believe Torgils instead of my brothers, but they behaved horribly after that incident, all the same."

"I hear you believe they spied on you," said Hakon. "But they have sworn to me that they are innocent, and I believe them."

"The spy confessed," countered Birger angrily.

"Yes, allegedly to your Lord High Constable who had planned treason against you and Sweden, and you believed him again!" retorted Hakon.

Birger sat looking into the glowing fire. Hakon was pacing back and forth in front of the hearth waiting for Birger to respond.

"You should make peace with your brothers," counseled Hakon gently. Put all this behind you and start anew."

"I still believe my brothers spied on me, and I cannot forgive that, whatever their reasons," said Birger stubbornly. "I am returning Nykoping castle and that is more than they deserve."

"I have something else to discuss which relates directly to the subject of peace in Scandinavia," continued Hakon.

Birger listened to Hakon relate the situation in Northern Halland without indicating how he felt about Erik gaining control of the three invincible west coast fortresses.

As Hakon finished, Birger said calmly, "Erik might well suit Erik Menved better than Count Jakob did. And if the rebels are returned to Denmark to stand trial again, I am sure that Erik Menved would agree to your suggestion."

"Still, there is the problem of my maternal inheritance which is a matter I do not consider closed," Hakon added.

"I am sure Erik Menved wants to solve that, too."

"If he is open to that, I see no real difficulty in our countries coming to terms. All we need is a meeting."

"I will take care of it," said Birger. "I will dispatch a message to Erik Menved requesting a meeting between the two of you." Birger rose abruptly from his chair. The shock of discovering Torgil's treason reflected in his eyes as he hastened from the hall.

Alone in his chamber at Gullbergshed, Birger felt utterly despondent. King Hakon and his men-at-arms had left for Norway, and prior to their departure neither he nor Hakon had mentioned Erik or Valdemar again, but now Birger was alone with his thoughts.

He had approached Count Jakob during the visit to satisfy himself that the count had indeed told the truth. He had asked Jakob to speculate on whom he thought could have overheard his and Lord Torgils' plans. Since they had always taken precautions, the count could come up with only one possibility: Lord Torgils' friend, Abjorn Sixtensson. That had convinced Birger. For why else had Torgils so vehemently insisted on having Abjorn expelled and his property confiscated?

He now had to face the fact that he had misplaced trust in one who had planned to betray him and Sweden, and he would have to start relying on others for advice. If only his brothers had not spied on him. Or had they? Torgils could certainly have lied about the spy's confession. Still, Birger could not accept his brothers' innocence on faith alone. It had cost him such anguish to push them out of his life that he could not risk taking them back, only to experience another heartbreak. Oh God, he prayed, give me some irrefutable proof, one way or the other.

He felt lonely and cold, even in front of the blazing fire. He yearned to sit near Martha, and to hear her talk about simple, everyday events. This futile war had kept him from her for months, and he wanted nothing more than to be home again.

His reverie was interrupted by the unexpected arrival of Bishop Nils. Birger felt a rush of gratitude, as if God had heard his plea and had sent someone to whom he could turn.

He greeted the bishop warmly. "What brings you here, your Excellency?"

"To congratulate you on the peace treaty with your brothers, and to bring you loving greetings from the queen."

"I was just about to give orders for our return to Stockholm. How is my family?"

"They are well, and eagerly awaiting your return."

"For a moment I thought you were bringing ill tidings," said Birger relieved.

"On the contrary. Following the archbishop's recent death, may his soul rest in peace, the Church Council met and designated me the new Archbishop! I am here to receive your blessings, as well," Bishop Nils said with a slight bow.

"You certainly have my blessings. The Church could not have made a wiser choice," said Birger as he kissed the ring of the man he had known all his life.

"Thank you, your Majesty. I am on my way to Strangnas where the bishops will sign the petition to the Pope to confirm me as Archbishop, and I was hoping you would accompany me there on your way to Stockholm. It would lend moral support to the Church, and to me, if you would witness the signing ceremony."

"It would be my pleasure," said Birger enthusiastically. Lord Torgils had always advised against ceding power to the Church, so he perversely relished adding, "I think it is time to grant the Church her former privileges. In your honor, I shall do it now."

"Your Majesty!" exclaimed the bishop, delighted that the coveted moment had finally arrived. He sat down by the fire, giving his thanks to God for touching the king's heart. But mostly he was grateful that the king had decided to act now which would assure him, as the new Archbishop, of a consolidated following within the Church.

As Birger rode over the southern bridge to enter Stockholm, the pale April sun was shining over the island city. He felt elated that he had done something counter to Torgil's wishes by visiting Strangnas, and the urgent desire to get home without delay caused him to spur his horse on, outdistancing his escort. Stockholm castle's sentries spotted him and called out his approach as he neared the castle. He rode into the courtyard and dismounted just as Marta came running to throw herself into his arms.

"We have been apart for too long," she complained, while at the same time laughing with happiness. "I am so relieved the war is over. I have heard that Erik and Valdemar will soon return and rule their dukedoms as before. Is everything all right again?" she asked without waiting for an answer. "Magnus and little Erik cannot wait to see you. They have grown so while you were away. You should see them on their ponies, or with their bows and arrows." Marta took a deep breath to be able to continue.

"My sweet one," laughed Birger. "You do not have to tell me everything that has happened during the past months in one breath."

"I am so happy to have you back again," she exclaimed exuberantly. "I cannot help myself." Birger put his arm around her shoulders to lead her into the castle. She looked up as she suddenly felt him stiffen. He was gazing across the Great Hall to where the Lord High Constable stood.

"Welcome home, your Majesty," Torgils called. "I trust you had a good journey."

"I did. It was quite interesting," Birger responded. "Especially my stay in Strangnas. I shall tell you all about it, but now I will spend some time with my family," he added curtly.

"Can Erik, Valdemar, and Kristina come and visit us, now that all this is over?" Marta asked later that evening while resting on Birger's arm in her large bed.

"We shall see," said Birger noncommittally as he pulled her warm body closer to his. "We shall see." Marta did not like the uneasiness his response gave her. Maybe the war was over, but the quarrel was not. Still, she did not want to think about that tonight. Instead, she turned and put her arms around Birger.

Lord Torgils could not fail to notice a change in the king's behavior towards him. At first, he thought the dukes had somehow regained the king's confidence, but when they failed to attend the next council meeting he thought the cause must lie elsewhere. He soon realized that Bishop Nils had gained influence over his former pupil when the king decided to cease taxing the Church. Torgils became even more concerned when one of the noblemen in the King's Council died and was not replaced by his son or relative as had been the custom, but by a member from a powerful church-loyal clan.

As an added burden in Torgils' life, Hedvig had decided that their country estate was too quiet once the house had been redecorated and the gardens rebuilt, so she insisted on spending more time in Stockholm. While Torgils was busy with affairs of state, she kept a circle of young knights bedazzled by her beauty and biting wit. Torgils had long since resolved not to become jealous since he suspected that was the very reason she kept them around. He had also discovered that when she got enough attention from others she did not demand as much from him, or as many expensive gifts. At times he could not decide which was the more difficult task--to manage the affairs of Sweden, or to manage Hedvig.

When the messenger handed Kristina the scroll that bore Valdemar's seal she sought out a quiet spot to open it in the orchard outside Roskilde castle beneath a shady tree. While she was relieved to receive the message, she also felt angry that she had heard so little from Valdemar for many months.

She frowned in annoyance as she broke the seal and unrolled the scroll. Valdemar wrote:

> *Dearest Kristina,*
>
> *My lateness in writing you is unforgivable, since I understand that you must be anxious to know what is transpiring in Sweden. Please forgive me and let me try to tell you all that has happened since my last letter. You might have heard the wonderful news that Erik Menved has approved of Erik as Northern Halland's new ruler, as Count Jakob can no longer afford to keep his ravaged lands, and Erik has signed a document swearing allegiance to the Danish crown. Because of this new relationship, Erik Menved has requested that Erik and I be present in Helsingborg where a retrial of the 'rebels' accused of murdering King Erik Klipping will take place.*
>
> *Never have Erik and I worked so hard as we have this spring. Luckily, we had our treasury chests with us and could start our work immediately. An added bonus was the pile of gold we found after the fire in Lodose. It has been very helpful as food had to be purchased and collected in Norway and Sweden and then shipped to Varberg and Hunehals to be distributed to the people. Seed had to be located in time for the spring planting. As midsummer is slowly nearing, and as we ride across the countryside, we are met with smiles of gratitude*

from the peasants. The farmers have toiled tirelessly; and as a result, the midsummer harvest feast will be a spectacular celebration.

Although we have thoroughly enjoyed rebuilding this new territory, I am urging you not to join us here in these rugged fortresses, but to stay comfortably where you are until it is time for us to return to Nykoping together. I pray this letter finds you well. Until we meet again, my dear wife, may God bless you and keep you safe.

Your devoted husband, Valdemar.

The Danes had settled in their large castle and the Norwegians had already raised their tents when Erik and Valdemar arrived in Helsingborg. Both monarchs had brought unusually large armies for what seemed to be a display of military might, but the number of soldiers had a markedly different purpose. There had not been a tournament between Denmark and Norway for many years, and every knight in either country wanted to be there for the occasion.

At the edge of the Norwegian tent city stood a large canvas-covered pavilion, separated from the rest and heavily guarded. It held the Danish noblemen accused of murdering Erik Menved's father who were about to face trial. Count Jakob was among the accused because King Hakon had agreed that he would stand trial with the others. Hakon knew that he had no choice in the matter if peace were finally to be achieved, but he had confided to Erik and Valdemar that Erik Menved had promised to be lenient.

When the day for the trial arrived, it was unseasonably warm. The judges and the accused alike suffered from the heat in the pavillion where the proceedings took place. Erik and Valdemar were almost lulled to sleep in the stifling tent.

They were, however, not impressed with the fairness of the trial as it seemed clear that the Danish judges had already decided on the guilt of the accused. The court took several days of testimony from witnesses which, in Erik's mind, did not fully prove that the accused were guilty. Luckily, as both the dukes and King Hakon had a vote in the sentencing, the rebels did not receive the death sentence that the judges advocated. They merely lost their ranks and estates and were banished from Denmark. At first, Erik thought this a light sentence in view of the fact that the rebels had already lived outside their native country for eight years without income from their estates; but then he realized that King Hakon could no longer protect them. As a result, their only chance for a decent life was to find some German state, hostile to Denmark, willing to offer them a position and a home. After the trial, when Hakon suggested that an exception be made for Count Jakob to live at one of Hakon's country estates as long as he never appeared at the Norwegian court, Erik Menved agreed.

The following day, both kings decided that the alliance between their two countries need not be delayed, provided negotiations on the inheritance issue would actively proceed. King Hakon was given the Danish island, Hjelm, as a pledge of Denmark's good faith until his maternal inheritance could be permanently settled.

The new Scandinavian brotherhood was celebrated for three full days. The grand tournament was won by Mats Kettilmundsson, the only Swede participating--a fact which thoroughly pleased Erik.

On the final day, Erik and Valdemar found a moment of privacy to thank Kristoffer for the invaluable information he had provided during the war. "It was but a small favor," objected Kristoffer. "I, however, am impressed by what you two were able to accomplish. You are in a most enviable position."

"Without your help, we might not be where we are. We know we owe you a favor."

"I shall remember that," Kristoffer promised.

Erik Menved also expressed his admiration for the way Erik had gained his new preeminence. "You are in quite a different position from when we spoke a year ago. Then you had lost everything, and now you have allies everywhere. Most importantly, you have made a devastated Northern Halland bloom again."

"We have had invaluable support from King Hakon," Erik answered modestly. "Without him we would still be sitting in Kungahalla brooding over our misfortune."

"The only item remaining is to make peace with your brother."

"That will not be easy," said Erik sadly. "Birger is so convinced that we spied on him that he persuaded even you."

"Birger presented a most convincing case; but Birger, like me, must be impressed with your accomplishments. He might be more willing to put the incident behind him now."

"We shall see," said Erik, unable to disguise the bitterness in his voice.

"We certainly have had our share of good fortune," Erik conceded, while lounging in his tent outside Helsingborg castle. Valdemar nodded. "Still, we will never regain influence in the Swedish Council until we eliminate Lord Torgils as Birger's advisor."

"From what I hear, Torgils' position is not as secure as it was. Maybe Count Jakob's confession had some impact."

"If we could prove to Birger," replied Erik pensively, "that the spy was not ours, Torgils would be finished for good. The bishops would never have admitted that the spy served the Church while they were trying to regain their privileges. Now that they have regained them, they might be willing to tell Birger the truth to have the Lord High Constable removed."

"Are you suggesting Bishop Nils would be willing to tell Birger if, indeed, they sent the spy?" Valdemar asked.

"We must persuade him to."

"The consequence for Torgils will devastate Kristina."

"Yes," Erik admitted sadly, "I know."

"Your Excellency. What can I do for you?" King Birger asked Bishop Nils as the churchman settled himself in front of the fire in the Great Hall at Stockholm castle, holding his customary cup of wine.

"The winter is going to be harsh this year, I can feel it in my bones," the bishop complained as he massaged his right leg. "I am on my way back to Upsala . . . and I need to clear my conscience before I am sworn in as Archbishop."

"You have never had any dark secrets to hide, of that I am sure," said Birger as he sat down.

"Every man has his secrets, your Majesty. I came here to make a confession, and to receive your forgiveness before I don the archbishop's miter. Some time ago, the Church realized that Lord Torgils was the hindrance to fulfillment of the pledge you made to Her at your coronation. In order to find something which would help us weaken his position, we placed a spy at your court."

"You placed a spy?" gasped the king.

"Yes, your Majesty. I am not proud to admit it, but we were desperate. And we did obtain some useful information--such as the fact that you had given Lord Torgils the right to repossess Church land. That gave us the chance to initiate the process of excommunication which resulted in our keeping our properties."

"And the spy?" asked the king in a tremulous voice.

"He was a devout and loyal priest. May God have mercy on his soul," said the bishop.

"My God!" whispered the king as he buried his face in his hands.

"Forgive us, your Majesty. But he was placed to spy on Lord Torgils."

"What have I done?" moaned the king.

"What do you mean?" asked the bishop, feigning ignorance. His lengthy discussion with Erik and Valdemar had aquainted him with every detail of the brotherly feud.

"So much pain could have been spared had you only come to me earlier."

"This is the first moment I felt able to confess to you. I had put the entire incident behind me as it was done in the name of Holy Mother Church, but now, as I am to become the head of the Church of Sweden, I had to tell you. The Crown and the Church should be close, and I did not want anything to stand between us, even if you would never have known about it. But, I deeply regret that we did unintended harm."

"The armed conflict with my brothers was the result of my believing they spied on me," said Birger as he took his hands away from his face and looked at the bishop.

"You believed the dukes spied on you? Your own brothers?" asked the bishop, hoping he was not overplaying his part.

"Lord Torgils convinced me!" exclaimed Birger. "He wanted my brothers out of the way as they knew something which he feared I would believe. He had to discredit them."

"The situation can be mended," said the bishop softly.

"How can they ever forgive me?" cried Birger in agony. "They came to me time after time to tell me that they were innocent, only to be humiliated. What kind of a man am I who cannot see right from wrong?"

"You are mortal like all men, your Majesty. And as a man you can ask forgiveness. You can make amends. You would not have acted so harshly if you had not loved your brothers as much as you do. So now let that love work to bring peace with them."

"But will they forgive me?" asked Birger desperately.

"That, only you can discover. I am saddened to have caused this. Please forgive me."

"You are forgiven . . . Not only will I feel that I can trust you in the future because you have confided in me, but you have given me a chance to be close to my brothers again . . . if only they will let me."

Chapter 23

Kungahalla

It was during a cold autumn afternoon as Erik and Valdemar played chess in the hall of Kungahalla that they heard thundering hoofbeats nearing the fort. Erik rose and went over to one of the wall openings to observe a large group of knights under the Swedish royal banner rapidly approaching their stronghold. He motioned to Valdemar to follow him into the courtyard.

Birger was the first to ride through the portal. Erik took immediate umbrage at his large mounted column, but then Erik noticed that the knights were not Birger's usual escort. Their replacements had been chosen from church-loyal clans or families Birger personally held in high regard, not from families close to Torgils. Erik's initial displeasure softened, and after inviting Birger into the hall Erik dismissed the servants and loitering knights with a curt gesture of his hand. The three brothers sat down at one of the tables--Erik and Valdemar on one side and Birger on the other. They did not look at one another, and no one chose to speak. Erik could feel the tension build, as they were totally alone for the first time in a year and a half. Birger sat nervously twisting his signet ring. He seemed eager to talk, but at the same time unsure of how to formulate what he wanted to say.

Erik and Valdemar kept their silence until Birger finally blurted, "I am ashamed of my false accusations. I took Torgils' word against yours, and I can not express how embarrassed and furious I am over my own stupidity . . ."

"Why this sudden change of mind?" Erik asked, coldly.

"Bishop Nils wanted to begin his tenure as Archbishop with a clean conscience, so he admitted that the Church had planted the spy." Birger paused, anxiously studying his brothers who showed no emotion. "As you probably know, Count Jakob has confessed that he and Torgils did, indeed, plan to create their own kingdom. Everything you told me was true. And I, like a fool, did not believe you."

Erik took a deep breath as he looked Birger steadily in the eyes. "You not only refused to believe us, or even listen to us, but you repeatedly humiliated us. And in front of Lord Torgils!"

"I was so hurt, Erik. When I thought that you and Valdemar had spied on me, I behaved like a lunatic."

"That behavior might be excused in others, but you are a king," said Erik. "You involved our country in a civil war because you were duped by a man who repeatedly lied to you."

"I know," lamented Birger. "I have no excuse. And I cannot explain why I followed Torgils' lead so blindly. All I can offer are my most sincere and humble apologies, and my promise that I will do anything to make up for the way I treated you. Anything!"

Erik knew that however furious he felt, this was the moment for which he and Valdemar had prayed these many months. But he was not about to let Birger off so easily.

"How can you possibly make up for the pain you have caused us? We lived like exiles, and now you come with a sheepish 'I am sorry,' expecting us to forget all that has happened? And when will you turn on us next?"

"I do not expect you to forgive me simply because I ask. I want to make amends, and you may demand anything which will prove to you how sincerely I regret my actions."

Valdemar could no longer contain his anger that had smoldered for so long. He eyed Birger with open hostility.

"What will you do about Torgils?"

"I not only want the Lord High Constable to lose his position. I want him to lose his head!"

"You mean that?" asked Valdemar with skepticism in his voice.

"I have never been more serious. Torgils planned to commit treason against the crown. He has to be executed."

"If you are willing to go to that extent," said Erik solemnly, "I will try to forget what has passed."

"God bless you," exclaimed Birger as he stood up to embrace Erik. When he turned to put his arms around Valdemar he could no longer contain his tears. "I have missed you so," he said holding

Valdemar close to him. "Thank you for giving me a chance to rectify my mistakes," he continued as he reached again to enclose Erik in his embrace. "I have been only half a man without you."

Erik was unmoved by Birger's words. The old warmth and caring simply were not there. He turned aside to fill their cups before the brothers touched metal against metal.

"To my brothers," said Birger.

"To the King," responded Erik and Valdemar, each wondering if Birger heard the hollowness of their words.

Later that night, Erik noticed that Valdemar, like himself, was unable to sleep. He patted Valdemar on the shoulder and motioned for him to follow. Moving quietly between snoring knights, they left the sleeping quarters and descended to the empty hall where the fire was still glowing on the hearth. "This is what we hoped for, Erik, still I cannot forgive him!" Valdemar exclaimed as he angrily tossed some logs on the fire and sat down heavily on a bench. "I am so furious, that all I want to do is to strike him."

"I know . . . I have the same feelings. But we must suppress our anger if we want to regain our influence in Sweden."

"I know that. But I am aching to tell him what I really feel--that he is a weakling, and utterly unsuited to rule a country. At the same time, I know that I cannot say anything, or we will be living in this pigsty for the rest of our lives," Valdemar said as he swept aside some clean-gnawed bones which fell from the cluttered table into puddles of ale on the floor.

"I wonder if we can make him believe that things are suddenly normal between us?"

"If he could believe Torgils' lies, he ought to believe anything!" sneered Valdemar.

"Birger wants to execute Torgils for treason. Let us concentrate on that and put aside our personal feelings. Then we shall see how things develop."

"You are right, of course, but I am not sure that I can control myself."

"Please try, Valdemar. And think about what we have accomplished. We won! Birger is now the one begging. Once his closest advisor is gone, to whom will he turn? To us, of course."

"I want us to arrest Lord Torgils together," Birger suggested the following morning. "And I want to do it right away. That is the reason I brought so many soldiers with me."

"When is Torgils coming west?"

"He will be here within the week. He is planning to spend the holidays at Lena."

"There is less chance he will be forewarned if we have to travel only a short distance with so many men," noted Valdemar. "Does Torgils know that you are here with us, Birger?"

"I do not think so. I told him that I would visit Erik Menved."

"It is set then," Erik said grimly.

Valdemar rode swiftly along the snowy forest path, followed by his escort of four knights. The only sound to be heard in the stillness was the muffled beat of hooves in the deep snow.

Finally, Valdemar saw Torgil's estate, Aranas, lit up in the distance. He knew Kristina had been waiting there for months, and that she would be startled by his unannounced arrival. Under normal circumstances he would have treasured the welcome sight of his destination after a long and freezing ride; but now, with the mission he had to perform, he dreaded seeing the inviting smoke curling up from the roof. As he and his men rode into the yard, two stable boys rushed forward to take their horses, and the housekeeper opened the door to see what the commotion was about. "Duke Valdemar! We were not expecting you," she exclaimed as she curtsied. "The duchess is taking her supper. Would you like something to eat?"

"Yes, please. And see that my men are provided for."

Valdemar handed the housekeeper his heavy mantle while he stomped the snow off his boots on the mat of fir boughs spread before the threshold. When he entered, Kristina rose slowly from her place at the table. He had not seen her for over a year, and his heart skipped a beat when he saw again how lovely she was. He stopped and bowed low to her. She stood with familiar graciousness; her willowy body encased in a dark green tunic that set off her fair skin and blond curls that crept out from under the toque. Her eyes sparkled in surprise over his arrival as she lowered herself in a wifely curtsy. What he would give to see that warm smile last, but he knew it would not be there for long.

"My lord and husband! What a welcome surprise," she exclaimed. He saw her look expectantly over his shoulder toward the door.

"I came alone, and I am sorry that I gave you no prior warning, but there are reasons for that," he explained as he kissed her cheek. "I hope your ladies will not mind leaving us for a while," he said as he turned to the women taking supper with Kristina. "You might enjoy the company of the gentlemen I brought with me," he added kindly.

Ragna and the rest of the ladies giggled and withdrew to a table at the far side of the hall, followed by the servants who had hurriedly cleared away their table settings. The housekeeper then set a place for Valdemar and left him with Kristina.

"Kristina," he said wearily. "I do not bring good news." He stopped, unable to continue.

" What has happened?"

"Most of it you know, or have guessed, and the rest I wish I did not have to tell you."

He moved closer and took her hand in his. As gently as he could, he told her the full story of her father's role in the war between the brothers. While he was talking, she did not take her eyes off his face but gazed at him pleadingly as if to beg for a happy ending. It did not come. "My father will be executed?" she whispered in utter disbelief.

"He has committed high treason, Kristina. And there is only one punishment for such a crime," Valdemar said, avoiding her eyes.

"I do not believe that you will do that. He is my father. I am your wife." Valdemar sat silently staring at the tabletop. "The king could pardon him! You could talk to Birger," pleaded Kristina, her voice broken by emotion.

"Do not forget what he has done," Valdemar said softly. "Not only to the crown, but to Erik and me. It has been decided, so do not ask me, Kristina. There is nothing I can do."

"Of course, you can. If only you wanted to." When he did not reply she sat motionless, staring at him. The pleading look was gone, and unbearable sadness took its place. "My father was the only parent I truly knew," she said finally, her eyes filling with tears.

"I shall do everything I can to make it easier for you," said Valdemar gently. "I will give you a divorce . . ."

"You will take everything from me!" exploded Kristina, her voice suddenly shaking with anger.

"I give you no happiness, Kristina. I was never a husband to you, and I wish you a fuller life. Our marriage was a political act, as will be our divorce. And Birger wants it."

"Finally, you will be rid of me. Is that not so, Valdemar?"

"Why do you say that?"

"You were never my friend after our marriage. You always tried to avoid me. While you were kind to me, I could feel your coldness, so do not come and tell me we are divorcing for political reasons. Had you been my true friend you would not have cared what Birger thought about me as a traitor's daughter, you would have stayed faithfully by my side. You hate me, but you have not the courage to tell me."

"You could not be more wrong . . ."

"A woman can feel when a man does not want to be close to her," she said bitterly. "At least have the decency to tell me the truth. You owe me that."

Valdemar looked into her flashing eyes. "The truth is that I love you, Kristina. And I could never earn your love in return. There was always Erik." He saw her take a deep breath as the anger left her eyes. She opened her mouth to speak, but he interrupted her. "The truth is that I cannot live so close to you, knowing that you want someone else. And I want you to be happy. Since you cannot find happiness with me, you should have your freedom to find it with someone else. That is how much I love you."

He saw her eyes again fill with tears. "If you had given us a chance, Valdemar. If you had let me be your wife . . . bear your children . . ."

"It was not to be. We cannot change the past, but we can do something about the future. You can start a new life. You have my love and best wishes," he said as he lifted her hand to his lips. "Naturally, you shall keep your dowry, and I will give you an estate."

"We will divorce then . . . for the good of the country, but who would marry me now? Who would want the daughter of a traitor, the discarded wife of Duke Valdemar? Who would want to give me his love and children? Who?" asked Kristina.

"I will make sure everyone knows that the royal family holds you in high esteem, regardless of your father's crime," said Valdemar lamely, knowing full well the truth of what she was saying. Even though she would be left with a fortune, she would not be a good marriage prospect. Some minor nobleman would, of course, marry her for money, but that would be the last thing she would want--another loveless marriage.

"Still, I suppose being alone is better than living with my father's murderer!"

Valdemar pulled her gently into his arms. She rested her head against his chest and cried like a lost child. He was convinced that he was doing the best for them both by divorcing her. She cried for a long time, and when her tears finally stopped, she looked at him and said, "I never knew it was possible to feel so lonely."

"Would you like to return to Denmark and be with Ingeborg—to be away while this business is going on?" asked Valdemar.

"No, I will go to my father," said Kristina stoically. "Maybe I can comfort him."

"Do you think you have the strength for that?"

"Yes. I know now how it feels to be alone, and I want him to know that someone is standing by him," she answered resolutely.

"If that is what you want, why do you not stay with Rikissa, at Santa Klara's convent in Stockholm? You will be with someone who loves you," said Valdemar, relieved that his sister would be there to support Kristina during the difficult days ahead.

"I will do that," she said, drying the tears she again could not hold back. "I think I must sleep now. I am exhausted." She stood up on unsteady legs while Valdemar supported her.

"Just leave me in front of the fire," she requested.

"I will eat something and not leave until dawn, in case you need me," Valdemar said as he helped her into a large chair close to the hearth and bent over to kiss her gently on the temple. He gestured to Ragna to see to her mistress. Then he left her side and sat down with his knights.

Kristina requested more wood on the fire, and that her small silver chest be brought to her. Slowly she opened it and took out the tapestry that the wise old woman had given her. She unfolded it to look more closely at the hunter holding the wounded deer in his arms. The doe's beautiful head was hanging lifelessly, but Kristina had the notion that the hunter nodded at her kindly as she drifted off to a fitful sleep.

A few days later, Erik and Birger reached the designated meeting place two miles from Lena where Valdemar would join them. Their armed escort now consisted of almost a hundred mounted knights and soldiers. Erik spotted Valdemar waiting for them in a clearing of the woods. He had dismounted and was pacing back and forth to keep warm. "Have you waited long?" called Erik.

"I just arrived," Valdemar called back.

Erik and Birger quickly dismounted and went up to their brother. Birger's face was somber when he said to Valdemar, "There was no other way to solve the problem. It would be politically unwise for you and Kristina to stay married. She must have understood that."

"Yes, she understood," said Valdemar curtly as he turned his back and walked towards his horse. He hated Birger that moment even more than when he had seized Nykoping. He wanted to stay married to Kristina even if she was still in love with Erik. Who but he could protect or love her better? He could still see her tear-drenched face looking incomprehensibly at him. In one moment they had stripped away her security and devastated her existence, and Birger talked only of politics. He felt his hands clench into fists, and he had all he could do not to turn around and hit Birger. "We should be on our way," was all he could say.

"Absolutely," agreed Birger, relieved that Valdemar seemed to have resolved the situation without any complications.

However, Erik could sense that there was more to the meeting.

"Tell me. What did she say?" he asked anxiously as he gave Valdemar a leg up to mount.

"We will divorce. For the good of the country," Valdemar said disdainfully as he spurred his horse to the head of the column.

When they arrived at Lena, the Lord High Constable himself came out into the courtyard. Erik wondered what was going through Torgil's mind when he beheld the large force of men at arms and the dukes' banners flying behind the king's, but the Lord High Constable did not betray his thoughts as he cordially greeted them. He shouted orders to prepare the midday meal and invited everyone into the warm hall. Torgils guided the king and the dukes to be seated away from the knights and soldiers, before offering them wine, which they refused. He looked inquisitively at them as he poured himself a cup.

"You look solemn, my lords. What is troubling you?" he asked finally.

Birger looked like a small boy as he faced the man who had for so long controlled his life. Erik could feel how difficult it was for Birger to tell the Lord High Constable who had been like a surrogate father that his days as the most powerful man in Sweden had come to an end. That his life had come to an end.

"I am here, Lord Torgils, with my brothers, to arrest you for high treason," Birger finally began with more assurance than he obviously felt.

"I see," said Torgils slowly as he sat down opposite them. "What are the charges?"

"You did at one time conspire with Count Jakob of Northern Halland to annex part of Sweden and create a kingdom of your own, and you falsely accused Erik of placing a spy at my court when you knew the spy was sent by the Church. Both incidents have been confirmed through conversations with Count Jakob and Bishop Nils," said Birger losing all hesitancy.

"I see," repeated Lord Torgils.

"Is that all you have to say?" demanded Birger angrily.

"There is not much to say, is there?" replied Torgils as he emptied his wine cup and refilled it again. Birger was incensed by Torgils' refusal to act beaten or to show the slightest bit of fear. Now, when he clearly knew that his life was threatened, he was still the immovable statesman he had always been.

"Since this will probably be the last conversation we shall have, your Majesty, let me give you some advice," Torgils continued without emotion. "Whatever I have done these many years, I did to preserve the stability of our country. It is difficult to relinquish power when you are wielding it successfully, so when I saw my position weakening, I reacted like any man would; I tried to counter that development. In the final analysis, I was unsuccessful. And that is that." Erik, Valdemar and Birger sat in silence. "My most cogent advice though," said Torgils, refilling his cup, "is to warn your Majesty about what power can do to any man. It is a potent drug of which one can never get enough. I am a prime example, which qualifies me to point out another who would resort to any means to gain it. You had better keep a watchful eye on your brother!"

"You have insulted and accused Erik for the last time!" hissed Birger, venting the full force of his anger.

The Lord High Constable smiled, "Keep in mind what I have said. I am impressed by what Duke Erik has accomplished during this past year," he concluded as he emptied his cup and looked over to the other end of the hall. "I think they are ready with supper. Let us eat before we leave. I assume we are going to Stockholm."

Lady Hedvig arrived at Lena two days after her husband's arrest. She entered the hall with six of her favorite knights, only to find the place cold and dark.

"What is going on? Hello, is any one here?" she shouted in the darkness.

One of the servants came running through the kitchen door carrying a lighted candle.

"Where is the Lord High Constable?" she asked impatiently. The servant stood stuttering. "Get the fires going, and light the candles! Are we supposed to freeze to death? And get someone who can tell me what is going on. Get moving!" snapped Hedvig as she snatched the candle from the servant. She started lighting the candles on the long tables, and one of the young knights put a taper to the wood logs on the hearth. A handful of servants came rushing with more candles and firewood to finish the work the travelers had begun. The major domo bowed deeply.

"I am sorry, my lady, but we were not expecting you. We did not think you would be coming here after they took his lordship away," he said apologetically.

Hedvig heaved a sigh of annoyance. "What are you talking about?" The major domo told Hedvig as much as he knew. "I will be damned! The old devil is in real trouble!" Hedvig said shaking her head in disbelief. "I thought he was indestructible. Listen," she continued, turning to the young knights after dismissing the major domo. "I want to know what is going on. Go to Stockholm to find out the latest news. The one who returns with the most thorough report gets a special treat," she said winking her eye. "However, you stay here and protect me," she ordered as she pointed to a tall, blond knight who bowed with a happy grin. The other men booed her choice, but she waved her arm and pointed to the exit. "Go, go . . . and hurry back." The knights scrambled for the door.

"How about coming over here," Hedvig beckoned to the blond knight.

She slowly started to take off her cape. Eagerly he went towards her, but she walked past him and sat down in a chair. She stretched out a boot-clad foot, motioning for him to remove the boot, which he obediently did. Then he leaned forward to kiss her.

"Not so fast, my pet. Start by kissing my foot and you work your way up very, very slowly." She sunk down in the chair and closed her eyes with a contented sigh.

Stockholm 1306

Kristina arrived in Stockholm during a blustery January snowstorm. She was shivering from the cold as she entered Santa Klara convent where Rikissa greeted her. As soon as she saw Rikissa's spacious chamber she realized that she had become the Mother Superior. The room could belong to no one else, with its high, vaulted ceiling, large window, and few but fine pieces of furniture. It contained only a small altar, a desk, some stools and a narrow cot by the far wall. Above the altar hung the most beautiful crucifix Kristina had ever seen, crafted in gold and encrusted with precious stones.

"It was a gift to the convent from Ingeborg," Rikissa explained in response to Kristina's gaze. "Come, sit down. I have been worried about you, ever since I spoke to Valdemar. I pray we can give you the support you need."

They were interrupted as one of the sisters entered with herbal tea. "We live simply here, and you are welcome to share our daily routine, or to live by your own schedule, as you please," said Rikissa as she poured the tea that smelled of mint and camomile. "Valdemar did not give me any details, but I would like to know all so I can be of help to you."

Kristina looked at Rikissa whom she had not seen for many years, but now, as they finally sat together, it seemed as if no time had elapsed as she gazed into those calm gray eyes. But rather than speaking, Kristina began to cry uncontrollably. Rikissa reached out and pulled Kristina close to her. "That is good," she whispered as she rocked Kristina in her arms. "Cry. Let all the pain drain out."

Her tears welled from the very depth of her being, and she cried for a very long time with Rikissa's comforting arms enveloping her. Finally, Kristina collected herself and related all that had transpired during the past two years.

"I cannot accept that my father has to be executed. He could return everything the king has given him and be allowed to live in the countryside where he would bother no one."

"You know in your heart that your father would not be removed from power that easily," said Rikissa. "He has many allies, and the country could end up in war again. I understand Birger's decision, even if I do not approve of it."

"I wish I could do something to save my father's life, but I do not even know how to begin," said Kristina sadly. "Am I allowed to visit him?"

"Yes, I have obtained the necessary permission for you," Rikissa replied. "But for now, I think that you should rest after your journey. I will take you to your cubicle."

That area was like all the other sleeping cells in the convent, just large enough for a narrow cot and a chest to hold the few belongings of the nun living there. Despite the sparse accommodations and the chill in the cell, Kristina slept through the night without nightmares. The following morning, after prayers and a sparse meal in the refractory, she set out for Stockholm castle to visit her father. Rikissa accompanied her as far as the convent gate, which she unlocked, and then she embraced Kristina warmly. "Go with God. And may He give you strength," she said as she made the sign of the cross.

Slowly, Kristina walked through the lanes of the awakening city. She took the shortest route, which led across the square where the merchants were opening their shops and setting up their stalls. She remembered when she and Ragna had stolen away from the castle, feeling so adventuresome while they browsed through the stalls. Such a different feeling from the one that now weighed her down. She walked over the drawbridge leading to the castle and noticed the look of surprise on the faces of the castle guards as she passed by unescorted. Instead of entering the castle by the customary wide portal, she went around to the side where two sentries guarded a narrow wooden door. She handed them her note of permission, which one of them brought inside, while she waited in the bitter cold. Eventually the jailer emerged, bowing profusely and beckoning Kristina to enter. She followed the fat, clubfooted man down two flights of stone steps before they reached the main cellblock. She could see yet another flight of steps leading down to the lower dungeons and the domain of the Master of the Chamber.

"Lord Torgils has been given a very nice cell, nothing in the dungeons," said the jailer congenially as if he were an innkeeper describing the accommodations. The prison was cold and damp. Its only source of warmth was an open fire in the jailer's quarters where a couple of guards were playing a board game. The jailer limped along a torch-lit corridor, past thick wooden doors, until finally he stopped at the last one. He unlocked it with a large key. "I shall look in on you in a while," he said "and if you want to stay longer, I will come back later."

He shoved open the heavy door and let Kristina enter before he closed and re-locked it. The cell was lit only by one small, barred opening in the wall near the vaulted ceiling. It took Kristina some time to accustom her eyes to the darkness before she could see the shape of a man resting on a hay-covered platform running along one wall. She realized that her father had already been in this dark, foul-smelling cell for weeks, and her heart ached.

"Father, are you asleep?" she asked softly as she approached. The figure sat up at the sound of her voice. His hands flew up to smooth his hair and to straighten his clothes.

"Kristina? Is that you?"

"Yes, father. I have finally come to visit you. It took a little time, but I wanted everything to be arranged at Aranas before I left. The servants have been paid, and I told them to stay and wait for the king's orders." Kristina prattled nervously, not knowing what to do. She saw that her father had lost weight, and his eyes had deep shadows beneath them and his beard was greyish and unkempt.

"I am sorry that you have to see me like this, Kristina. You should not have come. You should remember me the way I was. Not like some caged animal," he said sadly.

"But I want to be with you," she said, sitting down on the wooden platform next to him.

"Thank you, my dear, I do appreciate that, but you should know that I feel sad for you, not for me. I knew this could happen. It was a risk I always took, and I have to confess that I never thought about what it would mean for you. How have you been treated since my arrest?"

"My marriage to Valdemar is being dissolved."

"That coward!" Torgils hissed with fury.

"No, father, do not say that. We were not happy together. This is an opportune moment for us to go our separate ways. Valdemar is being very generous, he is not only returning my dowry but has given me an estate as well."

"Thank the Lord, you will be a wealthy woman, and I can rest in peace knowing that you will never want for anything material. Still, I have robbed you of your good name and for that I am devastated."

"You are not afraid of what is awaiting you?" she asked softly.

"I am, deep down. But it is a fate I have lived with all my life. I played a game few men are privileged to play, and I was a winner for many years. Now the game is over, and since I despise a bad loser, I shall try to be a good one. People actually enjoy a man going proudly and fearlessly to his execution. They are willing to believe he had justice on his side. I do not want my grand-children to be embarrassed by me," said Torgils as he stroked Kristina's hand and added, "Come now! We are getting sentimental, and I cannot afford such luxuries in my solitude." He stood up and turned his back towards her.

"Can I do anything for you?" she asked.

"Do not visit me again. It hurts too much to be reminded of what I will lose. Never to see your beautiful face again . . ." his voice broke.

"But I want to be with you!" she cried out.

"It is better if you are not. Let me keep a little dignity. I love you Kristina, more than even I knew. You have been a dutiful and loving daughter, as was your sister until she passed away, and I thank you for the years we have had together. I am sorry it should end this way. I hope you can find it in your heart to forgive me one day." He walked over and banged on the door, rubbing his hand over his eyes. "Jailer, Jailer!" he called. His voice echoed down the corridor. As they stood silently facing each other, they could hear the limping footsteps of the jailer approaching.

"If you should need me, send a message to Santa Klara where I am staying. Please!" begged Kristina as she threw her arms around her father.

Torgils drew her close and rocked her in his arms. He felt the most unbearable pain spread in his chest as he released her upon hearing the key turn in the door. He numbly watched her back out of the cell.

Bishop Nils was alone with King Birger after having proudly witnessed his friend Lord Knut Jonsson sworn in as the King's Chancellor. The composition of the council was slowly changing, much to the bishop's gratification.

"I do not feel right about Lord Torgils being buried in unhallowed ground even if it is customary for those executed," said Birger. "Could the Church permit him to rest in hallowed ground?"

"That could be arranged," answered the bishop. "But it will delay the execution, because Lord Torgils must be alive when the dispensation is granted. And Church petitions take time. Consider my own case. I was nominated as archbishop almost a year ago, and I still have not received final authority to put the miter on my head."

"But if I convinced Lord Torgils to leave part of his estate to the Church could the dispensation be expedited?" wondered Birger. "I do not want to delay the execution. His followers are restless, and chances for rebellion exist as long as he is alive."

"I appreciate the situation, your Majesty, but I cannot hurry the tedious procedure. However, I do have a suggestion. If the execution goes ahead as planned, Lord Torgils will be buried in unhallowed ground; but after some time we will quietly move him to the Franciscan monastery in Stockholm . . . in appreciation of his generous donation to Holy Mother Church."

"Then, that is how we shall do it," said Birger, relieved that he would not have Torgils' eternally restless soul on his conscience.

"What do you want?" asked Lord Torgils as a young monk entered his cell with a document in his hand.

"The king requests that you sign this last will and testament," said the monk handing Torgils the scroll. The jailer entered carrying a small desk and a candle that he placed in front of Torgils, and then took several steps back to wait in the shadows. It took Torgils some time to get used to the candlelight before he unrolled the document. As he read it, he started to laugh.

"This is comical! Why should I, who have fought the Church during my entire political life, want to leave a large part of my estate to her?" he asked. "Once I am gone, the king can do what he wants with my properties, but I will not leave them to the Church!"

"I neglected to say that you will rest in hallowed ground if you sign the testament," added the monk.

"So that is it," said Torgils sarcastically. "His Majesty does not want my soul on his conscience. But you can tell the king from me, Father, that having my soul on his conscience is part of the game!" The monk looked quizzically at Torgils who returned the document. "Just tell the king what I told you, he will understand. And, please, leave me alone."

The monk departed with the unsigned document as the jailer removed the desk and re-locked the door.

The following day the door to Torgil's cell opened again. This time the looming shape of the Master of the Chamber filled the doorway, permeating the cell with that eerie smell of slow death.

"Good day, my Lord," he said with a smile stretching over his grotesque face. "I have been charged to ask you to sign the testament with which you were presented yesterday." Lord Torgils looked at the document the Master held in his hand and took a deep breath. The game had come down to some basic moves!

"I suggest you sign it, Lord Torgils," the Master urged in a threatening manner as he unrolled the document on the small table the jailer had once more placed before Torgils.

"You have a way of convincing me that signing it would be wise." Torgils took the signet ring off his hand and pressed it into the wax the jailer melted with the candle's flame.

"Thank you, my lord," said the Master before rolling up the document again. "I would not have liked to work on you after you have been so generous to me in the past. Thanks to you, I now have a beautiful young wife to keep me happy."

"I am glad to have played a part in your good fortune," said Torgils, pitying the woman whose parents had doubtless sold her to the Master for a tidy sum.

The day of Lord Torgil's execution inevitably arrived. It was a cold but sunny February day. Torgils had slept surprisingly well. The long wait for this day had been so excruciating that its final arrival felt like a relief. The last meal had been satisfying, and he had been allowed to change his clothes for the occasion. He had even taken a tepid bath and washed his matted hair and beard. He pulled on the fresh tunic bearing his coat of arms embroidered with gold and silk. To his great surprise, he felt no fear.

He had been patiently awaiting the arrival of his guards and the customary priest who was to accompany him on his final journey. As he heard the uneven footsteps of the jailer, he reached into the hidden side pocket of his tunic and pulled out a few of the gold coins he had managed to get when his servant came with the fresh change of clothes. The jailer unlocked the door and entered the cell.

"I am sorry it had to end this way, my lord," he said earnestly. "I kept hoping for you."

"Thank you for what you did for me while I was here," said Torgils as he placed the gold coins in the surprised jailer's hand. "Do me one last favor. Go to Santa Klara convent and ask for my daughter, Lady Kristina. Tell her how much I appreciated her courage in coming to visit me. Tell her that I am not afraid."

"Of course, my lord, I shall give her the message. And . . . thank you . . ." said the jailer overcome by the amount he was holding in his hand.

"It is time, is it not?" asked Lord Torgils, turning the jailer's attention back to the business at hand.

"Yes, my lord, it is. Please follow me." He quickly slipped the gold coins under his tunic before leading the way down the corridor where two guards and a monk awaited. Together, they mounted the two flights of steps leading up to the narrow entrance door. "Remember, it is very bright outside, so get used to the light slowly. Close your eyes when we get out. I shall help you into the wagon," whispered the jailer who intuitively understood how important a commanding performance was to the Lord High Constable.

Torgils was grateful for the jailer's help as he climbed into the wagon, feeling the sharp pain from the light pierce his half-closed eyes. At the insistence of the jailer, one of the guards chained Torgils' hands together in front, rather than behind his back, so that he could hold on to the side of the wagon and not fall. Never in his life had Torgils purchased so much dignity for so little gold. He was deeply touched by the jailer's concerns, and the thought occurred to him that he must have failed to notice many such things in his life. The gestures most assuredly had been there, but he had never paid them any heed.

Despite the cold, Torgils did not feel the biting chill. He noticed only the warm rays of the sun touching his face as he raised it up. Soon he became used to the light, and he treasured everything he saw. All shops had been closed and most of the inhabitants of the town were already at the place of execution. But the older people who could not easily climb the steep hills watched from their doors and windows in silence as they heard the monotonous beat of the death drum. The drummer boy who was riding an old horse in front of the prisoner's wagon obviously felt important to be preceding such a distinguished man to his execution, and he was striking his drum with greater vigor than usual.

As Torgils passed through the Big Square, he saw several members of clans who had been close to him during his reign. As he caught their eyes they bowed deeply to pay their final respects, and he returned their bows with gratitude for their coming to bid him farewell. He felt even more confident after this incident, and he straightened his back and lifted his head higher to make everyone who knew him feel proud of him. All along the way to his final destination, Torgils found familiar faces. He was overcome by this show of support, and as he finally entered the place of execution, he did not have to pretend his resolve to die as a man of courage.

As the wagon rolled onto the field among the throngs of people, a hush spread over the area, and the wagon progressed in silence towards the executioner's platform. As Lord Torgils stepped down from the wagon and the guards unchained his hands, the crowd started to whisper and comment about the condemned man. Torgils unhesitatingly climbed up the steps to the platform and calmly stood in the middle of it, as tall and imposing as ever. His strong face was at peace, and his every move exuded his lifelong habit of being in command.

The executioner, dressed in black and with his face covered by a hood, stood waiting quietly by the block against which rested his long-handled ax. The large, crescent-shaped blade reflected the sun as he bent down on his knee in front of the former Lord High Constable.

"Forgive me for what I am about to do," he said as custom prescribed.

"You are forgiven," said Lord Torgils in a strong voice, which was heard by everyone in the silence. Torgils reached into his tunic pocket to remove the customary coin that he was to give to the executioner as a token of hiring his services, making his forgiveness complete. Instead of presenting the usual copper piece, Lord Torgils handed the executioner a gold coin. The crowd drew their breath and started cheering.

The executioner tied a strip of dark cloth over Torgil's eyes and led him to the block where he guided him to kneel and gently placed his head on its surface. Torgils felt the cold wood touch his cheek, and for the first time raging panic coursed through his body like a bolt of lightning. He was not ready to die as he had thought! He felt an irrevocable will to survive overpower his being as the ax fell swiftly to sever his stately head.

The crowd roared as the ax stuck in the block, but quickly grew silent once again.

Chapter 24

The three royal brothers sat waiting in uncomfortable silence in the audience chamber of Stockholm castle with untouched chalices of wine before them. Birger nervously tapped the table, while Vademar began to pace the length of the chamber until at last they heard rapid footfalls approaching in the corridor. The door opened, and a young knight appeared, bowing deeply.

"The Lord High Constable is dead," he announced as he straightened up and backed out of the chamber.

Birger walked over to his brothers and lifted his chalice. "May he rest in peace."

"Amen," mumbled Erik and Valdemar.

Erik would always remember that moment as the time when he began to feel fully in charge of his life--as if all restrictions had been lifted and he finally was his own master. He guessed that his brothers felt the same way.

"Now it is just the three of us," smiled Birger emptying his chalice.

Erik and Valdemar drank the toast, unable to look Birger directly in his eyes.

The jailer, eager to carry out Lord Torgils' final request, hurried off to find Lady Kristina. He had trailed behind the cart to the place of execution and had been present during the Lord High Constable's final moments, so he was deeply moved when he arrived at the convent.

"Your father was brave, my lady. You should've seen him," he said when he met Kristina in the convent garden. "The crowds went wild. It was the best execution ever! Begging my lady's pardon," he added quickly when he saw Kristina wince. "But you don't often see a man meet his death so bravely. His lordship asked me to tell you that he was happy you came to visit him. He said to tell you that he wasn't afraid."

Kristina's mouth quivered. "I am glad he was not angry that I came to see him."

"Oh no, my lady! I know he wasn't. But some men are funny like. They don't want anyone to see 'em when they're defeated," the jailer added as tears began to well up in Kristina's eyes.

She nodded silently, then thanked him before she rushed down the corridor to her cubicle. She collapsed on her cot. Her whole body ached, and she had only one singular thought. She did not want to live further. Her world had fallen apart, and she did not even have the strength to cry anymore. Then, from the depth of her soul came a howling shriek of loss so loud it pierced the peaceful stillness of the afternoon prayers.

She heard the rustle of the nuns' cassocks as they came running to see what was amiss. She saw their anxious faces surround her and she could hear their concerned questions, but she was unable to speak. When Rikissa finally arrived and asked the others to leave, Kristina still could not find her voice.

"Talk to me, Kristina. Let me help you," Rikissa pleaded as she pulled Kristina close to her. The warmth of that embrace and its loving empathy finally brought forth Kristina's tears again, and she cried as she had when her mother died and when she had learned that she would never marry Erik. Her tears flowed for the death of her father and for all the things she had lost in her life. But how ever much she cried, the pain would not abate.

When at last she had no more tears, Rikissa laid her down gently on her cot. The herbalist arrived with a chalice of hot, calming liquid that Rikissa had Kristina swallow.

"Try to sleep if you can," she urged. "I shall go to the chapel and pray for you. God, in his mercy, will soften your pain with the passage of time, but for now you have to get through the night. Call if you need me." Rikissa covered Kristina with a blanket and leaned over to kiss her forehead. "I shall watch over you, and God will give you strength."

Later that night, after the evening meal in the Great Hall had finished and the Hall had emptied except for the three brothers, Erik sat down by the fire, shaking his head in disbelief. "It seems Torgils will be remembered as a saint rather than a traitor," he said as he slumped back in his chair.

"Even Knut Jonsson, our own witness, confessed that he had never seen anyone face death with such composure," observed Birger. "People like to create heroes, but this time they picked a traitor to idolize. The gossip will soon die down. Now I have to subscribe some documents which have been on my desk for days, so please excuse me," Birger said as he left with an unusual spring to his step.

"Torgils' death seems a great relief to Birger," noted Valdemar. "He appears quite different."

"You would too, if you had been a king, and under Torgils' heel for so many years," said Erik. He looked at the fire pensively. "Poor Kristina. She must be heartbroken for her father. And the divorce? You never did tell me how she reacted to that."

Valdemar gazed at Erik for a long time before he answered. "She has lost her status, her father is dead, and her name will forever be linked to a traitor. How do you imagine she reacted?" He shoved his chair back roughly and paced before the fire like one wrestling with demons. "I do not know if you have guessed, but I love Kristina. Needless to say, she does not love me. She still loves you." His voice choked, unable to continue. Then his words came haltingly. "Because of that, we never consummated our marriage . . ." He looked up and found Erik staring at him in disbelief.

"I became more and more unhappy, since she and I could not even be the friends we always had been because of what I felt for her. Kristina was unhappy because she was not married to you . . . and because she did not bear any children." Valdemar came around the fire-pit and sank down in his chair. "It has been horrible for both of us. Still, just having her near was all I wanted . . . but now I will have not even that."

"Valdemar!" Erik burst out. "I had no idea . . ."

"How could you? You were wallowing in your own self-pity. And what difference would it have made if you knew?" asked Valdemar, his voice trembling with emotion. He closed his eyes. "You could have done nothing to ease my pain."

Erik remembered moments in the past when he and Kristina had expressed their love for one another, by words, glances or gestures, and he felt guilty towards his ever-loyal brother.

"You must have hated me," he said.

"Why should I hate you? Neither you nor Kristina could help how you felt. My pain came from my hope that she might learn to love me one day. But that did not happen."

Erik felt guilt choke him, realizing that if he had not shown his love to Kristina over the years, she might have turned her heart to Valdemar instead. But he had kept their love alive by his selfish need that she would never stop caring for him. What had he done to his brother? What had he done to her? "I am so sorry, Valdemar," was all he could whisper.

"I told you. It is not your fault," said Valdemar staring resignedly at the floor.

Erik was about to protest further when urgent footsteps could be heard nearing the Hall. Through the vaulted doorway their sister, Rikissa, entered, her robes flying about her, her face fraught with worry. Erik and Valdemar both stood up, alarmed at her unexpected entrance. She had not been back to the castle since the day she had left it.

" Kristina," she exclaimed, short of breath. "She tried to take her life!"

The brothers hovered about their sister as she sank onto a bench.

"What?" exploded Valdemar.

"Is Kristina all right?" Erik urgently asked.

"She is alive," Rikissa replied once she had regained her composure. "But she is deeply despondent. She has lost all will to live. I do not know what we can do for her."

"How did she try to kill herself?" asked Valdemar incredulously.

"I thought she had retired, but instead she went to the refractory and took some poison from our medicine shelf. Luckily, one of the nuns saw her, so we were able to prevent her from swallowing much of it. Had she not been seen, she would surely be dead!" Rikissa concluded.

"And now? How is she now?" Erik asked urgently.

"She is sleeping. The herbalist who tended her said that she did not take enough to be fatal. But her agony must be unbearable. How else," exclaimed Rikissa crossing herself, "could she have contemplated such an unpardonable sin?"

The Hall was silent as they looked at each other helplessly. "You must go to her, Erik," said Valdemar almost inaudibly. "You are the only one who can help her."

"I think Valdemar is right," agreed Rikissa, unaware of the pain etched on Valdemar's face as he turned away.

But Erik had not missed it. "I do not know . . ."

"Do you not care at all?" asked Rikissa indignantly. "She loves you, and she always trusted you. You might not care about her anymore, but I know that you did once."

"That is not it," interrupted Erik while he stared at Valdemar's back.

"Go to her," insisted Valdemar without turning.

Rikissa looked from one to the other. "Well?" she demanded with an enquiring look.

"I shall go," said Erik as he hastened towards the courtyard.

"I thought he still cared," Rikissa ventured.

"He does, more than you know," Valdemar muttered hoarsely.

Erik rode with abandon through the lanes of the quiet city. He almost ran down two carousing soldiers who seemed oblivious to their narrow escape, then his horse kicked over a water barrel as he turned a sharp corner. By the time he careened around the final corner he felt almost sick with self-recrimination over how Torgil's execution had touched Kristina. He reined up outside the convent and hurriedly tethered his mount before he began to pound on the heavy door. He waited impatiently until he heard a soft voice ask him his business.

"I have been sent by the Reverend Mother to see Lady Kristina," he said sternly. "I am Erik of Sweden." He heard the creaking of a large key turning in the lock before the oak door swung slowly ajar. He pushed it open and looked down at a young novice. "Take me to her!" he commanded as the girl obediently hurried before him down a dark and silent corridor.

The light from her candle threw gigantic shadows on the walls as they moved along. The only sounds he could hear were his heavy boots echoing against the stone floor. The nun stopped in front of a cubicle, then wordlessly handed Erik her candle before she continued down the corridor. Cautiously, although his heart was beating fast, he entered. Kristina was sitting in the darkness on her cot, her head down.

"Kristina," was all he could say.

She looked up, and he could see the naked pain on her face. At first, she did not comprehend who he was, but then her eyes focused for a brief moment before they became dead again and she whispered his name without emotion.

"We are leaving," he said as he looked around the cell for a place to set down the candle. "Where are your cloak and boots?"

She pointed stiffly to a chest whose lid he opened to find her mantle and boots. He knelt down to pull on the boots before he rose to gently drape the cloak around her.

"Stand up, my love. You are coming with me!" Obediently, she stood on unsteady legs. He lifted her into his arms and walked back the way he had arrived. He saw two candles moving in the corridor, held by two elderly approaching nuns.

"I am Erik of Sweden," he repeated. "The Reverend Mother told me to take care of Lady Kristina."

"She said nothing about you taking Lady Kristina away from here," said one of the nuns anxiously. "She is not well, you know."

"That is why I am taking her," said Erik as he proceeded towards the door, kicked it open, and continued out into the cold night. Carefully, he placed her feet on the ground before he mounted his horse, then lifted her up in front of him. He wrapped her cloak tightly around her then enclosed them both with his own mantle before spurring his mount toward the Northern Gate.

Kristina had no idea how much time had passed since she had heard about her father's death. She remembered that Erik had come to carry her away. She had intuitively known that it was he when she heard his footsteps shatter the stillness of the convent. She had had no will to resist when he lifted her and carried her into the cold winter-night, nor had she wondered where he was taking her.

They had ridden for hours, and she had fallen asleep resting against him. Though the night was cold, she had not felt its icy chill, only his warmth surrounding her. Then they had arrived at a place that looked like a large hunting lodge. He had carefully placed her on a bed by the wall and covered her with fur skins before he prepared a fire in the fire pit. The next thing she remembered was Erik tenderly lifting her head and forcing some warm broth into her. She wanted to thank him, but no words came, and she fell back into a troubled sleep.

How long she had slept, she did not know. It could have been hours, even days, but when she awoke she felt his arms about her, holding her protectively against him. Finally, she was in his arms, but she could feel no joy in it. All she felt was emptiness, as if her heart had been torn out of her body. She wanted to cry but tears would not come, and she fell back once more into her restless slumber.

The next time she awoke she was alone. She felt panic at the thought that Erik had left her. Her mouth was dry, and it was with difficulty that she called out his name. She heard some movement, and he was there by her side.

"How long have I slept?"

"For two days," he said as he stroked her cheek.

"I am hungry. " Gently, he helped her sit upright so she could swing her feet over the side of the bed. The room was spinning before her eyes.

"We are in Abjorn's hunting lodge, which is mine to use now that he is living in Norway. It is quite comfortable." He helped her to her feet and they walked over to the fire where he motioned for her to be seated in a large fur-covered chair. "What would you like?" he asked. "The old couple who tend this lodge have arranged quite a feast for us."

"Something to drink," she said, looking over to where she saw beverage containers.

"Rest, Kristina. You are my guest," he ordered, noticing her attempting to rise.

She looked around the lodge consisting of one room with a low ceiling. Along one wall were several beds, and in the center was an excavated fire pit with a heavy black cauldron suspended above it. The earthen floor had been covered with stone slabs on which thick fur hides had been spread. The room was cozy and manly, with the walls crowded with stuffed trophies. Large bear heads were mounted alongside those of moose, deer, elk and wolf. They all looked down at her with seeming sadness as Erik handed her a mug of warm apple cider.

She drank long and deeply, craving every drop of the sweet liquid. Erik refilled her mug before he sat down beside her. "How do you feel?"

"I . . . I do not know. Empty. . . Tired. . . I cannot describe it."

"Will you try?" he asked as he slowly coaxed her to eat a piece of bread smeared with honey. Grappling with words, she haltingly told him how she had experienced the loss of her father--a man who had had little time for her, but who nevertheless had loved and protected her. Losing him had made her feel utterly vulnerable, especially since Valdemar had withdrawn his protection by divorcing her. As she spoke, Erik fed her some food that had been prepared for them, but she seemed oblivious to the fact that she was chewing and swallowing.

Her words came more easily as she related treasured conversations and incidents with her father, until finally the tears burst forth and her body began to tremble uncontrollably. Erik quickly scooped her up in his arms, took her over to the bed where he pulled fur skins over them, and then drew her close while he rocked her to sleep in his arms.

When she next awoke, Erik was sitting near the fire pit with his back towards her. Reassured by his presence, she closed her eyes again. She felt totally exhausted although she must again have slept for many hours, and she could feel that her face was swollen from tears. But the sadness that had so overpowered her the night before had been replaced by a smoldering anger. The people for whom she cared the most, those who had been closest to her, had actually ordered her father's execution.

She sat up in the bed. Her movement caused Erik to turn to her and smile.

"Do you feel better?" he asked caringly. She did not reply, and his smile faded.

"You killed him. You killed my father," was all she could utter.

Erik was silent for a moment before he answered. "You are right, of course. We, or should I say, Birger, ordered his execution because he had committed high treason against the crown."

"You could have saved his life!" she shot back.

"You have lived at court all your life, Kristina. You know that your father could not remain alive if Birger were to rule unopposed. I am mortified over the impact Torgils' death has had on you, but there was never any other option."

She sat silent in the knowledge that he was right, but she did not know where or how to vent her anger, and again gave in to tears.

Erik came over and knelt down on the floor beside her. "I wish there had been another way. If it makes you feel better, then blame me, because I was the one who informed Birger about your father's treason." She fell back again and buried her face into the pillow. "Do you want me to tell you what transpired? Every little detail, so that you will know what really happened?"

"Valdemar told me," she mumbled into the pillow. "But, yes, tell me again."

Erik pulled her up from the bed and sat her down in the comfortable chair with a cup of mint tea from which she drank absentmindedly.

Patiently, he related the events of the preceding years, and when he was finished her anger had dissipated and she could feel the emptiness returning.

She sighed. "My father said he knew the consequences of his actions--that death might be his reward. But he acted anyway."

They were interrupted as the door opened. A small, bent woman entered.

"The young lady is awake I see," she said as a smile spread over her kind and wrinkled face. "That is welcome, as I have fresh baked bread and some ham and boiled eggs."

She deposited her burden on the table, item by item, which made Kristina realize she was famished.

"Let us take a walk," Erik suggested after they had finished every last morsel of their meal. He helped her with her boots, and then wrapped her fur mantle tightly around her. She realized that she had no headdress with her, so she drew the mantle's hood over her head.

Erik put on his own boots and mantle, and then opened the door for her.

It was a bright and glorious winterday, with pristine snow covering the ground and cloaking the trees. Kristina took a deep breath to fill her lungs with crisp, clean air, and she felt it invigorate her pain-racked body. The bright daylight made her squint for a moment, but once her eyes adjusted, she reveled in the sun glittering on the snow which made it seem like millions of diamonds had been scattered on the ground. They walked down towards a frozen lake that they circled at a surprisingly brisk pace. They did not speak during their walk, yet Kristina felt strangely renewed when they returned to the hunting lodge.

The old woman had tidied the cabin in their absence. A fire was burning briskly, and a basket of apples stood on the table. Before Kristina had even taken off her mantle, she took one of the red cellar-stored fruits and bit into it with relish. "The walk did you good," said Erik as he bent down to help her remove her boots. "But now it is time to rest."

Enveloped by the warmth and coziness of the cabin, she fell asleep in front of the fire, drained from the physical exertion as well as the myriad emotions that swirled within her.

When she awoke the old woman was quietly bustling around the cabin preparing the evening meal. The door stood open wide through which Erik and an old man entered, their arms laden with firewood.

"Good eve to you, my lady," smiled the toothless man as he deposited his burden by the fire-pit. "We shall have another pretty day on the morrow. The sky is filled with stars."

Kristina smiled at the kindly old retainer as he disappeared out of the cabin.

"I think you have everything you will need," said the old woman as she surveyed the table. "Enjoy the meal. Call for us if you want anything else. Sleep well," she added as she left.

Kristina eagerly surveyed the bounty on the dining table and walked over to sit down next to Erik. "What a feast," she said as she fingered a piece of fowl from a platter and attacked it with gusto. She noticed Erik was suppressing a smile. "What is wrong?"

"I never knew you had such an appetite."

"Neither did I, but my body seems to crave it."

"I am glad you are hungry."

Kristina loaded her tin plate from the different platters. She savored every mouthful and finally sat back with a sigh. "I do not think I shall eat again as long as I live."

Erik laughed. Kristina did not join in with him, but rather sat looking into the fire with vacant eyes. "What are you thinking of?" he asked.

"About our childhood. Despite your stern mother, it was a wonderful time."

"That is what adults often say of their childhood, but I do not remember it was all that happy for any of us. Duty was all that mattered."

"Perhaps you are right," she said as she began to think back over the years. She shuddered when she thought about her childhood fear of the dowager queen. She thought about her deep friendship with Ingeborg and Rikissa whose departures had left her feeling so lonely despite Marta's presence. Why she and Marta had never bonded quite as closely she did not know since they shared so much on a daily basis. And she thought about her loveless marriage to Valdemar.

For hours she told Erik everything she had experienced, and for the first time she held nothing back. She spoke of her sister who had died in childbirth some years before and the fact that she was now totally alone. He listened to her outpouring like a priest listening to a confession, but he had no redemption for her pain or losses, no remedy or brew that would miraculously heal all wrongs.

When, finally, she ran out of words, Erik wore a sad smile. "I told you. We were not that happy, except for being with each other." He looked towards the fire that was barely glowing. "It is time for you to go to bed."

When she awoke the following morning Erik was gone, and the old woman was tiptoeing around the cabin, doing her chores.

"Where is Duke Erik?" Kristina asked anxiously.

"He went hunting, my lady. He should return in time for the midday meal."

Kristina put her feet on the floor, stretched her arms above her head, and yawned. As she lowered her hands into her lap she noticed how rumpled her tunic was. Her hands flew up to her hair that felt matted and disorderly. She realized that she had not thought about her appearance for days, and that she had been totally oblivious to anything but her pain.

"Do you have a tub, Anna?" she asked the old woman whose name she had heard Erik mention.

"We most certainly do. I have a large kettle of water heated." Anna filled a small wooden tub with steaming hot water and then added some cold until she was satisfied with the temperature. Kristina undressed and sat down in the tub, her knees close to her chest. Anna took a brush and started scrubbing Kristina's back with gentle movements. The water felt good, and Kristina sank down as deep as she could. With Anna's help, she washed her hair and soaked in the water until it began to cool.

"Let me clean your clothes," said Anna as she pulled out a chest from under one of the beds. "Lady Borg left some of her things here, if I remember right."

She pulled out a linen underdress and a brown wool tunic which she helped Kristina put on. The clothes were too short and too wide, but they were clean and Kristina enjoyed the feeling of the cool linen on her body. Anna motioned for her to be seated so that she could brush her hair in front of the fire.

"You are so kind," said Kristina who was enjoying the pampering. She closed her eyes as the brush ran through her hair.

Kristina would never forget the look on Erik's face when he entered the cabin some time later. His eyes shone with pleasure at seeing her sitting by the fire. His gaze ran over her body when she stood up to greet him, and he did not seem to mind the oversized dress.

"What a difference!" he exclaimed touching Kristina's flowing hair with a loving gesture. He added, almost shyly. "You look beautiful." He deposited three rabbits on the table and then turned to Anna who only then, he realized, was in the lodge. "These are for our evening meal."

Anna emptied the tub water outside the door and cleaned off the wet floor. "I will take care of those," she promised as she picked up the catch and left for her own cabin.

The day passed leisurely. They took another long stroll, after which they visited Erik's horse to give it a good rubdown. The animal was kept in a small, crooked stable leaning up against the tiny cottage that was occupied by Anna and her husband.

Later that evening they again talked about their childhood. Erik recounted his own feelings and experiences, and soon she realized that he now felt as lonely as she did. "The last of my family to whom I felt close was Valdemar, and now I feel as if I have lost him, too. How could he ever forgive me for depriving him of the possibility of a happy life with you? Had I only known how he felt."

"What would you have done differently, then? How could you have made me love him and not you?"

"I could have made you believe that I no longer had any feelings for you, and you would have turned to him with an open heart."

"I do not think that would have changed anything. You must realize that not even I had any idea that he cared for me in that way. I only knew that he was unhappy in our marriage. I believed that he could not love me. Had I come to love him, my life would have become even more painful since we would no longer be married."

"Had you loved him he would never have divorced you whatever Birger may have thought about it. He only wished you to be happy."

She sat silent, her eyes filling with tears. "We are all so wounded," she whispered.

"Yes, but now you are free to start a new life."

"To do that I must have the desire, which I lack. I only want to sleep, never to wake."

"Do not say that," he admonished her softly. "You will surely want to live a full life again, given time. You look tired," he added as she sat staring vacantly into the fire. "Go to bed, and rest. Tomorrow will be better. " Obediently she rose to walk over to the bed. "Get undressed and get under those warm covers," he ordered, as if she were a small child.

While he turned his back and put some logs on the fire she pulled off the tunic and underdress and crept under the covers. It felt wonderful to put her head on the soft, clean down-filled pillows. She closed her eyes and began to slowly drift off to sleep when Erik carefully, so as not to disturb her, lifted the covers and slid in next to her. He put his arms around her and pulled her close to him. She felt his warm, strong body cradling hers, and before she fell asleep she thought that it should always have been like this.

Once again a nightmare woke her, and she must have called out in her sleep, because Erik was leaning over her, speaking softly and reassuringly. "I am here, Kristina. You have nothing to fear." She opened her eyes and looked into his. For the first time since her father's death she felt an emotion other than sadness. It was a yearning to embrace life anew, a desire to live.

Erik began to gently kiss her face. She turned her head so that their lips met--first in a gentle kiss, then in a passionate one, followed by many more. Erik's hands slid over her body, making an exquisite heat spread through her limbs, when suddenly he gently pulled away from her. "No, Kristina. I would be taking advantage of you in your present state . . ."

"You stopped us before," she said as she drew him back to her. "This time there are no excuses. I have lost my good name and position. I have lost my father. I will not lose you."

His eyes looked searchingly into hers and she smiled. She showed no hesitation.

The night that followed would be forever etched in her mind. She lost her virginity with little pain, and like an initiated woman she celebrated their lovemaking with every fiber of her being. Erik was gentle, and she relished feeling every part of his strong body. For the very first time in her life she felt free, carefree, almost reckless.

"You take my breath away," Erik said as the morning light filtered in through the tiny windows. He traced a line along her back and over

416

her hip, admiring the perfection of her slender body. She slowly turned around on her back and looked at him.

"I had no idea it could be like this," she whispered glowingly.

"Nor did I," he smiled back. "But we must make up for lost time."

They were asleep when Anna entered the cabin to prepare their morning meal and light the fire. They did not see the knowing smile on her face when she saw the pillows thrown all over the floor and the bed linen twisted around their arms and legs. As quietly as she could, she lit a fire, filled the large cauldron with water to be heated, and set the table for their meal. Then she quietly slipped out and closed the door behind her. A few hours later when Erik awoke, he thought for a moment that he had dreamed the events of the night before, but there she was, sleeping on his arm with a contented look on her face, his beloved Kristina. He filled with joy simply looking at her. Slowly, as if she sensed his gaze, she opened her eyes.

"I love you," she said as she closed her eyes again and snuggled into her pillow.

He smiled as he pulled the covers over her. He noticed the fire burning briskly and was surprised that he had not been awakened by Anna's presence. Trained as a soldier, he was normally alarmed by the slightest sound. But he was feeling no threat from anyone or anything here in the middle of the forest. He pulled on his shirt, went over to the table and sliced off a piece of cheese. It tasted better than he could ever remember, and he quickly ate several eggs, followed by half a loaf of bread and a mug of beer. He sat down before the fire to which he added several logs, savoring the simple joy of the moment.

He realized that the time had come to discard all the frustrations and disappointments he had ever experienced. This was a time to celebrate the love he had felt ever since that day Kristina returned from her two-year stay in Denmark. He must always have loved her . . . but now . . . what a night it had been. He felt his body react at the very thought of it. He was ready to return to bed once again. But he stopped himself. Kristina needed her sleep, and they had time to celebrate their newfound passion later. Or had they? With that thought came a fear so alarming that his heart skipped a beat and almost began to hurt. In truth, they did not have that much time. This was but a stolen moment for them both.

He refilled his mug with beer and stared morosely into the fire. As he was destined to become King of Norway, it would be utterly unfair to keep Kristina as his mistress until his wedding with Princess Ingeborg six years hence. Furthermore, if he and Kristina had any children they would be considered bastards, and she and they would never be able to live a decent life once he left her. How ever much he wanted her beside him, his love for her would not allow him to ruin her life. On the other hand, he could break his betrothal to Ingeborg, but that would certainly enrage Hakon to a point that the now peaceful balance promised for Scandinavia would be shattered. He had no choice but to honor his commitment. He felt anguished when he turned and looked over at her sleeping face. How could he ever let her go? He shook his head. He could not allow himself these thoughts. He had to put them aside and be there for her, to give her every part of his heart, body and soul to heal her pain.

"Erik," he heard her voice call. "How long have I slept?"

"Long enough," he said as he returned to the bed and pulled her close to him.

Never had the forest looked more beautiful and serene, the snow so white and soft under her feet. With her hand in Erik's, Kristina savored every moment of their leisurely amble around the lake. She could see their footprints in the snow from their earlier walks. She felt as if they owned this part of the woods, and that no one else could ever trespass into their magical world. It was theirs alone, forever, far from all duties. Seeing a hawk fly high in the sky and a white hare cross their path without making any sound in the snow, she felt a deep gratitude to Erik for making her feel again, and for loving her.

"What are you thinking?" he asked.

"That I am alive."

"That is a good beginning," he smiled as he bent over and kissed her cheek.

She turned her face towards his and they locked in a long kiss.

"Do you think the snow is too cold to lie in?" he asked her with a grin.

She smiled mischievously. "I will race you back to the cabin," she taunted as she tore herself loose and ran towards the lodge. Laughing he followed her, allowing her to arrive before he did.

"You are out of condition," she called breathlessly as she turned around to see him behind her.

"It is your fault," he said between breaths. "But come inside and we shall see how lacking my condition really is."

Neither of them was aware of the passage of time. The days and nights floated together, forming a limitless sequence of wondrous moments. They hunted together, they argued moves over their self-made chess set, and they took rides on Erik's horse that seemed content to carry the two of them. They took active parts in the household chores and were jubilant when Anna and her husband returned from a neighboring estate, their sled laden with the wonderful bounty Erik's gold coins had purchased.

Having stocked the lodge for weeks to come, they whiled away their time building a huge snowman as they had done when they were children. This time they did not have discarded armor with which to dress their knight, so the proud figure got a tree branch for a sword, a kettle for a helmet and a wooden lid for a shield.

"He is magnificent," laughed Kristina and curtsied before the creature. "We welcome you, Lord Protector of the Deep Forest, and charge you with shielding us from all evil." Kristina dragged Erik inside the cabin where they warmed their frozen hands by the fire. Suddenly Erik lifted his head and listened. "What is it?" asked Kristina anxiously.

"I thought I heard hoof beats. But do not worry. Nobody can harm us with our Lord Protector outside," Erik said lightheartedly. But he could feel fear seeping into his mind. Not that anyone would harm them. It was simply the arrival of someone, anyone, who would bring reality into their lives.

They stared at each other as they heard a voice order the old man to take care of a horse. They remained frozen when they heard a knock, but finally Erik moved towards the door. As he opened it, the tall shape of a man bent down to enter.

"Mats!" exclaimed Erik. "What are you doing here?"

"I have been looking for you everywhere," Mats replied as he embraced Erik. "You appear in excellent health," he continued.

Then he saw Kristina. Displaying no surprise at her presence, he walked over and took her hands in his to kiss them. "I apologize for barging in on you like this, but King Birger has called a special Council meeting--which is of crucial interest to you, Erik."

Kristina, who had remained speechless until then, asked in a small voice, "Would you like something to drink?"

"Thank you, but it is late, and I have to start back before it gets too dark."

"Mats, please have a drink with us," Erik insisted. Kristina hurried out of the cabin to fetch some wine which had been left to chill in the snow.

"How long has it been, Mats, since Torgil's execution?" Erik asked once they were alone.

"Three weeks," replied Mats with a quizzical look as Kristina returned to the cabin and filled three mugs with an unsteady hand.

"To your good health," said Mats as he lifted his cup and emptied it in one continuous swallow. He observed his two friends drinking their wine with dreamlike expressions. "I do have to leave. The meeting is in two days," he said. He noted the look of shock on Erik and Kristina's faces. "God bless you both," was all he could add as he bent over to exit the cabin.

"Have a safe journey," Erik called out after him. As they listened to the hoof beats fade in the distance, neither of them moved or said a word. When the silence was total, Kristina collapsed on a stool. "Two days," she whispered. "Only two days."

Erik could not reply. His worst nightmare was about to be realized, and the pain was greater than he had anticipated, even though he had tried to prepare himself for this moment. He went over to her and pulled her up to hold her close.

"Dear God, how I love you. I do not want to live without you." He lifted her and brought her over to the bed. Slowly he undressed her without taking his eyes off her as if to remember every detail of her body. When she sat naked before him she gestured for him to take his own clothes off, and while he did she studied his every movement, every part of the body that had relit the fire of life in her once-dead soul. Gently and tenderly they embraced each other, and without their usual haste and hunger they came together, their eyes locked, sharing the exquisite sensation of loving without boundaries.

When they were spent, they lay silently facing each other for a long time before Kristina spoke. "We knew this moment would come; yet we succeeded in blocking it out of our minds for all these many days. God gave me a gift when he sent you to heal me. You showed me that I want to live again. For that I will be eternally grateful. And the only way I can give thanks for that precious gift is to go on and live my life as fully as I can. How I will be able to do that without you, I do not know . . . but I will try because I love you, and I know that you love me . . . and I do not want you to be sad because of me. And you would be, if I broke down again. I saw the pain and love in your eyes when you carried me out of the convent, and those feelings were what brought me back from that dark place where there was no hope. I have had these days with you, and I am deeply grateful because I know I have had more than most people ever dream of. It has to be enough . . ." She swallowed unable to continue.

"I will never be happy without you," Erik objected.

"You will," she smiled sadly as she reached out and touched the wolf's tooth which still hung around his neck, "I can promise you. My mother taught me that. I thought my life was at an end when she died, but then I got to live with your family, and everything had meaning again. When I lost my father, you patched me together . . . and now I can go on."

"Where will you go?" asked Erik in a hollow voice.

"I will live in Smaland where Valdemar gave me an estate."

"Far away from Nykoping," said Erik, looking pained.

She did not answer, but she put her head on his arm. She wondered how she could talk so bravely when her life was being shattered anew. Still she felt indestructible, knowing how glorious life could be when one was loved in this way.

They slept little and spent every moment close to one another, as if the moment of parting would suddenly arrive if they separated for even a second. Despite their brave resolve, they both knew that leaving each other would be the most difficult task they had ever performed. When they finally stood outside the cabin to say farewell, neither would make a move to end the anguish.

"We might never see each other alone again," Erik said. "It seems insane."

"Remember," she replied softly. "What we have had together will make us stronger. We know that we are truly loved--whatever happens."

He kissed her gently, and then quickly mounted his horse, reining it around to face her one last time. As they looked at each other both started to smile.

"I love you," he said simply.

"And I love you," she answered.

He spurred his horse and took off down the path.

She stood looking after him for a long time. Suddenly, all her bravery left her, and her legs felt weak. She staggered, falling to her knees on the cold ground.

"Erik, Erik . . ." she whispered as the chill of the snow seeped through her mantle.

Chapter 25

Perspiration glistened on Erik's forehead and lathered the flanks of his mount as he pulled up from a full gallop on the road to Nykoping castle. Once his horse fell into a walk, Erik exhaled a deep, impatient sigh. Though weeks had passed, he could find no respite from the agony of leaving Kristina. Her loving eyes were etched in his mind, continuously haunting him. At night he would feel her arms entwine him only to awaken ensnarled in his bedding. He forced his thoughts back to what had transpired after his return to Stockholm castle.

Valdemar had been waiting for him, pacing the castle forecourt anxiously. Even from a distance Erik's heart was pierced by the look of pain that filled his brother's eyes. "Where have you been? Why did you not send me word?" Valdemar asked.

"I have been with Kristina, Valdemar.

"And is she well?" Valdemar inquired in a controlled voice.

Erik could see how agonized Valdemar was. And yet he knew that any dishonesty would only fuel the jealousy that he could read in his brother's heart.

"I wish that I had not hurt you, Valdemar; but I cannot wish that I had not been with her. These last weeks I saw her heal from her devastation over her father's death, and she and I had the chance of coming to an understanding of the inevitability of our duties."

"How pleased I am for you," said Valdemar coldly.

"Not for me as much as for Kristina. Had you seen the depth of her despair--she had no will to live."

"But you remedied that, I am sure."

"Valdemar," begged Erik. "What saved her was a secluded period of time when she could find and give vent to her innermost feelings. A time when she could feel love from someone she cared about."

"You mean someone she loved," said Valdemar fiercely.

"Yes, from someone she loved." Suddenly Erik turned away and his voice became hard. "Maybe that person could have been you, had you not insisted on divorcing her . . ."

"That is a low blow! You did not marry her in the first place because of duty to our country, just as it was my duty to divorce her for the very same reason."

Erik turned looking pleadingly at Valdemar. "I am sorry, but I could not stand to see the pain in your face and know that I caused it. I love you, brother. Can you forgive me?"

"I have done that already because I understand . . . but that does not dull the pain I feel."

"As God is my witness, I will do whatever is in my power to repay you for the hurt I have caused you." Erik went over and put his arms around Valdemar who sank into his embrace with an agonized sigh.

"Let us try to put all this behind us," Valdemar mumbled.

Erik gratefully replied, "Thank God that you are still in my life. I felt as if I had lost everyone."

Since that moment, he and Valdemar had spent all their waking hours together, determined to heal the breach that had torn them apart. They gratefully discovered that their deep fraternal bond had survived, however difficult it was for them to broach certain subjects.

Now as Erik slumped over his tired mount, he reflected back on the Council meeting at which Nykoping castle had been officially returned to him. The action was taken after Birger expressed profound regret that it had ever been confiscated, as well as his assurances that his brothers had his total support and trust.

Erik's thoughts turned to a private moment after the meeting during which Birger had lightly inquired, "Is Kristina feeling better?"

"I hope so," Erik had said, his heart resonating at the thought of her.

"Marta sent Ragna, along with an armed escort, to accompany Kristina to Smaland," Birger had said with obvious relief that a political embarrassment had been averted. Erik wondered if Birger was aware of what had transpired between him and Kristina. Whether he did or not, Erik had felt relieved that he did not have to discuss it with Birger.

Now that he was again in residence in Nykoping castle, it looked quite bare without Kristina's belongings, all of which had been packed and sent to her. Still, wherever he gazed he was reminded of her. He would imagine her turning the corner of every corridor, only to realize that was just wishful thinking and that she would never again return. He had been no pleasure to be around when Valdemar and their friends convened after evening meals, but he was the master of the castle and no one questioned his morose behavior.

Now, as he walked his mount slowly over the drawbridge into the courtyard, he noticed dozens of horses tethered there. "Whose are those?" he asked one of the stable boys.

"I do not know, my lord. But the riders' banners were those of Sweden's most powerful clans," replied the groom apparently impressed.

"Have our visitors been served refreshments?" asked Erik of a servant who met him in the doorway.

"Duke Valdemar has seen to it, my lord."

The first visitor Erik spotted was Lord Abjorn, his exiled chancellor. "You are back!" cried Erik as he hugged his friend.

"Yes, finally," said Abjorn, happily returning Erik's warm embrace. "I have just been to see the king, and he has returned my estates with a profuse apology."

As Erik looked around the Hall he saw many familiar faces. "I see no introductions will be necessary," he said with a broad smile. He walked around to greet the knights, each the head of an influential Swedish noble family, all of whom had been close allies of the late Lord Torgils. Some like Arnvid Gustavsson and Birger Persson had legendary names that flashed through his mind as he shook their hands.

After taking a chalice from a servant, Erik put his arm around Lord Abjorn and called for everyone's attention. Raising his goblet he said, "Welcome to Nykoping, one and all. Valdemar and I are honored to receive you."

"Hear, hear," murmured the knights before they emptied their cups.

"I suspect, however, that you have a reason for coming. Please sit down and tell us what we can do for you," Erik said, gesturing to the long tables.

After the knights seated themselves, Arnvid Gustavsson rose. He was a tall, squarely built man who had been an awesome jouster in his prime. As a reminder of his prowess he carried a long scar diagonally across his face. Upon first meeting him, one became fascinated by the perfect line traversing his features. It was hard to understand how he could have kept his nose. However, once he began to speak, his authoritative baritone made the viewer concentrate instead on his every word.

"I have been elected to speak for us all," Lord Arnvid pronounced solemnly. "We are mourning the death of our good friend and benefactor, Lord Torgils Knutsson. As of this moment, we still do not know the exact reasons for his having been accused of treason. We have heard only rumors; but whatever the reasons, we feel they cannot justify his execution."

"Let me enlighten you on the causes for Lord Torgils' demise," interrupted Erik, "To tell the whole story would take too long, so I shall summarize. Lord Torgils did, at one time, conspire to detach a part of Sweden and establish his own kingdom. This has been proven beyond any doubt, and his treachery was forestalled only by a fortuitous move by the king." The knights expressed audible surprise, but Erik lifted his hand to quiet them before continuing. "Lord Torgils was also the direct cause of the schism between the king, Duke Valdemar, and myself. He accomplished this by a blatant lie, which unfortunately was proven only long after the fact. In other words, he deliberately caused the war between the king and us, which cost our country much grief. The King's Council, when furnished with all the relevant details, supported the king, and Lord Torgils was justly executed."

The knights spoke amongst themselves until Lord Arnvid motioned for silence. "Thank you for allaying our fears. We suspected that the Church had instigated a political murder, which brings us to why we are here today.

"The king has restored to the Church the privileges which it enjoyed during your father's reign; and while this, in and of itself, is not alarming, the leanings of those men recently elected to the King's Council are. They are from Church-loyal clans, which means that the Church is not only gaining wealth, but worldly power as well. While Lord Torgils was alive, we were united under his leadership;

but following his death, rival factions developed amongst us as we attempted to elect a new leader. This is the reason we have come to you, Duke Erik. During the past year, you have impressed us with your accomplishments, so we would be honored if you would consider assuming the leadership of Sweden's noble clans."

Erik sat back in his chair, trying not to show what he was feeling. He had experienced nothing but sadness for so many weeks, and this request made life stir within him again.

"My lords, I am honored! But you speak for only some of the clans," he said.

"We, who are present, represent the largest clans in the country; and we have many others supporting our request. We chose not to come here all together since such a large group would create undesirable rumors if you rejected our offer. Furthermore, you should know that every one of the chiefs to whom we have spoken would drop their current choices in your favor," said Lord Arnvid.

"Then I would be extremely honored to serve," said Erik humbly.

"I will be most pleased to host the official election at my estate. Shall we say, middle of May?" Lord Arnvid concluded with a bow.

Consenting murmurs were heard from the delegation. Lord Abjorn proposed a toast to the resurgent strength of the nobles under their new leader. Everyone stood up, raised their cups, and solemnly exclaimed, "The Duke of Sweden."

"I am delighted for you, Erik," said Birger after another Council meeting at Stockholm castle had concluded and the brothers had sat down for some hot wine and private discussion in Birger's chamber. "It is a great honor to be asked to lead the noble clans."

"I have not agreed yet, because I wanted to discuss it with you first," said Erik, smiling winningly. "One obvious advantage to my accepting their offer would be that I could act as an intermediary; to allay their misgivings of you, since lately you have only added Church-loyal men to the Council. Furthermore, were I their leader, you would know their thoughts and plans."

"Those are all good reasons for you to accept," nodded Birger approvingly.

"So, if I accept," continued Erik. "Do you think it would be a good idea to make my first appearance a commanding one? To ask them to show their commitment and loyalty to their king and country by bringing their men-at-arms to full preparedness, testing their willingness to fulfill their quotas."

"That would certainly challenge them," said Birger, but Erik noticed a hesitant expression on Birger's face. Naturally, he might be concerned that his younger brother would control the largest army in the realm. But as Birger's feature softened, Erik knew that he had decided to trust his brothers as they had openly turned to him for approval. "In my experience, the nobles often fall short of their quota, yet they insist on keeping their tax-free status. They should learn from the outset that they must meet their obligations," Birger added quickly.

"I am glad you agree. Naturally, I will not state it quite that way," said Erik knowing that Birger would receive reports from the upcoming meeting.

"You have to convince the nobles to do it for their own good, to give them the proper motivation," nodded Birger. "What one has to do to get things done!"

Birger's last words were almost drowned out by loud and urgent voices in the corridor. The door flew open and Marta entered in an agitated state.

"Birger! Lord Lars has abused his position as Panter. Instead of giving the leftover trenchers to the servants, he has given them to people outside of court."

"Are you sure, my dear? There must be some misunderstanding."

"No, there is not. I want you to strip him of his title for this!"

" Even if he is guilty, that would be far too harsh a punishment."

"He is a thief! Anyone who steals from the king should be executed. I think that I am being lenient."

"I shall talk to him. Do not upset yourself so. I am sure his actions can be explained."

"You can talk to him now," said Marta as she gestured towards the open door. "The king will see you, Lord Lars," she called in a triumphant voice as she sailed out of the chamber, oblivious to Valdemar and Erik's presence. Through the door entered a young knight. He bowed deeply to the royal brothers and then stood with his eyes nailed to the floor.

"I assume you heard the Queen's accusations," said Birger, annoyed at the interruption. "What do you have to say for yourself?"

Erik looked at the young knight with interest. His coat of arms, embroidered on his tunic, showed him to be the son of one of their late father's most trusted friends whose banner had flown beside King Magnus' and Lord Torgils' in many a battle, and Erik immediately grew skeptical of Marta's accusations. Although Lord Lars' father was no longer alive, the young knight would surely do everything in his power to prove his clan worthy of the King's esteem. He already had earned the honorable position of Panter, despite his youth.

Lord Lars looked uncomfortable under Birger's scrutiny. "The Queen tells the truth. I have taken bread from the castle."

Birger looked taken aback by the knight's frank confession, while Erik could no longer keep silent.

"Why did you do it? A knight can do nothing more reprehensible than to steal from his lord."

"I know, and I deeply regret that I had to do it," blurted the knight.

"Had to? Your family is hardly starving, and if they were, I would gladly help the son of a cherished friend of my father," said Birger looking bewildered.

"It was not for me or my family, your Majesty."

"For whom, then?" asked Birger.

"I noticed that there were always extra trenchers and loaves of bread left over, even after the servants had taken their fill; so rather than letting them sell it for their personal profit I gave it to the poor."

"You gave it to the poor?" asked Birger incredulously.

"Once a man has been branded for a crime, it is hard for him to earn a livelihood since no one wants to hire his services. But many such men have families that are starving. I should have asked your permission, but I was not sure that it would be granted." The knight's words tumbled out as he looked pleadingly at Birger. "I hired a few of them so that they could earn a living, but once that became known, more and more came to me, and I could not hire them all. Do not misunderstand me, I would not want to hire all since some are genuinely bad; but because their children are suffering, I felt that they needed to be nourished more than the purses of your servants needed to be fattened. Still, that was not for me to decide, and the fact remains that I have stolen from you," concluded Lord Lars.

Birger stood silent for a few moments before he called for a guard. "Escort Lord Lars to the keep, and have him confined until I call for him," he said as the young knight bowed and left.

"He is both a thief and a savior," smiled Erik. "What will you do?"

"I will let you know on the morrow," answered Birger curtly as he left the audience chamber.

Erik became worried when he saw a smug smile on Marta's face when she arrived in the Great Hall for supper. But it was much later before he and Valdemar had a chance to ask Birger about his decision. "The man has stolen from me while he enjoyed a position of great trust, so he deserves to lose his title and privileges."

"Of course, he should be punished, but to strip all honor from so distinguished a family is too much, Birger," intoned Erik. "His old mother will die in shame, and his younger sister who is about to be betrothed to one of your knights will surely never marry."

"He should have thought about that before he acted."

"I do not believe that you feel this is fair, Birger. Marta has persuaded you to punish him this way," Valdemar said softly.

"My wife is in charge of the household," countered Birger defensively. "I have to listen to what she wants . . . and she has been under such pressure lately . . ." Birger's voice trailed away.

"I do not know what has been worrying Marta, but you should not punish him so drastically if you want to appear just," Erik insisted.

Birger looked torn as he rose from his seat beside the hearth and headed for the stairs. "It is late, and we have an early hunt in the morning," he called over his shoulder.

After the hunt, Birger held an open audience where he rendered judgment on Lord Lars. The young man was stripped of his title and privileges and banned from court. A few hours later when Erik saw the young knight ride off with his sister to live out their lives in shame on their family estate, his sister was hunched over on her horse, overcome with grief.

The spring day was chilly. Kristina leaned against the wall of Solang, her beautiful new home, savoring the last rays of the afternoon sun with her shawl wrapped tightly around her. In her hand she held the lengthy message she had just received from Marta. It was the first communication she had had from any member of the royal family during the months she had been living at Solang. The peace she had begun to find in the deep forest of Smaland was shaken by her friend's words.

Dearest Kristina,

How I have missed you! Nothing has been the same since I learned that you would not be visiting us any more. I find that intolerable, but political considerations seem to dictate everything. Yet, I need you desperately now. Let me tell you what has transpired so that you will understand why you cannot deny me.

Bishop Nils came to visit us a few days ago, and I can recall every word of our conversation: "I have no doubt whatever, your Majesties," he told us with conviction, "Little Prince Erik is a special child of God. Even though he is not yet five, he understands much beyond adult comprehension. He is not interested in the things that normally fascinate small boys like horses, weapons and games. He sits and listens to stories from the Holy Book for hours and makes comments that are astoundingly astute. Your Majesties, please allow the prince to be raised by the Church. He is surely one of God's chosen."

Birger took my hand before he replied to Father Nils: "This is not the first time you have pleaded with us, Bishop Nils, and we have thought about it for two years now. The queen and I have decided to let him go with you. We know that he is special, and he should have the full attention of the Church."

Bishop Nils responded with an unusually warm smile as he said: "I am so pleased you have come to that conclusion, your Majesties. I will personally undertake his education, and he will live with me in Upsala."

And now he is gone, Kristina. I know we made the right decision, and that he will be happy with Bishop Nils; but my heart is breaking. He is such a sweet and good child, and I will miss him every moment. Magnus also misses him, and it would lift our spirits if you came to be with us. You have Birger's blessing, since he knows how much Magnus cares for you. Please come and spend Saint Michael's day with us at Hatuna. I cannot bear the thought of knowing that you are all by yourself on that day. Please say yes, my sweet Kristina. I am in agony. I send you all our affection. Marta R.

Kristina sighed deeply. How could she refuse Marta? Would she have the strength to stay calm if Erik were there? These thoughts kept churning in her head until she found herself shivering in the chilly air. Hurriedly, she went inside.

She smiled the moment the door closed behind her. Solang was so peaceful that both she and Ragna had fallen in love with their new home at first sight. It was situated on a hill overlooking endless forests, which gave the impression it was floating on a low cloud. Because it had been neglected over the years, she had been fully occupied since her arrival restoring it to its original condition. With her ample dowry returned to her, she could easily afford to do the much-needed repairs. She was satisfied with the results as she looked around the tasteful hall that was smaller and more intimate than those to which she had been accustomed. It boasted a large hearth, walls draped with colorful tapestries, and thick and richly embroidered curtains shielding the beds. The heavy wooden tables were so highly polished they gleamed in the light of the fire. Torches burned in new and artfully shaped wall brackets; and two chandeliers hung from the high ceiling hosting a multitude of flickering candles. It was warm and inviting, and Kristina felt its calming influence.

Of course, she had to go to Marta and Magnus. They needed her. And she would avoid being alone with Erik--if he should be there.

"The head of every important clan has committed to you, Duke Erik!" Abjorn proclaimed jubilantly as he strode into Erik's audience chamber.

"Excellent. Could you summon Mats and Valdemar and then post guards around the corridors so that no one can come within earshot?"

When the four men sat down together, Erik began quietly, "What I am about to say must stay between the four of us." Valdemar, Mats and Abjorn nodded their assent.

Erik reached down and scratched the head of one of his hunting dogs that lay stretched out by his chair. "I think you already know what I am going to say . . ."

Mats interrupted him. "You are going to overthrow your brother!"

Erik smiled sadly. "As God is my witness, until Birger forced us to flee our own country, I never considered the idea. While I always thought that I could be a stronger ruler, I certainly did not need the Swedish throne to prove it, especially since I expect to wear the Norwegian crown one day. But when I saw how easily Birger was manipulated by Torgils, my brother's inability to discern the truth, and how he allowed his emotions to guide him; I became convinced that he was unfit to rule. He lacks compassion and strong moral direction. Apart from the hardships Valdemar and I had to endure, the people suffered needlessly because of the armed conflict he instigated. Their larders were emptied, and many were forced into military service. As a result of the war Sweden's coffers were drained.

"And now, when I saw how harshly he dealt with Lord Lars, simply because Marta demanded it--so that he would not upset her or suffer her recriminations-- that confirmed he is unfit to rule. Maybe it could be viewed as a trifling incident, but he destroyed a good man who actually had laudable motives, as well as his innocent family. Any lesser punishment would have served as a warning to others. Nor did it gain Birger any political advantage. It was a mindless act. Eventually the people will turn against him. I have to take over before something far worse happens. Fortuitously, as if by God's will, I have just been given the means to do it!"

"How, exactly, will you proceed?" inquired Abjorn.

"First, we have to find the right moment to take Birger prisoner and make all his fortresses surrender--which should not be difficult with the nobility's large army," said Erik.

"With all due respect," interjected Mats. "I do not think it would be wise to take the king prisoner. As long as he lives, there would exist a threat from his followers. I suggest we stage a battle. Even the most ignorant peasant knows that you fought against each other last year, so a new battle would not surprise anyone. The king might simply perish in the fighting."

"Never!" objected Erik. "I will not kill my brother! Yes, he is an ineffectual king and I want him deposed, but not harmed."

"I am sorry," argued Mats, "but it would be a mistake to let him live. I have great respect for your logical mind, but now you are allowing emotions to control you. As long as he lives you will never have total power in Sweden."

"I agree with Mats," said Abjorn.

"Why? My father imprisoned his brother after he overthrew him, and that did not cause any upheaval."

"Your uncle Valdemar ceded the Pope too much power over Sweden, which no Swede could tolerate. He also conducted a disgraceful love affair with a nun. Your brother has done nothing so reprehensible," argued Abjorn.

"I will not kill Birger, nor any member of his family!" Erik protested.

"I understand how you feel," interjected Valdemar. "Still, I can see what Abjorn and Mats are saying. The same arguments that required Torgils' execution, hold true now. And we both agreed in Torgils' case; but since I, too, do not want Birger killed, why not give him a chance to abdicate in your favor? The army you will command will be a strong inducement."

"I doubt Birger will abdicate," answered Erik pensively. "He is proud and stubborn. I think he would rather die than submit to me. Yet, it is certainly worth a try."

"A king can abdicate, but later change his mind," warned Mats. "What you are contemplating is politically naive. As your advisor, I must point out that if you wish to rule Sweden, your brother should be killed, not imprisoned or left at liberty in, for example, Denmark, whether or not he has abdicated. His followers will surely align against you."

"What do you really need the crown for?" asked Abjorn. "You already wield enormous power. Why risk it all for the dubious glory of being called King?".

"Believe me when I say I care not about the crown. It is Sweden that concerns me. Birger is simply not a capable ruler," insisted Erik. "He should not be king!"

"The price of a throne is high," said Abjorn. You must decide if you want to pay it or not. Still, you should know that both of us," Abjorn gestured towards Mats and himself, "are more than your loyal servants, we are your friends and that is why we speak our minds."

"I know that, and I understand that your advice is politically sound, but . . ."

"The idea of an overthrow is so timely," observed Valdemar. "Erik Menved is again preoccupied with fighting the Germans. He will have no forces available to aid Birger. There is no question that you could succeed in taking over Sweden."

"How can we let the moment pass?" asked Erik as he looked at Mats and then at Abjorn.

"I have done my duty by pointing out the dangers inherent in the king's survival," said Mats. "Still, I will follow you."

"As will I," said Abjorn.

"It is easy for me to agree," said Valdemar.

"Then, my lords, I think we just might have the perfect opportunity to capture him," said Erik as he went to his desk to retrieve a small scroll. "Our cousin, Valdemar of Holstein, recently sent us an invitation to spend Saint Michael's Day at his estate, Hatuna, here in Sweden. He intends to invite Birger and Marta as well for the small family gathering. The place is ideal since it is close to Stockholm, and not well guarded. The holiday is five months hence, which gives us ample time to prepare. What do you say?"

"Hatuna it shall be," Mats agreed. "How will you hide the preparations from the king?"

"There is no need for secrecy," said Erik confidently. "I have already explained to him that the nobles must meet their quota in the service of the crown. However, our ultimate purpose cannot be known to anyone but the four of us."

"Look at them," whispered Erik excitedly. "They are here to a man."

Erik leaned towards Valdemar who was sitting beside him on a large canopied platform overlooking Lord Arnvid's tournament field. The clan leaders sat facing them on benches ready to swear their allegiance and fidelity. Erik knew that the rituals would be long and tedious since every clan leader would have to repeat the oath, but the importance of the occasion overcame his boredom. When the nobles finally rose to unanimously approve their new leader, Erik felt relieved after sitting motionless for so long. When he stood to speak, the crowd went wild with enthusiasm. No one could remember such solidarity for a new leader. Not only was he a prince, to them he embodied the exemplary knight--tall, strong, and courageous. Erik motioned for silence, but to no avail. After a while, he began to speak and only then did the crowd quiet down to hear what he had to say.

"I am proud that you have chosen me as your leader. I will do everything in my power to serve our cause well."

"Hear, hear," chanted the crowd.

"For the past sixteen years, the nobles have been a strong and stabilizing force in Sweden under the leadership of the former Lord High Constable, Torgils Knutsson."

"Long live the memory of Lord Torgils," someone called from the rear, and the sentiment was echoed by the others.

"Lately," continued Erik, "there has been increasing pressure from the Church. While we can understand their desire for tax relief, we feel that they should occupy themselves with the kingdom of heaven, rather than ours here on earth." He smiled as he quoted Torgils.

"Hear, hear," shouted the audience enthusiastically.

"Men whose primary interest is in the strength of the Church are receiving positions in the worldly King's Council. That creates tension and divides the Council members."

"Yes, yes," the crowd agreed.

"We should not stand idly by while more church-loyal men become members of the Swedish Council."

"No, no," the audience roared.

"We have to show unity. We have to show that we are a mighty force to reckon with."

"Yes, yes," screamed the crowd.

"In four month's time, every one of you will have your quota of armed men in combat readiness," Erik insisted firmly as the crowd became silent. "I am asking for much. But it is vital that the king knows how committed you are to the protection of our country. If you can impress him with your unity, the next member elected to the King's Council will not be a man close to the Church!" shouted Erik.

After a moment of silence, the crowd jumped up and cheered.

"In order to gain something, one has to give something," called Erik at the top of his lungs. "Will you be ready in four months with the proudest army Sweden has ever seen?"

"Yes, yes," screamed the crowds. Some young knights rushed towards the platform, grabbed Erik, and hoisted him up on their shoulders to carry him among the men. "Duke Erik, Duke Erik," chanted the crowds until some of the regional leaders made the knights put Erik back on the platform. Erik raised his arms to silence as the men retook their seats.

"I appreciate your support, but your enthusiasm will surely wane as you pursue this costly project," continued Erik. "Remember, we are beginning a new era together. While I have the ear of the king--and that is the main reason you have chosen me--I cannot convince him of our united strength without your cooperation. Words alone will not sway him. He has to see for himself what you are capable of. And when he sees that, I will not even have to speak!"

"Four months. Four months," the chant began as Erik stepped down from the platform to lead the way to Lord Arnvid's home where supper was to be served before the afternoon's tournament games.

As Erik walked beside Lord Arnvid, the distinguished nobleman smiled warmly. "You are a born leader, your Highness. To require a task so demanding as your first act is courageous. If you succeed, you will lead with total authority. If, however, you fail . . ."

Erik realized that he had never even considered that possibility.

Chapter 26

The fall leaves had become a multihued, blazing frame around Nykoping castle as the regional chieftans of Sweden's nobles rode up in mid-September to report on the state of their preparedness. It was a proud group of leaders that settled in the Hall. All but a few clans had completed their assigned tasks. Erik realized that at that moment, thousands of men-at-arms stood ready to follow his command. "This exceeds my wildest expectations," he exclaimed. "You have done a remarkable job, my lords!"

"You inspired us to think beyond our personal concerns, to pursue our common interests," responded Lord Arnvid.

"Thank you, but it is you who have done the arduous work," Erik asserted to the thirteen men sitting around the table. Older and more experienced than he, they ruled like minor kings over Sweden's most powerful clans. Erik felt slightly intimidated before he reminded himself that, although he was young, he was born a prince and was now their elected leader. He remained silent for only a moment longer before he asked "Could you have the troops ready for inspection in two weeks?"

The men looked at one another. "We can be ready," Lord Arnvid answered after receiving affirmative nods from each of the regional leaders.

"Then I am swearing you all to secrecy," Erik said. "Two weeks from now there will not just be an inspection but a call to march." The men reacted with surprise and curiosity. "We are taking over the rule of Sweden since King Birger has failed to do the best for our country. You, yourselves, noted that he was no longer seeking guidance from men who have clearly shown their worth, but is following the advice of whoever happens to be close to him. He is my brother, and I love him; but he is not suited to rule. I do not want to shame him, but I can tell you that the costly internal war we suffered was caused by his accepting counsel from someone who shamelessly lied to him without his thoroughly examining the proof presented. And the recent incident with Lord Lars, though certainly not as significant, still upset us all because of its unreasonableness. That was caused by the queen, whose counsel my brother blindly followed. A king can obviously do whatever he wants, but his decisions have to be sensible if he is to be an effective leader. Valdemar and I, like all of you, want a strong and peaceful Sweden whose strength can be turned against a foreign foe, not squandered on petty grievances like the one the king pursued against the two of us." He fell silent to let the men absorb his words.

"Will you become our new ruler?" asked Lord Arnvid.

"God willing," Erik replied resolutely as he stood up to bring more carafes of wine over to the table, the servants having been barred from the Hall.

While the leaders conferred with one another, Valdemar joined Erik at the end of the hall to allow them free discussion. Both knew that the decision had already been made, but their youth required that the older men should feel they had made their own decisions. It did not take long before Lord Arnvid called them back.

"We have chosen you as our leader, Duke Erik, and we shall follow you."

Kristina was in high spirits when she rode up to Hatuna, dismounted and entered the Hall. After embracing her hosts, Kristina sat down beside Marta, accepted a cup of cinnamon tea, and related enthusiastically to her all the projects and tasks she had undertaken at Solang. "But I am so happy to be spending the holy days with you, Marta. It is my reward for being such a hardworking farmer."

Kristina noticed when she was speaking that Marta appeared somewhat ill at ease. Finally, Marta ventured, "Birger has invited Erik and Valdemar here, but you may not want to see them."

Kristina remained silent only for a moment. "I prepared myself for that possibility. I cannot hide away forever. I have found such peace and happiness in my new home that I feel much stronger now. I may stay by myself the first evening just to get used to the idea of being under the same roof with them."

"You decide, Kristina. But no one is happier than Magnus and me that you came."

"I have to be honest, Erik. I am nervous," admitted Valdemar riding up alongside his brother on the road to Hatuna. "I feel almost sick."

"Do you want to turn around and forget the whole thing?"

"Of course not. But after all these months I thought I was prepared, but now I feel shaky. After all, Birger is our brother. Why not just make certain he listens only to us, and that he does not make any major mistakes?"

"The three of us were closer than most brothers even dream of. But he threw that intimacy away when he turned on us. I, too, wish we did not have to do this, Valdemar, but we must act before he further harms our country."

"You are right, but I simply do not want to confront Birger."

Erik did not comment as Valdemar again fell in behind him and rode on in silence. When they saw the lights of Hatuna, Erik signalled Mats who was riding close behind them.

"You know what to do?" he asked tensely when Mats rode up alongside.

The marshal nodded calmly.

"Good luck!" Erik called as he wheeled his horse into the yard. He dismounted and strode into the hall of Hatuna where Birger and Marta were seated by the fire. Little Magnus was engrossed in playing with his carved wooden knights and horses. Alf was standing by the king's chair, observing Magnus' toy-soldiers charging imaginary forces on the stone floor.

"Oh, there you are!" exclaimed Marta when she saw them enter. She stood and went over to greet them. "We just found out that cousin Valdemar has taken ill and will remain in Holstein, so we will celebrate St. Michael's Day without him."

"That is too bad," said Erik, grateful not to have to detain his cousin as well. He kissed Marta on the cheek. She went over to greet Valdemar when Erik noticed Bishop Nils enter the hall. Damn! He would have to arrest him as well, since he needed to preserve the element of surprise for as long as possible. Not that he feared a public outcry over the king's imprisonment, but he knew that detaining the archbishop-elect could cause serious repercussions. He silently cursed their luck.

"What a surprise to find you here," he said stiffly as he greeted his old teacher.

"I am happy to be included in this family gathering," replied Bishop Nils with a kindly smile. "I have just reported on little Prince Erik's commendable progress in Upsala."

Erik and Valdemar embraced Birger with pretended cheer and then excused themselves to wash.

"We have to detain Bishop Nils, too," Valdemar complained in a hoarse whisper the moment they left the hall and headed for a private sleeping chamber--an unusual luxury in an estate in Sweden, but one their cousin had built to conform to continental standards.

"I know. It is too damn bad, but we will release him as soon as all the fortresses are under our control. By that time, Birger's imprisonment will no longer be a secret."

"That could take months!"

"Let us hope it will not be that long," said Erik as they reached their assigned chamber.

Before the evening meal, Alf of Smaland left the hall to check on the birds that were to be used for the morning hunt. The birds were perched peacefully on their wooden poles after having devoured their evening meal. Alf extinguished his candle and was about to leave the aviary when he heard voices outside.

"Word just arrived that the soldiers who were housed at the neighboring farms have been captured," said one low voice. "As soon as the king sits down for dinner we are to disarm any soldiers who are not in the hall."

"How many are there?" asked another hushed voice.

"We estimate about thirty," answered the first voice. "And most of them are over at the guardhouse playing cards and drinking beer. Some of our own men have joined them and are just awaiting the signal."

"What about the servants?" asked the other voice.

"We will try to avoid them, so they will not alert anyone in the hall."

The voices trailed off as the men moved away from the aviary.

Alf started back towards the main house, assessing what he had just overheard. Since he knew all about the feud between the brothers, he reasoned that Erik had decided that he would no longer allow his brother to control his life, or the country. Alf knew that he could not stop whatever had been set in motion even if he alerted the king, since there were too few men to protect him. He did not know what Erik intended to do to the king, but he wanted to protect Magnus whom he had grown to love like a son. Thank God, little Erik was safe in Upsala. It would be hard enough to escape with one youngster, let alone two.

Alf entered the hall where the guests were assembled, listening to a bard singing a ballad. He caught Magnus' eye and gestured to him. The boy left his place on the fur skins and came over. "Listen, we are going to play a game," Alf whispered. "I have waited until now to test you on things we have learned together. And this is the night!"

"What do I do?" asked Magnus eagerly.

"First, I want to test your ability to make people believe what you say. In this case it is not going to be true, but I want to see how convincing you are. Tell them you are not feeling well, and that you want to go to bed for the night."

"But I want to stay here with my uncles," Magnus protested weakly.

"This is also a test of obedience," said Alf as he pulled himself to his full height.

Magnus nodded with a conspiratorial grin on his face. "Mama!" he whined as he approached Marta who was applauding the bard's performance. "My stomach hurts. The supper is so late tonight that I got hungry. I went to the kitchen and ate a whole basket of apples. I feel awful."

"Oh, little boys. Will they never learn?" scolded Marta dotingly. "Master Alf!" she called. "Please see that this little rascal gets to bed right away."

Magnus kissed his mother with a look of intense suffering. "Come along," ordered Alf sternly. "Sleep is the only cure for eyes bigger than one's stomach."

"Good night," called Magnus as he was dragged away feigning a look of misery.

"Was I good?" he asked eagerly as they rushed along the corridor to his chamber.

"You were very good," said Alf as he opened the door and closed it behind them. "Now, to the next step. We will be chased by Duke Erik's soldiers, and our job is to evade them."

"Oh, Uncle Erik is in on it too. What fun!" exclaimed Magnus. "So how do we get away?"

Alf did not have time to answer before Kristina unexpectedly entered the room. She stopped in surprise at finding them there.

"I just came to tidy up before you went to bed, Magnus," she said, hesitating as she sensed the tension in the room. "What is going on?" she asked, looking from one to the other.

"Magnus, put on your warmest hunting clothes and a pair of walking boots!" Alf commanded. Magnus ran towards his clothes chest to do as he was told.

Alf rushed to his own chest while pulling off the tunic he was wearing, oblivious to Kristina who was following him. She appeared equally unaware that a man was disrobing in front of her. "What is going on? Please, tell me!" she pleaded.

"Listen," whispered Alf in her ear after he selected the proper clothes. "I have to take Magnus away from here immediately. Duke Erik is going to capture or kill the king; I do not know which. But I do not want Magnus to be harmed. Everyone thinks the lad has taken ill from overeating, so they will not disturb him until the morning. Magnus thinks we are playing a game, so he will do whatever I tell him. He is not afraid, only excited."

Kristina stared at him with tumultuous emotions. The man she loved was going to capture the man who was her king. Her loyalty lay with Erik, and always would. But if Magnus, the boy she had known and loved all his life, could be harmed she had to protect him. "Where will you take him?" she asked.

"To his uncle, the King of Denmark."

"I shall come with you!" she announced without hesitation. She did not want to be in Sweden while all this went on. She had conflicting loyalties, and she could think of no one she would rather be with than Ingeborg. "The dukes' men will be searching for you and Magnus. Since they do not know that I am here, they will not look for a family traveling together!"

"That is a clever idea," said Alf almost falling in his haste to pull on a boot. "But are you up to traveling under these circumstances? This will not be an easy journey."

"You forget that I, too, love Magnus," Kristina replied. "I shall get my cape and a pair of good boots."

"And some money, if you have any!" called Alf softly.

"What are we waiting for?" whispered Kristina as they finally stood in the dark, close to the aviary.

"We cannot cross the yard without being seen," said Alf quietly. "But I expect that there will be a commotion shortly when the dukes' men overpower the king's soldiers. No one will be looking this way then."

"This is the best game I have ever played!" whispered Magnus excitedly.

"Remember that we have to win! Do exactly as I say," commanded Alf.

Time crawled by while they waited. Finally, they heard loud voices from the guardhouse, and the sounds of metal clashing against metal. Alf grabbed Magnus' hand and whispered to Kristina, "Quickly now!" Crouching low, they ran across the open yard, out of the illuminated area, and along the dark road. Kristina had never run so fast, and her breath was coming in short gasps. After what seemed like an eternity, Alf dragged Magnus off the road and they all crouched down behind some bushes. Kristina could hear the sound of her heart thundering in her ears. She gratefully sat down to catch her breath. The lights at Hatuna were shining behind them, but she could see no movements around the estate.

"I think we have made it," said Alf who was not even breathing hard.

"We were not followed!" exclaimed Magnus, sounding disappointed.

"Hopefully, no one will look for us until morning, so we should use the time to rest, because God only knows when we will be able to sleep again. We cannot approach nearby farms because the dukes' men could be there. We will follow the road towards the inn we passed on our way here. It should only be a few hours walk."

"A few hours!" exclaimed Kristina.

"A family seeking night quarters should be of no interest to the dukes' men if they come around to inquire. They would never think we would use a public inn in the first place."

The supper was almost over when Erik abruptly stood up and clapped his hands. The large doors to the hall burst open and forty knights with drawn swords rushed in to take up positions behind each male member of the king's entourage. A few of the king's knights made an attempt to unsheathe their weapons, but were quickly disarmed. Johan Brunkow actually bared his knife while rushing to Marta's side, but a blow to the head rendered him unconscious. An awesome silence followed the sudden clamor. Bishop Nils stood up and opened his mouth in protest but sat down again when Erik placed his hand heavily on his shoulder.

"You are under arrest, King Birger!" Erik announced, surprised at how thin his voice sounded.

"For what crime?" Birger asked.

"For waging civil war without just cause! You are being arrested as a traitor to Sweden!"

"Well, well," said Birger slowly.

"What is all this about, Birger?" asked Marta in a falsetto voice.

Birger turned to his wife who appeared nearly hysterical. "I wish to withdraw with the queen," he said calmly. "I assume there is little else I can do to prevent this so-called arrest, knowing that you control the largest army Sweden has ever assembled. And imagine, I believed you did it to serve me."

"I did it to serve Sweden. Gullibility has always been your weakness," countered Erik coldly.

Birger shrugged his shoulders before he gently helped Marta, whose face had turned ashen, from her chair. "Let us go, dear." He turned to Erik once more. "When are we leaving?"

"Tomorrow morning."

"Let us rest until then, and do not wake Magnus."

"He will not be disturbed, but I have put a guard by his and Master Alf's door," said Erik.

Birger guided his wife out of the hall toward their chamber that was already guarded by two sentries. "I want to see if Magnus is all right," Marta whispered anxiously.

" Do not wake him, my dear. He needs his sleep," Birger counselled gently.

"Yes, you are right," she conceded as Birger led her past the guards into their chamber and closed the door. Alone together, Birger gestured for her to sit down in a chair.

"I think the time has come for me to tell you everything which has transpired between me and my brothers. I did not want to burden you with all the details before, but now I must. Here, my dear. Have a cup of wine. It will make you feel better." He was surprised at how calm he felt even though his hands shook as he handed Marta the goblet.

Three hours later Kristina could see the lights from the inn in the distance. She was grateful beyond belief. Her feet were aching, and she cursed her pampered existence that had not prepared her for something as simple as a long, fast walk. Magnus was still disappointed that they had not been followed. Alf kept reminding him that was fortunate because the knights had horses, which they did not. Magnus went along with that logic, but he was disappointed nonetheless.

As they neared the inn, Alf turned to Kristina; "You have done well."

Kristina blushed. "You are kind. I know that you have walked slowly on my account, but I shall improve."

"When we get to the inn, let me do the talking. The way you speak will mark you as nobility, and people will begin to wonder. Just confine yourselves to 'yes' and 'no', and if you have to say anything else, mumble your words. It is natural that as the man, I will do the talking. And if I give orders as husband to wife, please obey."

Kristina nodded. "I understand."

"And you, Magnus, address us as 'Mother' and 'Father,'" Alf continued.

"Yes, Father," said the prince with an angelic smile.

The three travelers entered the tavern. The proprietor rushed forward to greet them. He studied his guests gratefully. This was, indeed, a provident evening with such respectable late arrivals. The proprietor judged Alf to be a wealthy merchant traveling with his family.

"Good evening, my good man," Alf began. "Can you lodge me and my family for the night, and serve us some supper before we retire?"

"With pleasure," answered the proprietor as he led the way to a table close to the fire that was reserved for travelers who were able to pay for the best in the house. "My boys have taken care of your horses, I assume?" asked the proprietor as they sat down.

"We were travelling with my business partner who was in a dreadful hurry to get to Stockholm. My wife felt so tired that we decided to spend the night here rather than ride on in the dark. My partner took our horses with all our goods and baggage, so that he could get to Stockholm quickly with the horses lightly laden. This means that we will have to purchase horses from you. That is, if you have any to sell."

"Yes, I do!" said the proprietor eagerly, mentally calculating the highest price he could ask.

Alf ordered their dinner, and once the proprietor had placed a pitcher of beer on the table, they were left alone. Kristina admired the way Alf handled himself, confidently and with an air of assurance. She began to relax; certain that he would handle any problem that might arise.

"How much money do you have?" Alf asked as he poured some beer for Kristina.

"Three gold coins, and a few silvers," Kristina answered.

"Good," said Alf, taking a drink. He grimaced at the bitter taste of the cheap beer. "I have become spoiled at court," he added.

"It tastes heavenly to me," said Kristina as she took a deep swallow.

"I have two silver coins," Magnus proclaimed proudly. "My very own. But you can have them, if it is part of the game."

"If we need them," said Alf. "I have only one gold and some silvers. But we should easily make it to Denmark on what we have between us, if we are not robbed on the way."

They had not realized how hungry they were until they were served their supper. It tasted better than any meal Kristina could remember. Magnus was especially happy, since Alf told him to forget his table manners and eat as he pleased. Afterwards, the proprietor's wife pointed up a narrow staircase to their room. "But there is only one bed!" Kristina exclaimed.

"And we are only one family," Alf said. "Be glad we got our own room and did not have to sleep in the dormitory. Come now" he ordered kindly.

Kristina obediently did as commanded. Once in the small chamber she removed her boots and her hunting hose that she had on beneath her dress. She placed them over her tunic and mantle on a chest. Still wearing her dress, she crept in on one side of the bed and pulled the covers up to her nose. Magnus crept in next to her and fell asleep at once. Alf was the last one to lie down on the other side of the bed. Not surprisingly, Kristina fell asleep within minutes.

Erik and Valdemar sat before the hearth in the hall of Hatuna pondering the night's events. Both felt exhausted but unable to sleep.

After Birger and Marta had withdrawn, the king's entourage had been taken to the guardhouse with the rest of the prisoners. Bishop Nils had retired to his chamber under guard just before Mats arrived and reported on the successful rounding up of all the the king's men in the vicinity. Detailed instructions, which had been prepared in advance, were already en route to the regional leaders. Within days, every fortress in Sweden would be under siege if not already captured.

Erik knew that the nobles would be thrilled at the prospect of having their leader as Sweden's ruler. Whatever their conscience or loyalty to the crown, most were too power-hungry to stand by a king who was exhibiting growing favoritism towards the Church. He stared into the flames, confident of a virtually bloodless coup.

"It is understandable why Erik and Valdemar cannot forgive me," Birger said as he concluded his explanation to Marta. "I hoped they would, once Torgils was executed, but I was mistaken."

"You are the king!" Marta persisted.

"That makes little difference now, Marta. My brothers are in control of a vast army, so they are the masters of this country."

"Ask your allies to help you!"

"By the time they learn what has happened, it will be too late. We both know that your brother is embroiled fighting the Germans and cannot come to my aid. It is better that we accept the fact that Erik and Valdemar are the new rulers of Sweden."

"How can you take it so calmly, Birger?" Marta chided.

"I have no choice. I am grateful that we are alive. They should have killed us."

"Maybe they will kill us tomorrow!"

"They would have killed us immediately if that were their intention. How I hated them when I thought they had betrayed me, yet loved them at the same time, and they seem to feel the same towards me."

"I am afraid," Marta whimpered as she began to cry.

"Do not be," consoled Birger as he pulled her to her feet and put his arms around her. "We have each other, and that is what matters. Nothing will happen to us, except that I might not be king anymore," he said, gently rocking her in his arms. He only wished what he was saying would prove true. As he held her close, his heart was pounding with fear at the probable fate of his sons.

Chapter 27

"Get up. It is time to leave!" Alf's command punctured Kristina's dream world. She reluctantly opened her eyes, only to remember that they were on the run. When she looked out the small window she saw it was still dark outside.

"It is early, but we must be on our way. I have bought two horses from the innkeeper. Hopefully, he will not provide information about us for fear someone will discover that he overcharged us."

Kristina looked around. "Where is Magnus?"

"He is breaking fast in the tavern. Join us when you are ready," Alf replied as he left the tiny chamber.

Kristina left the bed to quickly pull on her tunic, hose, and boots. From a small pouch that hung from her belt she took a comb to untangle her hair, before donning her headdress. With her cloak over her arm, she descended the steep stairs to the tavern. Magnus waved from their table. "Good morning, Mother," he called.

"Good morning, dear," she replied as she sat down, admiring the little actor's performance. Since Alf had already settled with the innkeeper, they left right after their meal. The horses awaiting them were not the proudest of their species, but Kristina silently thanked the Lord that she would not have to walk. The stable boy helped her mount, while Alf pulled Magnus up in front of him on the other horse. "We shall seek a ship bound for Denmark once we get to Stockholm," Alf called as they set off. "It will be the fastest and safest way to travel. If we are lucky, we might find one sailing today."

Neither Birger nor Marta had slept when the guard knocked on their door and announced, "Your Majesties. We will depart in one hour."

"I shall go and wake Magnus," Marta offered.

"I will come with you," said Birger. "I do not want him to be frightened when he learns what has happened." Birger walked past the guard who stood outside their door and down the corridor, followed by Marta. "We would like to talk to our son alone," he told the guard outside Magnus' chamber before they entered. He closed the door, walked over to the bed, pulled the bed curtains aside, and reached toward the covers. "He is not here!" he whispered.

"Neither is Alf!" she whispered back. "They probably are breaking fast in the hall. Come, let us find them." As Birger started towards the door, his eyes were drawn to a piece of parchment on top of Magnus' clothes chest. "Wait!" he said, as Marta was about to open the door. "Look at this." He picked up the note and read it aloud, "We are taking Magnus to safety. Ninnie."

Marta turned with a bewildered look. Then her face lit up. "Alf and Kristina have taken Magnus away! God bless them."

Birger gave a sigh of relief. "This means Erik will not be able to imprison our entire family. That will be a blow to his plan. The people might rise against him in favor of a rightful heir."

"Where do you think they have gone?" asked Marta who was holding the note.

"I do not know. But I trust Alf will find a safe place," Birger replied.

"We must keep this to ourselves, so they can get a head start."

"Good thinking, Marta. Destroy the note."

"No, Birger, please. Let me keep it as a reminder that Magnus is on his way to safety."

"All right but hide it well."

"I promise," Marta said gratefully as she folded and placed it in a pocket of her tunic. "Just touching it will give me strength."

Birger suddenly exclaimed, "You realize that Erik has no idea that Kristina was here! He will not be looking for a threesome. It was lucky that you offered her your room last night. Now all you have to do is to go there and pack your things together with hers and no one will be the wiser."

"What do you mean?" demanded Erik of the sentry who had guarded Alf and Magnus.

"Just as I said, your Highness," the sentry stammered. "I knocked on the door, and when no one answered I went in. It was empty! I swear, your Highness, that no one except the king and the queen has been in or out of that room since I was posted there last night."

"Then they must not have been there when you took your post." Erik said as he dismissed the guard with an impatient sweep of his hand.

"That is a serious setback," said Valdemar pacing by the fire.

"We shall postpone our departure and send out search parties. They should not be hard to find since they must have bought or stolen horses in the vicinity."

It was late in the afternoon when one of Lord Mats' soldiers returned to Hatuna. "There is no trace of Master Alf and Prince Magnus. We have not heard about any stolen horses, either."

"Were any horses purchased in the area last night?" asked Erik impatiently.

"Only by a family--a man, wife and child--who stayed at an inn a few miles from here and continued this morning on horses they bought from the innkeeper," the soldier replied.

"That could hardly be them; sleeping peacefully at a public inn," observed Valdemar.

Erik and Valdemar were surprised when Marta and Birger joined them for supper, but presumed they were curious about how the search for their son was progressing.

"Why should I keep you in suspense?" said Erik. "We have not found either Magnus or Alf."

Marta consumed her supper with unusual appetite. After the meal, when Marta and Birger stood up to leave, Erik noticed Marta's hand fiddling with something under her tunic. "What do you have there?" Erik asked, as he went over and pulled her hand out of her pocket. Her fingers were clasped around a piece of folded parchment, and he was about to let go of her arm when he noticed her petrified look. He took it from her, unfolded it, and read it aloud. "Ninnie is Magnus' nickname for Kristina, " said Erik slowly. Then he turned to a soldier by the door. "You had better hurry after that family who stayed at the inn. Alf is not alone with Magnus. Kristina is with them! "

After arriving in Stockholm Kristina and Magnus spent most of the afternoon in a dark pew of the cathedral, while Alf went to the harbor to look for a ship bound for Denmark. Magnus fell asleep and after a while, the peace of the church lulled Kristina to sleep as well.

She woke when she felt Alf's hand on her shoulder. "The only ship I could find to take us to Denmark sails the day after the morrow. "

"I hope we can hide until then," whispered Kristina.

"When are we going to eat? " Magnus asked as he awoke to their whispers.

"I know a tavern close by. It should be quite empty now. "

The tavern was warm and cozy, and Alf found them seats in a dimly lit corner. Kristina began to relax once she finished her second cup of beer. The food was simple, a hearty pork stew that Kristina thought tasted heavenly. Magnus, who ate two full portions, did not disagree.

When they had finished their meal and walked out onto the street, Alf suddenly tensed. In front of the stable where they had left their horses, three soldiers bearing Duke Erik's colors stood talking to the attendant who was nodding.

"Three of Duke Erik's soldiers have just entered our stable, " Alf whispered. "Turn around and start walking toward the docks." When they reached the corner, they saw four of Duke Erik's soldiers walking along the wharf, a sight that stopped them dead in their tracks. As they turned to go back up the street, the first soldiers emerged from the stable onto the street.

"We are surrounded! " Alf said under his breath. "Quickly, come here! " He pushed Kristina into a doorway and hid Magnus between them beneath their long mantles. "If we pretend to be lovers they might just pass us by. " Alf gently embraced Kristina and placed his lips close to hers so that he could see along the street. The soldiers from the wharf turned up the street and called to the others. "Any luck? "

"Yes, those are their horses, all right, " shouted a soldier near the stable. Alf could feel Kristina stiffen in his arms and Magnus anxiously move between them.

"We will stay here in case they come back for them," the soldier called.

"All right," acknowledged one of the group standing at the end of the street as he motioned his men to continue along the quay.

"By now they might know that there are three of us," whispered Alf.

"I cannot breathe," mumbled Magnus as he struggled between them.

"We must get away quickly so you will have to be uncomfortable for a while longer," Alf warned as he put his arm around Kristina's shoulders and positioned Magnus in front of them, still hidden by their full length capes. "You have to keep in step with us so that it looks as if we were just a couple on an evening stroll. Can you do that?"

"Of course!" answered Magnus, his voice muffled by cloth. The bulky shape of two lovers emerged from the doorway into the street. They moved towards the harbor in the opposite direction from that taken by Duke Erik's men.

"Maybe we could ask the captain of the ship bound for Denmark to hide us for the night," said Alf. He stopped abruptly as he noticed a group of Duke Erik's men heading toward them from the far end of the harbor. "There are soldiers everywhere!"

"Maybe we should turn around," suggested Kristina. "We might be able to slip by the soldiers at the stable if they are no longer in the street."

"Let us try," Alf agreed. But as he turned, he saw the four men in the distance who had gone in the opposite direction along the quay begin to head back towards them.

"Now we are really trapped!" he whispered. "Let us try to find another doorway." Their three pairs of feet scurried past invitingly lit taverns and closed storefronts until they found a shallow doorway. "This is not ideal, but it will have to do," whispered Alf as he observed the armed men approaching from the end of the harbor closing the distance.

As Alf stood embracing Kristina in his arms, he was sure the soldiers would not be fooled this time since there were no deep shadows in which to hide. As the men approached, he prayed they would be busy looking elsewhere. Suddenly, he felt the door behind his back swing open and the three of them tumbled into the house. "Welcome," spoke someone in a hushed voice.

"We followed them to Stockholm, your Highnesses," reported a knight, still short of breath. "We have located their horses, and my men have learned that they booked passage on a ship sailing for Denmark the day after the morrow."

"So that is where they are headed," said Erik with an appreciative nod. "I knew that Master Alf was a resourceful fellow."

"In the meantime, my men are trying to find them, if not today then when they attempt to board the ship."

"Have you looked in Santa Klara convent?" asked Valdemar.

"Yes, your Highness," answered the knight. "The Mother Superior was not pleased about our visit, but they were not hiding there. We searched quite thoroughly."

"Then we will leave for Stockholm first thing in the morning," said Erik. "Thank you for your report. " The knight bowed as he left the hall. Erik turned to Valdemar "We have them cornered now. All routes are well covered."

Despite his strict orders not to harm the fugitives, he still worried that some overzealous soldier might hurt Kristina. He hoped they would be captured quickly so he might know she was safe.

Birger entered the hall at that moment. "Do you think that your physician could give Marta something to help her sleep? She is quite upset."

"I will find him," said Valdemar, leaving Erik and Birger alone.

"I understand your actions," Birger began slowly. "But Marta does not. If you have not yet captured Magnus, could I tell her that? It would make it easier for her to rest."

"We have not yet captured Magnus."

"Thank you," said Birger, turning to leave.

"Wait! I would like you to sign this document," said Erik as he walked over to a table littered with papers to look for the right one. He found it and walked towards his brother. "It is an order to the commandant of Stockholm castle to surrender in order to avert needless bloodshed."

Birger smiled, "You might want my crown, but I will not help you get it!" he said as he turned on his heel to leave the hall.

"Again, you are not thinking of the people," Erik shouted after him. "Why let them suffer unnecessarily?"

He got no answer. Birger was already gone.

Kristina turned to look at the stranger who had addressed them. The wise old woman was smiling kindly. "What can I do for you this time?"

"Who are you?" asked Alf, as the old woman closed the door and locked it behind them.

She beckoned them toward the fire; "I am just an old woman trying to assist fellow travelers in their wanderings." She chuckled as she offered them a seat by her large table.

Alf surveyed the cozy room while Magnus stared in fascination at the owl on the mantel blinking its huge eyes. On a bench sat two black cats whose steady gaze followed the visitors' every move.

"This is the wise woman who once told my fortune," explained Kristina. "She foretold everything terrible that has happened to me since then."

"Oh, but I also told you that you would be happy in the end," mused the old woman.

"I am afraid that we did not come to have our fortunes told," said Alf. "I do, however, want to thank you for your most timely invitation."

"I knew the soldiers were looking for someone. They have been searching for hours, and the way you were huddled in my doorway, I figured it was you they were after. But I never expected to find an old friend," she said with a kindly grin.

"Could you find it in your heart to let us stay until we board a ship to Denmark the day after tomorrow?" Alf asked as he accepted a cup of herbal tea from the old woman.

"Of course. But in return, you must tell me what is afoot," she replied as she joined them by the table.

"I do not know if I can," said Alf hesitantly.

"You can trust me. Once I take someone under my protection, as I did when this lady came to see me some years ago, I would never betray her or him," as she nodded toward Magnus. "You have my word."

"I believe you," said Alf after glancing at Kristina, who nodded her approval, "and I follow my instincts." Alf told the wise old woman who they were and explained the predicament in which they found themselves. He carefully explained, as he winked at her, the "game" to test Prince Magnus. The old woman nodded her understanding. When Alf finished, she shook her head in amazement.

"I did not realize that I had foretold Lady Kristina's divorce and Lord Torgils' death, because I did not know to whom I was speaking. And Prince Magnus, handsome as can be, here in my humble home," she continued. "Maybe I could have guessed you were Alf of Smaland if you had with you your bow and quiver. You are a legend among the common folk." Alf was amazed to hear that so many outside the royal household knew who he was.

"I will be honored to help you, and I shall get you to safety some-how," the wise old woman promised. "By now the soldiers must surely know of your plans. So, we have to get you out while your pursuers are still waiting to seize you when you head for the ship. When you do not show up there, they will start looking for you in earnest, and then not even I could hide you."

One of the yellow-eyed black cats jumped up on the bench on which Magnus was sitting, climbed majestically into the prince's lap, and started purring.

"That is quite a compliment, Prince Magnus. He does not like strangers, you know. And a black cat is good luck, contrary to what people say." The old woman chuckled as she stood to light a torch from the fire. "There is a bed in my weaving room. Is that suitable?" she asked Kristina.

"You are so kind," replied Kristina, hoping she was not blushing over the suggestion that the three of them share a single bed. "I am so tired I could sleep on a stone floor."

"Before you retire let me give you some more of my special herb tea," the old woman said as she took the kettle off the fire and poured them all another cup. "It will make you rest peacefully."

It did as the old woman promised. It was light outside when Kristina awoke, refreshed from a dreamless sleep. To her great surprise she saw that both Alf and Magnus were still sleeping, so she quietly crept out of the bed and pulled on her clothes. Despite her efforts not to disturb them, her movements alerted Alf who sat up. He looked worried when he realized that it was light outside.

"My goodness. I have not slept like this since I was a child. The old woman's tea does have a relaxing effect," he said as he pulled on his tunic and boots. He looked at Magnus sleeping in the middle of the bed, blissfully hugging the big black cat. "There were more of us in bed than I thought," he observed wryly as he and Kristina left the weaving chamber. The old woman had baked fresh bread, and the aroma filled the room.

"Did you rest well?" she asked.

"I have never slept better," said Kristina.

"Or later," Alf added.

"Just as well. There is nothing we can do now, anyway," noted the old woman. "Look out the window and you shall see what I mean."

Groups of soldiers were standing in different locations all along the harbor and on the docks. Alf knew that they would never be able to leave the house without being detected. "I have not been idle, though," the old woman assured them as she put the fresh bread on the table with butter, cheese, and pieces of cold meat. She served them steaming hot tea with a floral aroma that they gratefully sipped.

"I have spoken to my friends who have told me that the soldiers are looking for a young couple and their son who have stolen some valuables from Duke Erik. It is common knowledge that the thieves will try to escape on a ship for Denmark. Unfortunately I was right, you cannot go aboard that boat. To make matters worse, they have offered a large reward to the person who helps catch the thieves."

"How can we escape, then?" asked Kristina anxiously. "We are hemmed in from all sides."

"Not quite, my dear," the old woman said with a chuckle.

Erik raised his arm to bring the mounted column to a halt. Mats rode up to join them. "The town is under our control," he reported. "The commander refused to surrender, so we have the castle under siege. We shall be joined by more troops once the nobles receive their orders. Then, it is merely a question of time."

"It is unfortunate that the commander is unaware of the size of our armies or he would have capitulated at once," said Erik. "But now, we have to take the king and queen to Nykoping. Are the ships ready to sail?"

"At your command," answered Mats. "I shall meet you at the dock." He wheeled his horse around and galloped back towards the town.

"Now you know the plan," said the old woman. "It is the only way we can get all three of you out together."

"You must have truly loyal friends to take such risks when there is a reward on our heads," exclaimed Alf gratefully.

"They have known me for a long time, and I have done them many favors," the old woman allowed. " But now, get ready. The king, the queen, and the dukes have arrived in the harbor, and everyone's attention is focused there."

Kristina felt a great sense of relief at the news that Marta and Birger were alive, but she still wanted Magnus out of harm's way. She knew all too well about political murders.

Magnus hugged the big black cat affectionately. "I wish I could take you with me," he said sadly, as the cat rubbed its head against the boy's hand with a loud and contented purr.

The old woman opened a narrow door in the wall beside the large cupboard, lit a torch that she handed to Alf, and gestured for them to hurry through. On entering, they found themselves in a huge barnlike structure filled with wooden crates of every conceivable size.

"This storehouse belongs to a man who allows me to stay in my house rent free because I look after it for him," explained the old woman. "But the real reason is because I once told his wife that she would get a child when she had given up all hope, and it turned out I was right."

"I have heard that you are always right," said Kristina.

The old woman smiled humbly. "This warehouse faces the street running parallel to the harbor, so we are safely away from the soldiers." When she opened up the large double doors at the other end of the warehouse, they could hear the grinding wheels of a horse-drawn cart on the cobblestones outside. Soon an old and emaciated horse entered through the open doors, drawing a rickety wagon. An old man in frayed clothes led the horse by its muzzle.

"The Death Wagon!" gasped Kristina. She could feel her skin crawl at the sight of the rickety equipage, which caused men, women, and children to cross themselves whenever they saw it rolling down the streets. The wagon, accompanied by the old undertaker who the town folks jokingly called Charon after the mythical ferryman to hell, collected the corpses of those without the means for proper burial, or of strangers who had no one to claim them. Extra busy when epidemics ravaged the populace, its daily destination was a mass grave outside the town. To ride the Death Wagon at the end of one's life was to be as close to damnation as one could get.

"It is the only wagon they will not inspect at the gates," said the wise old woman.

"I've scrubbed it special today," said old Charon. "It's as clean as the king's own floor. An' the cover's never been used 'efore," he concluded with a toothless grin.

"It is our one chance," said Alf. "Come on, we have to get going." He jumped into the cart and lifted Magnus after him. He looked down at Kristina who stood frozen with horror on her face. "I am sorry, Kristina, but it makes sense," he said firmly.

"He is right, my lady," said the wise old woman as she gently nudged Kristina towards the wagon. "You listen to him."

"Come on, Ninnie," urged Magnus, not understanding her reluctance. But then he had never seen the wagon loaded to capacity with stiff bluish arms and legs sticking out from under its cover. Kristina hesitantly climbed in beside them.

"Good bye, dear lady," Alf said to the wizened old woman as he offered her some coins.

"You owe me nothing. I did this for an old friend," she replied, smiling at Kristina. "But now you must do as Master Alf tells you, my lady, or I will have failed."

"Thank you for everything," said Kristina as she laid herself down on the wagon bed as the old woman helped Charon pull the tarpaulin over them.

"Put your hands under you so they do not accidentally stick out should the cart lurch on the bumpy streets," the old woman advised. "They look far too healthy to belong to a corpse."

The old woman carefully checked the covers before she motioned Charon to start on his journey. "God speed," she called after them as the cart pulled out of the warehouse. She closed the doors, praying they would reach Denmark safely. Last night her fizzing black powder had shown strong configurations of adversity.

"Does this mean I am dead?" whispered Magnus under the covers.

"No, but you might be, if you do not keep quiet," admonished Alf sternly.

Even though the old nag did its best, the journey seemed endless, as they were jolted about on the hard wagon bed. They could hear little boys call Charon foul names along the way, and Kristina could imagine the people crossing themselves as the accursed wagon passed by. As the sounds of merchants hawking became fainter, Kristina assumed they were approaching the southern gate. Suddenly the cart came to a halt, and she could feel her heart pound faster. From the conversation ahead of them she guessed that guards were searching all wagons leaving the town. The cart jerked forward, but then stopped, and they waited, hardly daring to breathe.

As the cart moved forward once more, she could hear a guard call out, "Another load of unfortunates, eh, Charon? You certainly have a steady business! Hey, wait!" he called as the cart began to move once more. "Those boots look too good to bury." The guard was obviously coveting Alf's hunting boots that must have jerked free of the cover.

Charon held back the horse, "If you wan' the plague, take 'em," he replied. "I just picked him off a ship."

"Oh, get on your way!" snapped the guard with fear in his voice. As the cart started moving once more Kristina drew a deep breath and felt Magnus' grip on her arm relax.

The trip to the mass grave was slow since the wagon had to climb the southern hills. Through the slats, Kristina could see the place of execution where her father had lost his life, and she felt her heart constrict in sadness. When the wagon came to a final stop, Old Charon pulled the cover back.

"'Ere we are!" he said proudly. "Went smooth as a bishop's sermon." Stiffly, they stood up and climbed over the railing to the ground. "Look like mourners jus' in case anyone's 'ere," said the old man, "My 'elpers are off today."

Alf looked around the hollow where they were standing. No grass grew there since the ground was continuously being dug up. Charon and his men would dig a gaping hole where they would bury some bodies and cover them with several feet of dirt. When it was time to bury the next group of unfortunates they would dig back down a bit, put the bodies in and cover them in turn. Some crude wooden crosses marked a few of the graves where the victims had died from some common disaster like a widespread fire or an epidemic. The place lacked even weeds, and the trees surrounding the hollow were wispy and colorless.

Alf jumped as he heard horses approaching.

"Should be Fjodor," predicted the old man calmly. A young man straddling a strong stallion galloped into the hollow leading two fine horses behind him.

"These horses are from my mother and father," the young man announced as he dismounted. "The wise old woman asked us to bring them to you. Unfortunately, we cannot afford to give them to you, but a silver for each would be fine."

"That is much too little," said Alf. "These are really fine horses."

"Three silvers are what my father bade me ask."

"What has the old woman done for you?" inquired Kristina.

"Her medicines saved my father's life when he was deathly ill, my lady," the young man answered. "My mother says that we would not have lasted a year without him, because at that time we were ten children at home."

"The wise old woman is remarkable," mused Alf as he handed the young man a handful of silver coins. "No, keep them," he said as Fjodor protested. "And thank your parents from us."

"God bless you. Have a safe journey," called Fjodor as he ran out of the hollow.

"And thank you," said Alf as he turned to Charon to put some coins in his hand.

"Don' wan' your money. T'were a favor to the old woman. I, too, owe 'er my life."

"Then let us say that the money was for cleaning the wagon and getting a new cover," said Alf as he helped Kristina up onto a big, brown mare.

"For that I thank you, m'lord," said the old man with his toothless grin.

"By the way," said Kristina. "Do you know the name of the old woman?"

"No, can't say's I do," said Charon. "Never thought about 'er havin' a name. Never heard 'er called anythin' but 'the wise old woman.'"

"Thanks again," said Alf as he lifted Magnus up onto his horse before mounting the big stallion himself. "And give our warmest thanks to the wise old woman."

"Will do. An' God speed," old Charon called as he waved from his barren domain.

October made its entrance with sparkling colors and a bright sun. It was late in the afternoon, but most farmers had not yet started to return from the fields, so the main road was empty before them. Alf made the decision to risk riding the open road since they needed to gain as large a lead on their followers as they could. Kristina marveled at the beauty of the multicolored trees while relishing the wind in her face. How wonderful life was, despite the fear lurking in the back of her mind. She wanted to savor the moment, knowing Magnus and Alf were safely beside her.

After a couple of hours of hard riding, Alf guided them off the road down to a small brook where they dismounted. Alf and Magnus began to dry off their sweat-covered horses with clumps of dry grass.

"Look," exclaimed Magnus who was wiping down Kristina's mount. "The two saddlebags on this horse are filled with food!" They found bread, cheese and cooked sausages in one bag, and in the other were two large containers filled with fresh apple cider.

"Fit for a king," said Alf as they brought their bounty to the edge of the brook where Kristina had collapsed against a large stone. She imbibed deeply of the cider and sighed with contentment. While permitting their horses to graze and drink from the brook, they finished their meal in silence, savoring every bite.

Kristina's euphoria over their successful escape was dampened by the knowledge that their pursuers knew where they were headed. Alf had reasoned that Erik's men would limit their search to Stockholm until they failed to show up for the ship. Thus, the old woman had given them a day's head start. Though they had kept to the main road and had met several travelers on their way, Kristina prayed that no one would remember them. Riding fast, and with their hoods up, they might even have been mistaken for three men.

Alf had explained that the duke's men could easily outride them since the soldiers had the advantage of obtaining fresh mounts when needed. However, if they could stay ahead of their pursuers, in six days they could reach the forests of Smaland, which Alf knew like the back of his hand. There, Kristina felt confident, no one would find them. And from Smaland they could easily cross into Denmark.

Kristina was certain that Erik wished them no harm, but merely sought to apprehend Prince Magnus. But she was also well aware that as it was not he, himself, who was in pursuit and in a confrontation with his soldiers they could be hurt or killed.

"It is time to go," Alf ordered, interrupting her train of thought.

"All right," said Kristina bravely as she limped over to her horse. She had ridden all her life, but not such long distances at urgent speed.

Magnus needed no prodding to go on. He was eager to win the game. But soon he, too, would tire, and there was nothing as difficult to inspire as a tired child. They packed the remaining provisions into Kristina's saddlebags and resumed their southward flight.

As night fell they turned off the main road onto a path leading down into a valley. Alf stopped at the second small farm, dismounted and pounded on the farmhouse door. He politely asked for lodging and something to eat. The farmer's wife, eager for his money, offered the bed in the main house; but Alf insisted that the hayloft would suffice, and that they would take their supper there as well. So tired was Kristina that she almost lost her balance when she dismounted and stood on her feet again. Alf and Magnus led the steaming horses into the ramshackle barn and rubbed them down, while Kristina gave them hay and water. When they had almost finished, a farmhand came to offer help, but Alf met him in the doorway since he preferred his traveling companions to remain unseen.

"How many fer eatin'?" asked the farmhand.

"Four, please," said Alf, knowing that they could use the extra food later. "And give this to your mistress," he added as he handed the boy some coins.

They climbed up a rickety ladder into the hayloft where a pale half moon shed some light through an open hatch. Alf found a spot where the hay was softly packed, and he showed Magnus and Kristina how to arrange the hay into comfortable beds. For the first time since making their escape they relaxed. They were laughing and throwing hay at one another when the farmhand called from below. "Supper's here!" Alf climbed down the ladder and saw that his coins had impressed the lady of the house. There were cups of hot soup, loaves of bread, fresh apples, and a tankard of beer. "Thank your mistress most kindly," he said to the lad.

"There's a bucket over in the corner, and you can get water from the well," said the boy as he sauntered off towards the farmhouse.

With Magnus and Kristina's help, Alf got the food up to the loft where they enjoyed their meal to the fullest. Almost before he had finished eating Magnus fell asleep. Alf gently placed him in a hollow in the hay and covered him. "He has been really good," said Alf. "Never once complained."

"But that would spoil the game," Kristina said with a smile.

They woke at dawn, washed up, ate some of the remaining food, and after brushing each other clean of hay, the fugitives finally felt ready to face the day. They saddled their mounts and headed toward the main road. After cantering steadily throughout the day with only minimal intervals of rest, they spent the following night in another hayloft off the main road. Kristina wondered how she would ever manage to ride again, so stiff was she.

Anxiety kept Alf awake. He reasoned that Duke Erik's men must already have sent search parties along the southern road that by the next night would be breathing down their necks. With only one more day of relative safety, they were still far from the forests of his Smaland. Alf finally fell into a fitful sleep in which a fearsome monster stalked him at every turn.

The following day they were forced to take frequent rests since Kristina could not sit her horse for more than an hour at a time. Although Alf could see how she was suffering, she persevered. Magnus, on the other hand, enjoyed riding with elders who treated him as an adult.

As evening approached, they realized they were nearing Linkoping. Kristina pointed off to the side of the road. "Do you see that large house over there? It used to belong to my father. While I was never fond of his widow, Hedvig, maybe she will give us a place to sleep tonight."

When they rode up to the estate the housekeeper came out on the front steps, eying them suspiciously. Kristina pulled off her hood, and when the housekeeper recognized her, she curtsied as she exclaimed "Welcome, Lady Kristina!"

She quickly ordered a stable hand to tend the horses. "I shall tell Lady Hedvig that you are here, my lady."

They dismounted to follow the housekeeper into the hall where they were met by a deep growl. Kristina smiled in recognition. "Odin! Come here, old friend. It has been a long time." The huge mastiff began to wag his tail and padded forward to greet them. A fire was burning on the large hearth and candles were glowing everywhere. It seemed they had arrived just in time for supper.

"Well, lookie who is here. My little stepdaughter!" cooed Hedvig as she sashayed towards them. Then she added, gazing at Kristina's companions, "Master Alf and Prince Magnus, too. Now this is intriguing!" Preceding them with her characteristic sensual sway, she led the way to chairs by the fire. Her long black hair hung loosely down her back, which Kristina found most unseemly for a widow. "You look like you could do with some food and rest," she observed as she poured them wine, and for Magnus a large cup of apple cider, while gesturing for them to sit down. "Whatever are you up to now, dear Kristina, traveling with the prince and his companion without a chaperone?"

"It is a long story that we will be glad to tell you if we may count on your hospitality for the night--as well as your promise to keep our visit a secret," answered Alf.

"You can stay as long as you please, and I will not let anyone know," Hedvig said with a radiant smile. "You have no idea how desperate I am for interesting company in this Godforsaken part of the world. Let us eat, and then tell me everything."

Kristina soon realized that Hedvig was a truly charming hostess. She listened attentively to Alf's story, she poured them delicious wine; and even Magnus, still believing they were playing the game, became quite animated while contributing his share of their adventures. Kristina longed for a bath but was reluctant to leave Alf with this seductress.

"What an adventure!" concluded Hedvig when they had finished recounting their tale. "I felt no love for any of the royal brothers after they confiscated Torgil's wealth and I became the shunned widow of a traitor. Discontented as I am, I can hardly go back to my father, so I am stuck here. Kristina, you are after all my stepdaughter, so your secret is safe with me."

Hedvig then suggested that Kristina should take the bath the servants had prepared, and that Magnus should go to bed. Both victims protested, each for their own reasons; but Hedvig prevailed. Kristina enjoyed the hot bath behind a curtain, and before retreating to her own bed tucked Magnus into his.

"Is Lady Hedvig the most beautiful lady you have ever seen?" the young prince asked.

"Yes," admitted Kristina reluctantly as she envisaged Hedvig's enthralling green eyes drawing Alf under her spell while they sat talking in front of the fire. "We have to rest now," she admonished Magnus gently. "We still have a long way to go before we reach Denmark."

When Kristina awoke, fully rested in her comfortable bed, she almost forgot that she was on the run until she heard Hedvig laughing intimately with Alf and Magnus.

"I hope you had a good rest, my dear," said Hedvig in greeting as Kristina drew open her bed curtains.

"It is after daybreak and we should be on our way," Alf interjected. "Thank you so . . ." Alf never got a chance to finish the sentence as the pounding of horses' hooves was heard. He quickly ran to the window in time to see three of Duke Erik's knights followed by six soldiers riding up. "They are here!" he said coldly.

"Do not worry," cooed Hedvig calmly. "I have already ordered the servants not to say that you are here, or they will be severely punished. They never doubt my word, so they will obey. Now, collect your belongings and hide in my room. I shall invite the knights to have their morning meal with me, and I will see that all their soldiers get into the kitchen for some food."

As if by magic, servants came rushing to remove cups and knives from the table to make it look as if only one person had enjoyed a leisurely repast. Hedvig nodded with satisfaction. "I gave the servants their instructions last night, so your escape is already planned. Now get going!"

Kristina, Alf and Magnus raced back to their respective beds that the servants had already remade to look unused. There they retrieved their few belongings before racing towards Hedvig's room, while heavy knocks could be heard at the front entrance.

Hedvig held open the door to her chamber while holding the collar of the fearsome-looking Odin.

"Now listen carefully. Odin will stand guard outside this door. When you hear me come to feed him that is your signal to get away. Climb out my bedroom window and run along the brook until you reach the forest. Your horses are tethered there. And worry not, you will get a head start of at least several hours," Hedvig concluded with a lascivious grin. The knocking on the front door became louder and more insistent.

"How can we ever thank you?" Alf asked.

"Oh, we shall find a way," answered Hedvig with a provocative smile. She closed the door behind them. "Stay, Odin! Guard!" she commanded, whereupon the dog obediently sat in front of the door.

"Patience, patience!" she called out as she approached her front door. "Stop this noise!" she added irritably as she opened it and faced three young knights.

"Sorry, my lady. But we were not sure you heard us," said a comely knight as he gazed wide-eyed at the raven-haired beauty who had opened the door. "Lady Hedvig?" he asked hesitantly, recognizing the widow of the former Lord High Constable.

"What is your errand here?" she replied icily.

"We are looking for fugitive thieves; and our orders are to search every house along the main road. We did not know this manor was yours."

"Well, you are welcome to search my house," said Hedvig with no reluctance.

"Thank you, Lady Hedvig. Please forgive our intrusion," said the young knight as he and his two companions entered the house. They went around the hall looking behind the bed curtains. As one of them approached Hedvig's chamber, Odin stood up and bared his teeth with a threatening growl.

"He will not let you enter my private chamber . . . without my permission," said Hedvig sweetly. "But I might consider giving that permission if you behave yourselves and share my lonely morning meal." The three young knights eagerly sat down at the table, unable to take their eyes off their hostess. Maybe the rumors about her appetite for young men were true. They were certainly not going to pass up the opportunity to find out.

As the housekeeper entered the hall with fresh bread and a platter of cold meat, Hedvig said, "Invite the soldiers into the kitchen and give them something to eat."

While Hedvig enjoyed her second meal that morning, Kristina, Alf and Magnus inspected the ample food supplies she had left for them. Hedvig had even provided fresh clothes for Kristina. As Alf and Magnus listened by the door, Kristina changed into the clothes which she realized were of fine cloth, lined with expensive fur. In her heart she regretted everything negative she had ever thought about Hedvig.

They waited for what seemed like an eternity. Finally, they could hear Hedvig offer Odin some scraps of meat. Alf opened the window and jumped out before he lifted Magnus out and set him firmly on his feet. He then eased Kristina down with the rest of the provisions and closed the window behind them. Crouching low, they ran along the brook towards the forest where they found their horses. They decided to lead the animals through the forest for several hundred yards until they were out of earshot of any soldier venturing out of Hedvig's kitchen. There they mounted up and once more headed south.

Hedvig had made good her promise. They did not see anyone following them for the rest of the day. During rest periods they hid off the road but with Alf placed to observe anyone traveling on the main thoroughfare. At nightfall they were unable to find a farm, and since there was a full moon Alf suggested that they keep moving. Despite the hard day's ride and although they and their horses were exhausted, they persisted until Magnus nearly fell asleep in his saddle.

They dismounted in a hidden forest clearing where they unsaddled their horses and Alf spread their saddle blankets on the soft, mossy ground where Kristina collapsed with Magnus' head in her lap. The horses found fresh water from a small pond at one end of the clearing then began feeding on the long, soft grass. Hedvig's food was tasty, and a few sips of her fine wine soon put them in good spirits. The fire, which Alf adroitly made using dry wood he had gathered in armloads from the forest floor, quickly dispelled the chill of the night. Kristina must have fallen asleep sitting by the fire because the only thing she could remember was Alf gently taking Magnus from her, and then laying her down on a bed of dry grass and covering her with a saddle blanket.

She awoke with a feeling of panic. It was light, and she was alone. She sat up slowly, her body stiff from the ground chill. Their horses were tethered close by so she realized Alf and Magnus could not be far away. She walked in the direction of the main road figuring that they might be scouting for their pursuers.

"Ninnie! I am over here," Magnus hissed from behind a bush near the road. "Alf is trying to find out if Uncle Erik's soldiers have come this far," he whispered as she drew close.

She spotted Alf sitting on a stone by the roadside appearing to rest after a long walk. She could hear the squeaking wheels of a horse-drawn cart coming towards them from the south. Soon she saw a tinker's wagon drawn by an old nag, and beside it walked an equally old man cursing under his breath.

"Good morn' to you," said Alf as the irate tinker came abreast and stopped.

"'Tis hardly a good morn' when one is treated with such disrespect. I was just stopped by soldiers. They searched my wagon and left it a mess," the tinker complained.

"Would you like something to drink?" Alf asked as he produced a bottle of Hedvig's wine.

"'Tis kind of you," said the tinker, somewhat appeased as he reached for the bottle. "You must be a clever thief or a wealthy man to have such fine wine," he said appreciatively after taking some hefty swigs. "'Tis only found in the finest houses."

"A clever thief, I am," answered Alf as the tinker took another deep draught. "Why did the soldiers stop you?"

"Have no idea. They didn' take nothin', which was a blessin'."
The tinker crossed himself and took another slug followed by a burp.
"But they made such a mess o' everythin'."

"Who were they?" asked Alf innocently.

"They wore a royal coat of arms, and I think they should have better things to do than bother an old tinker."

"I have heard rumors that the royal brothers are feuding again," tested Alf.

"Makes no difference t'me who rules as long as I can go 'bout my business."

The two men idly chatted about weather and trade until the tinker had emptied the bottle. "Now that you know I am an outlaw I would appreciate if you kept my whereabouts to yourself," said Alf.

"T'was good of you to share your drink with me. You can rely on my silence," chortled the tinker as he took the reins and started to walk away. "Maybe they were looking for you, eh?" he said with a laugh before he began to hoarsely sing a ballad tune.

Alf stayed where he was until the tinker had disappeared down the road. Then he quickly went over to Kristina and Magnus who were still hiding behind their bush. "We have to lead our horses through the forest until we get past the area where the soldiers are. We will lose some time, but we have no choice."

They returned to the glen where they packed up, saddled their mounts, and began their walk. The forest was silent and dark, and they had to pick their way between huge boulders, trees, and fallen logs. Although their progress was painfully slow, after several hours Alf estimated they were safely beyond the roadblock. They turned again towards the main road where they remounted and once more cantered south. They rode with only short periods of rest. Every time Alf detected people they would get off the road and hide until the travelers had passed. At dusk, while turning off the main road in search of night quarters, they heard the sound of many horses fast approaching. Kristina and Magnus pulled their mounts in among the trees while Alf cautiously crept to the roadside and crouched down behind some thick foliage.

Once the riders galloped past, he reported back, "Those were Duke Erik's men! Now they are both behind us and in front of us!"

"Then we must rest and discuss what to do," suggested Kristina, sounding much more cheerful than she felt. Until now, it had been easy to pretend to Magnus that it was just a game, but now she had begun to feel real fear. She could not show that to Magnus, lest he figure out that they were hunted in earnest. Without any mishaps they could reach the sanctuary of Alf's Smaland forests by the following midday, but now only a miracle would get them through.

Alf decided they could not risk staying at a farm, so they would have to sleep outdoors again. Kristina sighed, remembering how uncomfortable and cold she had been the night before but accepting the wisdom of his decision. After finishing their supper from Hedvig's generous food supply, they sat by their small fire trying to figure out their plan of action.

"Tomorrow, we must take our chances and just keep riding on in the hopes of reaching Smaland forests before anyone catches up with us," said Alf resolutely.

"But how can we possibly escape the soldiers if we stay on the main road?" asked Kristina.

"If the first search party, or parties, are riding south ahead of us, they are likely to keep riding for at least a day," said Alf. "The next party ought to be half a day behind the one we just spotted, and if we are lucky we can stay between the two. We should take that chance and ride at full speed."

"It sounds frightening," said Kristina.

"We can do it, Ninnie," insisted Magnus. "We escaped a much scarier trap in Stockholm."

They bedded down on some dried branches that prodded and pricked Kristina through her saddle blanket and clothes, but she knew it was advisable to keep some distance from the damp and cold ground. Despite her discomfort, she soon fell asleep.

They awoke early, ate their morning meal in silence, and quietly led their horses back to the main road where they resolutely spurred their mounts toward the forests of Smaland. They did not encounter any of Erik's soldiers for several hours. Finally, they could see the edge of the forest looming ahead in the distance, and they began to cheer in triumph.

"I think we will make it!" But Alf's words came too soon. Just then they could hear the faint rumbling of horses on the road behind them.

"Ride for all you are worth. Follow me!" called Alf. He spurred his mount on, and Kristina and Magnus followed his lead. The thundering of hooves grew nearer; and when they reached an open stretch of road Alf looked back over his shoulder in time to see a large group of Duke Erik's soldiers galloping around the bend. The leading knight spotted the three riders in front of him and signaled his men to maximum speed.

As Alf neared a crossroad he spotted another group of Duke Erik's soldiers approaching from the side road. The knight leading this contingent, which undoubtedly was the one that had passed them the day before, visibly reacted to the three galloping figures by increasing his speed. Alf, Kristina, and Magnus still had a head start, but it steadily diminished as they raced for the safety of the dark forest. By the time they reached the first stands of trees, Kristina, who was bringing up the rear, could hear the wheezing of the horses behind her.

As they rode in among the trees she could hear Alf shout, "Stay close!" A few hundred yards into the forest, Alf called a warning before he veered his horse sharply to the left onto a small, narrow trail leading upward. Both Kristina and Magnus managed to rein their horses and turn behind him. The pursuers, who were not forewarned, rode on before they could rein in enough to turn, almost running into one another. Those few moments afforded the fugitives the small lead they desperately needed.

Once again, Alf veered sharply to head for some huge boulders. He rode between two large stones through an opening so narrow that his boots scraped against the rocks on either side. Guiding his horse between two more huge boulders, Alf turned again to ride on as if he were attacking a labyrinth, closely followed by Kristina and Magnus. Their pursuers were able to follow them through the first two passages; but then they got stuck in dead-end corridors too narrow to turn their horses, and the riders to the rear ran into those ahead. Soon the cursing and shouting of soldiers could be heard as they tried to back out of the stone trap. Alf led his companions through one passage after another until they reached the summit of the rocky slope. There they dismounted to observe the commotion below.

"We are safe," exclaimed Kristina with a sigh of relief.

"Not quite," growled a gruff voice behind them.

Chapter 28

"Move, and I will slit your throat!" the gruff voice threatened. Alf froze with a knife-blade against his neck. He was immediately surrounded by a motley band of highwaymen. They were young, hardened, and wiry; and he knew that if he made any sudden move, the knife would sever his jugular.

A fierce-looking brigand held Kristina's hands from behind, but she was first to protest. "This man is Alf of Smaland."

"And I'm the King of Sweden!" mocked the tall rogue holding Alf against his knife.

"I swear by the Holy Virgin. Do you not recognize him?" queried Kristina as she looked from one to the other of the dozen bandits surrounding them. "If you do not, then take us to someone who does. Do you want his life on your conscience?" A murmur of discussion ensued.

"Let us take him to Old Hans," declared the leader. "He knew the real Alf."

"The woman is lying to save their lives," protested one of the men. "Let us take what they have and finish them off."

"Not so fast! This man knew his way through the boulders. I want to know who he is. We can always kill him later," the leader said as he motioned for someone to tie Alf's hands behind his back. Alf was shoved ahead roughly, followed by Kristina and Magnus who were not judged dangerous enough to have their hands bound. Three of the outlaws led their horses as they began to make their way through the trees.

Kristina drew a deep breath as she walked into the silent forest. So awed was she by its magnificence that her anxiety seemed to ease. It resembled a green cathedral, with most of the tall pine trees canopied only at the top, forming a green translucent roof supported by tall branchless trunks, which reminded her of church columns. Pale sunlight spilled through the high boughs and shone to the ground where a carpet of soft, thick moss silenced their steps. The same moss grew like plush green velvet on the stone boulders making them resemble large pieces of furniture haphazardly scattered by some disorderly giant. Everywhere mushrooms spread their contrasting colors into the restful verdancy. Kristina marveled at the yellow clumps of chanterelles and the lovely red stands of poisonous white-dotted toadstools. As she turned her head, a shy doe froze and remained utterly still as they passed by. A small rabbit zigzagged in front of them on the forest path, frightened by a hooting owl overhead. Kristina almost forgot they were prisoners as she walked amidst this enchanted forest filled with peace and beauty.

After walking for an hour, they emerged through an opening among the trees into a clearing where small huts hemmed the perimeter of an open circle. Their approach must have been observed, as their party was clearly expected when they entered the tiny village.

Old Hans stood at the far end of the circle, surrounded by his outlaw band. His harsh outlaw life had prematurely aged him, and though he was stooped and grey, his arms and body were hard and muscular. A number of disheveled women and filthy children stood nearby viewing the visitors with open curiosity.

"You know this man?" asked the leader as he pushed his prisoner toward Old Hans.

The wizened figure leaned forward, his weak eyes squinting. As he moved closer to investigate, his face lit up in a toothless grin, "If he were not dressed like a well-to-do yeoman, I would swear he was Alf of Smaland."

"That is his claim," said his captor.

"Untie him! If it is he, we shall know soon enough," Hans announced. "Give him a bow and an arrow."

Once his bonds were removed Alf massaged his wrists to get the blood flowing. Everyone stared at him intently. Was he, indeed, the legend of the forests, the hero of whom endless tales were told?

One of his captors handed his bow and quiver to Alf, but kept his knife unsheathed should Alf try some trick with the weapon. Alf calmly notched an arrow on the bow string and let it fly across the open area into the door of the largest hut. He quickly let a second shot whiz off in the same direction, which split the first arrow along its shaft. The silence was complete before everyone started cheering and ran up to touch their hero. "Welcome, Alf of Smaland," Old Hans intoned ceremoniously. "You do us honor by your visit."

"The visit was hardly voluntary," Alf mumbled as he threw a sharp glance at the tall outlaw who now looked quite sheepish. "But we are grateful to be here, rather than in the clutches of those who were pursuing us."

"Come, tell us about it, and have something to eat," Old Hans prompted proudly, motioning the visitors toward his hut that was now distinguished by two arrows. "These arrows may not be removed!" he announced as he opened his door.

Old Hans and six of his trusted men sat down with Alf, while the women attended Kristina and Magnus. After introductions all around, Alf told of their flight to Denmark. On hearing his tale, Old Hans offered to have them guided to the Danish border, but suggested one day's delay to allow the time needed to contact other outlaws in the forest. Once every band knew that it was Alf who sought their assistance, the fugitives would travel swiftly and safely.

Kristina was surprised at how unimpressed these bandits were on learning Prince Magnus' identity. Whereas Alf was treated like a king, Magnus was merely looked upon with curiosity. Kristina had to admire how well Alf handled his newfound prominence. He spoke to the men and women of the village with his usual humility, warmth, and calm assurance.

Despite the chill of the October night, the villagers insisted on preparing a feast around a large bonfire in the center of the village. All their stolen and prized possessions were brought from hiding, and Alf and Kristina ate off silver plates and drank from golden goblets. The food was hearty, simple, and tasty. Kristina especially enjoyed the mushroom stews the women had expertly prepared.

While the villagers had heard the ballad extolling Alf countless times, they eagerly called for it to be sung after supper as they lingered by the fires. One young man, with the encouragement of those assembled, started to sing in a strong clear voice.

Who is the lad with the furrowed face?
The lad in hunter's green

Who one fine day will take his place
Beside the king and queen?

And far awide will spread his fame
Like fire to the sea
"They call him Alf," knights will exclaim
"Alf of Small Country."

His quills like summer lightning fly,
He'd strike a leaping flea;
No eagle has so sharp an eye
As Alf of Small Country!

Young man sober, young man sad
Who will be the luck-struck lad
Who one day soon will be clad
All in finery, ah yes, all in finery?

Who tills the cruel unyielding earth
With crops pathetic small?
And who has wife with child to birth,
No horse to help him haul?

And when her sister comes to stay
To help his birthing wife;
Whose babe lives through not e'en one day
Then loses his wee life.

Who has borne this knife sharp pain
With heart that did not wince;
Who's this man so poor and plain
Who'll raise instead the prince?

Young man sober, young man sad
Who will be the luckstruck lad
Who one day soon will have had
High authority, ah yes, high authority?

"His name is Alf," the sister said
To soldiers rough and free;

"Please leave him grieving for his dead
And let his poor farm be."

"But this place we do commandeer
The mercenaries spoke;
And with both deadly sword and spear
They did the sister poke.

They pushed her to the attic high
And had their way with her;
And all could hear her keening cry
For heartless beasts they were.

Upon the stored-up food they fed
When her they'd made with child;
No longer fit to sweetly wed
The suitor she'd beguiled.

Young man sober, young man sad,
Whose wife's sister has gone mad
And threw herself from yon high crag
To lie there lifelessly, ah yes, to lie there lifelessly

Whose wife had grieved a year and then
Too weakened to arise;
Did never speak a word again
And died before his eyes.

Who nailed her in the wooden crate
And dug the six-foot hole?
"They call him Alf," the old priest said,
"God bless his sorry soul."

"His quills like summer lightning fly
He aims them at the moon;
And as the mourning months go by
He knows not night from noon."

Young man sober, young man sad
What misfortunes he has had;

But whose life will turn to glad--and glowing.
Could it be? Ah yes, glowing it could be.

Who all alone in densest leaves
Roams danger-fraught dark wood?
And lies in wait for evil thieves
Who'd butcher all they could?

Those who ride through forest black
Where e'en the fearless flee;
Cry out for rescue from attack
And everywhere is he.

His quills like summer lightning fly
With speed no eye can see;
"They call him Alf," rescued maidens sigh
"Alf of Small Country."

Young man sober, young man sad
Who will be the luck-struck lad?
Who'll estates with fortunes add
To his property, ah yes, to his property?

The king a royal match did hold . . .
Who chanced to pass nearby?
And of this contest to be told,
And who did ask to try?

His quills like summer lightning fell
He shamed all others' skills;
And from the king he won full well
The winner's golden quills.

Who will tutor their son to shoot?
The king and queen agree;
And teach him other skills to boot!
Alf of Small Country.

Young man sober, young man sad
Who will be the luck-struck lad

Who will become himself a tad
Of Sweden's history? Ah yes, of Sweden's history!

Magnus, who had joined the village children high up in a huge oak tree overlooking the gathering, shouted and applauded from above. Alf, who was clearly flattered though more than a little embarrassed, thanked the singers. The young men in turn insisted on hearing stories about Alf's life at the king's court.

Alf obliged and held the outlaws spellbound with the tales they coaxed from him. When Alf finally insisted on retiring, Old Hans offered the use of his hut. Exhausted, the travelers stretched out on fresh straw mattresses and covered themselves with warm, soft fur hides. Quickly they were lulled to sleep by the comforting glow of the fire in the small floor pit and by the singing of the outlaws still outside.

Erik had mixed feelings as he pondered the news of Magnus' escape into the forests of Smaland. While he was disappointed at not having the heir to the throne in his grasp, he was greatly relieved by the knowledge that Kristina was unharmed. Erik had also received reports from the regional leaders charged with capturing the royal fortresses. Most of the forts had capitulated at the sight of his vast forces, but the commanders of Stockholm, Borgholm, and Kalmar castles were still obstinately refusing to surrender. Nevertheless, his plans were going well enough, so he decided that it was time to release Bishop Nils.

"I sincerely regret having had to detain you," he said when the archbishop-elect was brought before him a while later. "But you understand why I had to do so. By now, however, it is common knowledge that the king is imprisoned, so you are free to go."

"I do not relish my captivity, but it redounds more to your disadvantage than to mine," replied the bishop testily. "I am in no rush to leave, so I will stay until the entire populace has learned of my imprisonment."

"You do not wish to leave?" asked Erik as he studied the bishop's stony mien.

"That is correct. Unless you can convince me of the wisdom of your suggestion."

"And how could I do that?" asked Erik uneasily.

"The Church would like to retain the advantages recently gained under your brother. If you get to rule with the nobles' support, I fear the Church could lose her privileges again. Still, if you assure me those privileges will be maintained and that you will add more church-loyal members to the Council, I would be happy to leave Nykoping without informing anyone that my stay here was involuntary."

"I have no interest in your offer. If you do not leave of your own free will, I see no alternative but to extend your stay here as my guest."

Johan Brunkow sat with Queen Marta beneath the iron-barred window of her and King Birger's prison chamber in Nykoping castle; the same chamber where old King Valdemar had been incarcerated. On the same floor were held Lord Johan, several knights, squires, and ladies-in-waiting, all of whom could move freely within its confines.

Marta had been crying for hours, but finally Johan's words of comfort seemed to reach her, and she dried her tears. "I do not know how I would survive without you, dear Johan. The king cannot listen to my concerns all the time."

"Your Majesty, I am happy to be of support," the young champion knight said earnestly. "I understand how you worry about Prince Magnus, and that you need to talk about it. If my humble presence is of help, I am pleased."

Since their imprisonment Marta had started to confide in him. Not only was she worried about Magnus, but also about her husband. At night she thought she could hear guards ascending the stairs to lead Birger to his execution. She realized that these sounds might be imaginary, but she could not sleep as she waited for the door to their chamber to burst open.

"The dukes will not kill their brother. Of that I am certain," Johan assured her. "And the dukes have given orders that Prince Magnus must not be harmed."

"But it might happen anyway," she said as tears welled from her eyes.

"Have courage, my queen," Johan urged. Magnus and his companions have eluded the dukes' soldiers so far, and they should reach Roskilde very soon."

"I pray you are right, Johan," she said while her hands trembled in her lap.

"Who goes there?" demanded one of the sentries at the gates of Roskilde castle.

"Prince Magnus of Sweden," the youngster shouted back with surprising authority before Alf could even speak. "I am seeking my uncle, the King of Denmark. Open up!"

The sentry compliantly stood aside and signaled for the gates to open.

"Not bad," chuckled Alf to Kristina as they entered the courtyard.

In the Great Hall where the tables had been set for supper, the king and queen were watching a game the courtiers were playing by the fire.

"Prince Magnus of Sweden," a steward by the door formally announced. Queen Ingeborg wheeled around. "What a wonderful surprise!" she exclaimed as she rushed forward to greet them. Then she noticed the condition of their attire that had suffered from more than just road dust.

"Please excuse our appearances. We have fled for our lives," Kristina whispered when the king joined them so that Magnus could not hear, "Dukes Erik and Valdemar have imprisoned or maybe even killed the king and queen. With us is Master Alf of Smaland who is responsible for guiding us here safely. Magnus thinks it is all just a game."

"You are certainly welcome," said King Erik Menved, displaying no reaction to the news. "You might want to refresh yourselves before you tell us of your adventures."

"I shall accompany you," said Queen Ingeborg as she led the way to the guest quarters while Erik Menved turned back to join his other guests who eagerly gathered around him to hear the news. "The dukes have taken over Sweden. I wonder if Marta and Birger are still alive?" Erik Menved ruminated aloud.

He failed to notice the brief flicker in Kristoffer's otherwise vacant stare.

Kristina enjoyed every moment of her tepid bath. She was happily humming to herself when Ingeborg entered, followed by Lady Brigitte who had some clothes over her arm. "Kristina, dear, I have brought you one of my favorite tunics. How was your bath?" Ingeborg inquired as she hovered over Lady Brigitte who was arranging the clothing on the bed.

"Heavenly, thank you. It was blissful to shed all that grime," Kristina replied as Ingeborg gestured her lady-in-waiting to leave the room.

When the door finally closed, Ingeborg was bursting with curiosity, "Apart from everything bad going on, you have no idea how happy I am to see you . . . and with that handsome man . . . Now, tell me everything!" She sat down next to Kristina like a little girl demanding to be told a story she already knew had a happy ending. After Kristina was finished Ingeborg exclaimed "Alf is truly a hero."

Kristina nodded and asked "But how are you?"

"I still have no idea who tried to poison me, nor have I gotten with child again. But one day, if God be willing, I shall have a son."

"In the meantime, you will enjoy being around Magnus. He is a brave and sweet child."

"I am looking forward to that," said Ingeborg warmly as she helped Kristina don the lovely tunic. "You look a lot better now," she said as she scrutinized the result.

"I hope so," smiled Kristina, realizing how bedraggled she must have looked when they arrived.

Alf had already washed, changed, and privately recounted their flight to Erik Menved when Ingeborg and Kristina entered the Great Hall. As the queen joined her husband, he whispered in her ear to which she smiled and nodded. Erik Menved then gave hushed orders to his marshal and called for attention as he motioned for Magnus to stand beside him. He put his hand on the boy's shoulder and his expression became serious.

"Lords and ladies. Before we enjoy our supper, I want to thank a very special man for bringing my nephew here to us." The Great Hall fell silent as the king continued; "Prince Magnus' safe arrival is due to the bravery of one man--Alf of Smaland." The king turned to Alf who looked uncomfortable at the attention being focused on him. "Many of you might have heard of him as he is a legend in Sweden. He was born a common man, but he has risen to the trusted position of Prince Magnus' companion. Besides having received an education suited for a prince, he is the best archer known today and well versed in knightly skills. He is, in all but title, a noble and honorable knight. Come forward!" Erik Menved gestured for Alf to kneel before him. He took the double-edged sword his marshal handed him, and let it gently touch one and then the other of Alf's shoulders. "I dub thee knight. Arise Lord Alf of Smaland!"

"Hear, hear," cheered the voices around the Great Hall.

"On your banner you will carry a golden arrow on a field of green," Erik Menved announced as Alf stood up to bow deeply to the Danish king.

Ingeborg added, "Lord Alf, I have the pleasure of sitting beside you tonight."

Alf's eyes met Kristina's for a moment, and she saw them glow with gratitude and pride as he seated himself at the queen's side.

"It was not really a game was it?" asked Magnus who came to stand beside Alf. "My uncles have taken my parents prisoner, and they are ruling Sweden now. Is that not so?"

"Yes, Magnus. I am sorry we did not tell you the truth."

"You thought I would be frightened?"

"Yes, we did. Will you forgive us?"

486

Magnus looked down at the floor before he answered. "I am glad you did not tell me because I would have been afraid. But now, when I know what really happened, I am worried for my parents."

"From all we know, Magnus, they are safe. Your uncles and your father care for one another even though they disagree, like most brothers do at times, and I do not believe that your parents will be hurt." Alf was proud at how convincing he sounded when he saw Magnus relax. He prayed that this time he was telling Magnus the truth.

Alf turned to look for Kristina but did not see her at the dais table. He thought for a moment that she might have retired but then he spotted her sitting at a lower table listlessly staring down at her food. Alf was surprised over her placement, but on second thought he realized why. The daughter of a traitor and discarded member of Birger's family would not have been seated even in that position had she not helped bring to safety the heir to the Swedish throne. He could feel her deep humiliation, and he would have liked to go and sit beside her, but he could not move from his seat until the king or queen bade him to do so. He turned to Queen Ingeborg beside him and saw that her eyes, too, were fixed on Kristina. The queen felt his look, and a sad smile washed over her face.

"How do you think I feel to have my most beloved friend welcomed this way? But there is nothing I can do," she explained.

Alf said nothing, but his heart constricted as he looked at Kristina. His emotion was so strong that, for the first time, he dared to think the obvious. He was deeply in love with her. It was as if the brief ritual of being knighted had given him the right to accept his emotions. He was no longer a woodsman who had fallen into the fortuitous position of being the companion to a prince. Now he was a knight with the right to pursue the hand of a lady. Then he stopped himself. Kristina would not welcome his feelings. She loved Duke Erik. Nevertheless . . . a lady did need the protection of a man.

Erik knew that the time had come to inform the regional leaders about Bishop Nils and Magnus. He had dreaded this moment because he was unsure of how to break the unwelcome news without dampening, or perhaps even losing, their support. He surveyed the Hall at Nykoping castle where the regional leaders were celebrating the fact that Sweden was firmly under Erik's control and the coup had been almost bloodless.

To reward their support, Erik had granted the regional leaders generous tracts of land from estates formerly belonging to Torgils. After these preliminaries, which seemed to greatly impress the beneficiaries, Erik announced that Valdemar, like himself, would thenceforth be called Duke of Sweden rather than Duke of Finland. Observing Valdemar's reaction, Erik could see that he was touched by this demonstration of devotion.

But now the dreaded moment had arrived. The only way to impart the news was to be forthright, and to speak with confidence. Erik took a deep breath before he rose to survey the expectant faces of his followers. Calmly he related Bishop Nils' unanticipated presence at Hatuna.

"We did hesitate when we discovered the Bishop at Hatuna, but we proceeded according to plan because of our lengthy preparations, and the fact that all of you had evinced such a strong desire to thwart the Church's growing influence in the Council. However, I am solely to blame for this misadventure."

There was a murmur among the men as they discussed the unwelcome news and Lord Arnvid conferred with his closest allies. After much discussion Lord Arnvid lifted his hand for silence.

"Again, I speak for all of us when I say that this is deeply disappointing, but as the situation now stands, and until the populace grows accustomed to their new ruler, the risks of freeing the archbishop-elect outweigh those of detaining him. I suggest, therefore, that we allow the bishop to grow mellow in confinement and put our trust in Duke Erik to deal with the situation as it develops." To which all voiced their agreement.

"I wish that were the only bad news I have to impart," said Erik once the Hall grew quiet. "The morning after our attack we discovered that Prince Magnus had escaped; and if he is not already there, he will soon join our brother-in-law in Denmark." A decidedly more agitated murmur rose among the men. Erik raised his voice to be heard over the din. "Against all odds, Alf of Smaland managed to slip away from Hatuna with Prince Magnus. How he did so is a mystery, but

I admit that I admire their escape since we spared no effort to arrest them. Again, I deserve the blame."

Heated debate continued among those present, until finally Lord Arnvid called for silence and spoke again. "What has happened cannot be changed. Again, we rely on you, Duke Erik, to deal with this problem."

Erik knew that he had gotten off lightly. "I am grateful for your confidence. I will do whatever I can to make the best of the situation." He sat down feeling despondent. His aim had been to unite the country, and these unfortunate mishaps could easily lead to its being torn asunder.

"I see you have found my favorite spot," exclaimed Kristina when she discovered Alf sitting with his back against a secluded tree in the arbor below Roskilde castle.

Alf jumped up and smiled. "It is peaceful here, though a bit chilly."

Kristina shivered in a sudden gust that whirled multicolored leaves around the trunks of the trees. "I hope I am not disturbing you."

"You are most welcome," he said as he gestured for her to sit down on his mantle that was spread on the ground. "I have not seen much of you these last days."

"I have been spending all my time with Ingeborg and Magnus," Kristina replied demurely.

"You look like you have something on your mind," he said as he settled beside her.

"I am no longer welcome anywhere," she began, and he could see her eyes well up. "But why were you sitting here, Alf?" she asked to change the subject and quell her tears.

"I was contemplating the fact that I may never be able to return to Sweden again."

"I dream about returning home to Solang. Away from these people and their icy scorn. Ingeborg is doing what she can to protect me, but I am miserable here. I will write Erik and Valdemar to ask them to allow us both to go back. But while I am here I will help and protect Ingeborg," she added. Then she explained about Ingeborg's many miscarriages and their suspected cause. "If Duke Kristoffer were not around the next time she is with child, maybe everything will work out," she concluded.

"But like you, Kristina, I do not foresee his absenting himself from the center of power."

"I am so certain it is him. He is such a vile man."

"You have good instincts, Kristina, so I shall keep an eye on him. I have already gone hunting with him and his friends, and they have invited me to join them again."

"Thank you," she said as she studied his calm, strong face. "I am grateful to have you near, especially now."

"I will always be there for you," he said as they sat quietly together.

"Ask the king and queen to join me and Duke Valdemar," Erik ordered a guard. Erik was rereading the message just received from Kristoffer when the door was flung open and Birger and Marta entered the Hall. Erik felt pity on seeing Marta's pale face deeply lined from lack of sleep.

"Please sit down," he said as he gestured toward a bench by the fire. "Magnus arrived safely in Roskilde accompanied by Alf and Kristina."

"Oh, thank God."

Marta crossed herself and began to cry with relief.

"And that is not all," Erik continued softly. "Alf was knighted by Erik Menved for rescuing them!" Birger looked pleased since Erik Menved, by this gesture, was showing where his allegiance lay. Erik guessed Birger was already dreaming of Danish armies invading Sweden to set him free.

"Forgive me," whispered Marta between sobs. "I would like to go back to my room."

"Of course," said Erik as he called a guard to escort her.

"Thank you for informing us as soon as you knew," said Birger. "From my window, I saw the messenger arrive just a short while ago."

"What I have done, I have done for political reasons," Erik said simply. "I have no desire to cause you any heartache. Still, the best thing would have been if Magnus had been brought back here. Now Marta will miss him."

"You might well be right," agreed Birger as he stared at the floor.

"Would you care for some wine?" Valdemar asked to break the silence.

"Please," Birger responded as the worry for his son drained away, leaving him flooded with relief.

"Sweden is now ruled by me and Valdemar, and the only thing I do not have is your title," said Erik as Birger was handed the wine.

Birger took his time before speaking. "My title as King of Sweden will be mine for as long as I live," he said quietly. "And that title should belong to Magnus one day. But if you want to call yourself king, you need only to ignore my refusal. Who will disagree with the man who commands Sweden's armies?"

"You know why I took over the leadership of Sweden."

"I tried to rectify my mistakes," Birger protested.

"I do not need your crown. I can rule Sweden without being King. I can only hope that one day that title will be mine because I will have earned it."

"Then the people will have to give it to you, because I will not!" said Birger as he drained his cup. "And do not delude yourself that you will be a better ruler than I was. Your motives are purely selfish!" Birger stood up and slammed the door as he left.

Chapter 29

Nykoping 1307

Erik grunted in frustration as he fought the blanket that ensnarled him. Although he was tired and drunk, he could not sleep. The last two fortresses under siege had finally surrendered--an event he had just celebrated, following which he retired to his chamber with one of the girls who had danced for the boisterous crowd. Although he had coupled with the wench, his only desire had been for it to end. As he lay awake listening to her rhythmic breathing, he realized how utterly hollow he felt. Here he was, the undisputed ruler of Sweden, yet the realization left him joyless. He could think only of Kristina. Without her he had lost part of his soul. The knowledge that she loved him was what kept him going, day by day. He was jarred from his reverie when the girl rolled over next to him. Again, he noticed how pretty she was. Yet, all he could think of was the warm glow on Kristina's face when she had slept beside him. He turned away emptier than ever.

He forced his thoughts to politics. In the event that Kristoffer would ever replace Erik Menved as King of Denmark, he could easily be toppled as he would quickly prove himself unfit to rule any kingdom, much less one as powerful as Denmark. Erik guessed that the Danes would welcome another leader once they tasted Kristoffer's cruelty, and that new leader could actually be himself. Erik allowed his train of thought to continue. In the event of Hakon's death once he and Ingeborg of Norway married, he might actually rule all of Scandinavia! The mere thought was an elixir. It was time to visit Hakon again.

Erik studied Valdemar and Hakon slouched in large fur-covered chairs by one of the fire pits in the Great Hall of Akershus. They were enjoying the silence of that castle while its occupants were deep in sleep. Despite his and Valdemar's exhaustion from their long journey to Oslo through a February snowstorm, they cherished this hour alone with Hakon.

"Kristoffer informed us that Erik Menved was so incensed when he learned of our coup that he began to ready an army to come to Birger's aid," Erik began, breaking the comfortable silence. "In spite of Kristoffer's warning, we were totally unprepared when the Danes attacked, and we were unable to offer much resistance. Fortuitously, Erik Menved decided that a truce was in his best interest. All he really wanted to show us was that our position in Sweden is not invincible, or that Birger is not without allies. The result was that we signed a one-year truce."

"His visit had little impact, then," Hakon noted.

"It had a great impact on Birger and Marta, who expected to be liberated. They could not understand why Erik Menved made only a gesture, not a serious effort."

"Well, you can hardly blame them. Speaking of Erik Menved," Hakon said, nearly spitting out the name of his neighbor and supposed ally. "You two are not the only ones he attacked. Without provocation, he broke our peace treaty by burning the island of Hjelm that he had given me in lieu of my maternal inheritance. He is a liar and a snake. I was a fool to believe him. I even withdrew my protection of the Danish refugees so that we could all exist in peace. Meanwhile, he got everything he wanted, and I ended up with nothing!"

"We, like you," Erik confided slowly, "would be much happier if he were not around."

"With a neighbor like Erik Menved, we shall never have peace, " Hakon said as he slammed his cup down on his armrest, spilling its contents on the polished wood.

"I know someone else who is eager to be rid of him," Valdemar chimed in. "Our new neighbor who finally has taken up residence in his dukedom, Southern Halland."

"Kristoffer!" Hakon uttered with a smirk.

"For all his depravity, he would be easier to countenance than his brother," Erik opined.

"Decidedly!" Hakon nodded. "As most of Erik Menved's armies are still engaged in Northern Germany this could be the perfect time to act against him! What a tempting thought. But as a starter, I will infuriate him by once again offering sanctuary to the Danish refugees. I have missed my dear old friend, Count Jakob, here at court."

The men grew silent, savoring the thought of a tranquil future without Erik Menved.

When Erik returned to Nykoping a few weeks later he found a visitor clad in a priest's robe awaiting him in the Hall. Father Olov had come from the Archbishop's rectory in Upsala, and he was looking chagrined to have been kept waiting for days. Erik presumed that he was there to negotiate Bishop Nils' release.

"Come, share our supper," Erik suggested as he greeted the priest. He could see that Father Olov was reluctant to participate in any social ritual, and that he wanted to get his business over with as quickly as possible. "We can talk while we eat," continued Erik without waiting for a response. Father Olov, looking grim, sat down at the dais, while the knights collected in the Hall, noisily discussing the visit to Norway.

"What can I do for you?" Erik asked as he scrutinized the emissary. Father Olov looked youthful, but Erik estimated that he was older than his smooth features suggested, as his cropped hair was flecked with grey. Looking into his eyes, Erik discerned resolve and tenacity.

"I am here to discuss the release of the Archbishop-elect. You must realize the level of anger directed towards you for what you have done. I cannot conceive what it will take to get the Church to forgive your barbaric conduct."

Erik smiled. "And you must know that Bishop Nils is welcome to leave any time he wishes. Your leverage to extract something from me is considerably less now than that which Bishop Nils wielded six months ago. Those who at first reacted violently against his internment appear to have forgotten about his predicament. I know that a small group is still trying to have him released under circumstances discrediting us, but the generous harvest and the resultant prosperity have rendered even the most avid agitation ineffectual."

"Do not underestimate the power of Holy Mother Church."

"I do not, and I know that we must appease Her if we are to rule in peace, so I will tell you what I will do. I will raise tax money for the building of a cathedral in Upsala, and transfer the estate, Øn, which formerly belonged to Lord Torgils, to the Upsala congregation."

By the priest's expression, Erik could see that his offer came as a surprise. Clearly, the priest had counted on a protracted negotiation since from the time Erik had been in control of Sweden, not one single clan had taken up arms against him, and the populace spoke of him with trust. Fully aware that Bishop Nils could have walked away with nothing, Father Olov was unable to hide his pleasure over the offer. Erik knew that both terms benefited Bishop Nils personally, since he would get the glory for building the cathedral and derive the income from Øn. "In return, the Church must agree not to interfere in future affairs of state. In writing," Erik added softly. Father Olov nodded his agreement.

When Bishop Nils and Father Olov left Nykoping castle the following morning, it was with sadness that Erik and Valdemar stood at the window in the audience chamber watching the two men depart without a farewell. They knew their lifelong friendship with Bishop Nils was lost forever.

Erik and Valdemar immediately noticed how anxious Kristoffer was when he greeted them in Motorp on the Swedish-Danish border. Kristoffer, through his chancellor, Anders Hojby, had already laid out his plan for ousting Erik Menved. For their armed participation, Sweden and Norway would receive generous parts of the Danish province of Skane. Erik, Valdemar, and Hakon had already approved the plan in principle, and had even begun to ready their armies in secret.

Kristoffer was nervously moving about his tent while he offered them the two most comfortable chairs. Erik was startled by the change that had taken place in Kristoffer's appearance. During the past year, with few challenging responsibilities, Kristoffer's waking hours were spent scheming against his brother and he seemed habitually in a foul temper, as he was a nasty drunk and rarely sober. Erik noted the lines of bitterness and boredom that deeply etched his face.

"My brother is still trying to force his German allies back into line," Kristoffer said as he downed his cup. "The sooner we attack, the more certain we can be of surprising him."

"I know that you want to seize the moment, but if you conquer Denmark, can you keep it?" Erik asked.

"Well . . ." Kristoffer began as he adjusted his girth to lean forward.

"The sure way of staying in power is to have support from the Danish nobility," Erik interrupted. "When Erik Menved's army returns from Germany, you will face a force larger than ours combined, so you must have strong allies. Do you know how many men will follow you, men who are loyal and not just paying lip service?"

"I have not been able to approach any of them personally, as they could betray my plans. But from what my spies tell me, we can count on many to follow us once we strike."

"How many is many?" asked Erik sharply. "Half of them, or ten out of a hundred?"

"I do not know . . ."

"Erik became the leader of the nobles before he attempted a coup," Valdemar interjected. "They felt their position in the Council was threatened so they had something to gain from a shift in leadership. What can you offer your nobles that is better than what Erik Menved is now providing?"

"They are unhappy with the frequent and costly wars," Kristoffer answered lamely.

"Whoever is king will face the same problem. Denmark must control her neighbors because it means collection of tribute, pure and simple. You have to offer something for which the nobles will turn against your brother, " Erik insisted.

Kristoffer remained silent. Erik could see that he was struggling to find a valid reason other than his own voracious desire for the crown. Then with a glint in his eye he looked at Erik. "I am amazed how you could tolerate my brother on the throne after what he has done to Kristina." Whatever he knew or did not know about Erik and

Valdemar's feelings for Kristina, Kristoffer's comment had the desire effect. Erik leaned forward with narrowing eyes.

"What has he done?"

"He has made it clear that Kristina is no longer to be respected because of her father's treason and the fact she was ousted by the Swedish royal family through her divorce. She has been relegated to the women's quarters, and she eats at a lower table."

"Kristina has stayed in the women's quarters before," Erik objected.

"She was a maiden then, and that was appropriate. She is a mature woman now with the need of direct royal patronage if she is to have any position at our court."

"I cannot imagine that Ingeborg would not stand by her," objected Valdemar.

"It is the king's word that counts," Kristoffer insisted.

Erik sat back. He felt almost physically ill at the thought that Kristina would continue to suffer for his and Valdemar's actions. He realized with horror that she probably thought that she could no longer return to Sweden since she had helped Magnus to reach Denmark. He had to invite her back. Yet he needed to answer Kristoffer's challenge without letting him know how deeply this news had affected him.

"If you want to rule Denmark, you have to figure something out," he said, wanting Erik Menved deposed more than ever. "Because I want to prevent Erik Menved from freeing Birger, I am willing to support you, despite the risks. We can only hope the nobles will rally behind you once you conquer Denmark.

"There is one other matter," Kristoffer added cautiously, as he studied Erik. "As we agree that secrecy is essential, I can hardly prepare my troops in Southern Halland. Could I use Kungahalla as my base of operations?"

"I cannot see why not," said Erik after reflecting for a moment.

"Thank you," said Kristoffer, looking relieved. "I have been in a quandary over how to ready an army without my brother finding out."

"One last question, Kristoffer," Erik said casually. "Was it you who burned the town on the island of Hjelm?"

Kristoffer stiffened. "Why would I have done such a thing?"

"You needed to fuel Hakon's anger to get him to support the ousting of your brother."

"It was an accident. Some fires spread out of control. I have explained that to Hakon."

"Well, he does not believe it, and neither do I," Erik said lightly.

Kristoffer did not reply, but his lips spread in a churlish grin.

"It is good to have you back," King Hakon declared warmly as he embraced Count Jakob in his audience chamber. "Nothing has been the same since you left."

Count Jakob refrained from mentioning the obvious--that he had had no choice in the matter--and seated himself in the chair to which Hakon motioned. "I am here now, and that is all that counts," Jakob said. "Much has happened in the past two years," he continued, hoping that the king suffered a bad conscience for having caused his dear friend to be banished for so long.

"It certainly has," agreed Hakon, seemingly unmoved by Jakob's travails. "The balance of power is now tipping in our direction for a change."

"If your prospective son-in-law could place a puppet on the Danish throne, it would seem that way."

"What do you mean?"

"If Erik Menved were replaced by Kristoffer, it would follow that Kristoffer would be beholden to whoever helped him gain the crown."

"Erik, Valdemar and I are all helping him. He would be grateful to all of us."

Jakob prayed that he was not overdoing it, but he knew that his candor was a trait the king appreciated. And he had no other choice. He had to stop Erik from usurping Erik Menved. As long as Northern Halland remained Danish territory Erik Menved would allow Erik to manage it, but he would never allow Erik to claim it as his own. Kristoffer, on the other hand, would deed the area to Erik if he became king. And once Northern Halland actually belonged to Erik, there would be no chance for Jakob to regain even the smallest part.

"I do not foresee that you would benefit as much as would Erik," Jacob ventured. "Erik is acting as if he will be King of Scandinavia. I might have been away from court for a couple of years, but I still hear rumors. Did you know that Kristoffer is readying his troops at Kungahalla?"

Jakob enjoyed seeing Hakon's eyes flicker in surprise. "It is my fortress. Erik would never allow anyone else to use it without asking my permission."

"Well, he has in fact, and such action does not demonstrate much respect for you, your Majesty. But then he might feel that he does not have to show you any, since he could easily eliminate you once he has removed Kristoffer from the Danish throne. The Danes will thank him for getting rid of Kristoffer once they discover what a ruthless ruler he can be. It seems only logical that if Erik is ruling Sweden and Denmark, and eventually is expected to rule Norway, he might find it inconvenient to wait."

"I hardly believe that!" said Hakon dismissively.

"Then why would he let Kristoffer use your fortress without your permission? It seems as if he does not deem you someone to reckon with."

King Hakon sat silent for a while. "Maybe Erik is behaving haughtily, but I am sure that is all it is," he said finally, but without the same conviction.

"You know him so much better than I do," smiled Jakob ingratiatingly. "But I would be a poor friend if I did not tell you what I hear." Hakon nodded uneasily.

Erik was in high spirits as he neared Akershus castle. He did not even mind the dry road-dust that kept swirling in ever-thicker clouds around him. He simply drew the scarf tighter around his mouth and nose while he listened to the cursing of his men in the hot afternoon sun.

Upon arriving at the home of his future father-in-law, his mood was enhanced further by a relaxing hour in a steaming hot tub scrubbing the grime off his body and out of his hair and ears. His sense of wellbeing made him oblivious to Hakon's solemn mien when they greeted each other. "Before we speak of anything else," Erik began, handing Hakon two scrolls. "Please read these. The first is a letter to me, the second is a copy of my reply."

Hakon slowly read the first message that was written by Kristoffer.

"Dear Erik,
Erik Menved just made peace with his German allies in Fermen on the first day of June. He opened those negotiations in early May, making me wonder if he knows about our plans which took shape around that time. While we have worked hard to prepare our troops, we are not yet ready. Should we strike before my brother returns, or should we wait until we can mount a massive assault? I am in urgent need of your advice. Yours faithfully, Kristoffer"

Hakon then read Erik's answer.

"Dear Kristoffer,
I share your concern, and I am equally disappointed. We have to wait, but if we--you, Hakon, Valdemar, and I--stand together, we can still accomplish what we had planned. I shall be ready by early fall, and I will soon leave for Norway to check on the situation there. In the meantime, continue preparing for what will be a victorious war. Yours, Erik"

"Our situation has changed drastically since we last met," Hakon began.

Erik quickly replied, "But I still believe that we can be successful. With our combined strength we surely can defeat the Danes."

"Maybe," agreed Hakon, "but I have decided that my armies will not participate!" Erik sat stunned. "For me, the game is no longer worth playing," Hakon continued in a measured voice attempting not to show his anger. "Had Erik Menved still been involved in his German wars I might feel differently, but he is not. Kristoffer has a crown in the offing. You stand to consolidate your rule of Sweden. But I have nothing of comparable value to gain, so count me out."

"Without you, we cannot win this war."

"I do not really care!"

"Why do you say that?" asked Erik. "Have I done something to offend you?"

Hakon looked directly into Erik's eyes. Erik's steel-blue gaze met his without wavering, only with innocent query. The resentment Count Jakob had carefully nursed suddenly welled forth.

"You think everything is due you," Hakon began. You have succeeded in making the Swedes embrace you, and now you think we should all bow to you, me included. You took it upon yourself, without even the courtesy of consulting me, to lend Kungahalla to Kristoffer. I allowed you to use my fortress during your confrontation with Birger as a gesture of support. This hardly entitles you to treat it as your own."

"I never thought it was. I... I..."

"I know! It never even entered your mind. I assume you think Northern Halland is yours, as well?"

"It is under my rule," countered Erik lamely.

"It belongs to Denmark, and its rule was handed to me by Count Jakob. I chose to let you rule it; so, if you think it will be yours permanently, you should think again."

"I did not mean to offend you. Kristoffer needed a place to conduct his military preparations in secret."

"And you lent him *my* fortress."

Erik stood up to face Hakon. "Hakon, you know that I never meant to offend you. You should not allow your anger with me to stop our preparations," he pleaded.

"I am not participating!" Hakon declared turning away, showing that he considered their conversation finished.

Erik was shaken as he walked down the corridor. If Erik Menved invaded Sweden with all his armies within the next two months, Erik would have great difficulty defending it. As originally planned, it had seemed virtually impossible to lose, and now he knew that there was no way to win.

With long strides he entered the Great Hall where his knights had joined their Norwegian comrades. He noticed that the Danish "rebels" were back, and the Hall was noisy as old friends were reunited. Erik nodded to the left and right as he walked among the throng trying to locate Mats. Finally, he found him at the far side of the Hall and gestured for him to follow towards the guest quarters.

"That is a blow," Mats dolefully agreed after Erik had, in a strained voice, related his conversation with Hakon.

"I know that there is nothing I can do to change Hakon's mind," concluded Erik with a sigh. "Especially, as he is right. He does not have as much to gain as do we and Kristoffer. And I was stupid not to have sought his permission before lending out Kungahalla. I am sure he would have agreed."

"Maybe you should let him know how you feel."

Erik decided to ask Hakon's forgiveness, but the king had left to hunt. Erik waited for many hours, but then he felt obliged to leave as he had already announced his departure and did not want to look ridiculous by staying on. Besides, he suspected that Hakon would not change his mind no matter what he said.

Erik mounted his horse. He had only a short ride from his camp in Markaryd on the Swedish side of the border to meet Erik Menved who had called for a parley in Danish Orkelljunga. After an uneventful trip through the dense forests Erik emerged in a glen where he dismounted outside the meeting tent. Erik Menved appeared dwarfed in size by Erik when they shook hands, but his authoritative manner left no doubt in anyone's mind who held the upper hand. Before they took their places, Erik Menved held up his hand to halt the men who had begun to follow. "My lords. The duke and I will talk privately before we commence our meeting. Take some refreshments in my tent. We shall summon you when we are ready."

"We should discuss Kristoffer's dream of wearing the Danish crown," Erik Menved began as he sat down in his chair without taking his eyes off Erik. "You, if anyone, know it is only natural to nurture such a dream. But unlike you, dear Erik, he is no threat to any throne." The king smiled coldly. "Even if, against all odds, he is successful in getting rid of me, his own allies would be the first to recognize his glaring weaknesses, and they would quickly rise against him. But

Kristoffer, inspired by your success, is blind to that simple truth and he wants to forge ahead."

Erik Menved looked steadily at Erik who tried to appear calm, which was difficult as he was uncertain as to how much the king knew of his own involvement with Kristoffer.

"Kristoffer is my brother, and despite his treasonous ambition, I am concerned for his welfare. I do not want those loyal to me to act against Kristoffer, or those with grievances against me to side with him to create an opposition camp. I doubt they could ever pose a real threat, but it would be an irritation we could well do without."

"Are you the only one aware of his designs?" Erik asked, his voice measured. "Others might have heard rumors."

"If so, I will downplay the seriousness of Kristoffer's intentions. To dream does not mean to pursue. I will talk to him, and I promise you that if he does not want to lose Southern Halland, he will behave."

"You are probably right. And as you are no longer fighting with your neighbors . . . I doubt he will try anything now. "

Erik Menved interrupted him coldly. "Erik, I am not a fool. I knew about the armaments that were under way in Sweden and at Kungahalla. Once I learned how extensive the preparations were, I had no choice but to make peace in Germany before you were ready to strike. And although I am disappointed that you would ally your-self with Kristoffer, I am here now with a simple suggestion of how to solve our present situation." Erik felt humiliated by Erik Menved's disdainful tone and wanted to say something in his own defense. But Erik Menved continued without looking at him. "Your reason for supporting a change of ruler in Denmark is to prevent my invading Sweden to free Birger. But if you free Birger and allow him some minor compensations, I would have no reason to invade Sweden, would I?"

"What minor compensations do you have in mind?" asked Erik.

"Why not give Birger Lord Torgils' domains in Linkoping and Vaxjo counties? I know you have already deeded away many of Torgils' properties, but you still have those. Naturally, Marta's dowry would remain hers. What do you say?"

"I assumed this meeting was about negotiations between Sweden and Denmark, not Sweden's internal affairs."

"As I know all about your plan to oust me," the king continued, "I certainly do not view Birger's freedom as an internal Swedish matter, and I am offering you the undeserved courtesy of bringing this up in private. Never forget that the Danish army is quite a force to reckon with--especially when it is supported by some of our allies from Northern Germany. I am still not proposing that Birger be returned to power, merely to a decent life. I am also thinking of my sister."

"I doubt if he, or they, would be content with that, once they are free."

Erik Menved ignored Erik's comment. "Without setting Birger and Marta free, there will be war, Erik. It is as simple as that." Erik Menved stood up to signal the end of their private talk. "I have to attend another meeting, so we do not have time for final negotiations now. I suggest that we settle on a period of truce and then meet back here in a few months to decide on the precise terms. Agreed?"

"Part of those terms must be the release of Birger?"

"Absolutely. As you did not kill him, you must have known that this moment would come." When Erik did not reply, Erik Menved sent word for the members of the meeting to join them. The final negotiations, it was agreed, would take place before the coming Christmas at the same location with each party bringing no more than two hundred men. Erik was charged with informing his allies "whoever they may be," of these decisions.

On the trip to Kungahalla Erik could feel his future crumbling around him. If Birger were set free, his followers would enthuse and rally. Intrigues and unrest would follow, and Sweden would be weakened. Perhaps even to the point that Erik Menved's armies could once more place Birger on the throne. Everything Erik had accomplished would be wasted. These thoughts were still swirling in his mind when he saw Kungahalla looming up against the darkening horizon. He dismounted and entered the familiar stronghold.

"I have been worried about you," Kristoffer began as he rose from his place by the fire. "Your message said you would be here much earlier. Did something go wrong?"

Erik noticed that no servants were present, a sign that Kristoffer was brimming with curiosity to hear how Erik's meeting with his brother had gone. Erik sank down by the table and poured some wine into a silver goblet.

"I am as hungry as a wolf," Erik began as he looked over the table laden with dishes of food.

"The table was set for you," said Kristoffer as he pushed a platter of venison closer to Erik.

Erik took a generous helping. He enjoyed being back in Kungahalla, though the fortress still resembled a pigsty. As he devoured his meal he gave Kristoffer a terse summation of what had taken place in Orkelljunga. "Maybe we thought we would rule Scandinavia," he said with a forced laugh, "but now we know better."

Kristoffer nodded morosely. "Not only does my brother retain the upper hand, but you have a quarrel with Hakon." He poured himself another chalice of wine and burped loudly after he downed it in one long swallow. "Either I must remain content with my dukedom and you must set your brother free, or we have to plan some drastic action. Should you be interested in the latter option, I have a suggestion," Kristoffer added.

"Which is?"

"The element of surprise . . . It worked in Birger's case. We could do the same when you meet my brother in a few months." Erik waited for Kristoffer to continue, but the Dane just smiled broadly while allowing his suggestion to sink in.

"If we capture Erik Menved would you imprison him or kill him?" Erik asked.

"He must be killed," Kristoffer said with conviction. "His death could be arranged so as not to arouse suspicion. We must find a scapegoat among his enemies to blame. Once he is dead, the Danish nobles would rally behind me quickly enough."

"I could not kill Birger. Can you really kill your brother?"

"Surely you jest! My brother has done nothing but make my life unbearably dull."

Erik tried to stop straying to the delectable thought of remaining the unopposed ruler of Sweden, with Birger locked up and Kristoffer as a friendly and grateful neighbor. "If you were successful, Kristoffer, our problems would be solved. On the other hand, the plan could have terrible consequences if it failed."

"I know who the culprit will be," chuckled Kristoffer suddenly. "One of my oldest friends hates my brother for what he once did to his family. His sentiment is well known, and the only reason that he has not been expelled from court is because of me. I think the time has come for Lord Rolf to repay me for all these years of privilege under my protection," Kristoffer mused. "We will kill Rolf and place him, along with the murder weapon used to kill my brother, in the royal tent. My brother's corpse will hold the weapon used to kill Rolf who finally sought his revenge, and Erik Menved died defending himself."

Erik cringed at the idea of Kristoffer not only killing a brother but sacrificing a lifelong friend, as well. But neither seemed to bother Kristoffer in the least. On the contrary, he looked enormously pleased with his idea.

"There is one disadvantage, however. I cannot help with the preparations. I have just received a message from my brother ordering me to return to Southern Halland and not to leave unless he explicitly requests it. If I do not obey he will know that I am up to something, and I will lose my dukedom--and with it, my army." Kristoffer remained silent for a moment. "But we must go through with it, Erik. I cannot be dictated to by my brother for the rest of my life. Neither do you need your inept brother to be free to meddle in your affairs." Erik sat pondering the scheme. "And you will not have to soil your hands, Erik," continued Kristoffer. "I shall do the dirty work before you even get to the meeting. All you have to do is to bring a substantial number of men, as we cannot be sure how many soldiers will escort my brother. For the present, my men will pretend to disarm while they are actually doing the opposite, and my dear brother should suspect nothing. And afterwards, when it is all over, I promise you the full extent of my gratitude. You will not be disappointed!"

Erik still was not ready to give his commitment to Kristoffer's plan.

"Why do you hesitate?" asked Kristoffer. "If you were willing to fight a war, why not eliminate my brother in a far easier manner?"

"It is underhanded."

"Was not the imprisonment of your brother underhanded?"

"That was different," objected Erik. "He was an ineffectual ruler. Your brother is quite the opposite." Despite his objections Erik could not quell the memory of Birger's hatred and insults, and of his own feelings of desperation as he and Valdemar fled Sweden. He would never accept Birger interfering in his affairs again. He also remembered what Kristoffer had told him about Erik Menved's humiliating treatment of Kristina at the Danish court.

"I will join you," Erik finally decided.

Erik attacked the young knight with more ferocity and greater speed than his opponent had anticipated from someone older. The knight took a few quick steps backward to get out of Erik's reach before he stumbled and fell on his back. As he looked up he could see the dukes' eyes shine with fury through his visor. Erik felt the adrenalin pump through his system at the sight of the younger man vanquished at his feet. Day after day he had practiced at arms and this was the best opponent he had just left in the dust of Nykoping's courtyard.

"You are a great swordsman, my lord," the knight huffed.

Erik pulled off his helmet and threw it to the ground. He was surprised at his own single-minded urge to best any man wielding a sword. His eyes softened as he reached down to help the knight to his feet. As he pulled him up he could hear horses thundering over the drawbridge, and when he turned he saw Mats and his escort rein in their mounts on the far side of the courtyard. Erik walked over to greet his marshal. " Is Hakon supporting us this time?"

Mats caught his breath and dismounted before he answered. "He will not send an army."

"Damn him!" grunted Erik. "He wants to get rid of Erik Menved as much as we do, but because he is angry with me he will not participate."

"He does, indeed, want to get rid of Erik Menved. He will help us monetarily."

Erik's anger subsided. "That is something. But he must not believe that we can succeed, or he would participate himself."

They entered the Great Hall and sank down in the chairs in front of the fire.

"I have openly called off our military preparations because of our truce with Denmark," said Mats as he pulled off his boots and warmed his feet close to the flames. "On my way back, however, I met with our most trusted regional leaders and they are keeping small contingents ready to converge on Orkelljunga at the appointed time. And do not worry," he said quickly when he saw Erik open his mouth. "I disguised myself and the meetings took place at remote places. I am confident that Erik Menved's spies will have little to report."

"Lord Alf," called Erik Menved as he motioned for Alf to join him for a stroll towards the water below Roskilde castle. "I need your help!"

"Whatever I can do," said Alf bowing to the man who had knighted him.

"A few weeks ago, I met with Duke Erik to discuss continued peace between Sweden and Denmark through the release of King Birger." Erik Menved then confided to Alf how Hakon, Kristoffer, Erik and Valdemar had plotted to depose him from the Danish throne. "They must be disappointed to have their plan exposed," he mused. "Anyway, we are to meet in December, but I do not trust my brother, or Erik. They have too much riding on my downfall, so I need your help."

"I have no reliable connections at Duke Erik's court."

"That is not what I have in mind. I have my own sources, but they will not be likely to learn much because Duke Erik will be extremely cautious. No, I need your help in keeping me informed of any military movement within Smaland around the time of our meeting."

"I have the best spy system available--the outlaws of Smaland, your Majesty. If you will arrange to have messengers at specific points along the border, I shall see they get what information we gather."

"I knew you would prove to be worthy of my trust, Lord Alf."

The meeting between Erik Menved and Erik was scheduled to occur on the seventeenth day of December. Early on the preceding morning, Erik Menved had set out for the final ride to the Orkelljunga meeting place. At the same time, various Swedish contingents began moving toward the Danish border. The moment the first armed men entered the forest of Smaland, the news of their coming was already on its way to the Danes along a human chain the outlaws had formed through the forest. The sighting by the first observer was passed on to the next by means of messengers stationed in a straight line so they could shoot an arrow with a message to the next relay point faster than soldiers could ride the narrow, winding road at full gallop. By the time Erik's first troops reached Markaryd, a Danish messenger was already on his way to Erik Menved.

The Danish monarch was not concerned over the first report. Erik had the right to bring two hundred men, and the soldiers in Markaryd had not yet reached that number. Erik Menved continued traveling, but subsequent reports of soldiers at various points along the border caused him to halt. Something was clearly afoot. Erik Menved decided to send a pair of trusted knights ahead to Orkelljunga to ascertain Kristoffer's involvement. In the meantime, he would await further developments at a nearby estate belonging to a friend.

Kristoffer was all smiles as the two Danish knights rode into camp. If, as the knights informed him, the king was not far behind, everything would proceed according to plan. The knights pretended to be inspecting everything for the king's arrival while keeping an eye on Kristoffer. Once finished with their inspection, they settled down for a friendly drink.

As the hours passed, Kristoffer became progressively more edgy, which he tried to conceal by pretending to get intoxicated while his friend, Lord Rolf, was indeed getting seriously drunk. Kristoffer saw that as an added bonus. He would be easy to deal with.

As the hours dragged by, Kristoffer desperately tried to figure out how to warn Erik about the delay of the king's arrival. If Erik rode into the camp with more soldiers than expected before Lord Rolf and Erik Menved were killed, the situation would turn against them.

As Kristoffer stood up to heed the call of nature, he noticed that two knights followed him to do the same. When he went to his tent to get some special wine, it was no mere coincidence that one of the knights suggested that he help carry the precious liquid. It was impossible for him to be alone for even one moment in order to send someone to warn Erik. As the night wore on, Kristoffer no longer had any doubts that Erik Menved suspected foul play. His brother had not appeared, and his two knights were watching Kristoffer's every move. He decided to become drunk in earnest. He did a good job of it, and soon he was sound asleep in his tent, flanked by Erik Menved's snoring knights.

Erik could feel blood pumping in heavy surges through his neck veins as he spurred his horse on. The pitch-dark December night was bitter, but no snow had fallen. He was following behind Mats who had insisted on being the first to enter the Danish camp should an ambush await them. They were riding as fast as they could on the path with the aid of torches held high over their heads. As Erik looked back he could see an endless column of flickering lights snaking its way through the murky forest.

When they finally reached the meeting place where the sentinels had already been overpowered by Erik's scouts, the Danes were rudely awakened by the Swedes riding in among their tents. It did not take long for Erik to discover that all the soldiers in the camp belonged to Kristoffer and that Erik Menved had never arrived.

"What in hell happened?" Erik asked Mats furiously. "If Erik Menved was not coming, why did Kristoffer not warn us? We did not have to give ourselves away by disabling sentries and storming into the camp full force!"

"Go to Kristoffer's tent and you will find the explanation," suggested Mats who had already been through the camp.

Erik understood all too well when he saw Kristoffer passed out between two knights dressed in Erik Menved's colors. Even if

Kristoffer had wanted to, he could not have sent a warning. But were Erik Menved's knights in Kristoffer's tent because the king knew his brother was involved in a conspiracy, or only because he suspected it? If Erik Menved was uncertain of his brother's involvement, there was little to gain by giving Kristoffer away.

"Where is Erik Menved?" Erik asked as he shook one of the Danish knights. He looked angrily at the dazed man. "Why is your king not here?"

The knight stood up, punchy from his drunken state, attempting to give excuses. Erik cut him short. "I do not understand what you are trying to say. What I do understand is that Erik Menved is not here without even the courtesy of informing me of his altered plans. You can all consider yourselves under guard until I have an explanation."

The Danish knights were taken aback by Erik's flaring anger which was exactly what he intended as he needed time to consider his next move. He was not sure that he could turn the tables and make himself appear the aggrieved party. "Detain the soldiers in the meeting tent and the two knights in the king's tent!" he instructed Mats.

Mats, who grasped Erik's reasoning, quickly called out his orders. Despite his stupor, Kristoffer sensed the cover Erik was offering him.

"What is going on here? How dare you?" Kristoffer screamed as Erik's soldiers dragged him away to the king's tent. "My brother will punish you for this villainy!" Erik was impressed with the performance, considering the hangover Kristoffer must have been nursing. But there was little else to applaud. Lost was the chance to prevent Birger's release. The Danish nobility might be tired of the high cost of wars, but if they suspected Erik of arriving at a peace meeting with the intention of harming their king, they would find new resolve to part with their money.

He ordered his men to search the area in case any of Erik Menved's soldiers lay in wait, and for the majority of his own men to return to Sweden so the Danes would not realize how many more than the agreed number he had brought with him.

"I do not think we fooled them," Erik muttered when Mats rejoined him after having posted guards around the entire area.

In the morning Erik had Kristoffer and his men, as well as Erik Menved's knights, assemble in the center of the camp. "I am insulted by your king's lack of common courtesy," he barked loudly, "However I am letting you go, all of you. But before I do, I demand that you, Kristoffer, Duke of Southern Halland, publicly swear not to retaliate against me, now or ever, for having detained you."

Kristoffer raised his hand and pledged his oath. Slowly Erik and Kristoffer shook hands. Without even moving his lips Kristoffer whispered a barely audible "thank you." Then gruffly and loudly, he bid his farewell.

Chapter 30

Roskilde, Denmark 1308

Kristina heard the long blasts of a ship's horn announce its arrival. She rushed to the window in time to see a Danish troop barge nearing the dock below Roskilde castle. It was a large, open vessel with soldiers and weapons covering every inch of the deck. Banners from various Danish clans fluttered in the wind along the railings. The distance was too great for her to recognize any individual, nor could she spot the banner she was seeking. Anxiously, she rushed down the corridor and the stairs.

She was not the only one to have heard the ship's heralding. The courtiers in the Great Hall were heading for the doors, while throwing on mantles to shield against the biting winter winds. Young wives rushed ahead with eager expectation written on their faces, followed by older courtiers who moved with the dignity of those who had witnessed many homecomings of fathers, brothers and sons. Kristina was surprised at the intensity of her fear as she quickly strode toward the dock. She reminded herself that this was the first vessel to return, and that she should not be disappointed if Alf was not aboard, but she hastened her steps nevertheless. She noticed immediately that the ship carried no wounded--which indicated a peaceful expedition--as casualties were often sent back on the first ship. She searched eagerly for Alf's distinctive green banner. Finally, to her great relief, she spotted it by the aft railing. As Alf came down the gangplank she threw her arms around him and hugged him fiercely.

"Thank God for delivering you back safely," she laughed with relief.

"If this is how you greet me when I never even got a chance to fight, how will I be met if I return with battle wounds?" he asked with an amused smile.

She felt a little embarrassed by the spontaneity of her welcome, but as she looked into his eyes she could see that it pleased him. "Let us take a stroll in the orchard. I need to get my land legs back."

They walked in silence. Snow patches were hugging the bases of the apple trees that stretched bare branches towards the silvery sky. "What happened?" she asked as she pulled her cloak tightly about her.

"Erik did not come to sign a peace treaty. He descended upon the Danish camp with the obvious intention of capturing, if not killing, Erik Menved," he replied. "But Erik Menved never made it to the campsite. He is safe and well."

"Why would Erik attack him?"

"Erik Menved insisted on King Birger's release as a condition for peace between Denmark and Sweden, so Erik hoped to obviate that necessity. For the first time since seizing the rule of Sweden, I feel he made a serious miscalculation. Not only must he now free Birger to avoid all-out war, but he has made a powerful enemy of Erik Menved. Rumor has it that Erik Menved suspects Kristoffer of being the real culprit behind Erik's treachery, so we may not see Kristoffer at court for some time."

While Kristina had always believed Erik to be infallible and had cheered his every action, she could not condone the fact that Erik had allied himself with a brute like Kristoffer. Nevertheless, questioning Erik's actions, even in the slightest, made her feel as if she was betraying their love. "You arrived here safely, Alf, and for that I am grateful."

"I understand how betrayed you must feel," Ingeborg confided to her husband who had made every effort to hide his fury over Erik's sneak attack, as she was suffering from a devastating headache. But she knew him well and could sense the depth of his anger. "Are you sure that it was a premeditated scheme?" she queried.

"I have no doubt, Ingeborg, and every instinct I possess tells me that Kristoffer was behind it. Incensed though I am, I can still understand your brothers not wanting to share power with Birger. With me out of the way they would not have to. But that my own brother would actually want me dead . . ." his voice trailed off. "Erik would never allow his brother to be killed, no matter what danger that posed."

Ingeborg realized that this was the perfect moment to impart her own suspicions about Kristoffer, but her husband looked so miserable that she hesitated to do so.

"Kristoffer was not always like that," Erik Menved continued. "We were close as children, but that changed when I became king. Our father's murder was not the first assassination in our family, and from what I can see, it might not be the last." His voice broke. "Still, Kristoffer is my brother. However, I cannot countenance him now. I do not want him here at court."

Erik Menved's face was contorted with anger and sadness. His suffering was so evident that she almost forgot her blinding headache. "Shall we try again to start a family of our own?" she asked as she reached out and touched his arm. "To rear a new generation with love, and security."

He leaned forward and pressed his lips to her hand. "There is nothing I wish for more."

Ingeborg's monthly flow was late by three weeks and she knew that she was with child again. She was filled with joy as she pulled the bed curtains open, stuck her feet into her shoes, and wrapped her thick robe around her. She quickly washed up, drew on her clothes, and was humming to herself when she noticed a light flicker outside her window. When she looked out she could see only a single torch moving towards the castle. Seeing no banner and only a single man, she surmised he was a messenger. In the pale light she caught a glimpse of the crest on the messenger's tunic that belonged to Kristoffer. Was he coming back? If he was hoping to return she had to know in order to prevent it. She entered the Great Hall as the messenger arrived. He bowed deeply when he saw her. "I bring a message for the king."

"I will give it to him," Ingeborg said as she took it from his hand. "Go to the kitchens and have something to eat. I will let you know if the king needs to send a reply."

She went up the stairs, slowly and with the dignity befitting her rank. She had never read any of her husband correspondence behind his back, but her fervent desire to finally give birth to an heir emboldened her. She broke the seal and read Kristoffer's pleading words to his brother to allow him back at court. The letter was well crafted, and she felt sure her husband's heart would have softened at Kristoffer's pledge of eternal devotion.

Slowly she walked back to her chamber torn between loyalty to her husband and the need to give Denmark a crown prince. By the time she entered her room she had no doubt about what to do. "Good morn," she smiled at Lady Brigitte and Kristina who were setting up the morning meal. "I need your help, dear friends," she said as she sat down at the table to show them the letter.

As months passed their vigilance paid off when the three women intercepted two more communications from Kristoffer. But Ingeborg's luck ran out one day when she and Erik Menved were standing in the courtyard as a messenger arrived. She could do nothing but watch as her husband read the missive from his brother. She saw his eyes soften before he put it down.

"Anything interesting, my dear?" she asked.

"It is a very contrite letter from Kristoffer. He wants to return to court. I suppose that we cannot keep him away forever. You should read his letter. It is quite moving."

"I would prefer if he came back after I have our child. I do not like the way he always stares at me, as if he wants me to lose the babe."

"In your present condition you are overly sensitive, Ingeborg," said Erik Menved kindly.

Ingeborg knew that it would do no good to argue if she was not ready to tell her husband of her suspicions. But she had, after all, succeeded in delaying Kristoffer's return for many months. She felt confident that this time she would give birth to a healthy child.

The sudden storm broke in full fury as Kristoffer's ship left the safety of the harbor to make the voyage to Roskilde. In no time at all, the wind had built to ferocious strength; and the ship, tossed about by irrational gale winds, cavorted on the choppy waves. Even though Kristoffer had withdrawn to the relative warmth of the captain's cramped quarters, there was no escaping the ship's movements or the heaving sensation in the pit of his stomach. God was surely punishing him.

During the preceding months he had repeatedly written his brother to beg forgiveness for having been so misled by Erik. "I had nothing to do with Erik's plans," he had written. "At the time, I was simply looking for a close friendship, and did not realize how much Erik had to gain if you were no longer king. I was shocked about Erik's ambush in Orkelljunga. Could you find it in your heart to forgive your penitent brother for having had the poor judgment to befriend Erik?" When Kristoffer penned his first effort he had felt abashed at his duplicity; but as he dispatched successive drafts, he came to believe his own words. Erik had seduced him. He was nothing but a victim! Yet seemingly endless months passed without a reply. Clearly, Erik Menved had not been swayed.

When Erik Menved finally responded to his last letter by inviting him to visit Roskilde, Kristoffer drew a deep sigh of relief. Isolated in Southern Halland for what had seemed like an eternity, away from court and shunned by the nobility, he had yearned to return to Roskilde if for no other reason than to escape his wife. Despite the fact that their marriage had produced three sons, it remained nothing but a political alliance as he had little affection for her. Euphemia, on the other hand, felt that life at the Danish court was the only thing that made her existence bearable. Having to listen to her endless nagging had driven him almost insane. But now he had avenged those insufferable months by refusing to bring her along to Roskilde. She had cried, implored, screamed and threatened--all to no avail. The thought of her, left behind and pining for her friends at court, made the violent heavings of the ship almost bearable.

Dusk was falling when Kristoffer arrived at Roskilde. He was utterly grateful when at last he entered the warmth of the Great Hall to find the court assembled for supper. When his brother came forward and embraced him, he almost cried. "God bless you," he whispered.

"Let us never again mention what happened," said Erik Menved as he held his brother at arm's length, looking him in the eyes. "But from now on I demand total loyalty. Do you understand?"

"I do. And you have my unswerving devotion," Kristoffer pledged unabashedly.

"Good," said Erik Menved as he walked towards Ingeborg by the dais table. Kristoffer saw that she was far gone with child. She met his gaze with a faint, triumphant smile. He knew he had to conceal his disappointment over her condition, so he greeted her warmly. When they stood together, a hush fell over the crowd. Why the brothers had been estranged, no one knew for certain, but the incessant rumors had been close to the truth.

"Let us never forget that the duke is my brother," announced Erik Menved as he put his hand on Kristoffer's shoulder, "and welcome him back to court."

"Hear, hear," called those assembled.

As Kristoffer took the position of honor beside his brother, he once again felt secure and promised himself that henceforth he would be much more careful.

Birger, with Johan Brunkow at his side, presented himself promptly at midday in Erik's private chamber in Nykoping castle. Erik, Valdemar, Mats, and Abjorn, who were already seated around the table, greeted them solemnly as they took their places.

Erik felt a pang of conscience at the sight of Birger's pallor. A year and a half in prison had taken its toll. His brother had lost weight, and there were deep, dark circles under his eyes. Even his hair looked colorless. It would be good, thought Erik to himself, if Birger spent some time outdoors to regain a healthier appearance before others saw him. The way he looked now, everyone would pity him.

"Well, let us talk about why we are meeting today," Erik said after a moment of silence. "At this point in time, it would benefit all of us if you were set free. When I say 'set free' that is all I mean. You will not resume the rule of Sweden," continued Erik.

"I understand," said Birger looking almost faint from relief. Erik knew that Birger was deeply concerned about Marta's state of mind as he had repeatedly pleaded for her freedom, claiming that it would be the only thing that would save her sanity.

"You will have to swear allegiance to us as rulers of Sweden; to stand by us, to defend our country and promise never to turn against us. You will swear to this on the Holy Bible. If you break your oath you will have to answer to God and His Church. Only if Valdemar and I die childless, will you rule again. We shall call a meeting of the Council to settle all the details, such as what part of Sweden you will keep as your estate. Do you have any questions?"

"No, I do not," said Birger.

Erik was surprised by his brother's readiness to agree to the terms of his release. But then, his immediate goal was to be free. Later the restrictions would chafe, and he would surely curse himself for having been so accommodating.

"Congratulations!" said Johan excitedly as they left Erik's chamber. "This is the best news we could bring to the queen."

Birger lengthened his stride to cross the courtyard and took the stairs two at a time before rushing into their prison chamber, his face bright with happiness. "We shall be freed!"

She looked at him. "We can leave? We can see Magnus again?"

"Yes, yes, yes," shouted Birger. "We will be freed!"

Marta sat down on the bed and gazed into space with a vacant stare. "Maybe they are just saying that. They might kill us as we leave, and then tell everyone we tried to escape."

Birger felt the elation drain out of him. Silently, he turned and left the chamber with both fists clenched at his sides. When he saw Johan Brunkow in the corridor he took him aside.

"Thanks to Erik Menved, Martha and I are free. He has always been a loyal friend. We should go to Roskilde and thank him."

"Well, it is a good idea to go to Denmark for several reasons," said Johan encouragingly. "You must be longing to see your son again, and I think it would be beneficial for the queen to be with your sister."

"Would you suggest it to her, Johan? I cannot talk to her right now. She is always so negative, and I might lose my temper."

"Duke Kristoffer has returned to Southern Halland," Lady Brigitte reported as she handed Ingeborg a large skein of silk. "

"I shall leave now so the ladies can come in," Kristina interjected as she placed an embroidery frame in front of Ingeborg.

"Oh, Kristina. I do not want you to go. They can sit elsewhere and work."

"No," protested Kristina. "They become even more resentful towards me when you and I spend time together."

"Has anyone done anything to hurt you? Just let me know who, and I will punish her."

"They are very careful not to comment or act openly," replied Kristina, recalling the nasty little tricks the courtiers had played on her. Her best tunics had been slashed, her bed soiled, and her pillows emptied of down. She had not told Ingeborg about these pranks so as not to upset her. Still, once Ingeborg delivered a healthy baby, Kristina would leave for Sweden whatever Erik and Valdemar thought of it.

"Lady Brigitte has told me that they are making your life miserable," continued Ingeborg. "I will talk to my husband again."

"Please, do not bother. The king has shown me as much support as he can under the circumstances," Kristina said as she picked up her embroidery frame and left the queen's chamber. In the corridor she was met by hostile glances from the ladies waiting to be summoned by their queen. Kristina hurried down the corridor and into the Great Hall where she seated herself beside one of the fire pits, away from the knights who were gambling at the long tables and the ladies needle-pointing by the other fire. In a way, she did not mind sitting among the lesser nobles where she could listen to the gossip. In the beginning the courtiers had whispered among themselves, but by now they had grown accustomed to her silent form bent over her needlework and so paid her little heed. She was idly listening to the talk around her when Alf entered the Great Hall to enthusiastic greetings from the men at the tables. He was accorded the same respect and affection here as he had been at the Swedish court, despite the fact that he acted as her protector. Declining the invitations to join their games, he came over and sat down beside her.

"I have a message for you from Duke Erik," he whispered as he slipped a parchment scroll into her lap. His heart constricted at seeing her face light up. "The poor fisherman who brought it had been waiting for days to find either of us. You had better throw it in the fire after you read it. Erik Menved would not condone such correspondence."

Kristina looked around to see that no one was watching. She broke the seal and opened the scroll.

My beloved Kristina,

It has come to my attention that you are being poorly treated at the Danish court. I hope you know that you are always welcome in Sweden and that I harbor no ill will towards you for bringing Magnus to Ingeborg. I know how much you love him, and I would not have harmed him, just as I have not harmed Birger and Marta. This is all politics. Again.

I do not know when this message will reach you as I have no easy way of getting it to you, but when it does arrive I pray it will find you well--or as well as can be expected. Do come back, my love, where you will be safe from scorn. Valdemar and I have made it abundantly clear that you are under our protection. There is not one day passing when I do not think of you. You have my love for eternity. Erik

Kristina felt her hands tremble and tears come to her eyes. To hold his heartfelt words, written by his hand, was more than she could endure. "Must I burn it?" she asked.

"Your situation is bad enough, Kristina. Imagine what would happen if you were found communicating with the enemy. Of course, you must destroy it."

Kristina looked at the date below Erik's signature. The message had been on its way for two months and she was grateful that it had reached her at all. She read it through again, slowly, savoring every word, before she threw it on the fire where it rapidly disintegrated into nothing. She dried her eyes. "Erik says I can go to Sweden whenever I want."

"I was sure that he would," said Alf.

"Is the fisherman still here?"

"He is staying until you are ready with your answer, if you want to send one."

"I shall tell Erik that I will gladly go back once Ingeborg gives birth, and that I want you to have the same opportunity. I can feel that you do not like it here. Why, I cannot understand, as the ladies dote on you and the men constantly seek your counsel."

Alf did not respond at first. What could he say? Tell her that the court's treatment of her was making Roskilde intolerable for him? After a moment he said, "I wish for nothing more than to return to Smaland, but I am not so sure Duke Erik would welcome such a request, not even from you."

"We have nothing to lose by asking. I shall go to the library and pen my reply."

"Please, be careful. Do not let anyone catch you."

Kristina silently slid into the library and looked around the huge book-lined chamber. Fortunately, the monks who normally worked there had gone to morning mass, leaving her quite alone. She went over to one of the writing desks and sat down. Again, she was grateful for having been educated with the royal children, enabling her to write her own messages without the need of a scribe.

While she composed her reply, she felt as if she were with Erik again. She could see his face and hear his strong, gentle voice. But her initial pleasure quickly turned to pain. She thought she had learned to live away from him, but the impact of his words had shattered her composure and acceptance of their situation. All she could think of was his body against hers, his mouth over hers, and the longing that had built up for almost two years. Her emotions took her breath away, and she started to cry. But she quickly realized that she had to control herself if someone were to enter the library. Her tears had to come later. Shakily, she penned her message of gratitude for being able to return and requested the same for Alf. As she was about to sign it she added, "You will be part of me to my last day of life, and after that; but I must start living without thinking of you constantly. It is simply too painful." She signed her name and pressed her signet ring into the hot wax she dripped to seal the scroll. She must finally accept the fact that they would never be together again, perhaps never even to see each other again.

She returned to the Great Hall where Alf was immersed in a game of chess. She took her seat by the fire and continued to embroider the coverlet she was making for the royal crib.

"Have you finished your message?" Alf asked as he sat down beside her after his game.

"Yes." She discreetly removed the scroll from beneath her tunic and slid it over to Alf who hid it in his sleeve.

"It is on its way," he said as he stood and left with purposeful strides.

Once outside the castle, he walked towards the water. He moved quickly, but not so fast as to attract attention. When he was shielded by some weeping willows he stopped and studied the scroll in his hand. He noticed that the wax had loosened at one end and he realized that he could easily peel it open and see what Kristina had written. He was burning with curiosity. Maybe she was no longer in love with Erik, allowing him to finally tell her how much he cared for her. But then it might be a love-letter, and he knew that he could not bear the confirmation that she still loved another. He sighed as he lowered the parchment and resolutely moved along the water's edge to find the fisherman.

As Birger and Marta rode away from Nykoping castle, Birger looked back at their former prison. Its high grey walls rose forbiddingly against the morning sky, resisting the brightness of the day. He felt a shiver down his spine, as if the castle were gripped by some evil spell from which they had narrowly escaped.

Marta also felt as if the force that had held her in its grasp had finally released her. For the first time in almost two years she appeared happy. She inhaled deeply of the fresh air and beheld the scenery around her. They both could feel spring bursting forth and nature's rebirth carrying over to them. As Birger turned, he noticed a glowing smile on her pale face. Again, he was struck by that tender feeling he had experienced so often before their imprisonment. He reached out and touched her gloved hand. She smiled back at him with tears in her eyes.

Birger felt better than he had in many months. Dozens of the nobles who had remained loyal had joined them on this trip. The column rode throughout the warm spring day and stopped at a small inn for the night. As Birger drifted off to sleep after making love to Marta for the first time in many months, he felt blessed. Their love-making had been as passionate as in the beginning, and as tender as only longtime lovers can make it. Though he was not the ruler of Sweden, with her in his arms he felt power and peace.

Marta disembarked the ship and greeted her brother and Ingeborg while she eagerly looked for her son on the dock near Roskilde castle.

"I told Magnus that you would probably come on the morrow. He has looked forward to your arrival more than you can imagine. He is playing with his friends over there," said Ingeborg as she pointed down the shoreline. Marta unceremoniously left the welcome commit-tee and ran towards the sounds of laughter and screaming by the water's edge. There six boys were scampering in the shallow water, floating small model Viking ships in fierce battle.

Marta spotted Magnus immediately. He had grown tall for his eight years. The passage of time was clearly written on his face, and she was painfully reminded of how long they had been parted. She stood silently savoring his presence. He must have felt hers as he slowly straightened up and turned around.

"Mother?" he whispered at first. "Mother!" he called as he leapt toward the shore and ran towards her. Marta could not fight back her tears when he rushed into her arms. She realized that he consid-ered himself grown up now, and that it would be unmanly for him to succumb to displays of emotion, nevertheless his tears mingled with hers. Birger joined them and the three of them huddled together with their arms around each other.

Birger and Erik Menved sat alone in the Danish king's chamber, sharing a private moment before joining the reception festivities. Erik Menved read aloud the new treaty between Sweden and Denmark. "A year and a half!" lamented Birger, unable to mask his disappointment.

"I came here to ask your help in negotiating a more acceptable solution for me and your sister, but I cannot live in Sweden with no power."

"Further negotiations with Erik and Valdemar are impossible now. Without the imminent threat of war your brothers have no reason to change their agreement with you." Birger's face fell. Erik Menved added, "Still, you can be sure that I have not forgotten what your brothers tried to do to me, and I shall move against them the moment this truce runs out. You have my word on that." Birger's eyes became soft with gratitude.

Erik Menved sat pensively for a few moments. "Count Jakob's son, Nils, was taken prisoner while fighting against me on the side of his German cousin," he said finally. "King Hakon has intervened, requesting Nils' freedom. I sent some trusted men to mediate who, while visiting the Norwegian court, heard that a rift has developed between Hakon and Erik. If we could get Hakon on our side, we might even get you back in the circle of power sooner."

"If only we could," sighed Birger.

"I think it would be worth my while to meet with Hakon, and if, indeed, a breach does exist between him and Erik, we shall add some fuel and hope for a raging fire."

Erik Menved and Hakon arrived in Viken accompanied by only a few men who, in order not to betray their identity, flew no royal banners. Hakon had been intrigued at Erik Menved's insistence on secrecy; and his avid curiosity, which outweighed his dislike for the Danish king, had made him comply with the request.

"You wanted to talk," Hakon said.

"Since our representatives were to meet here anyway, this seemed as good a time as any," said Erik Menved, smiling kindly. "And to take first things first, I will be pleased to have young Count Nils returned to his father's care if they both swear not to act against Denmark in the future."

"If that is all you require, it is extremely generous of you," said Hakon settling back to hear the real reason behind his enemy's generosity.

"The situation in Scandinavia has changed since we last met," Erik Menved began. "Your prospective son-in-law has taken over Sweden, and my ally has lost his throne. That must gratify you, while it obviously displeases me. King Birger is now in Roskilde requesting my help to regain a voice in the affairs of Sweden."

"I knew he was free, but I did not know he had gone to Denmark."

"I intend to help him."

"Why are you telling me?"

"If Erik could rely on no armies other than his own, he might accede to my suggestion."

"Why should I forego my allegiance with my future son-in-law in favor of Birger?" asked Hakon, incredulously.

"I could offer you something Erik could not," Erik Menved replied softly.

"And what would that be?"

"Northern Halland," Erik Menved continued. "As we have not yet settled the question of your mother's inheritance, and as her particular properties are located far from Norway, I am sure you would find it more convenient to have land adjacent to your own borders instead."

Hakon started laughing. "The last time we made a bargain you burned the island you had given me in lieu of my mother's inheritance. Why should I listen to you now?"

"I am truly sorry that happened. Believe me when I tell you that I had nothing to do with those fires. I have no proof, but I strongly suspect Kristoffer was behind them."

"I cannot pretend that I am disinterested in your proposal. Still, why would Erik not give me Northern Halland if I asked for it? After all, it was I who arranged for him to rule it in the first place."

"Even if he did offer it to you, I would not approve of your ruling any Danish territory."

"I see," mused Hakon.

"And there is more to my offer. If we become allies, we could actually return Birger to his throne if we found that to our advantage. If you would then allow your daughter to marry Crown Prince Magnus, she would not only be Queen of Norway, but Queen of Sweden as well!"

"You are not offering anything that my daughter does not already have."

"I do not want more wars. With your support, I could accomplish my goal with merely a threat, and you could finally claim Northern Halland. And at the same time, I am suggesting another way to the Swedish crown for your daughter. It sounds like an ideal solution, especially since I have heard that you and Erik are not on the best of terms."

Hakon looked impassively at Erik Menved, impressed by his incisiveness, but knowing it would be a mistake to show any real interest. "I will think it over," he said coolly, leaving Erik Menved to wonder if the alleged feud had been nothing but a rumor.

Erik and Valdemar sailed back to Nykoping from Stockholm after a week of Council meetings followed by nightly carousing at the Black Cat. Erik's mind had not been on affairs of state since receiving Kristina's note with the request for Alf's safe return to Sweden. Naturally, he would grant what she asked, as Alf had merely carried out his duty. But Erik had been devastated by the last lines of the message. Kristina was writing her final farewell. The comfort he had had in knowing that she loved him as much as he loved her vanished in an instant as jealousy consumed his being. Had she found another? Was she in love again? The demons were ripping at his heart.

Erik was still morose when they entered the courtyard of Nykoping castle. As they slid down from their mounts, a servant informed them that a Norwegian knight had arrived two days earlier. "Show him to my chamber," ordered Erik.

When the visitor entered, Erik was surprised to see that it was the younger cousin of one of King Hakon's trusted knights. Erik asked, "Rangvald, what are you doing here?"

"My cousin sent me," Rangvald began. "Two weeks ago, a meeting was arranged in Viken to negotiate the release of Count Jakob's son, Nils, who had been captured by the Danes during the last war in Germany. My cousin was one of the Norwegians who accompanied Count Jakob to the meeting. Two unexpected parties arrived at the last minute, one from Denmark and one from Norway, carrying no banners except those of their captains. The men being escorted were housed in tents befitting powerful men, and it turned out that the visitors were the Kings of Denmark and Norway!"

"What?" said Erik sitting up in his chair.

"They met for one night and left at dawn the next morning."

Erik and Valdemar stared at each other with the same thought in mind. Why had Erik Menved met with Hakon just after Birger had arrived in Roskilde? And in total secrecy.

"There is no doubt?" asked Erik.

"My cousin knows Hakon well, and he saw Erik Menved as he left in the morning."

"What secret business could the two of them have?" Erik asked pensively.

"Well, they must have decided to let Count Nils go free because the meeting adopted that resolution," offered Rangvald helpfully.

"And what did Jakob pay for his son's freedom? His entire fortune?" asked Valdemar.

"He and Nils promised never to act against Denmark."

"A cheap price," Erik noted suspiciously. "Erik Menved obviously made the gesture to get something from Hakon in return. I am eternally grateful to your cousin and to you, Rangvald," he concluded with a dismissive bow.

"Birger has probably asked Erik Menved to help him regain power, and Erik Menved could have asked Hakon to stay out of an impending war," ventured Erik after the Norwegian had left.

"Or could Erik Menved have asked Hakon to turn against us?"

"Maybe. But even if Hakon is furious with me for lending Kungahalla to Kristoffer without permission, that is hardly sufficient cause for him to take up arms against us."

When the following morning another Norwegian messenger arrived, Erik ordered Rangvald to remain in the guest quarters to avoid being seen by his countryman.

Erik handed Valdemar the message after reading it. "Hakon wants to meet us at Kungahalla in ten days. I suppose we will learn what the secret meeting was all about."

Meanwhile Rangvald, suffering pangs of guilt, longed to get away from Nykoping without delay. Back in Norway, one of Erik Menved's spies had approached him to propose that he arrange for the dukes to learn of the meeting. When Rangvald had asked why, he was merely offered a handsome sum of money. As a third son, with no prospect of land or fortune, the inducement had been irresistible.

Chapter 31

"I am here with nothing but good intentions," Hakon declared. "All I want is for you to return Kungahalla to me and Varberg fortress to Count Jacob and we will forget the past."

Hakon and Erik were alone in the hall of Kungahalla fortress. Erik just stared at the Norwegian. He had hoped that Hakon would tell him about his secret meeting with Erik Menved but Hakon had said nothing. How could Erik return the strategic fortresses to Hakon if he was now allied with Erik Menved?

"What is your concern?" asked Hakon, becoming exasperated. "We are supposed to be allies."

Yes, thought Erik, and as allies you are supposed to tell me about any dealings with my enemy. If you do not, I can only surmise that you have something to hide.

"Whatever it is, tell me!" implored Hakon, trying to hold his temper.

How can I? thought Erik. It would be the same as accusing you of treachery. So, he kept his silence, praying Hakon would tell him what had transpired during the meeting.

Hakon shifted uneasily in his chair, and Erik could see that he was at his wit's end. "You do not even give me the courtesy of a reply." Hakon stood suddenly, drew a deep breath and then he exploded. "I have had enough of your lust for power! Not only do you want to control my fortresses. You want to rule all of Scandinavia! I have been extremely patient with you, but from this moment on we are no longer allies. You may consider your betrothal to my daughter broken. And I will take back my fortress by force if I must!"

The king glared at Erik, then turned on his heel and stormed out of the hall. Erik could hear him call for his horse and the sounds of his soldiers scrambling to follow. After much shouting and scuffling about, Erik heard the Norwegians thunder over the drawbridge.

"What happened?" asked Mats who had descended the stairs at the sound of Hakon's departure. Erik explained, to which Mats responded, "You should have told Hakon that you knew of his meeting. Maybe nothing came of it, so he did not consider it of any import."

"Even so, he should have told me about it. As he did not, I can only assume they discussed something he does not want me to know," insisted Erik. "If there is one lesson I have learned, it is to trust no one."

"Hakon has never crossed you. He has always been a loyal friend. Maybe you should have given him a chance to explain."

"It had to come from him. How can I part with Kungahalla and Varberg if I do not trust him? Do you not think it strange that he wants the two fortresses back right after that meeting?"

Birger spotted Marta and Ingeborg under a shade tree outside Roskilde castle observing Magnus and his companion practice at arms. Ingeborg gestured for another bench to be brought on which Birger gratefully settled. He recounted how he and Erik Menved had just met with three of Hakon's most trusted men in Copenhagen. The Norwegians had presented an outline of a contract granting Hakon legal title to Northern Halland in lieu of his Danish mother's estate. In return, Hakon promised to support Erik Menved and Birger against the Swedish dukes as well as to change the marriage plans for his daughter. "The wonderful news," said Birger with a broad smile, "is that Princess Ingeborg of Norway is to marry our Magnus!"

"But she is betrothed to Erik," protested Queen Ingeborg.

"Not any more! A quarrel between Hakon and Erik has broken the betrothal. One day, our son might be the King of Sweden and Norway!"

"What a surprise!" exclaimed Marta. "And a wonderful one at that!"

Magnus was told about his splendid marriage alliance later that day. "I suppose it is good," he opined with a serious mien. "But do I have to marry Princess Ingeborg now?" he asked apprehensively.

"No, you will wait until she is of age," answered his mother.

"Oh, good," said Magnus, much relieved. A few years seemed like a lifetime, and he would not have to think about it for now. "If you will allow me, I have to tend to my hunting birds," he said and raced out of the room.

"I am so glad he fully understands the honor that has been bestowed on him," jested Birger as he put his arm around Marta.

Kristina had been counting the minutes between Ingeborg's cramps for several hours, and from their increasing frequency and strength it was clear that she was ready to deliver. A feeling of hushed energy filled Roskilde castle where courtiers were pacing the Great Hall and the corridors. Wagers were being quietly made on the time of delivery and the sex of the child.

Ingeborg had only allowed Marta, Kristina, the physicians, and Lady Brigitte to be with her. Not until the actual moment of birth would the bishops and members of the Council be admitted.

"How does it look?" asked Kristina as the surgeon came to her side after again examining Ingeborg.

"Everything is going well. We will not have long to wait."

Kristina checked on the hot water and clean cloths for the last time before she sat down to hold Ingeborg's hand. Suddenly Ingeborg's moans became piercing screams and Kristina moved aside to allow the physician access to the bedside.

"Call for the witnesses," he ordered as he placed Ingeborg in delivery position, seated against a huge pile of pillows. He pulled down a curtain that had been rigged from the ceiling to afford her privacy. Kristina reflected on how civilized this delivery was in comparison to what Marta had had to endure in Sweden with all those men looking on for hours.

The delivery went quickly, and when the surgeon pulled out the child he slapped its bottom gently. Once the baby's cry pierced the expectant stillness the courtiers' faces lit up in smiles. The surgeon cut the umbilical cord before he invited the king to examine the infant.

"A boy," cried Erik Menved jubilantly as the witnesses offered their felicitations. Lady Brigitte and Kristina covered Ingeborg with a fresh sheet and pulled aside the curtain, so all could see the infant resting in Ingeborg's arms, its little face contorted by crying. Once the men had satisfied themselves that an heir had been born, they filed out of the chamber.

"Bless you, my sweet wife," whispered Erik Menved as he bent down and kissed Ingeborg on the forehead. "This is truly the happiest day of my life."

Ingeborg looked down on her child with immeasurable tenderness, her own face awash in tears. "At last, my little one. I never dreamt it was possible to feel such happiness."

"He is a beautiful baby," said Lady Brigitte as she gently took the child to clean and dress it.

Six nights later the royal crib was placed in the Great Hall for the courtiers to view the infant prince. During all the excitement over the birth, Kristina had been ignored, and even her worst tormentors had left her in peace.

"I think this is a good time for me to leave," she said standing at Alf's side and watching the courtiers pay their homage.

"I cannot go with you, as we have not yet heard from Duke Erik."

"I am sure that he has no objection to your coming back to Sweden, Alf."

"I shall escort you home, but then I must return."

"I have gotten so used to having you near that I cannot fathom what life will be without you," she said softly. He felt his heart leap, but he quickly cautioned himself not to read too much into her words of friendship. "I shall talk to Ingeborg tonight. I am sure she will understand," Kristina said resolutely.

The opportunity came after the celebrations were over and Ingeborg and the baby had returned to the queen's chamber. Once the little prince had been nursed and tucked into his crib, Kristina and Ingeborg sat down together.

"You know that I want you to stay, Kristina; but if you have to leave I understand, and I wish you all the best. Still, I shall miss you. But please do not leave until after the baptism on the morrow."

Kristina nodded, knowing how important it was for Ingeborg to have the child christened to protect it from sorcery. She walked over to the crib to bid the baby farewell. As she bent over his little body she was struck by his stillness. She could feel her heart constrict in fear when she saw no movement or breathing. "Ingeborg," she said hoarsely.

"What is it?" asked Ingeborg as she came over to the crib.

"He is not breathing!" whispered Kristina.

Ingeborg bent forward and touched the child before she picked him up and held him close to her cheek to feel his breath. Kristina could see all color drain from Ingeborg's face as she stared at her baby in panic. Kristina turned and ran down the corridor to find the surgeon monk. She had to rouse him from his sleep, but once he saw her face he quickly rose to follow her through the silent castle. They found Ingeborg standing immobile in the middle of her chamber with the child clasped tightly in her arms. Father Gregory tried to pry the baby from her, but she held him fast.

"My baby is fine. He is just sleeping very quietly," she whispered.

Resolutely, he took the little body from her and listened for a heartbeat. Time was suspended as they waited for some sign of life. After what seemed like an eternity he shook his head.

"I am sorry, your Majesty, but he has been called to his heavenly Father."

"No!" screamed Ingeborg. "No! No!"

Kristina held Ingeborg close while Ingeborg's cries pierced the silence again and again as she struggled from Kristina's embrace to pick up and hold the little body. "Why?" she cried as she slowly rocked the child. "Why?"

Kristina felt utterly helpless. Her heart ached for Ingeborg who was pleading to an unanswering God when Erik Menved entered the chamber.

"What is going on?" he asked when he saw his distraught wife pacing the floor and hugging her child. Then he looked demandingly at Kristina.

"The prince is dead!" explained Kristina.

"Dead? How can that be?"

"I do not know, your Majesty," said Kristina in a quavering voice. "He was in his crib . . . he just stopped breathing."

"No one who is perfectly healthy just stops breathing. That is ridiculous," he said as he walked up to Ingeborg. "What happened to my son?"

"God is punishing me," whimpered Ingeborg as she held the baby close to her cheek.

At that instant the physician, who had left for a few moments, reentered with a cup in his hands that he held out to Ingeborg. "Please, drink this your Majesty."

Kristina held out her arms to take the child so that Ingeborg could drink the potion, but she stubbornly clung to her baby. Erik Menved took the cup and pressed it to Ingeborg's lips, forcing her to empty it.

"What happened, Father Gregory?" he asked, his face now ashen from the realization that his son was dead.

"I do not know, your Majesty. Both ladies were here when the prince passed away, and neither seemed to have noticed anything unusual. Lady Kristina discovered what had happened when she went to bid goodnight to the child."

"Did you do anything to him?" Erik Menved asked Kristina accusingly in his agony over the unexplained loss of his son.

"Nothing, Your Majesty," stammered Kristina, looking in the direction of Ingeborg for support, but the queen was whispering to her child without paying any heed to their discussion. "I did nothing but discover that the prince was no longer breathing."

Erik Menved walked over to Ingeborg to try to calm her, but she did not respond to his gentle words. His face was filled with despair when he turned towards Kristina.

"A child cannot be healthy one moment and dead the next. There has to be some explanation. You shall be put under guard until we have sorted this out," concluded the king.

"Please, let me stay to help the queen," pleaded Kristina.

"You leave her in peace," said Erik Menved, his face now hard. "Guard!" he called.

Kristina had sat in a guestroom for hours watching the candle burn down and crying over the tragic death of Ingeborg's child. At last, out of sheer exhaustion, she had finally lain down and slept. When she awoke she could hear people moving about in the corridors, speaking in hushed voices. She went to the door to listen to what was being said. She stiffened when she heard the word 'witch-craft' mentioned. Did they think she had killed the child? No, that was impossible. They all knew how much she loved Ingeborg. But as she listened at the door she realized that that was exactly what they believed. She felt a sudden dread since she had heard about witches subjected by the church to unspeakable methods of torture. None of those accused, to her knowledge, had ever survived their ordeal. She was panicked because she had no doubt that some jealous courtiers would press for an inquisition. And they would have the king's ear, since in his anguish he seemed to blame her for the death of his son. The only comforting thought was that Ingeborg would surely come to her defense once she regained some composure.

Alf was aghast at the venomous mood in the castle that morning. While shock and sadness over the little prince's death were rife, some gloated that Kristina had been found out for what she was--a witch. Finally, when he could no longer stand listening to all the outrageous slanders about Kristina's secret sacrifices to the heathen gods, he decided to seek out the king to plead that he end the insanity.

When the king saw Alf enter the audience chamber, he gestured for everyone to leave the room. The large chamber emptied out slowly, and Alf could sense that the king was impatient.

"There is no explanation for my son's death other than witch-craft," Erik Menved began. "Do you know how long Lady Kristina has been practicing?"

"I have been shocked to hear these accusations thrown about, and I am surprised that you give them credence, your Majesty. You must know that Lady Kristina is no witch, and that she would never do anything to harm Ingeborg. They are like sisters."

"Yes, that has been puzzling me, but then who can understand how a witch might act?"

"Your Majesty, do you seriously believe such vicious gossip from people who are desperately envious of Lady Kristina's closeness to the queen? Have you spoken to Queen Ingeborg and heard her version of what transpired?"

"She does not understand how the child could have died either. And even if she thinks Kristina is innocent; as a witch, Kristina could make her believe anything. No, I am becoming more and more convinced that we must begin an inquisition. I have spoken to the Archbishop, and he concurs."

Alf was stunned. But then, the king had to lash out at someone to lessen his pain, and Alf could sense that he had closed his mind and heart to reason."

Please, let me speak to Lady Kristina, your Majesty. I might be able to discover the truth."

"It would be a blessing if she confessed of her own free will. Go and talk to her, and I shall pray for guidance and decide how to proceed on the morrow."

With a heavy heart, Alf accompanied those the king had directed to take him to where Kristina was being held.

"Alf!" whispered Kristina as she threw herself into his arms. "What is happening?"

He related what the courtiers believed, and of the king's suspicion, as well. "I know you are innocent, Kristina, and I will get you out of here. But we do not have much time."

"How can you get me out with the room so well guarded?"

"Trust me, Kristina. We will soon be far away. I promise." As she looked into his eyes she believed him--perhaps because she desperately wanted to, but also because he always seemed to find the solution to any problem. He gently kissed her hand and whispered, "Have courage."

Back in the Great Hall, Alf looked for Duke Kristoffer's close friend, Lord Anders. He found him drinking with his friends by the fire. "Can I see you for a moment?" Alf asked. Anders rose to follow him out into the warm night.

Now that the dastardly deed is done we have to get her out of here so she will not break under torture and tell who asked her to poison the prince," Alf confided in a hushed tone.

"What are you talking about?" asked Lord Anders dumbfounded.

Alf nodded appreciatively. "Duke Kristoffer did not even tell you! Well, I suppose he wanted to protect you if you were questioned."

"I do not understand . . ."

"It was Duke Kristoffer who employed Lady Kristina. It was a brilliant plan as the queen trusts her implicitly. What we had not counted on was the swiftness of her detention. We have to get her out of here tonight so that she will not break under torture."

"But how . . . ?"

"There is no time for questions if you want to protect Duke Kristoffer."

Kristina stood by the window peering into the darkness. As the hours had crawled by, she had become less and less convinced of Alf's infallibility. She began to wish that she had some poison with which to end her life before the ordeal began. She could never confess to something as ungodly as witchcraft, so she had to face the awful truth that she would die in excruciating pain. And even if she confessed, they would still torture her to exorcise the evil spirits.

When she heard the key turn in the lock her heart leapt in anticipation. Through the door came Lady Stina, Lord Anders' younger sister. Kristina was surprised that she would be the one to bring her some food since Lady Stina had been harassing her since her arrival, which in itself had never bothered her, as she wanted nothing to do with anyone close to Duke Kristoffer. She guessed Lady Stina had been sent to further deepen her humiliation.

As soon as the door closed behind her, Lady Stina put down the tray of food and pulled out a tunic and head dress she had hidden under her own tunic.

"Quickly, remove your clothes and put on these."

Kristina stared at the tunic which was identical to the one Lady Stina was wearing. It was the same flamboyant orange and yellow signifying Stina's clan. "Hurry! We have but little time." Kristina came out of her stupor and did as she was told. As she adjusted the head-dress, Lady Stina smiled in appreciation. "We are the same height. Pull the toque closer to your face and look down, and no one will suspect it is anyone but me in that tunic. My brother is waiting for you at the end of the corridor. He will take you to Lord Alf."

"What will happen to you when they discover that you are not me?"

"I shall tell them that you bewitched me," giggled Lady Stina nervously as she emptied the tray of its food. "Be on your way."

"But why are you helping me?" asked Kristina, afraid for a moment that this kind gesture was a trap.

"Because I am grateful for what you have done. Now, go!"

Lady Stina gave the empty tray to Kristina and pushed her towards the door. Kristina was too stunned to reflect on what Lady Stina had said, so she lowered her head and held the tray protectively close to her face when she passed the guard who barely glanced at her. It took all her willpower to walk at a normal pace though she was bursting to run down the empty corridor. She realized that her liberator had timed her departure with the evening meal and that most of the courtiers and servants were in the Great Hall.

At the end of the corridor Lord Anders stepped out of the shadows and motioned for her to follow him downstairs. As they reached the bottom of the stairs Lord Anders made a right turn leading to a small door, which he unlocked. As they closed the door behind them they heard voices in the corridor. Kristina's heart was pounding with excitement over her narrow escape, and with anxiety over how they would make it across the open areas undetected. As Lord Anders took the tray that she still grasped in her hands and put it down on a serving table, he smiled. "You look just like my sister from the back, so walk slowly beside me towards the water, and everyone who sees us will believe that we are out for a stroll."

Kristina had to control herself to take one measured step after another. Then they heard a voice behind them in the dark. "Lady Stina, Lord Anders. May I join you?"

Kristina froze at the sound of King Birger's voice.

"It would be an honor," she heard Lord Anders say as he discreetly nudged her. With her back still towards King Birger she curtsied deeply and continued to walk slightly ahead of the two men. She remained silent through the walk, which was the way she was expected to behave as a woman of lesser rank. She listened impatiently to the two men discussing the tragic death of the little prince.

"I have difficulty believing that Lady Kristina is a witch as I have known her all my life," sighed King Birger. "But then witches are said to be able to dupe anyone." Kristina felt her heart constrict. Even Birger, who had been like her brother throughout their childhood, had fallen prey to the ridiculous rumors and forsaken her! She felt tears begin to well. When King Birger excused himself to return to the Great Hall she again curtsied deeply with her head averted. Once the Swedish king had entered the castle, Lord Anders turned and walked away from the dock and along the water's edge. After a time, they came to a dense stand of trees overhanging the water where Lord Anders whistled softly.

Alf came out from under the foliage holding out a bundle of clothes to Kristina.

"Here. Change into these and return Lady Stina's tunic to Lord Anders."

She ducked under the screening branches to do as she was told, while Alf thanked Lord Anders for his help. "Tell no one, not even Duke Kristoffer, about our spiriting away Lady Kristina. What a person does not know cannot be used against him, and we must protect the duke, as well as ourselves."

Kristina heard Lord Anders' consenting murmur and profuse thanks as she pulled on the nondescript tunic Alf had provided. She emerged and handed the yellow and orange garment, along with the headdress to Lord Anders. "Thank you for your help," she said gratefully. "I do not know why. . ."

"We have to hurry, Kristina," Alf broke in as he forcefully guided her towards a boat hidden by some heavy underbrush.

"Safe journey. And thank you both . . . " Lord Anders began.

"Do not mention it," Alf interrupted again as he helped Kristina on board and pushed the skiff away from the shore. He sat down, grabbed the oars, and began to row with steady strokes. Kristina saw Lord Anders walking briskly back the way they had come.

Her mind in turmoil, Kristina sat in the bow, gazing back at Roskilde as it slowly receded from sight. She began to shiver, not from the cool evening breeze but from the relief of narrowly escaping torture and death.

"No one will know that you are gone until the early morrow," Alf exclaimed. "There is a good breeze favoring us tonight, and once we hoist our sail, we shall be well ahead of any pursuers--if they would even know where to look." He laughed softly. "I can imagine how Lord Anders will play his role if he is found out: he had no idea that the woman with whom he was walking was not his sister. How cleverly he had been duped by the wicked witch!"

"You told Lord Anders and his sister that I killed the prince?"

Alf nodded. "It was the only way I could get their help. Yes, I lied, and I would gladly do it again. And whatever else it would take to keep you safe," he added.

She felt tears of gratitude fill her eyes until utter exhaustion overtook her. Alf stowed the oars, let the wind fill the unfurled sail and tightened the lines as the boat picked up speed. "Thank you, God, for sending Alf to my rescue," she whispered. She also offered a prayer for Ingeborg and the poor little babe before she was drawn into a deep slumber.

"We have been incredibly fortunate not to be captured," Kristina concluded as their small craft made its way into the harbor of Lodose.

"I do not think they bothered to look for us," said Alf. "They were most likely relieved to be rid of a witch rather than to have to deal with her. You could have cast further spells on them, you know."

She laughed. "You speak as if you believe I really am a witch."

"I am simply trying to see it from their point of view." Alf maneuvered the boat towards the dock, lowered its sail, and secured it to the pier. He helped Kristina up onto the dock and looked around. "We need to sell this little boat so that we can buy two horses."

Alf located the harbormaster who directed him to a fisherman at the quayside tavern. After inspecting the trim little vessel, the fisherman and Alf shook hands on the sale and both went back to the harbormaster who arranged for Alf to receive his money.

"That was easy," exclaimed Kristina who had followed the transaction from a distance.

"It is not often a boat like this can be bought for the price I asked, and the harbor master was pleased to lend the fisherman the money until he can pay it off--with high interest, I venture."

The next place they visited was a stable behind the harbor where they found two strong, fine horses. This time the negotiations took longer, and it was not until late in the day that Alf finally closed the transaction. "We have to stay here for the night," he said as they sat at the harbor inn eating their simple supper.

When she finally bedded down in the inn's only private chamber she wondered why Alf had insisted on her sleeping alone in its big bed. They had shared every accommodation imaginable in the past, and now she felt confused as sleep overtook her.

"This is Solang," Kristina proclaimed proudly as they rode up to her home several days later. Even as she said the words she was filled with a wondrous calm. Just seeing her home again made her feel safe.

Solang was especially lovely at that time of year with the surrounding trees blazing their brilliant colors before their winter sleep. Alf and Kristina dismounted to walk around the house towards the dark and tranquil lake. The field sweeping down to it was carpeted with multicolored leaves that danced in the wind. Calls from wild ducks flying south in disciplined formations broke the silence of the surrounding forests.

"It is just as beautiful as you said," Alf remarked.

She turned towards him as his voice sounded thin and unnatural. "You like it?"

"It is lovely," he added. "It suits you."

She pointed out the fine landscape and out-buildings that made Solang so precious to her. She told Alf of the abundant game, of the deer that grazed close to the house at nightfall, and of the huge owls that flew across the lake on silent wings. Exuberantly, she ran around the house to open the front door. It flung open and Ragna emerged onto the steps, opening her arms to jubilantly embrace her mistress.

"You are home. You are home," was all she could repeat as she hugged Kristina. When she looked up and noticed Alf, she smiled. "How nice to see you again, Master Alf."

"Lord Alf. He is a knight now."

"Welcome then, Lord Alf," beamed Ragna as she pulled Kristina inside. "We have kept everything ready for your return. I have dusted and aired the house most every day for the past two years. I knew that you would come home one day. I will get you something to eat and drink . . . I will fill the washbasin so that you can clean up."

When Kristina and Alf had finished the fine supper Ragna prepared for them and were sitting outside the house looking at the sun set over the lake, Alf remarked sadly, "It is time for me to depart."

Suddenly Kristina realized that she had been dreading to hear him say those words, and now when he uttered them she knew she did not want to hear them.

"I have something to show you first," she said. She walked into the house and returned with a small leather chest from which she took a piece of cloth, slowly unrolling it in front of him. Alf saw that the square tapestry piece depicted a hunter with a doe resting in his arms. "This is what the wise old woman gave me when I visited her the first time," said Kristina. "She foretold my future then, and all her predictions have come true. I was just waiting for the final one to be fulfilled."

"It is lovely work," said Alf appreciatively as he took the cloth to study it closely. "She really has captured the man and the animal. It is so lifelike, you can feel how the doe wants to jump up." He stood and looked at Kristina. "I dread long farewells, so I will leave you now. I shall remember you just as you are this moment." He smiled gently as he backed away, putting a finger to his lips when she opened her mouth to say something. The smile turned sad when he walked out of her sight. Kristina sat very still as she heard him call for his horse and bid his good-bye to Ragna who had come out of the house. As she listened to their muted voices she looked down at the tapestry. What had Alf said? That the doe wanted to jump up? The deer was dead. She had looked at the tapestry countless times.

She gasped when she looked at it again. Her heart began to race when she saw the alert look in the doe's eyes; the same eyes that had been closed in death when the wise old woman had gifted it to her. Then she had felt like that lifeless doe. But now she realized the obvious--the wise old woman's final prediction had come true. The doe's transformation mirrored her own. She wanted a full life again, and she wanted to live it with Alf.

She jumped up in panic when she heard the hooves of Alf's horse on the gravel. "Alf!" she screamed as she ran around the house. As she came around the corner she saw him mounted, waving to Ragna who was closing the door behind her. "Alf!" she called as she ran up to him and seized the reins of his horse. "Please, do not go. Stay here with me."

He looked down at her searchingly.

"Please do not leave me. I need you."

"Do you ask me to stay as a protector, or as a man?"

"As a man," Kristina whispered.

Alf dismounted and stood in front of her. "Then you must already know, I love you with all my heart." He gently pulled her into his arms, stroking her golden hair as he held her tightly to him--the hunter with his beautiful doe.

"I have news," announced Kristoffer as he entered the hall at Kungahalla, throwing his cloak on a bench. "I can hardly wait to share it with you." He sat down looking quite pleased with himself.

"Finally, your sister gave birth to a boy . . ."

"That is good news!" exclaimed Valdemar.

"Unfortunately, the child did not survive more than a few days."

"What happened?" Erik asked with consternation.

"According to Ingeborg and Kristina who were present when the child died, the baby just stopped breathing. Naturally, no one could believe that is what really happened, so Kristina was accused of being a witch."

"Kristina? A witch?" cried Erik. "That is ridiculous!"

"My brother considered holding an official inquisition into the events, while Ingeborg was vehemently against it. If she succeeded in talking him out of it or not I do not know, but Erik Menved never had a chance to inform Kristina of his decision, because she vanished into thin air, along with Lord Alf." Erik could feel the imaginary steel band that had tightened around his chest slowly loosen. "Exactly how they disappeared has been a topic of much speculation. Some say that Lady Kristina assumed another woman's form and simply walked away from the castle. Others claim that she flew away like a crow before the morning sun came up. But they all believed that she bewitched Alf to help her."

"One has to be insane to believe that Kristina would kill Ingeborg's child," said Valdemar angrily.

"Well, she got away safely. But that is not all of my news. It seems that Prince Magnus is now engaged to Princess Ingeborg of Norway!"

"What?" was the only response Erik could muster. He had never thought that Hakon would put his threat into action, but obviously he had.

"The official betrothal will take place next year."

"Hakon has obviously not forgiven you for lending Kungahalla to Kristoffer," Valdemar commented.

"I was the cause of your falling out?" asked Kristoffer, surprised.

"It was more than that, and it is too late for any regrets," Erik said as he stood up to walk towards the stairs. Without a word of explanation, he bounded up the flight of steps and walked out on the parapet. Instead of feeling anger towards Hakon for acting on his threat, Erik felt relief, as if he had been sprung from an invisible trap. He was no longer to become King of Norway. He was not to marry Princess Ingeborg. Once that reality had fully sunken in, he ran back down the stairs and through the hall where Valdemar and Kristoffer watched him with quizzical expressions.

"My horse!" he yelled as he raced out into the courtyard.

Time and time again Erik had visualized his arrival during his long ride to Solang. He had ridden without stopping, other than to change horses, and he had not slept for days. Those mental scenarios had kept him awake and in the saddle.

He had pictured how he would gallop up to the house and simply call out her name. He would rush forward and take her in his arms as she came out of the house, her sweet face filled with surprise. He would whisper into her fragrant hair that he was free to do what he wanted with his life, and that they would never again be parted. Or he could ride up quietly, tether his horse away from the house and knock on the door like a gentleman, giving her time to collect herself from the moment she heard his voice addressing her servant until he stood before her. Then he would tell her. Whichever way he decided, he knew how she would look at him, how her eyes would fill with light and how sweet would be her smile. He spurred his horse forward on the rough forest path leading towards her house.

When he finally spotted Solang in the distance it was dusk, and servants had already lit the torches in the hall. Against every instinct, he slowed his horse, dismounted, and led it towards the house. Still out of earshot, he tied the animal loosely to a tree so that it could drink from a small brook running close by the narrow road. He walked towards the house that looked temptingly inviting, with smoke curling up from its roof and light spilling out of its windows. As he drew near, he could not resist going up to one of the windows to peek in.

By a table close to the fire Kristina sat with her head bent over an embroidery frame. She wore a simple head cloth over her fair curls that spilled out from under it, framing her delicate face. The flicker from the fire made her appear angelic, and she smiled as she spoke to someone beyond Erik's line of vision. From the shadows, Erik saw Alf emerge to place his hand on her shoulder. Erik smiled in relief. Alf was there to protect her. Then Erik's heart froze, and his breathing stopped. On Alf's hand shone a gold band, and when Kristina lifted her hand to touch Alf's, Erik could see that she, too, was wearing a similar band on her left ring finger.

Erik staggered backwards. Kristina and Alf had married! He realized that he had never, not even for one moment, considered the possibility that Kristina would not be waiting for him. How arrogant and self-important his assumptions had been. Kristina had to marry and be protected to survive the hostility directed at her for her father's treachery. Alf was now a knight and quite suitable to marry; and, Erik grudgingly admitted to himself, one of the few men he respected and admired. He stumbled away from the window and collapsed in the grass. The devastation of again losing the chance of spending his life with Kristina made his whole body weak, almost numb. He sat with his face buried in his hands, barely able to breathe.

When duty had directed his fate and forced him to live without her, he had accepted it begrudgingly, but now . . . Still he could have rejected the hand of Princess Ingeborg when it was offered. He could have done that with one single word, but for the sake of Sweden he had accepted. He had no one to blame but himself. But now Hakon had broken their alliance, leaving him with nothing. He felt his over-powering sadness slowly change to fury.

Chapter 32

"I have told you what I am willing to do. Now, get out!" Erik bellowed.

The peasant cringed and backed out of the Hall of Nykoping castle. Valdemar, being the only other person present in the Hall, could not repress how he felt about his brother display of abusive anger.

"This has to stop, Erik! You must get hold of yourself! The poor man was asking for nothing more than any fair master would provide. He has traveled across the country to save his family from starvation."

"I did not turn him down, did I?" snarled Erik.

"You did not have to humiliate him. If it was only this man you mistreated, it would be one thing, but you have been insufferable since you learned Kristina had married. You must come to terms with that and stop attacking anyone who gets near you."

Erik put his head in his hands like a child being scolded, but Valdemar was unstoppable in venting frustration that had been building for months. "Yes, Hakon violated his oath by breaking your betrothal to his daughter; but would you have laid siege to Akershus as you did, if Kristina had still been waiting for you? No, you would have thanked him. Your passion to attack him prevented us all from foreseeing the inevitable--that after months of freezing weather and of staring at that cursed, invincible Daredevil tower, we would suffer a humiliating withdrawal."

"We had a strong force. No one could have predicted such harsh weather, countered Erik.

Valdemar ignored his brother's remark and continued to warm to his theme as he paced before the fire. "It was hardly surprising that Hakon, besieged in his own lair for all that time, would decide to counterattack. The waste he laid to our lands! Our poor farmers were stripped of their meager winter rations to feed his army. And then we had to counterattack in turn. It has been nothing but a series of futile assaults that served no purpose, other than venting your and

Hakon's anger. You have acted as irresponsibly as Birger--caring not about the people."

Erik knew that Valdemar was correct. He had caused nothing but suffering.

Erik began to think back on the events contributing to his misery. Before they even had had a chance to travel to the peace parlay in Oslo, Lord Abjorn had been felled by a Norwegian arrow, confined to his estate to recover from his wound that would not heal where he was fighting for his very life. Erik and Valdemar had abandoned everything to reach his sickbed. Abjorn lingered near death for several days before they reached his estate in Knivsta. There he lay, surrounded by his family, drained, pale, and utterly weak from his festering wound. Still, he smiled wordlessly to greet his friends. They had been with him only an hour when he closed his eyes, grasped Erik's hand, and inhaled a final labored breath.

"You have lived a good life," Erik had whispered to his deceased friend. "You had the respect and admiration of your peers, Valdemar's and my total trust, the love of a good wife and your children. You can close your eyes in peace, my friend."

From that day on, Erik recalled, he had been unable to fall sleep without downing a large carafe of wine, and not even then could he sleep until early morning. Valdemar had, on more than one occasion, been awakened in the night to find Erik bent over him, dripping candle wax on his pillow. When Valdemar had anxiously inquired what was afoot, Erik had smiled crookedly, mumbling that he only wanted to make sure that Valdemar was there.

Now, in the Great Hall of Nykoping, Erik snapped back from his reverie when Valdemar stopped pacing and said sympathetically, "It has been a miserable time, Erik, and I know how much you have been suffering, but you must take charge again."

"What can I do to help you?" Valdemar finally asked. "You cannot just sit here staring at the fire. You cannot go on like this."

Erik looked up at his brother with deep sadness. "I know, but I cannot feel anything, except numbness and occasional anger."

"You could start by attending the peace meeting in Helsingborg. Rid yourself of these resentments that have so engulfed you, help to mend fences with our neighbors, and negotiate a permanent peace between all the Scandinavian countries."

"I will try, Valdemar. I will try," Erik uttered in a hollow voice.

Marstrand, Denmark 1310

On the sixteenth day of May, King Hakon officially declared the betrothal of his daughter, Princess Ingeborg, to Prince Magnus of Sweden. He signed the declaration on the tiny island of Marstrand where his ship had sought safe harbor from a storm.

Hakon thought to himself. His beloved daughter, was wise beyond her nine years, and always serious about her duties. He could picture her attentive little face, and he knew that she would ask him all sorts of questions following the proceedings when he returned home-- questions which he sometimes could not answer with anything but the standard phrase "that is tradition." She had grown up with the knowledge that she was to marry the much older Erik of Sweden, and now, suddenly, she was to marry instead her contemporary, Prince Magnus. While Hakon knew that it would suffice, as it always had, to explain the change was to benefit Norway, he still felt that he owed her a more honest explanation. But could he admit his anger was the reason for the change?

While the violent storm held Hakon prisoner on the small rock island for three days, his keen sense of loss over Count Jakob's sudden death only increased with the dismal weather. He donned heavy layers of clothing to walk the craggy windswept cliffs, watching the towering waves crashing against the rocks. It took nearly an hour to walk around the island, but so restless and frustrated was Hakon from sadness, that he turned and circled in the opposite direction. When he finally returned to the cabin of his ship his face was wet from ocean spray and tears, but he felt as if he had put to rest the devastating pain of Jakob's death.

Once the storm abated, his ship weighed anchor for his meeting with Erik Menved.

"We still have a problem," Hakon insisted after he and Erik Menved had gone over their agreement. "Erik unfortunately has a legitimate claim to my daughter's hand and I can hardly blame him for attacking me. They have been betrothed ever since Ingeborg was born, and many of my nobles are in an uproar over the switch in wedding plans. They insist that Erik, himself, must disavow any claim or there could be a revolt."

"Would you trust me to handle that when we meet Erik in Helsingborg?" Erik Menved asked softly.

"Only if I know what you are planning," answered Hakon bluntly.

"My reasoning is simple. The three Swedish brothers must be on friendly terms again, or else we will never have peace in Scandinavia. This last war cost me dearly--because I supported you--both financially and in my relations with my nobles. When Erik was betrothed to your daughter, a schism in Swedish allegiances ensued: Birger's was to Denmark; and Erik's--and therefore Valdemar's--were to Norway. However, if Erik were to marry a Danish princess, all three would have a tie to Denmark that would unite rather than split them. And as Birger's son will marry your daughter, Norway will be similarly allied."

"But you do not have any children to marry off," protested Hakon.

"My younger sister, Rigitze--may her soul rest in peace--was married to Prince Nils of Werle and they had a daughter," said Erik Menved with an ingratiating smile. "Princess Sofia is now seventeen, and no suitable alliance has been found for her yet. This would be the ideal match."

"I am not particularly enthused about another of the Swedish brothers marrying into your family," muttered Hakon.

"But dear Hakon, we are trying to create a stable situation in Scandinavia, are we not?"

"That is our goal, but I have serious reservations about the means you are suggesting."

"I can understand that, but it was you who broke the betrothal between Ingeborg and Erik. And you made the final decision that she would marry Magnus. Erik must now look for a bride, and Sofia is the perfect choice. That is, if Erik is willing to relinquish his claims on your daughter."

"His attack on Akershus has been devastating to Norway," said Hakon with a sigh. "If his marrying Sofia is the price for peace and giving up any claim to Ingeborg, so be it!"

Erik and Valdemar's ship sailed into Helsingborg harbor late in the evening. Immediately upon docking they went ashore to their encampment.

Later that night a human shadow moved close to Erik and Valdemar's tent. The man, who was wrapped in a long, dark cloak, stood outside the tent listening to the voices within before entering. "I am glad you are alone," said the man as he closed the tent flap behind him.

"Erik Menved!" exclaimed Valdemar.

"In person," said the king as he pulled off his cloak and sat down on a bench opposite Erik and Valdemar. "Are you going to maintain your right to marry Ingeborg of Norway, at this meeting?" he asked bluntly.

"I certainly will," confirmed Erik.

"I thought you might feel that way," responded Erik Menved. "Therefore, I have a proposal to make. If you forswear the right to Princess Ingeborg's hand, I shall be honored to offer you my niece, Sofia of Werle, as your bride!" Erik shook his head, but Erik Menved held up his hand. "Do not reject my offer so quickly, Erik. Sofia is not only well dowried, she is beautiful and intelligent. Many have been her suitors, but no one has been successful because her father has set very high standards for her future husband."

"What is her dowry?" asked Erik, looking disinterested until he heard the figure. "That is impressive! Still, Ingeborg comes with a crown."

"It is a crown Hakon does not want you to wear, and he is adamant about that. You can, of course, press your demands, and they will be tried in a Scandinavian court where four of its six members will be Norwegians and Danes. I doubt you will be successful."

"And it could take years. By the time the court decides, Hakon and I might well be friends again," Erik said with a smirk.

"Maybe, maybe not. But to make my offer irresistible, I will give you back Northern Halland."

"But you gave Northern Halland to Hakon to make Hakon switch his allegiance," said Erik, looking at the conniving king. "How can we both rule it?"

"Listen, Erik. I want peace in Scandinavia at any price. If Northern Halland induces you to accept my offer to marry Sofia, it is worth risking Hakon's wrath, as there is little Norway can do against the united front of Denmark and Sweden."

"Hakon will surely object" Erik replied.

"He is not coming here," grinned Erik Menved as he stood up. "He took sick a few days ago. He is ill with a high fever, and his physician has advised against any travels before the fever has broken. In his message he requested we go ahead, keeping the points in mind which he and I have discussed. I see no reason for canceling the meeting."

"I will give you my answer before we meet," said Erik as the Danish king drew his cloak around his shoulders and nodded his farewell.

The meeting commenced the following morning after the arrival of Prince Nils of Werle, Princess Sofia's father. The first item on the agenda was to outline a final peace treaty between the three Scandinavian countries, the basis for which was the two proposed marriages. The details were argued back and forth, and not until the following afternoon was everything settled. Erik knew that injustice was being done in Hakon's absence, but in his anger against the Norwegian king he made no objection when Erik Menved granted him sovereignty over Northern Halland. He had, after all, withdrawn his claim to Princess Ingeborg, just as Hakon desired.

After the final documents were signed, the participants turned to the division of Sweden between the three brothers, which was another of the conditions for a peace treaty. The Danish and Norwegian kings felt that Birger's present domains were too small. After days of negotiations, Sweden was divided into two parts: one-third for Birger and two-thirds for Erik and Valdemar, whose shares would be hereditary and who would rule jointly. Birger was given most of the eastern part, including the island of Gotland, the Viborg fortress and its environs in Finland, Nykoping castle which he wanted more than anything else, as well as Visingso castle and Stegeborg fortress. Erik and Valdemar were assigned the western part of Sweden, plus Kalmar county and the island of Oland, as well as the fortresses of Stockholm, Kalmar, and Borgholm on the east coast of Sweden, and the major part of Finland. The brothers would sit jointly in the Council and support each other against common enemies.

After the meeting, Erik and Valdemar went to Birger's chamber in the castle.

Birger's face brightened when they entered; "I was just coming to see you."

"Birger, this is a special day for all of us," Erik began slowly. "We have been through difficult times, but now they must be left behind. I want you to know that we are pleased with the new division and the fact that we will rule Sweden jointly."

Birger remained silent, but he was visibly moved. "You could have killed me," he said finally, his voice trembling. "That would have been the most logical action. I was much to blame for our quarrels. It will take time for us to trust each other again, but I shall try my very best."

"As will I," said Erik as they embraced. To his surprise, he found that he truly meant it. The brothers clung to each other. Valdemar felt his vision blur as he put his arms around both their shoulders. Silently they stood together before they slowly released each other.

"I shall miss you so much, Marta," said Ingeborg. "It has been wonderful spending these two years together here in Denmark. I wish you did not have to go. When Magnus leaves it will be as if I were losing my own son. His mere presence has helped me cope with not having children of my own. But now . . . oh, listen to me going on," said Ingeborg, close to tears.

"I shall miss you, too," said Marta. "And I dread returning to Sweden. I still fear for our lives."

"Marta, dear," exclaimed Ingeborg, "my brothers have had serious disagreements, but they want to put it behind them. So why should Erik and Valdemar harm you now?"

"They imprisoned us," said Marta feeling her hands start to shake.

"I believe my brothers want to respect the treaty," said Ingeborg as she sat down next to Marta. "Power and honor is what men live for, and each one of them have compromised to keep their honor. There is a real chance for a lasting peace now. You must remember, Erik is the undisputed ruler of Sweden, not Birger. Erik has no need to harm him," Ingeborg continued.

"Birger is still the king," Marta insisted.

"That title is the only thing Erik does not have, and had it been important to him, he would have taken it four years ago. Why can you not let go of your fears?"

"My father was killed," Marta whispered with tears in her eyes. "It will happen again. I know . . . I can feel it."

Ingeborg embraced Marta to comfort her, but her shivering became ever stronger. Ingeborg called to Lady Astrid who was outside in the corridor. "Get the physician and the herbal monk right away!" Lady Astrid ran as fast as her aged legs would carry her.

She returned with the physician and the herbal monk to find Ingeborg still cradling Marta in her arms. The physician bent down to look gently into Marta's eyes. He touched her neck, and finally took her trembling hands in his.

"A mild solution of henbane, and let us get her to bed," he ordered. Marta obediently drank the potion before she fell back on the pillows, grimacing at its bitter taste. "Let me know when she awakens," the herbal monk whispered to Lady Astrid who was hovering by the door.

"What happened, your Majesty?" the physician asked as soon as he was seated with Ingeborg in her chamber.

Ingeborg related what had transpired, and how Marta had always feared becoming a victim of assassination. "Since coming to Denmark, she has had similar spells. She denies that these incidents occurred, but I saw them myself."

"Well, I found nothing physically wrong with her, so I am convinced the problem lies within her soul. We all know that evil spirits can invade a person and make them behave in unusual ways. I do not find it strange that someone becomes frightened and suspicious after living through a father's assassination, but after so many years acute fear normally abates. It must be evil spirits. People become susceptible for various reasons, and evil spirits are quick to take over. That is, of course, more common among women who are of the weaker sex."

"What can we do to help her?"

"Normally, we prescribe exorcism when the victim has lost all self control, but that is hardly the case with Queen Marta as she is mostly lucid and only suffers occasional attacks. That, in turn, means one of two things: either the evil spirits are weak, or Queen Marta is strong. Whichever is the case, I shall prescribe a mild solution of bittersweet nightshade for a few days. It will calm her, and when she regains her strength she should follow a program of devout prayer and fasting. I hope, with God's help, that will heal her."

Ingeborg went to find Birger. "A spiritual invasion could explain her behavior," Birger said after hearing his sister's explanations. "When we were imprisoned in Nykoping, she was always frightened and saw deceit in everything. The only one who seemed able to deal with her was Johan Brunkow. Without him we both would have gone mad. But she seemed so much better after being here with you and Magnus, I was sure that she had overcome her worst fears."

"I suspect that Marta became frightened because she is going back to live in her former prison. Can you live somewhere else?"

"I must live in Nykoping Castle to show that I am back in the circle of power," said Birger in a voice that forbade objection. "Once there, Marta will realize that we are not under any threat."

"It is not a wise decision, Birger. You might need to prove something to yourself, but it is terrifying Marta. Why not live at Visingso? It is such a happy place."

"We shall live there, too. But our main residence will be Nykoping," Birger proclaimed with finality.

The physician at first reduced, and then discontinued Marta's sedative drugs. As she displayed no recurring symptoms, Birger, who was impatient to return to Sweden, decided that she should do her fasting and prayer cure there. Although Marta was heartbroken to leave her brother and Ingeborg, she smiled bravely as she, Birger, and Magnus, together with their retinue, boarded their ship. Ingeborg on the other hand went to her chamber and stayed there for three days, crying over the loss of Magnus, her almost child.

"I should have known that I could not trust Erik Menved," hissed Hakon in cold fury.

He was sitting at his desk in his chamber at Akershus speaking to young Lord Val, the son of Count Jakob, who stood by the window. Val Jakobsson had been a longtime friend of the scribe who copied the final peace agreement in Helsingborg.

"The content of the document certainly explains why Erik Menved has not sent me a copy," Hakon continued. "Imagine, the main reason I considered a marriage between Ingeborg and Magnus was to finally rule Northern Halland! And now it has been deeded to Erik."

"But, your Majesty," interjected Val, "it is said that Duke Erik refused to withdraw his claims on Princess Ingeborg's hand, which is what you insisted on, unless he received some consideration for doing so. Northern Halland must have been it, because he is now betrothed to Princess Sofia."

"Maybe I could swallow Erik Menved's deceit had he finally given me my rightful inheritance in southern Denmark, but he did not even that. He left me with nothing. Again!" Hakon banged his fist on the table. "With Denmark and Sweden allied, they can field five men against each of ours, so he knows there is precious little I can do. That liar!"

"But there is a balance, now that your daughter is betrothed to Prince Magnus of Sweden," Val said soothingly.

"I do not like the odds. Prince Magnus is the son of the least powerful player," grumbled Hakon. "I wish things had remained as they were."

Chapter 33

Marta gazed up at the ceiling of her tiny cubicle in Santa Klara convent that glistened with moisture from the dampness. She noticed droplets had collected on the crucifix above her narrow cot. She was deadly tired, so when the persistent bell tolled for morning prayers she sighed in despair. Then, suddenly, she smiled. This was the last time she would be jarred from only a few short hours of sleep to sit through long, monotonous prayers in the damp and frigid chapel. Today she would be departing the convent where she had been staying for more than two months during which she had obediently taken part in every facet of the daily life of the sisterhood. And while she had felt at peace in its quiet and repetitive daily life, she longed to be home with her family again--especially after hearing from Birger how he felt to be working again with his brothers.

Birger had waxed more exuberant than he had in years upon returning to Nykoping from his first Council meeting in Stockholm. "Erik and Valdemar not only treated me with consideration but with respect. You can go to the convent for your cure with the knowledge that there is true peace between us," he had assured her enthusiastically. Even while she lived at the convent, weekly messages from Birger described his continuing satisfaction, so with the passage of time she experienced progressively more resentment at her voluntary incarceration.

At the convent her spells of fear had erupted rarely, and, thank God, only when she was alone. She had not told Rikissa of them or mentioned them in her confessions. And, yesterday, at last, she was pronounced healed from whatever had invaded her body and soul. She felt a pang of conscience for concealing the truth, but the thought of going home was irresistible. After all, her spells were much less severe. This morning a special prayer would be offered in gratitude for her divine cure. As she hastened toward the chapel, she heard Rikissa's unmistakable footsteps behind her. By this time, she knew the walk of every nun.

"I thank our Lord for your recovery," Rikissa began with pleasure in her voice. "If you keep saying your prayers, I am sure no evil spirit will invade you again." Rikissa maintained a long moment of silence before she stopped and put her hand on Marta's arm. "Are you truly well, my dear?" she inquired softly. "You must be certain because if you leave prematurely, what you have done here will be to no avail. When we pray at our service this morning I want you to search your soul, Marta. It is dangerous to hide the truth from our Lord, as it will give strength to the evil spirits . . . if they still lurk within you," she said as her eyes bore into Marta's with such penetrating force that Marta quickly lowered her gaze.

She knows, thought Marta. Somehow, she knows. But I cannot stay here any longer. I have suffered enough. I have seen my husband dethroned, my youngest son taken from me and given to the Church. I have been imprisoned and possessed by demons. I deserve happiness now.

"They are gone," Marta said aloud as she willed her eyes to steadily meet Rikissa's.

"Then I am happy for you," smiled Rikissa.

Birger proudly watched his sons play together in the courtyard of Nykoping castle. Little Prince Erik, who was progressing in religious studies beyond the archbishop's fondest hopes, had returned for a visit with his family. Despite his serious mien he was a fun-loving child who obviously adored his older brother. Magnus, usually the ruthless attacker in military games, softened around his brother as he patiently instructed him in throwing horseshoes at a metal stake. The boys were howling with triumphant laughter as little Erik managed two successful ringers in a row.

Birger watched with satisfaction as he sat with his back against the tower wall. Not only did he have his sons at home, he was delighted over the change in Marta since her return. She appeared quite calm and at peace, and she still followed a strict regimen of prayer. Birger realized that he had every reason in the world to feel content with his life.

Yet, somehow, he did not. Discontentment had begun to gnaw at him ever so subtly. He had become more and more aware of the fact that he would never again wield any meaningful power. The real power belonged to Erik, and although his own proposals and opinions were heard politely, they never altered the final outcome. And what was worse, he knew there was nothing he could do to regain his former stature. The Church's troops would follow him if he turned to arms, but they were no threat to Erik's forces, and Erik Menved would certainly not welcome a plea for further intervention. Birger's Chancellor, Knut Jonsson, had confirmed this time and time again. His only consolation was that he, not his brother, held the title King of Sweden.

When he had visited Archbishop Nils in Upsala earlier, he had placed with him for safekeeping by the Church all the official regalia including his crown and his scepter, not to be released without his, or Marta's, or in case of their deaths, Magnus' permission. Birger realized it had been a childish gesture, but he also knew that the Archbishop relished having the symbols of the crown under his control.

Marta had immediately become anxious when she caught him packing up the precious pieces. Did this mean he expected an attack on his family? If not, why was he taking them to Upsala? He kept reiterating that placing them in the safekeeping of the Church was a simple gesture of faith until she finally appeared to accept his assurances.

Erik was bursting with anticipation when he sat down with King Hakon in Stenso in Northern Halland. Hakon had requested the meeting, and Erik was hoping that they could heal their breach.

"I can understand why you were so angry when we last met," Hakon said after Erik had explained his version of their disagreement. "A meeting between Erik Menved and me did, indeed, take place, and it is unfortunate that it caused you such anguish because

I did not accept his suggestion then regarding Ingeborg and Prince Magnus. If I had only told you of the meeting, we could have avoided all that animosity. But dear Jakob stoked my anger against you quite successfully. I am sorry, Erik."

"I am equally to blame. I misinterpreted your silence, and I insulted you. I should have told you what I knew."

"We have been allies too long not to have at least one misunderstanding," said Hakon as he stood up to embrace Erik. Erik returned the hug with warmth, impressed as always by the Norwegian's straightforward manner.

"Now, let us talk about the future," Hakon began as they seated themselves once more. "Frankly, I do not like the position I find myself in. I preferred the balance of power that prevailed while you were betrothed to Ingeborg, and I wish things were as before. I propose that you marry Ingeborg as originally planned."

Erik stared at Hakon. After their quarrel, and the new marriage arrangements, he had given up any hope of ever ruling Norway. "It is not exactly honorable to break betrothals," continued Hakon, "but it was equally dishonorable for Erik Menved to go back on a promise of land exchange. He has, however, finally granted me my inheritance. All the same, our original marriage plans would suit both of us better, would they not?"

"You need not go to such lengths to restore our ties, Hakon. You have my friendship in any case," said Erik.

"I know. But . . . I always wanted Northern Halland, and now it is legally your territory. Once you become King of Norway, it and all of your lands in Sweden will become allied to Norway. Ours is the best political alliance Norway can have."

"You certainly tempt me," said Erik. "However, I must consider my relationships with Birger and Erik Menved."

"Erik Menved is at war again, and Birger has no powerful allies apart from him. Neither of them will relish these changes, but there is not much they can do just now."

Erik nodded slowly. "I want to talk it over with Valdemar first."

Valdemar left the game table in the hot and smoky Great Hall of Akershus castle. He was impatiently awaiting Erik and Hakon's arrival. He assumed their meeting had gone well as Erik had sent him a message asking him to meet them in Oslo, something which would have been inconceivable had the talks gone badly. Valdemar walked across the drawbridge, and down towards the water that surrounded most of the castle. It was a hot summerday, and he squinted his eyes against the sun while trying to spot the royal ship.

He stopped abruptly when he heard someone crying. He looked around. The sound came from behind some bushes near the water's edge, and he quietly walked over. As he looked over the top of the greenery he could see a young woman sitting, hugging her knees and crying with abandon. Next to her lay a piece of rumpled parchment.

"Can I be of help?" Valdemar asked softly as he moved the branches aside and stepped down to where she sat. Startled by the sound of his voice, she looked up to eye him suspiciously. "I do not mean to disturb you. But you sounded so terribly unhappy," he explained to the beautiful young girl, suddenly embarrassed at having intruded on her grief. Her hair was a light flaxen color, partly braided, and the thick braid was fastened around her head like a halo, while the rest of her hair cascaded down her back. She studied him with her wide-set blue eyes without responding. "Shall I leave you, or would it help to talk to someone?" he asked.

She took a deep breath. "I do not like to be alone when I feel like this. It makes me cry the more," she replied in a soft and melodious voice. Relieved by her answer, Valdemar seated himself on a stone a bit away from her. He pointed to the parchment on the ground.

"Did you receive bad news?"

"It is my List," she smirked with obvious disdain. "One suitor appears to be worse than the other."

"The one you want is not on the List?"

"It is not that I love anyone. I do not. But from what I have heard of these men, not one would be to my liking."

"Will you let me look at it? Maybe what you have heard is exaggerated. I might know one of your suitors and I think him a fine fellow."

"You can look," she said as she retrieved the parchment and handed it to him.

Valdemar started to read the names and noticed they each were princes from North German principalities, so he immediately realized the girl was Princess Inga, the daughter of Hakon's older brother, the late King Eirik of Norway. He knew of her but they had never met as she had lived away from court with her mother. "It is an impressive list," he said cautiously. "I understand now why you must make the right selection. It is not just for your own and your family's future, but for Norway, as well."

"Their likenesses have been sent to me, and not one of them is pleasing, or displays character."

Valdemar had to agree that none of the names conjured up a handsome visage since he had met all the princes at some point in his life. "The prince of Mecklenburg is a fine hunter," he remarked, remembering the fifteen-year-old boy skillfully downing a deer on a hunt in Denmark. "And the prince of Wismar has a lovely voice," he added, recalling his fine tenor from the chapel in Lubeck. But then, most likely the prince had long since outgrown it.

"None of those talents foretell a good husband, do they?" asked Princess Inga unhappily.

She began to cry again. Valdemar racked his brain to find something positive to suggest. Finally, he said, "As we both know it is for the good of Norway, we should try to find out as much about them as we can, just so that you can make the wisest choice possible."

She looked up at him, and he was touched by the soft smile of gratitude that spread over her face. "Would you do that for me?" she asked. "A total stranger."

"Then let us be strangers no more." He smiled back, feeling something warm spread inside, a feeling he had not felt for a long time. He was disappointed that his own name was not on her List. But then, Norway urgently needed an alliance with one of Erik Menved's closest allies. "I am Valdemar of Sweden," he said as he rose from his place to bow to her.

"And I am Inga Eiriksdotter," she said as she rose to curtsy to him. He was stunned when he saw her stand to reveal a graceful, comely and curvaceous body. She was lovely. Valdemar was about to say something when he heard a horn heralding the arrival of a ship.

He turned and spotted the royal Norwegian ship sailing towards the castle.

"I must go and meet my brother," he said reluctantly. "He is arriving with your uncle. But later, let me help you." He leaned over to kiss her hand that felt warm and soft resting in his. His lips brushed her skin as he looked into her eyes.

"Whomever I marry, I hope he will be as chivalrous as you," she uttered softly as she flashed her innocent woman-child smile. He left her with long strides, but part of him remained with her, gazing into those blue eyes, seeing her face slowly change from sadness to a smile. All at once, he wondered what she thought of him. He must seem ancient--twenty-seven years old and her senior by thirteen years. That was probably why she had been so trusting, allowing him to enter her private world. He felt foolish thinking that she could find him attractive in any way other than as an older kinsman.

The royal ship had already docked by the time he arrived, and Hakon and Erik were busy greeting courtiers who had assembled on the quay. It was clear from their demeanor that they had patched up whatever past differences they had had.

Erik's eyes lit up when he saw Valdemar, and he rushed over to embrace him. With his arm draped over Valdemar's shoulder they started walking towards Akershus. "You will never guess what Hakon suggested," Erik taunted while looking challengingly at Valdemar who shook his head. "Hakon again wants me to marry Ingeborg!"

He related their conversation and waited for Valdemar's reaction. "That is great news, Erik! And Hakon is right. There is not a lot Birger and Erik Menved can do about it just now. Congratulations!"

"I have not formally accepted Hakon's offer because I wanted to talk to you about it first."

"What objections could I possibly have? The crown of Norway is what you have always wanted."

"Well, let us sleep on it. I should give my answer on the morrow."

Though the Great Hall was filled to capacity, Valdemar spotted Inga immediately. She was standing beside her cousin, Princess

Ingeborg. Both girls were fair haired and comely, and despite the fact that Ingeborg was three years younger, she looked far more at ease with the boisterous crowd than did Inga. Still, it was that shy gentleness that had attracted him to her in the first place. He made his way across the room. Inga's face lit up as he neared. She leaned over and whispered something to Ingeborg who turned her head to scrutinize him.

He bowed to them. "Greetings. And my warmest congratulations," he added, looking at Ingeborg. "Once again, we are destined for kinship."

"So, I have heard," Ingeborg smiled with the just right amount of grace and warmth.

She will make a grand queen thought Valdemar, before his eyes were drawn again towards Inga. "You look quite recovered," he smiled.

"I am, indeed. Thank you," Inga smiled back.

Valdemar noticed that Ingeborg was studying them while she listened to their polite, everyday conversation.

"Excuse me. I must find my mother," she said, sensing the moment to leave them alone.

Valdemar, who was at a loss for words, was rescued by Inga. "We have been placed together for the banquet. Shall we be seated?"

Valdemar nodded as he followed her up to the dais table where servants pulled out their chairs. Despite his earlier moment of awkwardness, he found it easy to converse with her. She showed an interest in everything and she seemed eager to learn. He found it quite exhilarating to share some of his experiences; to find her following his every word with admiring attention. He found that he had so lost himself in their conversation that he was utterly taken by surprise when the royal ladies stood to leave.

"I shall see you on the morrow," Inga said. He was warmed by her beguiling smile as he bent to kiss her hand. Then she was gone.

Valdemar sat back in his chair looking around to see if anyone had noticed how lost he had been to all but her for the preceding hours, but no one seemed to have paid any heed. He settled back with his wine chalice, relishing the thought of seeing her the next day.

"So here you are," Erik noted as he stepped out on the parapet to find Valdemar leaning against the castle wall, waiting for him. "What is so secret that we could not talk about it at the table?"

"You asked me if I had any thoughts about your acceptance of Hakon's marriage proposal. Well, I do," said Valdemar taking a deep breath. "I want you to accept it only if, at the same time, I can marry Princess Inga!"

"What?"

"I want to marry Inga. I truly like her, and I think she likes me."

"This is news, indeed. But I am afraid there is not the slightest possibility that Hakon would sanction such a marriage. He will gain an alliance with Sweden through Ingeborg, and he needs one with a North German principality through Inga."

"I know all that, Erik. But for once, this is something I want." Erik looked at his brother in silence. "All my life I have lived in your shadow," continued Valdemar. "I have never minded it; you are the natural leader, and besides, we think alike. Most importantly, I love and trust you. I do not regret for one moment following you. Now, finally, I have found someone I could love, and I will not throw that chance away, if she will have me."

"But she must marry one of the German princes for the sake of Norway. I do not know what could persuade Hakon to change his mind on that."

"I know it will be difficult," said Valdemar looking straight at Erik. "That is why I asked to be alone with you, because this is the one and only thing I have ever asked of you."

Valdemar brushed past his brother to run down the stairs, leaving Erik with what seemed an impossible task.

"So, Erik, what is your decision?" asked Hakon with a smile as he pulled on his boots.

Erik and Valdemar stood in Hakon's private chamber. They were dressed in their hunting gear and ready for the day's hunt. "Something has occurred, Hakon," Erik began, "Something I knew nothing about."

"What is that?" asked the king as he picked up his other boot off the floor.

"You need an alliance with Sweden and one with a German principality."

"Correct."

"The only way that can happen is if Valdemar marries Inga and a German prince marries Ingeborg!" Both Hakon and Valdemar stared at Erik in surprise. "Valdemar has fallen in love with Inga and wants to marry her. He has never asked me for anything, so I know how strongly he must feel. Not even the promise of the throne of Norway can deter me from giving him the one thing he wants, so I hope you find this suggestion a favorable solution to Norway's needs."

Hakon sat silent while Valdemar swallowed hard and stared in amazement.

"Most of my men know, and highly approve, of your becoming betrothed to Ingeborg again, Erik. They were not happy with the idea of Magnus as her future husband. I cannot possibly disappoint them again," said Hakon looking helpless.

"I am sorry, Hakon, but I see no other way to accomplish your goals."

Hakon turned to Valdemar. "Does Inga want to marry you?" he asked.

"I hope so."

"I shall find out," Hakon concluded as he pulled on his boot with agitated motions.

The door to Queen Euphemia's chamber burst open and Ingeborg rushed in, slamming the door behind her. Inga, who was alone in the chamber working by her embroidery frame, looked up.

"Is it true?" Ingeborg asked tensely. "That you are in love with Duke Valdemar?"

Inga blushed. "How do you know? I have not told a living soul."

"I just listened in on a conversation between my parents. My father said that Valdemar desires to marry you, if you want him. My mother is to ask you how you feel."

Inga looked as if she would faint. "He . . . he wants to marry me?"

"Yes. Do you want to marry him?"

"Oh, yes. He is the kindest man I have ever met."

"Do you know what that means for me?" asked Ingeborg. "It means that I will not marry Erik, but one of those boys on your List, or someone equally horrid."

Inga looked close to tears. "If I tell your mother that I do not want to marry Valdemar, will you marry Erik?"

Ingeborg stood silently before she answered. "I do not want you to lie to mother. If you love Valdemar, you should marry him. I do not love Erik, so I have no right to ask you to sacrifice your feelings. Still, I very much want to marry Erik for his power and position. But perhaps we can find a way for both of us to get what we want."

"Yes, my dear, Inga wants to marry Valdemar," said Queen Euphemia in response to her husband's question. Hakon was sitting in a bathtub in the middle of his chamber, washing away the grime from the day's hunt. Euphemia picked up his towel, which was thrown on a stool next to the tub and sat down. "Inga seems very much taken with him."

"You should have warned me this was going on," grunted Hakon.

"I did not know. As surprising as it might seem to you, I do not know everything that goes on here. Inga seemed surprised herself over her sudden feelings."

"Father!" Ingeborg's voice called as she came rushing into the chamber, slamming the door behind her. "Father, does Inga's marriage to Valdemar mean that I cannot marry Erik?"

"Nothing has been finally decided," said Hakon gently as he looked at his daughter who seated herself on a stool.

"Good. Because I want to marry him!"

Hakon sighed deeply. "Being the daughter of a king carries certain obligations . . ."

"I have always tried to fulfill whatever is expected of me, Father, but I do not want to marry any of the Germans princes. I want to marry Erik!"

"You have told me that he could be your father, and that you are not in love with him," countered the queen to her daughter who was speaking well beyond her years.

"I am not. How could I be? I have only met him twice. But I like him. He is strong. He is powerful. And he is righteous. He is willing to give up the throne of Norway for the happiness of his brother. I admire that."

"As do I," agreed Hakon, motioning to his daughter to add hot water from the cauldron hanging over a small fire in the corner. As she did so he sat back, enjoying the warmth. Ingeborg hung the cauldron back before she turned to him.

"Ever since I learned to talk, you have discussed politics with me, Father. It would be a mistake for me not to marry Erik. He is more powerful than any of those North German princes. If he marries Sofia of Werle, Norway has lost him as a principal ally. True, Erik and Valdemar are close, and Erik will always respect Valdemar's wishes on Norway's behalf. But he will primarily be allied with Denmark if he marries Sophia of Werle, which is exactly what you wanted to prevent when you again proposed he and I should marry."

Hakon looked at Euphemia who sat openmouthed, listening to her precocious young daughter planning the future of Scandinavia. He could not stop himself from smiling with pride.

"Furthermore, Father, if we marry, Erik will most likely outlive you and become king of Norway, but if both Erik and I die and leave no heir behind, who will be king then? If Inga, a Norwegian king's daughter, marries Valdemar, he--a Swedish prince--would be the perfect pretender to the throne!" The parents looked at one another and then back at Ingeborg. Hakon broke out in hearty laughter that rolled along the corridors of the castle like thunder.

Chapter 34

Nykoping, Sweden 1312

As Marta strode up the hill toward Nykoping castle, she felt invigorated. Spending a sunny fall day outdoors instead of within its gloomy chambers was truly energizing.

The two years since their return had been peaceful ones. Her now ten-year-old son, Erik, had been inducted into the Church, her thirteen-year-old, Magnus, would marry Princess Ingeborg of Norway the following year, and Birger appeared to be content with life. She had experienced only minor panic attacks, and those she had hidden successfully from everyone around her. She was actually smiling as she entered the courtyard with Lady Astrid trailing behind her with labored breath.

"Look, your Majesty," Lady Astrid called as she pointed toward the courtyard, "Your brother's colors!"

Marta had already caught a glimpse of the red and white Danish banners. She hastened towards the Great Hall to learn what news had been brought. Upon entering the Hall her eyes had to adjust to the relative darkness. Soon she was able to discern Birger in deep conversation with Danish emissaries by the fire pit. She realized that the visitors were knights, and not mere messengers. As she wondered what was afoot, she tried to suppress the familiar panic. When Birger noticed her, his face broke into a smile. "Would you excuse us while we read King Erik Menved's message?" he said to his guests.

Marta sank down into her large chair, settled back against the soft pillows and looked at him expectantly. Birger broke the seal and began to read aloud:

"Dearest Sister and Brother-in-law,

This is written in haste since I must return to the battlements as soon as possible as we are still under attack from the Hanseatic cities' armada. We have held them at bay for months now, and I trust that they soon will see the futility of their endeavor and leave. Still, I had to write you the latest news of which I am sure you are unaware. I have just found out that there has been a double wedding in Oslo. Valdemar married Princess Inga and Erik married Princess Ingeborg."

"How is that possible?" exclaimed Marta bolting upright in her chair. "Ingeborg is betrothed to Magnus!"

"Let me read on," Birger muttered.

"King Hakon has broken his treaty with us by sanctioning these marriages. In a way, I myself am to blame for not sensing the depth of Hakon's displeasure with me for deeding Northern Halland to Erik, which I had promised him previously. Had I been more generous towards Hakon this might never have come to pass. Still, your son and my niece, Sophia of Werle, have been openly humiliated, and it follows that we must retaliate. But at present I cannot find enough men to send north to fight for our honor. I am afraid that we have to parlay to see what we can extract from your brothers as compensation for breaking this latest treaty. I am sad to bring you this unsettling news, but I am sure that we can find suitable alliances for Magnus and my niece elsewhere.

Yours, Erik Menved R."

Birger lifted his eyes to see Marta staring at him uncomprehendingly. "I do not understand how Ingeborg could marry at this time," she said slowly. "She is not yet of age."

"They probably received a dispensation from the Church."

"But why is Erik doing this? To humiliate us? It is an outright act of hostility."

"Marta, my dear, you must remember that Erik was betrothed to Ingeborg for eight full years, so if you see his present conduct as hostile, then we treated him exactly the same way when Magnus was promised the alliance. In both instances, it was Hakon who made the decision to serve his own purposes."

Marta studied Birger who appeared calm and reassuring. Nevertheless, she could see his jaw tighten, a sure sign of his latent anger.

"You are too kind, my love. Of course, your brothers are behind this," Marta angrily blurted out. "You do not want to believe that your brothers could wish you ill, but our son could have become King of Norway, and they forestalled that. Again, little by little, they are eliminating any influence you have, or which Magnus could have in the future."

Her words made his jaw tighten more as he tossed the parchment on the table. She could see that he was struggling to control his emotions, but his voice broke when he spoke. "Perhaps I was gullible when I thought that my brothers and I could live together in harmony. While I accepted that Erik was the ruler, I felt that I could make a contribution, and Erik and Valdemar made me feel as if I did. They must have known for some time that they would marry the Norwegian princesses, and they never shared that with me. They still have not told me. I suppose that I no longer merit their confidence."

Marta felt triumphant. Despite Birger's protestations, she had always known that Erik and Valdemar harbored some secret agenda. Exactly what their plans were, or why they had not acted before, she did not know, but she was certain that they were slowly and deliberately moving towards the destruction of her family. She suddenly felt her hands tremble, her heart pound, and an overpowering sense of fear pervade her. She clasped her hands tightly in an effort to suppress their shaking and to breathe normally.

Birger, who had turned his back towards her, stood staring into the fire.

"Erik and Valdemar have never forgiven me for siding with Lord Torgils against them. I believed my two years in prison would count as penance, and that we could begin anew. But we will never again be the brothers we once were. Although it would have been difficult for them to tell me about Hakon's change of marriage plans, it was surely easier for them to just get married, because once the weddings had taken place there would be nothing Erik Menved or I could do. I understand that, but I still would have liked them to tell me."

Marta listened as Birger continued to ruminate aloud, his voice becoming harder, while her hands continued to shake. "Their aim seems to be my gradual removal from the circle of power, so they can one day stop dealing with me altogether." When Birger finally turned to face her, he was aghast at her ashen and trembling countenance.

"Marta! Marta! Calm yourself," he pleaded contritely as he knelt by her side. "Summon the surgeon monk!" he yelled at a page who quickly rushed away. "Do not be afraid," he pleaded as he took Marta's hands in his. "I was only venting my hurt and disappointment in my brothers."

"They will kill us," she whimpered.

"Never, my dear. They may continue to diminish our power, but that is all that will happen." She was shaking from head to foot when the physician and Lady Astrid arrived to gently lead her away to her chamber.

Birger sat down heavily. As he stared into the fire he felt a surge of fury rise within him. Again, his brothers were making him pay for his failings. They were vengeful not just toward him but also toward his family. He had to stop them. But how?

Archbishop Nils listened attentively to Birger's laments as he lounged comfortably by the fire in the Great Hall of Nykoping castle sipping his favorite wine.

"Ever since that day the queen has not been herself," Birger continued. "She requires our food to be tasted, which was done only sporadically in the past, and she insists that I always ride with a large armed escort, even while hunting. Her visit to Santa Klara helped only temporarily." Birger hesitated for a moment before he continued. "Erik, Valdemar, and Hakon have met with me and Erik Menved, and they assumed all the blame for the broken betrothals. They expressed their most sincere apologies. They handsomely compensated Prince Nils of Werle, as well as me. I have tried to explain to Marta that they want only to live in a peaceful Scandinavia. But she does not believe them."

"From what you tell me," said the archbishop, "she is deeply troubled. Still, there is help for her." While he spoke, he was scrutinizing Birger's distraught countenance and wondering if the king was prepared to face reality. "There is but one way to drive out strong spirits permanently."

"You mean by torture?" Birger asked with a shiver as the archbishop nodded. "There must be some other way than exorcism," he protested.

"Her evil spirits have resisted gentler methods."

"But flogging is monstrous," Birger objected.

"I understand how you feel, your Majesty, but we are dealing with forces beyond our comprehension--evil forces which must be fought by evil means."

"I cannot allow Marta to be tortured. I cannot even contemplate it. We must try a new regimen of prayer and fasting."

"I will pray for its success," said the archbishop skeptically.

Kungahalla, Norway 1313

"We have to start preparing for my wife's arrival," Erik told Mats as he threw his hawk into the air. It spiraled skyward and slowly circled above the glittering waters outside Kungahalla fortress. "It was a blessing," he continued "that Hakon wanted Ingeborg to first come of age before both she and Inga left Norway to come to Sweden. I am not all that eager to assume the role of a devoted husband, but now that her arrival is imminent I will do my best to make the marriage a good one. We should arrange a splendid banquet and tournament to welcome her."

"Will Valdemar and his bride be arriving with Ingeborg?" Mats queried.

Erik smiled. "Yes. It will be good to have Valdemar back home again. While I can understand that he did not want to part from Inga leaving her in Norway, he has stayed there far too long."

"Will you invite King Birger here to welcome them?"

"Yes, we are family after all, " said Erik. "Since Valdemar and I are now married, we will have to set up separate households and divide our lands. Logically, I should have the western parts since they border on Norway, and Valdemar should take the eastern properties, like those in Finland, Stockholm and Oland."

"That sounds like a wise solution," agreed Mats."

Erik nodded sadly. "I do not relish living apart from Valdemar," he said, feeling again that he was becoming estranged from everyone important in his life.

Amidst much commotion, the Norwegian royal vessel eased in to gently dock at Kungahalla where its gangplank began to be lowered. Erik scanned the deck for Valdemar, and when he spotted him he waved happily. The moment the gangplank was secured in place he went aboard to greet King Hakon's representative who was there to formally discharge his ward.

"I hereby deliver Duchess Ingeborg to the safety of her husband," the Norwegian proclaimed, bowing deeply.

Erik looked with full attention at Ingeborg. She had grown since he had last seen her, and she appeared quite mature for her twelve years. He had not remembered how pretty she was with her slender figure and pale blond hair. She had her father's dark eyes, which presented a striking contrast to her fair complexion. Those eyes looked back at him with decisiveness and intelligence, an impression further supported by the strong line of her mouth. She carried herself with great dignity as she regarded Erik with a serious mien and a curtsy to deliver her short speech with poise and sincerity.

"I am honored to have arrived in my new country, and I know I shall be happy here."

"The honor is Sweden's," offered Erik as he bowed low in return. Erik then acknowledged Inga. Again, he was struck by her gentle shyness until she flashed a brilliant smile in Valdemar's direction. Erik felt his heart constrict. She looked at Valdemar just the way Kristina used to look at him so long ago. Valdemar interrupted his thoughts by hugging him warmly, and again Erik was reminded of how desperately he had missed his brother.

The two couples approached the ship's railing to wave to the crowd that had assembled at the quayside. All attempts to keep the well-wishers away proved futile, and some soldiers who tried to restrain the pressing throng from coming onto the dock were unceremoniously pushed into the water.

"Are you tired," Erik asked Ingeborg as they disembarked. "Would you like to rest before the evening's celebration?"

"Thank you, but I am too excited to rest even if I tried."

The young duchesses were ushered to sumptuous tents pitched especially for them outside the fortress where they were formally introduced to their new ladies-in-waiting. After greeting everyone, they bathed and finished dressing before setting out on horseback for the tournament arena, led by thirty mounted knights. Erik rose from the dais where he was waiting with Valdemar and the other guests as they approached. He noticed how confidently erect Ingeborg sat in the saddle and, despite her tender years, emanated an indefinable air of dignity before the two duchesses dismounted and stepped up onto the dais.

When Ingeborg greeted Mats, she smiled warmly at him. "Will you fight in my honor today?" she asked as she pulled her colors from her sleeve.

"I am deeply honored, my lady, but I will not take part in the games today," replied Mats, bowing.

"Mats claims he is too old for this sort of sport!" taunted Erik.

"Could I not persuade you?" asked Ingeborg softly. "It is my very first day in Sweden."

Mats heard the soft command in her voice and knew he could not refuse. "I shall do my best, but I cannot assure you of victory. I am an old man now."

"I know you will win. Good luck!" she said as she tied her colors around his arm.

Mats shot a glance at Erik as he stepped off the dais. This was not just a pretty little girl. This was King Hakon's daughter!

Ingeborg had something personal to say to each of the guests, and everyone sat down nodding their approval behind her slender back. They also had a warm smile for Inga who was obviously too enthralled with Valdemar to pay much heed to anyone else.

It turned out to be an exciting tournament with outstanding competitors from both Sweden and Norway from which two finalists emerged. Mats had to fight a strapping young Norwegian knight. Erik could clearly see how tired Mats was from the qualifying bouts, but he persevered and finally emerged victorious.

"You have a good eye for a champion," Erik complimented Ingeborg as they rode back to the castle.

"He has been your champion for years" she said modestly. "I just followed your lead."

Erik smiled at her flattery. "But you made him fight. He was not going to, you know."

"All one has to do is to ask in the right way. Men will do anything if it has to do with their honor." Erik decided not to comment. Instead he turned away to conceal his amusement.

The sumptuous banquet that followed lasted six hours. The entertainment was lavish; and Ingeborg obviously enjoyed herself, commenting on everything. As the ladies later withdrew, Erik went over to Valdemar. "I like Inga," he said warmly.

"She is wonderful! And having had the opportunity to spend time with Ingeborg, I have come to know that she is a real lady."

"That she is," said Erik with conviction. "She was born a queen, no question about it. I got everything I wanted in a public wife."

"I hope you will get along privately as well," said Valdemar as he readied to leave the banquet. Erik was in no hurry, so he refilled his chalice; but after a while he could feel that he was expected to go, so he had no other recourse but to leave the festivities.

Ingeborg was waiting for him in her tent, sitting curled-up in a chair draped in furs. "I hope the accommodations are to your liking," he began. "The fortress is not a place for ladies."

"Thank you. Everything is perfect. It was a lovely banquet," She flashed a bright smile to hide how exhausted she was. "I wanted to talk to you, if you are not too tired," she began cautiously. When he nodded and came over to sit down next to her, she continued. "This is our first night together, and I know what is expected of me. One makes love to have children, and such behavior is blessed by the Church. Therefore, I thought I should tell you that I am not a woman yet." She blushed. "I mean . . . I have not yet had a monthly flow. But if it would please you to make love to me anyway, you are perfectly welcome . . ."

"Are you telling me that you do not want to make love until we can produce a child?"

"Well, if we could wait until we can have a child, I would not mind," she said quietly.

He started laughing and for once, Ingeborg was at a loss for words.

"Listen," he said solemnly as he regained his composure. "I know you think that men will do anything if you ask them the 'right' way. But this is the wrong way with me. Do not try to manipulate me. We must be friends if ours is to be a good marriage. If there is something you do not want to do, I will never force you, because then we would not remain friends."

Her eyes filled with tears. "I have displeased you. Forgive me."

"No, you have not, Ingeborg. I am just telling you not to try to maneuver me with transparent arguments."

"But everyone plays games. No one at court ever says what they think or feel."

"I know, but between husband and wife, like any true friends, it is essential to be honest. One needs at least one person to trust."

"Then you are not angry because I am afraid to make love? I know so little about those things," she added reluctantly, hating to admit her ignorance on any subject.

"You mean you do not know everything?"

He regretted his sarcastic tone when he looked at her crestfallen childlike expression.

"Well, you said we were going to be friends," she bit her lip. "That I have to trust you . . ." She hesitated, and he could see the determination return to her eyes. "But make no mistake, I know an awful lot!"

"I do not doubt it." He smiled at her need to be in control in an alien, adult world. "I admired the way you handled yourself today. You seemed quite confident, and that is the mark of a true lady."

"Thank you," she said, beaming at the compliment. "You did too."

She was quietly for a while before she asked: "Should we sleep in the same bed?"

"The rest of the world does not need to know what we do or do not do."

"Would you turn around, please," she said as she stood up. He turned towards the tent opening as she undressed and crept between the sheets. "I am ready," she called.

He stood up and walked over to the bed. "I have to get undressed too."

"My eyes are closed," she said demurely.

He smiled as he pulled off his clothes and joined her in the warm bed. "Sleep well, my wife," he said as he pulled himself up on an elbow and kissed her chastely on the forehead.

He took her hand and squeezed it gently, but he could feel that she had already fallen asleep, safe and secure in her childhood world. He lay sleepless through the dark hours, missing the warm touch of love that had so filled his being for a few short weeks of his life.

Chapter 35

"It was a splendid welcoming celebration at Kungahalla," Birger read aloud before he paused to look up at Marta who was embroidering in her chamber at Visingso castle. He put aside the parchment that he held in his hand and just stared into space. The castle was silent around them, and he could see dusk approaching through one of the narrow windows. He always felt at peace here in Marta's room, but now he was becoming agitated.

"Read on," Marta prompted without pausing in her stitching.

"I would have liked to have been there with my brothers," Birger mumbled.

"It was impossible for us to attend, you must see that. It would have seemed as if we approved of Erik's ill-begotten marriage."

Birger paced the floor loudly lamenting his fate, while Marta became increasingly agitated. Her hands began to tremble, and by the time Birger noticed she was shaking uncontrollably.

"My God!" he exclaimed. Then he called for Johan and her ladies-in-waiting. "I cannot open my mouth without her going into hysterics!" he muttered as Johan came rushing in. Birger left her room furious with himself for his failure to control his temper, knowing how badly she took the slightest negativity.

"This can not go on, your Majesty!" Johan Brunkow said upon returning from Marta's chamber where she was finally resting with the help of a sleeping draught. "She has had too many of these spells lately."

Birger decided he had to summon the archbishop.

"I will not go!" Marta screamed hysterically when the physician monk entered her chamber. She was sitting on her bed, dressed in traveling clothes, her face streaked with tears.

"Marta, it was you who decided that you should do this," Birger reminded her as he sat down next to her, taking her hands in his. He looked pleadingly at the physician who offered Marta a calming potion. "You will feel much better after you drink this," he prompted kindly.

"I will not drink it, and I will not go!"

"Listen, your Majesty," Johan Brunkow pleaded as he sank to one knee in front of her. "When you get this upset, you get an attack. Please drink this and then we shall talk about it."

"All right, Johan," she responded to his caring voice, gesturing for the cup that she drained before tears again flowed down her cheeks. "You all think I am insane."

"No, your Majesty," Johan objected gently. "But you are possessed by something which makes you appear deeply troubled. You have to drive it out so that you can be yourself, and again enjoy those who love you. Have you not had enough?"

"Are you sure it will work? I am so afraid."

"Of course, you are frightened, but the evil spirits are equally afraid. If you are just a little stronger than they are, they will be forced to leave you."

"Are you absolutely sure?" She turned her head to look pleadingly at Archbishop Nils.

"God will cure you," he answered with conviction. "You have always been a devout woman. He will surely not abandon you now."

Marta stood on unsteady legs. "Let us go then," she said in a thin voice as she leaned on Johan who gently guided her from the room. Birger followed them down to the Great Hall where Marta stopped him. "Let us say our farewells here."

"Dearest, you know that I want to go with you, but the archbishop insists that you face this alone. You will be in my thoughts every moment you are away, and I shall pray for you, my love. Do not for a moment forget how much I love you."

"You still do?" she asked through her tears.

"Yes, and forever," he said as he kissed her hand with great tenderness. She smiled weakly as she followed Archbishop Nils and Johan out the door, leaving Birger in the dark and empty Hall. He turned and ran to the parapet to see Marta and her entourage board the barge that was to take them to the mainland and the convent.

Birger was unaware of the fact that he was crying out loud as tears ran down his face. But he was aware of how deeply he loved her. She was his life and he did not want to live without her. The guilt of allowing her to go through this torturous ritual had weighed on him day and night, and he was panicked by the very thought that she might not survive it. All this was his brothers' fault! Had they not imprisoned him and Marta, had they not played political games that had so frightened Marta, she would never have fallen victim to evil spirits. That he had played the very same game did not cross his mind. And now his brothers would cause Marta inhuman agony. He would never forgive them for that.

The following day, without the benefit of the calming drug, Marta awoke in a nun's cell on a narrow cot with the realization that there was no reprieve from the horrid pain and humiliation she was about to suffer.

She rose, threw off the thin wool blanket that covered her, and went over to try the door to see if there was any means of escape. The door was locked, so all she could do was to wait for her tormentors. Even though she found the waiting unbearable, it was far too soon when she heard muffled steps. A key turned in the lock before the Mother Superior entered, closing the door behind her.

"I, alone, know who you are, your Majesty," she said kindly as she came over and took Marta's hands in hers. Her grey eyes were filled with empathy as she continued. "The sisters know exactly what to do. You will never see their faces, nor will they answer if you speak to them. It is not that they are callous, but if they help you in any way, it will destroy the chances of driving out the evil spirits. Only you can do that through your own resolve and God's help."

"I am so frightened. Will I have the strength?"

"God helps his children. Just believe in Him, and you will prevail."

The Mother Superior gazed at the petrified queen and prayed that she would win her lonely battle. "Get undressed and don this robe," she ordered as she handed Marta a simple brown woolen garment. "The nuns will be with you shortly."

"Do not do this to me!" pleaded Marta in panic. "Let me out of here!"

"You realize that it is not you speaking now, but evil spirits who are panicked over what will happen to them if they are driven from their sanctuary in your body. They will become unprotected and utterly defenseless, especially here in a convent where God's presence is overpowering. Have courage, my child, you will live a full life again."

The Mother Superior leaned forward and kissed Marta on the forehead. "May God bless you," she whispered before she straightened up to leave the cell. Marta heard the key turn.

As if in a trance, Marta undressed. She pulled on the rough woolen robe and tied a rope around her waist to secure it. She sat down on her cot to wait in the silence. Soon she heard steps. The lock turned. The door opened, and a nun with a hood pulled down over her face stood in the doorway gesturing Marta to follow her. Marta stood on legs that buckled. She took a deep breath to fight the panic that filled her being. It is only the evil spirits, she thought to herself. They are more afraid than I am.

Outside the door six other nuns met her with deeply cowled hoods shadowing their faces. The nun who had summoned her led the way, gesturing for her to follow. Marta walked slowly, followed by the others on silent feet. At the end of the corridor, they passed through a portal leading to a stone spiral staircase. Marta could not keep track of how many times the winding stairs turned as they descended deep below the convent. At the foot of the stairs, the lead nun set forth down a damp and narrow torch-lit hallway. They turned several more corners before she stopped at a thick wooden door that she unlocked. She gestured for Marta and the others to pass through, then re-locked the door after they were all inside a large stone chamber. Marta had to take a few more steps to the floor on which stood just one piece of furniture--a long, thick wooden bench.

The first nun silently gestured for Marta to disrobe and to lie, face down, on the bench. Marta numbly obeyed. She felt two of the nuns bind her hands to the sides of the bench while two other nuns bound her feet to its surface. She saw two of the nuns on either side of her, each with a whip in hand. The whips had thick, short handles with thonged leather tails.

The nun at the head of the bench intoned a prayer before she crossed herself and stepped back from Marta's vision. She must have given the sign because Marta cried out in pain as the first lash bit into her back. She was given no reprieve as the next lash from the other side landed lower down on her back. The pain became even worse as the lashes began to strike places that had already been hit. Marta lost all sense of time, unable to concentrate on anything but the excruciating pain. She could hear the nuns breathe heavily from their labor, and she realized that other nuns took turns with the whips. She started to plead and cry for mercy--but none was given. As the punishment continued she felt increasingly dizzy. Suddenly she heard a scream that could only have come from the throat of a dying animal. That scream, she realized before she surrendered to a blissful blackness, must have come from her.

When she awoke she was alone in her cell, lying face down on her cot. Her first sensation was the intense burning on her back, buttocks, and thighs. She tried to move, but the slightest movement caused intense pain. She drifted back into a blessed state of unconsciousness. When she next awoke she noticed a mug of water and a piece of stale bread on a wooden platter below the cot. With great effort she lifted the cup to her mouth long enough to take a sip of water. But the act was so painful that she put the mug down with a whimper, and mercifully fell back into darkness.

The dreams came as clouds floating on an endless sky. She was a small child again, standing by the huge doors of Roskilde castle. A pallet was carried into the Great Hall by six gaunt figures concealing a prostrate figure on the wooden boards. When they set it down and withdrew, she saw that it was her father. He was not moving, and he was covered with blood.

She was awakened by her own screams. It was light in the cell, and she assumed that she must have been unconscious throughout the night. As she moved her arm to reach the mug of water on the floor, she realized that she was covered with a thin, coarse wool blanket. The blanket heightened the pain, and she made an effort to remove it;

but the blood from the wounds had dried to the woolen surface, and the blanket stuck to her skin. She ceased abruptly from the horrendous pain, but then she thought it better if her wounds were exposed to air rather than putrefying under the coverlet. With tears of resolve she tore it away. The naked slashes burned so intensely that she was grateful for the chill of the damp cell. With great effort she drew her legs up and tucked them under another blanket, which was folded by the foot of her cot, in the hope of retaining some body heat. The effort made her lose consciousness again.

Time must have passed, because the pieces of bread on the platter changed shapes and did not seem stale to the touch. She never ate any. She only drank the water and cursed every moment of consciousness and pain. Now and then she sensed humans nearby. She could hear the murmur of prayers, but she never saw anyone.

She floated in and out of her dreams. Once again, she was back in the Great Hall of Roskilde castle. Slowly she moved towards the pallet and kneeled beside her father's corpse. She leaned over to look at his beloved face. As she bent down to kiss his forehead, his features changed, and she realized she was looking into Birger's face. She screamed . . . without a sound passing her lips.

"I want to see the archbishop," Marta demanded in a strong and authoritative voice.

The young nun who was about to leave the cubicle after having delivered fresh bread and water stopped in surprise to look into Marta's clear and focused eyes. She scrutinized her carefully before she left the cell, half-running.

"Your Excellency," she said as she burst into the chamber where the archbishop had been staying for several days. "The lady is asking for you."

"How is she?"

"She looks alert, your Excellency."

"That is encouraging!" he said as he hurried down the corridor. He entered Marta's small cubicle where he seated himself on a low stool. He reacted with an involuntary shiver when he saw the hideous, inflamed wounds on the queen's frail back. Having to repeat the treatment on her chest and stomach would be horrible, but if she had not repelled her invaders, that would have to be done.

"Your Majesty," he whispered softly after the nun had withdrawn.

Marta opened her eyes and looked at him calmly. "I thank God for delivering me from evil."

The archbishop studied her skeptically. After receiving such punishment, most victims pretended to be cured to avoid further torture. It was not difficult to detect those, but Marta, with her calm demeanor and absence of any fear in her eyes appeared to be telling the truth.

"Praise the Lord!" he sighed as he crossed himself and went over to open the door. "Summon the herbalist immediately," he ordered the young nun who had been waiting outside.

The Mother Superior concurred in the archbishop's assessment. Seeing the festering wounds on Marta's back, she knew that her nuns had carried out their duty as instructed; and the clarity of Marta's speech, her impressive calm, and a fervent desire to attend chapel, were proof of her cure.

"We shall thank God on your behalf today. Sister Clara will administer ointments, as well as give you something to eat. You must rest and regain your strength. Tomorrow will be soon enough for chapel."

God had freed her body from the evil spirits. Of that, Marta had no doubt. And he had replaced them with insight. That simple insight, which she had only faintly perceived before, was that she had a mission. She had always suspected that Birger's enemies would stop at nothing to harm him. They were everywhere and had conspired in unseen and devious ways to frighten her, to make her appear insane. They had hoped she would be flogged to death, and once she was out of the way and unable to protect Birger, they would kill him and their children. She was the only one who perceived the threat, and now she would outwit and fight them with every possible means at her command. She could not let them know that she was aware of their designs. She would let no one know. Not even Birger.

"It is a glorious miracle, your Majesty," Johan Brunkow called to Birger who had been waiting anxiously, and who had raced to meet him the moment he returned to Visingso castle. Birger's eyes were filled with worry and red from lack of sleep. "The queen has been pronounced cured!" Johan said jubilantly. " I have not seen her myself, but the archbishop assured me that the treatment was successful."

"Thank the Lord," whispered Birger as he crossed himself. He could not remember ever feeling such fear as he had over the past days--fear that he would lose Marta to that dark world which had threatened to engulf her. He would be totally bereft without her unwavering love and support. The prospect of having her back as her old self filled him with such joy that he promised himself he would do anything she wanted. Anything to keep her smiling at him as she had before.

Visingso, Sweden 1314

On her first day home at Visingso castle, Marta took out her favorite jewelry box and sat down in front of the small fire in her chamber. She was exhausted from the celebration Birger had lovingly prepared for her homecoming. She would have preferred to go straight to her chamber as the wounds on her back were far from healed, and still burned every time she moved, but his look of rapture over her return had silenced any objections she might have expressed. She could not bear to disappoint him.

Slowly she opened the box, which was filled to the brim with her treasured mementos. She had always felt that her very being resided in that box, along with her precious memories. How ridiculous, she thought as she stood up, turned the box up side down, and without hesitation, emptied its contents into the flames. Her life now belonged to God and his Holy commandments. She did not need childish and comforting reminders to feel strong, or to do what He expected of her.

"Please do not cry any more, my love," Birger pleaded as he put his arms around Marta.

"How can I stop? Archbishop Nils was one of the few friends I made here in Sweden. His death came so suddenly, and I cannot get used to the fact that I will never see him again."

"I, too, will miss him."

"I want to go with you to Upsala for his funeral," she sobbed into his chest.

"It is a long journey, Marta, and the weather is miserable."

"I have to bid him my final farewell," she insisted.

The funeral was a lavish affair attended by every churchman in the country and representatives from all the noble clans. Erik and Valdemar participated as well. After the two-hour service they and Birger left for a Council meeting in Stockholm. Marta and Johan Brunkow stayed behind to await Birger's return.

While it had been important for Marta to be present at the archbishop's funeral, her visit in Upsala had a far more important purpose. Full of resolve, she set out to do her work.

"You will be so proud of me, Birger," bubbled Marta ebulliently in the archbishop's luxurious quarters behind Upsala cathedral that had been allocated to Marta during her stay. "During the weeks you spent in Stockholm, I have found our new candidate for archbishop!"

Birger was a captive audience sitting in his bath as she buzzed around him filling his tub with hot water. The private chamber, with its splendidly wide, heavily draped bed and myriad of fine rugs and tapestries, boasted a huge fireplace under a deep stone hood. This novel architectural idea from the continent freed the room of smoke and the customary draft from a ceiling hole, while filling it with welcome warmth. Birger, who had been stiff with cold from his trip, wanted only to lounge in the tub in silence, but from Marta's excitement he knew that was not going to happen.

"All the bishops were here for the funeral, and I took the opportunity to talk to each and every one of them. It did not take me long to discover the two bishops Erik and Valdemar are supporting for archbishop. When I spoke to them, as a queen seeking spiritual solace, I could clearly see why your brothers favored them. Not only are they intelligent and devoted to the Church, they are also smooth politicians, and utterly supportive of the dukes. Should either of them be elected you might no longer have the total backing of the Church," Marta warned.

"But after many careful interviews, I found our man. Do you remember the priest who negotiated the archbishop's release from Nyköping when we were incarcerated there? His name is Olov, and he has risen to the position of administrative bishop. He is very clever, and he has been close to our beloved Archbishop Nils for many years. Olov has no love for the dukes after their imprisonment of the archbishop, and he is extremely well-connected within the Church hierarchy as a result of being posted here at the seat of the Swedish diocese."

Birger listened as Marta extolled Olov's virtues as well as those of other possible candidates, and after she was finished, Birger had to agree with her choice.

"I knew you would feel that way, so I have very carefully begun to put his name forward to the different members of the Church council, as well as to the chieftains of the church-loyal clans. From what I have heard from Johan Brunkow and Knut Jonsson, my suggestion has been eagerly taken up as a religious woman's intuitive preference."

"I am proud of you, Marta," smiled Birger. "I could never have spoken to the different bishops without my ulterior motive becoming apparent. Do you think Bishop Olov has a chance to be elected?"

"He has few enemies, which I think has been the key to his success so far. I do think he has a good chance, and if, indeed, he is chosen, you will continue to have the Church as a strong ally."

Birger sighed with pleasure as he sank further down into his tub causing the water to rise dangerously close to the edges. Marta, oblivious to his movement, added more hot water, which immediately overflowed onto the precious carpets.

"You have always told me how important it is to know whom you can really trust. Can you trust your closest advisors?" she asked.

"Most of them," he answered pensively.

"The only one I trust is Johan Brunkow," she said softly. "He stood by us all through our imprisonment and during my illness. Never, but never, has he wavered."

"He has been a loyal friend, closer than anyone, even my chancellor, Knut Jonsson," Birger agreed. He also remembered that of all of his advisors, none had given him any encouragement or hope of becoming a ruling king again. None, that is, except Johan Brunkow.

"I want to make Johan Brunkow my chancellor, Marta," Birger announced proudly several weeks later.

"That is a wise choice," Marta replied, not in the least surprised by the decision. "I hope that you are absolutely sure. Your advisors will tell you that he does not have a great deal of experience, and the position carries an awesome responsibility."

"I am sure," answered Birger, confident in the knowledge that he had made the decision on his own. "Johan is clever, and most important, he is absolutely trustworthy."

"What position will you give your present chancellor?"

"I do not know," said Birger hesitantly. "Whatever I give Knut Jonsson will be a step down, and he is bound to take it badly. But he keeps on saying that nothing can be done about my situation, and that I should be grateful to retain my title. Johan Brunkow, on the other hand, understands how I feel."

"I am so glad that you have made your decision, my dear," said Marta gently, inwardly exulting over the first piece of her plan falling into place.

Chapter 36

"He is beautiful," cooed the Queen of Denmark as she bent over her nephew cradled in Duchess Ingeborg's arms. "He looks just like you, Erik."

"Magnus does have my coloring," Erik agreed as he looked down on his son of less than a year who had slept peacefully through most of the trip to Denmark.

Prince Magnus Erikson had been born in Norway where his doting grandparents wanted to keep him permanently. While Erik did not care where his son grew up, he had become extremely attached to the infant and consequently took him along on trips whenever he had to perform his duties. Furthermore, it seemed appropriate for the little prince, even at his tender age, to meet the rest of his family as well as the leading nobles and churchmen of Sweden.

"He is a fortunate child," slurred Duke Kristoffer as he moved closer to the little prince, his wine-rancid breath causing Duchess Ingeborg to wince and turn her head. "One day he will become King of Sweden and Norway, the lucky little cuss."

As Kristoffer reached out with his fat fingers to grab hold of Magnus' little hand, Duchess Ingeborg stood up. "He needs to be fed," she declared before she escaped from the Great Hall, closely followed by the queen.

Erik watched the departure of his sister, his wife and their son, but his mind was on Kristoffer's words. When Erik had first beheld his new born he had a premonition that his son would become not only the King of Norway, but of Sweden as well. The feeling had been so strong that with it had come the realization of the absurdity of Birger remaining king in name only. He cursed himself for not claiming the title when he had Birger incarcerated.

"Come sit by the fire," Kristoffer suggested, interrupting Erik's thoughts as the Dane eased his heavy frame into a high-backed chair and reached for a wine chalice resting on a nearby side table. He waited for a servant to fill Erik's cup and to leave them alone together before lifting his own. "May your son grow up to rule in peace," he said as he drained his chalice in one swift draught.

The passing years had been unkind to Kristoffer. His hair fell in greasy tresses around his puffy face. His watery eyes betrayed utter boredom. Only his mouth displayed any character--it was thin and cruel. His elaborate ducal chain was sorely out of place on his badly stained tunic. "I am sure that it has not escaped you that my brother is not here to greet you," smirked Kristoffer while refilling his own cup. "His official excuse is that he is sitting in judgement today and tomorrow. Still, I am sure that he could have taken a few moments away from those duties to welcome his brothers-in-law, if he had felt so inclined. Personally, I think he is still perturbed with you for marrying Ingeborg of Norway."

"I do not think a man like Erik Menved sulks for five years over foregone marriage alliances. He makes the best of things, and goes on from there," objected Erik.

"You do not know my brother as I do. He is still holding a grudge because he suspects me of being involved in the attempt on him at Orkelljunga ten long years ago. Thanks to your silence he has no proof, but his suspicions have never waned. Some months ago, he found out about some of those who plotted with me then, and he had them executed. They did not inform on me either, being aware of what I would do to their families had they spoken of my involvement."

Kristoffer rose on unsteady legs and excused himself to heed the call of nature. Erik decided not to await his return but went instead to seek out Erik Menved. When Erik reached the richly appointed audience chamber it had just been cleared of the king's advisors.

"I am sorry not to have greeted you personally," Erik Menved said with a much warmer smile than Erik had expected after Kristoffer's ruminations.

"I understand you were sitting in judgement today. One cannot interrupt such proceedings for visitors."

"I am glad you understand," said Erik Menved as he enveloped Erik in a warm embrace. "It was no snub to you. Of course, I have been angry with you for breaking our treaty, it is true, but that is all behind us now. I congratulate you on your son and heir. Something I sorely lack since your poor sister has suffered no less than fourteen miscarriages," he added ruefully. He gestured for Erik to be seated beside the long, polished table next to his own high seat. "Not having an heir is especially troubling when closest in line for the throne is that power-hungry, dissolute brother of mine. That is why I have him here where I can keep an eye on him."

After a long pause Erik ventured to change the subject.

"When Birger and I reconciled after his imprisonment, would you have interfered had I taken the title of King, while allowing Birger to rule one-third of Sweden as his dukedom?"

"I do not suppose that I would have risked an all-out war for him merely to retain the title, when you were in fact the ruler."

"I was only curious."

"You are not thinking of making that change now, are you?" Erik Menved asked.

"I have no immediate plans," Erik replied evasively.

"Do not have *any* plans, Erik. I implore you. Enjoy the peace. No one needs the grief of conflict and war, especially between brothers. Maybe I have grown old," Erik Menved added sadly. "I did once love the thrill of it all." Erik merely smiled. For his son, he would fight any war.

Queen Ingeborg of Denmark gazed gratefully as the door to her chamber closed behind the last fleeting skirt of her ladies. "Finally, Ingeborg, we can be alone," she said to her sister-in-law who was nestling little baby Magnus into an elaborately embellished crib. The child was fast asleep after a long day of adulation and unfamiliar surroundings.

"Your ladies did not seem pleased at being dismissed," Duchess Ingeborg observed as she straightened up, satisfied that her son was resting comfortably.

"You know how they are. They hate to be excluded from even the most trivial occurrence. And in a way, I suppose I have always been rather distant. I find it hard to trust anyone, or to make new friends."

"Just like me, then."

The two women's' gazes locked, and they smiled in understanding. The queen sat down by the small fire and drew a chair close beside her. The peace of the beautiful chamber enveloped them as they sat in comfortable silence before the flickering flames.

The queen turned to look at her sixteen-year-old sister-in-law. They had never met before this day, which the queen already regretted, as she immediately liked her. While Duchess Ingeborg had a comely and childish face, she exuded the self-assurance of one far more mature, and from her lively conversing during the supper that evening it was obvious that she was well informed on worldly affairs, about which she spoke with both wit and insight.

She similarly had opined about womanly topics with the same keen interest, and she was attired in the latest continental fashion--a more elaborate headdress than was common in the north, as well as a tunic entirely embellished with embroidery rather than just at the hem, wrists and neck--that left a favorable impression on the ladies who had studied her attire with admiration and envy.

"My brother chose wisely," said the queen finally. "I am impressed by your carriage and manner."

"Thank you for your praise, dear sister, but my actions are merely instinctive. My father always said that I was born to be a queen." The duchess' open smile was without boast or pride. "I hope that I will be of support to Erik in years to come."

"I have not been of much help to my husband," confided the queen with a sigh. "If anything, I have caused him problems. I have given him no heir; and I certainly have not endeared myself to the ladies at court as you must surely have noticed--and consequently not to their powerful husbands. But my husband has stood behind me nevertheless, and at least I have their grudging respect." The queen looked away to hide her eyes that had filled with tears. "Though not having a child is the hardest fate of all."

"I can well imagine that," said the duchess with genuine concern as she looked over to the crib where her son was sleeping peacefully.

594

"Still, the blame for failing to have a healthy child is not mine alone. I was a victim of sorcery and poisoning. Once those malevolent forces had been set in motion, my poor body became weakened, with the result that I have had miscarriage after miscarriage, two stillborn children, and one child lost before he was a week old. My husband is still fervently praying for an heir; but as for me, I am finally through with tears and futile hope. I would go insane if I concentrated my every waking thought in that direction."

"But who would wish you ill?"

"Duke Kristoffer."

"Are you certain?"

"I no longer have any doubt. While I have no absolute proof, I know of too many circumstantial connections for it not to be so. I finally approached my husband with my suspicions, but understandably he does not want to believe them. Kristoffer is his brother, after all . . . Oh, how I detest that man."

"He is a loathsome looking character," ventured the duchess, recalling some of her father's conversations on which she had eavesdropped over the years. "I have heard that he desperately covets the Danish throne, but I had no idea that he would resort to such diabolical means."

Hesitantly at first, but then with her words eagerly tumbling forth, the queen told of her years at the Danish court. "How utterly alone you must have felt," exclaimed the duchess empathetically when the queen had finished her story.

"Had it not been for Lady Brigitte, and for Kristina, I would have gone mad. Now I have become resigned to whatever happens in the future."

They went on talking for hours. When the duchess rose to take the baby back to her chamber, Ingeborg asked anxiously, "Have I spoken too much? I wanted your visit here to be a happy one, and now I fear I may have spoiled it."

"You have done no such thing. If finally speaking of your woes has eased your mind, I am honored to have been the one in whom you chose to confide, and I shall pray that you never have to lay eyes on Kristoffer again."

Erik had to admit that he had been lucky to wed Ingeborg. She had assumed her role seriously, and she wanted to learn all about his duties and obligations. During the first year of their marriage she had taken to being present on days when Erik sat in judgment, something Erik's advisors, courtiers, and the populace considered a caring and considerate gesture on the part of their Duchess. But she was not just an ornamental presence. She soon became an active participant in the discussions of the cases that preceded and followed the judgments. At first, Lords Mats and Arnvid were somewhat uncomfortable with her impromptu comments, but they soon forgot her gender when she presented her arguments in a well-reasoned manner and even came to value her astute observations. They had, therefore, not been surprised the first time they found her curled up by the fire when Erik's Council met, even though no outsider was allowed in the Hall during those meetings. She sat quietly gazing into the flames while stroking Erik's favorite hunting dog stretched out beside her. Mats had given Erik an inquiring look, but Erik had simply shrugged his shoulders and then seated himself for the meeting. The men had soon forgotten her presence, and from that day on she had been present during every Council meeting. The only thing disturbing Erik was that his dog had become far more devoted to her than to him.

It had not taken long for Ingeborg to begin to offer her opinions to Erik in private, and while they were obviously those of a young and inexperienced novice, they were insightful and often creative. Erik found himself listening to her, and even asking for her input. Still, he was careful not to appear the fool in front of his men by openly discussing matters of state with her.

Throughout the first year of their marriage, Erik had chastely kissed her cheek before they went to sleep. The wenches at the tavern close to Varberg castle satisfied his needs, and apart from awaking with Kristina on his mind, he had had little to complain about.

Once a month he would travel to Stockholm for meetings. Upon returning from one of these trips, Ingeborg blushingly informed him that she had entered the state of womanhood, suggesting that they approach their marriage in a suitable manner. Erik had all he could do not to laugh at her demurely constrained initiative; although he solemnly agreed to claim his marital rights with little excitement at the prospect, as he looked upon her as a younger sister. Still, they had to produce an heir, as he was occasionally reminded by courtiers looking questioningly at her still slender figure.

Ingeborg assumed the role of mistress in the same way she had approached the role of duchess. She was determined to perform it well. Little by little she coaxed Erik into explaining what could be done besides mere copulation. As Ingeborg put it: "There must be more to it than this!" Always the avid pupil, she had gone about her task with eagerness and energy. Erik smiled, grateful for such a spirited partner.

When Erik entered their chamber, Ingeborg was seated on the bed, busily brushing her hair. Erik was still peeved at Kristoffer for trying to enmesh him in his schemes, and his head had started to pound from the wine. Ingeborg had her back to him, so she could not see how downcast he looked. "Erik, I have spent the past hours with your sister, and we must help her," she began as she put down her brush and quickly braided her long hair. She turned around. "What is wrong? You look positively ashen."

"I drank too much," Erik replied evasively.

"Then you should rest," Ingeborg said. "But first we must talk about your sister."

"What about my sister?" he asked. It took the better part of an hour for Ingeborg to tell Erik what Queen Ingeborg had endured during her years at the Danish court. Her rendition was filled with empathy, and by the time she finished, Erik had forgotten his lethargy and was pacing the spacious guest chamber with angry strides.

"I had my suspicions and Lady Kristina was certain of it, but I never wanted to believe that Kristoffer could fall so low as to victimize a woman. He has flagrantly violated the code of chivalry, and for that he deserves to pay with his life."

"What I do not understand is why Erik Menved has done nothing about his brother," Ingeborg wondered from inside her under-dress that she was removing. She tossed it on a stool and walked naked to the bed. "All your sister ever wanted was for Kristoffer to leave court."

Erik gazed with admiration at his young wife's strong and supple body. All at once, he realized that he was not quite as tired as he had thought. He began to undress, and quickly crept into the bed beside her. "I will have a talk with Erik Menved on the morrow," he promised as he reached out to fondle her beneath the covers.

"Tell me about Kristina Torgilsdotter."

"What do you want to know?" he asked, withdrawing his hand.

"Your sister seems to adore her."

"She grew up as one of us," he said curtly. "We all adore her." He could feel the queasiness return. He turned on his side to extinguish the bedside candle. "Let us sleep now. I will have to wake early to join Erik Menved as he sits in judgment. Rest well, my dear."

"You, too, husband," she yawned as she snuggled against his back.

It took him a long time to get to sleep.

The next morning the Great Hall was crowded with courtiers pushing and shoving to find a space on the benches to watch the judgments. Erik made his way through the throng heading towards the king's chamber.

When he entered, he found Erik Menved alone, placing the weighty crown on his head.

"This thing always makes my head ache," the king muttered as he turned to Erik.

"I am here to talk about Kristoffer," Erik began, "And I will be blunt. You should permanently exile him to his dukedom."

"And what do you think he will do then behind my back? Stay content as a wealthy landlord, banned from participating in court intrigues he loves so dearly?"

"If you demand exhaustive tribute from him, he will not have the means to raise an army large enough to threaten you. Furthermore, without money to spread around he will not be able to incite his neighbors and recruit allies. He will be rendered harmless."

Erik Menved's face filled with sadness. "You have spoken to Ingeborg?"

"No, but my wife did, and she is convinced that Kristoffer was responsible for many, if not all, of her miscarriages."

"In the past I could never bring myself to believe that Kristoffer was behind any act so low, but lately I have been less sure," Erik Menved admitted after a long silence.

"As I said before, I will not come between two brothers, but I do suggest that at long last you act to make life tolerable for your wife."

"I will heed your advice," the Danish king promised solemnly after a long pause. Then his face broke into a grin. "Remember how Kristoffer punished his wife by refusing to let her come to court after I brought him out of exile last time? Well, this time I will permit her to stay on with us when he leaves."

A few weeks later, Erik's ship pulled into Borgholm harbor on Oland. Ingeborg was delighted at the prospect of once more feeling firm ground beneath her feet. The weather had been stormy for the final three days of the voyage, causing their ship to heave and toss and spilling their belongings all over their cabin. When she sighted Valdemar and Inga she called out and waved excitedly, and the moment the gangplank touched down she rushed to embrace Inga with tears of happiness.

"I do not often get seasick," she explained as they walked off the dock, arm in arm. "But this time I would have gladly died rather than feel so ill."

"You can rest as long as you want," said Inga, her expression one of concern on seeing Ingeborg's pallor.

"Congratulations on your son," Erik said warmly to his brother as they walked toward Borgholm castle that was now Valdemar's main residence.

"I trust you understand that this reunion is solely to admire each other's precious offspring," Valdemar bantered as they entered the castle courtyard. Once they were seated comfortably in Valdemar's chamber, Valdemar resumed the conversation in a more somber tone.

"I have encountered some serious problems during these last years. It all started with the election of the new archbishop," he recalled. "Birger succeeded in having Bishop Olov elected by mounting an unexpectedly well-coordinated effort. I tried to thwart it using every means at my disposal, but I started too late. So, after the election, I detained Olov to prevent him from traveling to the Pope for final confirmation.

That only worked for a while. Then I tried to block his annunciation by forbidding it to take place in Upsala cathedral that lies within my domain. When the Church, not surprisingly, decided to do it there anyway, I revoked their right to collect taxes, which effectively stopped them from going ahead. But then the Danish archbishop offered to have the annunciation in Lund cathedral. After that, Olov launched a campaign against me for interfering in Church affairs. I found it easier to live here on Oland, rather than to stand my ground in Stockholm, so close to the Church's seat in Upsala."

"But why did you work so hard against his election and then his installment? Our candidates could not match the support Olov had. Why did you not just let it go?" Erik asked.

"I felt it was vital to have an archbishop with an allegiance to us, and Olov had displayed nothing but hostility. And Birger had been behaving strangely. He forced his advisors to sign yet another loyalty oath after his surprise appointment of Johan Brunkow as chancellor. I had a feeling Birger was up to something, so I did not want to let the Church align solidly behind him."

"You think he is preparing some action against us?"

"Yes, I do. He has begun to levy new taxes in his dukedom, to the great despair of his subjects, I might add. Which indicates only one thing--that he intends to raise an army."

"I have heard about those new taxes, but he could never pull off a coup."

"I agree, but he might try."

"Birger is not that unrealistic, Valdemar. Even if he hires mercenaries, he poses no threat without the Danish armies; and Erik Menved is our ally now. Birger will continue to be a malcontent, but nothing more."

"I pray you are right."

The summer fields bordering the sea were ablaze in color from millions of wildflowers through which Erik, Valdemar, Mats and Arnvid rode with abandon at full gallop until they reached a clearing where Valdemar's servants had set out a variety of delicate foods on a wooden table under a shady tree.

"Too much exercise for this old man," Arnvid reluctantly acknowledged as he collapsed on a bench with a sigh of relief. The four knights settled down at the food-laden table, breathing heavily from their ride and laughing at each other's lamentable condition.

"Remember when we never got tired," Erik recalled, still looking fit for his thirty-five years.

"That is what all old folk say," noted Mats in jest.

The hard ride had made them hungry, so they devoured their meal in silence. When they had finished and were resting in the grass beneath the tree, Erik spoke in a serious vein.

"Many things have changed lately. Most importantly, Valdemar and I have become fathers. And soon I shall have another babe."

"Hear, hear," mumbled the men as they drank to the small princes and the child to come.

"My son will become King of Norway one day, but who will rule Sweden?" Erik continued. "Is Birger's son to become the next king? The son of one who is king in name only? That would be a travesty. I should, of course, have taken the title when I imprisoned Birger, but then I never cared what people called me - king or duke. I was the ruler in any case. Now I do have a son, and I might have another, and one of them is entitled to wear the crown of a country that I have ruled these many years. And Valdemar's son deserves to be next in line should anything happen to them. I would like Birger to cede the title of his own free will."

"He has little chance to keep it if you want it, Duke Erik. Nevertheless, I think he will fight for it," noted Arnvid.

"I agree," added Valdemar. "Birger will never yield his precious crown. He has even placed it with the Church for safekeeping. It is the last symbol of power he possesses."

"I mean to have the title," vowed Erik. "Having just met with Erik Menved, I doubt he will interfere even if he does not approve. We just have to figure out how I can convince Birger to let the crown go without creating more animosity."

Icy winds howled outside Borgholm castle, while inside in the Hall the fire pit was piled high and burning briskly. The two little princes were busy crawling on large fur rugs in front of the fire and throwing wooden soldiers and carved animals at each other, accompanied by howls of jubilation when one of the objects found its intended target.

"Ingeborg, if you want to be with your mother in time for your baby's birth, we must set sail in the next few days," Inga counseled. "It will not be long before the ice freezes over, so we should delay no longer."

Inga was cut short when Erik and Valdemar noisily entered the Hall and began shaking snow from their capes.

"The first snow," announced Erik. "I cannot remember when it came this early."

"We were just discussing our departure for Oslo," said Inga.

"I am afraid that Erik and I cannot come with you, dear," said Valdemar. "We just received an invitation from Birger and Marta to spend the Christmas holidays with them. It is important for us to go since it gives us a chance to be together in a friendly atmosphere, hopefully to persuade Birger to relinquish the crown."

"Oh," was all an extremely disappointed Inga could manage to say.

"When you are finished, you can join us in Oslo," said Ingeborg before she sank heavily into her chair.

"Can you manage such a long trip yourself?" asked Erik, looking down at his wife.

"Absolutely. I might feel clumsy and resemble a bloated badger, but otherwise I am fine. The baby is not due for weeks. My only regret is to leave Borgholm. I have been so happy here."

"That pleases me more than I can say," Valdemar enthused warmly. "Let us drink a toast to our time together here."

They raised their cups, looked into each other's eyes, and drank together in silence.

The invitation to spend the Christmas holidays with Birger and Marta had come as a complete surprise considering Kristina's diminished social standing after her father's execution, but Alf and Kristina decided to attend. They rode up to Nykoping castle on the day before the holiday banquet so as to arrive ahead of other guests and afford themselves a chance to talk privately with Marta and Birger. They found the royal couple in the Great Hall supervising the preparations.

"Everyone should have a gold chalice," they heard Marta admonish a servant. "All of our guests should feel special on this occasion. Take those silver cups away."

Kristina and Alf made their way among the tables that filled the large chamber to capacity. "Kristina! And Lord Alf," called Marta as she noticed them approaching. "You are early. How nice," she continued as she embraced Kristina and accepted Alf's cordial bows. "You must help me, Kristina. You were always so capable in these things."

Birger greeted Kristina and Alf in the same effusive manner so uncharacteristic for both the king and queen. "Let us go upstairs and sample some of the dishes we will enjoy at the feast. Kristina and Alf followed Birger and Marta who never ceased instructing servants as they made their way upstairs.

"We will be filled to capacity on the morrow so everyone will have to sleep in dorms, but tonight I can offer you a private chamber," Marta explained as they passed the open door to the audience chamber. "Even this room will sleep guests."

Kristina observed a huge heap of freshly filled straw mattresses stacked against a wall next to piles of down pillows and blankets that would be spread out on the floor the following night.

"I shall be delighted to help you," Kristina offered as they entered the king's chamber where the servants had set out plates filled with tidbits from the banquet dishes.

"Let us see if you approve," gushed Marta as she lifted one plate and smelled its contents with a sigh of satisfaction. They enjoyed sampling the food and tasting the different wines, and Kristina could see that Marta had done her utmost to ensure that the banquet would be a memorable occasion.

During the rest of the hectic day Kristina found no opportunity to speak to Marta privately, and when she joined Alf later that night in the chamber she had once shared with Ingeborg and Rikissa, she had little to report.

"Marta has changed so . . . almost beyond recognition," she confided. "She seems pleasant and kind, but like an actress performing a well-rehearsed play. She used to be so easy to reach. She was emotional and vulnerable. But not any more."

"The king seems very much like his old self," responded Alf. "Maybe more energetic than I remember, but then they both seem to enjoy readying for the feast, which might explain their mood."

"Something is just not right, that I can assure you. I have lived with them. I know them."

"That was ages ago, Kristina. Things change."

"I know. But what I am sensing is not just change."

"One should never argue when a woman claims she senses something strongly."

Chapter 37

Although it was still early afternoon, the winter darkness was falling rapidly as the dukes and their escort approached Nykoping. Flakes of snow swirling lazily down lightly dusted the road. Once the riders entered the castle courtyard, preparations for a sumptuous banquet became evident. The smell of roast pig, broiled lamb, and tempting whiffs of baked apples hung in the air. The singing of scullery maids and the bellowing of a beleaguered cellarer could be heard through an open kitchen door. The scene reminded Erik of holidays long past, when his father was alive. He could remember falling asleep under a banquet table amongst the dogs. He had felt secure there, comforted by the sound of voices mixed with music and laughter. He remembered waking in the early morning hours, watching a hand wend its way under a skirt beneath the table. It had been great sport to jump up and surprise the hand's owner, and to receive a generous coin as the price for silence.

Erik's reverie was cut short when Marta appeared in the courtyard, followed by Birger and Johan Brunkow.

"Erik and Valdemar! Welcome. Your dear wives could not be here. That is too bad. We shall miss them, but we are so happy that you could come," she enthused with open arms to embrace her brothers-in-law. "And Lord Arnvid, welcome. All of you, welcome!" she called as she waved to the large group of knights and squires massing behind the dukes. "Come in and warm yourselves," she said as she took Erik's arm to lead him into the Great Hall.

"We have not spent Christmas together for many years," Birger added as he put a welcoming arm around Valdemar's shoulders.

"Lord Arnvid," Johan Brunkow said cordially. "Did you have a pleasant journey?"

Arnvid nodded. "Although a cup of hot wine would make it perfect."

"Then follow me, gentlemen," Johan replied. As was the custom when entering a friendly house, the knights removed all weapons, except their long, decorative knives that hung from their belts. Johan detected, however, that most of the dukes' knights carried extra knives in their bootstraps. This was not unusual among traveling men-at-arms, and just as the guests had to trust their host by discarding major weapons, so the host had to trust his visitors with minor ones.

As Erik entered the Great Hall he noticed that nothing had been spared to make the banquet memorable. On the tables, placed on large silver platters, he could see brazed peacocks and swans with their tails spread, and swans with their feathers silvered and their beaks gilded. Marta proudly explained that the ovens would be baking pies to contain small, living birds, which would fly out as the crusts were cut. Erik saw a wondrous 'cockatrice'--the head and forequarters of a small pig attached to the body of a capon--on the dais table, and on a table in the corner stood a magnificent fountain spurting three different kinds of wine.

The entertainment seemed no less spectacular with musicians, jugglers, acrobats, contortionists and trained animals mingling among the guests. Marta excitedly told him that they had been brought from afar and that a nativity play would be performed before the final dishes of sweets and candied fruits were presented.

When Erik turned his attention to the many guests assembled in the Great Hall, he spotted Kristina. She stood across the room; her back turned to him, speaking to a group of ladies. He watched her whisk away a curl escaping from under her headdress with her slender hand, a gesture so familiar that he felt his throat constrict. He excused himself to Marta and pushed his way towards her, wondering what he should say. He had not seen her since the day he had gone to Solang. Despite the passage of many years she looked as lovely as ever. Thinner perhaps, but more mature with her head held high.

She must have felt him approaching, for she slowly turned around to face him, her eyes widening. He could not prevent his smile from exhibiting the depth of his pleasure at seeing her.

"Kristina," he bade endearingly as he took both of her hands in his and kissed them. "How wonderful to see you again."

"Erik," was all she said although her eyes filled with warmth. She became oblivious to the many people around them as she stood gazing at him with her hands in his. She was shockingly unprepared for the strength of her emotions at being near him again. He was, if possible, even more striking than before, his face more mature and his features still perfectly chiseled. The lines the passing years had cut around his eyes only enhanced his warm smile. It seemed like just yesterday when she had stood outside the hunting lodge, watching him through her tears as he disappeared astride his steed.

"It has been so long," she struggled to say as she began to feel short of breath.

"It has," he agreed. He wanted to pick her up in his arms and spirit her away from the crowded Hall.

"Duke Erik, it is a great pleasure to see you again."

Erik turned to face Alf of Smaland. Alf was smiling with his usual openness, without a trace of suspicion or jealousy.

"I, too, am pleased to see you," Erik said as he shook Alf's hand.

Erik hoped he sounded sincere, and with the right amount of warmth over greeting them together as man and wife.

"Valdemar and I just arrived," he added while trying to regain his composure.

"And Duchess Ingeborg?" Alf inquired as he looked around the Great Hall.

"She and Duchess Inga have traveled to Oslo for the holidays, and will unfortunately not be here with us," Erik explained.

"We had looked forward to meeting them both," Alf replied graciously.

Kristina is feeling something for me still, even though she clearly lives in a comfortable marriage, thought Erik. She has not forgotten our promise to always love each other, notwithstanding everything, and everyone else.

"Duke Erik," interrupted the Bishop of Skara as he neared the threesome. "I would like to introduce you to our two new bishops." Though Erik had savored the moment with Kristina, he was grateful to break away, as he did not know how much longer he could retain his facade of politeness. He bowed to Kristina and Alf, and then followed the churchman.

It took a long time for his heart to resume its normal beat, and he was glad that he did not have to contribute much to the conversation with the priests. While he stood listening without hearing their words, he emptied his chalice several times in the hopes of quelling his turbulent emotions. It worked well because after a few cups he began to enjoy the simple fact that he was in the same room with Kristina. He must not, and would not, say or do anything that would harm her marriage to Alf. To savor her presence was all he had the right to do.

As the reception continued, Erik again was charmed by Marta's exuberance and warmth, and Birger's overt efforts to make him feel welcome. He noticed that Valdemar, too, was enjoying seeing their many old friends. It was only Arnvid and Johan Brunkow who appeared tense amidst the jovial crowd.

Finally, the king called for prayers, and everyone set off for the chapel. A small choir sang, and one of the bishops conducted the long holiday ritual. While filing out of the chapel Alf made his way towards Erik. He was about to place his hand on Erik's arm when he saw Marta approaching. Quietly, he allowed himself to melt into the crowd.

Once they were back in the Great Hall, the guests resumed their drinking and merrymaking. Some of them had even snatched a brief nap in the chapel, and all were ready for a long night of celebration. The trumpets sounded their fanfare; whereupon the king and the queen, followed by their brothers and most honored guests, took their places on the dais, while the rest sat along tables now filling the entire Hall.

"What a lovely banquet," said Erik appreciatively to Marta who was seated beside him. He noted that she looked positively radiant. "You have spared nothing."

"It is a good time of the year to celebrate," she smiled warmly. "I have but one problem. I have had the servants trying to find sleeping space for your men. But as you can see, we have many guests, and you brought quite a few knights. In order not to have to move any of our guests, would you mind if we quartered your men in town?"

"Not at all," obliged Erik. "I just hope they can find their way there after all this wine!"

"That is one reason I do not want the ladies to go any further than a flight of stairs," she laughed as she gestured to Johan Brunkow who came over. "Duke Erik has no objection to his men staying in town, so could you please inform his captain where they will be lodged. And send some of our own men to guide them there. That is, if there are any sober ones around."

"Of course, your Majesty," smiled the chancellor as he withdrew.

"Do you want all of our soldiers lodged in town?" whispered Arnvid at Erik's shoulder a few moments later. "Do you want to stay here totally unprotected?"

"We are here to enjoy ourselves, Arnvid. Stop worrying."

So merry was the celebration that no one wanted to retire. The servants moved the tables closer to the walls and the guests began dancing. There was much laughter and playful screams when they all joined in the torch dance. Each participant carried a taper that he or she tried to keep from being blown out by others while maintaining their position among the dancers. If one did not succeed, one had to leave the dance and join the cheering crowd. Finally, there remained only three strapping knights, one of whom simply toppled from exhaustion at blowing out so many candles before the last two decided to call it a draw. Once the commotion died down, a famed storyteller began to recount his fabulous tales to allow the guests some rest before they resumed dancing.

Birger, who had collapsed on a bench after a wild serpentine dance amongst the tables, downed yet another chalice of wine. He could not remember ever feeling so good as he did this night.

He smiled at his former chancellor, Knut Jonsson, who had landed on the bench next to him, panting heavily. "What would you say if I told you that I plan to imprison my brothers?" Birger whispered excitedly.

"Surely you are not serious, your Majesty!" exclaimed Knut with a nervous laugh. "That would be a most dishonorable act. Are they not here in your home as invited guests?"

"They imprisoned me. Remember?" Birger snapped.

"They did, but not while you were a guest in their home," Knut whispered into Birger's ear to make himself heard over the din.

"What is the difference?"

"It is a matter of honor, your Majesty, but the most important difference is that you do not have the armies to stage a successful coup. They did. Please, do not even consider it. Their forces will overpower you, and you will lose everything! This time even your life."

"Not if I kill them! Who will their armies fight for then? Their infant sons? I think not! Erik's son will be King of Norway, that is enough for him."

Knut looked searchingly at the man whom he had served with unquestioning loyalty throughout his life. Though Erik had proved to be the better ruler by far, Knut had faithfully stayed with the crowned king, but now he doubted the wisdom of his choice. By according the king fair treatment, the dukes had won the respect of the nobles and most of the bishops. If Birger harmed his brothers, he would never rule in peace. "If you kill them, your Majesty, I doubt the people will accept you as their leader."

"Ridiculous! I am their king!"

"Please listen to what I am saying, your Majesty," Knut pleaded, "I cannot participate in an act which will destroy you."

"Then so be it. I can manage without you. However, everything has to appear normal. And you are not to divulge any of this. Not to anyone. Is that understood?"

"Yes, your Majesty," the former chancellor mumbled as he sunk deeper on the bench. The king was his liege and master. He had to obey.

"I have had no opportunity to warn either Erik or Valdemar of your suspicions," whispered Alf as he drew close to Kristina who stood observing the dancers.

"Neither have I," she said, not wanting to confess her fear that she might be unable to approach Erik again without openly revealing how strongly their encounter had affected her.

"We should keep trying to draw their attention, but if we do not succeed, I will go and see them once they retire," said Alf.

It was early in the morning when the last guests withdrew to their crowded quarters. It was still dark outside, and the snow had stopped falling. Erik and Valdemar retired to their childhood chamber in a drunken stupor where they stripped off their clothes and fell naked into bed to be immediately overtaken by deep sleep.

"It was a fabulous feast, Marta," Birger commented as he stood by the fire in her chamber.

"Yes, it was a lovely occasion," she agreed as she looked impatiently at the door. The person she expected finally entered.

"Everyone seems asleep, your Majesties," Johan reported in a hushed voice.

"I have changed my mind," Birger blurted out suddenly. "I do not want them killed. Just take them prisoners."

"That is most unwise, Birger," Marta objected. "This country will be divided as long as they are alive. You know that!"

"They are my brothers! Seeing them here tonight as when we were children, I knew I could not kill them. But I shall not be merciful. Put them in the deep dungeon, Johan."

"Listen to yourself," said Marta. "You hate them. Why not end this charade, once and for all?"

Birger turned to Johan. "Take them to the dungeon." Obediently, the chancellor turned and left the room.

Lord Arnvid was still half awake, so it took him but a moment to realize that something was amiss when he heard the sound of horses nearing the inn where he and some of his men were billeted. "Wake up!" he called to the six knights who were sleeping in the same room. "Horses approaching!"

One of the knights stumbled to the window that overlooked the yard of the inn. "They are wearing the king's colors," he called. "I thought all of the king's men were drunk tonight."

"Most of those we saw were," agreed Arnvid bitterly. "But these knights likely have not had a drop. We are in for trouble."

"But why would the king's men attack us?" asked another knight as he pulled on his chain mail and drew his sword from its sheath.

"I cannot tell you. But they are too many for delivering a message. If they intend to attack us we will have to take them on, and then ride to the castle as fast as we can. Go wake the others."

Silently, Arnvid's men prepared for the onslaught. When it comes, thought Arnvid, we will have a momentary advantage since the attackers will be surprised to find us ready and waiting for them.

Some of Arnvid's men slipped out of a window and prepared to attack the king's men from behind if they entered the inn. That would have been a clever move had not the king's men who stormed the entrance outnumbered them by three to one.

Arnvid leapt down the narrow stairs and vaulted over the banister to join in the fighting. He was so furious at the sneak attack that to his own amazement he found the strength to overwhelm two of the king's soldiers. But the moment their leader saw what he had done he ordered Arnvid overpowered. As Arnvid was set upon from all sides he felt two swords enter his body simultaneously. He was surprised that it did not hurt as much as he had imagined, but he felt his knees buckle before he slowly sank to the ground. He landed in a place that was black and soft, and all he could hear were the triumphant shouts of his enemies.

Despite the many copious cups he had imbibed, Knut Jonsson could not sleep. His bedding, along with several others', had been placed in Johan Brunkow's room. Their incessant snoring was not the only reason for his sleeplessness. The fact that Johan Brunkow had not come to bed worried him, since it could only mean that this was the moment when the king's plan would be carried out. How can I just lie here and do nothing he thought. What is about to happen is wrong for Sweden! He rose silently from his mattress, tiptoed around the sleeping men, opened the door to the corridor, and hearing no sound, slipped out of the room. Stealthily, he made his way down the corridor towards the chamber where he knew the dukes were sleeping.

"Everyone should be asleep by now," Alf whispered as he rose stiffly from a bench in the Great Hall where he and Kristina had waited. All around them were sleeping men and women who had not made it to their beds. Alf quickly kissed her on the forehead before he quietly exited the Great Hall to make his way up the stairs and along the corridor towards Erik and Valdemar's chamber. He hesitated for a moment when he thought he heard a sound behind him, trying to ascertain from where the sound had come. When he heard nothing further he cautiously continued down the corridor, but before he had taken many steps he felt an arm around his throat and a knife blade at his back.

"Do not move or make a sound," a voice whispered. He froze and kept absolutely still. The man who was holding him in an iron grip forced him toward a door leading out onto the parapet. "Open it!" the voice hissed in his ear. Alf obeyed and felt the cold air as the man pushed him out onto the walkway and pulled him around to get a look at his face.

"Lord Alf! I am sorry. I did not recognize you. You appeared to be up to no good. Forgive me," said Knut Jonsson as he sheathed his knife.

"I am sure it looked that way," Alf said as he rubbed his neck where Knut had pinned it in a viselike grip. "But what are you doing up at such an hour?"

Knut felt he could no longer keep silent and told Alf what the king was planning.

Alf interrupted him. "Listen! We are not the only ones up at this hour." Sounds of muffled footsteps could be heard in the corridor, and Alf made a gesture to go back inside.

"Stay here!" urged Knut holding onto Alf's arm. "There is nothing we can do now!"

Neither Erik nor Valdemar heard the chamber door open, but they became aware of the flickering torchlight.

"You are under arrest," Johan Brunkow announced from the foot of the bed.

Still drunk and sleepy, Valdemar grabbed the knife from under his pillow and lunged at the nearest figure. Erik, who realized the chamber was crowded with fully armed knights, called out, "Stop! They are too many."

Valdemar attacked nevertheless and succeeded in getting his blade under his intended target's throat mail before two other knights pulled him off and struck him with their metal gauntlets. Valdemar sprawled to the floor.

"What the hell is going on here?" he shouted angrily as he pulled himself to a standing position. "Are you all insane?" In response, one of the knights manacled his hands together with iron cuffs, while two others pulled Erik from the bed and similarly restrained him. The two dukes stood naked in the middle of the floor as movement could be heard in the corridor. Those standing by the door parted to allow the last arrival to enter.

King Birger Magnusson stepped imperiously in front of his brothers and looked them in their eyes. "Remember your little game at Hatuna?" His face was quivering with uncontrolled rage. "Now you shall learn what it is like to be humiliated by your own flesh and blood! Take them away!" he roared.

Johan gestured to the soldiers flanking the dukes to move them out of the room. Still naked and barefoot, the two brothers were prodded along the corridor by their captors, down the stairs and through the Great Hall, between tables and sleeping bodies.

Kristina sat motionless in the shadows, looking on in petrified silence as Erik and Valdemar were brutally herded past her towards the door. She wanted to stand up to object, but she was paralyzed by their abject humiliation. Not a sound or movement betrayed her presence as Erik and Valdemar were taken out of the Great Hall and across the icy courtyard towards the dungeon tower.

Only Birger remained behind in Erik and Valdemar's chamber, still dimly lit by a lone torch that had been left in a wall bracket. How he had relished the sight of his brothers being dragged away like common criminals!

Suddenly, a figure emerged out of the dark corridor. Birger turned to peer into Knut Jonsson's ashen countenance.

"Now, finally, I am the master of my country!" Birger boasted, pounding his chest.

"With all due respect, your Majesty," responded the former chancellor morosely, "now you have lost it for good."

Without another word, Knut turned his back on the king he had served so faithfully. He strode down the corridor past Alf, down the stairs and through the Great Hall, across the courtyard and out the castle gate. He cursed himself for stopping Alf who had been on his way to warn the dukes. They might have escaped had he not interfered. Knut continued into the cold night air without even feeling its chill.

When Alf re-entered the Great Hall, Kristina was standing in the center of the large space. To her surprise, not one of the guests had been awakened despite the knights' marching through their midst. "Erik and Valdemar are now Birger's prisoners," Alf whispered.

"I know. I saw them being taken away. The king is repaying them for what they did to him at Hatuna," she mumbled.

"This is far worse. I fear he is planning to kill them."

"Why now? I thought they were finally at peace with each other."

"The king wants to retain his title and rule Sweden alone. I wish that I could have warned them." He then told her how Lord Knut had interfered.

"You did what you could," she murmured.

"But I might have saved them."

"Maybe we still can. I will speak to the queen."

Shivering from the bitter cold of the courtyard, Erik and Valdemar were relieved to enter the relative warmth of the tower. They were pushed roughly into its large circular space with its thick wooden floor, in the middle of which a grate-like trapdoor made of heavy metal bars lay open. Above the trapdoor stood a large winch and crane. One of the guards bearing a torch put his foot into a loop at the end of the rope dangling from the crane and was winched down into the bowels of the tower. Another guard followed before the two dukes were forced to descend in similar manner, not an easy task while manacled in heavy iron fetters. Sixteen feet below they landed on the dirt floor of a circular stone dungeon about twelve feet in diameter. There the two naked brothers' necks and ankles were fettered by iron chains to opposite walls dripping with moisture. Between them glimmered a small pool of water where dampness from the cell had collected. They were left in darkness as the two guards were winched up, torches in hand. They could hear the loud clang of the trap door closing over their heads, and the metallic sound of a key securing the massive lock.

"Why is Birger doing this? If he plans to kill us, what point is there in treating us like animals?" asked Erik when the silence became oppressive.

"He is bitter," said Valdemar. "And he wants to humiliate us before he kills us."

"We let him keep his dignity when he was our prisoner."

"It is so cold," Valdemar complained, shivering in the frigid dampness.

"Maybe he is planning to have us freeze to death."

"Whatever his plan, I do not understand what brought it on. If the banquet had been less elaborate, I think it would be easier to forgive him," Valdemar quipped with maudlin humor.

Lord Knut Jonsson held a large mug of hot spiced tea gratefully clasped in his two hands as he sat by the fire in the inn. He was surprised that he had been allowed to leave the castle, but then the guards were used to his coming and going. The fact that he had not been properly dressed for the weather, or that he left on foot, had not concerned them. He, himself, had been too angry to realize how cold it was outside, feeling only the urge to flee that accursed place. On the way to town he had encountered the king's men returning with Erik's soldiers as their prisoners. He managed to duck behind some shrubbery at the side of the road to avoid being seen.

The inn was still in disarray. The innkeeper, his wife, and their servants were attempting to put the place back in order. They had righted the heavy tables that had been toppled during the fight and had collected the broken pottery, bottles, and glass which had littered the floor.

"What a mess!" complained the innkeeper's wife as she came down the stairs. "It will take a lot of work to put this place completely aright."

"Stop carping. It could have been worse," admonished the innkeeper as he patted the coin-filled purse the king's captain had tossed him.

Upon entering the inn, Knut had been horrified to discover Arnvid's corpse still lay where he had fallen close by the corpses of three more of the dukes' men and five of the king's soldiers. The innkeeper's stable boys moved the bodies out to a shed to await collection for burial, while Knut ordered a wagon to bear Arnvid's body to the harbor for shipment back to his home. Knut resolved to be on the same ship. He had to reach Mats in Stockholm.

"Innkeeper!" he called to the busy proprietor. "Do you know if any more of the dukes' men are lodged elsewhere in town?"

"No, my Lord, but I could find out."

"Please do. And if you find any, bring them back here. Also send word to a tailor that I need a warm mantle."

The innkeeper bowed and called out orders to his servants, two of whom raced down the lane to inquire about strange knights in town and another to find a tailor, all grateful to escape from further cleaning chores.

Within the hour Knut had purchased a fur-lined mantle from a local merchant who was glad to sell one of his finest garments before the day's trade had even begun. Soon thereafter, three men entered the tavern and cautiously approached the former chancellor. "We heard you are looking for Duke Erik's men. We are sworn to Lord Mats and we are staying here incognito."

"Keep it that way," said Knut. "The dukes were taken prisoner some hours ago. I do not know if they are dead or alive. I am about to return to Stockholm with the body of Lord Arnvid, and I shall inform

Lord Mats of what I know. In the meantime, try to learn further details before you report back to your marshal."

"With all due respect, Lord Knut, you are one of the king's men. How can we trust you to deliver the message to Lord Mats?" one knight asked.

"You have a point there. Why not accompany me? However, one of you should stay behind to learn what has become of the dukes."

"We will all come with you. We have more men here."

Later that morning the banquet guests, oblivious to the sinister events that had taken place while they slept, gathered for another sumptuous meal before they set out for their respective estates. The king, the queen, and the two dukes still had not appeared by the time most guests had departed, but nobody thought that strange. It was their royal privilege to do as they pleased.

"I shall go and see the queen now," Kristina said to Alf after learning that Marta had awakened. "Once she finds out what has happened, she might dissuade Birger from harming Erik and Valdemar." She hurried off in the direction of the queen's chamber.

Marta was breaking fast by the small fire as Kristina entered. The chamber had not changed much. The tapestries, carpets, and bed curtains were new; but they were of similar colors as Queen Helvig's had been. Kristina felt like she was visiting the past, and it might just as well have been the dowager queen sitting there, remote from the rest of the world.

"Good morning," Marta exclaimed with a radiant smile. "Did you sleep well? Come sit here by me. Have you eaten yet?"

"Yes, thank you," Kristina replied nervously. "I have heard some distressing rumors which I am sure cannot be true, but I wanted to ask you."

"What, my dear?" asked Marta calmly as she dipped a piece of bread into a small silver pot of honey. Maybe I should say nothing, thought Kristina. She might get one of her spells. Still, Erik and Valdemar's lives are at stake.

"I have heard that the dukes have been imprisoned," she uttered finally.

"Yes?" answered Marta as she took another slice of bread and broke it into smaller pieces.

"You know about it?"

"Naturally, my dear. Why should I not know?"

"I am surprised that you take it so calmly. I even heard that they are to be killed."

"I wish that were true," sighed Marta as she took a sip of herbal tea. "But Birger has turned so sentimental . . ."

Kristina felt her mouth go dry. "But why do you want them killed, your Majesty?" she asked, trying to make her voice sound firm.

"I am surprised you ask. You, of all people. They killed your own father," responded Marta as she carefully scrutinized the different jams in the silver jars. "They wanted to eliminate my husband and our sons. We simply could not sit by and allow that to happen, and we were fortunate to act before they did. This time they would not have been satisfied with just our imprisonment. Of that, I am certain." Calmly, she made her choice of jams and spread a spoonful of the sweet preserve on her bread.

"How can you be so certain they meant you harm?" asked Kristina desperately. "I thought that you had put the old strife to rest."

"Since when did you start meddling in politics?" Marta demanded as she scrutinized Kristina across the table. "I never thought you were interested."

"I am not . . . really," said Kristina, not knowing what to say. Her heart was pounding. She was no longer talking to the woman she had cared for like a sister. Something had happened to Marta.

"Anyway," continued Marta sweetly. "All of this does not concern you, does it? It is simply affairs of state. Since I suppose you are planning to leave today, I wish you God speed."

"Thank you," Kristina replied lamely, feeling obliged to continue the bizarre exchange. "It was a lovely banquet last night. Simply beautiful."

"I am so glad you enjoyed it," gushed Marta. "And do give my regards to Lord Alf. Magnus is so very fond of him. Kind of you to look in on me."

"Goodbye, your Majesty," said Kristina. She stood immobile for a moment after closing the door behind her. As a child she had been fearful of the mistress of the Queen's chamber. But that fear was mild compared to what she now felt for its current occupant.

Time passed slowly in the darkness as Erik and Valdemar kept asking each other the same questions but were unable to find any new answers. To keep warm they moved about as much as their chains permitted, dozing fitfully from the wine they had consumed during the banquet, always to awaken to the brutal cold.

"If Birger plans to keep us alive, he must deal with our armies, against which he stands no chance," said Valdemar.

Suddenly, they heard the large key turn in the lock and the trap door lift open. Someone was being lowered holding a flickering torch.

It was Kristina who wedged her torch into a wall bracket. Instinctively, Erik and Valdemar shielded their nakedness from the sudden light. Kristina avoided looking at them as she set the tray she was carrying onto the dirt floor along with booties, blankets and woolen tunics. She looked around the dungeon that was now dimly lit by the flickering torch. It comprised a grim and ghastly hellhole, a place to which one would only consign one's most hated enemy. Even her father, who had been accused of treason had not been treated in this manner. She shuddered at the thought of what awaited Erik and Valdemar.

Shaken with emotion, she reached for the tray she had brought. "Some food and drink," she said as she handed them bread and cups of tepid herbal tea. Erik and Valdemar, who were shivering from the cold, gratefully sipped the tea but left the bread untouched.

"It is a miracle that I could come," she rambled on to distract herself from her dread-filled thoughts. "There must be at least a hundred soldiers around the tower. They materialized suddenly out of thin air. Luckily, since Ragna's father is the jailer, he smuggled me in. But he cannot allow me more than a few moments. We have to hurry. Come, let me help you."

She knelt down beside Valdemar and carefully assisted him to dress. It was difficult because of the iron fetters. To get the tunic over his chains, she had to stretch and rip the thick fabric. She succeeded in pulling booties on his stiff, cold feet and finally wrapped him in a thick wool blanket she had carried with her. "God bless you, Kristina," whispered Valdemar as he pulled the blanket tightly around him.

"What can I do for you?" she asked, nearly in tears, as she again looked around the dungeon.

"Get word to Inga that I am alive," Valdemar pleaded. "Tell her that I think of her every waking moment."

"I shall bring her the message myself," Kristina promised as she stood up and looked over to Erik who was struggling with his tunic.

"Let me help you," she offered as she bent down to assist him. She relished feeling his strong and still-so-familiar body as she pulled the tunic over his head and down over his chest. She was embarrassed by her feelings, but she enjoyed touching him as she slowly pulled the soft boots on his feet. Carefully, she wrapped him in a blanket, holding her arms around him a moment longer than necessary.

"Thank you, my love," whispered Erik as she sat back on her heels. "I could never wish for anything more wonderful than to see you again, even if it is only for a moment." She looked at him as tears began to stream down her face. "Do not cry, Kristina. We will get out of here."

She felt reassured by his voice to which she had always listened with trust and belief.

"I love you with all my heart," Erik whispered, taking her hands. "And I was glad to see how much Alf loves you, and how much you care in return. I can feel that you are safe and happy, and that is all important to me. Now I know my love can never be a burden to you, only knowledge to strengthen you, should you ever doubt yourself."

"I will be there for you, if I possibly can," said Kristina, devastated in the knowledge of how little she could do for him now. "Every moment of every day I will pray for you." She looked into his eyes and ached with the sudden realization that this could be the last time she would look into those loving blue eyes.

"Lady Kristina!" a voice could be heard from above. "You better come up now."

Slowly their faces drew closer and she felt his lips on hers. The kiss was tender and tasted of the salt of her tears. Deeply now, and with passion of a lifelong love, he kissed her, holding her as if he would never let go. Again, they heard the hushed but urgent plea from above.

"Lady Kristina. You must come up now," Ragna's father warned more urgently.

"May God bless you," Kristina whispered as Erik again took hold of her hands.

"Thank you for everything," he said as he inverted her hands and kissed the palms before he gently released them.

"Thank you, Kristina," echoed Valdemar.

She stood up and reached for the torch in the wall bracket. Then she put her foot in the loop of the rope and tugged on it. Slowly she was winched up. Taking the light with her and not daring to look back, Erik and Valdemar were once again left in total darkness.

Kristina sneaked out of the tower the moment the jailer motioned that it was safe to stand with her back against the cold stonewall. No one seemed to have noticed her exit, but she stayed where she was, attempting to look inoccuous while she surveyed the courtyard where soldiers were loitering everywhere with servants passing amongst them bearing pitchers and platters. Kristina hardly saw them as her mind flashed back to the first time she had watched the brothers at weapon practice there.

It had been a day as cold as this one, and she had had to pull her demure red cape tightly around her as she watched them wield their swords. How they had smiled at one another as they strained against fatigue to complete the prescribed moves. Afterwards, they had slapped each other on their backs, sharing each other's success in finishing the full routine.

"Want to cross swords with me?" Erik had asked as he looked challengingly at his brothers.

"Of course," responded Birger and Valdemar as they attacked Erik in unison.

"I did not mean both at once," Erik had protested as he tried to parry their thrusts.

Their laughter was heard all over the courtyard as Erik tried to evade them by jumping behind water barrels and woodpiles, but they finally caught up with him and pinned him to the ground.

"Oh, I beg you to spare my life," Erik had pleaded between spells of laughter.

"What do you think?" Valdemar had asked Birger, looking serious. "Should we spare this villain?"

"We will be chivalrous and save his miserable hide," Birger chuckled as he reached out to pull Erik to his feet. Still laughing, and with their arms around one other, they had left for their lessons with Father Nils.

Kristina became aware again of the cold stonewall at her back, and of the courtyard filled with servants and soldiers. Good God! How had it come to this?

Chapter 38

"Are they dead or alive?" bellowed Mats as he paced aimlessly back and forth in the Great Hall in Stockholm castle.

"I know not," answered Knut Jonsson. "Some of your men stayed behind to find out."

"Why your sudden concern about the dukes' well-being?" demanded Mats who had been eyeing Knut with suspicion.

"Their imprisonment or deaths will not benefit Sweden. On the contrary, it may foment another war, so I want King Birger stopped before he involves Denmark. That is my main concern."

"That is truly your reason for alerting me?"

"As God is my witness," Knut swore solemnly.

"I believe you," said Mats after studying the older statesman whom he had long admired. "And you, Lord Alf, who served in King Birger's court and were knighted by his Danish ally, why are you here to support the dukes?"

"What was done to the dukes was not merely underhanded, they were treated despicably; and as a ruler, Duke Erik is far superior to King Birger."

Mats had only to observe Alf's totally open demeanor to know he was speaking the truth. Mats grimaced in anguish over the loss of his friend. "If Erik and Valdemar had not traveled to Nykoping, they would not be imprisoned and Lord Arnvid would still be alive. But what is done is done. Now we must liberate them. I will order the regional leaders to immediately assemble their armies. At the same time, I will warn every fortress belonging to the dukes to be on the alert for attacks by the king's men. That will get things moving while we plan our strategy."

The three new compatriots worked tirelessly through the ensuing days and nights to prepare an army to free the dukes. On the third day, news reached Stockholm that Erik and Valdemar were still alive.

Early the following morning Mats heard a commotion outside his chamber.

"We are under attack!" someone shouted in the corridor. "Everyone to the battlements!"

Someone began pounding on the marshal's door, and without waiting for a response, the commander of Stockholm castle entered.

"I heard you," said Mats, rising from his desk chair and holding up his hand to stop the man from repeating his message. "Our attackers will learn that we were ready and waiting for them, and that we will not surrender. Inform them that armies are being assembled everywhere and will soon be moving to free the dukes. That should induce them to cease their attack here in Stockholm, go back and prepare to defend Nykoping castle."

Disappointed that news of the dukes' imprisonment had traveled faster than the king's army, the message had its desired effect. Johan Brunkow immediately withdrew from Stockholm, as his only hope of capturing that fortress had been to take it by surprise.

The vessel that had borne Kristina and Ragna to Oslo was a small one, heavily laden with huge sacks of sheared wool that offered them no privacy. Kristina was grateful, however, that its cargo at least had provided a soft and warm place to bed down at night. They had to take the first ship sailing to Norway, and the trim little vessel was a lucky choice as it had cut a swift passage through the winds and swells.

When the two women disembarked they walked slowly along the dock to regain their land legs. Although Kristina was aware that the captain had demanded too much for their passage, he had shielded them from his lusty-eyed men. But here in the harbor they were unprotected. Drunken sailors called out obscenities or reached out to touch them. Resolutely, Kristina and Ragna picked up the pace on the short walk to Akershus castle.

"Who goes there?" called a sentry from the parapet above Akershus' gate.

"Lady Kristina Torgilsdotter of Smaland," Kristina replied. She was amused at the soldier's dubious expression as he stared down at the two disheveled ladies without even an escort. "I assure you that Duchess Ingeborg will want to see me immediately, she added." Her air of authority got the gatekeeper to act. Kristina and Ragna quickly crossed the drawbridge and passed under the gate that was raised.

Kristina had never been to Akershus, but she had heard it vividly described by Erik and Valdemar many years earlier, so she was able to unerringly head for the doors of the Great Hall. They entered the large chamber where the royal family and the courtiers were taking their supper. No one seemed to pay them any heed as they entered. Kristina quickly led the way between long tables towards the dais. From their placement, she could easily determine who was who, although the only one she sought was King Hakon.

She was momentarily taken aback when she saw how much the king had aged. Then she realized he was close to fifty. But his appearance was due to more than old age; he did not look in good health. Her heart sank at the thought of the tragic message she had to deliver.

"Your Majesty," she began as she stopped and curtsied in front of the dais. Despite the fact that she was still breathing heavily from their brisk walk, she continued, "you might remember me from many years ago. I am Kristina Torgilsdotter." She pointed to the snakeskin purse she carried at her waist.

"My dear lady, of course I remember you. I owe my life to you," the king declared as he rose with some effort to greet her.

"May I please speak to you and the Duchesses in private," Kristina pleaded, unwilling to lose any time in delivering her news.

She noticed the slender figure of a lady at the dais rise slowly and look at her in alarm. That has to be Duchess Inga, thought Kristina as she noted the woman's placement. She also noticed a younger woman, sitting beside the king, lean over towards her. Erik's wife.

"What news do you bring?" Duchess Ingeborg inquired.

"Come," interrupted King Hakon as he gestured for his daughter and niece to follow him and Kristina down a corridor and into the large audience chamber. When he had closed the door behind them, he sank down on his throne, "I fear you bring bad tidings."

"I do, your Majesty. The dukes have been imprisoned by King Birger."

After allowing a moment for that to sink in, Kristina related the details of the banquet night. Inga broke into tears, while Ingeborg began to pace the chamber. Out of empathy, Kristina omitted from her report that Erik and Valdemar had been incarcerated in the deep dungeon rather than being confined in the guest quarters.

"I shall ready my armies immediately," King Hakon said, looking at his daughter.

"No, dear Father, do not interfere. This is an internal struggle between a powerless king and the actual ruler of Sweden. It should be settled between their armies. If you become part of it, the Danes will have every right to come on the scene, which will make the confrontation larger than necessary." The king pondered Ingeborg's words. "Erik's forces can rapidly field more than twice the number Birger has. It is merely a matter of time before we win," Ingeborg added.

"But they could be killed in the meantime," lamented Inga.

"All I know is that the dukes were alive when I left," Kristina reported.

"I am going back to Sweden," exclaimed Inga, wringing her hands.

"As am I." Ingeborg stepped in front of her father. "Sweden is my home now, Father, and I shall do what I can to help my husband."

The winter sun cast its rays bleakly on the snow-blanketed courtyard of Nykoping castle where a messenger dismounted his sweat-covered steed and headed for the king's chamber on unsteady legs. He had been riding for countless hours and was exhausted.

"I bring news from the King of Denmark," he intoned formally as he handed Birger the scroll, bowed low, and withdrew.

"And what does my dear brother have to say?" Marta asked impatiently from her place by the fire. "I hope he is sending a huge army to convince that mulish commander of Stockholm castle of his stupidity. Imagine, refusing his own king access," she snarled as she embroidered an intricate pattern of rose-colored flowers. "I simply do not understand how anyone can defy you."

"The nobles have heard rumors that my brothers are still alive, and they consider them the rulers of Sweden," said Birger patiently as he broke the seal on the message.

"You should have killed them! You still can!"

"If they are not seen in any of the customary royal prison apartments, rumors will soon circulate that they are dead. A little patience, my dear, and then there will be no reason for their followers to resist."

"I hope you are right," she said as she began to choose from among the multicolored threads.

"Listen to this!" said Birger as he read through the message. "Erik Menved will send six hundred men immediately under our son Magnus' command. He says that he will consider sending more soldiers later."

"That is speedy action," said Marta approvingly. "It will be Magnus' first command now that he is eighteen years of age. I knew that we were wise to arrange his visit to Denmark at this time." She smiled proudly as she picked the correct shade of pink for the dainty flower on which she was working.

Suddenly the door burst open, and Johan Brunkow entered with only a curt bow.

"A large force of the dukes' men are on their way here," he reported. "They will arrive in a matter of hours. Your Majesties must depart at once."

"Lord Mats gathered his armies faster than I thought," Birger said after reflecting for a moment. "But you are right, Johan. We cannot be stuck here when they place the castle under siege. My dear," he turned to Marta. "I am afraid you do not have much time to pack, so take only what is most important. We shall be back before long." He forced a smile.

"I detest the idea of fleeing," sighed Marta as she stood up. Upon reaching the door she looked back at the two men. "I want to repeat what I have said before: Erik and Valdemar should be killed!"

The room was silent. Only the rustle from her dress could be heard as she exited.

Johan spoke softly. "The queen is right, your Majesty."

"You seem to have forgotten that I do not want to kill them!"

"I have not forgotten. But even if you keep them hidden, your Majesty, someone will find out that they are still alive and get word to their men who will not rest until they are freed."

"That will be a long time from now, if ever. This fortress is well stocked and can sustain a siege for more than a year, and by that time I shall have Sweden united behind me. My brothers can do little against me then."

"With all due respect, your Majesty; the dukes have powerful allies and most of the Swedish armies. They will not be merciful."

Birger drew a deep breath. "See that everything is ready for our departure to Stegeborg fortress," he ordered as he turned away from his chancellor.

Left alone, Birger stared into the glowing fire. What should he do? His whole being resisted the inevitable. His father had not killed his brother, and his own brothers had not killed him when they took over the rule eleven years earlier. Had they killed him at Hatuna, Erik would have been the unchallenged King of Sweden today, instead of Birger's prisoner. Dimly, in the back of his mind, he could hear his ex-chancellor predicting that he had lost Sweden forever. But that would never happen! He was the king and his people would follow him . . . or would they, while Erik lived?

Birger allowed his emotions to wane. He had a clear choice. He could kill Erik and Valdemar and hope to rule the country in peace, or he could let them live to pose a threat. But then, what kind of life would they have? Chained in darkness, cut off from the world; was that better than dying? It would almost be a favor to put them out of their misery.

For a brief moment he felt encouraged by the thought that killing his brothers would be sparing them a dreadful fate, but he quickly reminded himself that it was he who had created their hell. He felt as if the walls were closing in on him, and he began pacing the chamber. As he strode past the window he gazed at the large key to the dungeon's trapdoor hanging close by. He had given strict orders that it was to hang there at all times, to be removed only if the jailer had to descend into the pit. His eyes were always drawn in the direction of the massive metal object, and rarely--if ever--was he unaware of its existence in the room. Slowly, he walked over and took it off its hook. He started towards the door, opened it, and walked slowly down the corridor, all the while staring at the heavy object in his hand.

He had to kill them! Yet, to give the order for their execution seemed impossible. He opened the narrow door to the parapet. The outside air was biting cold, and the vapor of his breath formed a thick cloud around his face. He moved along the walkway, clutching the massive key in his hand. He stopped and looked down at the dark river swirling past the base of the fortress. The water was coursing swiftly along its channel, breaking up the ice that had formed between the stones and tree roots along the shores.

He looked at the key again, and then felt his arm pull back in an involuntary motion before he hurled the key in a wide arc over the parapet into the dark and swirling river.

He would not have to give an execution order! Nobody would have to lay a hand on Erik and Valdemar. He felt a rush of excitement mingled with fear as he stared into the water that had swallowed the key to his brothers' lives. He felt a sensation of lightheadedness as he turned to go back into the castle.

"Are you ready, dear?" asked Marta who was pacing impatiently before the doors in the Great Hall.

"I am ready," he answered, reliving the moment and the sensation in his arm as the heavy key flew from his hand and spiraled through the air. "Now we can depart!"

"Have you made all the necessary arrangements?" she asked as she threw her mantle over her shoulders.

"Everything has been arranged," he answered as he started for the door to their waiting sleighs, oblivious to Marta's triumphant smile.

The garrison's soldiers stood in tight formation, awaiting Birger's orders. In an impassioned speech Birger exhorted them to defend the stronghold to their final breath, and he admonished them severely that no one was to enter the dungeon. The jailer who was standing by the door to the dungeon was puzzled. If no one entered to feed the prisoners, they would die! Maybe the king only meant that none of the soldiers should go near the dungeon. The little jailer discreetly approached Johan Brunkow who was already mounted beside the queen's sled.

"Did I understand correctly?" he asked. "No one at all is to enter the dungeon?"

"You heard correctly. Absolutely no one! And furthermore, you are not to speak to the prisoners. If you do, you will pay with your life!"

"I understand," muttered the jailer as he returned to his place by the dungeon door. He shivered at the thought of the dukes starving in that miserable pit. That kind of treatment preserved no dignity at all. Royal blood entitled one to a decent execution, something of importance. The jailer was deeply disappointed in his king.

Nykoping, Sweden 1318

When Mats' armies swept down on Nykoping castle it was prepared and well defended.

"We are too late!" Mats cried in frustration. "All we can do now is put the fortress under siege while we assemble a force strong enough to storm it. We must hurry. If the dukes are still alive, every moment will be agony."

Lords Knut and Alf, who were at Mats' side, grimly nodded, knowing that it could take months to ready an army and build war machines strong enough to successfully storm the formidable redoubt.

"We should leave now for Skara to meet with the duchesses and the regional leaders to plan our final assault," the marshal added as he pulled off his helmet to stare at Nykoping castle's towering granite walls.

"I am so hungry it hurts," groaned Valdemar in agony. "We have not been fed for days."

"I know," sighed Erik. " Maybe they have decided to starve us to death."

"I cannot believe that," objected Valdemar weakly. "If Birger wanted us dead he would have executed us."

"He placed us in this horrible pit. I do not put it past him to let us die slowly. Nothing he does surprises me anymore."

"If that is his plan, I do not want to think about it," moaned Valdemar. "There must be a perfectly logical explanation for the lack of food and water. They may be preparing for the onslaught of our armies, and the jailer has forgotten about us in the midst of everything."

"Valdemar, days have gone by without anyone coming here."

"They will be here soon. You just wait and see."

Duchess Ingeborg sat at a dressing table in Skara castle looking into her mirror. She saw the tired face of an eighteen-year old woman staring back. She took a deep breath to collect herself for the meeting. Just then she heard the door open and Inga appeared, looking equally drained.

"Almost everyone is here. We are waiting for Lord Mats to arrive," Inga explained, trying to sound efficient. "I have offered hot drinks and food to those waiting. Are you ready?"

About fifty noblemen were standing around the Great Hall when the two duchesses entered. Silence fell over the company as Mats, who had just arrived, came forward to greet them. "We are all mortified at what has transpired," he began.

"Lord Mats, are you offering us condolences?" Ingeborg demanded bluntly, as she stood erect in front of the tall marshal. Mats noticed Inga blanch, and he quickly retorted, "All reports indicate that the dukes are alive."

Inga drew a deep, grateful breath as Ingeborg announced in a loud voice, "My lords, let us start the meeting." Mats was again impressed with her ability to take command in such a natural way. The men set down their goblets and seated themselves at the long tables. The two duchesses sat alone at a smaller table facing them.

Mats reported the events of the past weeks. He recommended that Knut Jonsson be permitted to join the council, reasoning that the king's former chancellor had proven his new allegiance by his actions. He asked the same permission for Alf of Smaland. The nobles and the duchesses nodded their agreement, whereupon Mats invited Knut and Alf to take their seats with the others. Mats then explained the urgent need to storm Nykoping, as well as Stegeborg fortress where Birger was rumored to have barricaded himself.

"May I add a small piece of information," said Ingeborg when Mats was finished. "Just as we left Oslo, we found out that Erik Menved is sending a force under the command of Prince Magnus to support King Birger."

A murmur broke out among the men. Mats held up his hand. "Let the duchess finish!"

"We therefore need three strong armies; one for Nykoping, one for Stegeborg, and one to confront Prince Magnus and the Danes,"

Ingeborg continued softly, but with an edge of steel in her voice. "We have at our immediate command armies garrisoned at Varberg, Hunehals and Kungahalla. Naturally, most of those are needed to defend those fortresses, but the combined force we can field from there will most likely outnumber Prince Magnus' knights." The men stared in amazement. Here was an eighteen-year-old marshal dressed in female clothing! "Well, what do you say?" she asked as the silence continued.

"I think I speak for all of us when I say that I am impressed by your analysis of the situation and the actions you have proposed," Mats responded with sincerity.

"Hear, hear," chorused the men in the hall.

"I will be in charge of the western regions, Birger Persson of the eastern regions, and Lord Alf will lead the forces from Smaland, " Mats announced. "I also propose that we start construction of heavy catapults, storming towers, and ramrods. When we strike Nykoping, we must have every possible advantage. Time is of the essence. Several weeks have already passed since the dukes were imprisoned. We know that they were alive when King Birger left Nykoping, and if the king had planned to kill them, it is logical to assume that he would have done so before he left to be certain the executions were carried out. But from now on we will not get any information, as no one is going in or coming out of the castle. My lords, I am not criticizing the speed with which we are assembling our forces, but from the dukes' point of view we are proceeding at a snail's pace. I beg of you, extend yourselves to the limit."

"Hear, hear," chorused the nobles as Birger Persson raised his arm to be recognized.

"Before we conclude this meeting, I want to ask the Council for its ruling on a matter of great importance," he began. "I have no doubt that we will be victorious in our assault, but we have no guarantee that the dukes will be alive when we take Nykoping castle. Of course, we believe they will be," he added, looking quickly in the direction of the duchesses. "But if they are not, God forbid, we must elect someone to act as interim ruler before the next king is elected. If we do not choose that man right here and now, we might face internal strife later."

"Hear, hear," called the assembly.

"My suggestion for interim ruler is Mats Kettilmundsson!" roared Birger Persson.

"Hear, hear!" agreed the men as they pounded the tables in unison.

"Are we agreed on the election of Mats Kettilmundsson as Chancellor and interim ruler of Sweden, or do you have other candidates to suggest?" asked Birger Persson.

Silence reigned before the entire assembly shouted. "Lord Mats! Lord Mats!"

The new Chancellor was visibly moved as his right hand grasped the haft of Gram and he rose to bow his acceptance. His left hand absent-mindedly stroked the white patch of hair at his temple as he recalled his father's proud smile when he took Gram from its scabbard for the very first time.

When the furor finally quieted down, Ingeborg stood. "We wholeheartedly support your election, and so would our husbands, had they been here," she said as she bowed her head toward Mats.

Mats bowed back before facing the assembly once more. "I shall return immediately to work on the construction of the war machines. So, my lords, if there is nothing further to discuss I bid you farewell!"

As Mats was about to mount his horse, Inga came rushing out into the windswept courtyard. "Please, Lord Mats, may I have a word with you?" she called anxiously.

"Of course! But please step back inside," he suggested as he noticed her shivering in the cold.

"No, I do not want to take even one moment away from your effort to save Erik and Valdemar," she protested. "But I have heard rumors that they are being held in a dungeon and not in the quarters where King Birger was imprisoned. Is that true?"

Mats knew the rumors were correct, but he had hoped they would not reach the duchesses' ears. As they had, he felt he had no choice but to be truthful. "I am afraid that the reports are accurate, my lady. But have no fear, we shall liberate them safe and sound," he said with more conviction than he felt.

Inga turned pale and gasped at the confirmation she had hoped never to hear. "My God," she whispered and started to cry. "But do not let me delay you. May God go with you," she implored as Mats spurred his steed out of the courtyard, followed by his men.

Chapter 39

"We are being starved to death!" Erik mumbled. That he finally said it aloud had not precluded him from constantly thinking it during the preceding days. He felt untouched by the realization, but his anger rose when he added, "Birger is a coward. He could not face our public execution."

Valdemar was silent for a long time before he spoke. "Thank God, at least the hunger pains have gone."

Erik tried to focus on the euphoria that had begun to overtake him. Memories of Kristina and the short time they had together were coming easily now and seemed incredibly real. He did not have to conjure up her face or try to remember a specific episode. He could actually feel her touch and smell her hair. He could hear her lovely laugh.

"We have to write our wills," said Valdemar, interrupting Erik's dreams again.

"I suppose so," answered Erik drowsily, trying to hold on to the picture of Kristina resting in his arms.

"They must allow us to write our wills," persisted Valdemar. "I know they can hear us through the small grate in the tower door even though they have pretended not to hear our pleas or our bribes. But to write a will is a dying man's right. Jailer!" screamed Valdemar. "Jailer! We demand the right to draw our testaments! Jailer!" Valdemar screamed until he became hoarse and quieted down. "Bastards!" he muttered angrily under his breath.

Later, they heard banging on the thick metal grating section of the trap door before the jailer's voice called down to them, "I will send down what you need to write your wills."

They could hear the winch turning as the jailer lowered parchment, quill, and ink in a small basket atop which was set a lit taper. Valdemar's chains, when fully extended, allowed him to grab the basket. The taper almost became extinguished as it was being lowered but revived when Valdemar held it still.

"Call for me when you are ready," yelled the jailer as his footsteps died away.

For the first time, in what they felt was an eternity, they saw light again and were temporarily blinded by the soft flame. But as their eyes became accustomed to it, again they could behold their miserable prison. Heaps of excrement lay by the walls, and the pool of water in the middle of the floor from which they had drunk so gratefully when they no longer were receiving food or drink, was dark brown and filthy. But the worst shock came from looking at each other.

"My God!" whispered Valdemar with panic in his voice. "Erik, you look like a ghost! Ashen. You could be a hundred years old!"

Erik lifted his eyes to view Valdemar and experienced the same painful shock. Valdemar's face was covered with an unkempt beard and was deeply lined, like cracks in dried grey plaster. He had dark circles under his bloodshot, unfocused eyes. His hair was matted and colorless.

"Good Lord!" exclaimed Erik in horror. "What has become of us?"

"I am glad we had no light before," said Valdemar in an attempt to lessen the terror they both felt.

"We are dying," whispered Erik as he studied Valdemar's unfamiliar, haggard countenance. "Whatever else I may have tried to tell myself, now I know. We shall die here, in this dungeon."

Completing their task took longer than anticipated. The jailer had to lower another taper when the first one went out. Erik found it hard to hold the quill, so painfully stiff were his hands from the cold. Valdemar took over the writing when Erik gave up, and he had an equally difficult time. Still, the two men struggled on with their task. Together, they tried to remember those for whom they had cared during their lifetime, and to bestow appropriate rewards for past loyalty. When they finally were finished, Erik leaned back, feeling absolved.

"Valdemar, I do not want to look at you again," he said in a thin voice. "I want to remember you as you were. Would you mind if I blow out the candle?"

"Absolutely not," said Valdemar gratefully. "There is no beauty to behold down here. I also prefer the darkness."

"Jailer!" called Valdemar, as he crawled towards the basket with the parchments in his shaking hand. Erik blew out the flickering flame and they fell back against the cold stonewalls.

As they heard the jailer draw near, crank the winch, and receive the wills up through the trapdoor's grating, Erik could not resist calling out, "Is the castle under siege?"

The jailer did not reply. Erik felt a mindless fury well up within him as he screamed. "We know we are dying, so show us a last bit of human kindness by telling us how long we have been without food and water, and if the castle is under siege. What pleasure can it give you to make our last moments more horrifying than they already are?"

"It is not I who wish to treat you ill. I am helping you under pain of death. The key to the dungeon door and this grate is gone. I had to break both locks so as not to ignore your last wish . . . You have been without food for more than four weeks now; and yes, the castle is under siege," the jailer added before they heard him walk away from the trapdoor.

"Thirty days without food," mused Valdemar wondrously. "I thought it was months."

"Time is a strange thing," mumbled Erik as he floated into another vision of Kristina."

"We were happy here once," said Valdemar, feeling the same euphoria. "I miss my Inga. And our son."

"Thank God that we each have something to think about, something wonderful to remember. It might even keep us alive until our people take the castle," was Erik's wistful reply.

As more days and nights passed, Erik and Valdemar felt the life force slowly ebbing from their bodies. They rarely spoke to one another, sensing that even the slightest effort would bring them closer to the end.

Erik opened his eyes, but he was still enveloped in darkness. Then he remembered where he was. He shivered in the merciless cold and pulled the tattered blanket closer to his body. He smelled the fetid dampness of the earth floor and the bodily wastes which he had tried to excrete as far from his resting place as his chains would allow, and he realized that he was no longer revolted by the stench. It was now part of his small and hellish world at the bottom of this dark, deep hole. He massaged his wrists and ankles where the heavy shackles had chafed and sighed deeply as he curled against the frigid stonewall.

Slowly the fog lifted from his brain and a mix of defiance and anger coursed through him. How could their own brother treat them like tortured animals? Erik suddenly found strength in his fury as he screamed at the top of his lungs, "Birger, curse you! If we die, you will never enjoy another happy day! As God is my witness, you will pay for this!"

Leading a splendid column of knights with his son by his side, Birger, at thirty-seven and fully dressed in heavy armor, could feel his years. The weight of the metal was wearing him down, and he was aching in every muscle after riding for only a few hours. He felt old. He turned to look at his son riding beside him. The nineteen-year-old Magnus sat tall and erect in the saddle. His helmet covered his long honey-brown hair, but his strong profile was clearly visible beneath his raised visor. He looks like my father, thought Birger. He is showing all the signs of a powerful leader, and I would not mind dying in battle if I knew he would wear my crown.

Suddenly one of their scouts came riding up at full gallop. Birger raised his hand, and the signal to halt was passed down the line. "Your Majesty, there is an enemy force just ahead," called the scout as he reined in his mount. "I estimate we are almost double their number, so we can make a frontal attack if that would be your Majesty's wish."

"Lord Johan, prepare to attack!" he commanded as his blood began to pump faster. He would show his brothers' men that he still was a force to be reckoned with!

The dukes' armies were waiting--warned of the king's approach by their own scouts--on a field next to the small village of Karleby. With a thunderous noise and a cloud of dust, the two mounted armies clashed in the middle of the field. Birger stayed in the midst of the battle, overtaken by an irrepressible urge to kill each and every one of his adversaries. Magnus and Johan Brunkow, who were fighting beside him, shouted their consternation over his reckless involvement, but he was not deterred.

The battle lasted for hours, and dusk began to gather. Birger realized that darkness could save the dukes' men which he could not allow to happen! He thirsted for a victory, something survivors would talk about in fear and awe. He summoned his marshal and ordered him to torch the village so that they could finish their battle by firelight.

"Father!" called Magnus next to him. "We do not have to burn the peasants out of their homes. We have already won this battle."

"Burn the village!" ordered Birger as he eagerly spurred his horse on to engage the enemy anew.

The fighting ended with a resounding victory for Birger. Exhilarated, he sat on a stone by the edge of the field, looking at the dying embers of what had once been the small village, and listening to the cries of the women and children huddled together in the snow. He could hear the screams and moans of the wounded, and the scraping of shovels digging graves for the many that were no longer in pain. Although many of the dukes' men had managed to flee, he was not unhappy. Word of his mighty army would spread!

"You were wonderful, my son!" he exclaimed proudly as Magnus came by holding his chest.

"I think I have some broken ribs, but I shall live," Magnus explained as he left to seek the surgeon.

"This place is frightfully uncomfortable," Marta complained as Birger entered their small screened-off space in Stegeborg fortress.

"It was built as a fortress, not as a dwelling," Birger explained as he walked over to the small fire grate where Marta sat embroidering. "But its defenses are strong, and that is what matters."

"I do not understand what is happening, Birger," she continued bitterly. "It is as though we are prisoners here. Your brothers are gone, so why are we still in a state of war?"

"Many do not yet consider me the ruler of Sweden, and they have taken up arms to free Erik and Valdemar."

"But they must be dead by now!" she objected.

"Dead or alive," Birger said evasively, "their followers know not which, so they will fight until they know."

"So why did you not order a public execution?" she asked irritably and not for the first time.

"Well, I did not, and the rumors about them being alive are hard to quell. We shall have to fight until the truth is known."

"And then?" she asked as she looked up from her needlework. Birger remained silent for a long time before she continued, "Why did you put yourself in such a predicament? It could all have been avoided!"

"Perhaps I should not have seized my brothers in the first place," he retorted.

"You had to! There was no other way," she insisted. "They would have killed us!" Then she took a deep breath. "I am sorry, Birger, I do not mean to nag, but I cannot stand being confined in this place with the constant clamor of arms around me. It is unnerving."

She was interrupted as Johan knocked on the door and entered.

"You must get ready, your Majesties," Johan Brunkow pleaded. "Your brother's troops are on their way here and you must leave before the fort is placed under siege."

"Where should we go? To Denmark?" Marta asked anxiously.

"We shall go to the Swedish isle of Gotland which is still loyal to me," said Birger. "There we will prepare an armada to attack from the sea if they put Stegeborg under siege."

The door flew open and Magnus walked in. "You should leave immediately," he said looking from one parent to another. "I will assume command of the fortress."

Birger looked at his son and was about to object when he realized that his family would appear to be cowards if they all left and allowed a non-family member to command Stegeborg.

"Is that what you want to do?" Birger asked.

"Absolutely."

"Then your mother and I will go with Lord Johan to Gotland and raise a fleet to aid you," concluded Birger without facing his son.

"We are being hounded like animals," exclaimed Marta.

"This is war, Mother," Magnus replied softly. "You better get your things together."

"Yes, my dear," she agreed, soothed by her son's appeal. She stood up and carefully collected her most precious possessions to put them in her traveling chest. Everything that was transpiring was God's will, and even if He were testing them now with adversity, He would ultimately deliver them as Sweden's rightful King and Queen. Nothing was easy. Marta knew that all too well. She had a mass of scars on her back to prove it.

Mats had just fallen asleep from sheer exhaustion on the narrow cot in his tent outside Nykoping castle when he was awakened by the sound of an approaching horse. He reached for his sword and moved toward the tent opening, his eyes searching the open meadow before him. Across the field he spotted a lone rider approaching at full gallop, long dark garments flying. He took a deep breath in surprise and curious anticipation when he realized that the somber attire was that of a nun. He put down his sword and stepped out of his tent.

"Rikissa?" he called as if he were seeing a vision.

Rikissa reigned in her horse before him and slid down. Mats tethered the animal by his tent. When he turned to look at her, his heart constricted. Her face was contorted with worry and lined with exhaustion, but she looked strangely unchanged from the last time he had seen her so many years before. Her lovely gray eyes conveyed her deep concern.

"You must attack now, Mats. My brothers are in deadly peril."

"You rode all the way from Stockholm to tell me something I already know?" he asked, perplexed.

"You have forgotten that I can feel when those close to me are in danger. My brothers are dying, if they are not already dead. I know. I could never tell you face to face of my accursed ability to sense these things. As Kristina and Erik must have told you it was these feelings that led me to enter the convent. When you were fighting in Finland I lived within you, all through your deadly combat, with such intensity that even you could sense me. I promised our Lord that I would serve him if he spared your life that day. He did, and I have kept my promise."

Rikissa saw a wan smile spread over Mats' face. "I was so worried that you had stopped loving me," he said at last.

"You were so wrong," she whispered looking down on the ground.

Slowly, Mats pulled her faded and tattered colors from his tunic pocket and held up the swatch of silk without a word. He saw her eyes fill with tears.

"I am always praying for you," she said in a trembling voice. "And I shall continue to do so. But before I return to Santa Klara, I beg that you believe me when I tell you that you cannot delay a moment longer."

"I was waiting for some war machines to be readied and the last group of soldiers to join us, but as your intuition is so strong we will attack on the morrow." He was silent for a moment before he added "Seeing you again after these many years—and hearing from your own lips why you left me--I feel reborn." He bent down to kiss her forehead and enfold her in his arms.

"May God keep you safe," she whispered softly.

Mats stood alone in the middle of his tent after Rikissa's departure. His thoughts were in disarray while he tried desperately to concentrate on the task ahead. He poured himself a cup of wine and then drained it as he gazed upon his armor, shining and ready on its stand. His squire had done a fine job of polishing both his armor and his magnificently plumed helmet, evidencing his newly elevated status as Chancellor.

Mats had one last thing to do before retiring. Setting down his goblet, he walked over to a chest by the tent wall. He opened it and took out two gold-embroidered, fur-edged mantles. He carefully draped the garments over a bench before he lifted out Erik and Valdemar's ducal chains and placed them over the mantles.

"Tomorrow, you will wear these again!" he promised solemnly.

"Wake up, my lord!" shouted an agitated knight who burst into the king's chamber at Nykoping castle.

The fortress commander sat bolt upright in the royal bed. Next to him slept the scullery maid he had requisitioned to relieve the monotony of the siege. "What is it?" he barked.

"We are being attacked!"

The commander sprang from the bed, pulled on his armor, and followed the anxious young knight towards the parapet.

"Sweet Christ!" he whispered as he surveyed the host of war machines and thousands of armored figures standing motionless below. Shakily, he crossed himself. "I had expected a large army, but not this!"

"Look!" The young knight said, pointing at a tall, plumed figure riding toward the gates. The warrior stopped on the other side of the moat and called out in a stentorian voice,

"As Chancellor of Sweden, I order you to surrender!"

"It is Mats Kettilmundsson, the new chancellor!" exclaimed the commander as he walked over to a spot above the gates where he could look directly down at the challenging figure. Then he shouted loudly,

"As the Commander of Nykoping castle, and as the servant of the King of Sweden, I dare you to attack!"

"It is my duty to inform you that we will take no prisoners! Review our forces and consider!" taunted Mats.

"We do not stand a chance," whispered the young knight.

"We will not surrender," called out the commander resolutely.

"But it will be outright slaughter!" objected the young knight.

"Will you spare our civilians if we give you the dukes?" the commander shouted.

"We will," Mats shouted back, euphoric at the thought of being reunited with his friends.

"Then we will give you the dukes," the commander called out as he left the parapet. "This will give us the precious time we need to have every single man at his post fully prepared," the commander explained as he rushed down the stairs, barking his orders.

Mats wheeled his mount and gestured for a squire to bring forward the dukes' horses, their mantles and chains of office.

The army stood waiting for what seemed like an eternity. Then the creaking of chains was heard as the drawbridge was lowered. The heavy gates opened slightly, and Mats held his breath as he waited for his two friends to emerge. Instead, two squires came through the gates, half-running, carrying a pallet between them. On the pallet was the shape of a man covered with a blanket. The pair moved quickly across the drawbridge and deposited their burden on the ground. Following them, two soldiers placed a second pallet beside the first. Then all four ran back into the castle whose gates slammed shut as the drawbridge was raised.

Mats stared in disbelief at the motionless forms, then spurred his horse forward and dismounted beside the pallets. He pulled off his helmet and kneeled on the ground. Invoking a silent prayer, he gently lifted the blanket off the nearest human shape.

In front of him lay the decomposing corpse of Valdemar. Numbly, Mats rose and pulled the other blanket down to reveal Erik's remains. He straightened up to his full height. Appearing far more composed than he felt, he gestured for some squires to approach, and with their assistance draped the bodies in the golden mantles and placed the ceremonial chains around their necks.

"The former ruler of Sweden, Birger Magnusson, has committed a most heinous crime. Fratricide! In front of us lie his victims, our masters; the chivalrous Dukes Erik and Valdemar of Sweden." Tears were streaming down Mats' face--if from grief or indignation, or even from the putrid stench of the corpses, he did not know, nor did he care. The full force of his fury surged forth as he roared to his men at the top of his lungs, "I made my promise of not killing the civilians because I thought the dukes were still alive. But now we shall not leave one man alive, or one stone resting on another. After you have bade the dukes farewell we will destroy this cursed place forever!"

A roar, as from a thousand wounded animals, rose from the throats of the soldiers before they began to file by their dead leaders. When all stood back in their original positions and the corpses had been moved to the chancellor's tent, Mats unsheathed the legendary Gram, raised it on high, and screamed a single word to signal the attack.

"Revenge!"

Though the catapults had ceased hurling their stones and fireballs, dust and smoke were still billowing around the broken and scarred walls of Nykoping castle. The eerie silence, which followed the thunder of battle, hung like a pall over the area. All that could be heard were the cries of wounded and dying men. Mats fell to his knees to thank the Lord that the battle had been brief and decisive.

He stood, gathered up his sword, and slid it back into its scabbard. He began to climb the piles of stones that had once been a proud fortress wall. He entered the main courtyard where not one of the wooden dwellings was left intact and found black smoke rising from the remnants of the Great Hall. There, among the bloodied and motionless bodies of the fort's defenders, Mats' men stalked, checking the corpses scattered everywhere. If any were found alive, the soldiers would quickly run swords or lances through their defenseless bodies.

The once mighty tower, which had been bombarded for hours with heavy stones, was almost leveled. As Mats neared its skeletal remains, he heard loud moans coming from beneath a pile of rubble. Mats kicked away some stones to discover the jailer buried under heavy rocks. He stared at the badly wounded man crushed beneath the stones, then bent down for a closer look.

When he saw the jailer's eyes flicker he asked, "On whose orders were the dukes murdered?" The jailer was breathing laboriously and moving his dry and bleeding lips slowly without making any sound. "Answer me! Who killed the dukes?"

"It was . . . the king . . . he ordered us . . . not to feed them. On the penalty of death."

"That you obeyed those orders has cost you your life," snarled Mats as he unsheathed his sword and swiftly dispatched the wounded man.

Mats could feel the bile rise in his throat as he peered down into the now-gaping dungeon where his friends had died a slow and torturous death. He clenched his jaws and turned away as fury consumed him.

"On to Stegeborg!" he roared when he saw Birger Persson approaching. "We must not waste one precious moment."

The sun reflected like diamonds on the gentle waves of the lake below Solang as Kristina strolled along its peaceful shore. The cloud-free sky was even brighter than the colorful flowers she had collected in her basket to adorn her table.

It had been quiet in her secluded home while Alf was away fighting for Erik and Valdemar's freedom. She had not heard from him in months, which was to be expected in times of war, but she had been waiting for him to return every day for weeks, so she had not ventured far from the house. But today, for the first time, she had walked out into the field on the other side of the lake to gather the multihued flowers that flourished there, and she was returning with her basket full.

As she neared the house she could see Ragna waving to her. She hurried her steps. By the time she reached the kitchen door, Ragna came forward carrying a scroll and a small box in her hand. "One of Lord Mats' messengers . . .." she began.

"Is Alf all right?" asked Kristina anxiously.

"Yes, the messenger told me that he is on his way here," Ragna reassured her.

Kristina placed her flower basket on a worktable, sighed in relief, and then crossed herself before she took the scroll and the small box out into the garden. She sat down on a bench on the side overlooking the lake. She leaned back against the wall, feeling her pent-up concern over Alf's well-being drain out of her body. Thank God, he was safe.

Slowly she unfurled the scroll to read Mats' message. She noticed that it was dated several months earlier.

"Dear Lady Kristina,

It is with great regret that I inform you of Duke Erik and Duke Valdemar's deaths. Although we were successful in storming Nykoping castle we were too late to save them. God have mercy on their souls."

Unable to continue, Kristina dropped the letter into her lap. She felt her tears begin to flow. Though her hands felt like lead, she lifted the message to resume her reading.

"The box I send you contains the item that Duke Erik left to you in his will. I deeply sympathize with your loss of our beloved friends.

Yours, Mats Kettilmundson, Chancellor of Sweden

She was shaking when she opened the small leather box. When she saw what it held, she could no longer deny the truth of Mats' letter.

She had felt so confident that Erik and Valdemar would be liberated that she had never allowed herself to contemplate any other outcome. Doubled over, her hands covering her eyes, she began to sob with abandon. Her body shook from a loss so profound that it tore at her very soul.

When Ragna heard her piercing cries, she ran outside the house in panic. She found Kristina standing with her hands pressed to her chest, her eyes closed, and her mouth opened in a heartbreaking scream. As Ragna rushed to put her arms around her mistress she saw the leather box had fallen to the ground, and beside it a silver chain attached to a large wolf's tooth.

Epilogue

The summer day was warm, and a gentle breeze was blowing over Mora Mead outside Upsala where the Council, the powerful noble clans and leaders of the church, had assembled for the election of a new Swedish King.

Lord Mats Kettilmundson, Sweden's interim ruler, stood beside the King's stone trying to concentrate on the events of the moment, but his mind was wandering towards the past and his fruitless pursuit of King Birger. . . . In record time he had repositioned Sweden's armies and war machines to attack the king's last stronghold at Stegeborg. But the King and Queen had already left. Its young commander, their son Prince Magnus, quickly realized that the fortress could not withstand such a formidable force, and surrendered the stronghold--and himself--in exchange for safe conduct for his men.

Once Birger's loyalists were defeated, Mats returned to Stockholm for the elaborate and emotional funeral of the two dukes. The moment they had been interred, he again went on the attack--this time against Birger's strongest ally, Erik Menved, whom he forced to sue for a three-year peace—the latter offering to no longer take up weapons in support of Birger if Mats would break his alliance with Duke Kristoffer. But even before Mats signed the treaty he ordered the execution of Johan Brunkow. When Mats saw the bewildered look on Brunkow's face as he was being led to his execution he almost felt pity for the faithful doomed warrior.

With Birger's most important supporter neutralized, Mats had set sail with a sizable fleet to capture Birger on Gotland, to which Birger and Marta had fled. But, as before, the royal couple slipped away just days ahead of his arrival. Their destination was the Danish court that they reached in time for the Christmas celebrations. Although Erik

Menved would no longer defend Birger with armies, he welcomed them warmly to live at his court.

Upon his return to Stockholm, Mats learned that King Hakon had died suddenly causing Duke Erik and Ingeborg's three year-old son, Magnus, to become the King of Norway. And today the Swedes were to elect their new king. Mats surveyed the people massed around the King's Stone. He pulled himself out of his reveries and raised his hand to quiet the assembly. "We are gathered here today to elect a new King of Sweden," he began. "I have found consensus amongst you as to who that should be. I am therefore placing before you one candidate only--the son of Sweden's last ruler--Magnus Eriksson!"

Silence reigned over the green meadow. Mats went over to Magnus, bent down and lifted him up. Holding the small prince high above his head he strode over to the King's Stone and placed him on its granite surface. Then he knelt before the boy. There, my little prince, Mats thought sadly, you now have all for which your father ever longed.

"Long live King Magnus!" Mats called. "Long live the King of Sweden!"

"Long live King Magnus!" roared back the crowd. "Long live the King of Sweden and Norway!"

The Author's Note

Writing historical fiction is like riding on a history train. You know what happened at every station through dates and events like marriages, births, coronations, wars, treaties and legal contracts. But what happens on the ride is all yours! Fitting the two together is the hard part!

I have based my research on many historians for the time period and much on the doctoral dissertation by Sverker Rosen "The feud between King Birger and his Brothers". However this source, and most others, was written long after the facts. The most contemporary writing I found is The Erik Chronicle in versed rime, probably composed in the early part of the 14th century, in order to glorify Duke Erik. (It is suspected by some historians that it was commissioned by Mats Kettilmundson.) So no sources seem totally reliable. But the second word in Historical Fiction is just that, Fiction!

I have mostly my husband, Erik, to thank for the book to be finished. He lovingly and doggedly urged me to write and edited over the years, while much was happening in both our lives.

I also want to thank Miranda Cowley who guided me through a major part of the book a long time ago when she worked with Sterling Lord's Agency.

My thanks go to Bespoke Covers for creating the moody cover, to Robb Allan for creating the genealogy charts, and to Bob Reiss for teaching me about book publishing.

Finally, and very importantly, the Ballad of Alf (sung by the outlaws of Smaland) was written by my talented sister-in-law, Joan Javits Zeeman.

The Folkungs of Sweden

as this story begins
(some dates approximate)

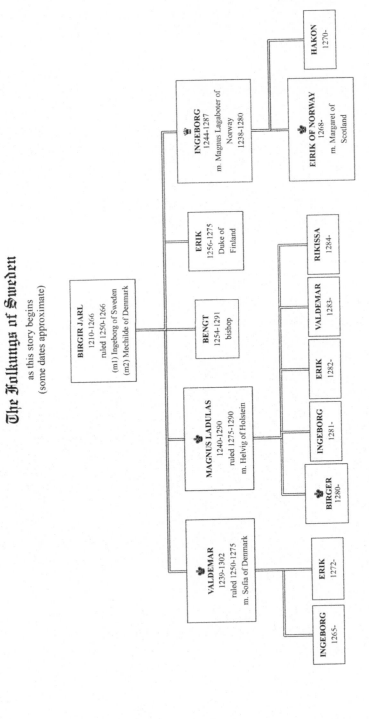

BIRGIR JARL
1210-1266
ruled 1250-1266
(m1) Ingeborg of Sweden
(m2) Mechilde of Denmark

VALDEMAR
1239-1302
ruled 1250-1275
m. Sofia of Denmark

MAGNUS LADULAS
1240-1290
ruled 1275-1290
m. Helvig of Holstein

BENGT
1254-1291
bishop

ERIK
1256-1275
Duke of
Finland

INGEBORG
1244-1287
m. Magnus Lagaboter of
Norway
1238-1280

EIRIK OF NORWAY
1268-
m. Margaret of
Scotland

HAKON
1270-

INGEBORG
1265-

ERIK
1272-

BIRGER
1280-

INGEBORG
1281-

ERIK
1282-

VALDEMAR
1283-

RIKISSA
1284-

The Relationships between the Royal Houses of Denmark, Norway, and Sweden

as this story begins
(some dates approximate)

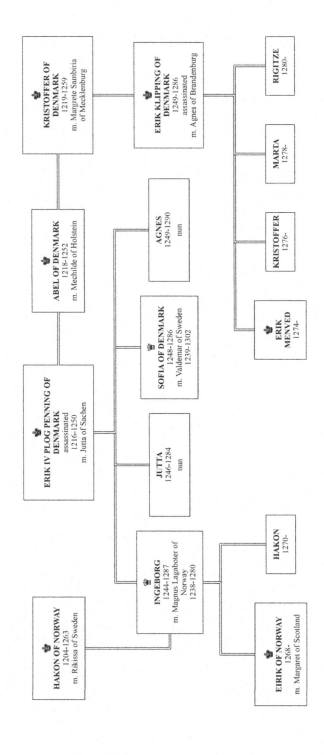

HAKON OF NORWAY
1204-1263
m. Rikissa of Sweden

ERIK IV PLOG PENNING OF DENMARK
assassinated
1216-1250
m. Jutta of Sachen

KRISTOFFER OF DENMARK
1219-1259
m. Margrete Sambiria
of Mecklenburg

ABEL OF DENMARK
1218-1252
m. Mechilde of Holstein

ERIK KLIPPING OF DENMARK
1249-1286
assassinated
m. Agnes of Brandenburg

INGEBORG
1244-1287
m. Magnus Lagaboter of Norway
1238-1280

JUTTA
1246-1284
nun

SOFIA OF DENMARK
1248-1286
m. Valdemar of Sweden
1239-1302

AGNES
1249-1290
nun

EIRIK OF NORWAY
1268-
m. Margaret of Scotland

HAKON
1270-

ERIK MENVED
1274-

KRISTOFFER
1276-

MARTA
1278-

RIGITZE
1280-

653

Margaretha Espersson Javits was born in Stockholm, Sweden. After graduating from Teachers College in Stockholm she left for the United States where she earned her Doctorate in Psychology and Higher Education at Columbia University. She served as an Assistant Dean in its School of General Studies for several years before leaving academia to work at a leading advertising agency in New York. She accompanied her US Ambassador husband to Europe for eight years before returning to the US where they now reside in Palm Beach, Florida.